Fiona Walker, whose novels have been Sunday Times best-sellers, leads the field as the voice of young, media-aware women. She lives with her husband and two dogs in an idyllic cottage in Oxfordshire.

Praise for *Kiss Chase*:

'Simmering sexual tension and steamy escapism'
Daily Mirror

'Fast, fun and furiously entertaining'
Birmingham Post

'Fast-paced, racy and fun'
Today

Also by Fiona Walker

French Relations
Well Groomed
Snap Happy
Between Males
Lucy Talk
Lots of Love

Fiona Walker

KISS CHASE

CORONET BOOKS
Hodder & Stoughton

Copyright © 1995 by Fiona Walker

First published in Great Britain in 1995 by Hodder & Stoughton
First published in paperback in 1996
A Coronet paperback
A division of Hodder Headline
This edition published in 2003

The right of Fiona Walker to be identified as the Author of this Work
has been asserted by her in accordance with the Copyright,
Designs and Patents Act 1988.

30 29 28 27 26 25 24 23 22

A CIP catalogue record for this title
is available from the British Library

ISBN 0 340 63515 0

Typeset by Hewer Text Ltd, Edinburgh
Printed and bound in Great Britain by
Clays Ltd, St Ives plc

Hodder & Stoughton
A division of Hodder Headline
338 Euston Road
London NW1 3BH

For the Second Mum, the Fairy Godmother,
the Golden Curls, the Sunny Scunny Babe and
the Best Dressed Window Dresser in London.

I

'*At the third beep the time sponsored by Accurist will be three-twenty-five precisely . . . beep . . . beep . . .*'

'Yes we offer a fully comprehensive service. Let me tell you a little bit about it – '

'*. . . time sponsored by Accurist will be three- . . .*'

'– and of course we provide a back-up cover which enables our clients to – '

'*. . . and ten seconds . . . beep . . .*'

It was always the same. Phoebe Fredericks had been working in telesales for three weeks precisely . . . beep . . . beep . . . beep . . . and it was getting on her nerves. She generally started calling up the Speaking Clock after lunch. By that point she would have exhausted all the 0891 numbers she could find in the free magazines that had been handed to her at the tube station that morning: Tarotline, Recorded Horoscope, Dial-a-Date. (Oh, those poor lonely hearts; little did they know she was trying to sell insurance over their mumbled descriptions of a caring D-cup blonde with a sense of humour.)

Phoebe found selling to the Speaking Clock annoying. She had to hold the phone very close to her ear to stop the beeps being audible to her manager, who was wont to prowl around behind the sales team whispering: 'Good call, sweetheart!' and 'Ask for the business! Get the bastard to buy!' Holding the ear-piece so close gave Phoebe a headache and heated her earrings to Regulo 8. But anything was better than cold calling.

'Yes, we do. That is available for very little extra cost and is inclusive of VAT. Would you like me to pencil you in for that option now?'

'*At the third beep . . .*'

'Well, if you choose to buy it today we can offer you a special package.'

'Good call!'

Phoebe's shoulders were suddenly pulverised by the enthusiastically damp hands of her boss, Trev. One of his many motivational ploys was the team massage.

'Close on him, sweetheart. Close!' he hissed as his pudgy thumbs almost dislocated several of her joints.

'Er . . . tell me, sir, for what reason is that?'

'*. . . and forty seconds . . .*'

'Yes!' Phoebe could feel Trev's hot, excited breath on the back of her neck. It made her spine try to hide in her stomach. The man must have marinaded overnight in Paco Rabanne. Her eyes were beginning to water.

Thank you, God! Phoebe smiled. *Call Waiting* was flashing on the LCD panel in her phone.

'Of course, I fully understand. What a shame . . .'

The fingers tightened on her shoulders; Paco Rabanne was joined by Chicken Tikka as Trev's breath quickened. Phoebe's back gave an uncontrollable shudder of revulsion.

'*. . . precisely.*'

'And you too. I certainly will. Take care and thank you for your time.'

'*. . . beeeep . . .*'

'Why the fuck did you lose the sale?' The pudgy fingers scrabbled for a cigarette.

'Can't speak now, Trev.' She smiled, trying to get the feeling back in her shoulders. 'I've got a call waiting. Good afternoon, Phoebe Fredericks speaking.'

'Hello, Freddy. It's Virginia Seaton. Saskia's mother.'

'Good grief – Gin! How are you?'

'Oh, not so bad. Look, I'm sorry to bother you at work like this – your mother gave me the number.' She sounded odd somehow, tense and high-pitched, not her usual effervescent self.

'Please don't worry. I'm here to deal with these sorts of problems,' Phoebe simpered, aware that Trev was still hovering, ears flapping like Dumbo taxiing around Heathrow.

'What? How was New Zealand, Freddy? Or have I called at an awkward time?'

Trev started to move off, hoicking up the back of his pin-stripe trousers with a pudgy hand.

'Not at all.' Phoebe swivelled round on her chair and pretended to be looking for a file. 'New Zealand was terrific – I can't believe it's been a whole year. I'm so sorry I haven't been in touch since I got back, but what with getting a job and finding a new flat . . . I've tried calling Saskia, but I always get her machine. Is she away with this ravishing bloke she wrote to me about?'

'Er, no.' Gin cleared her throat awkwardly.

'He sounds divine. Whirlwind romance, weekends in Tuscany, diamond ring in a glass of vintage Dom Perignon by the Seine – I bet it'll be the wedding of the decade!' Phoebe sighed wistfully, staring at Giles, the office Romeo, and wondering how long it had been since she'd fallen in love. A year. Not since the Major, Never Spoken Of Disaster. Oh, to be whisked off her feet like lucky, beautiful Saskia. But she'd always got the men and Phoebe was forever stuck with their cheesy friends.

'. . . still there? Freddy?'

'What?' She snapped out of her daze. Giles was staring back at her wolfishly. Gulping, Phoebe swivelled into the filing cabinet again. 'Gosh, sorry, Gin. Is it my measurements you wanted? Saskia mentioned about the bridesmaids' dresses in her last letter. I was going to ask her if she'd mind re-thinking the orange and purple caftan idea. I mean, I know the seventies are back in fashion, but – '

'Oh, Freddy!' Gin let out an exasperated laugh. 'You haven't changed one bit, have you?'

'I'm sorry?'

Trev, fresh from a fumble with his secretary in the stationery cupboard, was closing fast, his tie askew under his four-ply chins. Giles, whizzing backwards on his swivel-chair as if he were reversing a Lamborghini out of an SW1 parking space, offered Phoebe a bite of his tuna and sweetcorn bun with a caddish leer. She shook her head.

'Look, Freddy,' Gin suddenly sounded urgent, 'what are you doing this weekend?'

'Well, Fliss and Stan have organised this sort of reunion barbecue,' she muttered, trying to ignore Trev mouthing 'Is that a personal call?' 'Why?'

'Would you like to come down to Berkshire?' Gin was almost pleading. 'Saskia's here.'

'She's with you?' Phoebe banged her head on the filing cabinet in surprise. Giles was draped seductively over the partition, offering her half his scotch egg now.

'Yes.' Gin coughed uneasily, as if afraid of being overheard. 'She's in a bit of a state.'

'But I . . .'

'*Phoebe!* A word in my office, *if* you can spare a moment.'

Phoebe froze, noticing Trev was clutching an itemised phone bill and something that looked suspiciously like her P45.

'Of course I'll come down,' she told Gin hurriedly. 'And you never know, I might even outstay my welcome.'

'You what?' Fliss turned around, a lump of clay dripping mud from one outstretched hand on to the worn carpet as Phoebe slunk guiltily around their shared Islington flat.

'I got the push,' she repeated nervously, flicking on the kettle.

'Already?' Fliss rubbed her forehead, streaking it with red clay which matched the titian corkscrews straying out from under her headscarf. 'Damn! I bet Stan you'd last at least a month.'

'That was generous.' Phoebe poured an inch of coffee granules straight from the jar into a mug then slopped kettle water on top, not bothering to stir. 'How much?'

'Ten quid. Stan got it right – he gave you a fortnight.' Fliss raised one ginger eyebrow as Phoebe scuttled past. 'And the electricity bill came today – I could have used the winnings.'

'Great.' Phoebe sank down on the sofa, bringing her knees up to chin level as yet another spring gave way. 'How about I pretend I kept the job longer?'

'No good. He knows someone you work – *worked* with. Miles something.' Fliss scrunched up her freckled face as she returned to her sculpture.

'Giles,' smiled Phoebe, blowing the froth from her coffee and watching Fliss work. It was one of her all-time pleasures. Fliss attacked fifty pounds of wet clay like a battered wife a pillow at a self-assertiveness course, but the end result was inevitably breathtaking.

'Yeah. Stan says he fancies you.'

'Stan's always fancied me.' Phoebe deliberately misinterpreted Fliss's words.

'No, this Giles character fancies you.' Fliss was already becoming lost in contouring the emerging shape of two clay thighs. 'Stan offered to set you up at the barbecue. We reckon you need a pretty man to help you get over The Corps. Stan thinks you're still infatuated . . .'

'What's wrong with the studio this time?' Phoebe butted in quickly, then grinned to hide her discomfiture. 'How many times have I told you about bringing your work home, darling?'

'No water.' Fliss shrugged, examining her maquette, which looked like something young mothers pick up from parks in pooper scoopers to prevent their toddlers catching toxicaria. 'And Geraldine's welding half a car to a shopping trolley, so the noise is deafening.'

Fliss was trying to forge a path as a sculptress, funding her chosen career with waitressing jobs, and occasional secretarial work for a party planner called Georgette Gregory. She worked from a communal grant-maintained artist's studio in Camden Lock, sharing the damp converted archway with two ex-convict welders, a cockney artist called Stan MacGillivray, and a would-be Damien Hirst who was currently in the process of freezing his sperm daily to create an ice-sculpture taken from a mould of his private parts. Fliss's broad Mancunian accent and tendency towards extreme bluntness often puzzled people who, taking in the luscious red curls, snub nose and red pepper freckles, assumed that as an artist she'd waft about in smocks drying flowers all day. Phoebe adored sharing a flat with her. Fliss could change a plug, build shelves and plumb in a dishwasher in less time than it took the average man to climb into a boiler suit. And she was always trying to set Phoebe up with her dishy mates.

'There's a couple of messages for you on the phone.' She waved her hand vaguely at the clay-encrusted telephone.

Slopping coffee, Phoebe struggled out of the sofa and pressed the play button.

'Hello, this is Phoebe's mother, Poppy Fredericks, speaking . . .'

Phoebe groaned. Her mother always treated answermachines as if they were secretaries.

Not listening to the message, she turned back to Fliss. 'Anyway, I can't go to the barbecue. Some old friends have asked me down for the weekend.'

'What?' Fliss was pummelling a couple of spare tyres out of the clay.

'In Berkshire.' Phoebe briefly listened as her mother moved on from the atrocious weather in Hong Kong to give a brief lecture about getting in contact with her sister.

'. . . of course the idiotic girl is still dallying with The Thing, you know . . .'

The crackling message moved on to describe a dinner party which Chris Patten had attended. Phoebe ignored it again. Poppy refused to acknowledge her younger daughter Milly's boyfriend as anything other than 'The Thing' – which, considering he was really called Goat and sharpened his teeth with a file to frighten people, wasn't terribly insulting. For Poppy.

'Who in Berkshire?' Fliss turned around, her eyes narrowed. She even had freckles on her eyelids.

'I said, some old friends of the family.' Phoebe was dying to name-drop about Saskia Seaton's fiancé, Felix Sylvian, but thought better of it. Fliss might try to muscle in on the invite too. It had been known.

'Nothing to do with The Corps?' she asked lightly.

'No!' Phoebe snapped, her cheeks draining of colour like a dishcloth in bleach. 'And don't fucking well call him that!'

Fliss shrugged, watching her friend's face. 'Stan's right. You are still in love with him.'

'I am not!' Phoebe was prevented from launching into a spitting defence by the answermachine giving a loud bleep to signal the end of her mother's message. There was a brief pause and then another voice began – brittle with tears and venom but still ringing with hautesse.

'Hello, Freddy. This is Saskia Seaton. Mummy tells me she's invited you down for the weekend. Look, I – ' there was a pause as the receiver was muffled for a few seconds '– please don't come. That's all. Just don't come. I don't want you here.'

Phoebe stared at the phone in silent amazement. She barely heard the message from Stan asking her to a private viewing the following week, or from her chum Claudia saying hello. One final message was brief and to the point.

'Freddy, it's Gin. Please ignore anything Saskia might have said to you on the phone. I gather she's been in touch. We're all dying to see you – just let me know what train you'll be on. Sorry about Saskia. She got rather the wrong end of the stick about something. Tony sends his love. See you tomorrow.'

Fliss whistled excitedly. 'She sounds like Penelope Keith. This is all very intriguing. Can I come too?'

'No.' Phoebe rubbed her temples in bewilderment.

Virginia and Anthony Seaton, known to friends as Gin and Tonic, were very close chums of Phoebe's parents, Ralph and Poppy Fredericks. Friends since the pendulum-swinging and rune-reading sixties, the foursome shared an off-beat sense of humour, capacity to drink all night and a leaky canal barge into which they'd once all piled at weekends. And amongst their respective children were two girls who shared exactly the same birthday. It stood to reason that they should become cronies.

But 12 August was the only thing Saskia Seaton and Phoebe Fredericks had in common. For most of their childhood, they had loathed one another. Curvy, snubnosed Saskia was the youngest and prettiest of four sisters; bright, wildly precocious, utterly spoiled and very, very charming. Phoebe had two gorgeous, scruffy elder brothers, a natty line in hand-me-down dungarees, a demon little sister and the social graces of the Dulux puppy fresh from a slurry pit: friendly, scatty, enthusiastic, but hopelessly ungroomed.

When Saskia and Phoebe were sent to the same boarding school in Chester they'd formed rival cliques. Yet each term they'd travelled up together, their trunks nestling companionably in the boot of either Phoebe's parents' rusty Landrover (known as the Dinosaur), or the Seatons' latest flashy Mercedes. And every holiday they'd suffer the humiliation of being invited to one another's houses, where one or several of the rival clique would inevitably be in situ to make life hell. Saskia's visits were slightly easier because both Phoebe's brothers were madly in love with her, dispensing hospitality and Pimms in abundance. Saskia's three elder sisters, however, were completely indifferent to Phoebe. On the few occasions they registered her presence, they treated her with the same bored irritation they would a school hamster that it was their turn to look after during half term. Saskia, however, took great pleasure in making Phoebe's visit as hellish as possible, bullying the gangly, timid little girl into terrified submission.

Then Ralph Fredericks – a six-foot six industrial architect and devout rugby buff – accepted a long contract overseas, the first of many. He and his elegant wife Poppy became virtual expatriates as they moved between time-zones with little more than a crackling intercontinental call to the school to pass on their new address. Occasionally Phoebe sat on fifteen-hour flights with her younger sister, Milly, to join them for holidays. Mostly, she spent the yawning gaps between school terms with the Seatons, to the horror of Saskia and her sisters. Saskia merely redoubled her efforts to make Phoebe's stays unpleasant. Jealous of Phoebe's close relationship with her mother, Gin,

Saskia enlisted her sisters' help in the ritual goading and teasing which the adults never witnessed.

Phoebe grew to dread her birthday each year, when she and Saskia would share a party. If it weren't for the fact that she adored Gin and Tonic Seaton, Phoebe would have kicked up a stink long before they shared their appalling eighteenth, when Saskia spent all night plugged to the lips of the local Sandhurst stud – on whom Phoebe had shed tears, wasted her best poems and for whom she'd forked out for a Valentine for over a decade. The next day Saskia had phoned him and told him that she had suddenly found out her best friend, Freddy 'Krueger' Fredericks, had a honking great crush on him so she couldn't possibly see him again, finally adding that he kissed like a slug trapped in a vacuum nozzle.

After school, with considerable relief, they went their separate ways. Saskia spent a bomb at Pineapple, had collagen injected into her lips and, installed in a plush Battersea flat by her parents, went to a London drama school. Phoebe took a place to read English at Exeter, fell in love with every be-ponytailed drop out, partied furiously, achieved a lousy degree and, moving back to London and into a shared house in West Hampstead, worked her way through six jobs in as many months, dreaming of becoming the next Edna O'Brien but writing nothing more than the odd rubbery cheque. Temping at the headquarters of a tabloid newspaper for a week, she met and fell in love with Dan – a funny, charming and utterly addictive renegade whom all her friends referred to as The Corps because he was a corporate lawyer and far older, wiser and more married than her. He pursued her mercilessly, told her his marriage was a wreck, and then dropped her like a used condom when *Private Eye* devoted three lines to the story, naming Phoebe as the 'alleged leggy and libidinous new love-interest for celebrated Street of Shame "Libel Detector"'. He was convinced his wife would find out.

The storm blew over in less than a week with The Corps sidling daily through his old front door, chocolates and flowers held up like shields and his amazed wife emerging to kiss him on his two faces, blithely unaware of the scandal.

But the Fredericks family, finding out the full story from a hand-me-down *Private Eye* in Hong Kong, had been appalled by Phoebe's behaviour, issuing instructions to one of her brothers to invite her for a year in a different hemisphere to hush up for good the affair. When Phoebe refused to go, Poppy Fredericks had cut all links until she caved in.

Phoebe had only seen Saskia Seaton once before setting off to spend a year with her elder brother, Dominic, who lived in New Zealand.

At the time, Phoebe had a new, very dishy boyfriend called Stan – Fliss's artist friend – who was giving her second thoughts about going to the opposite end of the globe to live in an Antipodean vineyard. Stan was wildly romantic: a starving artist with a mane of lion blond hair. He virtually lived at the ICA, drank vodka for breakfast and talked about Existential Chaos Theory in reverent tones while taking Phoebe for jellied eels on the Isle of Dogs. He was also the complete opposite of The Corps and consequently as comforting to rebound on as a padded trampoline.

Desperate to impress him, Phoebe booked tickets for a very dingy fringe play called *Mort et Misère*, advertised as 'avant garde, polemic performance art that will redefine your spiritual boundaries'.

It took place in a tiny, darkened room above a pub in deepest suburban Putney. Apart from a couple of lesbian drama professors and a stray drunk from downstairs, Stan and Phoebe were the only audience.

To the accompaniment of a greasy-haired anorexic banging a tambourine against her bony hip, eight hunch-backed figures wearing plastic bin-liners, with paper bags on their heads, shuffled on stage and started moaning incoherently.

Meanwhile the juke box downstairs worked through AC/DC's full repertoire of hits. Or it could have been one song played over and over again, Phoebe found it hard to tell.

After about ten minutes, the drunk got up and, groping noisily in the gloom, staggered to the door. The lesbians paused from taking notes, looked over their John Lennon specs at each other and tutted. Stan started snoring loudly. Phoebe got the giggles.

About two hours later, the play ended with all the actors taking their bin liners off and, stark naked apart from their paper bag helmets, hitting each other with raw mackerel while the anorexic almost broke her tambourine in Bacchic ecstasy.

Phoebe prodded Stan in the ribs and he woke up, yawned loudly and squinted at the fishy flagellation on stage.

'Nice tits.' He nodded in the direction of an actress with a much smarter paper bag than anyone else. In fact, on close inspection it turned out to come from Harvey Nichols Food Hall. She also had a very familiar birthmark, shaped like a sea horse, on her left leg.

'My God,' Phoebe muttered, almost falling off her chair in amazement. 'It's Saskia.'

Afterwards, trying to prize Stan away from his fourth pint of London Pride in the bar downstairs, Phoebe felt five ringed claws clutch her shoulder.

'Freddy Krueger!' shrieked a voice.

Phoebe spun around, ready to express total surprise so as not to embarrass Saskia by admitting she'd seen the bin bag orgy. Then her jaw dropped.

Saskia had always been beautiful. She had the sort of cheek bones women in America remove most of their teeth to achieve, the glossiest mane of slippery blonde hair and huge, cobalt blue eyes like the priciest chips on a roulette table. Built in the Joely Richardson English Rose mould, she had a perfect, elongated size-twelve figure that would have made Laura Ashley weep with joy – just the right height for the hem of a chintz smock to finish at the ankle. Her pink and white complexion made Princess Diana look like a Greek goat herder in comparison.

But instead, smiling at Phoebe was a glorious raven-haired siren with hypnotic eyes the colour of Parma violets. She wore an all-in-one Marlboro-red hot-pants catsuit and enormous fashionable clod hoppers at the end of her endless tanned legs.

'Saskia!' Phoebe gasped in awe. 'You look sensational. You've changed – '

'Whatever you do, don't let on my hair's not natural,' she hissed into Phoebe's ear, casting a wary eye over her shoulder to where a gaggle of actors were kissing each other's cheeks and holding hands.

'I think you'll have to shave your minge to make people believe that,' grinned Stan, laid-back as ever, eyeing her birthmark with lazy interest.

It was Stan's rude directness that Phoebe liked, but he did have a tendency to go a bit far. And Saskia could be absurdly sensitive. Bracing herself for a flurry of bitchy crushing remarks, Phoebe was amazed when Saskia merely shrieked with laughter. She *had* loosened up.

They talked for hours. Or rather, Saskia did. Phoebe yawned, ate the lemon in her Coke and ground her teeth on the pips as Stan observed Saskia in much the same way as he would gaze at a mesmerising, incomprehensible Miro in the Tate.

By half-past eleven, he was on to his eighth pint and glazing over.

We *would* find ourselves in a pub with extended licensing hours, Phoebe thought glumly. But even she had to admit she was fascinated.

Saskia had changed more than just her hair colour and contact lenses. She'd picked up that thespian tendency to touch the person she was speaking to. Phoebe's fingers turned blue as Saskia gushed on about their 'crazy' schooldays, with all those '*fab*ulously bizarre' parties. Yet, despite this new-found chumminess, Phoebe realised you could slice steel on her ambition.

'I had a test with Ken Russell last week,' she enthused, speaking loudly enough to cause whirlpools in most of the pints in the pub. Phoebe charitably assumed it was her drama training which made her project her voice so much.

'Really?' Stan grinned lazily. He never lost his cool.

'Yeah.' Saskia lit another cigarette. She'd got through almost half a packet. 'He's doing a screen adaptation of Eliot's *Waste Land*.'

'Fucking antiquated crap,' Stan yawned, impassively watching Saskia's cleavage deepen as she leant forward to tap her ash.

'No one gives a shit about twenties neo-sacrilegious symbolic subversion any more.' His eyelids batted in boredom, although Phoebe knew he was relishing the wind up.

To do her credit, Saskia didn't flinch. Phoebe was impressed. She just smiled and started telling them a story about being chased across London by an enraptured RSC director.

'He wanted me to audition for a Coward revival – Tom Conti's going to be in it. But I'm not willing to channel myself into mainstream West End yet. I find experimental theatre far more broadening.'

It was only after the bell for last orders had rung that Saskia asked what Phoebe was up to.

'New Zealand!' she shrieked when Phoebe told her, her purple lenses nearly rotating as she widened her eyes. 'Oh, how awful, darling. I mean, I've only just found you again, Freddy, and you're scooting off to shear a lot of flea-infested ewes.'

'Dominic's a wine-grower.'

In the end, Saskia insisted on swapping addresses.

'It says Hounslow, but it's much closer to Richmond, actually,' she said, thrusting a beer mat covered in her illegible scrawl under Phoebe's nose. 'Promise you'll write and let me know everything. And give my love to that gorgeous brother of yours.'

Phoebe didn't expect to hear from her again. No doubt Poppy would soon write with news of Saskia's impending stardom, relayed via Gin Seaton.

In the taxi on their way back to Stan's grotty Brixton flat, Phoebe braced herself for jealous demons and asked him what he thought of Saskia.

'Fucking screwed-up toff.' He shrugged indifferently. 'Decent legs, but I preferred her with the paper bag on. At least you couldn't see her mouth moving.'

Oh God, she loved him for that.

But it didn't really come as much of a surprise when the first letter Phoebe received from Saskia was a gushing apology for the fact that she was now dating Stan. What surprised Phoebe more was that she'd bothered to write at all. And then keep on writing.

Sporadic letters, sometimes no more than a postcard, sometimes eight leaves thick, and always postmarked from a different part of London, wound their way to Dominic and Vicky Fredericks's isolated farm, often months late.

Until then Phoebe had never believed distance makes the heart grow fonder. She liked regular gossips, lots of chummy meals and two-hour phone conversations. Saskia's letters were a revelation.

She took life on the chin at a reckless, whistle-stop pace. Her stories often appalled Phoebe. She could be totally amoral, utterly unforgiving, and very, very kinky. But her unending enthusiasm, ambition and humour kept Phoebe alive through the tiring, back-breaking months she spent with her brother. She supposed Saskia treated her as a sort of confessional – a listener on the other side of the globe, safe from prying flatmates and jealous lovers.

Any news Phoebe gave in return was pathetically scant. How could telling Saskia that they'd repaired twenty miles of ring fence and found a new recipe for roast lamb compare to her writing that she'd met and fallen in love with one of the most successful, lusted-after and oh-so-eligible heart-throbs in London – the some-time playboy, some-time model Felix Sylvian? And what's more, he was utterly obsessed with her, had thrown in a well-chronicled relationship with his MTA partner and was planning to marry Saskia a month after Phoebe was due back from New Zealand.

Her delirious, infectious happiness made Phoebe tingle. She simply lived for the next letter. Saskia was wildly indiscreet about their sex-life, repeating kiss for slap every sizzling detail about his penchant for knotted silk scarves, voyeurism, crème fraîche, exhibitionism and dressing up. But it was the romance that made Phoebe shiver. She didn't believe other men ever did things as totally unexpected, imaginative and bohemian as Felix Sylvian.

*   *   *

Rattling on a slow train through leafy Berkshire stations with their red painted lamp posts, lurid Quick Snacks and modern glass waiting rooms, Phoebe was not at her merriest. Now jobless and broke, she had no way of paying her part of the rent on the shared flat. She'd fobbed Fliss off with a vague excuse about still transferring dollars from Wellington, but with red phone, electricity and gas bills pinned pointedly to Phoebe's empty food cupboard, things were getting desperate. To cheer herself up she'd booked a haircut and emerged from the ultra-trendy Covent Garden salon with a very light head and cold neck vowing never again to say 'I want something different'. She looked like a schoolboy; her sleek brown hair cut to an urchin's three inches. Fine for petite, curvy women with pretty faces; Phoebe was almost six foot, very gangly and, although her eyes were the same green as the inside of a kiwi fruit and her mouth had once been compared to Julia Roberts's by a drunk on the tube, she had a nose like a falcon's beak and a long, scrawny neck that either had to be buried in a polo neck or surrounded by a flattering cloud of hair.

It was Wimbledon week, mid-summer and the train – a modern electric-door type with eye-watering upholstery and no windows – was stifling. Phoebe's polo neck already felt like a woolly noose. Beside her, a teenage girl was chewing gum with squelchy salival squeaks and listening to the men's semi-finals full-blast on her Walkman.

Plink . . . plop . . . plink . . . thwack . . . grunt . . . plop . . . audience gasps as the lob goes up . . . smash . . . OUT! . . . groan.

Phoebe shot the girl a grouchy look, noticing that she had a stud shaped like a clenched fist through her nose. Phoebe hoped she didn't have hay fever; she could puncture an innocent member of the public if she sneezed.

She edged closer to the window just as they whooshed into a tunnel. Her face stared back, naked without its veil of hair. Next to Saskia's slender curves, slithering mane and glorious chest, Phoebe reflected, she'd look like a Dickens character wandering into a Jackie Collins sex scene by mistake. She prayed Felix

Sylvian wasn't down for the weekend, then told herself off for being so vain.

The tannoy gurgled into life with a baffling submarine-to-HQ coded message.

Translating 'Hssskkbreich' as Hexbury, Phoebe pulled her featherweight hat-box from the overhead luggage shelf. She had virtually no clothes with her. Returning in high sulk over her shaved head, she'd bunged her overdue laundry into the machine without noticing that Fliss had left the dial at boil wash after shrinking her new Levis. Now Phoebe had a dozen Sindy-sized knickers, several toddler-fit shirts and two skirts which, given a frame, would make terrific lampshades.

Anyway, she told herself, if the drought continued, it would be too hot for more than shorts and a sun-top. And she already had a reputation in the Seaton house for being an utter slob.

But, just in case, she'd vengefully nicked two outrageously sexy dresses from Fliss's wardrobe.

2

Too early for the returning Friday night commuters, the platform at Hexbury was almost deserted when Phoebe stepped off the train. Two women clutching classy bags of shopping clicked away from First Class on high court shoes. A BR guard lit a cigarette and eyed Phoebe with interest.

Probably bisexual, she thought, miserably running a hand through her new crew cut. God, it was short.

She wandered towards the car park and gazed around hopefully. Even the taxi rank was empty. Rows of shiny BMWs in the *Season Ticket Holders Only* enclosure waited like pony lines at a polo match for their masters to return with a space age remote-control key. Phoebe searched for a flashy Merc.

A woman was standing beside a battered Golf, her wiry grey hair on end, ancient yellow cords rammed into green wellies, creased sun top showing a lot of loose mahogany skin. She looked at Phoebe curiously.

Trying to work out what sex I am, no doubt, Phoebe thought crabbily. She yanked up her cycling shorts and tried to look cool. Gin was notoriously late for everything, she told herself. She'd be totally wrapped up in her garden at this time of year, not noticing time flying as she whizzed around dead-heading and weed-pulling, inspired no doubt by a recent visit to Chelsea Flower Show.

'Freddy?'

Phoebe spun round to see the welly woman peering at her

questioningly. She had a red-veined face like port-soaked Stilton – though it had once undoubtedly been very beautiful – and merry, faded blue eyes.

'Gin?' Phoebe's voice faltered.

'My dear, it *is* you. Gosh!' Phoebe was enveloped in a hug. Gin smelled comfortingly of fading Miss Dior and potting shed. But the hair against Phoebe's cheek seemed to have turned from the colour of sun-bleached straw to pepper overnight, and she felt as frail as a rag doll that had lost most of its stuffing.

'I didn't recognise you!' she laughed, pulling away to look Phoebe in the face. 'Tony always told me you'd become a swan', Gin touched her cheek in amazement, 'and so you have! Gosh, but you have!'

Phoebe was burning with embarrassment. Her mother had always taught her to return one compliment with another. Yet Gin looked so old, faded and unkempt whereas she'd been the most elegant woman alive when Phoebe had last seen her. For the whole of her childhood she'd idol-worshipped Virginia Seaton. In two years she must have aged a decade.

'And you look well too,' she lied, far too late.

'Don't talk rubbish,' Gin dismissed her, hooking her arm through Phoebe's and towing her towards the tatty Golf. 'I look a sight. I need you to make me stop rushing around and sprawl around by the pool reading glossies and talking non-stop like we used to, remember?'

'Of course I remember.'

'It's just that things have been so hectic lately, what with the wedding plans and then the awful – of course, you don't know. I'll – damn thing!' she cursed as the car alarm went off.

'Bloody thing's new, you see,' she yelled over the din. 'Can't work it out yet. Oh, bother!' She ran a hand through her peppery hair and it stood up even more.

Finally the alarm shut up, more because it chose to than from anything Gin had done.

'Awful old banger, isn't it?' she complained as they sank into cracked leather seats.

'I think it's lovely.' Phoebe laughed in amazement. 'Believe me, the only car I've been inside in the last year is a rusty Moke with no suspension. And since I've been back in London, I've had my bicycle wheels nicked twice.'

'Oh God, am I being a frightful snob again?' Gin looked genuinely appalled as she crunched the gears into reverse. 'It's just I'm so hatefully reactionary these days. And since Tony's lost so much money – bottom's fallen out of the property business since the recession, you know, and he's a Lloyd's name – I'm finding it terribly difficult to adjust. I wish I was your age again.' She glanced at her reflection in the rear view mirror and grimaced. 'Gosh, it was so easy then.'

They lurched forwards in a series of kangaroo hops and then accelerated at breakneck speed out of the car park.

At least Gin's driving hadn't changed, Phoebe thought as her knuckles whitened on the seatbelt.

As they sped up the bumpy pot-holed drive towards Deayton Manor Farm, the Seatons' square-shouldered, brick-and-flint house, three Labradors and a yapping Jack Russell came tumbling out of the open front door. Narrowly missing running over the most grey-muzzled of the Labradors, Gin pulled the Golf up at a rakish angle beside a dusty Range Rover and they got out to a rapturous canine welcome.

'That's Reg's now really,' she nodded towards the Range Rover, 'but Tony likes it kept in front of the house – silly old fool. Since he lost his licence, he decided it wasn't worth keeping a large car running. Reg drives him to the station in it.'

Phoebe walked towards the house, trying to look as dignified as possible with two Labrador snouts glued to her crotch.

Inside, it was blissfully cool and just as she had remembered it – grand, tatty and eccentric. A battered keeper's check deerstalker was still balanced on the bust of Julius Caesar in the hall, and a faded British Ensign draped over the portrait of a particularly ugly ancestor, because one of Tony's great-aunts had once had a heart attack while looking at it. Passing through to the back lobby, Phoebe even recognised the pock-marks on the panelling where her brothers had knocked a cricket ball against it years ago.

'Please ignore the utter shambles – strawberry jam in progress,' Gin apologised as they went into the kitchen. She paused by the back stairs and shouted up, 'Sheila! The rest of the dog food's in the boot of the Golf. Come and say hi to Freddy when you get a chance.'

The Seatons' kitchen was huge, messy and old fashioned, and hadn't seen a fitter wielding a tape-measure in its two-hundred-year life. Gin always referred to it as her organised chaos. Although old and ugly enough to be classified as archetypal rustic chic, none of the furniture matched. The high, chipped-tile walls were lined by stain-blotched benches and tables, cupboards without handles, a fifties washing machine, seventies dishwasher, shuddering fridge, an ancient four-door Aga loaded with drying tea towels, and two cracked enamel sinks of differing heights, all shoulder-to-shoulder like a decrepit city skyline. The enormous scrubbed yew table in the centre of the room was as warped as a tricky golf green – Phoebe knew from experience that if one rolled a marble from the high end, it would spiral and slalom its way to the opposite one. Surrounding it were chairs of every shape and wood, from a bent-backed classic to a folding canvas director's chair with 'The Boss' emblazoned on the back. A psychologist would have had a field-day analysing why people chose to sit in each different one.

Phoebe selected a wood-wormed one with a shredding wicker seat and sank down on to it, realising she felt fifteen again. The combined smells of baking, jam-making, wet dog and drying laundry stirred up childhood memories as vividly as looking at an old photograph. For many summers this had been her refuge; she had stayed here for hours with Gin, chatting, laughing and nibbling biscuits as an escape from the Seaton daughters' spite.

'Is Saskia here?' she asked, fiddling with a strawberry.

'Still in bed, I should think.' Gin shook the kettle before opening the Aga hot lid. 'Tea or coffee? No, I know. It's horribly early for a proper drink, but I think we can get away with Pimms, don't you?'

'Well . . .' Phoebe glanced at the kitchen clock. It was just past four. Maybe Saskia and Felix were holed up for a long love weekend, she wondered. 'Did she have a late night then?'

Gin shrugged. 'I don't know, darling. She creeps around the house like a ghost – didn't get up at all on Wednesday.'

'Hello, Fred.'

A jolly red face appeared around the door to the back stairs, clutching a pile of sheets. The Seatons' housekeeper, Sheila, was as short, stout and rounded as a Beryl Cook lady, with an unruly mop of blonde corkscrew curls and a penchant for the most incredible spectacles. Today's were huge, pink-tinted round ones with mother-of-pearl frames that balanced on the end of her sunburnt snub nose, forcing her to hold up her head like a tubby seal balancing a ball.

'Sheila!' Phoebe leapt up, giving her an enormous hug. The little woman came up to her chin.

'Mind these,' Sheila laughed as she gathered up the sheets, squinting at her over the specs. 'I can't believe it's you. Don't she look good, Virginia?'

Gin nodded, smiling. It had taken her almost a decade to persuade Sheila to stop calling her Mrs Seaton, but no inducement would persuade the housekeeper to call her employer by her nick-name. 'It just don't feel right,' she always complained. Yet she ruled the house; bossing Gin around like a mother hen, lending her back copies of *Hello!*, and throwing away her secret supplies of comfort chocolates which broke the constant diet.

'You giving the girl alcohol at this time?' Sheila clucked, watching Gin tug some mint through the garden window. 'You'd rather have a nice cup of tea, wouldn't you, dear?' She shot Phoebe a shrewd look.

'Anything liquid suits me. Can I go up and see Saskia?'

'Of course.' Gin rolled her eyes. 'What am I thinking of? Poor old Saskia's bound to want you all to herself for a while. You run up and pop your head round the door, Freddy.'

Wondering if she should ask whether Felix Sylvian would be in there too, Phoebe headed towards the lobby.

'Here, take these.' Gin handed her the two glasses of frothy Pimms.

Phoebe could hear Sheila tutting as she headed through to the main hall.

'She knows then, does she?' she quacked, clearly itching for a gossip.

'Oh my God!' wailed Gin. 'I quite forgot to warn her – poor Freddy!'

Trailed by two panting dogs, Phoebe bounded two steps at a time up the huge, curved staircase with its death-trap carpet which still hadn't been properly rodded and was now as threadbare as the elbows of a schoolmaster's ratcatcher.

As a child, Phoebe had been wildly jealous of Saskia's room. Set at the front of the house with huge sash windows, it looked out over acres and acres of farmland almost to the next county. Even when Saskia went through a rebellious stage in her teens, painting the walls black and draping tie-dyed muslin mosquito nets everywhere, it had remained lighter than Phoebe's Laura Ashleyed north-facing cell at the tiny cottage her parents had owned in nearby Froxclere.

She tapped lightly on the door, but there was no answer.

'Saskia? Saskia, it's me . . . Freddy. Can I come in?'

Still no answer. Aware that being caught *in flagrante delicto* was one of Felix's fantasies that Saskia had written to her about, Phoebe cautiously pushed the door open a fraction.

The heat was stifling. As she peeked in, she could see nothing for gloom and cigarette smoke. A thin leg of light poked out between the drawn curtains.

A den of siniquity, no doubt, Phoebe thought nervously.

Then, pushed by two anxiously scrabbling dogs, she practically fell into the room.

'Saskia?' she muttered, blinking through the fug as her eyes fought to adjust. She could feel Pimms, cool, sweet and sticky, soaking through the front of her T-shirt.

Phoebe suddenly felt very gauche. Despite her letters, Saskia might still regard her as the brat out of hell. Her coming here had been Gin's idea, after all.

'Over here,' came a muffled croak from the bed.

The dogs thundered across the litter of discarded clothes and dive-bombed Saskia's duvet. Phoebe picked her way across the room more cautiously. Far from being a love den, it looked more like somewhere recently vacated by orgying rugby players. A pair of knickers wound themselves around her ankle like a cotton jellyfish as she dodged strewn tape boxes, food wrapping, magazines and Coke cans. Tripping over an electric cord, she sent a mug of cold coffee flying.

'Oh God, sorry!' Phoebe started to mop it up with a make-up-stained towel.

'Leave it.' Saskia pushed the dogs away and heaved herself upright.

Phoebe glanced up. Looking Saskia in the face for the first time in a year, she was certain she wouldn't have recognised her if they'd passed in the street. Through a haze of smoke and shadows, a sad, fat, lard-coloured face dissolved into tears.

'Sasky!' Phoebe propped herself on the side of the bed and gave her a hug.

Saskia must have put on two stone. Her hair, corded with grease, was now two-tone, the light roots inching into the black like a wasp's back. When she wriggled away from Phoebe, her eyes were tiny and bloodshot, sunken into deep shining char-coal caves from lack of sleep. Her face was almost grey. Two huge spots, attacked by savage finger nails, were the only colour on her pasty cheeks, like jam blobs in school semolina.

'I wish you hadn't come, Fred,' she sniffed, reaching shakily for her cigarette packet, although a barely smoked one was still smouldering in the brimming ashtray. 'I spent all today dread-ing it, hoping you'd miss your train. Please go back to London. I know that sounds beastly but I hate people seeing me like this.' Her face crumpled again.

'Shh,' Phoebe handed her the half-full Pimms glass and pushed the dank hair back from her friend's face so that she could take a slug. Saskia flinched away from her like a small child about to have a graze attacked by cotton wool dripping in iodine.

Phoebe was groping desperately for something adequate to

say, but found the stifling silence as impenetrable as the first slot at an Alcoholics Anonymous meeting. Instead she sat in silence, waiting for Saskia to pull herself together, wishing she was better at coping with tearful people. Beyond hugging them and locating a tissue, she'd always been a hopeless counsellor with distraught friends, cracking clumsy jokes in an attempt to cheer them up and saying all the wrong things. She couldn't stop herself staring at Saskia, appalled at the change, horribly aware of her own burning curiosity.

Saskia was wearing nothing but a tatty red towelling robe, its pulled threads giving the impression of an old fox's pelt. It reeked of stale cigarette smoke and unwashed occupancy. The chintzy duvet was coated with ash, sweet wrappers, old Sunday supplements and two trashy novels, their spines barely bent. A letter had been ripped to shreds and spread like confetti over one pillow.

The claustrophobic, airless fug began to pierce through Phoebe's temples.

'Can I open a window?'

Coughing as she lit the quivering cigarette, Saskia shrugged.

'Don't open the curtains!' she yelped as Phoebe pushed up a stubborn sash.

Phoebe leant out and breathed a heavenly lungful of warm summer air tinged with a distant tang of bonfire. At the far end of the freshly striped lawn, the crumbling brick and flint garden wall was wearing its tangles of ivy like a shredded string vest.

Giving Saskia a few seconds to recover unscrutinised, Phoebe watched as Sheila's portly husband Reg packed armfuls of privet cuttings into a composter. He'd removed his shirt to work, but his forearms and neck were so seasoned and brown compared to his pale, fleshy midriff that he looked as though he were still wearing one. As he turned back towards the house, he caught sight of Phoebe watching him and struck a mock body-builder's pose. Phoebe laughed.

'Revolting, aren't I?' Saskia's voice wobbled behind her.

Turning back, Phoebe quickly shook her head. 'Just very, very depressed,' she replied quietly, moving back towards the bed, horrified by her tactlessness.

'No wonder he dumped me,' Saskia's voice rose to a shrill whine, 'I'm utterly, utterly disgusting – rank, putrid, stinking, grubby, sour, squalid . . . disgusting!' She collapsed into a sobbing heap.

Taking her cigarette before she set light to the paper tinder littering her bed, Phoebe held her heaving, unhappy body until she stopped crying.

'What happened, Saskia?'

But Phoebe couldn't get another word out of her.

'How is she – did you have a good chat?' Gin asked hopefully when Phoebe came down with ten fingers full of mug handles.

She shook her head, setting the mugs in the largest sink with a series of clanks.

Gin sat down at the vast, pitted kitchen table and lit a cigarette, offering Phoebe one.

'I know, I promised I never would,' she apologised irritably as Phoebe refused. 'But, Christ, I need it at the moment.'

She sounded accusing, but Phoebe knew she was merely angry with herself. Once on over forty a day, she and Phoebe's mother had both made New Year's resolutions to give up about five years ago. Poppy Fredericks – hopelessly lacking in will-power – had sneaked the odd Silk Cut in the garden throughout January and finally admitted defeat when her husband bought her a packet of extra strong mints and a bottle of scent for Valentine's Day. Gin, however, had stuck to her promise without relapse.

'How long has Saskia been like this?' Phoebe asked, sinking into a paint-splattered chair beside her.

'Ever since Felix pushed off.' Gin raised her eyebrows and sighed. 'She's not always as bad as today – when I told her you were coming it sort of exacerbated the situation. You met Felix, didn't you?'

Phoebe shook her head.

'No, of course, you were away.' Gin hopped up and headed towards the dresser.

Like a fat, lofty old man stooping to avoid a beam, the

Seatons' oak dresser was the size of a double garage door and tilted forwards alarmingly. As ever, it was heaving with clutter – framed photos, unmatched crockery, rosettes, dog leads, recipe books and seed packets – so that it resembled a white elephant stall at a school fête awaiting price stickers. Gin dragged open a drawer with some difficulty and its contents sprang upwards as if breathing out. Tipping several postcards on to the floor, she extracted a silver photograph frame and took it back to Phoebe.

'The agonising thing is, we all liked him so much. There, that's at the annual Wellbeing barbecue. They looked so divine together.'

Of course, Phoebe thought, they would look spectacular. Felix, on the occasions she had glimpsed his photo in newspapers or magazines, possessed the carved-jaw elegance of some sixteenth-century knight, both devilish and seraph-like, plus those endless muscular legs just made for doublet and hose. His eyes couldn't just smoulder – they razed clothes off and made libidos spontaneously combust.

He and Saskia were standing in front of a billowing cream marquee, hot from dancing. Saskia was swathed in crotch-length chiffon layers that looked hand-woven on to her body, her purple contact lenses brimming with happiness, a huge smile showing teeth as white and even as King Wenceslas's castle grounds. Beside her, Felix Sylvian's ravishing face was animated and laughing in a way that hundreds of moody modelling shots had never shown. He was quite simply beautiful. Floppy blond hair falling over his forehead, bow tie pulled undone and dress shirt open, he looked more beddable than a twelve-tog duvet.

'Why did it end?' asked Phoebe, noticing a pile of wedding invitations spewing from the drawer which had hidden the photograph.

'Didn't Saskia tell you?' Gin looked surprised. 'I thought she might. You've always been such chums.'

Phoebe winced. Gin had no idea how much Saskia and she had once loathed each other.

'You see, none of us really knows,' Gin went on. 'She refuses to say. All I know is that he virtually begged Saskia to marry him – you know how terribly stubborn and independent she's always been, never short of dishy boyfriends. But secretly she absolutely adored him. She kept him stewing for a few weeks, but it came as no surprise when she finally accepted. Tony threw a huge party which we could ill afford – your parents came down for it; Ralph was in London at the time. Then, about a month later, Saskia and Felix flew to Italy to escape the wedding plans, came back to London for some film première, and she was here two days later, totally distraught, saying it was all over.'

'She didn't say why?'

'Not a word.' Gin stood up and started loading the mugs into the dishwasher. 'It was terribly awkward because Zoe's marriage had just fallen apart and I had her weeping around the house plus the three little monsters. Having two daughters in distress, I just couldn't cope. Tony talked to her, but he just seemed to make things worse. I suppose I rather let her get on with it.'

'And she hasn't heard from Felix since?' Phoebe asked in amazement.

'Oh, she nearly drove us all mad trying to track him down,' Gin sighed, revving up some more Pimms. 'But I gather not. And he certainly hasn't been in touch. You should see her bolting to answer the phone every time it rings or waiting like a terrier for the post. Nothing.'

She plonked a frothing glass in front of Phoebe, who was fanning herself with the unread *Upper Selbourne Parish News*. 'I'd suggest we go for a swim, but the pool is full of slime.'

Phoebe picked a piece of apple from her Pimms and sucked it thoughtfully. Everything about the Seatons seemed to be decaying.

'She looks awful, doesn't she?' Gin said sadly. 'Every morning, I find the fridge open, half its contents missing and dirty plates stacked in the sink. Tony had his cellar valued by Sotheby's last week – he was thinking of selling it – and found huge gaps. She'd been nipping down and whipping Châteaux Petrus and Latour to guzzle in her room. Such a ghastly waste.

But when I tried to confront her about it, she threw the most frightful wobbly, denying it. She hides the empty bottles in her wardrobe. I bought a whole load of cheap Sainsbury's plonk the other day in desperation, but she refuses to touch it – still pretending it's not her.'

Gin put her head in her hands, rubbing her forehead as if trying to erase the deep furrows worry had etched there.

'Has she seen a doctor?'

Gin sighed with an exasperated smile. 'He prescribed some awful tranquilliser things. One night she took eight and we were scraping her off the ceiling. Tony flushed them down the loo. The doctor suggested counselling, but she won't leave the house. When we got some ludicrously expensive psychiatrist chap in, she locked herself in the bathroom. In the end, he spent all afternoon chatting up Zoe. I think she's been out to dinner with him a couple of times.'

'Is Zoe still here?' Phoebe asked, looking at various stick-man drawings of 'Granny Double Gin' pinned to the door of the freezer with fruit-shaped magnets.

Gin shook her head. 'Thank God. Those children are un-bearably spoiled. No, she and Charles are back together because a messy divorce would blot his political copy book – he's hoping for a post in the Treasury if there's a reshuffle – but it's still very sticky.'

Phoebe tried to hide her relief. Zoe had been the most spiteful of the Seaton sisters. She'd once locked Phoebe in a stable with three angry geese, only letting her out when she promised to put cowpat on her face and be her slave for a week. Phoebe hadn't seen her for years, although Dempster occasionally mentioned her marriage problems when he had space to make up. No doubt childbirth and six years shackled to a chinless Tory MP in Buckinghamshire would have mellowed her somewhat, but Phoebe wasn't keen to test it.

Suddenly it struck her what a mistake it was to have come. Saskia's letters may have invested her with an illusion of new-found respect, but her childhood loathing and jealousy had merely been a blacker shade of the same emotion. In writing to

Phoebe, Saskia hadn't really extended the hand of friendship at long last, she'd been showing off her ring. Now the charmed life had been shattered, she wouldn't want Phoebe around to dish out pity, however much of it she felt.

'Gin, I really don't think Saskia wants me here,' she said, unable to look her in the eyes.

The pause was as sticky as Gin's jam bubbling on the Aga slow plate. Phoebe could hear Sheila whistling *Copacabana* upstairs. In the distance, a car door banged making the Jack Russell scuttle, growling furiously, into the lobby.

Gin looked at her watch. 'That'll be Reg setting off to fetch Tony,' she muttered curtly. 'If you want to go back, you'd better run out and stop him. He'll give you a lift. There's bound to be a London train soon.'

The voice was icy with contempt, and Phoebe suddenly realised why her father had always been rather intimidated by Gin. She could cut someone dead if she felt they'd let her down, switch off as abruptly as a DJ zapping a rude caller on a radio phone-in.

Phoebe heard the Range Rover start with a throaty diesel cough, but she didn't move.

'Go on then!' Gin snapped.

Phoebe wavered, unable to leave. It was like a beloved headmistress telling a pupil she was expelled. She couldn't bear the thought of Gin despising her, yet she was totally torn. Leaving now would save the agony of exposing the real truth later; the fact that Saskia probably still hated Phoebe and certainly didn't want her popping up with a tissue and a one-line-joke at her moment of grief. And Gin would undoubtedly be far more distressed to realise that the years of chummy, jolly jape-loaded, Enid Blytonesque holidays had in fact been tortuous survival missions of sleepless, tearful nights and plots to run away. Phoebe could never risk letting her discover how ghastly the Seaton girls had once been to her; Gin would be devastated.

But as Phoebe finally rose in defeat, Gin burst into noisy sobs. Frozen in amazement, Phoebe stood by the table uselessly, tears stinging her eyes. Seeing Gin cry was one of the most agonising sights in her life, as sad and unexpected as the Pope suddenly marrying La Cicciolina in a Las Vegas Elvis chapel.

'Oh God, how utterly awful of me,' Gin sobbed, leaping up and snatching some kitchen roll to blow her nose. 'I'm sorry, Freddy – this must be so embarrassing for you. We're all in such a state. I've been so worried about Saskia, but with everything else falling around our ears, I've been next to useless. She absolutely hates me now, feels I've let her down, which I have.' She blew her nose noisily and looked out of the kitchen window, fighting to regain her composure.

Phoebe opened and shut her mouth like a tapped mussel, totally helpless with confusion.

'Please stay,' Gin begged, her voice wavering in distraught tremolo. 'You're absolutely my last hope.'

Phoebe was in a sun-drenched guest room unpacking her scant luggage when Tony Seaton arrived home. Through a broderie anglaise curtain of wistaria, Phoebe watched him emerge from the Range Rover and head towards the house. She caught her breath.

She'd expected him to look thin and drawn, like Gin. He'd always been a lean man, obsessed with competitive sport and keeping his cholesterol down. But straitened times had affected him like his daughter; his Oxford stripe belly was hanging over his pin-stripe legs and the jacket of his single-breasted suit clearly wouldn't do up over his midriff. Most shocking of all was that, in the brief glimpse Phoebe had of his set face, his handsome, patrician features had completely disappeared in a red-veined expanse of flesh.

Phoebe didn't want to meet him again, intimidated by the gloom that seemed to be making the walls of the Seatons' house close in like a black and white B-movie. So she fiddled around in her room, swapping the Pimms-stained polo neck for a faded purple T-shirt, washing her newly shorn three-inch urchin's cap of hair and trying to make it look anything other than butch, and painting her toe nails crimson, which looked horribly tarty, before realising she hadn't brought any polish remover.

She needn't have worried. When Gin called her for supper, Tony wasn't in evidence.

'He's having a tray in his study tonight,' she told Phoebe rather tetchily. 'He's positively buckling under paperwork. But he sends his apologies and says he'll pop his head round the door later to say hello.'

From Gin's downcast face, Phoebe got the impression that he'd promised no such thing.

'I hope cold salmon's okay,' she apologised. 'Sheila's been too busy to cook today. Try and get Saskia to come down and eat something, will you, darling?'

But when Phoebe knocked on Saskia's door, there was no answer. She tried the handle and it was locked.

'Saskia, please come down and eat something,' she pleaded. 'We don't have to talk or anything.'

Phoebe didn't catch the muffled response.

'Sorry?'

'I said, piss off!' the voice hissed with venomous hostility. 'Fucking leave me alone.'

When she went to bed, Phoebe found a note shoved under her door. The huge, spiky writing was unmistakable.

Freddy. I can't face anyone at the moment, least of all sad bitches like you. You never liked me, so why grub around looking for gossip now? Just piss off back to London and get a life.

That night, while Phoebe snivelled like a self-pitying toddler, Saskia tried to kill herself. Had Phoebe not drunk so much wine with Gin at supper, she probably would have succeeded.

3

Gin travelled to Casualty with Saskia in the ambulance. Because Tony wasn't legally allowed to drive, Phoebe ferried him to St Luke's, Hexbury, in Gin's Golf.

Almost certain that she was still over the limit, panic and terror raging in her stomach, Phoebe's reactions felt erratic and sluggish.

It was the first time she'd spoken to Tony since arriving. Such a horrible reunion.

'You found her?' His fingers were drumming a military tattoo on the dashboard as they pelted along the deserted lanes, left far behind by the wailing ambulance.

'Yes.' Phoebe shuddered at the memory; stumbling tearfully towards the Seatons' main bathroom instead of her little guest one because she'd thought, rather childishly, that she might catch Saskia on one of her midnight feast forays and confront her about the note.

It had taken Phoebe several seconds, wavering in the door, to comprehend the scene. 'So much blood,' she kept hearing Lady Macbeth rattling histrionically in her head. 'I never knew he had so much blood in him.' And then she thought: How odd. Saskia was one of the messiest, untidiest people she knew, yet she'd cut her wrists in the bath. Totally uncharacteristic to be so thoughtful. 'A little water clears us of this deed.'

'Watch out!' Tony bellowed as a deer shot out in front of them, crossing from nettle-choked verge to verge in a split-second, its eyes shining with terror as Phoebe swerved to miss it.

She started to cry. Not huge racking sobs but a sort of frozen, shivering ache that allowed her to keep on driving as if on autopilot, the tears sliding down her cheeks, her nose running, lips quivering, knuckles white on the wheel.

They soon reached the outskirts of Hexbury. Lots of empty roundabouts to negotiate, drenched in yellow neon light which dyed the serried ranks of flowers in their centres artificial shades of sludge brown.

Tony barked the directions like a simulated voice in a car computer.

'First left, second exit, get into the right-hand lane, last exit. Christ, do you want to kill us both? Stop here. We'll swap.'

Tony, huge and bull-necked, stormed out of the car and round to the driver's door while Phoebe clambered over the gear stick.

She knew that she should have offered quiet reassurance and support, but by the time they reached the hospital, she loathed Tony and his slab-like, grey face. He seemed furious that her screaming had woken him in the middle of the night and was treating his daughter's horrific bloodshed as some sort of irritating teenage misdemeanour, like an early hours phone call from a party requesting a lift home. He wasn't the courteous, laughing, handsome man Phoebe had once wished her own father to be; he was a monster, and, full of illogical indignation, Phoebe blamed him totally for Saskia's state.

They were herded into a brightly lit waiting room, given frothy opaque coffee in plastic cups and told to wait. Gin was already there, sitting forlornly under a poster of a grinning teddy bear with a stethoscope. Tony immediately whipped out his cellphone and rang a consultant friend to try and get Saskia transferred to a private ward as soon as she'd been treated. As he paced the room, waiting for the great man to get out of bed and answer the phone, he lit a fat, stinking cigar, his jellylike chin ramming the phone into place as he struck a match.

Phoebe glowered at him and put her arm around Gin's shaking shoulders.

'She didn't come round,' Gin was muttering, her face pale grey, the frilled cuffs of her nightie sticking out of a worn old jumper as she frantically fished in them for a handkerchief. 'The paramedic kept going on about how much blood she'd lost, asking me over and over again what type she was, and I couldn't remember – it's all my fault. If she dies, it'll be all my fault. I just couldn't remember . . .'

She put her head into her hands and started to cry. Her nails were bitten almost to nothing, her fingers dry and calloused, the skin ingrained with soil from gardening.

After half an hour a harassed nurse popped her head around the door to check the Seatons were okay.

'How's my daughter?' Tony demanded, so forcefully that the girl flinched.

'They're seeing to her now,' she announced in a quaking voice.

'You mean they've only just got around to dealing with her?' Tony's voice almost seared the hessian paper from the walls. 'What sort of fucking place is this? Get the consultant in here – I want to talk to him.'

The nurse didn't move.

'Tell the man I want to see him. NOW!'

She took a slow, deliberate breath. 'She's in with your daughter, sir. If you want more coffee, there's a machine by reception. We'll let you know as soon as there's any news.'

His hackles well and truly raised, Tony kicked up such a stink that he and Gin were ushered off to see Saskia within five minutes.

After a while, for something to do, Phoebe went to get herself another coffee. Feeding twenty pence pieces into the whirring machine, she could hear a familiar voice barking into a mobile phone nearby: 'No, it's all right, Guy. Damn fool girl just scratched herself with a bit of glass. Looked far worse than it was – her friend panicked and sent us all into a bloody riot! Yup, bit of a hysterical sort. No, they're keeping her in for ob. and she'll be home tomorrow. Yeah, it is. Gin's talking to them now. Damn fools want to get the social services in and some bloody shrink. Quite. Thanks for the help anyway. Love to Helen – sorry to bother you. See you at The George next week.'

Phoebe left her coffee sitting behind the machine's plastic flap and headed for the curtained cubicles. A brusque nurse pointed her towards Saskia's.

'She's pretty heavily sedated, so don't expect much of a gossip.'

Saskia was so pale that her regulation white gown, stamped across the chest with *St Luke's* like some witty t-shirt slogan, made her skin seem almost blue. The hollows around her eyes were even darker and the whiteness of the room made her two-tone hair look even greasier.

She looked absurdly like a tennis player – the thick bandages around her wrists resembling the sweat bands tossed into the crowds by serve-volleying heroes at Wimbledon. Although the nurses had washed away as much of the blood as possible, it still stained the skin of Saskia's hands and splatters punctuated her sheets and pillow like homework marked by an angry teacher.

Yet she was strangely beautiful. Her face, lying back on the pillows, appeared slimmer; the chubbiness sinking back from long, slanting cheekbones and heart-shaped jaw. Phoebe almost recognised her again. She had a vision of Sleeping Beauty, slumbering deeply and peacefully as she waited for her prince to wake her with a kiss. Only her prince had hightailed it with an ugly sister or something, so she was left with Phoebe.

Then Sleeping Beauty ruined it all by groggily opening an eye and looking at her with unfocused eyes.

'Mummy?'

'No, it's me. Freddy. How are you feeling?' Phoebe took her hand.

'Ouch!' Saskia howled in pain as she whipped it away. 'I feel fucking lousy, what do you think?'

Phoebe bit her lip.

'What are you doing here anyway?' sighed Saskia irritably, turning her face away.

'I found you.'

'Great.' The sarcasm in her voice was slurred by drugs but nonetheless stinging. 'Didn't you get my note? I wish you'd just piss off and leave me alone.'

'Saskia . . .'

'I didn't want you to come, you know,' she went on, her voice rising shrilly. 'It was Mummy's idea. She always liked you more than me anyway. Fucking bitch! I just wanted to die – why didn't you let me die?'

She was crying now, her hands clasping at the pillows like a film heroine clutching the edge of a cliff as she slides inevitably towards her doom.

'Saskia, please – ' Phoebe put a hand on her neck. It was drenched in sweat.

'Don't touch me, you bitch!' Saskia screamed, almost falling out of bed in her attempt to get away from Phoebe.

A crisp swishing of curtains announced the arrival of the nurse.

'I think perhaps you'd better leave,' she ordered briskly. 'Miss Seaton seems to find your presence upsetting.'

Phoebe left close to tears, not understanding what she'd done to make Saskia detest her so much.

Saskia came home the next day. Bizarrely, it seemed to be something Gin and Tony dreaded. Until lunchtime on Saturday, they were more their old selves than Phoebe could have imagined. Gin even put on a bit of make-up and a stylish cream silk dress.

'From better days,' she announced airily. 'Pointless really, when the dogs will probably scrabble it to shreds, but I felt I needed cheering up. And this dress has always made me feel rather Garboesque.'

Tony scoffed cruelly at this, but his general good humour and generous dispensing of Gordon's was a vast improvement on last night's unsympathetic fury.

That changed when Gin set off to fetch Saskia. Tony stomped off to his study, gloom rising like the tide-mark on a storm-whipped cliff. Phoebe begged Gin to drop her at the station on her way to the hospital.

'Don't talk nonsense, darling.' She smiled rather tautly. 'Saskia's delighted you're here. She really needs you at the moment. I do think it would be rather selfish to scuttle off at the first true test of your friendship. Come on, Freddy – you're made of sterner stuff than that.'

She left Phoebe mouthing like an astonished goldfish. At least she hadn't asked her to go too, she thought bleakly.

4

'Sorry, darling, I'm going to have to blow you out tonight – Mitzi's come back from New York early. Terribly short notice, I know. I really hate to screw up your numbers.'

'Sure you do.' Susie Middleton wedged the phone receiver under her chin and swung the metal strap of her watch around her narrow wrist so that she could read its face. 'So can you recommend a dashing semi-detached man I can put next to Portia Hamilton at an hour's notice?'

'Nope.'

Susie rolled her eyes and snapped open her Psion without much hope.

Centring the marble ashtray on his Milan-designed coffee table, Piers Fox stood back and examined the effect, a neatly man-icured finger pressed to his lips, entranced to see it without the addition of Topaz's massed cigarette butts. After a few seconds, he crouched forwards and rotated it forty-five degrees so that it created a geometrical contrast to the square, granite-topped table. He then flipped the matchbooks upright and into a fan so that they revealed their exclusivity – Bibendum, Quaglino's, Daphne's and The Ivy.

Momentarily satisfied, he sank back on to his white hessian sofa, hooked one silk-socked ankle across the other knee and shook out the pink section of yesterday's *Evening Standard*.

When his American wife was away, Piers delighted in his own

pedantry and perfectionism – luxuries Topaz took equal delight in undermining when in situ.

Although the finished result was stunning and much-envied, Piers occasionally wished his lusting, resentful friends could see the by-products created to get Topaz Fox on the road. Catering packs of cotton wool, tissues and baby buds would be left swimming and swelling in the steamy, flooded bathroom along with towels treading water and blonde hairs wrapped around the soap, toothpaste, shampoo bottle and lavatory seat. Clothes were left furled and crumpled like a slain couture army on the floors of both dressing room and bedroom; padded hangers lay in a tangled mass by the bed; shoes – seldom in pairs – footprinted their way from room to room. And an asphyxiating cloud of Panthère would linger at ankle level, like the rising vapour of a swamp. Topaz called it 'layering' her scent. As far as Piers could tell, this required a layer of the stuff to be in continual, miasmic view while she got ready to go out.

Yet there was something erotic and eerie in her ability to re-invent herself from scrawny, ribby schoolgirl into shimmering, slithering Lorelei with the application of cosmetics that cost triple figures per ounce and had to be Fed-Expressed from Macy's. And Piers found it doubly exciting when, at the end of the night, the sex siren wiped herself away with yet more elixir-soaked cotton wool and the schoolgirl climbed into his bed.

The phone rang but Piers didn't look up from the *Standard*, letting the machine pick it up instead. Disappointment that it wasn't Topaz tightened his pulse-points like manacles. He half listened to one of the minor celebrities on his books rant tearfully that all Piers had set up for him recently was a vox pop soap powder commercial and a slot on The Big Breakfast's Handy Tips. Thankfully, the machine cut him off after thirty seconds.

Piers glanced up at the wooden ceiling, staring at a spot-light for so long his eyes started to water. Topaz had been away three days and had not called him once. Hardly surprising, he reflected. Their last conversation – if it was possible to call a twenty-minute monologue broken by the occasional 'But,

Topaz . . .' such a thing – had left his ears ringing like an unanswered phone. Topaz, when angry, had a disconcerting ability to paint the air blue, her nails pink and the town red simultaneously.

'I wanna baby, Foxy,' she had announced rather suddenly and horrifically on the morning of her departure to do a French *Elle* editorial shoot in New Orleans.

'What, my darling?' Piers had bided his time as he shaved, but found spots of blood appearing through his light beard of foam like first shots in the October Massacre.

'A little baby. Everyone's having them now,' Topaz explained as if she were discussing a skirt length or haircut.

'Really?' Piers tried not to catch her eye in the mirror.

She'd just climbed out of the shower and deliberately allowed the dark red towel to slip from beneath her elbows. Her slender, waifish body, oiled with wet droplets, slithered around the bathroom as she collected chemicals for phase two of her morning ablutions. White-blonde hair lay like a thick rope of wet satin down her back-bone, dropping between the pronounced shoulder blades so that the end, neatly banged like a horse's tail, dripped water on to the small of her back.

'I've thought all about it, honey,' Topaz went on dreamily, stretching her hands behind her neck and rolling her head. 'I wanna little girl called Velvet. It won't stop my career – Yasmin le Bon still models and she's always whipping out Pampers.'

'What about all the travelling you do, darling?' Piers pointed out smoothly, although one hand clutched the chrome Conran washbasin with knuckles as white as his flashing teeth.

'Hell, Foxy, once I get some really decent acting work, I won't have to worry so much,' Topaz said dismissively, squatting down to attack a manicured toe nail with scissors. 'I'll structure my movie schedule around Velvet, like Demi Moore or Phoebe Cates. And you can look after her, too, honey. After all, you work so much from home. Wouldn't it be just great? You didn't get the chance for real early paternal bonding with your other kids.'

Cleaning his razor blade in frothy water and chewing his

bottom lip to pull flat his chin, Piers rolled his eyes in despair, then, noticing Topaz watching him, hastily pretended that he had an eyelash in one.

Earlier that year, he'd finally given in to her goading and secured Topaz a couple of screen tests for small, deferred payment continental films. Both directors had phoned him afterwards and asked if it was his idea of a joke, to which Piers had steelily pointed out that he didn't have a sense of humour as it wasted time. Unable to tell Topaz, he had been forced to pretend that both projects had folded.

Piers's real fear, however, lay on the fourth floor of Harrods, a shop called the White House and in the windows of Mothercare. Babies frightened him more than spiders, heights and dirt. The idea of producing more children brought large beads of nervous sweat bubbling to the surface of his forehead and made his heart pump so fast that the spots of blood in his shaving foam started to join together. He already forked out crippling maintenance on his three children from two previous marriages, and had fought an expensive paternity suit on a fourth from a long-term girlfriend in the States. The wondrous, exciting glow of becoming a father had lasted only until the first sleepless night with Piers's first-born and hadn't re-emerged since, despite the birth tanks, nannies, Mozart quartets and video cameras subsequent births had in attendance to entice him. At forty-three and in possession of a higher cholesterol level than a battery hen-house, he guessed that repeating the nappy-filling, teething and potty-training process stood every chance of being life-threatening.

'Velvet will be my best friend,' Topaz announced blissfully, reasserting a long-standing fear Piers had that all women metamorphose into trainee mothers-in-law during their first labour. 'We'll wear the same clothes. Do you think Yves would design her a little dress, Foxy? Wouldn't that be a scream?' She started massaging her scalp with essential oil and lavender water, her huge amber eyes tipped up serenely like a praying first year in a convent school.

Topaz was just twenty and, Piers felt, far too young to be

getting broody. He assumed that her maternal fervour was part of the latest craze echoing through the modelling world.

'Paula Yates has just brought out a great new post-natal exercise video,' she carried on, ignoring his stricken face. 'And Mommy really wants us to start a family.'

Realising the Shelzners were in on the baby pitch, Piers nearly passed out. The thought of the combined force of Topaz's twenty-stone mother, and undoubtedly Pa Shelzner as well, making him have a sperm count, take out an account with Hamley's, register with pre-Montessori and take Topaz's temperature daily, gave him the same instant shrinking sensation in his underpants as the prospect of a communal shower with the West Indian cricket team. What she told him next turned the shower freezing cold and gave the Old Trafford audience, including both his ex-wives and their new partners, a full frontal view.

'You what?'

'I haven't been using contraception for two months, honey.' Topaz vigorously rubbed green gel into her forehead, afterwards breaking a small pink capsule and dabbing its oily contents around her eyes. 'I wanted it to be a surprise.'

'You mean you're already pregnant?'

'Who knows?' she chirruped, her gold eyes sparkling with excitement. Then she pushed out her plump bottom lip and cocked her head winningly. 'You *do* want us to have a little baby, don't you, Foxy?'

Piers took a deep breath and told her that no, he wasn't sure if he did. Not this year, anyway. Not, he thought privately, until he'd found a bloody good vasectomy clinic.

That was when the storm broke. Topaz spun around the flat like a clothes-collecting tempest as she threw boxes of cosmetics, laundry-serviced shirts and endless Calvin Klein undies into her leather suit-carrier. All the time her beautiful, hornet-stung mouth yakked, whinged and spluttered expletives, wails, shrieks, whines, sobs and threats like a spoilt child told for the twentieth time that she can't have eight ponies and Luke Perry for Christmas.

It was an enormous relief when Piers had spotted her furtively shoving a week's supply of Tampax beneath a pile of tissue-wrapped Joseph leggings. She'd left with reddened eyes and no kiss, kicking over his favourite rare six-foot cactus before she slammed the door.

Now the sexual anticipation that usually dug into his loins like Deep Heat on a groin injury when she was away working was strangely absent. He'd hoped to feel immensely relieved at having the flat to himself for once, without a working dinner or celebrity networking bash to attend. But instead he was feeling bored and restless.

He put on a Billie Holiday CD which he knew Topaz would have hated (Puccini and INXS were the only vogue sounds on the circuit at the moment), and wandered over to the huge floor-to-ceiling window that stretched the entire length of the flat, broken only by narrow metal uprights and the nautical running rail at waist height.

In front of him, London stretched out into a heat haze, metalwork and windows glimmering in the evening sun like the tacky gilt embossing on the cheap postcards sold from kiosks opposite Buckingham Palace. The lengthening square shadow of his building bobbed on the surface of the Thames, breaking the shifting cross-hatches of sunlight. Taller than those on either side, it stretched like a bullish boxer's head beyond broad, square shoulders of neighbouring blocks. To the left, the shadow cast by the first pointed roof of Tower Bridge stretched almost as far as the base of the second tower, and tourists in an open-topped bus were craning out to gape down at a boat full of tourists gaping back up at them from the river below.

Piers had bought the Shad Thames warehouse conversion after his second marriage fell apart in the mid eighties, but before realising how much money the divorce settlement would pare off his bank statements. During the following years, he had watched its value escalate with far more pleasure than his children's growth brought him. And he still loved it now, despite the fact that his would-be Canary Wharf had become a great, yellow albatross around his neck. It was inconvenient as he no longer worked in the City floating films on to the markets to secure backing, but within the entertainment industry itself, working from a tiny office off Wardour Street. Yet, as he stared across the Square Mile, he knew he was happier with its jabbing geometrics than the curving, elegant terraces and leafy squares of the glitterati's favourite postcodes.

Even though it was a Friday night, Piers sank down at the wicket-length blackwood dining table and snapped open his portable Macintosh before firing it up. He could feel the familiar tightening of his neck tendons, as if they were being cranked in on a pulley, and a nervous spurt of adrenaline shot like neat caffeine into his bloodstream. He knew he needed a very big deal very quickly or his company's udders would be pointing at the clouds. He was currently living off the crumbs of publicising soap stars and politicians' mistresses, much as he had been since setting the company up three years earlier. He'd signed up some terrific talent during that time, but either they were too unknown to be risked across the Atlantic, bringing in bread and butter from BBC dramas and continental mini-series, or they were poached from him by bigger, established, usually American, agencies the moment Piers kick-started their careers; Hollywood, having grown bored with rebellious tattooed New Yorkers, was currently lusting after Merchant Ivory types, brattish British blue-bloods with pretty faces.

Topaz's income was currently paying the mortgage and, if she really persisted in the acting-and-having-babies phase, their only means of survival would be for Piers to clinch a really huge deal with one of his naive unknowns whom he could screw an enormous cut from.

The first file he accessed brought a smile to his face for the first time in several days. It was Felix Sylvian's.

Piers heard his phone ringing twice before the machine picked it up, but didn't bother to cross the room. All his business associates knew that he worked by returning calls when he had time, or that – if it was urgent – they could catch him on his mobile.

The phone rang again and was picked up by the machine.

Within seconds the pattern repeated and went on for over a minute. Someone was simply pressing their redial button.

Unable to concentrate on the screen in front of him, Piers cursed and crossed the room. It must be Topaz – probably keen to continue the baby argument. He'd have to pretend he was going out. Gazing back at the computer screen as he picked up the phone, he almost wished he was.

'Yes?' he snapped.

'Piers?'

'Yes?'

'It's Susie Middleton.'

'Who?'

'Elect Models.'

'Oh, yes. Yes, of course.' Piers hooked his fingers under the phone and carried it back to his computer. 'Is this urgent?'

'Yes – am I catching you at a bad time?' Susie's voice was deep and merry, the sort that made business contacts lean into their phones.

Piers looked out across shimmering London and wondered when wasn't a bad time. Billie Holiday had sung her compact disc swansong and the flat suddenly felt clinical and empty without Topaz slithering into a sofa and lighting a cigarette. One of the reasons he adored their combative relationship so much, her constantly trying to distract him from his work and make him notice her, was because they invariably ended up in bed. And these days, sex revitalised Piers's flagging enthusiasm for his work far more than a coffee break.

'Look, I know this is seriously short notice, but are you free tonight?'

Piers turned 'no' into an inaudible grunt and thought about it. It would make a welcome change to be bought dinner for once, instead of yanking out the corporate Amex after signing a deal on a napkin which would fall through the following day.

'Why?'

'Because I want you to flirt with someone.'

Now that was even more welcome.

*   *   *

Portia Hamilton noticed him immediately and prayed that he was there for her.

Arriving later than she'd planned because she always forgot how far away from the Fulham Road Totteridge was, she entered Susie's sumptuous yellow-stripe drawing room just as the six or so couples were chasing the ice around their second gin and tonics and talking loudly enough to disguise the sound of rumbling stomachs. Standing to one side of the huge open fireplace, looking both aloof and gloriously indifferent to the twittering, glittering small-talk, was a devastatingly attractive man.

Giving her a hug and a huge drink, Susie swept Portia into a group of gushing PR types, but Portia remained curiously aware of his presence, one corner of her eye scanning his outline like a grazing impala aware of a leopard stretched out on a distant rock. Tall, angular and impeccably dressed in a dark suit and waistcoat, he had a lustrous mane the colour of rain-soaked October bracken and a glorious beaky nose. His eyes – huge, dark and focused – watched the face of the man he was talking to as if he were a method actor absorbing research. His companion was classic media: redframed spectacles, bright blue jacket and tie loud enough to be seen by satellite. The red-haired man reminded Portia of a champion red setter at Crufts – arrogant, groomed, admired and very aware of it – standing next to the bow-decked toy dog in reserve.

Just as Portia was describing what she did for the fifth time to an eager Chanel-wearing fashion columnist, the introduction came.

'Portia, I don't think you've met Piers Fox, have you?' Susie raked back her bobbed blonde curls and put one hand on Piers's shoulder, her gold bangles jangling. He stiffened almost imperceptibly. 'Piers, this is a gorgeous chum of mine, Portia Hamilton. She thinks up features and interviews for *Élan*, so be very nice to her. Piers is a startlingly clever agent, Portia – he represents everyone from movie stars to industry chiefs, making sure they're either always in the papers or never in them, depending who his client is.'

Creasing her eyes at them both, Susie backed away to check on the situation in the kitchen.

'So you're a publicist?' Portia asked, watching his eyes. They were utterly mesmerising: dark, bottle green and as cold as verdigris marble.

'Of sorts.' He looked over her shoulder and squinted against her cigarette smoke. 'I represent mostly actors, for work as well as just publicity.'

'So do you spend lots of evenings scouting for talent at theatres?'

'No.' Piers glanced at her as quickly as he would flick his gaze over a hopeful's ten-by-eight that came with the morning post. He noticed that her blonde hair, wound into a tight chignon which pulled at her cheeks like a new facelift, had been streaked almost white at the front to look sun-bleached.

'Theatrical work doesn't interest me,' he explained, wincing at the fussy striped walls, 'although I do have some contact. I work almost totally within television and film. My business is three-quarters PR, the rest agency.'

'Isn't that unusual?' Portia noticed a slight mid-Atlantic twang lightening the drone of his deep, dry voice.

'In this country, unique.' Piers gazed out of the window, across to Totteridge Green where couples walking dogs and toddlers were clutching bags of breadcrumbs as they headed towards the little pond in the last, slanting rays of sunlight.

'Is it an idea you picked up from the States?'

'No, I thought it up myself.' Piers glanced at her with mild irritation.

'Fox is a wonderfully apt surname.' Portia, torn between annoyance and fascination, felt she was coaxing blood out of a stony silence.

'Yes?' Piers raised a red eyebrow without interest. This line of conversation was guaranteed to make him crabby.

Portia laughed edgily. 'With that glorious titian hair, you're just born to persuade people. Are you sly, Piers Fox?'

'No.' He downed his mineral water and then looked across to

the door, where Susie was hanging half-in and half-out, having a gossip with one of her guests.

Christened plain Peter Fowler, Piers loathed the thought of anyone finding out that he'd changed his name by deed poll while at university. In the early seventies – a time when children were being named Amber, Sorrel, Jet and Jade – Fox had seemed rather a witty and striking second name. Now Piers deeply regretted it.

'Oh.' Portia's huge grey eyes dropped from scrutinising his hooded gaze and she ran a manicured nail around the rim of her glass.

Oh God, I'm supposed to be chatting her up, Piers thought miserably. He wished he hadn't come out now. The moment he'd walked through Susie Middleton's door, she'd lynched him with a business enquiry about Felix Sylvian. Felix was still under contract to one of Susie's clients, a German design house, for whom he was facing a cologne ad campaign. Not that he really counted as a professional model: he worked so seldom and for such high fees. A spoilt, infuriating dilettante like his father, he relied on his charm, looks, money and boundless enthusiasm to propel him through every heavily guarded door to the bouncy castle of privilege, jumping happily over far more worthy hopefuls' feet, which had been wedged in there for years. The tabloid press seemed to love him; the big ad agencies, the top photographers, high-flying marketing directors and the best magazine editors still lusted after him. Now the Germans wanted to shoot their Christmas commercial and Felix was stalling because Piers had said he'd got work lined up for him. He hadn't. Piers had been deliberately evasive to Susie, but felt jittery.

Turning back, he studied Portia Hamilton without interest. She was in her late-twenties, he guessed – although she had the nervous, quivering manners of a schoolgirl desperately out of her depth in her first pub. She was exceptionally slim – her shoulders had shadowy hollows and creamy peaks of bone – and her strappy green silk dress barely seemed to touch her flesh as it dropped in a lightly tailored curve the length of her body.

Her gamine face was dominated by huge expressive eyes with long, sooty lashes that curled like gift-wrap ribbon. She had a refined, slightly Roman nose and the broad, intelligent sort of mouth that Piers always associated with French New Wave film heroines who spent a lot of time arguing voraciously in black and white, lounging beneath a crumpled sheet in bed and inserting endless unfiltered Disque Bleu between white teeth.

Although undoubtedly attractive, she was not Piers's type – too bright, nervy and fragile, clearly in need of bolstering flattery and charm, neither of which he was adept at.

'Known Susie long?' he asked gruffly, wondering how long it would be until he could politely refuse coffee and shoot home on the pretence of phoning Australia.

Portia looked up at him, her eyes blinking thoughtfully. It suddenly occurred to Piers that she hadn't, as he'd assumed, been gazing at the ground in chastened, shy embarrassment at his abruptness. She looked as though her thoughts had been leagues away, dwelling on some deep distraction.

'Years,' Portia admitted, then dropped her voice. 'Although it seems to shorten these days with each telling, depending on how much Susie and I are knocking off our ages.'

Piers almost smiled.

'My sister Zoe and she were in the same year at school together,' Portia went on. 'Susie used to roll up in the holidays wearing cheesecloth caftans and twelve-inch platforms. My father caught us all smoking a spliff in the potting shed once and somehow – God alone knows exactly, because he was really hopping – she persuaded him to share it with her. He couldn't talk for two days. Claimed it was laryngitis. She's marvellous.'

Piers flashed a stiff smile. Schoolgirl pranks in the potting shed were about as far detached from his childhood as *Brideshead Revisited* from an Emile Zola novel.

Realising his discomfort, Portia quickly turned the conversation to the more inane topic of an impending royal wedding. But Piers merely glazed over even more – his interest in royalty being restricted to helping the odd author publicise an unauthorised biography.

'*Élan*'s a society magazine, isn't it?' he butted in, deliberately sounding as though he'd barely heard of it before tonight.

'I suppose you could say that,' Portia replied carefully, guessing his back was coming up faster than a mule with a new saddle.

'Lots of pictures of aristos' weddings and features on Dai Llewellyn's latest pranks.' Piers raised a withering rusty eyebrow. 'Does it sell any copies other than to Kensington dentists for their waiting rooms?'

'None.' Portia's lips curled into a tight smile, 'That's why it's published quarterly, so there's a new issue out for every check-up.'

As soon as another media couple drifted up to swap gossip, she escaped to the kitchen to roll her eyes at Susie.

'So?' Susie looked up from whisking olive oil and balsamic vinegar, her face flushed with effort. She blew blonde curls from her nose.

Portia nicked a roasted cherry tomato from the salad and groaned. 'I thought you said he was Croesus, Hyperion and Dennis Quaid all rolled into one? He strikes me as more like Neil Kinnock in a toupee.'

Susie giggled. 'I'm afraid the Greek god cocktail, Dan, had to back out at the last minute. Piers is his replacement.'

'Don't tell me he's gay!' Portia howled, waggling a cauliflower floret.

'No.' Susie poured the dressing over the salad, then cursed. 'Shit! I wasn't supposed to do that till the last minute – now it'll go soggy.' She sucked her finger and looked back at Portia. 'But I'm afraid he's married. Then again,' she grinned wickedly, 'so was Dan.'

Portia groaned. 'You've decided I'm so desperate, I'm destined to be a significant other woman, haven't you?'

Susie shrugged. 'All the loveliest men are married – it's a fact.'

'Yours is,' Portia lit a cigarette. 'Ernest the Enigma.'

'He's not called Ernest,' Susie sighed, accustomed after so many years of prying from Portia to protect the man she refused to name. 'Look, you know I don't condone pursuing married men per se. It's just that – '

'So he's called Percy?' Portia grinned between nervous puffs. 'And you just want some other lonely divorcée to share Christmases and weekends with?'

Susie narrowed her eyes for a split second then laughed. 'Actually I'm seeing him this weekend. We've got a Sunday morning assignation.'

'Gosh, how sordidly exciting. Do tell more.'

But Susie's eyes dropped to her soggy salad with her usual secrecy and she hastily changed the subject. 'Do you really hate Piers that much?'

'He looks divine,' Portia admitted, 'but so icy cool he could go undercover as a halibut on ice in Billingsgate market.'

'Chat him up.' Susie removed Portia's cigarette and threw it into the waste disposal.

'What!'

'Seduce him over dinner, I dare you. Dinner at Quag's if you succeed.'

'I have no desire to be humiliated, thanks.'

'You won't, and you'd be doing me a massive favour.' Susie flashed her wickedest grin. 'I'd love to have a bit on the side in reserve when it comes to Mr Wily Fox. He's proving a pain in the neck to persuade to relinquish Fe— one of my biggest earners.'

'Fuck off! I'm not some strumpet pulled out for a bit of Cold Fish War blackmailing,' Portia hissed.

'And besides,' Susie carried on, ignoring her, 'you fancy him like mad. It's written all over you – like a Moschino dress.'

As ever, Susie had invited too many people to fit comfortably in her cosy elm-panelled dining room. But no one seemed to mind as they sidled laughing around the six-inch gap between the table and the wall, knocking picture frames into jaunty angles and prising themselves into seats like contortionists folding their bodies into wine casks. Chairs had been brought in from other rooms to pack fourteen people around the long Victorian mahogany table which was almost buckling under its weight of colourful Heal's tableware and fat, flickering candles in wrought iron holders.

Piers was crammed into a squat leather-backed side chair which left him feeling like a dwarf between the Chanel-decked columnist and Portia Hamilton, who were sitting on normal-height dining chairs. Space was so tight that their arms continually interlocked like Scottish dancers as they reached for glasses of wine or pieces of bread. At the opposite end of the table, the blue-jacketed media man reached for a candle to light his fag and knocked over a glass of wine to shrieks of laughter.

'By the time we've eaten all your delicious grub, Suse, we'll be wedged in for a fortnight,' he hooted.

Piers bristled, immensely uncomfortable. He loathed people who smoked between courses, and there was absolutely no sign of any mineral water on the table, just enough bottles of Chablis to float a full oil tanker.

'You've got breadcrumbs on your chin,' Portia whispered into his ear, her eyes still facing front like a guardsman chatting on duty.

'Thanks.' Piers wiped them away angrily with his napkin.

'Are you all right? You seem terribly tense,' she said in a low voice, putting her thin elbow on the table and resting finger and thumb against her forehead as she turned to face him. The gesture pulled one pale eyebrow up into an almost caricatured look of enquiry.

Piers stared at her, amazed by her impudence. She had disturbingly clever eyes, he noticed, that could look haunted one moment and mirthful the next.

'I could have asked you the same thing earlier,' he said huffily. 'You were firing questions at me like Walden.'

Portia laughed and fingered her wine glass. 'First knight nerves,' she muttered, smiling to herself. 'I always get them.'

'What?'

'I was nervous because I find you extremely attractive,' she said honestly, her huge grey eyes not flickering from his, 'and I was trying to figure out whether your complete disinterest was hiding the fact you felt the same way about me, or just because you think I'm a neurotic spare thirtysomething?'

Piers didn't flinch, his face completely shuttered, like a Manchester corner shop. 'And have you made up your mind?'

'I'm about to,' she murmured, looking up and smiling as Susie brought in the first course to flattering whoops.

Some time between the wild watercress soup and steamed turbot, Portia Hamilton slipped her hand between the thighs of the man on her left. It wasn't in itself an original advance; restaurants and dining rooms throughout London are filled with people eating with their right hands and determinedly not looking at the person to their left. But Portia's fingers were so practised and so delicate, they could have been reading Anais Nin in Braille as they traced their way up Piers' inner thigh. As her nail bumped up the teeth of his fly zip and then drew it down by the metal tongue, she popped a nugget of bread into her mouth with her right hand and talked to the PR girl opposite about the difficulty of fitting an Aga into a first-floor flat.

Piers made no acknowledgement of the action at all, but by the time the red fruit salad was completing a second circuit, he was picking at his food like a vegetarian at a pig-roast. He didn't refuse coffee and bolt home to phone the Southern Hemisphere. Instead he drew the heat of the froth through his front teeth, looked at the woman on his right and shivered. The last time he'd been picked up was when his mother waited at the school gates; he had never, in twenty-seven years' active sex life, been seduced by a stranger. The feeling of helplessness and squirming excitement was not altogether pleasant but it was utterly intoxicating, like the first downward plunge of a ferris wheel.

Smiling at him, Portia asked if he had a busy week ahead. Piers watched her red tongue moving between curling pink lips and cool white rows of teeth, and wanted to taste them all.

'Very busy,' he replied gruffly.

Turning away, Portia removed her hand from his crotch and selected a cherry from the untouched, uncollected bowl in front of her. She sucked its tip thoughtfully, nodding sympathetically as the man to her right whinged about taxi drivers who thought taking a fare to Richmond was as troublesome as ferrying someone to John O'Groats via Lizard Point. Starting to tell him a story about getting a cab to Heathrow on a Bank Holiday, she nibbled the end off the cherry between sentences.

As Piers fought to regain his composure and fumbled to do up his zip unnoticed, the Chanel-wearing columnist to his left tapped him on the arm and asked him what he thought of the future of the British film industry. Whipping his hand back on to the table, Piers took a breath to answer and then suddenly gulped a second one, filling his lungs to near-explosion point.

The moist, bitten end of cherry had just been inserted through the still-open flies of his trousers and his underpants and was being rolled very slowly around the tip of his penis.

Piers swallowed and gazed at the two rather bloodshot eyes looking enquiringly at him.

'Do you think deferred payment films are the answer?' the woman asked helpfully as the cherry slid down the thick, taut vein at the back of his cock.

'No,' Piers finally answered with a loud gasp, as enough compressed air to keep a diver underwater for a day burst out of his lungs.

Getting to the part of the story where she and her fellow passenger had jumped out of the taxi on the M4 hard shoulder, Portia deftly removed the cherry and popped it in her mouth.

'Piers . . .' she said in a throaty whisper, her eyes again performing their guardsman out-front routine.

'Yes?' he croaked, praying she hadn't brought her car with her and needed a lift home.

'I hope you don't mind my saying,' interrupted the columnist in a far louder whisper, which caused the chattering table to hush very slightly, like the muting effect of the fire curtain going up in a theatre, 'but your flies are undone. Thought you'd like to know.' Hiccuping slightly, she lurched off to the loo, knocking three paintings off the wall and upturning her coffee cup with her quilted handbag as she went.

Puce in the face, Piers fought to pull the zip over his erect crotch and scraped in his chair so that his stomach was flat against the table.

Biting back amusement, Portia caught Susie's eye. Four blonde eyebrows shot up as they exchanged a momentary look only very old friends would be able to decipher.

'Have you brought a car?' Piers asked Portia, picking up on the guardsman trick as his dark green eyes scrutinised a guttering candle in the centre of the table.

'No,' she whispered, shooting his pulse into triple figures. She selected another cherry and popped it into her mouth. 'I'm being collected at midnight. I'm catching the first flight to Milan.'

'On a Saturday?' Piers' voice was hoarse with disappointment.

'I'm going to lunch.' Portia smiled, delighted with her lie. She was planning to spend tomorrow in the flat, not eating, doing sit-ups, applying fake tan and shaving every inch of her body except a three-by-three-by-two triangle. Then she would phone Susie and get her to tell her absolutely everything she knew about Piers Fox and – if she was feeling brave enough – his wife.

As hefty brandies started prompting rowdy anecdotes from Susie's guests like a post-prandial truth drug, Piers drew a silver ball-point pen from his jacket and wrote three numbers on one of Susie's exquisite linen napkins. One was his office, one was his home and the third was his mobile. Each was accompanied by a range of times and days neatly contained within swirly brackets.

Portia took the napkin, dabbed her French New Wave heroine's lips and dropped it on to her lap with a happy smile. The temptation to wink at Susie was almost too much to bear. Instead she picked up a chocolate mint and nibbled it as she turned to the man on her right for a chummy chat about the forthcoming royal wedding.

At midnight, Susie's guests still hadn't moved away from the table. Fingering empty coffee cups and replenished brandy glasses, they chattered and cackled, arranging lunches they would have to cancel the moment they consulted their diaries. They picked wax off the encrusted candlesticks, roaring with laughter and shrieking with delight as they gossiped loudly, squeezing one another's knees, arms and occasionally cheeks to emphasise points. Ties, belts and tongues had been loosened, more wine had been fetched and it was clearly set to be a long night, as Susie's parties always were.

A loud buzz in the hall signalled that someone was outside the drive gates.

'Susie, darling, I must go – that'll be my cab,' Portia stood up to leave, kissing the man on her right before popping another dark chocolate in her mouth and stretching across to kiss Susie on both cheeks.

Turning to Piers, she held out her hand.

Piers shook it, gazing into her intelligent grey eyes and longing more than anything to follow her out and kiss her to near-suffocation, to press her narrow frame up against Susie's white walls with the entire length of his body and beg for her to come home with him. But he was far too proud, and far too frightened.

'It was lovely to meet you, Piers,' she murmured, stooping down and planting a cool kiss on his mouth.

At first, Piers thought she'd slipped her tongue between his lips and almost passed out with shivering excitement. But, as Portia straightened up and slid past him, he tasted mint and found his tongue wrapped around one of Susie's soft, melting after-dinner chocolates.

5

Sunday morning brought a storm crackling towards the Seatons' house from the east. As thunder hammered around the valley, Phoebe stayed in bed as long as possible, her duvet pulled up to her ears. Bad dreams riddled her half-conscious mind, obscured and distorted, like the view from the Gods.

By the time she made it downstairs, Gin was back from church and shovelling dry dog food into five huge ceramic bowls in the kitchen, watched by ten eager brown eyes above five drooling mouths.

'Saskia up yet?' she asked.

'I don't know,' Phoebe confessed.

'Oh, be a duck and check for me, would you?' Gin kicked the terrier away. 'Piss off, Tebbit, you're on a diet, little man. See if she wants to be included in lunch, would you? Tell her it's Beef Alexander. And Portia's coming down for the evening so that should be fun.' Something in her tone indicated nerves frayed to a laddered mesh.

Reluctantly, Phoebe trailed back upstairs. She approached Saskia's door fully expecting it to be bolted and electrified. Instead, as she knocked and tried the handle, it swung open. The smell of cigarette smoke, rancid food and unwashed skin was worse than ever, but this time the curtains were partly drawn, letting in shafts of dusty grey light. The room looked even more of a tip when illuminated, every surface littered with debris, dust, stains and ash like Miss Havisham's wedding table. But Saskia wasn't in there.

In a panic, Phoebe sprinted to the bathroom. She wasn't there either.

'Christ!' She rubbed her short hair in anguish as she wandered back out on to the landing, debating whether to raise the alarm, or whether Tony Seaton would say she was over-reacting and tell her to get a grip.

'I'm in here.'

Phoebe swung around to her right and noticed Saskia sitting on the bed in her own little guest room. She was wearing a pair of faded leggings, burst on the inside seams, and a long, shapeless black jumper, its sleeves pulled down over the bandages on her wrists. Her greasy hair was scraped back from her face with a rubber band from which rats' tails were already escaping. Yet the ghost of beauty still haunted her face. Her eyes, as wide and blue and liquid as distant lakes in an Austrian mountainscape, raked Phoebe's face.

Almost hollow with relief and compassion, she rushed forward, but Saskia held out her arm like a furious Milan traffic cop.

'Don't!' she howled, then lowered her voice an octave. 'Don't start crawling all over me with huggy, insincere questions and sympathy. I can't cope with it.'

'Okay.' Phoebe wavered in the doorway and asked quietly, 'What would you like me to do?'

'Sit over there.' Saskia jerked her head towards a narrow sofa under the window.

Feeling anger tugging at the tendons in her neck, Phoebe did as she was told.

'Your mother wants to – '

'I don't give a shit what the old bag wants,' Saskia snapped, pulling a cigarette out of the packet so violently it snapped. She tossed it irritably across the room so that it landed in one of Phoebe's discarded boots, and lit another. 'I want to talk to you.'

Not trusting herself to reply, she raised an eyebrow enquiringly.

'You know I didn't want you to come, don't you?' Saskia picked up Phoebe's sponge bag and nosed inside.

'You've made that pretty clear, yes,' she answered carefully.

'God knows why you bothered – I mean, I tried to stop you.' Saskia examined a tube of Rembrandt toothpaste moodily. 'And it's not as if we were ever really friends, as such.'

'No.' Phoebe thought about their recent letters, the scandalous confidences, gossip and glorious chatty descriptions, and bit her lip. Then she remembered back to their schooldays and to Saskia's spiteful, bullying hatred. The recollection made her shudder, suddenly feeling vulnerable and picked-upon again.

'Well, I've changed my mind.' Saskia drew out a Guerlain eye-liner and tested it on her arm, the cigarette dangling between her sulky lips. 'I'm glad you're here now.'

'Thank you.' Phoebe's sarcasm scorched across the carpet like a line of ignited gunpowder.

'Yes.' Saskia ignored it. 'I've decided you could be useful. I want to employ you.'

'You what?' Phoebe almost fell off the sofa in appalled amazement.

'I want you to do a job for me.' Saskia's voice was starting to waver, but she took a deep, shuddering breath and carried on. 'I've got money, you know. I can pay you. I realise Daddy must look washed up – I mean with the business floundering and this place for sale and everything. But I still have a private income.'

'The house is for sale?' Phoebe repeated in a whisper, not because she didn't believe it, but because it was taking several seconds to sink in.

'Of course, you've been away – you wouldn't know about the Seatons' steady decline.' Saskia stood up cumbersomely and shuffled over to a wastepaper basket to flick her cigarette. 'Daddy needs some cash assets to pay off debts. He's offering this place through his London office but no one's in the slightest bit interested in great freezing tombs like this at the moment. There simply aren't those sort of cash-rich buyers around any more. Just as well, he hasn't got round to telling Mummy yet.'

Poor Gin! Phoebe rubbed her temples. Parting with her beloved garden would be like cutting off a limb.

'Anyway, we're not talking about Daddy's problems,' Saskia said sharply, 'we're discussing my offer.'

'Offer?' Phoebe was finding it harder and harder to take in what she was saying.

'The job.' Saskia, flicking the cigarette continually with her thumbnail, turned her head away so that Phoebe couldn't see her face. She shambled across the room to close the door.

'What exactly is it you want me to do?' Phoebe asked.

Saskia was standing by the door in silence now, her forehead resting against it, fingers clutching her greasy hair as she battled not to break down.

'I want – ' Her voice, almost a whisper, disappeared into a series of gasping breaths.

Phoebe felt any traces of anger dissolve. She stood up and walked to Saskia's side.

'What?' she coaxed gently. 'What do you want me to do?'

'I want – no, I can't ask you. I want . . .' Saskia suddenly started sobbing; streaming, unstoppable tears that flooded down her cheeks. She looked up at Phoebe, her eyes tortured. 'I want you to seduce Felix for me.'

'What?' Phoebe gaped at her in bewilderment.

'I want revenge, Freddy. For what that bastard did.'

Taking a deep breath, Phoebe stretched out a tentative hand towards Saskia's elbow.

'I think you'd better tell me about it, don't you?' she prompted gently.

The stringy hair bobbed up and down. Another cigarette was inserted between two rats' tails and lit.

'We were due to go to this big première together,' Saskia started saying in a shaky, hurried whisper. 'Some friend of Felix's – a big star, bums-on-seats man – had top billing. It was the first high-budget British film in ages – American-backed of course – so absolutely everyone was due to be there: royalty, tons of film industry suits, celebs, other blue-blooded chips.

Felix is so frantic to break into acting, he was desperately excited.' She took a deep pull on her cigarette.

'We were staying at his father's London place then.' Saskia shuddered as the recent tears ebbed away. 'Jocelyn lives abroad now. It's a sweet little mews near Notting Hill, but Felix and his cronies have absolutely trashed it. I think there's only about six months to go on the lease, so Pa Sylvian couldn't give a damn. Don't think he gives a damn about anything much actually.' She mopped her nose.

'Wasn't he a novelist?'

Saskia nodded, pulling at her cigarette. 'Still is, although not all that obscure literary stuff that won him prizes in the seventies. He writes under a pen name now, Herbert Wilson.'

'The thriller writer?' Phoebe gasped in astonishment.

'Self-same.' Saskia shredded a corner of her tissue. 'No airport terminal is complete without a revolving stand of his schlock.'

'You were telling me about Felix?' Phoebe prompted carefully, aware that she'd pulled the conversation off to a tactless tangent. 'The première?'

'Felix.' Saskia rolled the word around her mouth like a sweet and then swallowed it down with a sniff, sliding her reddened eyes back to Phoebe. 'Felix didn't have any work on that week – we were virtually living from the bed – and everything seemed utterly hunky-dory. His agent, Piers – the publicity shark, not his modelling agency – had lined up a few key lunches. There was a pile of unread scripts by the bed. I'd bought *the* most drop-dead Westwood corset for the big night. Dylan – that's Felix's chief crony, he lives in the mews too – kept bursting into the room while we were having sex to recite another line of his best man's speech. Felix just laughed and laughed. God, I was so happy.' She started to cry again, frantically trying to find a dry corner of her handkerchief to swab her eyes.

'Then a few days before the prem,' she continued jerkily, 'a half-page filler appeared in the *Express* about Felix and me getting married – I thought he'd love it. There was a gorgeous pic of him on some Kenyan fashion shoot and a blurry passport job of me before I dyed my hair, looking very Greta Scaatchi.'

'You sent it to me,' said Phoebe.

'God, yes,' Saskia remembered, biting the soggy tissue and closing her eyes. 'I was writing to you that morning while Felix was still asleep. I went out and bought another copy and posted it off before I – ' Her face crumpled.

'You showed him the article?'

Saskia nodded. 'He's always raving on about no publicity being bad, and this piece was wildly flattering. But when I showed it to him, he got the most awful sulks, accused me of leaking the story to deliberately fuck up his career and then slammed his way out of the house. I couldn't believe it. When I got back from a wedding dress fitting that afternoon, he and his passport had hot-cloven-hoofed it. Dylan tried to pretend Felix had a last-minute job, but I knew he didn't. Dylan's always trying to protect Felix, but he's a lousy liar.'

'And that was how it ended?' Phoebe asked, rather flummoxed.

'God, no!' Saskia rolled her wet eyes. 'If only – then I might have preserved some dignity. He finally crawled back in the small hours a couple of days later – the day before the première in fact – and was all over me; incredible sex that went on for hours and hours. But he was really odd – I'd never known him like it – sort of detached and a bit frightening. He said he'd been to visit his father in Barbados and persuade him to come over for the wedding. But when I asked if that meant Jocelyn *was* coming after all, Felix bit my head off, telling me it was none of my business.

'When he came to bed that night he was really, really violent. I mean, he often skated on the edge during sex, but this time he actually hurt me quite badly, cutting my lip with his teeth and bruising my arms so much, they were almost black above the elbow.'

'You didn't walk out?' Phoebe asked in amazement.

'God, no.' Saskia looked as if she'd suggested doing a Bobbit with her nail scissors. 'Afterwards he cried into my stomach, his body curled up into a tight ball, apologising over and over again, telling me he loved me. And when I woke up he'd gone out jogging, leaving me covered with flowers like Ophelia and a lovely apologetic note tucked between my fingers. He must have done it while I was asleep. Oh God, I loved him so much for it.' She blew her nose on the sleeve of her jumper.

'That morning, the day of the première, I met my sister Sukey in town for lunch, then I had a hairdresser's appointment. We got quite tight and when I got back to the mews, Felix was in a divine mood. He'd bought a huge cake from Pat Val's and a vat of Moët and he was in the bath, reading through a script with Chopin blaring.

'He looked so lovely, stretched out in the frothy water like a beautiful, playful golden seal. I just raced in and told him how much I loved him. I wanted to yell it from the Post Office Tower, tattoo it all over my bum and splash it across billboards, buses and black-cabs!'

The tears were pouring again now. Saskia tried to mop them away, but the tissue shredded in her fingers.

'And then – and then he suddenly looked me in the eyes and told me very calmly that he didn't love me at all. That he never had, that he thought I was a stuck-up, selfish tart and that he'd only taken the relationship this far because he thought I needed teaching a lesson, but that he had absolutely no intention of marrying me. All the time he had this smug little smile on his face.'

'God!' Phoebe shook her head in horrified amazement.

'I – I thought it was all a huge joke. Felix's sense of humour can be dreadfully lop-sided. There he was, stretched out like Dionysus, telling me it was all over. I even laughed, but he just carried on explaining that when he'd first met me he'd found me quite attractive, but that I'd been such a bitch, really messing him about by playing hard to get and then rolling over like a puppy and opening my legs when he offered me a holiday and a couple of tickets to the opera, that he'd started to detest me and everything I stood for.

'I suppose he must have thought that I used him at first,' she looked up at Phoebe with desolate red-veined eyes, 'but the truth is I was just so intimidated by him I didn't believe he really fancied me until he offered that holiday. I tried explaining it to him, but he wouldn't listen. He just reared out of the bath and wandered stark naked through the flat, throwing all my stuff into suitcases and telling me a few more home truths – that I'm a lousy fuck, that I'm thick, philistine and bigoted, that I have a fat bum, cellulite and small eyes. He said I was bone-idle, ungrateful and sponged off people like the worst type of leech. He even told me I reeked like a dolphin's lunch. It sounds so like a joke now, but I thought he'd gone mad. I just cried and cried. He was a completely, completely different person.'

'It doesn't sound like a joke to me.' Phoebe shuddered, taking Saskia's cigarette, which had burnt down to the stub and gone out unnoticed.

'After he'd packed most of my stuff, he got out that bloody cake and the champagne from the fridge. I really thought that was the moment he'd tell me it was all a prank. I was spitting with anger. But, as he cracked open the Moët, he cheerfully told me he'd bought them to celebrate our pre-nuptial disagreement.

'Then, just as he was tearing my family to shreds – saying I was the cunt of the litter and my sisters were all slags – Dylan lumped in from work and asked what the hell was going on. Felix was still standing stark naked in the kitchen with me sobbing all over the table. When Felix announced that he'd sacked me, they had a flaming row. Dylan kept howling at Felix that he'd promised never to do it again and that Jasmin should have taught him a lesson. I hadn't a clue what they were going on about, but I was far too upset to ask. Then Felix threw a glass at Dylan and stormed off to get dressed.

'Dylan's so sweet – even though he had a pretty evil cut on his forehead, he gave me a drink, mopped my face and told me everything would be all right. So bloody Felix re-emerges and starts shouting that Dylan could have me if he fancied me so much, but the sex would be about as tantalising as a vegan barbecue. I threw the entire cake at him and howled anything offensive I could think of. In the middle of it, Felix literally threw my stuff out of the door, picked me up and carried me out of the house, dropping me on the cobbles and slamming the door in my face.'

'God, what on earth did you do?'

'I kept banging and ringing the bell, but they ignored me and carried on yelling at each other. So I started screaming until the next-door neighbour appeared and told me to shut up. In the end I went round to Daddy's office and wept all over a board meeting Sukey was chairing. She marched me back to her flat and I tried phoning Felix, but his bloody machine was on.'

'That night I sat ranting and sobbing and watched a television special about the première,' she went on between hiccups. 'Felix arrived looking absolutely stunning with Isabel Delaunay, the French actress. He was grinning from sideburn to sideburn and paused to tell a roving reporter that he and "Belle" were really looking forward to seeing the show. He'd known her for ages and she'd made no secret of fancying him like mad. My guess is he'd always planned to take her – she's a paparazzi headliner at the moment. All that sexy sleaze with brains. They never would have bothered filming Felix if he'd arrived with me. When I tried phoning the mews again, they'd taken the phone off the hook.'

Saskia shuddered. 'I went through hell trying to contact him, but he'd sloped off to France to shoot some little scene he had in a film then on to America for a Cola commercial. Piers Fox refused to take my calls at all. And Elect, Felix's model agency, told me that he had asked them not to pass on any more of my messages, and that if I "persisted in wasting their time, they'd contact the police". I felt like some sort of Hollywood stalker, it was so awful.'

'You poor, poor darling.' Phoebe stroked her arm.

'Then about a month later,' Saskia lit another cigarette with shaking hands, 'I saw him. Quite by accident. He was in Café Nero when I was walking past – blowing the froth off his coffee and laughing with a couple of friends I didn't recognise. He'd got a tan in the States and looked so unspeakably glamorous, like one of those Italian commercials. I just stood in the street and stared.'

'Did he see you?'

She nodded. 'He caught me watching him and just looked away – as if I were a total stranger. His face didn't flicker. We'd been living together for six months – we'd chosen our bridesmaids, for Christ's sake! I trusted him with my life. And then within twelve days he was cutting me dead and threatening to report me for nuisance calls. Then I found out something quite awful . . .'

Her face crumpled and she looked away, fighting for control again.

'That afternoon, I was so angry I went to see Jasmin – Felix's ex-girlfriend. She's a model – pretty thick but incredibly beautiful; very Seattle Grunge. She takes a lot of drugs to keep her skinny, and quite a lot of the magazines won't book her. They say she's got an attitude problem. Felix calls her the Waif-er Thin Bint.'

'Charming.' Phoebe perched on the end of the bed. 'What did she say?'

'At first she wouldn't even let me into the flat, but then she saw I'd been crying and guessed straight away. She was really, really pleased. Gave me a huge brandy and said she'd been praying that Felix would ditch me. She kept laughing and hugging me, as if I'd just got a terrific job. I came seriously close to cracking up, but when I said I was going, she went totally ballistic, throwing the brandy bottle through a window and starting to scream like a bimbo with a spider in her bed. I was sure she was going to knock my lights out. Instead she told me the truth. Felix had done exactly the same thing to her. On the day they were due to get married, she was having two bottles of paracetamol pumped out of her stomach in St Mary's. Her liver is virtually a sieve now.'

'Christ! *They* were going to get married?'

Saskia nodded. 'They'd been living together for two years, although they both worked abroad most of that time. He dumped her the day before the wedding and then totally disappeared for two months. He'd said some truly diabolical things. Later she discovered he'd been screwing around the entire time she'd known him. She also found out he'd slept with her mother.'

'Now you've got to be joking!'

'No.' Saskia closed her eyes. 'He's one howling shit, but he's so fucking irresistible no one ever says no. Jasmin reckons he's never been turned down in his life. What's worse, he seems to really get a kick out of totally decimating women's confidence. It turns out he'd done the same sort of thing long before Jasmin or me. All through school, university and even when he was bumming around Australia, he didn't just break hearts, he knifed them.'

'But why?'

Saskia shrugged. 'I guess it's like the ultimate prurient kick to him, some sort of power trip. Getting laid is too easy for him; he needs to play sick mental games to amuse himself. So he picks up a difficult, screwed-up woman and nurtures her – treating her like a demi-goddess, driving her wild in bed, focusing his life around her. For her, it's like stumbling into Eden on the Seventh Day. Felix makes her feel so incredibly good about herself, so confident and so cherished, she's high all the time, utterly secure in his love. And then he shreds her. He peels away inhibitions like a picture restorer lifting grime from an Old Master until it's beautiful and vibrant and wanted, before slashing a scalpel through the canvas so that no one will ever desire it again.'

The tears had stopped. Saskia just stared mindlessly, her expression frozen with numb misery like a corpse's face staring out from a glacier, her eyes almost closed from crying.

'I know what your perfect revenge would be,' Phoebe said cautiously, trying to shake her out of her torpor.

'Yes?' Saskia kept her eyes lowered.

'Go back into acting, work like hell, and make it.' She urged. 'You *have* got the talent. You know how difficult it is to get into drama school – particularly a great one like LADA – and you always were exceptional, even at school. All you need is a couple of years, grit, determination and balls. Make it into the West End, get a longer blurb in the programme than anyone else, flirt with Hollywood, and Felix will turn greener than a June conker.'

'No.' Saskia shook her head. 'I know exactly how to get back at him. Why do you think I've been telling you all this, you stupid cow?'

'What?' Phoebe was baffled.

'The trouble is . . .' she sighed, 'I know *you* can do it, but I'm not sure if I'll be able to cope.'

'What are you talking about, Saskia?' Phoebe asked in bewilderment.

'I want you to do exactly what Felix did to me . . .'

'*What?*'

'. . . to him,' Saskia finished, her face threatening to crumple into tears again at any second.

'No, Saskia – ' Phoebe started to protest.

'Wait!' she interrupted. 'Let me finish, Freddy. I just want you to hear the idea at least. You're so perfect for it. You're one of the few friends I have who's never met him. You're the best flirt I've ever known and you've got bags more confidence with men than I do – they always fancy you.'

'Now wait a minute . . .'

'Shut up! What I want you to do is engineer it so that you meet Felix – not hard as I know exactly where he hangs out. Then you get him to notice you. I can supply you with absolutely all the low-down on how to make him fancy you like mad: his favourite designers, music, films, restaurants. Everything. And I know how he likes women to dress, to flirt, to talk, what really turns him on and how to make him howl with lust.'

She paused for a few seconds.

'I lived with him for over six months, Freddy,' she went on, suddenly resolute and charged with excitement. 'One of his pet topics for talking about during sex was the other women he wanted to fuck. Or he and Dylan would spend an entire day discussing some girl's arse. It drove me mad at the time but, God, I never believed it could be so useful. You'd have him rolling over and begging to have his tummy tickled within seconds – and believe me, it reaches as far as his tummy! Just because I didn't turn out to be his ideal woman,' she smiled through a series of tearful hiccups, 'doesn't mean I didn't work out exactly what is. With a bit of tuition, you could be it.'

'And supposing I do?' Phoebe humoured her. 'Supposing I am. Then what?'

'Then,' Saskia's gaze scoured Phoebe's face, 'you play him at his own narcissistic game. When he falls for you, when he starts really trusting you and lavishing his gifts and attention, you dump him. As publicly and humiliatingly as possible. Tell him he's a lousy screw with a small cock, bad breath, thinning hair and an intellect as challenging as a tot's Tomy toy, then disappear out of his life totally.' She started to laugh. 'It can't fail. A huge, huge overdose of his own poisonous medicine!'

Phoebe watched Saskia giggling through her tears. Watched a girl she had once envied and hated so much it had been physically painful, now reduced to a heaving, tearstained wreck, her eyes dead with grief.

As far as Phoebe was concerned, Felix Sylvian deserved a quick trip to hell with Bacofoil wrapped around his privates for the way he'd ground his hand-stitched leather heels into Saskia's ego. And her plot was so gloriously vengeful it made hairs stand up on the back of Phoebe's neck. In theory. But given messy things like friends, feelings, sanity, job, and the difficulty of inflicting pain on a stranger, it sank without trace in emotional baggage. And besides, she was terrified he wouldn't fancy her.

'I can't do it,' she said, taking Saskia's hand and squeezing it apologetically. 'It wouldn't be fair. On you, as much as anyone else. You deserve time to get over Felix and win your confidence back – not prolong the agony by exacting revenge. Try to forget him.'

'I can't,' Saskia croaked. 'I don't think I ever will. Anyway,' she snatched her hand away, her reddened eyes flashing angrily, 'what makes you think this revenge is purely personal? Can't you see he's fucked up women all his life and will probably carry on doing so for as long as he can get eight inches of ego up? He's

a misogynistic bastard, Freddy.' She stood up, her voice rising to
a scream. 'Don't you think the future Saskias, Jasmins and God
knows who else deserve someone giving him a kick in the
undropped balls before he goes too far? What if his next victim
really does kill herself?'

'I don't think I could do it even if I wanted to, Saskia,' argued
Phoebe, indignant flames of anger leaping inside her. 'I'm not
all those things you set me up to be. I'm hardly a great catch –
no job, no background to flaunt, weird looks, grotty flat. If
you're looking for some sort of Virtual Reality blow-up debu-
tante then, sorry, I'm not your girl.'

Saskia looked at her for a long time, studied the huge mint-
green eyes and short, boyish hair, the slim, tanned legs that
could ride pillion on a Harley and still touch the ground, and
the clever, curling mouth shaped like Eros's bow aimed for a
long-distance shot. Phoebe looked glorious – grouchy, sexy and
crumpled, like a tall, skinny Beatrice Dalle. Felix would love her.
She was Saskia's best chance and she'd always been a soft touch.

Saskia cleared her throat and winced against another barrage
of hiccuping sobs. 'You won't do it because we've never really
been friends.'

'Saskia, that's ridiculous . . .'

'No, don't argue,' she howled. 'It's true, isn't it? We loathed
one another when we were kids. You only came down here this
weekend because Mummy asked you, and probably because you
wanted a good gawp as well. You just think I'm a sad fat cow
who wants to get her own back. Well, get out then.' She pushed
Phoebe towards the door.

'Saskia, that's total – '

It slammed in Phoebe's face.

'– rubbish,' she finished. She banged on the door, pleading to
talk to Saskia again, but the only answer was an angry brooding
silence.

6

The north London supermarket was cool, light and un-crowded, the concentrated silence broken only as the odd shopping trolley executed a hand-brake turn around tinned meat chicane into the dogfood straight.

Fliss leant her elbows on the handle of her trolley and whizzed around the aisles, coming to squealing wheely halts as she lobbed in plastic cups, seeded baps, hickory chips and charcoal.

Stan, who was helping to organise today's party, had insisted they set a strict price limit to the barbecue – the food quota being one-third of the drink allowance as always. He knew of old his friend's tendency to over-cater; Fliss adored parties and tried to hold at least one a month in the cluttered, shared Islington flat. It was, in fact, the reason her last flat-mate had moved out. Each time Fliss's extravagant parties were held, these chaotic, noisy gatherings grew larger and more frenzied as friends of friends heard how much fun they were, how much booze was shipped, how excellent the food was, and most importantly – how many good-looking, single people always roamed around flirting their socks (and occasionally other items of underwear) off.

Chewing her lip, Fliss paused by the fresh trifles and hoped her brother Selwyn's friends would turn up today. They always added an extra frisson to the parties – although Stan grumbled that they drank everything, phoned friends in Australia from the flat, bonked on the beds and then trashed the place. Fliss, who pointed out that Stan behaved almost exactly the same way himself, didn't much care: they were all, without exception, drop-dead gorgeous. They came from the planet of the beautiful people (Stan grouchily called them Intra-Venus Drips), that exclusive, elusive club which she had glimpsed through windows, stood next to on tubes, read about in gossip columns, but never been given membership to. When Selwyn brought his friends to one of her parties, Fliss felt she had been honoured with a guest pass into its hallowed corridors.

She'd left three messages on her brother's answermachine yesterday: one saying they were having a party, the second to explain who 'they' were, just in case he didn't realise, and a third to remind him where she lived, because he always claimed to forget.

Bugger Stan, she was going to lay on the best spread yet, she decided gleefully.

Outside, with fifteen splitting carrier bags in the boot and Kiss FM blaring from the car stereo, Fliss tried turning the key in the ignition one more time, heard the same sulky, bronchial cough, and wailed. She couldn't possibly struggle the one-stop tube journey and ten-minute walk home with so much to carry.

She thumped the steering wheel and then grumpily apologised to it. She loved her car – an ancient, rusting blue 205 called Honk. But these days Honk had been spluttering and dying more often than *King Lear* on a regional tour. Particularly as Fliss, overdrawn to the point of hiding from the bailiffs, had become more and more forgetful about filling him with petrol.

In the end, Stan answered her phone-box distress call and emerged from his rattling Beetle, eyebrows knotted together with irritation and anxiety. He'd lost his driving licence six months earlier when caught woozily ferrying a very drunken friend home from a party, and now kept his unused car near Fliss's flat in Islington as it had been broken into more often than the local Spar when parked outside his own flat in Brixton. This meant, however, that not only did Fliss borrow it whenever

Honk wouldn't start, regularly stranding it without petrol in
various parts of North London, but she also now regarded Stan
as the fourth emergency service, and expected him to risk a
hefty fine whenever she was in distress.

'I'll siphon enough petrol in for you to get to a filling station,'
he sighed resignedly. 'And if I get caught driving out here for
you, girl, I'll skin you – from the inside.' He stomped around
the front to open the boot. 'I'll get the hosepipe.'

'No, there isn't time, Stan,' Fliss was hopping from foot to
foot excitedly. 'I'll just bung a note under the wiper and we can
come back this evening.'

'You'll be over the limit this evening,' he pointed out bluntly.

But Fliss was already heaving carriers out of Honk's boot and,
as always forgetting that the Beetle's boot was at the front, trying
to ram them next to Stan's car battery.

'Oh, Christ,' he groaned as twelve French sticks jack-knifed
under the weight of lager party-packs. 'Why the hell d'you buy
all this stuff, girl? I thought we'd only invited a few old friends.'

'Ah, yes, well . . .' Fliss quickly grabbed the bag of exotic
meats and cheeses before he could nose into it. 'When Phoebe
said she was going down south, I didn't think there was much
point in just inviting her lot, so I phoned around a bit.'

'One of your brother's pack has turned up already,' he told
her as they waited in a queue of traffic to turn on to Essex Road.
'I hope that doesn't mean the rest of the buggers are coming?'

'Which one is it?' Fliss said nonchalantly, wishing she'd bothered to put on her make-up and change into something drop-dead
before coming out to shop. But it was only midday, and she'd told
everyone but her closest friends to come from two onwards.

'God knows, some pretty boy who said he'd come to the
party where Claudia stripped on the kitchen table.'

'She always does that,' Fliss pointed out, wracking her brain.
'He's not that blond god who caused complete hormonal havoc
on Rachel's birthday? The actor? What was he called – Fabian or
something?'

'Could be,' Stan said idly, knowing it wasn't but wanting to
see Fliss's reaction.

As expected, she flipped down the Beetle's sun-visor and moaned at her reflection. Her hair was at its wildest, battling like an unpruned, virulent privet against the sagging trellis of her hairclip. Her face was paler than ever except for an angry red nose and a new crop of freckles in a stripe which spread from ear to ear across the bridge of her nose as a result of the briefest of walks in the recent sun. Her eyes, huge and bloodshot from working too late in the poorly ventilated studio with a large bottle of wine, gave the impression of a rabbit in the early stages of myxomatosis.

'So have you given him a drink?' she asked anxiously. 'You haven't just left him to fend? He might try the home-made beer in the laundry cupboard and need his stomach pumped like Basil!'

'Hi there,' greeted a lazy, honey-rich voice, followed by a contented yawn.

Fliss turned from staggering through to the kitchen with the third drinks box to see a heavenly, seraph-like vision wandering barefoot through the door from the bathroom, rubbing blood-shot blue eyes.

For a second she mistook him for the deliriously beautiful hormone-wrecker, but, gazing in delighted wonder, she realised he wasn't as broad or quite as blood-fizzlingly unreal as the man who had practically brought a recent party to a standstill with his glorious, good-looking arrival.

His floppy hair was more white-blond than gold and his nose was longer and beakier. He had the pale, crumpled look of someone who seldom got out of bed unless he was tipped out; his white T-shirt was creased and untucked from his threadbare Levi's which were showing a lot of lean, tanned muscle through their copious holes. But, all the same, he had enough rug-pulling sex appeal to cause Fliss to clutch a chair for support and plot madly how she could get him to sit for some sketches.

'Hi,' she croaked, busying herself with her rustling bags to stop a horrible, predictable blush streaking down to her chest. 'You're well early, I'm afraid.'

A hand stretched over her freckled arm to grab an apple, brushing her skin with blond, downy hairs so that her nerve-endings ran amok. Close to, Selwyn's friend smelled delicious, like freshly baked bread.

He rolled the apple in long, bony fingers. 'I'm sorry I'm so precociously premature, but I was staying – er – overnight around the corner so I thought I'd just pop in. I couldn't remember your exact address, this is the third house I've tried – I had no idea you were having a party, or I wouldn't have been so presumptuous.' He seemed to like words that started with pre-, drawing them out with lazy arrogance like a long, melancholy lute strum.

He flopped down into a chair opposite Fliss and shot her a devastating, wicked grin which almost knocked her backwards. 'Staying overnight', said in that deep, playful voice, could only mean one thing, Fliss realised. And his clothes looked as if they'd been underneath whoever he was 'staying overnight' with.

'Stay for the barbecue if you like,' her attempt at smooth indifference came out as a breathless pant. 'I mean, the more the merrier, love,' she added quickly, flustered by her own total transparency. But that just made her sound like Norah Batty organising a WI charabanc trip to Cleethorpes.

She wondered why she hadn't noticed him at the party he'd come to before. But if it had been the same night that Blond God had visited, she reflected, no one would have noticed him. Whenever that party was talked about, the hormone-wrecker was the only guest anyone remembered at all.

'Terrific kitchen,' he murmured, gazing around at the chaos of tiles, clutter and fading trompe-l'oeil murals Stan had added when drunk one night and which the landlord had yet to see. 'Didn't see it last time for all the people.'

His eyes really were blue, Fliss noticed. The same almost artificial azure as a Caribbean bay on a holiday postcard. With his long, narrow, almost androgynous body, he'd be heaven to sculpt. He looked like a young, caddish knave from a medieval fantasy – he'd be utterly irresistible in green tights, long leather

boots and a doublet. A golden-locked Lochinvar, she thought
dreamily, wishing he would hoist her up on a horse and whisk
her away from making garlic bread and putting up Phoebe's
shelves.

'Are you okay?' he asked, laughing throatily and biting into
the apple with teeth as white as soap flakes.

'Huh?' Fliss glanced down with clouded eyes and noticed
she'd pulverised a red pepper between her reddening hands.

'I'm sorry, it's dreadfully rude of me but I can't remember
your name,' he apologised softly, blue eyes watching the downward progress of her blush with amusement.

'Fliss Wolfe,' she mumbled.

'God, of course! You're Selwyn's little sister. Stupid of me not
to remember.' He flashed the bewitching grin again. 'You don't
look at all like him.'

'No, well, I wouldn't,' Fliss hated explaining. 'I'm adopted –
our parents couldn't have any more children of their own after
Sel.'

'Oh, yes, I see,' he drawled, without much interest.

Which, Fliss thought angrily as she tipped out salad ingredients, is why Selwyn is tall and raven-haired and head-turning
while I'm short, solid and ginger!

'I'm Mungo,' grinned the pretty Lochinvar. 'And I'm dying
for a drink.'

With the vodka bottle open in front of him, he worked his
way through a packet of cigarettes Claudia had left on the table
and watched Fliss while she moved around the kitchen, parcel-
ling garlic bread, mixing up salads, making burgers out of
minced beef and egg, and lining up fork-pronged sausages ready
for the barbecue.

'God, that's marvellous!' he said over and over again, the
heart-melting grin flashing intermittently like a faulty neon
sign. 'How do you do that? . . . Have another vodka . . . Did
you study cookery? . . . Can I try some? . . . You've got a great
bum.'

The lower the vodka level went, the more complimentary he
got. Fliss, who normally shrugged off compliments with the

same amused embarrassment as she would an amorous Jack
Russell, was burning up with delight. Never had salads been as
well garnished or dressed, butter as garlicky, strawberries as
sugared or veggie cheese flans as neatly criss-crossed with sun-
dried tomatoes. Soon she no longer cared that she was still
wearing the old, stained jeans which made her rear look like a
rhino's or the striped t-shirt which had shrunk in the wash and
had a clay stain on one nipple.

One by one old friends arrived, trooped into the kitchen,
gawped at Mungo, complained about their hangovers and
trooped out again.

Among the new arrivals was her merry-eyed, grinning friend
Iain, the long-haul traveller she had been intending to set up
with Phoebe.

'Frizz!' he whooped, galloping through from the throng in
the sitting room and, quickly depositing several six-packs of
Dos Equis on the table, gathered her into a vast, swinging hug.
As she spun round, Fliss caught a brief blurred glimpse of
Mungo on each circuit, eyeing Iain thoughtfully. Perhaps, she
thought with almost delirious hope, he's jealous?

'Put me down, you great wassock!' she howled.

When Iain finally released her, she staggered back groggily
and thought what a shame it was that Phoebe wasn't there.
Having so far only spoken to him on the phone since he
returned from Peru, she noticed now how much a spell abroad
had improved him. A bit of a university nerd in his time, Iain
still possessed an unfortunate hooked nose and big, flashy teeth,
but he had broadened and filled out from a twiggy sapling to an
impressively long, slightly willowy tree. He was tall, tanned and
sun-streaked, his merry green eyes glowing almost incandes-
cently from a laughing face. Gone were the anorak and cords,
too. He was wearing a baggy black rugby shirt and cinnamon
jeans which brought out the tortoiseshell beauty of his hair. He
and Phoebe would look almost incestuous together, Fliss
realised, the physical similarity was so acute.

'You look as sexy as ever, Frizz babes.' Iain kissed her on the
forehead.

'Don't patronise me, you great wanker.' She shrugged him off hotly, then smiled in apology. 'This is Mungo – Mungo, this is Iain, an old friend from university.'

'Enchanté.' Mungo stared at Iain unblinkingly, his blue gaze glittering like a challenge.

Fliss took another swig of her Coke and winced. It said *Improved Recipe* on the side, she noticed, but she personally begged to differ. It seemed very chemical. She'd been so busy she hadn't noticed Mungo topping it up with vodka as she worked.

Smiling at him rather dubiously, Iain wandered out through the glass door to the balcony to introduce himself to Stan and help him set up the barbecue. Mungo's blue gaze followed his cinnamon bottom impassively.

As Fliss worked her way through another Improved Recipe Coke, Stan loped in and out of the balcony door, firing up the barbecue and reeking of Obsession for Men.

For the first time, Fliss noticed he was wearing his dreadful striped jeans, the ones he normally saved for a night on the town. Matched with his bucket-wide biker boots, they emphasised his long, stick-like legs and lack of bum. Instead of the normally shoulder-length, leonine hair, he'd slicked it back so that it shone almost pewter-grey against his scalp. And the black t-shirt he was wearing had toothpaste splatters on the front. Fliss thought he looked awful, and almost told him so. She was feeling horribly abrasive today, she realised with a start.

'I must go and change,' she explained woozily to Mungo, who was now reading Stan's Sunday papers, heaving each section into crumpled heaps at his feet when he'd finished it and ripping off a hunk of the Arts Review to mop up some spilled vodka.

Stan would hit the roof, Fliss thought. She could hear the entryphone buzzing again and someone shriekingly zap another guest in.

'You look terrific in just that.' Mungo narrowed his eyes and looked at her in a way that almost scorched her t-shirt off.

'Natural and sexy – like a cherub dressed for an orgy. But if you insist on changing, can I come and watch?'

Quivering with happiness, Fliss polished off her Coke without bothering to wipe away the frothy moustache of foam, and wondered if her period was due. Unlike women who mutated into Mrs Hyde, murdered their husbands and then bit heads off chickens at the point of menstruation, Fliss bloomed. Her tits swelled, her skin glowed, and she bubbled with sexual potential, getting turned on by the most ridiculous of things – ice-cream posters on tubes, coffee ads on telly, even old Carry On films.

''Lo,' rasped a gruff voice and Claudia walked in, wearing nothing but a cream t-shirt, her long glossy black legs shuffling in tiny, hungover steps as if she was wearing a kimono. She was carrying her linen flares, which were soaked through.

'Honestly, Fliss babes,' she croaked, 'I'm so fucking fragile, I just walked straight through the bloody sprinkler when I was cutting through the gardens. I din' even notice till I was ringing your bell. Can I bung these in the dryer, yeah?'

'Sure.' Fliss's tiny bubble of sexiness popped as she took the trousers from her friend.

Even when feeling as fragile as a wafer-thin toffee web over a brûlée, Claudia looked unspeakably seductive. Her long ropes of corded black hair fell almost to her tiny waist, her shrewd, clever eyes still held a trace of their usual brilliance and, even if it tasted like an unemptied pub ashtray, her mouth was as plump, red and kissable as the inside of a strawberry.

'Clods, honey!' Fliss greeted her brightly, swallowing down a dastardly, jealous urge to throw a tea towel over Claudia's head and push her out of the balcony door before Mungo noticed her. 'This is Mungo.'

''Lo,' Claudia croaked, hardly looking at him. Instead she staggered over to the fridge and stooped to pull out a carton of milk, showing a white Sloggi g-string between buttocks as perfect as peaches but considerably less hairy.

Shutting the fridge door with her bum she leant against it, closed her eyes and grunted. 'Did I get completely boxed last night or what? I danced for five solid hours and then threw up

on the night bus,' she groaned, flipping open the carton flaps
and taking a huge swig. To emphasise her point, she opened her
huge, tired eyes again and rolled them.

They landed on Mungo and stuck like a bluebottle on fly
paper.

''Lo, Mungo,' she growled huskily, flashing a grin as white
and as perfect as his own.

Fliss wanted to weep. She loved Claudia, who lived in an even
grottier converted flat just across their shared gardens, but
realised that her beautiful, predatory friend wouldn't imagine
that Fliss staked any claim on the blond Lochinvar. In fact Our
Cilla, in Claudia's eyes, was probably providing the set-up of a
lifetime.

But when Mungo smiled back, the flood-light wattage he had
afforded Fliss was dulled to a hand-held torch; he seemed totally
without warmth or interest.

Rather taken aback, Claudia fetched herself some Alpen and a
bowl and settled down at the table.

Fliss wrapped up the last Smartie-filled banana in foil and
bolted across the sitting room – now crammed with friends
breaking into cheap bottles of wine – to change in her bedroom.

Two minutes later she was howling with fury as she flipped
furiously through her wardrobe.

'Bloody Phoebe!' she hissed under her breath, noticing
several empty coat hangers rattling at the risqué end of her
carefully serried clothes. 'Why, why, why this frigging weekend?
Both my best bloody seductress kits – the cow!'

The fact that almost half her wardrobe was currently occu-
pied by her flatmate's clothes did nothing to pacify Fliss's
bubbling temper or to exonerate Phoebe. To nick one bed-
me dress could be the behaviour of an old friend who knew one
wouldn't notice. To nick two looked like deliberate sabotage.

The entryphone buzzer was going off as regularly as an
electric alarm clock now. Fliss hastily tipped all her clothes
out on to the bed and swam through them with her arms in the
hope of turning up a really eye-catching impulse-buy which hid

her appalling legs and made her look like she had a bust. A recent failed attempt to revive the sequinned boob tube surfaced in her search, along with a pair of mock-croc bell-bottoms bought in Oxfam which had induced spontaneous laughter on public transport on the only occasion she'd worn them. Her drop-dead leather bodice had deodorant-dusted armpits and the long suede skirt which had proven pulling power would be far too hot. In desperation, Fliss settled for a linen waistcoat she could get away with wearing nothing underneath and a pair of baggy black flares which lengthened her legs and flattened her bum.

Hooking them over a chair, she threw the rest of her clothes back into the wardrobe and kicked the door shut. Then she carefully made up her bed, telling herself she was a stupid, optimistic fool.

Grabbing her towel, she hurtled into the bathroom and showered, nicking tons of Phoebe's perfumed body-gel and extra-shine shampoo.

Back in her bedroom, she stood with a clean bra and knickers sticking to her damp skin, slapping Erace over her spots and a few selected freckles.

A knock on the door almost shot her into the ceiling. She knew she fell in love a lot, almost every day in fact, but she'd seldom felt this deranged sense of hope before.

'Yes?' her voice warbled like a yodeller warming up for the ultimate Alpine stretch as she grabbed her soggy towel and held it up to her chest.

'Brought you a drink.' Stan wandered in clutching a can and quickly averted his gaze. 'Thought you might want one before the rest of the marauding horde arrive,' he explained, searching around for an uncluttered surface to put it on. Giving up, he held it in her general direction, his head still turned towards the door.

'Thanks.'

Fliss took it, letting the towel drop. Stan had seen her in her undies hundreds of times when he'd dropped in and she was bolting around the house, late for their arranged drinks or for work and desperate to iron a shirt. It didn't stop him behaving like a gay abbot stumbling into a communal girls' shower whenever he saw her, but today she somehow didn't care. She flopped down on the bed and took a giant swig.

'Are Mungo and Claudia still gabbing away?' she asked, and then bit her lip for being so obvious.

'What?' Stan said incredulously, spinning around and then hastily looking in the mirror instead of at her.

'I think they're pretty well suited – they'd look ace together.' Fliss picked at her duvet cover. 'He's a nice lad.'

Stan, about to bite sarcastically into her ridiculous banter, stopped himself, his jaw suddenly hanging from its hinges. Fliss had absolutely no idea what a twisted little f-wit Mungo was, he realised angrily. That's why she'd been wafting around like Delia Smith on speed while the rest of them had lurked in the sitting room wondering how to turf him out.

'Suppose so,' he muttered and stomped out.

Listening to the door clunk shut, Fliss shrugged and took another huge swig from her can. It was the terribly sweet, strong lager they always bought in bulk because it was cheap and got everyone legless before their bladders topped up. In the past, there'd been endless queues for a drunken lurch around the loo at Fliss's parties, as guests who'd lost their ability to focus attempted to rid themselves of five cans of Heineken and half a litre of Lambrusco within an hour of deciding they needed a pee. But nowadays, with the discovery of the six-percent sweet soup, the loo queue usually only stretched a modest halfway into Phoebe's bedroom next door.

It must be because it was lunchtime, not evening, that it was already making her feel woozy, she decided. Or perhaps it was nerves. She'd never met anyone as sexy as Mungo and simply didn't know how to react. She took it all back about Blond God the hormone-wrecker – he'd never generated this sort of pube-frazzling excitement. But then again, hormone-wrecker hadn't so much as batted a divine blue eye in her direction, whereas Mungo had said she had a nice bum. Now, with the aid of her dressing-table mirror and a hand-held one, she examined it.

It was lightly dimpled with fat like rising bread dough, and one buttock was visible, glowing and goose-bumped with rare exposure where her knickers had slipped upwards.

Deflated again, Fliss flopped on to the edge of her bed and reached for her can, picking up her hairspray by mistake and trying to drink it. Her mouth puckered up in horror, as if painted with Stop and Grow. Giving her hair – and most of her forehead – a thoughtful squirt, she located the liquorice lager and sucked at the keyhole.

She wished Phoebe was with her. Phoebe was opinionated, fun and reckless and would bolster Fliss's confidence enough for her to make a move on Mungo.

Of all her friends, Fliss considered Phoebe the closest; she had missed her terribly during her year away. Phoebe was the only mate who treated her like a real, rounded person, not a caricature of matchmaking, kettle-fixing, DIY hyperactivity.

But Phoebe was, it had transpired, an old school tie girl, and had dropped everything to dash off to whoop it up at a friend's weekend party, reminiscing over gym slips, girdles and hoisting one's first bra up the flag pole on sports day. Fliss felt slightly resentful that her scummy London barbecue – to which Phoebe had been invited first – had been rejected so hastily. She'd been looking forward to Phoebe's re-emergence on their party scene; she had an abandoned, exuberant spontaneity that was as contagious as snorting giggles in a fifth-year sex education class. With Phoebe around – particularly after more than one thimble of wine – anything could happen.

With me around, Fliss reflected – particularly after a couple of swigs of vodka and half a can of lager – nothing could happen. Not unless she suddenly developed the courage of Madonna, the body of Elle MacPherson, the face of Kate Moss and the seduction routine of a dominatrix Mae West let loose in a Masonic lodge. Fliss's closest brush with seduction had been to close her eyes and hope. Her friends joked that she was a flame-haired man-eater, but the truth was that she usually resorted to getting plastered and pouncing on the men she fancied because they had never once pounced on her. Her technique still needed honing – her failure percentage was still in three figures – but fewer men screamed these days.

Today, I am going to change, she told herself. Today is the first day of the rest of my sex life.

Flumping on to her duvet and waiting for the room to stand still again, she swilled her can and started on the second half to get her in the mood.

Slicking his hair back, Stan tapped lightly on Fliss's door. When no one answered, he cautiously poked his head around it.

She was lying flat out on the bed wearing her bra and knickers, an empty can of lager clutched in one hand, a racket-shaped mirror in the other. Her huge eyes were closed, fluttering in a deep, distant dream, dark red corkscrews of hair winding out on to the pillows like party streamers.

Watching her for a moment like an indulgent nanny drinking in her sleeping infant and wishing she was young again, Stan sighed and then closed the door very softly.

As he turned around, he saw a covert, giggling couple stumble into Phoebe's deserted room, their clothes already scattering a creased path behind them like multi-coloured crazy paving.

Sighing with long-suffering resignation, he turned to go and walked smack into a very straight, creased forehead.

'Oi, watch it, mate!' He reeled back angrily.

'Ah, yes, sorry.' It was Fliss's friend, Iain, rubbing his sun-streaked hair and spilling liberal amounts of lukewarm party Liebfraumilch – one of the few drinks left – on to the flat's rush mats. 'I – er – I was looking for Fliss actually. Don't s'pose you've seen her, have you?'

Stan looked at him obliquely, bristling at the rich accent, as plummy as Robinson's extra-fruit jam.

'She's around,' he shrugged unhelpfully.

'Oh, right.' Iain gazed over one of Stan's wide t-shirted shoulders towards the throng of people. 'Haven't seen her – so many bodies here. Look, you couldn't pass on a message, could you? Only I've got to push off to see my parents in Suffolk and I only really came to see Fliss.'

'S'pose so.' Stan was bristling even more. The bloke was, he personally thought, a prat of the calibre that pranged his Golf for a hoot, read Jeffrey Archer without chagrin and wore his old school tie to interviews for graduate training in merchant banks. When setting up the barbecue earlier, Iain had stooped over the coals and prodded them rather uselessly, waffling on about a year spent in Peru, the size of the steaks and the women's tits to such a boring degree that Stan had sloshed on enough meths to practically raze those fluffy tortoiseshell eyebrows off. And, Stan realised, he was just the sort who always got honking great crushes on Fliss, which, because she had such a low opinion of herself, she seldom noticed. Unless, that is, they practically floored her with one of the rugby tackles they'd learnt in their exclusive public schools.

'Actually,' Iain was picking up on Stan's disapproval, 'I'll write her a note, if that's okay?'

'Yeah. Just make it quick, mate.' Stan didn't want Fliss waking up and stumbling out before he left.

He whipped a slim-line diary out of his back pocket and scribbled a note in stiff, childish handwriting. Ripping out the page, he folded it over twice.

'Great – thanks a lot, er, Stan. I'll see you soon maybe?' Iain handed the note to him.

'P'raps.' Stan took the note and grinned stiffly.

The moment Iain was out of sight, he read it.

'Yeah,' he muttered grumpily, 'that should do it.'

Then the side of his mouth twisted into a shrewd grin. Two weeks, he bet himself privately. And that's only because she's too kind-hearted to say no.

7

The longer she stayed with the Seatons, the more cracks Phoebe noticed in everything. They seeped like tiny veins throughout the house, splitting through polish on furniture, plaster on walls, marble fireplaces, gloss paintwork and the lichen grey mortar between the outside brickwork. Crevices mosaiced every flowerbed, hard with thirst, and chipped away the faces and fields in Tony's old, grubby oil paintings.

There was even a hairline split on the plastic loo seat in Phoebe's tiny guest bathroom, which had given her a blood blister. Sitting down was now becoming so uncomfortable that she felt like a naughty schoolboy fresh from six of the best before corporal punishment was phased out in favour of group detention and basket-weaving interaction sessions.

On Sunday evening, Phoebe ate with Gin and Portia around the bowed kitchen table. Saskia refused to emerge from her room and Tony had sloped off to the local pub with some neighbouring weekenders.

'He's looking terribly porky, Ma.' Portia pushed an undressed salad around her plate without enthusiasm. 'Is he drinking too much?'

'Of course he is, darling.' Gin, still hungover from lunch, was battling with a spritzer. 'We both are. Have some more cheese, Freddy.'

Phoebe gratefully hacked off another slice of brie and some smoked cheddar.

'Damn, I was hoping this would do for tomorrow night's cheese board.' Gin followed suit with some white Stilton. 'I suppose I'll have to dash into Hexbury and brave Sainsbury's after I pick up the trout.'

'Who's coming?' asked Portia, nibbling the corner of a piece of cucumber and watching jealously as Phoebe tore off another hunk of baguette.

'Oh, some friends of your father's I've never met – and Garth Drayson and his wife.'

'That old letch!' Portia sneered.

'He's a jolly nice chap,' Gin retorted. 'Just because he touches one's bottom when he follows one out of a room doesn't make him a letch. He's old fashioned.'

'So his wife must be positively pre-historic for groping Daddy at every opportunity,' Portia said nastily.

'Jilly Drayson's divine.' Gin took a huge slug of her spritzer and winced. 'She's just very tactile. And your father runs a mile when she's kissing hello – you know how embarrassed he gets.'

Portia raised one sceptical plucked blonde eyebrow and tossed her fork on to her untouched plate.

'Portia, you must eat something,' Gin grumbled. 'I don't want you frightening us by going haggard again.'

'I had a vast lunch, Ma,' she lied, lighting a cigarette.

Gin studied her face thoughtfully. 'You've met someone, haven't you?'

'God, Ma!' Portia slammed her lighter back on to the table irritably. 'I'm always meeting people – if I skipped a meal every time I had a date, I'd be hooked up to a drip by now. Look, I don't want to talk about it. Grill Freddy for a change.' Her huge grey eyes shifted mischievously to Phoebe. 'Yes, Freddy's very quiet tonight. Hasn't so much as squeaked a word. Saskia's been blubbering loudly all over the house with you in tow, Fred. You must have wheedled something more out of her than the bald facts about divine Felix trotting off with a French porn star?'

There was something slightly gloating and teasing about her tone, like an Agassi fan asking a Becker supporter who had won the men's finals, when she knew perfectly well that her hairy idol had conquered in straight sets.

'Not really.' Phoebe cleared her throat, guessing that Portia knew more about slithering Sylvian than she was letting on.

Later, as Phoebe helped Gin, Portia hooked her long, slender legs up on to one of the vacated chairs and scratched an outstretched black Labrador nose.

'I hear,' she said slowly, leaning back and watching Phoebe over her shoulder, 'that you had a bit of a flingette with a friend of a friend of mine.'

'Oh, yes?' Phoebe froze, a side plate hovering over the dishwasher.

Portia grinned wickedly. 'And I can hardly say I blame you – he's utterly drinkable.'

'Who was it, Freddy?' asked Gin, cramming two plates into the same slot without bothering to scrape off the hunks of crust still on them.

'I don't know.' Phoebe's eyes widened with fear as she watched Portia's playful, smiling face. She clearly meant Dan. How could she do this to me? Phoebe thought furiously. Gin seemed to be one of the few people not to have heard about the Dan disaster, Poppy Fredericks being too embarrassed by her daughter's errant behaviour to pass on that particular slice of family gossip.

'Well?' Gin quizzed, straightening up and wiping her hands on the back of her faded cotton skirt.

'Oh, honestly.' Portia flicked her ash towards the sink and missed. 'He's called Stan MacGillivray; looks like the Angel Gabriel, sounds like Sidney James and has a mind like Pablo Picasso. I met him recently because he was one of our magazine's Twenty Most Eligible Bachelors. Saskia and Phoebe have both dated him.'

'Stan was one of your eligible bachelors?' Phoebe gasped, not sure whether to be delighted that Portia hadn't meant Dan, or appalled that her magazine had located someone as off-beat, gorgeous and unexpected as Stan for their list. Although incredibly desirable, he was one of the least eligible men she could think of; he was never sober after midday or conscious after midnight, always turned up three-quarters of an hour late, stank continually of turps and used his hair as dental floss. Portia's magazine, *Élan*, was renowned for assessing people by their lineage, peerage and acreage; Stan's only title was a battered copy of the *London A to Z* and he rented about thirty square feet of bedsit.

'He was the token arty farty,' Portia explained, laughing at Phoebe's wide eyes. 'None of the team knew any artists, except the odd portrait painter, so I suggested Stan. He's tipped to be the next Damien Hirst media anti-hero. An artdealer friend of mine keeps raving on about him; even commissioned one of Stan's funny potato print paintings for his own flat.'

'It's abstract destructionilism,' Phoebe said huffily.

'Who is he, Freddy?' Gin polished off her spritzer. 'Is he dishy?'

'Very.' Phoebe sucked her finger and shrugged.

'Nothing on Felix, of course.' Portia pulled at a blonde strand of hair and examined it closely for split ends. 'Sasky dropped Stanley like a hundred-yard catch when Felix prowled into her life.' There was a touch of bitterness in her voice. Then she looked up at Phoebe and grinned. 'Ironic, really.'

Phoebe looked at her sharply, but Gin rammed a ninety-percent-wine spritzer under her nose before she could speak.

'Portia, can you stay tomorrow night?' she asked, sitting beside her daughter and nicking one of her cigarettes.

'And have my bum massaged by Garth Drayson's gold rings?' she sniffed. 'No, thanks. And put that out, Mummy, it's a disgusting habit.'

'Oh, please do.' Gin ignored her and flicked ash into a vase holding some drooping delphiniums. 'I might even be able to rustle up a hunky local – there's a very dashing entrepreneur just moved into the Fenshaws' old place. Keeps racing around the lanes in a flashy red Noddy car. He might be available, though I'm not sure if he's married or not – I haven't seen a wife in evidence at all.'

'No.' Portia examined her nails thoughtfully. 'I'm not into

unmarried men.' She looked up at Phoebe again, and this time the scornful message in her eyes was as clear as Windowlened glass.

Portia set off late the next morning, scattering gravel as she accelerated along the Seatons' pot-holed drive and out on to the lane without braking, signalling or glancing up from her search for a cassette in the glove compartment.

'Won't her office be furious with her for turning up so late?' Phoebe asked Gin, who was standing beside her, shading her eyes from the sun with a gardening-gloved hand as she watched her daughter climb the opposite verge to overtake the local milk float.

'Lord, no.' Gin, who was wearing an old khaki fisherman's waistcoat over her sun-top, fished around in one of its many pockets for a piece of wire. 'I doubt she'll go in at all today. They seem terribly casual about it. Portia says there's seldom a soul in the office for the fortnight after the magazine's put to sleep, or whatever they call it. And, as she's in Features Planning at Large, she works months ahead of copy dates anyway.' She stretched across a small cluster of dehydrated bedding plants and started to secure some sagging clematis to a drain pipe.

Deciding to have a shower, Phoebe wandered back into the house.

'Oh, Fred!' Gin called after her.

'Mmm?' Almost in the hall, Phoebe caught sight of Saskia dashing up the stairs with a packet of Frosties under one arm and her hands crammed full of chocolate bars, Sheila's Embassy packet and the bottle of twelve-year-old Islay malt Tony had bought for this evening's guests.

'Could you be an absolute angel and do me a massive favour?' Gin stretched into sight, her hands still busily tying the clematis.

'Of course.' Phoebe quickly looked away from the stairs.

'Could you possibly run along to the farm shop and pick up a few things for me? I'd ask Sheila but she's frantically mucking out the dining room, and I just haven't the time. There's a list on the kitchen table. Thanks so much, Freddy.'

Phoebe wandered into the kitchen, rubbing a lump of sleep out of her eyes. She'd spent the night swinging between uncomfortable and ludicrous images of chasing after Felix Sylvian, and the appalling, clamorous need to feel Dan's solid, warm body beside hers. As tiredness had assailed her rationality, the two had got horribly mixed up. It wasn't until she heard Reg setting off to take Tony to the station at six that she'd dropped into a bottomless pit dream about landing a job in a chicken-plucking factory where Saskia was the supervisor. The chickens had all looked just like Felix Sylvian.

It was almost midday, and the overhead sun had reached brain-boiling intensity. Phoebe swatted flies as she passed two summering hunters, nose-to-rump by a fence with bobbing heads and twitching tails as they sought the shade of a thin oak tree. The tarmac driveway leading to Upper Selbourne Farm burnt through her espadrilles and the piebald collie sagging next to the gate hardly lifted his panting head as two chocolate eyes followed her progress into a purpose-built glass-house with a huge blackboard offering Pick-Your-Own soft fruit, and ready-made hanging baskets at cut rate.

Saying hello to a girl with burgundy hair, kohled eyes, hotpants and Hunter wellies who was lounging by the cash-box listening to Classic FM, Phoebe grabbed a plastic basket and wandered around heaving in double cream, strawberries, as-paragus, lemons, fennel, and two mutant baking potatoes the size of bricks.

'You not from round here?' The kohled eyes asked, plotting her progress.

'No.' Phoebe smiled over a punnet of raspberries.

'Thought not.'

'Oh.' She took in the unfriendly gaze. 'Why's that?'

The girl shrugged, scuffing the rubber toe of her boots on a bag of new potatoes. 'You picked out all the stuff we have to buy in – 'part from those strawberries and taties. Got to compete with the supermarkets these days, see?'

Phoebe nodded, listening to a plinkety-plinkety version of Roderigo's Concerto d'Aranjuez advertising ice-cream.

Tempted, she pulled open a gaudy little freezer and selected a phallic-looking cornet. Then she grinned. Nestling beside the Zooms were a small stack of Galaxy bars, stocked for passing weekenders needing a choccy-fix. Tossing them all into her basket, she headed back to the welly-wearing vamp.

'I'll pay for the chocolate and ice-cream separately,' she explained. 'The rest is to go on Mrs Seaton's account – Deayton Manor Farm.'

The vamp's eyes narrowed into two smudgy bands of kohl.

'Mrs Seaton, you say?' She scraped a midge-bite on her arm with long, black-painted finger nails.

'Yes.'

'Dad!' the vamp yelled towards the far end of the building where serried ranks of geraniums and violets drooped on trestle tables.

A huge man appeared from behind a seed stand. He was wearing nothing but straining denim shorts, flip-flops, a flower-pot hat and a quilted olive waistcoat which gaped across his vast, tanned beer belly.

'Yeah?'

'Girl wants to put goods on Mrs S's account. Over at Deayton.'

Beer Belly scratched beneath his flower pot hat and looked at Phoebe's legs appreciatively.

'Tell her she can't,' he barked back. 'I've told Mrs S for the last time. If she don't pay her bill, she can't have more goods. S'final.' With a last leer at Phoebe, he turned back to his seeds.

The vamp looked at her smugly. 'Sorry,' she said, not meaning it. 'You'll have to put the stuff back.'

'It's okay, I'll pay with cash,' Phoebe said hurriedly, digging in her bag for her wallet.

The girl pursed her lips and started weighing things on an old-fashioned hanging scale, adding up the totals by hand on the back of a piece of flower-wrapping paper.

Paying, Phoebe decided that the small market garden could hardly present stiff competition to any supermarkets, however much Balsamic vinegar and sun dried tomatoes they stocked.

She could have fed herself for a month in London and still had change to rattle for the same amount as they charged for some veg, chocolate and an ice-cream. Even her local Europa offered better value.

She wandered back along the lane, licking her cornet thoughtfully and letting the thin striped plastic bag swing from her fingers. The hunters had shuffled off to a denser oak and were now nibbling one another's withers lovingly.

Pausing to watch them, Phoebe didn't notice the ice-cream melting in frothy rivulets down her wrist as her eyes misted over. I want to nibble Dan's withers, she thought childishly, letting self-indulgent tears begin to tickle the backs of her eyes. Blinking them determinedly away, she ambled back along the lane towards the house, groping under her skirt to straighten her rucked-up knickers and licking the running ice-cream from her other arm.

The Range Rover appeared so quickly and quietly, it was just metres away before Phoebe noticed it. As she hopped on to the verge, she waved, thinking it was Reg. But the driver was a woman wearing huge dark glasses, her sleek hair drawn back in a neat pleat, her mouth moving in constant, angry speech. Her passenger was buried behind an Ordnance Survey map, clutched with white-knuckled fingers. The dashboard in front of them was littered with estate agents' glossy details.

As the car drew level with Phoebe, it slowed and an electric window whirred downwards as the woman, still arguing furiously, leaned her head out.

'– probably missed it by now. Hang on, I'm asking this girl. Excuse me!' she shouted, as though Phoebe were two fields away although they were now practically nose-to-nose. Something about her honking, SW1 tone made Phoebe feel mischievous. She slouched into a wellied vamp pose and licked her cornet Lolita-style.

'Yeah?' she grunted in a terrible Berkshire accent. 'What d'ya want, like?'

If she'd been auditioning for The Archers, she would have been kicked into Kent.

'I'm afraid we're rather lorst,' the woman quacked. She was glossy and well turned out, with plenty of good quality gold jewellery and a navy silk shirt which looked as though it had been flown from Hong Kong seconds ago, swathed in tissue paper. A grey streak of hair sliced rakishly through the un-naturally even mahogany of the rest, running from her forehead to her French pleat like a seam. But she was one of those upper-middle-class women who, despite immaculate turn-out, is born to look like a horse; long nose, flat forehead, no chin and tiny eyes which even an expert application of Estée Lauder couldn't enhance.

'Where're you heading, like?' Phoebe rolled her tongue around the cone and batted her eyes in what she hoped was a shag-me-under-the-apple-cart way.

The woman blinked warily. 'What's the name of that damn place, darling?' she demanded archly over her shoulder.

'West Yealmford,' came a reply from deep within the map.

Phoebe's teeth closed around the ice-cream in shock. She could feel her face surging with sudden colour as a punch of pain in her stomach almost floored her.

'Yealmford?' she croaked, ice-cream clogging her throat.

'That's right,' the woman quacked. 'We're looking at a cottage there – fifth today actually, and we've got six after lunch. But as we're eating down here tonight we thought we might as well make a day of it. You heard of it? We're terribly late.'

Phoebe was feeling dizzier and dizzier. Not trusting herself to speak, she shook her head.

'Never mind.' Nodding dismissively, the woman put the car into gear and glanced up the hill at the Seatons' house, almost hidden from view by trees.

'Now that's more the sort of place I was thinking of, darling,' she brayed as the window went back up and the car started moving off. 'Much better than those poky little shacks. I think left now, don't you? That girl obviously hadn't a clue – actually I think she was a simpleton. Rather quaint, don't you think? Like Whistle Down the – '

As the car drew away, the passenger looked up from his map and across the field to the Seatons' house.

Standing in the lane, Phoebe watched his profile move away and felt her chest tighten into a pip of winded pain. It was Dan's profile. Dan's voice. Unmistakable, beautiful Dan.

As the car slid around the corner and disappeared from view, Phoebe howled with despair. Then she belted out the loudest scream she could. Throwing the ice-cream into the hedge, she dug into the bag, pulled out the first object that came to hand and hurled it at a nearby tree. One of the mutant potatoes made contact with the trunk and split apart, landing with two quiet thuds in a patch of meadowsweet.

Slumping down on a verge, Phoebe ate her way through six Galaxy bars, tears sliding down her burning face.

8

Back at the house, she threw down Gin's groceries next to Julius Caesar's bust in the hall then flew upstairs. Crashing into her tiny bathroom, she pulled off her shorts and vest top and stood under the shower.

In her dramatic mental scenario, the hot, steaming sheet of high-pressure water would blast away her unhappy, churning thoughts. Instead a lukewarm dribble spluttered through the heavy coating of lime-scale before turning cold and thinning to a dripping trickle. Phoebe rested her forehead against the cool tiled wall and clenched her eyes tightly shut. Razor-sharp metal clamps of jealousy were clenching every muscle into spasm, tearing flesh through skin and pulling her stomach up into her throat. The shower let out a couple of cold coughs and died.

Phoebe, her cropped hair plastered with Wash and Go, rinsed her head under the cold tap in the basin until it too puttered out. She then scraped a sponge over her body and washed her feet by coating them in soap, sticking them in the loo and flushing. Years in university digs had taught her how to survive appalling plumbing.

Dressed in one of Fliss's daft Gaultier Junior dresses, with bare legs and dripping hair, she wandered into the garden.

'You can't wear just that!' Saskia grumbled, prone in a frayed deckchair beside the slime-filled pool, wearing leggings and a t-shirt.

'Why not?' Phoebe stepped out of her dress and hoicked up the waistband of her knickers before sitting down beside her on a musty folding chair and tipping the straps of her bra off her shoulders. 'No one can see.'

'You make me feel like I'm in purdah,' Saskia tugged the hems of her leggings up until they cut into her legs just below the knees. 'Christ, you're skinny.'

'I'd lay down my life for a decent pair of boobs.' Phoebe splayed out her legs and closed her eyes against the sun.

'I'd lay down my life for good legs again,' Saskia sighed, listening to her mother roaring off in the Golf to stock up on cheese, *Tristan and Isolde* blaring from her open windows.

'And longer hair,' Phoebe added wistfully.

'Clear skin.'

'Firmer bum.'

'No cellulite.'

'No fillings.'

'Felix.'

'Longer nails.'

'Felix.'

'A job.'

'Felix.'

From six o'clock, Gin was in a frenzy of trout-stuffing, salad-chopping hysteria. Every action was accompanied by the tinkling sound of ice cubes hitting the side of her crystal tumbler of gin and tonic. The WNO belted *La Traviata* out of a crackling transistor tuned to Radio 3.

Sheila, having prepared her contribution to the dinner party in advance, laid the long oak table in the dining room and then shared a quick fag with Saskia outside.

'Looking forward to tonight?' Sheila cocked her head, listening to Gin whisking egg whites for the asparagus soufflé.

'I'm not joining them.'

'Oh,' Sheila knew better than to try and coax Gin's youngest daughter into anything. 'Freddy and you going to have a gossip upstairs then? Or going out to the pub?'

'No.' Saskia leant back as her mother shot past to throw eggshells into the outside wheely bin. 'I've got things to plan.'

'Oh.' Sheila held her cigarette away as Gin whisked back past to the kitchen. 'D'you know why your mother's wearing a headscarf?' she whispered. 'She's had it on since she came back from the trout farm. One of the hottest days of the year, too.'

'Haven't a clue.' Saskia tossed her cigarette at a drain and wandered inside to grab a tub of taramasalata and a bag of Kettle crisps on her way upstairs.

Tony was dropped off by Reg just after seven. He hurried inside, searched for his malt whisky, gave up, poured himself three fingers of Teacher's instead, and shot upstairs to change.

'Good grief!' he gasped as he walked into the bedroom and caught sight of his wife's rear view.

Gin was crouching over her dressing table, elbows on the glass top, wearing a knee-length navy slip over her bra and running a stubby coral lipstick around her mouth. Nothing unusual in that. Tony was familiar with his wife's tanned, slightly muscular body; the way the flesh of her upper arms hung like a baggy jumper from her bones and her back, covered in freckles and moles, creased like a tortoise's neck between her shoulder blades. And she never afforded herself the time to sit at her dressing table and apply make-up – could not if she'd wanted to, in fact, because the old piano stool that had once been there was now under three fat begonias in the window recess.

But what he hadn't seen before was that she was blonde.

'Is that permanent?' he asked in horrified amazement.

'Of course it is,' Gin dismissed him, not expecting praise. Admittedly, the hairdresser in Hexbury had gone a little wild. Having promised very subtle ash-blonde highlights and a Gloria Hunneford set, Cut Above had provided Gin with Princess Di gold and a severe Joan Bakewell bob. But the effect knocked off a good ten years, showed off her tan and was an immense confidence boost.

Making no further comment on it, Tony polished off his whisky, loosened his tie and stomped off to the bathroom.

Gin shrugged and wondered if she should go wild and apply some mascara. She'd had all the flattery she needed that evening. Catching sight of her returning from her bath earlier, Phoebe had stopped in her tracks, blinked, wolf-whistled and then, laughing incredulously, given her an enormous hug.

'I don't want you to stay upstairs with me.' Saskia placed herself firmly between Phoebe and the open door to her room, then started backing inside. 'I said, I've got things to do.'

'Like what?' Phoebe demanded.

'I'm working on a project,' Saskia muttered cryptically.

'But I came here to see you, not your parents' friends,' Phoebe pleaded. 'I'm going back to London tomorrow.'

Saskia pretended not to hear.

'And I don't think your father really wants me here,' Phoebe argued hopelessly.

'All the more reason to rile the old bastard.' Saskia started to close the door.

'We need to talk some more,' Phoebe tried another tack. 'About your revenge idea.'

'No, we don't!' Saskia snapped angrily. 'Either you say yes or you piss off.' And the door banged closed.

Phoebe sighed. She was getting very familiar with the wrong side of it.

Phoebe couldn't be bothered to change or put on make-up despite her sunburnt nose and cheeks. Instead she glared at her reflection in the rusty full-length mirror in her room, wishing she hadn't come to stay with the Seatons at all. She could have remained in London and hit some beloved wine bars, clubbed all Saturday night and had a lovely lazy barbecue with her friends on Sunday before slobbing out with Fliss and the papers. Then she'd have spent today pottering around central London on the pretext of finding another job.

Downstairs, she could hear Tony's booming haw-haw tones welcoming friends into the house with much back-slapping, wife-kissing and coat-taking. He hadn't sounded at all pleased earlier when she'd heard Gin tell him that Phoebe would be making up the numbers.

Fliss's dress would look ridiculously tarty to a bunch of old-school-tie professionals like Tony Seaton's cronies, Phoebe realised. Fliss was such a fashion victim, her clothes were usually only admired in about two streets and one club in Soho. The Gaultier dress was no exception: an asymmetrical, A-line, asexual, crotch-length gym slip made from thick black cavalry twill panelled with coarse, tight elastic which dragged it in around the chest almost like a liberty bodice. Phoebe loved it because it gave her the appearance of a cleavage and was amazingly comfortable. To be a true fashion victim one was supposed to wear a Bonnie Prince Charlie white shirt (definitely not ironed) underneath it. But it was far too hot, and her only white shirt was back at the Islington flat, boil-washed to a size six. Phoebe did, however, kick off her manky espadrilles and lace up her ultra-trendy long black boots, even though they'd probably frazzle her feet to a hot sweaty pulp. She then had to undo fifteen pairs of lace holes to remove one of Saskia's stubbed out cigarettes from the arch of her foot.

Bounding downstairs, Phoebe looked like a very tall Upper Third choirboy taking part in his boarding school's production of Moby Dick. But she felt it hardly mattered. She'd be polite for Gin's sake but, as she was unlikely to meet any of the guests again in her life, it hardly mattered if she freaked them out a bit.

Gin was whistling from the smartest drawing room to the kitchen as Phoebe jumped the last three steps and nearly landed on Tebbit.

'Oh, there you are, Freddy – gosh, you look simply gorgeous. I wish Tony had lined up a dishy chap for you.' She paused by the door and hissed in a loud stage whisper, 'You've got Garth Drayson's son, Huw, I'm afraid. He's pretty innocuous, but don't ask him anything about computers, for Christ's sake.' She winked, bringing her voice up to normal level again. 'Just go through. Tony will fix you a huge drink.'

As Phoebe approached the babbling room, she briefly registered a familiar, honking woman's voice amongst the general burble before Tony loomed out into the hall, stopping her in her tracks with his paunch. Gripping her arm like a manacle, he whisked her across to his study.

'I thought you were going back to London today,' he hissed, his three chins wobbling in fury above his pink and green Garrick tie.

'I decided to stay,' she said sulkily.

'So Gin tells me.' Tony's eyes narrowed as he took in what she was wearing. 'Christ, whatever possessed you to dress like that? You look like a fucking schoolgirl with a Saturday job at Madame Cyn's.'

'What business is it of yours if I do?' Phoebe snarled, loudly enough for the chattering in the room opposite to lull dramatically. She found his dictatorial, pompous attitude utterly exasperating. 'You're not my bloody father.'

Tony was twitching with anger, his forehead creased in agitation like a Shar Pei dog. 'True – and I thank God for that fact. But I'm a good friend of Daniel Neasham's, and I don't want you fucking up his marriage.'

'Who?' Phoebe croaked, feeling as if he'd put his hands around her throat and squeezed.

'You heard.' Tony's tongue lashed his teeth as he spat his words. 'Dan Neasham.'

'Oh, Christ,' Phoebe whispered, the reality of the situation pinching her ribs with agonising spite. Why the hell hadn't it occurred to her earlier? she thought furiously. The woman had even said they were eating in the area. It just hadn't registered.

'He's here?' she croaked.

Tony nodded. 'With his wife, Mitzi, who I happen to like very much.'

Phoebe put her face in her hands, desperate not to cry, her eyes peeking from above her index fingers. 'Gin doesn't know about us?'

'Of course not. No one bloody does, least of all Mitzi.' Tony pushed the door to as he heard his wife strolling back from the kitchen, ice tinkling. 'And I intend to keep it that way. Your being here is a complete fucking cock-up.'

'I'll go back upstairs,' Phoebe whispered hastily. 'Tell Gin I felt sick suddenly – too much sun or something. Say I've decided to go to bed. Anything.'

She realised she was physically shaking, her gut hollow with nerves. She longed to see Dan with every shuddering, leaping muscle. She felt like a rescue dog knowing her old master was in the next room and quivering with ecstatic, anticipated joy. But he had a wife. A living, breathing, French-pleated, grey-streaked wife, not just that oblique reference to a marriage early on in their affair. Mitzi the honking horse. Poor Mitzi, with her long nose and dreadful, patronising voice.

Tony looked at her, his slab-like face momentarily unguarded and astonished.

'Christ, you're still in love with him, aren't you, you stupid girl?'

Phoebe nodded. Tears blurred his heavy features into an oval blob in front of her.

'And I suppose you want to sell him the house?' She forced a half-smile and headed towards the door. 'Look, I'll push off – '

'I'll just see if I can find them – ' laughed a voice from the other side.

Phoebe walked smack into Gin.

'There you are, Freddy.' Gin, positively floating on half a bottle of Gordon's, didn't notice her stricken face. 'Why's Tony been hogging you?' She propelled Phoebe across the hall. 'Here, I want you to meet some lovely friends of his – '

They were in the drawing room now, being watched by a host of curious faces.

Phoebe fought a desperate urge to close her eyes. It would look so utterly awful, so bitchily planned. Dan would think she'd arranged it all: the invitation, the late entrance, the dress.

Fighting the urge to scan the room for him, she forced herself to concentrate on the other couple: Garth Drayson, a short, fat, grinning Welshman whose bloodshot faux-blue eyes dipped to her cleavage as often as his caraway toast hit the sour cream and gruyère, and his wife Jilly, much younger – blonde, gushy and kissy – with a Page Three body and skin tanned the texture and colour of a leather desk-top. They introduced Garth's shuffling son, Huw – his nose level with Phoebe's armpit – who was cripplingly shy, his bulging rabbit eyes remaining glued to her wacky, ridiculous boots.

'Oh, aren't they, er, trendy!' Jilly surged vapidly, following her step-son's gaze.

I've been chatted up in clubs purely as a result of wearing these boots, Phoebe remembered crabbily. But Jilly gave them the same amused, pompous glance that she would afford were Phoebe to have hopped in wearing long-haired seventies Yeti walkers. Phoebe wished she could stand behind a sofa. The Draysons were what her mother would snobbishly term artless-nouveau – lots of designer labels that one could wear outside: Lacoste and Ralph Lauren Polo shirts, Rolex watches, Versace jeans and Gucci bags. M and S comfort, Gin-style, was as alien to them as stainless steel taps and cotton sheets.

'Oh, you're such a big bear, Tonic!' Jilly, who clearly found standing next to Phoebe unflattering, sashayed towards Tony who was looking thunderous. Her high heels speared and lifted the Seatons' ancient, balding rug like a pastry chef's air holes. 'Give me a cuddle, you old devil – we've hardly said hello yet.'

'Are you a model or something, my darling?' Garth Drayson stretched up on tip-toes to growl into Phoebe's ear, his over-sized gold signet ring brushing the bare flesh of her thigh.

Opposite them, Huw's rabbit eyes narrowed and he stared at Phoebe's boots with loathing.

'Freddy's so talented she could do anything.' Gin smiled rather woozily.

'Yes, I thought when she came in, there's some real talent!' Garth laughed raucously, reaching for another slice of caraway toast and shooting Phoebe a wink that almost popped out one of his tinted contact lenses.

She winced and shot Huw a sympathetic look, which landed somewhere on his sweating, white forehead.

'Now where have that other lot got to?' Gin murmured, sounding very Miss Marple as she squinted across the room.

The sun, minutes away from dropping behind a hedge, was

slicing through the two high, grubby windows at almost a right angle. It made the inside of the room appear strangely grotto-like, the light deep and saturated yet illuminating little, just swathing whole corners in subterranean shadow.

Over Huw's rounded, dandruff-scattered shoulder, Phoebe could see the glitter of a gold earring as Mitzi Neasham, grinning broadly and artificially in the general direction of the room, was frantically trying not to move her lips as she hissed: 'It's the simpleton, darling,' to the man next to her.

'Ah, there they are! Freddy, meet Daniel and Mitzi Neasham.' Gin towed Phoebe across the room. 'Freddy's Saskia's best and loveliest friend,' she explained to the Neashams. 'This is a very rare treat as she hardly ever visits old fossils like us any more.' Gin beamed at Mitzi, who was settling into a patronising I-donate-to-Mencap smile. 'And Daniel knows Tony through his chums at the Temple, Freddy. He's a very high-flying legal eagle at Satellite Newspapers, I gather. What is it they call you, Daniel? The Libel Detector? Tony tells me stars quake in fear of going belly up when they sue one of your papers, because it costs so much if one loses.'

'They always lose,' he said mildly, his iron grey eyes tracing the side of Phoebe's face like a finger before smiling into Gin's.

She felt as though she was undergoing acupuncture to every single pore of her body. She knew she should hate him for being an adulterous toad, should be cutting her heart out as a pound of flesh for Mitzi, should in fact behave as politely and coldly as possible. But instead it was as if someone had dropped a box of fireworks inside her dress followed by a lit match.

'What are you having to drink, Fred?' Gin detected a sticky silence through her happy haze of juniper and decided to escape. 'Huge glass of white wine okay?' She bolted off before Phoebe had a chance to ask for mineral water.

Mitzi Neasham was still beaming out an indulgent, condescending smile which made her look like a donkey about to sneeze.

'Have you known the Seatons long, Frederica?' she asked in a slow, clear voice as if talking to a finger-sucking toddler at a gymkhana.

'Years,' Phoebe croaked, suddenly desperate to escape to Gin and the kitchen. 'I – '

'And you're friendly with Saskia? That's nice, isn't it?' Mitzi cocked her head to one side and crinkled her tiny eyes kindly.

She was the ultimate in smothering, mumsy do-goodness, Phoebe realised, watching her rapt face. Although undoubtedly a raging snob, who probably thought Medicare was a type of private health plan, her heart was as high-carat gold as her snaffle chain bracelet. She was the sort of person continually referred to as a 'brick', a 'trooper' and the 'salt of the earth'. Phoebe, who spilled more salt than a leaky Saxa container, wanted to toss her over her left shoulder.

'Yes, we went to school together,' she explained, refusing to let herself steal a look at Dan, whose jacket shoulder was touching his wife's padded one. He'd changed aftershaves, she noted. Instead of the icy, citric smell she always woke with in her lungs after dreaming of him, she could smell Mitzi's Chanel No 5 fighting a head-on battle with something very butch and cloying – all musk, spice and manly chat in the changing room. It was probably a Christmas present, she realised with a start.

She could hardly believe there had been a Christmas and his birthday since they'd last seen one another. The obscene, suffocating guilt that was pulling her eyes unwillingly towards the carpet and scorching the red sunburn stain on her cheekbones across to her jaw, made her feel as if she'd just slipped out of the crumpled bed in his Barbican flat that morning.

'One bucket of white wine!' Gin announced brightly, swaying in with Phoebe's glass and her own refreshed tumbler spilling their contents across her wrists.

Mitzi was looking at Phoebe quizzically. 'You know, I'm quite sure we saw you this morning,' she quacked. 'Asked directions. We've been house-hunting all day.' She turned to Gin who was pressing drink drips from her silk waistcoat with her shirt sleeve. 'Actually, it's hugely ironic, isn't it, Dan? We passed this place on the way somewhere and I said to him, that's *exactly* what I'd like – we've been looking at some really poky

little barn conversions and such. I had absolutely no idea this
was your house. I mean, we could have saved ourselves a tank of
diesel. Quite amazing, isn't it?'

'Yes, it's a beautiful house.' Gin sighed happily, misunder-
standing the implication. 'Tony and I are both devoted to it. We
moved here in the early seventies, you know – of course, it was
in a dreadful state then – and we haven't felt the slightest urge to
up-sticks since.'

Mitzi gave her an odd look. 'So why . . .?'

'Everyone all right for drinks, yes?' Tony loomed in hastily,
putting his hand on his wife's back so quickly that two ice cubes
and a slice of lemon hit the carpet.

'Actually, I'd love another cranberry juice, Tony.' Mitzi
crinkled her crows' feet again.

'Dan?' Tony's sunken rhino eyes bored into Dan's wide,
bright ones, which were watching Phoebe with hypnotised
interest.

'I'm fine,' he muttered, flicking his gaze across with the same
speed as a typist pressing the carriage return, his empty glass
clutched tightly in his hand.

'Er – right.' Tony was clearly desperate to defuse the situation. Help came in an unwarranted cloud of Lou Lou as Jilly
Drayson wafted up.

'I was just saying to Tony here,' she put five red-painted,
gold-ringed claws on Gin's shoulder, 'how much better you
look blonde, Ginny. Really suits you with that tan. When did
you take the plunge?'

Gin looked faintly embarrassed, but wildly flattered. 'This
afternoon actually,' she confessed. 'I was feeling such a dowdy
old bag, I decided I needed cheering up.'

'Don't we all?' Jilly cackled, cheerful in the knowledge that
she was almost two decades younger and far richer, therefore
the recipient of weekly facials and clay wraps. 'Do you have a
tint, Mitz?' she asked without a trace of bitchiness, just a keen
thirst for girl-talk.

'God, no!' Mitzi's receding chin almost inverted with horror
as she cast an anxious glance at her husband.

Despite her brash bravura, Jilly Drayson was one of those genuinely interested, chatty and uncomplicated women who draw the more inhibited, stuffy and modest ones out. Whilst professing to love talking about the arts, politics and charity, Gin and Mitzi had never been so animated. Soon they were confessing to sleeping in make-up, buying at sales and longing for the nerve to hit Harley Street's finest tuckers as Jilly's receptive, eager gaze drank them in.

She was wearing exactly the same shade of tinted lenses as her husband, Phoebe noted with interest as she slugged back her wine. She'd lay down fifty quid that they had matching jogging suits as well. And those tans definitely came out of a tube – of the UVA sun-bed variety.

God, I'm being a bitch, she thought wretchedly. Her nerves were rattling so much that her skin was crackling with static electricity.

'Right, cranberry juice,' Tony said to no one in particular, still hovering. 'Circulate a few bites, huh, Freddy?' he hissed, anxious to get Phoebe and Dan on to different rugs.

Phoebe nodded but, as Tony slid away, found her boots rooted to the spot, gluing her opposite Dan.

As she looked into his face properly for the first time in a year, she repeated a determined chant in her head . . . It's over, it's over, he scratches inside his ears with matches, he likes Clannad, it's over, he wears Y-fronts, he kisses with his eyes shut . . . it's over.

She forced herself to remember the utter humiliation she'd felt before leaving for New Zealand; the grieving, car-crash sense of loss, the degrading vilification from her friends and parents, the aching need to be free and frenzied and unruly again. She tried desperately to look at braying, giggling Mitzi and let compassion bleach out longing. But all the time her eyes were sliding deeper into Dan's with the same hairdryer-in-the-lungs delight she would feel if her hand were slipping inside his shirt.

He hadn't changed at all, she realised, as a scalding sensation of delight reinflated both lungs to bursting point. Everything –

his clothes, his tufted bitter-chocolate hair, his canyon-wide smile, shadowed at the corners where it stretched beyond his teeth into two acute triangles of affection, his crinkling cheeks and broad straight nose – was exactly as when she'd left them, like a beloved painting one returned to in a gallery and drank in with intoxicated rapture.

The urge to touch him was so compelling that the sofa squeaked noisily as she tried to step back further.

'You look so different,' he muttered under his breath, one corner of his mouth hooking up towards his ear in a curious half-grin.

'Do I?' Phoebe tipped the last of her wine down her throat without tasting it.

'Cranberry juice!' Tony bustled into the next group so loudly that, across the room, Huw dropped a miniature brass telescope on a George I lowboy violently enough to scrape away three years' worth of Sheila's beeswax.

Tony stiffened, his deep jowls rising in anger. But such was his desire to extract favours from Garth Drayson, he forced his most deal-clinching smile and laughed. 'Bless you, Huw,' he boomed congenially. 'For once I'll be looking at the French polishing cards in the post-office window with purely innocent motives.'

Garth almost fell into the fireplace with mirth.

Gin was now so tight that she missed the incident entirely.

'Tony, I was just saying to Minxy,' she touched her husband's shirt sleeve dreamily, 'wouldn't it be rather fun if Turandot met Don Giovanni? What do you think they'd make of one another?'

Tony flashed a terrified smile and once again hauled Phoebe into a corner, tipping the grey-muzzled Labrador on to Dan's Chelsea boots in his haste.

'Check on the bloody food, will you?' he demanded, his forehead moist with tension. 'Gin's totally plastered.'

About to tell him to piss off, Phoebe saw the desperation in his eyes and changed her mind. His future was riding on tonight, she realised. And that meant Gin's, Saskia's and all the Seatons' happiness.

Nodding, she turned to go.

'And Phoebe.' Tony beckoned her back, glancing around like a night watch-man about to light a fag. 'I have to ask you this – please, think of it as a favour to Saskia.' His face was so sunken with worry that his old features were almost surfacing from the swamp of flesh.

'Yes?'

Tony dropped his voice to a wheeze. 'Lay off Dan and chat up Garth and his son a bit,' he pleaded. 'They both fancy you.'

Phoebe held Tony's wet-eyed gaze with her own.

'I'll check on the food,' she said flatly.

Forcing herself not to look in Dan's direction, she walked out and followed the smell of burning through the side-lobby and into the kitchen.

'Christ!' She backed away as she opened the top oven of the Aga, fanning the air in front of her in an attempt to clear enough smoke to discern what was burning. Eight blackened miniature ramekins were neatly lined up on a baking tray, sitting in pools of their sizzling, spitting contents. The top oven looked like the aftermath of a scene one closed one's eyes on in *Alien 3*.

With the aid of two oven mitts shaped like Thelwell pony heads – why did everything equine make her think of Dan's wife? Phoebe wondered bitterly – she dragged out the hissing starters and plonked them on the quarry-tiled floor.

'You'll burn yourselves, kids.' She batted the dogs' noses away and peered at the frothing pots. Several charred stalks poking out at jaunty angles told her that these had once been Gin's asparagus soufflés.

'Christ!' she muttered, straightening up and gazing around for inspiration.

The kitchen was afloat with spilling bags of flour, bottles of vinegar, olive oil, lemon peel, carrot tops, milk bottles crammed with parsley and yesterday's Style and Travel section of the *Sunday Times* liberally scattered with ring marks. Eight neatly foil-parcelled trout lay on a metal tray by the sink alongside half a dozen bottles of claret breathing the smoky air.

Phoebe found colanders of chopped vegetables under several tea-towels, a sizzling wodge of mustard-encrusted beef in the bottom oven and a vast lemon mousse in the fridge along with a furry tub of Philadelphia, four bottles of Hunter Valley, three eggs, some Hellman's and a withered ginger stem. But apart from half an acre of brie softening on the table and a frilly, variegated salad banked up in a crystal bowl, nothing immediately presented itself as an instant starter.

She flung open the larder and prayed that a giant pot of Fortnum's foie gras would be idling half-hidden on a shelf, left over from Christmas. It wasn't. Rows and rows of Sheila's chutney, some dating back five years, dominated the space. Gin never had the heart to throw them out. More bags of flour spilled their contents through the wooden slats along with ancient packets of sauce mix, icing sugar, dried fruit and breakfast cereal. Beneath the wire mesh window, several geriatric avocados were sinking into the wooden sill looking as if they needed some of Jilly Drayson's anti-wrinkle tips. Phoebe counted them and grinned.

'Guacamole, holé!' she laughed, remembering Fliss reduced to near-tears of frustration as she'd tried to teach her how to make the spicy green dip.

Grabbing them, Phoebe tore off peel as she waltzed back into the kitchen and threw their slimy contents into Gin's eggy food processor, squelching around to extract the stones from the brown-flecked pulp. She then extracted the tub of cream cheese from the fridge, scraped off the fluff, and up-ended that too, along with a good slurp of olive oil, a blob of mayonnaise and a tin of ready-chopped tomatoes. Feeling as smug as Mary Poppins with an Aqua-vac, she pressed the green button and waggled her plastic spatula excitedly.

The resulting sludge looked ideal for grouting tiles, gluing on shoe-heels and gunk-tanking guest celebrities on Noel Edmonds's light entertainment show. Apothecaries could have pyramid-sold and got rich quick if the recipe had existed in the Middle Ages. Just looking at it made Phoebe want to develop an eating disorder.

'Oh, God,' she wailed, backing away into a solid body.

Before she could take in what was happening, two warm hands had slipped beneath her skirt and cupped each buttock as firmly as a ski-lift heading up a black slope.

Breathing in a hot, musky tang, she knew it was Garth Drayson. She certainly wasn't going to stand for this. Swinging around, she slapped him firmly across the face with the plastic spatula.

'Christ!' came the low, fervid howl she knew of old, although she was more used to hearing it at the point of orgasm than after a right hook.

'Oh, God.' She covered her mouth with her hand and tried not to laugh.

Two watering, hurt grey eyes came level with hers and widened in shock.

'What the hell did you do that for?' Dan put a hand to his stinging cheek.

'I'm sorry.' Phoebe coughed back a cramp-like attack of giggles. 'I thought you were Garth.'

'Thanks.'

Dan's sulky scowl lifted into the old heart-stopping lazy grin. Phoebe's giggles burst and vanished like bath bubbles doused in talc.

'Oh, hell.'

She knew how Lot's wife felt gazing back at Sodom. She needed dark glasses to blot out the delight in his eyes. I'm not the salt of the earth, she wanted to yell, I'm a pillar of it.

Instead she blurted, 'I'm so sorry, Dan. I had no idea you were coming tonight.'

His gaze wandered over her body with the brimming, excited joy of a schoolboy spotting his first Aston Martin. A sparkler suddenly lodged somewhere in Phoebe's chest and skipped around inside her, shooting embers lower and lower down her body.

'I mean, if I'd had any idea, I'd never have come.' She fought to make her voice sound authoritative and unemotional.

'Christ, I'm glad you did.' Dan's eyes found hers again,

suddenly wide with forlorn sadness. 'I've missed you so much.' He touched her cheek incredulously.

Phoebe flinched away, terrified by the hot, excited flames licking at her stomach. Instead of the cold, angry self-loathing she longed to feel, the guilt-ridden publicity of their meeting was stirring up quagmires of churning, thrill-seeking recklessness.

She backed away until the kitchen surface hit the small of her back.

'Won't the others be missing you?' she asked more snappily than she'd intended.

'I'm here for a top up,' he murmured, following her. 'And right now I can think of something I'd far rather refill than my glass.' He stopped, his lips only an inch away from her mouth.

Phoebe looked into his huge, trust-me eyes and a long finger nail of lust quivered the length of her back-bone. Then they both burst out laughing.

'That's by far the corniest line I've ever heard you say.' She turned back to the olive sludge, deliberately breaking the frisson.

'I'm rather out of practice.' Dan hovered for a second, his breath touching the back of her neck before he moved away to fetch his glass from the table. 'God, what's that?'

Phoebe glanced over her shoulder and saw him gazing at Gin's charred ramekins which had cooled enough for the dogs to be lapping tentative tongues at the rims.

'Asparagus soufflé,' she sighed, shovelling her mend-all paste into a large ceramic bowl.

'Don't tell me you're proposing we eat that instead?' He watched the last of the khaki sludge land on her dress.

'What's wrong with it?' She wiped the blob away with her thumb and sucked it. Wincing in disgust, she almost threw up.

'Well, for one,' Dan stood beside her and spun the dish around so that the bold lettering on the side was visible, 'you've just put it into a dog bowl.'

'Oh, God!' Phoebe threw the spatula on top of the gunky guacamole and groaned. 'Where's Gin?'

'Still taking my wife on an operatic tour of her ferns, I should think.' Dan picked up the bowl and deposited it in the sink. 'Is this some sort of fish course?' He looked at the eight foil sausages.

Phoebe nodded.

'Look, bung these in the oven then.' He handed the tray to her. 'Just serve them as a starter – I'll head back and distract everyone for twenty minutes or so, try to stop Garth Drayson from licking out the dip bowls.' He leant into the fridge and took out some Chardonnay.

Phoebe stood watching him, clutching her tray of trout like a nervous waitress trying not to rattle the champagne flutes at a glitzy party. She was fighting a terrible urge to throw it down and pounce on him.

'Are you really going to buy this house?' she asked, desperate to numb her impulses.

He straightened up and shrugged, examining the wine label uncomfortably. 'I'm not sure.' He glanced around the kitchen, returned to the bottle and fingered the foil. 'With a place like this – that a family has grown up in and adored – it seems like adopting someone else's grown-up child. There's so much of the Seatons hallmarked everywhere. And it really is far too big for us.'

'They need the money,' Phoebe blurted, aware that she was being horribly indiscreet but incapable of keeping anything from him. Feeling unusually gauche, she shoved the fish into the oven to hide her burning cheeks.

'I know,' Dan sighed. He watched the back of her legs as she bent down, loving the apple-shaped hollow above the first curves of her inner thigh.

'Stop looking at my knickers,' Phoebe growled, grabbing the rail to pull herself upright.

'I really must get back,' he said, starting to move away, then paused and stepped towards her instead. 'One last thing, Phoebe?'

'Yes?' Looking around, she turned her face straight into his lips.

Knowing she should pull away, she felt the first light traces of his tongue slide from her cheek to her teeth and could do nothing but kiss him back.

Kissing Dan was like eating the first spoonful of ice-cream from the top of a new Häagen Dazs tub. Once started, it was almost impossible to stop. Dan was smiling, kissing and saying her name at the same time, all teeth and nose and tongue. Revisiting a long-lost sensation, Phoebe felt as if she was free-falling into a king-sized water bed in Paradise. Laughing between takes, their kisses got greedier and increasingly un-dignified as lust sidled off with their self-control.

'You're the loveliest, sexiest woman I've met in my life,' he muttered into her lips.

'Don't talk with your mouth full,' she murmured back.

'My tongue's completely tied.' He dipped back into her mouth again.

As his hand inched up under the hollow of her ear, Phoebe could feel the tiny circles of his shirt buttons against her chest and the hard fronts of his thighs pressing against her own. The sexual punch in her groin was so powerful, she felt as if she were wearing a crotch-strapped harness and being dangled from Concorde halfway across the Atlantic. When the icy bottle of Chardonnay he was carrying stroked the back of her thigh, she shivered with delight and let her fingers slip from the tailor-stitched lapels of his jacket down to the trouser bump of his pelvis.

They surfaced, gasping for air like children who've battled underwater to see who could hold their breath the longest.

'Oh, Christ.' Dan's springy hair tickled Phoebe's throat as he dropped his head onto her chest, smiling with delight. 'Where the hell have you been?'

It wasn't a geographical enquiry, just happy, relieved rhetoric.

Phoebe swallowed hard and willed herself to pull away, apologise, dust herself down and beat a hasty retreat. But some harpy inside her was curling her fingers into his waistband and pulling him as tightly to her as a fly zip in a pair of leather jeans. As Dan pushed her back against the Aga rail, his hand sliding down her throat, the Thelwell oven gloves fell off and landed on Tebbit's head.

Phoebe glanced down at them, thought about prim, honking Mitzi, and shuddered with self-loathing. But as Dan's lips found hers again, her body was still rattling down a bobsleigh run of wanton longing. She hated herself for her weakness, but she fancied him too much to be virtuous. His tongue curled around her eye tooth and slithered, cool and wine-flavoured, into her mouth. Phoebe took the bottle from his hand and dropped it into a nearby dog's bed, then traced the back of his thigh with shivering happiness. It was like rediscovering a long-lost diary of halcyon days.

'I think they're about to send out a search party,' a sardonic voice announced from the door. 'Garth Drayson is threatening to eat a pot plant. But I see you're staving off hunger by nibbling each other. Very enterprising.'

'Shit!' Dan dropped Phoebe like a flaming pan and spun back to the table, ducking his head.

As tears of guilt and embarrassment threatened to spill in a sudden, whooshing damburst of repentance, Phoebe gaped across the room.

It was Saskia, leaning against the frame of the door to the back stairs, glaring at her with unveiled contempt. She was wearing the old red dressing gown again, along with small wire-framed spectacles, bed-socks and three pens tucked into her drawn back hair. A cigarette smouldered between two yellow-stained fingers.

'Right then.' Dan coughed, hugely uncomfortable, stooping to retrieve the Chardonnay. 'I'll take this wine through.'

He paused at the lobby door and looked back at Phoebe, his roan eyes tortured with worry and the need to say far more than the split-second allowed.

'Say your bye-byes,' snarled Saskia.

'Don't forget the trout,' he muttered rather gutlessly and, shooting Saskia a poisonous look, went out towards the hall, where the chattering hubbub had been joined by the haunting beauty of '*O mio babbino caro*'.

Saskia walked into the centre of the kitchen, barely batting an eye at the shambles of burnt food and spilled ingredients around her.

'You're disgusting,' she spat, facing Phoebe over the bowed table where the brie was now sweating like a marathon runner.

The impression of Dan's belt buckle still indenting her stomach, Phoebe sagged back against the Aga and closed her eyes, not feeling the heat of the huge oven scalding through the fabric of her dress. She felt as if she'd just been shot – a frozen, deathly numbness she knew would turn to pain at any second. But if you stand in point-blank range, she reasoned, you don't expect a flesh wound.

'That was The Corps, I take it?' Saskia plucked at her cigarette with a shaking hand. 'Rather unfortunate, Daddy knowing him,' she rattled on, her words sizzling with venom. 'You didn't think to mention that he was Daniel Neasham, did you? No wonder Daddy wanted you to piss off. Looks great, wheeling in Daniel's ex-mistress and trying to get him to buy the house at the same time. Could knock a comma out of the asking price if glitzy Mitzi finds out.'

Phoebe covered her ears. 'Shut up, Saskia. Why the hell are you saying this?'

'Because I had no idea what a calculating bitch you could be.' Saskia flicked her ash into the drooping salad and narrowed her eyes. 'You knew all along, didn't you? No wonder you don't want to help me with Felix. You're hell-bent on leaping back into bed with desperate Dan, aren't you? It's probably why you came here in the first place.'

'Saskia, shut up!'

'He'll never divorce her, of course, you know that?' Saskia gloated. 'She's worth a packet – far more once her father croaks. And seeing as she herself's knocking on, that shouldn't be too long now.'

'Saskia, I – '

'Still, from the way you virtually had your legs wrapped around him, I suspect he'll be game for a couple of lunches in a seedy Kensington hotel, room booked in the name of Grandpa Smith,' Saskia went on. 'After all, if the freebies are on offer, he might as well grab the odd quickie.'

'Shut up!' Phoebe wailed. 'Why are you being so horrible?'

Saskia's eyes were brimming with tears. 'You really don't know, do you?' Then, like a slashed tyre, she flopped down at the table, ash tipping everywhere, completely deflated. 'You were my last hope, Freddy. You're brave and bolshie and could genuinely do it.' Her voice shook. 'I've always been so bloody jealous of you. I just prayed you'd do it. But why the hell should you? You don't even like me.'

Not moving from her scalding leaning post, Phoebe stared at her, blind with anger and humiliation. Saskia was completely obsessed, worshipping at the altar of Felix Sylvian so slavishly that she saw events only in its reflected light; her world turned on its axis. Nothing was important except in the context of how it was going to affect her plotted revenge.

'God, god, god, god, GOD!'

Clutching her empty tumbler, Gin flew into the kitchen and slithered to a wonky halt just in front of the charred tray of ramekins. Swaying dramatically, she squinted at them and howled: 'God!'

'I've put the fish in the top oven,' Phoebe told her, fighting to sound normal. 'They'll be ready any minute.'

'What?' Gin muttered, still staring tearfully at her tar-pool soufflés.

'The trout. I thought they'd do for the first course.'

'Yes, yes, I suppose they'll have to,' Gin sighed irritably, pitching slightly to the left. 'God, Tony's going to be so angry, drat him. I just totally forgot. I was chatting to Mitzi Neasham – such a lovely woman. Terribly keen to see round the house and so complimentary. She loves the garden.' She looked up at Phoebe and smiled, then suddenly looked concerned. 'Fred, are you all right? You're deathly pale.'

'Freddy wants to go back to London tonight,' Saskia announced before Phoebe could speak.

'What?' Gin's voice slurred slightly as she made a supreme

effort to sound sober. 'Don't be ridiculous, Saskia. We're about to eat. Freddy can't leave.'

'Freddy's not hungry,' she said firmly, glaring at Phoebe over her mother's shoulder.

'Nonsense,' Gin stared at Phoebe, her bright, drunken eyes glinting with annoyance. 'Don't be childish, Freddy. If you feel ill, just say. You can slope off to bed early.'

'I don't feel ill.' She glared back at Saskia.

'She just wants to go home, don't you, Freddy?' Saskia stood up and mouthed '*Dan*' like an evil, snapping terrier issuing a silent threat.

'What then?' Gin demanded as Phoebe stared at Saskia in silent confusion.

'I'll tell them all what the butler saw, Freddy,' Saskia murmured, shambling over to the wall phone. 'I'm sure Mummy's guests would be fascinated to know what goes on below stairs.'

'For Christ's sake, what are you both talking about?' Gin snapped, pushing Phoebe out of the way so that she could get out the trout.

'No, Saskia,' Phoebe muttered desperately.

'Oh yes I will!' she grinned, hooking the receiver over one shoulder and dialling out.

'I can't believe you would be as selfish as this, Freddy – ouch!' Gin started plucking foil from fish with her bare fingers, bristling with fury. 'What will the Draysons think? They had to bribe Huw to come and make up the dratted numbers with the promise of a new floppy chip for his computer or something. Now he's – ouch! – going to be sitting between an empty chair and Sheila's flower arrangement. Honestly, Freddy, it's bloody unfeeling of you.'

Phoebe wanted to throttle Saskia as much as she wanted to dissolve into a tearful heap in front of Gin and beg for a hug. But she did neither, standing by the fridge instead, frozen with horror. Over and over in her mind, she saw the awful scenario of Saskia swanning into the drawing room and telling a rapt audience that she'd just spotted Phoebe flattened against the oven by Mitzi's husband's mouth. It would be like the second act denouement in an Ayckbourne farce.

'Hi, Sheila, it's me. Is Reg there? Thanks.' Saskia rammed the phone under her chin and lit another cigarette while Sheila fetched her husband at the other end of the line. 'Hi, Reg. Look, I've a huge, huge favour to ask. Phoebe needs to get to the station to catch the last London train – yes, I know, it is cutting it fine. The thing is we're all in the middle of a dinner party here – oh, thanks, thanks so much, you're a darling. Okay, five minutes.' She put the phone down and spun round to shoot Phoebe a victorious smile.

Staring back disbelievingly, Phoebe turned to Gin who, hunched in exasperation, was picking off fish skin with the same drunken, jabbing intensity as a typist slewed after a lunchtime office booze-up.

'Gin, I'm so sorry,' she started, knowing any fabricated explanation would be hopeless. 'Please forgive me?'

Gin's fingers slowed over the fish and she rubbed her sweating forehead with the back of her hand but said nothing.

'I really have to go tonight – '

'Well, bloody well do it then,' Gin snarled, not turning around. 'You'd better go and pack your things.'

The coldness in her voice made Phoebe flinch. She's never going to forgive me for this, she realised miserably.

'What the fuck is going on in here?' bellowed Tony, storming in to grab another bottle of wine. 'We should have been sitting down an hour ago. Everyone's plastered.'

'Phoebe's got to go back to London,' Saskia announced cheerfully.

'What, now?' He looked at Phoebe, his sunken eyes bulging with fear. 'You can't do that. It'll look so bloody obvious.'

'*What* is everyone talking about tonight?' Gin shouted, spinning around so violently that a trout flew through the air and landed on the congealing bowl of guacamole in the sink. Too drunk to notice, she carried on furiously, glaring at her husband, 'First you're so bloody foul to Freddy she almost cries all over the guests. Then Mitzi Thing starts rabbiting on about this house being so perfect for them – as if it were on the bloody market which it isn't. Now Saskia's talking nonsense and dratted Freddy's decided to high-tail it back to London. And to cap it all,' her normally husky voice was shrill with emotion, 'someone's trying to poison my dogs!' She pointed at the sink where the green sludge was lurking in the ceramic dog dish, now garnished with undercooked trout.

Tony glowered at her impatiently. 'Shut up, dear, you're drunk. Saskia, get your mother a very large black coffee and change out of that dreadful dressing gown. Freddy, I want a word with you.'

'This family's a bloody shambles!' Gin wailed tearfully, now determined to vent her cirrhotic spleen. She swayed towards Tony and grabbed his sleeve, staining it with fish fat. 'No one talks any more, we all just hide in different parts of the house. The girls' lives are complete messes – apart from Sukey, who's too ashamed of us to visit any more. Even Freddy can't stand being here. We've no money, no social life, no affection for one another any more. Our first dinner party in months is a total disaster . . .'

'Because you get so fucking drunk before anyone arrives you're crawling around in front of the oven like a dinner lady slewed on port and lemon,' Tony snarled, pulling away from her grip without any sympathy. 'Phoebe, a word.'

His irate order bounced off Phoebe who was watching Gin, eyes hot with sadness.

Staggering back as if hit, Gin lurched for a few seconds and then grabbed the work top to steady herself, wiping away tears with her sleeve like a small child. Because she was so unaccustomed to crying, she had no idea what to do with herself when she was. She looked so utterly pitiful that Phoebe rushed over to comfort her.

'Get away from me!' she stormed, shrinking away just as Saskia had earlier that weekend.

Phoebe reeled back, her face burning with shame, crashing into Saskia who was lurking nearby to shoot out spiteful smiles.

'Hello, all.'

Reg's rotund, weathered face appeared around the kitchen door, grinning broadly in the hope of a drink and some cash for his efforts. He was wearing a lurid country-and-western checked shirt and jeans with bleached ironing-stripes down the front. Off-duty, without his flat cap, his bald head was as shiny and red with sunburn as a ripe Cox's Orange pippin.

'Christ, what do you want?' Gin hissed through clenched teeth, too drunk and upset to have taken in Saskia's recent phone call to the cottage.

Reg gaped at her in amazement. Firstly because his employer had never once, in over ten years, spoken to him like that. She could be bloody abrupt when she was angry with him, he reflected, but never snapped without reason. Particularly recently, when she'd owed him so much money. Secondly, she was blonde. It shocked him as much as the Queen suddenly getting a blue rinse and a Rain-mate.

Picking up on the atmosphere like a rabbit a fox scent, he shrank back against the door and fiddled awkwardly with his car keys.

'Lift to the station?' he stammered, sounding like a terrified mini-cab driver outside a gay S and M club.

'Phoebe, we must talk about this,' Tony was growling urgently.

'Freddy, don't go,' Gin suddenly pleaded like a child left at prep school on the first day of term.

Saskia, standing so close that Phoebe could smell stale cigarettes, whisky and the last faint traces of hair conditioner, dug her fingers deep into the flesh just below Phoebe's kidneys.

'I'll just get my stuff, Reg,' she muttered, unable to bear looking at Gin's stricken face.

Racing upstairs, she heard Dan's lovely mellow laugh echoing from the drawing room and felt as if someone was running a darning needle up and down her ribs. Battling not to cry, she threw the few items she'd brought with her into her hatbox, searched for her duffle bag which seemed to have become hooked on to a chair by some unknown poltergeist, and thundered downstairs.

Amused, confused voices were whispering in the drawing room now. Far louder than anyone else, Garth Drayson was telling a booming, unflattering story about Tony losing the sale of a vast former rectory because the Arab who wanted to buy it had asked if the church could be moved further away.

Phoebe hovered for a second, willing Dan to wander out in search of another drink. But, hearing Mitzi hee-hawing as Garth reached the bit where Tony had spoken to the vicar, Phoebe whimpered and shot back into the kitchen.

The Seatons were there, still in a state of crisis. Tony couldn't find the corkscrew and had tipped out the contents of three cutlery drawers on to the floor in his rage, Gin was trying to wipe sludgy guacamole from one trout, crying loudly, and Saskia was hissing something sotto voce to Reg who was shuffling backwards out of the door, desperate to escape.

When Phoebe tried to say goodbye and apologise once more, Tony and Gin completely ignored her.

Only Saskia, in yet another baffling mood-swing, suddenly became tearful.

'Please understand why I'm doing this, Freddy.' Clutching Phoebe's arm, she tried to hug her. 'Please don't hate me. I've given Reg something for you. You will think about it, won't you?'

For once it was Phoebe who twisted out of her grip.

'I hope you get over him soon, Saskia,' she said honestly. 'But I won't be your character assassin.'

She followed Reg, who was bolting along the shadowed path to the garages like a scenter in a drag hunt. Glancing back through the brightly lit kitchen window from the shadowy dusk outside, Phoebe saw Gin drop her head into her hands and sob.

Rattling to Reading on a slow, smelly diesel train, Phoebe took out the folder Reg had given her. Written on the front in Saskia's semi-legible scrawl was one word: FELIX.

Not even bothering to open it, she rammed it back into her bag.

9

Phoebe finally arrived in London after midnight. Too late to tube it from Paddington, she treated herself to a black cab, flopping back on to the plastic seat with her boots up on the fold-down one opposite. She gazed out at the wide London pavements, still polka-dotted with people, feeling only relief at being back.

They passed a huge office block, latticed with lines and lines of gridded windows where lights blazed here and there for the night-cleaners, making the frontage look like a huge, winking code on a sixties sci fi computer.

'Going out to a club, then?' the taxi driver was eyeing up Phoebe's outfit in his rear view mirror.

'No,' she said, praying he wasn't one of the chatty, opinionated 'did-you-know' racists who must come out of the womb as Bow bells chimed, all ready and willing to take the Knowledge. But this driver merely snapped his sliding partition shut with a grunt and unscrewed the top of his thermos at the same time as swinging the cab out on to the crowded Marylebone Road.

Digging out her purse as they crawled along towards Euston behind a Panda car, Phoebe realised that the meter already read ten pence more than she had. All her cash had gone on fruit and veg that morning. If she'd had any with her, she'd have seriously considered bartering a cauliflower and three strawberries per quarter-mile. Instead she knocked on the sliding glass door in front of her.

'I'll get out here.'

Shivering on the pavement, she upended the contents of her purse in the driver's hands (inadvertently providing him with a grubby Extra Strong Mint, her house keys and a coffee-machine token dating back to Trev and the P45 disaster). Claiming back her keys and telling him to keep the change, she raced off in the general direction of Islington.

What seemed like a five-minute stop-start from the top of the bus took over an hour trudging on her beautiful but impractical boots. Phoebe popped a blister with every step. And, still dressed in the Gaultier teaser, she attracted another horn-beep, wolf whistle or crude yell each minute.

Greeting the tall, thin Victorian house in Douglas Street like Mrs Danvers clapping eyes on Manderley after a fire-damage restoration job, she staggered up to their top floor door.

The flat was a tip. Fliss had clearly gone out in a raging hurry. And from the evidence on display, something of a lurve week-end had preceded it. In the darkened sitting room, two smudged wine glasses sat companionably beside a couple of empty bottles of Yalumba Creek in front of a pair of propped-up cushions. Two sets of dirty plates wearing identical twinned leftovers sat on a surface in the kitchen. A pair of unfamiliar red socks lurked, balled inside out, beneath what passed for their coffee table – a thick sheet of glass propped up on four piles of Fliss's art books. And two sports kit-bags were slumped by the skirting next to Fliss's bedroom.

Whoever it was, wasn't shy of preparing himself for a long away-game, Phoebe thought with interest. Fliss's last boyfriend had been so frightened of leave-a-toothbrush-here commit-ment, he'd scoured the flat for his possessions like a divorcé every time he left in the morning, just in case he didn't come back.

Collapsing on to the rickety, low-slung sofa and almost dislocating her jaw as her knees flew upwards, she sank back and closed her eyes. Her hot, throbbing feet felt as if they were quite literally growing and shrinking rhythmically at the ends of her stiff legs. And – more intriguingly – her bum felt very odd.

She shifted awkwardly. Then she squirmed sideways, twisted around, wriggled forwards and finally stood up, which, given the bottom-clamping seventies-design sofa, was no easy task. Digging beneath the huge silk shawl which Fliss had apparently deemed it seductive to drape over the sofa's usual wine-stained gold Dralon, Phoebe extracted a pair of stripy boxer shorts, a Zippo lighter, several coins, an empty foil condom wrapper and one of Fliss's most treasured fuck-me-pumps – five inches of solid rubber sole attached to about six feet of thin black suede strap which looked like an unravelled gut.

She must be keen, Phoebe thought, giving up on the sofa and hobbling through to the kitchen to hit the fridge instead. Those shoes made strictly limited public appearances due to their unfortunate side effect; they caused such blistering pain, Fliss walked around in bedsocks and Dr Scholls for weeks after a night out in them.

The thought made Phoebe acutely aware of her own distorted pinkies. If she didn't get out of her boots soon, her melting feet were going to start seeping through the stitching around the soles.

Selecting a carton of orange, and noting with interest that Fliss had even stretched to buying real butter, full-fat milk and – hugely shocking – Nutella (Fliss had watched '9½ Weeks' with the same rapt delight as a Born Again at a Billy Graham show), Phoebe flopped down in front of the open fridge door and spent the usual ten minutes undoing her laces. Once her feet were liberated – creased and reddened like newborn baby twins – she removed the salad tray and stuck them in the bottom of the fridge. The cool was bliss.

Half a carton of orange juice later, Phoebe lay back on the kitchen floor and looked up at the tiled ceiling. Dan's face gazed back like a Michelangelo fresco, surrounded by fluffy little cotton wool clouds, fat trumpet-playing cherubs and duck-egg blue sky, lightly cracked with Renaissance old age.

'I've missed you so much,' he murmured, his pepper-flecked grey eyes bright with love.

Phoebe scrunched her eyes tightly closed, but his face still stared at her, as if tattooed on the insides of her lids.

She was vaguely aware of voices drifting in from afar.

'Oh, Phoebe's back – that's her tart sack. She must be in bed. Brew us some tea while I have a pee. You'll love her, she's pretty wild.'

'So I can see.'

Phoebe opened one tentative eye, was almost blinded by light and clamped it shut again. Christ, it was cold. Her teeth were chattering. Although her body was still half-asleep, her mind sat bolt upright and reeled inside her head. She was aching all over, too, she realised as nerve endings started stretching, yawning, and sending grouchy messages brainwards. She was lying somewhere hard, sun-lit and very, very cold.

Oh my God, she thought, I'm flat out on a pavement. I've been sleeping rough on Islington High Street.

Now fully awake, she snapped her eyes open and registered a brief, unfocused shot of a white, tiled ceiling before a shadow fell over her and two speculative eyes the colour of unripe conkers homed into range, examining her face with surgical interest.

Operating theatre! Phoebe thought in a panic. Out of body experience during life-saving surgery. Anaesthetic not strong enough. Where was the pain? She couldn't feel her feet. Christ, they'd amputated her feet.

'My feet?' she managed to croak in a stricken voice.

'They're right here,' a hugely amused grin beamed out four inches below the conker eyes, 'next to a withered mushroom and some whiffy kidneys.'

Phoebe looked at him in horror. His face – rather an attractive one, she noticed in post-operative drowsiness – was swimming in front of her tearful eyes.

He had her feet. Oh God, don't tell me he's going to offer me them as a keepsake in a little jar like wisdom teeth or kidney stones? she wondered, appalled at the insensitivity of it. He may be a stressed junior doctor, reeling from another hundred-hour shift, but this was unethical and sick. He had the same sort of prank-playing, public school voice her brothers had once adopted when proffering fake severed fingers in matchboxes.

'Phoebe, what the fuck are you doing down there?'

'Fliss!' Phoebe craned her neck and saw a blur of red freckles behind her head. On closer inspection, they were dotted on two slender ankles plunging into green, woolly bedsocks. 'Where am I?'

'On the floor of our kitchen with your feet in the bloody fridge,' Fliss said bluntly. 'Which is effing unhygienic. The damn ice-box has melted all over my food, which has probably all gone off. And you're wearing the bloody dress I spent an hour looking for yesterday. It cost me a month's salary, that did.'

When distressed, Fliss sounded just like Ena Sharples on a gin binge.

'Oh.' Phoebe propped herself up on one elbow, knocking over the carton of orange juice. Squinting the length of her body, she saw two very white, very wet feet looking distinctly like morgue-fodder in the blue-white light of the thoroughly defrosted fridge. They were in direct contrast to her face, which suddenly felt as if it had been in a very hot oven.

'Were you drunk?' Fliss demanded, knowing that, when slewed, Phoebe had demonstrated an illogical urge to sleep in her wardrobe, on the kitchen table, in the bath and quite often on the floor. The fridge was a new and unwelcome variation.

'No, I don't think so.' Phoebe shook her head and examined a very large pair of docksiders shuffling menacingly less than a foot from her leg.

'This is Iain,' Fliss sighed irritably. 'Iain, this is my ex-flat-mate, Phoebe. She moves out tonight.'

'Hi, Phoebe.'

She looked up to see Conker Eyes grinning sheepishly down at her. He was a very Merchant Ivory mix of floppy walnut hair, dimples, boyish grin and chiselled chin, guaranteed to cause mayhem if trawled within sniffing distance of a girls' boarding school dormitory. His clothes were straight out of the Blazer old public school book of fashion – expensive cream chinos, white t-shirt, hand-stitched belt, navy blue Guernsey knotted around the shoulders. He had clearly only just stopped short of donning a pair of round tortoiseshell specs and carrying a teddy bear. The effect was far too Hugh Grant meets Michael Praed for Phoebe's taste, but he certainly had the sort of looks that left women with cricked necks wherever he went. No wonder Fliss had bulk-bought Nutella.

'Lovely to meet you, Iain,' Phoebe smiled, trying to muster dignity around her in the same way an interrupted adulterer gathers up a crumpled sheet. Flipping the fridge door shut in what she hoped was a casually nonchalant I-sleep-with-my-tootsies-in-it-all-the-time way, she looked up towards a glowering Fliss, keen to ingratiate herself again. 'Have you been out clubbing?'

'Till six.' Fliss rolled her still narrowed blue eyes. 'We've just had breakfast in that greasy spoon in Camden you like so much.'

'Fry By Night?' Phoebe perked up, glad that one of her recommendations had been taken up. She tentatively tried her feet for weight carrying and howled with pain.

'Yes.' Fliss studied her progress without sympathy. 'Charged us three quid each for an uncooked egg and burnt toast swimming in lard.'

'Yum.' Phoebe tried to look lip-smackingly unsympathetic back, but her eyes were only registering pain. The feeling was seeping back into her feet like battery acid on raw wounds. Pins and needles were rapidly being replaced by hammer and tongs.

'If you'll excuse me,' she apologised, making it on to all fours and twitching with agony, 'I'm going to have a bath.'

'You'll have to have a shower.' Fliss watched her shambling in a crab-like crawl to the door. 'Iain – er – broke the bath plug yesterday.'

As her knees moved from linoleum to carpet, Phoebe could hear them stifling laughter. But, like most new lovers, their attention span on anything other than each other's bodies was as short as a grenade fuse.

'I love the way you say that – bath,' Iain growled, mimicking Fliss's accent.

'And I love what you did to me in the barth yesterday,' Fliss purred, mimicking his.

'Well, at school I could hold my breath underwater longer than anyone else . . .'

Behind her, Phoebe could make out the giggling, slurping sound effects of a romping snog hitting top suction.

Had she been in a fitter state, she would have stuck her fingers in her mouth in a mock-puke. But it was all she could do to make it into the bathroom, strip off and clamber into the bath. Once there, she directed the shower nozzle at her feet and sighed with a shiver of relief as the stinging blast of hot water gradually defrosted them.

When she emerged again, Fliss and Iain were not, as she'd anticipated, shrieking with sexual athleticism behind Fliss's bedroom door. They were sitting drinking coffee on the sofa, their chins between their knees in the standard position. Both were dressed for work; Iain in a linen Blazer suit, old Etonian tie (Phoebe doubted it was his own) and very shiny brogues. Fliss was wearing her one and only flowery tea-dress as it was one of her secretarial days, her ginger curls sprouting from a purple silk scarf, feet plunging into wildly fashionable wooden-soled clog espadrilles and earrings that looked as though they could pick up West Coast satellite broadcasting dangling from her freckled ears. They made an incongruous couple – like Prince Charles shacking up with Molly Parkin. Phoebe secretly bet herself it would last about as long as her next job. If she ever got one.

'I'll just clean my teeth.' Fliss leapt up, shooting Phoebe a 'talk to him' look as she whisked past into the steaming swamp bathroom.

Something about her flat-mate's rolling blue eyes made Phoebe guess that, as ever, Fliss wasn't as keen as her latest amour would like. The only time she became truly hooked on someone was when they were completely indifferent towards her.

'Where do you work, Iain?' Phoebe asked politely, hovering on her way to her room.

'Sorry?' He looked up and nearly dropped his coffee into his cream linen lap.

He clearly wasn't very used to morning-afters in shared flats. His eyes gawped at Phoebe, who was wearing four towels – one turbaned on her head, one saronging her body and one wrapped around each foot. Her face was coated thickly with night cream to try and calm her sunburn, and she had a toothbrush poking out of her mouth.

'In the City?' Phoebe asked encouragingly, chewing her toothbrush.

'Hell, no,' Iain averted his gaze and feigned interest in a nearby cushion. 'I work for a charity based in Farringdon – we try to get funding for overnight centres for the homeless. I started there yesterday, actually. I've been in Peru for a year.'

'Oh.' Phoebe raised an impressed eyebrow. The voice might be straight out of Billy Bunter, but the job had definite Fliss kudos. He wasn't, however, blond or effete enough and close up his teeth were as big as Eeyore's. Two months, she revised thoughtfully, and staggered out to lie down on her bed.

Ten minutes later, she heard the door clunk and two hand-made brogues clatter down the uncarpeted stairs to the front door. Squinting at her clock – eight-thirty, middle of the night in her book – she braced herself for Fliss to come charging in on pretext of giving her a ticking off about fridge-fetishism, but really to have a gossip about Iain and, possibly, her own weekend with the Seatons.

But two minutes later the door clunked once more, followed by the unmistakable sound of clogs hammering against stairs.

Guessing Fliss would call in exactly half an hour, Phoebe snuggled deeper into her bed and cast an eye around the room, wishing she'd mucked it out before going away for the weekend. Although nothing on Saskia's scale of putrefaction, the tatty little box room was matt with dust and littered with clothes still shaped like their owner, lying where they had been stepped out of so that they criss-crossed the room in lines, forming paths to and from the wardrobe, the bed and the door like paperchase trails.

In a vague attempt to make their colour-blind landlord's seventies decor palatable, Phoebe had stuck a few arty posters on the walls, replaced the yellow and orange striped curtains with cheap rush blinds and raided the nearest florist for pot plants. But the recent heat had melted the Blu-tack so that the posters now bent at their waists, drooping towards the floor. The rush blinds had curled upwards and warped like dead leaves; the pot plants were just dead leaves.

Trailing her towels like an unravelling mummy, Phoebe wriggled to the end of the bed and threw all the discarded clothes within her reach towards her laundry basket, marvelling at how aerodynamic knickers were as opposed to bras.

Just as she was gearing up to test a pair of tights, the phone rang and she leapt for it before the machine intercepted, shooting one foot towel into orbit where it remained hooked on her Biba lampshade.

'You need a job.'

It was Fliss, panting like a dog in a sauna after the quickest recorded bolt from Islington to Kensington.

'That was fast. Did you go by Tardis?'

'Slipped the bus driver a fiver to ignore request-stops.' Fliss was turning on her word processor with a whirr of interference. 'And don't change the subject. You need a job.'

'I know.' Phoebe sat on the floor and curled her sore feet under her. 'Does La Gregory want another assistant to spear on her stilettos?'

Fliss laughed. 'Oh, Phoebe mate – be realistic. If I recommend you, and you last a week again, how does that make me look? And before you ask, no, I haven't heard of anything else.'

'So you mean Georgette *is* looking for someone?'

'Not exactly.' Fliss sounded cagey. 'She just mentioned that she might – and it's a very small might – be thinking about expanding into corporate work.'

'Mmm.' Phoebe chewed her nail thoughtfully, leaning back

against the bed. 'So when shall I come in? Can you help me invent a CV she'd approve of?'

'No, no, no!' Fliss growled, sounding genuinely horrified. 'I need this job – it pays for my clay. Shit! That's her chariot drawing up outside.' Her voice faded as she craned to look out of the window. 'Look, forget it, Phoebe. I'd love it if you worked here, but you and she would have a punch up before she asked for her first coffee. I must go – let's meet for a drink this afternoon. I finish early and the studio's got the plumber in.'

'You want to talk about Iain?'

'So I can't get any sculpting done.'

'And you want to talk about Iain?'

'And I'm dying to know all about your weekend in Wiltshire.'

'Berkshire. You want to – '

'– talk about Iain, yes.'

'Okay. Where?'

'The Vats, fourish. No, on second thoughts, come here and meet me – Georgette might just decide she likes you, she's batty enough. But under no circs say that I mentioned there's a job going. That's her cloven footsteps on the stairs. C'ya.'

The line went dead.

Humming thoughtfully, Phoebe replaced the handset. Now, a job with Georgette Gregory was to diet, dye and lie for, she mused – all those celebrity parties one would just have to pop in on.

Georgette Gregory was the most influential party planner in what Phoebe's mother termed the odd SWs. As in SW1, SW3 etc – or anything beginning with a K other than Kilburn and Kentish Town. No self-respecting hostess in Knightsbridge threw a bash for their finished, Vidal Sassoon-coiffed, Belville Sassoon-decked debs without Georgette adding her calligraphy to the place names, her flower arrangements to the tables, and her hired chef to the Moulinex. It was reputed (or at least Fliss had told Phoebe it was) that Jerry Hall, Shakira Caine or Madeleine Lloyd–Webber wouldn't dream of getting diaries together with fellow celebs for a party unless they had been assured of Georgette's undivided attention on any specified date. And Georgette, it was said, was the one who specified.

La Gregory was bound to be a thundering, pearl-clad Sloane, Phoebe decided, fingering a linen suit her mother had sent over from Hong Kong. Even Fliss, whose dress sense was notoriously off-the-wall, dressed like a former Miss Pears one day a week in her honour.

Three hours later, she looked like a founder member of the Women's Institute Crochet Team lining up for a handshake with the Queen Mother. Compared to the sharkskin hotpants she normally wore, her ensemble was as tame as goldfish slacks.

A neat cream wrap-around skirt was twinned with a very cropped white polo neck. Her bare midriff was covered by a navy Regency-pastiche Westwood jacket. Phoebe had even swallowed her pride and slipped into a pair of navy ballet pumps she'd once bought when recovering from an ingrown toe-nail.

Trailing through to Fliss's room where there was a full-length mirror, she hardly recognised the eager, scrawny gel who walked towards her. The only familiar thing about her was a cropped mane of glossy, razor-cut brown hair.

Halfway through whipping it into Shirley Temple shape with Fliss's curling tongs, the doorbell went.

'Yes?' If Phoebe stretched the flex of the tongs as far as it would go, she could just reach the phone intercom. Her hair sizzled and steamed into another whorl as she waited for the response, hating herself for the illogical day-dream that it might be Dan.

'S'us, sis,' rasped a hungover voice.

Phoebe dropped the tongs, which sparked blue into the carpet for a couple of seconds and then died with an ominous electric phut. Groaning, she leaned against the wall for support.

Only her little sister Milly had a voice like Barrie White with laryngitis. And the 'us' clearly meant she had her lanky lover Goat with her.

'What are you doing up at this time?' she asked grumpily. 'I haven't seen you before midday in nearly twenty years.'

'Shut up and buzz us in, you stupid cow – I'll die without coffee.' Minutes later, she arrived, panting, at the flat door.

'Spinning shit! Come up and look at this, Goat, you'll just die. Couldn't you afford the full perm, sis? Don't tell me that's fashionable? Looks awful.'

'Come in.' Phoebe leant back against the door as her sister wandered past in a cloud of Marlboro smoke and blown kisses.

Clad in leather jeans and a black mohair fish-net jumper shaped like jellyfish, Milly headed straight for the kitchen where she disappeared behind the swinging fridge door.

'Shit two – you and Frizzy Fliss on diets or what?' she rumbled from its deepest recesses. 'And something's definitely high in here. Did I tell you I got my navel pierced last week? I'll show you in a sec – it's gone a bit weepy.'

Milly re-emerged with Fliss's Nutella and went in search of bread, her spray-painted Docs squealing on the kitchen floor.

Phoebe ignored her and waited by the flat door for the sound of wheezing and clomping to materialise into physical form. It soon did as a greasy head of white rats' tails appeared around the stair turn, followed by stained Army trenchcoat and eighteen-hole scuffed Doc Martens tied with red laces.

'Hello, Goat,' Phoebe greeted her sister's boyfriend, averting her gaze from a pair of frayed, wrinkled jeans which looked as if they'd been towed around behind the Emmerdale Farm muckspreader for several episodes.

Shuffling past at forty-five degrees to the floor, Goat made a deep, grunting noise which burbled from the lowest regions of his throat and bobbed his Adam's apple, without manifesting into words. This, for Goat, was a lengthy monologue and Phoebe beamed, certain she was cracking through his shy exterior at long last. Eye contact was almost within her reach – although she had yet to prove Goat possessed two eyes beneath his Old English Sheepdog fringe and hanging head.

'We were just passing,' Milly said as Phoebe wandered into the kitchen. 'The old Matriarch Royal told me to check you were still alive in her latest bulletin from HK.'

She'd already cut six vast hunks of Fliss's malty grain and was flipping on the kettle with her elbow as she prised open the Clover tub. Meanwhile Goat had sunk, knobbly knees to goatee-bearded chin, into the sofa in the sitting room and was starting to flip through television channels.

'Bit out of your way, isn't it?' Phoebe narrowed her eyes mistrustfully at her sister. 'Tooting's hardly a stroll from Islington.'

Dressed in the usual funereal mourning for laboratory mice rights and River Phoenix, Milly was looking paler and grungier than an anaemic Suede groupie on a pot-holing package holiday. Slightly shorter and curvier than Phoebe, she had the same dark, straight hair and lime-green eyes, although these were heavily disguised with black war-paint. Her nose – sporting a hooped gold sleeper through one nostril – was sloping and pretty, unlike Phoebe's beaky one, and she had a mouth so perfect and rose-bud, it was shaped like an M sitting on a W.

'Ah, well. No, actually.' Milly was rattling through drawers for a knife.

'What do you mean – have you moved?'

'Er . . . no.' Milly started buttering the bread with a six-inch Sabatier. 'That is, not yet.'

'Oh, yes?' Phoebe raked her hair in angst. 'So when?'

'We've been given a week. They're demolishing the squat.'

'Poor you.' She tried to keep her voice even and objective, adding hopefully, 'So where are you planning to live next?'

Swinging round, Milly was clearly about to ask whether six electric guitars, two sleeping bags, a three-foot cactus and the most definitive collection of Morrissey tracks this side of Oxford Street HMV could be moved in by Thursday. But the words stayed in her throat and her jaw swung like a cat flap from its hinges as she caught her first proper full frontal of what her sister was wearing.

'Have you found God or something?' she asked croakily as her acid green eyes gaped at the ballet pumps.

'Of course not,' Phoebe said, huffily extracting the coffee from an overhead cupboard. 'I've got a job interview.'

'Another one? Matriarch Royal only just informed me on the grapes of wrathvine that you were panting down dirty 0891 sex-numbers.'

'Selling insurance,' Phoebe corrected archly. 'And it didn't realise my full potential.'

'Oh, I see.' Milly licked the knife, pink tongue tracing Fliss's oil-stoned blade. 'You got the push.'

'There was a difference of opinion, yes,' Phoebe bristled, throwing enough dark roast coffee into each mug to send a Café Häg fanatic into spasm.

'So what are you going for now?' Milly smirked, the M and W flattening into lower-case italics. 'Receptionist at the Virgin's Mission? Mary Whitehouse's cleaner? Avon lady?'

'Bob Geldof's PA,' Phoebe smirked back, just to rile her. 'It's my third interview. Just a formality really.'

Milly's mint-green eyes widened into dinner plates. 'You're going to work for Saint Bob? The altar at which I worship?'

'I might,' Phoebe shrugged. 'I haven't made up my mind yet. Fi Fi Trixibel loves me, but Peaches and Pixie are a bit wary.'

The curling tongs were declared dead and laid to rest in the exact position Phoebe had first found them, so as not to insinuate any flat-mate tampering. She was forced to resort to Velcro rollers which split her ends like a desk-top shredder and dragged precious follicles from her scalp. But the end result was undeniably chic; former Roedean head girl meets glossy business exec in South Molton Street. She even coiled one of Fliss's cream and navy scarves around her neck, tying it carefully to hide any traces of clay.

When she braved the sitting room again, Milly was immersed in something which – had Phoebe not known better – looked suspiciously like her university work. She didn't even look up from the piles of smudgy A4 papers littering her lap. Goat, a pointy red nose poking out from his bleached dreadlocks, was cackling over Sesame Street. The nose rotated towards Phoebe like a submarine periscope as she searched for one of Fliss's smaller portfolios which would pass as a slimline briefcase.

'You look wild,' he wheezed.

Phoebe nose-butted a cupboard in shock. Three words. And as unexpected as his declaring a passion for Julio Iglesias's 'Begin the Beguine'.

'Thank you, Goat,' she said, fighting to sound normal. She straightened up and smiled at the area of dreadlocks she assumed hid his eyes.

'Doncha fink, Mill?' He turned to his engrossed partner.

'Uh?' Milly gradually surfaced from her paperwork, menthol eyes luminous with excited preoccupation.

'Looks great, don't she?' Goat's shaggy hair was nodding at Phoebe like pampas grass in a gale.

Ten words. Phoebe was struggling not to shake his hand and declare the moment a miracle. But her eyes had caught sight of something familiar by Milly's leather-clad legs. Her own cavernous duffle bag was spewing Tampax, sweety wrappers and a loose-leaf *A to Z* like an overfull bin in a Ladies' lavatory.

'I can't believe it's him,' Milly murmured as she returned to the folder on her lap. 'How d'you fancy a threesome, Goat? Apparently this guy likes them. Phoebe, baby?'

'Yes?' Phoebe watched her sister with mounting concern. The last time she'd seen that lustful, rabid look was when Milly had emerged from seeing Purple Rain aged twelve.

'I want – no, I *must* – meet this man,' Milly groaned happily, plucking out a model's composite and holding it to her mohair chest. 'Oh God, he's not your latest? I've been in love with him for two years. He's the shrine beside Bob's altar.'

'Who?' Phoebe asked, knowing the answer.

'Felix Sylvian,' Milly laughed, amazed at the question.

Phoebe tried every trick she knew to turf Goat and her sister out of the flat before lunchtime, but they had the edge on her. Having travelled for six months in a double decker bus on the New Age Travellers' circuit, they could bed themselves down in the Highgrove pony paddock and not get budged. A small Islington flat was child's play.

Milly (named after their father's heroine, Millicent Martin) was precociously bright. She had left school at seventeen with four effortless 'A' levels and then announced her intention to learn a little of life by travelling with some friends for a year before she took up her place at Cambridge to read History. Her mother had been doubtful but, knowing Milly would merely double the hitch-hiking, bungee-jumping danger factor if crossed, feigned delight.

Milly had dyed her hair purple, packed two pairs of thread-bare jeans, three holey jumpers and a week's supply of t-shirts into a Tesco bag and phoned her boyfriend, Goat, who was then living in a Housing Association flat in Wandsworth. Two hours later, ignoring her mother's hysterical screeching, she had climbed into the front of a camper van and roared off in a cloud of puttering diesel fumes towards the West Country.

The camper had in fact broken down three miles away and Goat quickly declared it completely without pulse.

Oil-splattered thumbs out, Milly and Goat had hitched a lift on a sixties double decker bus – the Rolls-Royce of New Age

Travelling – belonging to an ancient hippy called Horatio. Both now agreed their luck had been formidable. Horatio was the mythical Magus maestro of the music festival circuit. Along with his two skinny lurchers, Cat and Donovan, and various hairy girlfriends, he could sniff out an unguarded Wiltshire field from the middle of Dorset. He had an irregular convoy of cronies who followed him in several other buses, caravan-towing bangers and camper vans, splitting up en route and then regrouping at each new location so as not to arouse suspicion from local police. And, most excitingly, he could roll a spliff as big as a parsnip. Goat and Milly stayed with him for six months.

By November, Milly had got fed up. A lot of the younger travellers had returned home for the winter, raves were now as few and far between as off licences in Saudi Arabia, and Horatio had just got hold of another lurcher, christened Joni, who'd pissed all over the bus and chewed up their sleeping bags. So Milly and Goat hitched to London, where they joined a group of Goat's oldest friends in a chilly squat in Worslade Road, Tooting, overlooking Lambeth Cemetery. They called them-selves the Wandsworth Poets Society, although the only writing they seemed to do was signing on the dole fortnightly.

In Hong Kong, Poppy Fredericks received a grubby, news-starved postcard from her daughter.

Dear Old Folks,

Living at this address now. No phone, sorry. Have decided not to go to Cambridge as Goat says it's full of inbreds, and there aren't any decent Indy gigs nearby. Have got place at Thames Poly instead, reading Druid History. Start next Oct. Send cheque. Love you both.

Milly – kiss, kiss.

That had been almost eighteen months ago. Milly had now completed a year at the newly christened Thameside University, funding her degree with occasional nude modelling for local evening classes and weekend work at Brixton McDonald's. Goat, who still proclaimed himself to be a professional poet, worked for a local second-hand record shop. They both spent several months a year travelling with Horatio.

Now that was a different line of attack, Phoebe mused as she made their fifth cup of coffee and ground her teeth malevolently.

'When are you going to stay with Horatio this summer?' she asked casually as she slopped coffee all over a tray carrying it back through.

Still wearing his trenchcoat, Goat – who had failed to improve on his ten-word record – had his only visible feature, his nose, firmly pointing at the lunchtime repeat of Home and Away. He held out his hand for coffee, but the nose target stayed locked on to a close-up of Pippa windsurfing.

Plumping on to a seventies tartan sag bag beside Milly, who was sulking because Phoebe refused to discuss the reason for the Felix file, she repeated the question.

'Not,' Milly said gruffly, lighting another Marlboro. 'He's in Ford Open with all the old Etonians. They arrested him at Stonehenge Solstice – Goat and I were pulled up ten miles off. The oinks raided Horatio's bus and found three mini hothouses crammed with blow-plants running off the battery. And he had enough resin blocks stuffed under the seats to build a drug rehab centre. Got six months, din' he, Goat? With an out-of-date tax disc and a dodgy brake light taken into consideration.'

Goat grunted his assent as Ailsa popped into the general store for some tinnies in front of his focused nose.

'They were light on the sentence because it turned out Horatio was at Bedales with the jury foreman, then Balliol with the judge.' Milly looked at her sister. 'Wasn't Felix Sylvian going out with Saskia Seaton?'

Caught offguard, she looked shifty and shrugged.

'Thought so,' Milly grinned. 'Matriarch Royal wrote to me about it. So why've you got a file on him?'

Phoebe nearly jumped out of her wrap-around as she heard an eerie, strangled wail across the room. It sounded as if Goat was having a cold turkey fit. But, spinning round, she saw that

Milly's boyfriend was simply slouching back on the sofa, humming along to 'You Know We Belong Together'.

'He loves that song.' Milly smiled fondly, reaching across to stroke his skinny white knee which was poking out of a frayed hole in his jeans like a knob of lard.

'. . . *belong together*,' Goat finished with a contented, whiny croak. The nose rotated towards Phoebe. 'Got any scrumpy?'

She shook her head apologetically.

'Phoebes?' Milly was gazing through her thickly painted lashes, her peppermint eyes at their most beguiling. As a wily child, she'd been able to spin her elder sister around her little finger as easily as silk thread on a bobbin.

'Yes?'

'Tell me why you've got all this stuff on Felix Sylvian, and Goat and I will go to the pub.' She grinned minxily. 'Let you get off to the Geldofs.'

Phoebe sighed reluctantly.

'And,' Milly drew the word out playfully, 'we'll tidy your flat before we go.'

Leaving Milly wafting a duster around like a gothic June Whitfield, and Goat sniffing Pledge thoughtfully, Phoebe explained how to double lock the door and post her spare keys through the locked letter box, then raced off to the tube.

Outside, the sun had weakened like an expiring Calor gas stove, and was winking feebly between gusting, shower-loaded clouds. The wind was whipping strongly enough to shuffle fast food litter along the pavements.

There was a student recruitment fair on at the Business Design Centre, and Phoebe fought her way to Angel tube through crowds of young hopefuls in new, shiny suits, clutching gleaming, boxy briefcases crammed with free info from accountancy and telesales firms.

As she waited in the queue for the escalator she could hear two eager girls discussing their prospects behind her.

'I've got a group interview with *Metalwork Industry* magazine next Tuesday, and then the *Vending Machine Journal*,' one twittered. 'I mean, selling space is practically advertising proper – I could easily move across to a copywriting job at DMBBMB & G. in six months.'

Listening in on their naive enthusiasm, Phoebe forced herself not to spin around and beg to differ.

'Quite,' the other girl was agreeing as she straightened her unfamiliar pencil power skirt. 'I mean, I was thinking that training as an actuary could put me in quite a favourable position when I finally get a place at law school.'

As they travelled down the escalator, crammed in a crocodile of hot, sweaty graduates loosening ties and stripping off jackets, the second girl pursued her line of conversation.

'Of course, corporate law is almost as popular as criminal these days – and there's a lot more money in it if you get hooked up to a really good, blue chip company,' she rambled, her Milk Round teeth barely cutting reason as she removed her brand new Warehouse jacket and hooked it through the strap of a handbag which still had its Real Leather tag attached. 'I'd love to work for someone like Conrad Black when I qualify. Newspapers are supposed to be one of the most prolific areas.'

Phoebe scowled broodily.

At the divide between the two platforms, she wavered, feeling briefcases ricochet off the backs of her knees as the teeming graduates fought to get past.

I am not going to try and see him, she told herself furiously. It would be hurtful and childish. I've shed that skin once and for all.

She turned to the left and stepped forward purposefully, staring fixedly at a poster of three blondes draped in gold bikinis printed like lottery cards. 'You Get A Lottery More with Us', boasted the red copy-line. It was an advert for the *News*, Satellite Newspapers' flagship tabloid.

Shivering with recklessness, Phoebe did an about turn and walked across to the opposite line. Feeling guilty, she spun around again and retraced her steps. For the next five minutes, she marched back and forth like a deranged sentry on duty, to the curious amusement of the gaggles of graduates. Finally, she stood by the northern-bound line, stared at the blondes again, and concentrated hard on the memory of Dan's paunch, his promised then forgotten phone calls, his last minute cancellations and the late evening guilt showers to rid himself of any trace of her scent before he crept back to Mitzi.

'He's a toad,' she said out loud, entertaining her onlookers even more.

Why was it then, she wondered minutes later, that when she was supposed to be heading for King's Cross to change on to the Piccadilly Line, she was in fact hurtling south towards London Bridge? Wasn't that two minutes' walk from Dan's company's Thameside office?

Get off at Bank, she told herself firmly.

As Bank slid past in a droning medley of 'Mind the gap' and 'Stand clear of the doors, please', Phoebe gnawed at a thumb nail and stared at her prim, two-faced reflection in the double glass window opposite. I dressed like this for Dan, she realised in horror, not for Georgette Gregory.

The train ground to a juddering halt at London Bridge and stood hissing with its doors open. Phoebe closed her eyes and thought hard about Dan's penchant for garlic and whiffy Irish stout.

I'll go and look at Tower Bridge, she decided quickly, hopping out as the doors closed. Then I'll cross over and get a bus along the Embankment. It'll be a form of exorcism.

The moment she was standing outside the tube station, shivering in the cold, she realised how foolish it was to have come here; she wasn't skipping the Yellow-livered Brick Road to freedom, she was glued to the spot on Memory Lane. She'd met Dan dozens of times in cafés and wine bars nearby, had shared stolen lunches in the little barge restaurants moored beside the City Pier, and once been totally flattened by a passionate kiss in the narrow alley which ran between two offices on Duke's Hill.

Opposite her, the wind was swinging the hanging baskets outside the pub Dan sometimes drank in with the hacks. Clouds were now huddling together for warmth as the wind sheered the summer glow from everybody's faces, replacing it with cold-pinched grimaces.

Feeling like a guilty teenager bunking off from school, Phoebe hurried along Toomer Street, crossing the road so that she would not have to walk directly outside the Satellite Newspaper building. But not even her best intentions could stop her gazing up at the row of gleaming windows on the top floor, their mirrored panes reflecting the darkening, turbulent sky. Having never actually been in the building, Phoebe had no idea which office was his. But Dan, who had vertigo, had mentioned that it was on the top floor, and that, when uninspired, he would stand at the back of his office and look from a safe distance across the bows of *HMS Belfast* and out towards the Tower of London, wondering what it would be like were he defending Lady Jane Grey or Sir Thomas More instead of a tabloid newspaper.

Phoebe's stomach flipped over with longing as she clutched the flapping, flimsy jacket around her and broke into a brisk trot towards the grey gates of Tower Bridge. Huge droplets of rain started to bounce off her shoulders and sting her face. Her hair – the curls already whipped into souffléd splendour by the wind – was rapidly plastering itself to her head. By the time she reached the bridge, she could barely see in the hammering deluge. She bounded blindly up the steps.

A car, turning on to the bridge from the direction of Shad Thames, squealed to a hand-brake halt opposite her and induced a horn-beeping cacophony from irate drivers behind.

Phoebe ground to an amazed halt as the window whizzed down and Portia Hamilton's blonde head shot out, leaning precariously across the passenger seat.

'Freddy!' she yelled, ignoring the increased tempo of horn beeps. 'I nearly didn't recognise you. Need a lift?'

Nodding, Phoebe plunged through a kerbside puddle and hopped gratefully in and they rocketed off before she'd even shut the door, terrifying an overtaking Saab on to the opposite pavement.

As they careered across the bridge, Phoebe listened to the rain now thundering a deafening drumroll on the canvas roof and ran her hands through her sopping hair, blinking drops from her eyelashes.

'Thanks so much,' she yelled over the blaring stereo. 'What are you doing so far east?'

'I could ask you the same question,' Portia said evasively, veering across the road as she turned down the stereo. 'God, it's stair-rodding now – I can't see a thing.'

Phoebe leant across and turned the wipers on for her; Portia drove just like her mother.

'I had a job interview,' she lied.

'Oh?' Portia cut up a taxi and almost killed them both. 'Are you going back to Islington? Because I'm heading for Fulham really.'

'No, Kensington,' Phoebe clutched the sides of her seat as they did an emergency stop at some traffic lights.

'Oh, I'll drop you off then.' Portia, waiting for the green light, revved the engine as if she were Andretti in an inferior grid position. 'Interview go well?'

'Not bad,' Phoebe grinned, realising she wouldn't be cross-examined. Portia simply wasn't interested enough in her to ask where and with whom she'd had her fictitious meeting. It was a relief; Saskia's streetwise sister would never have swallowed the Geldof line.

'Good job it's over,' Portia looked across at her and laughed. 'You look like you've driven through a car wash in an open-top. Is that a perm?'

Phoebe sulkily pulled down the visor and gaped at her reflection. Her hair was as flat as a corn circle on top and springing out in short, wild corkscrews at the side, making it look like a clown's wig. Her jacket shoulders were black with water and the thin linen skirt was plastered to her legs, sodden, crumpled and see-through. Georgette, the pearl-clad boot, would definitely not sanction the Miss Wet T-shirt look.

'Are you going back to your office?' she asked, frantically ruffling her hair as Portia crawled along with her front bumper rammed angrily into a dawdling motorist's exhaust pipe.

'God, no.' She swung out to overtake illegally, then swung

back as she caught sight of a police Metro in her rear view mirror. 'I'm going home for a shower.'

Phoebe, ricocheting off the side-window, raised an eyebrow, half in pain and half in amazement. Looking at her, she wondered if Portia had been into the office at all that day. She knew the staff of glossy magazines had a reputation for outré couture but she doubted even they rolled up to work in a black sequinned pageboy tunic and velvet opera coat. And the dishevelled, just-got-out-of-bed blonde mane looked suspiciously genuine. She had no tights on; her thin, glossy brown legs and bare feet jabbed at the pedals like Vincent Price on a hydraulic organ. A pair of suede court shoes lay discarded on the rubber mat, and her face was completely free from its usual professional make-up. She looked fresher and younger, her cheeks flushed rhubarb pink, her huge grey eyes shining and a lump of mascara-stained sleep trapped in the corner of one.

Saying nothing, Phoebe stared out at the grey rumpled Thames as they crawled along Victoria Embankment in heavy traffic. She recognised the signs, remembering only too vividly sitting on the tube with London's morning commuters, wearing last night's seductress outfit, no knickers and a soppy smile on her face.

'I'll go via Hyde Park Corner,' Portia announced as they whizzed around Parliament Square almost on two wheels, shooting off towards Victoria before Phoebe could protest. 'How was the dinner party last night?'

'Oh, fine.' Phoebe bit her lip as she opened her eyes again, wondering whether to mention her premature exit from Portia's parents' house.

'And is Daniel Neasham as dishy as my friend Susie claims?'

'Who?' Phoebe croaked feebly.

'Dan Neasham, the Libel Detector – he was there, wasn't he?'

'Oh, him – yes.' Phoebe squelched her wet toes around in the sopping ballet pumps. 'Nice bloke.'

'Susie tried to set us up last week,' Portia said blithely, gazing at her reflection in the rear view mirror and almost ramming the Sierra in front.

'Oh, yes?' Phoebe's voice sounded like the little old lady who'd swallowed the fly.

'Mmm.'

'But he's married.' She winced. What a ridiculous, hypocritical thing to say.

'I know.' Portia weaved in and out of the traffic banked up beside Victoria Station. 'But then, so is the one I'm seeing now. Come on, Freddy, don't look at me like that. You're hardly one to preach, darling. People in glass warehouse conversions throwing stones et al.'

Phoebe shifted awkwardly in the wet leather seat.

'Dan's wife's the only female at Keurtz-Cooper – the American bond house,' Portia said, changing lanes without looking over her shoulder. 'There's a saying in the City – something like: "it's easier to get camels to conga down Threadneedle Street than for a ball-breaker to enter the top floor of Keurtz's" – and yet they head-hunted her. Can you believe it? She's immensely powerful.'

'Mitzi Neasham?' Phoebe almost slid into the glove compartment as they hit another red light.

The honking horse, a high-flying banker? she thought in shock, gazing fixedly out of the windscreen at a sticker on the off-roader in front, declaring that its owner slowed down for horses. She had a sudden urge to leap out of the car, race to their window and yell at them to run one particular gold-jewelled equine over. All morning, Phoebe had been indulging in blissful images of Mitzi braying around Laura Ashley, honking in Selfridge's Food Hall, hee-hawing with the 'girls' over lunch and then driving the Range Rover back to Barnes to quack out the details of her 'hectic' day to a yawning Dan over solid, finishing-school cooking. Instead, she was probably taking a conference call, faxing Wall Street, talking billions of yen, scouring Reuters and telling her secretary to phone her husband and explain that she'd be late home again.

Phoebe was appalled at the degree to which jealousy had allowed her to distort and misjudge Mitzi into a gross, bounding, jolly caricature. Of course Dan wouldn't marry an ageing, chintzy charity chairwoman, she mulled miserably. And, despite love-deafened ears, she still remembered hearing the reverent, almost cowed tone in his voice when he'd made those oblique but nonetheless agonising references to 'my wife'. Phoebe felt as if she'd been punched in the face by an iron fist.

'Dan likes assertive women, I hear.' Portia watched Phoebe's washed-out face as the lights changed. 'I guess Mitzi didn't know he was up to his old dominatrix again last night. Dan must have been hopping with nerves.'

Phoebe turned to snarl at her, but she swallowed it back. Portia was looking incredibly smug, and Phoebe had no intention of adding to her satisfaction by showing how upset she was.

'Mitzi seemed nice.' She smiled back gamely, but her lip was wobbling like an ageing diva hitting top C.

'Don't worry.' Portia patted her wet knee with a slim hand as they queued to tackle Hyde Park Corner with hordes of fellow kamikaze motorists. 'I hear she likes sex once every other Black Wednesday – and not with her husband. Susie says she wears thick-gusset tights and support knickers, because it takes so long for Dan to prise them off, he gets too bored to move on to the waisty bra. And she's got legs like a scrum half.'

Phoebe was feeling horribly car sick. She swallowed a mouthful of neat bile as they hurtled past the Lanesborough. It occurred to her that she'd consumed nothing but liquids since her Galaxy binge the day before. Portia, gazing happily past her at the windows of Harvey Nichols, clearly thought she and Dan were getting back together faster than the Rolling Stones with a sell-out tour lined up by eager promoters. Somehow, despite herself, she couldn't deny it.

'And this bloke you're seeing?' she asked, anxious to get off the subject of Mitzi Neasham's underwear.

'I'd rather not talk about him,' Portia said evenly. 'Not yet, anyway. Too soon.'

She flashed Phoebe a conspiratorial smile which made her stomach heave even more. 'We mistresses stick together' it said, 'bits on the side unite.'

As they drew level with Harrods, Portia slammed on the brakes so hard they locked and the car slid into a jolting, angled halt.

'What's wrong?' Phoebe asked as the taxi driver behind leant on his horn.

But Portia didn't answer. She was staring at a huge poster opposite the store. A ravishing supermodel pouted back, slanting yellow eyes smudged with mascara, baby blonde hair pulled into two uneven pigtails, making her look about fourteen. The scattering of blonde freckles on her nose was as tempting as chopped almonds on cream. She was wearing nothing but a pair of men's Y-fronts and about half a million pounds' worth of Tiffany diamonds. TOPAZ FOX WEARS HER BEST FRIEND'S declared foot-high lettering.

'Portia?' Phoebe asked cautiously.

But she just rammed the car into gear and roared towards Kensington in stony silence.

The shower had lifted and the sun was dipping a few golden legs back out of the clouds by the time they swished along the wet road beside Queen's Gate. Brollies were going down like sleeping bats and wet jackets were being prised off shoulders. In front of them, a flashy yellow Porsche let down its power hood like a pram-lid and the driver donned racer specs.

Portia dropped Phoebe outside Kensington Market, her foot pumping the accelerator as if she was blowing up a flat tyre.

'Thanks so much for going this far out of your way,' Phoebe shouted over the din of straining engine.

'Not at all, darling,' Portia yelled back, still sulky but mustering a smile. She delved into the glove compartment and produced a battered leather Filofax. 'Look, write your number down, Freddy. We must meet up for lunch or something.'

Astonished, Phoebe took the organiser and flipped through for a spare millimetre to cram in her number. At least it was 0171; she had a feeling Portia was the sort of girl who expunged all 0181s from her address section, unless they were Richmond. Every letter of the alphabet was bulging with pages, some falling out with age, each over-filled with names and numbers written in a multitude of pens. F contained a frightening quantity. On the last page, there was just one word as a final entry, *Fox*, and about twelve numbers underneath.

The penny dropped with a pound-coin thud in Phoebe's head. Christ, Topaz Fox's husband was Piers, wasn't he? The one Saskia had mentioned was Felix Sylvian's publicity agent.

'Hurry up, I can see a wasp buzzing in,' Portia yelled, staring into her wing mirror at a traffic warden goose-stepping towards the BMW.

Phoebe hastily scrawled her details underneath Piers Fox's and handed the Filofax back.

'Ciao then, Freddy,' Portia smiled, raking her blonde hair away from her face so that she could see to pull out. It didn't stop a Mini almost spinning on the spot as it braked to avoid hitting her. She accelerated back on to Kensington High Street amidst a squealing flurry of rubber and flying puddles.

Phoebe knew that Fliss worked somewhere off Kensington Church Street, but as she raced to the opposite pavement, she caught sight of her rain-soaked reflection in Hyper Hyper's windows and realised she looked far too bedraggled to pop in uninvited. Georgette Gregory wasn't likely to welcome friends of her secretary dripping over her paperwork and oozing water from their ballet pumps on to her hand-woven carpets. Nor was she likely to tap her feet along to the sound of their stomachs rumbling out hunger drumrolls. It was only three-thirty, Phoebe realised, so she had time to cram in some food and a quick, invigorating drink whilst drying off.

In a side street, she found a dingy wine bar belting out Noël Coward tracks and ordered a bolstering glass of white wine and an omelette bap. The huge, frostbite-dry drink arrived almost half an hour before the bap, and Phoebe slugged it back, brooding unhappily about Dan.

Halfway down the glass, and Dan was picking up in the popularity stakes. The other half drained remarkably quickly and, deciding to indulge in a rare second glass, Phoebe was soon feeling deliciously tight.

Dan had the most beautiful voice, she thought dreamily. As smooth as maple syrup slipping down freshly buttered warm brioche. Every time she heard it, she wanted to slide off her chair and bite the carpet in delight, toes flexed with joy. And he had a lovely way of swinging his gaze between her eyes when he spoke to her, like a hypnotist with a gold watch on a chain. She also adored the way he purred like a huge, tickled cat when she kissed every tiny dark mole on his bare stomach.

Phoebe snapped out of her daze, realising she was attracting quite a lot of attention, having slid almost horizontal on her chair whilst pursing her smiling lips in daydream stomach kisses.

'It's a paunch,' she told herself firmly, draining her wine. Paunch, not stomach, she repeated to herself – not out loud this time.

She ordered her third drink just as the meal arrived. Spearing a forkful of salad, she then tried to locate her mouth, which seemed to be moving alarmingly around her face.

'Jolly good this,' she beamed at the waiter when he brought her a glass of wine the size of a Munich Beer Festival tankard, clearly deciding to save himself the legwork of fetching a fourth.

'Surprised you can tell,' he grinned, dropping his eyes to Phoebe's plate before moving away.

She dropped her eyes too and blushed. One complete, unbitten omelette bap sat on a bed of scattered frilly lettuce which her fork seemed to have distributed on to the ashtray, side plate, single-carnation-in-a-Perrier-bottle and all over her lap. There was even a piece hanging off one of her earrings.

Finding she'd lost her appetite, she took another slurp of wine and thought about Mitzi Neasham again. Thick-crotched tights and support knickers. She giggled, feeling better. Perhaps she'd just give Dan a quick call at his office. Check he was okay and apologise for rushing off yesterday. Yes, that could do no harm, she reasoned. After all, she needn't give him her new number.

She reached for her duffle bag to extract her address book and her fingers closed around the cool leather of Fliss's best A4 portfolio. Of course, her bag was at home, she remembered, her face flushing with shame and relief.

'Stupid fool,' she said out loud and, polishing off her wine like a marathon runner with a roadside beaker of water, went in search of a loo.

It was downstairs in the cellars. Somehow missing the last three steps and staggering towards a painted door, Phoebe lurched into the Gents without realising.

'Oh, Christ!' she yelped at her reflection in a four-by-six postcard mirror set, for once, at her height.

No wonder everyone in the wine bar – especially the waiter – had been looking at her as if she was sporting a stuffed moose head and wearing a spinning bow tie. Her hair had dried in even, frizzy spikes around her head, like a recently electrocuted punk, and her clothes were now corrugated with dried-in creases. The linen skirt had shrunk to an alarming degree so that it was not so much a wrap-around as a French maid's apron. And she *would* be wearing her new, ultra-trendy women's boxer shorts which poked out of the gaping side, making her resemble a very unstylish cross-dresser.

Dispiritedly, she tried to rake a comb through her matted hair, but it broke in two, one half shooting across the room and landing in something that looked suspiciously like a urinal. There was another one next to it, she noticed with slightly cross-eyed amusement.

'Now that's taking political correctness too damn far,' Phoebe snorted, running the tap and resorting to dampening her hair down. 'Probably got a Tampax machine in the Mens.'

Pondering this thought, she reeled towards the roller towel, hanging off it for a few seconds to regain her balance before using it to wipe off her rain-streaked mascara which had descended to nostril level. Still gripping the towel for support, she pitched left and blasted the soggy shoulders of her jacket with the hand dryer. Back at the mirror, she was relieved to see that the restoration job had salvaged some of the old sex appeal. She was now sporting a rather damp, rumpled, just-got-out-of-the-burst-water-bed look that, she felt, was bound to catch on fast.

About to leave, she remembered that she'd originally come in because she needed the lavatory, and ricocheted into a cubicle.

Voices drifted in from outside.

Lolling on her loo seat, Phoebe stifled a laugh. Two men were coming into the Ladies. Perhaps they were transvestites too, she mused.

Then reality struck her like a blast from a hot air vent in the face. She whipped back her ballet-pumped feet, which had been swinging about under the partition door, and held her breath.

'– came to Paris with us, stupid sod,' one voice drifted past her door and towards the urinals. 'So we told him to meet us at this dingy gay restaurant in the Latin Quarter, and the rest of us ate at Taillevent. He didn't reappear for two days.'

The second man snorted with amusement and then the unmistakable sound of recycled wine hitting the Armitage Shanks filtered through to Phoebe, cringing in her cubicle like a Mexican stowaway hidden in a cattle truck crossing the US border.

'Did you see that totally skulled girl upstairs just now?' laughed the first voice again.

'Christ, yes – the airhead dog with the bad perm,' replied a second, slightly deeper and gruffer. 'Totally boxed.'

In her cubicle, Phoebe stiffened.

'She was dying to be picked up, you could tell. Poor bint. Talk about deluded. Do you think she imagines for one minute she looks good in that sack thing? She was wearing men's pants as well, did you notice? And muttering to herself.'

'What a fucking weirdo,' Second Voice whistled, accompanied by the sound of a zip being fastened.

Phoebe fought the temptation to burst out furiously and confront them with the Tower Bridge saga, but grouchily decided complete cowardice was the most gracious option in the circumstances. She felt absolutely livid.

'The jacket was Westwood, though. Three years old and completely out, but Westwood. Sad bitch really – fucked up on drugs, I suppose,' First Voice mused, still recycling his wine. 'Talking of which, get the goodies lined up, Dyldo. I didn't come down here to swap lipsticks and bitch people up.'

Phoebe shrank back against the cistern pipes as the shadow of two legs appeared in the slat of light at the bottom of her cubicle door.

'I can't,' Dyldo hissed. 'There's someone in the bog.'

'Shit!' The second zip went up and two more shadows fell into Phoebe's shrinking patch of light.

Terrified that they'd spot her ballet pumps, she lifted her feet very slowly and silently in the air and held them shakily there, feeling her thigh muscles screaming with the strain. Then, in a moment of drunken miscalculation, she bashed them hard against the door, which rattled in its lock.

'Let's go,' hissed the huskier voice, and one set of shadows disappeared.

Phoebe bit her lip as the other set hovered for what seemed hours and then followed suit. Red with mortification, she pressed her burning cheek to the wall and found it glued to an old piece of chewing gum.

Mustering her dignity, Phoebe clambered back up the stairs to the bar and paid the bill for her alcoholic stupor, aware that several pairs of eyes were fixed on the back of her three-year-old, unfash Westwood jacket, two of which had recently been discussing her drug problem in the men's loo.

As she waited for her change from the grinning waiter, she turned and gazed around the brasserie, trying to work out who they had been. Several couples, still on very late lunches, were staring into one another's eyes instead of their office VDU screens. Two middle-aged women were shooting Phoebe furtive, amused glances from behind a cloud of Silk Cut smoke; a lone businessman in a tight chalk-stripe suit with dandruff-encrusted shoulders was smouldering at her lasciviously; a giggling threesome of trendy students were obviously sharing a huge joke at her expense. But the only two loo suspects were a pair of salesman-types with shiny expandable briefcases, shiny grey suits, shiny blue ties and very shiny balding pates. They both gaped at Phoebe with smug little salesmen's grins tugging at their shiny red mouths. One winked an insidious beady eye and a shiny little tongue poked out to dab a cold sore.

Phoebe narrowed her eyes like Arnie spotting Predator II in the bushes. Taking her change with a grateful smile, she left a pound on the bar and walked slowly out, stopping by their table and smoothly elbowing their wine bottle so that it tipped on to its side and poured House Red into one shiny grey crotch. The winking salesman squealed like a branded pig.

'Christ, I'm sorry,' she gasped in mock apology, grabbing a napkin and pretending to mop the red stain whilst carefully elbowing a water jug into the second crotch.

'Oh God, so, so sorry!' She backed off, her eyes rolling in merry angst. 'I'm just totally boxed out of my tiny little airhead today.'

And, flashing them both her most winning smile, she teetered happily on to the pavement outside where she weaved to a halt and drunkenly tried to work out where she was. Something to do with Fliss and a job, she remembered vaguely.

Behind her, two people were howling with laughter. Very familiar laughter, Phoebe realised. Laughter which she had just been sole party to downstairs.

'Oh God,' she moaned quietly, looking over her shoulder.

Sitting at a sun-drenched pavement table outside the café bar were two men nursing tiny espresso cups. One was short, chunky and dark with a crumpled striped shirt, chaotically untidy hair, kind, laughing brown eyes and a big, friendly grin like a panting Rottweiler. Beside him, two lengthy, muscular calves clad in strawberry jeans were propped up on the table with a battered copy of *The Caretaker* resting on them. The owner was wearing very dark Armani shades with tortoiseshell tops, had hair as shiny and blond as an open book of gold leaf, bone structure like a freshly kilned Rubens bust, and was roaring his head off.

It was unmistakably Felix Sylvian.

Close to, his lazy, feline, fallen seraph beauty was utterly breathtaking. Had she been Icarus, Phoebe suspected her wings would now be lying in two smouldering, feathery puddles on the pavement below her. She couldn't tear her eyes away.

'That was simply wonderful,' he drawled in a fathom-deep voice, wiping a sapphire eye under his specs with a long finger. 'Quite the most spectacular piece of ham acting I've seen since Leon the Pig Farmer.'

Phoebe's tongue felt as if it had been tied to her lower intestine. Saskia would weep if she could see the infallible Fredericks seduction technique now. What had Felix called her? A sad bint? Cowardice was definitely once again called for, she decided.

Shooting him a venomous look, she clutched her portfolio to her chest, covered her knickers, which were once again flashing, and stalked off on her shredded ballet pumps.

II

The sun was shrinking the last puddles on the pale grey Kensington pavements into dark, mottled stains by the time Phoebe found Fliss's office. Weaving up the immaculate marble steps towards a gloomy red-brick portico, Phoebe squinted thoughtfully at the rows of buttons lined up beside the squawk box. Most had neat brass plaques beside them: Kelleher's Design; Russell and Friedlander Chartered Surveyors; George Cubitt FLIA, ACMB, Financial Adviser. At the bottom of the row was a lacquered red circle with a small, dainty drawing of a wine glass and a corkscrew; *The Function Junction* boasted twirly, embossed gold italic writing, looping gaily through a party streamer.

Stifling a derisive snort, Phoebe buzzed and waited.

'Hang on, darling, I've only got half my bloody face on – oh, shit, there goes another lash!' screeched a voice. Definitely not Fliss.

Phoebe wavered uncertainly and then pressed again.

'I said – '

'Is Felicity there? It's her friend, Phoebe.'

'Christ, what a relief! I thought you were bloody Dennis. Come in, poppet. I think she's on the bog – or did I send her to see Harriet Johansson? God knows. Top floor – just – '

The loud entry buzzer obliterated the rest.

Inside a very grand galleried entrance hall, an ancient wire-vest lift rattled up the centre of a spiralling mahogany staircase to the fifth floor. Groaning like an octogenarian passing a kidney stone, it stopped with such a jolt that Phoebe felt three large glasses of white wine travel up to her throat and rinse her tonsils before swooshing back down to her stomach.

A narrow strip of lobby separated *The Function Junction* from Heritage Listings Renovation Co., the boundary clearly delineated by the change in framed pictures from thick, stripped pine ones holding water-colours of crumbling Sussex houses to silver-framed photographs of Georgette Gregory simpering between the shoulder pads of the glitterati. Phoebe had imagined her to be tall and big-boned, but evidence suggested she only came up to Imran Khan's elbow and was as lithe as an ageing, anorectic ballerina with gnarled toes from years of pouting into Nureyev's lips *à point*. And instead of a Baroness Thatcher sculptured hairdo and pussy cat bow, GG had a raven bob as sharply cut as a topiaried yew and a very startling line in haute trash fashion.

Phoebe knocked tentatively on a half-open, carmine-painted door and then walked into a reception area as red and glossy as the rows of nail varnish testers on a manicurist's counter. The walls were the same deep, shot crimson as the fake blood adored by the make-up artists of seventies Hammer House movies, a vast Persian rug spread in a rich mix of plum, raspberry and cherry compôte across the parquet floor, and a long, tomato gloss library table, stretching between clashing red doors, was coated with scarlet bowls overflowing with roses, carnations and azaleas like a florist's window on Valentine's Day. Two fat maroon leather Chesterfields crammed with scarlet scatter cushions faced one another across a red-stained pine coffee table which was loaded with cardinal-glazed vases and a bowl of china apples looking as though they'd been prepared earlier by Snow White's evil stepmother. Thick gilt frames were crammed on to the gory walls like a huge cubist mosaic, holding paintings of doubtful artistic merit, all of which were slapped with liberal licks of crimson lake or washes of vermilion.

The gaudy, eyewatering effect left Phoebe feeling as though someone had slipped a hallucinogen into the air conditioning, crammed an Alice band on her head and shot her through a looking glass. She knew without doubt that she wouldn't last a week sitting in the cochineal womb.

'Hebe – delighted. I'm George!'

A flurry of black John Richmond PVC and white silk dashed through the reception, clipping on a stud earring.

'Actually, it's Phoe—'

But the flurry had disappeared behind a slamming ruby door.

'Christ.' Phoebe sank into one of the maroon sofas, stood up again to adjust the shrunken linen skirt towards some form of modesty, and then sank down once more with a squeak of skin against leather. She wondered where Fliss could be.

The ruby door flew open again.

'Felicity tells me you're looking for a job?' Blotting lipstick furiously with a hunk of loo roll, the flurry dashed past a swinging damson-stained pine door, through which Phoebe briefly glimpsed a tiny kitchen in more shades of green than Jonathan Porritt's philosophy on life.

'Yes,' she replied vaguely, wondering whether to follow her, but doubting she could keep up. So Fliss *had* recommended her, she realised gratefully. Where on earth was she?

Georgette nipped back through the still-swinging kitchen door.

'I'm afraid I can't offer you anything . . .' she breezed, dashing through an open burgundy door and into an office entirely decorated in shades of blue.

Phoebe opened her mouth to query this, burped winily, and closed it tight again, letting a fruity Sauvignon Blanc float up through her nostrils.

'. . . because you're obviously far too provocative, darling,' Georgette went on, crashing about in the drawers of a navy-stained ash desk the size of most offices' conference tables. 'Shit! Where *has* that damned girl put my glasses?'

Phoebe watched Georgette's narrow PVC bottom in amazement as it stooped over the huge desk. She wondered what she'd just done that labelled her 'provocative'. Staggering in to *The Function Junction* and collapsing rather woozily into a settee hardly counted as one of her wildest entrances.

Tossing back her jet bob, which immediately fell into place again like the final take in a Vidal Sassoon ad, Georgette flapped over to some groaning royal blue shelves, filled almost entirely with blue leather-spined books. 'No, you're far too sexy, Hebe, I can tell at a glance. Felicity said you were rather quirky-looking, so I was hoping for someone rather more Dawn French or Caitlin Moran – voluptuous, witty and pretty. Business clients adore that earthy mumsiness tinged with a sharp mind.' She whisked over to an indigo cupboard. 'The sultry look just isn't cost-effective; smacks too much of ambitious PR girls that everyone gropes and grabs phone numbers off, and I can just about still fill that role. Believe me, it's . . . ah, here the blessed things are! . . . all about looks these days.'

To prove her point, Georgette appeared in the doorway of her blue office waggling a spectacle case and draping a slim, silk-sleeved upper arm against the frame whilst beaming at Phoebe. The effect was ravishing. She must have been the wrong side of fifty for several years, but still had the sort of mesmerising looks that would cause cab drivers to do rubber-burning U-turns on the Bayswater Road if she so much as lifted a manicured finger to signal them.

As slim as the sharpened edge of a blade, she had massive, black-rimmed brown eyes like a seal pup's and a wide, red-painted mouth which split into an uptilted crescent over the white peaks of her uneven teeth, spreading warmth across her pale face like an open log fire, and creasing up a retroussé nose with nostrils as perfectly symmetrical as inverted commas. Her black bob wasn't just glossy, it reflected the wire filaments in her office's overhead spot lamps. And her outfit was so superbly cut and elegantly tailored that, despite its ludicrous trendiness, it clung to her like Demi Moore's spray-on suit for the Liebovitz *Vanity Fair* cover.

Phoebe, still vaguely tight, couldn't take in much of what Georgette was saying. She merely gawped at Fliss's boss and wondered how such a vision of sylph-like splendour could possibly, as Fliss regularly reported, send out for triple bagels with smoked salmon and cream cheese for breakfast, demand two doughnuts with every decaff coffee, break into a fresh family-sized Milky bar daily and dine out more often than Craig Brown with copy to make up.

'Did you get that skirt at Nicole Farhi?' Georgette indicated for Phoebe to stand up with an impatient waggle of her thin, bony hand. Unable to stand still for long, she perched on the edge of the opposite sofa, swinging a thin PVC leg.

'Hong Kong.' Phoebe stood up reluctantly, revealing a lot of boxer short.

'Divine – I love it.' Georgette moved to the other sofa arm and creased her eyes. 'Shame you're not fatter really. But I want someone to face me up and do a lot of liaising, and it's amazing how many – Felicity'll be back in two ticks, by the way – companies think that caterers and party planners have to be fat to be doling out decent, generous measures of everything. Skinny ones look as if they skimp on the pudding. Do you work out?'

'What? Oh, no, I never exercise.' Phoebe was reminded of Julius Caesar declaring a need to be surrounded by fat people. Georgette's was the oddest employment strategy she'd ever encountered. Although on reflection, she mused, Georgette was just very odd all round.

'Amazing.' She hopped up and straightened the piles of glossy magazines on the coffee table. 'When I told Felicity – she's just popped out to deliver some menus to an old boot in Holland Park – that I was looking for a part-timer, she suggested you right away. Drinks!' She straightened up and vanished into the green kitchen again, leaving the door swinging frantically.

It took Phoebe several seconds to figure out what Georgette had just said. She had a way of interjecting one sentence with another quite different one, making her line of conversation harder to follow than Theseus's piece of string in the Minotaur's maze.

'That was kind of her.' She ducked through the swinging door and tried to adjust her watering eyes from reds to the smarting green viridity which themed every utensil in the shoe-box kitchen from the kettle to the mug-stand.

'No, it bloody wasn't.' Georgette was rushing around, leaving fridge and cupboard doors gaping as she haphazardly poured out two gin and tonics strong enough to render Olly Reed comatose. 'She said we'd probably loathe one another, but that if she didn't suggest you, you'd never forgive her. Told me you were always late, totally disorganised, took three hours for lunch and never lasted in a job more than a fortnight. Here, you might as well join me – I always need to be pissed to talk to Dennis, horrible old man.'

She handed a brimming glass to Phoebe, who forced a grateful smile and closed her nose to the rising gin fumes. Phoebe was furious with Fliss who, far from keeping schtumm as she'd said she would, appeared to have told the truth for once in her life.

'Anyway, I told Felicity you sounded bloody marvellous.' Georgette laughed, pressing past Phoebe and swinging back out through the door again. 'I hate wimps. They're always scared of me, and stupidly jealous as well. Fliss can come across as pretty wet – all those revolting flowery dresses she wears – but she's such a fabulous liar and so good at getting to grips with the air-conditioning, I can't bear to sack her. You seem . . .' Her voice trailed away.

Hopping after her, Phoebe found the reception and the true-blue office deserted. She tried the ruby door and walked straight into a glacier white loo. Backing out, she tried to follow Georgette's voice.

'. . . shame, really. But I can give you a couple of numbers that might prove fruitful. Don't suppose you could suggest a chubby friend who's good at charming people? Oh, there you are.'

Through a coral door, Phoebe found a sitting room decorated exclusively in mustard-field yellows, rendered agonisingly bright by the sunlight which sliced through three vast windows like Hollywood studio floodlights.

She blinked in the doorway.

Georgette was hovering beside a striped primrose chaise longue, fiddling with a custard bolster. She then raced over to a stripped pine writing desk and started scribbling down some numbers on a Post-it pad.

No wonder she's so slim, Phoebe thought as she carefully placed her drink behind a vase of garish tiger lilies and slumped on to a banana brocade sofa. Georgette Gregory emitted so much nervous energy that, if tapped into the National Grid, she could heat Leeds. Something about her manic, racy bonhomie and endearing egotism reminded Phoebe of Saskia the time she'd met her before leaving for New Zealand.

'Actually, there is a friend who might be interested in working with you . . .' she said cautiously, wondering whether she was being totally deluded or inspired.

'Don't make it sound such a ghastly idea.' Georgette snapped her pen closed and folded the piece of paper. 'If I advertise this job, Fliss will be scanning CVs for months.' She handed over the numbers and polished off her gin. 'Not a bad idea, really,' she mused, 'give her something to do other than read her horoscope, kill my pot plants and write letters to the Arts Council on my word processor. Bloody Pisceans. Your friend?' she demanded crisply.

Phoebe smiled. 'Oh, I'm sure she'd love to work with you, and she'd be incredibly good – but I'm not certain that she wants to move back to London yet. She's been through a pretty rough time lately.'

'Wonderful. I love sob stories. You must tell me sometime. Mention it to her and – don't you want this drink? – get her to call me. What's her name?' Georgette started to drain Phoebe's gin and tonic, moving towards a window.

'Saskia Seaton.'

Georgette's drink sprayed back out, drenching six inches of saffron curtain. 'Not one of Tony's girls?' She turned back to Phoebe.

Phoebe nodded.

'Christ, yes – how is the old bugger? – send her along.'

'He's well, a bit stressed maybe, but not bad.' Phoebe fought an urge to slag Toady Tony off as a bullying coward who was bored to death by his daughter's problems. 'Do you know him well?'

'No, not really. Shit!' Georgette rolled her seal eyes as the door buzzer went. 'That'll be the Menace.' She headed towards the door. 'Look, I'll go straight down. Hang on for Fliss here, poppet, and ask her to lock up. Lovely to meet you.' She dashed back in and kissed Phoebe on both cheeks, leaving two scarlet lipstick stains. 'Get Tony's daughter to call as soon as. And best of luck getting a job – I like your interview technique. Very natural. Tell bloody Dennis I'm coming down.' And grabbing a purple velvet jacket, she whisked out.

'Thanks for the numbers . . .' Phoebe called, but the lift was already passing another kidney stone as it groaned down to the ground floor.

The buzzer went again, and, picking up the entry phone, Phoebe gave it her best cerebrally-challenged receptionist's tinkling voice.

'She's on her way down to meet you, Mr Dennis.'

'Oh, right. Thank you, darling,' replied a voice as gravelly as a cement mixer chewing through some particularly stubborn road chippings. 'You new?'

'No – I'm just holding the fort, Mr Dennis, sir.'

'You sound quite lovely, m'dear. What d'you look – ah! George, darling!' The voice faded away.

Dashing to the window in the blue office, Phoebe waited a few moments and then saw the top of Georgette's shiny black bob appear at the bottom of the steps. Beside her was a head of white curly hair above two broad chalk-stripe shoulders.

As the grey-haired man waited for his slight companion to climb into a waiting Senator with dark-tinted windows, he glanced along Kensington Church Street and then up at the blustering little clouds shuffling in an impatient queue along the narrow strip of blue sky overhead. Phoebe held her breath and then whistled.

Drawing away from the kerb, the big car nearly ran over a girl who was crossing the road without looking, her burnt sienna hair escaping from a purple scarf as she gazed thoughtfully at a male jogger's Lycra bottom bouncing away towards Hyde Park. The car beeped and she jumped out of the way, waving happily so that the contents of her open satchel scattered across the near lane.

'You didn't tell me La GG was seeing Sir Dennis Middleton,' Phoebe greeted Fliss as she panted into the office minutes later, still trying to buckle her refilled handbag.

'What?' Fliss sank on to a leather Chesterfield beside her friend, her glowing cheeks matching the reception decor. 'You look rough – and that's my bloody scarf.'

'Thanks. Hi.' Phoebe kissed her hello and did up the handbag buckle for her. 'Are they an item then?'

Fliss rested her neck on the back of the sofa and blew red corkscrews of hair from her eyes. ''Course they are. She's been attending to the Honourable member for ages.'

Phoebe whistled. 'What does Lady Middleton think about it?'

'Pretty much the same as Georgette.' Fliss rotated her head towards Phoebe and grinned. 'Seeing as they're one and the same – oh, Phoebes mate, can we walk around the park before we have a drink? I've just seen *the* most gorgeous lad heading off – '

'I know.' Phoebe heaved herself up. 'And no, we can't. You'd never suit a fitness fanatic. Your idea of getting some fresh air is winding down Honk's window.'

Grumbling, Fliss shuffled around the office, switching on the answerphone and fax, turning off the lights, nicking pens, stamps and envelopes and complaining about the cost of getting Honk released from the King's Cross compound.

'To cap it all,' she bustled Phoebe out of the main door and dashed back in to set the alarm, 'I paid the astronomical release fee, kissed him hello, and the little bugger wouldn't start, even when I siphoned some petrol off a nearby Saab. In the end, the police had him towed to a garage for me – they've quoted six hundred ransom, or he goes in the compressor.' She ran out and locked the door as the alarm beeps sounded angrily inside the office. 'But there are compensations. Look.' She dangled a set of keys in front of Phoebe's nose. A gold key ring glittered with a distinctive insignia.

'You've got a Merc?' Phoebe gasped.

'Georgette's.' Fliss winked, punching the lift button. 'I told her a gang of six-year-old sub-criminals had vandalised Honk and, out of the kindness of her heart – the fact that she's got eight points against her licence and another speeding charge pending doesn't come into it, of course – she told me I could fetch her each morning on my way here and dump her off at night if Den can't pick her up.' The lift arrived with a shuddering moan and Fliss pushed Phoebe in. 'She's usually too pissed to drive at the end of the day, anyway. Meet you at the bottom, I'm getting fit.'

Eyed by a distrustful cleaning lady, Phoebe waited by a smudged brass banister for Fliss to pant down the last few flights, earrings jangling.

'Do you climb up them as well?' she asked in awe as they wandered outside.

'Get real, Phoebes.' Fliss donned some scratched sun-specs and headed towards Notting Hill. 'I'm trying to lay a jogger, not a Gladiator. Besides, I only decided to get fit five minutes ago. Let's walk really fast.'

'You did what?' Fliss gasped as she sat down beside Phoebe in Vats wine bar with a glass of house red and a Coke, her face still puce from the pace of their walk.

'I suggested Saskia to La Gregory.' Phoebe took a swig of Coke. 'She's all right, Fliss, you'll like her. She needs a break – and since Georgette had rather an odd impression of me,' she raised her eyebrows, 'I reasoned that I could at least do Saskia a favour.'

'Hmm,' Fliss attacked the foil on a packet of beer nuts, her faded blue eyes widening with familiar faux-innocence. 'I did my best to pitch you at GG, honest.'

'Sure.' Phoebe grinned.

'Okay, okay.' Fliss watched two young Hugo Boss-suited businessmen come into the bar with critical artistic appraisal. 'But, face it, Phoebe, could you work with her? She's hell. She gives dictation from her jogging machine then eats me alive if I accidentally add one of her comments like: "Fuck, I've only done three miles and I'm sweating like a bloody pig." She knocks back gin from ten in the morning then bawls me out for having half a lager at lunchtime, and the old bag always sends me out for doughnuts and loo roll if someone famous is rolling up, so that I never get to meet them. You'd think she was embarrassed by me – and after all the bloody effort I make to dress up, too.' She picked a hunk of dried clay from her freckled chest.

'I liked her,' Phoebe said honestly. 'Admittedly she's barking, but she's phenomenally energetic. She gave me some numbers to try, too – look.'

Fliss took the Post-it sticker and snorted. 'Yolande's PR company's so far down the plug-hole it's bobbing in the S-bend. Freddy Reisler's a possibility, but you'd have to sleep with him to get him to look at your resumé when he's trying to remember your name in the morning. Susie Middleton's hopeless – she's Georgette's step-daughter, runs a pretty impressive agency, but only employs ex-models or the toy-boys she wants to bed.'

'Susie Middleton?' Phoebe's memory was frantically trying to excavate a link.

'Yes.' Fliss shrugged dismissively and then leaned forward, her shrewd blue eyes searching. 'Why did you suggest Saskia to Georgette? You told me last week that she was a toffee-nosed arriviste who'd once drawn Hitler moustaches all over your David Cassidy posters and told your brothers you were having a lesbian affair with the Latin mistress.'

'That was before I saw her this weekend.'

Fliss dipped a finger into her wine and dabbed red fingerprints on to the white paper tablecloth.

'So you had a jolly gas swapping lower-fifth anecdotes about apple pie beds and losing your virginity to the tennis coach?' She tried hard not to show how hurt she'd been at Phoebe's sloping away to the Seatons. 'Made friends again over a school photo where you appeared at both ends?'

'Not exactly.'

Phoebe gave her a brief run-down of her weekend mopping tears and listening to Saskia's crazy revenge idea, carefully omitting the Dan encounter and her ignoble exit from the Seatons' house the night before. Nor did she mention Felix by name, knowing only too well Fliss's ability to spread gossip like flu through air conditioning.

'Christ!' Fliss swilled round the last inch of her wine. 'Poor old Saskia. He sounds a complete louse. Are you going to do it?'

Phoebe shrugged, wondering whether to blurt out her unfortunate brush with the complete louse earlier but deciding against it. The sad bint jibe was still causing a prickly heat of humiliation to sandpaper the surface of her skin. She snorkelled up some more Coke and watched straggling office workers trying to squeeze into the packed, chattering bar, edging briefcases and handbags between cramped, gossiping groups as they fought to get their proffered tenners within sight of the ten-deep bar.

'You've seen The Corps, haven't you?' Fliss asked suddenly.

Phoebe snapped her gaze up abruptly, fighting to keep her expression on the incredulous side of shock. 'What makes you say that?'

Fliss's pale blue corneas seemed to be melting into the whites of her eyes with pity, a trick practised so rarely and to such tremendous effect it was guaranteed to educe a confession faster than direct angle-poise lights and finger-nail extraction.

'Phoebe, you're my best mate. Just look at yourself,' she said gently. 'You're a wreck, you look as though you've not slept in weeks, your eyes are as red as your phone bill, and you're dressed in your Dan kit. I know you too well to believe it's just because you had a lousy weekend with a distressed friend. You look exactly like you did a year ago. Either it's The Corps back on the scene or your dog's died.'

'I don't have a bloody dog.' Phoebe shifted guiltily. 'I got caught in the rain.'

'Where?'

'Outside Dan's office.' Giving up, she looked at Fliss pleadingly. 'But I didn't try to see him. He was there last night – at the Seatons' dinner party. I had no idea.'

'Christ!' Fliss's eyes widened so much, they looked in danger of popping out of their sockets and landing in her wine. 'Did anything happen?'

'No.' Phoebe glanced away, hating herself for the memory. 'But it would have if Saskia hadn't walked in. His wife was there too.'

'Shit, Phoebe. What are you playing at?' Fliss, who could explode to rare and tremendous effect as forcefully as she could melt, sounded furious.

Phoebe put her hot face in her hands and shrugged. 'I'm a bit of a mess, aren't I?'

'You're coming completely unravelled, baby.' Fliss pulled Phoebe's hands into her warm grip and squeezed them kindly, looking her in the eyes. 'You're becoming lazy, you need to stretch yourself – get a fabulous job and a lovely, long, flirtatious romance to keep you busy. Stop trying to recapture rose-tinted spectres. Believe me, chuck, I've tried it and it never works. You'll twist yourself into a knot instead of tying it.'

'Once bitten, twice twisted,' Phoebe muttered sadly, then summoned a smile. 'So where do I find this fabulous job and flirty romance? The *Loot* classifieds?'

'I'll set you up,' Fliss offered, lifting her glass and resting her nose on the rim so that it snubbed up comically.

'No, thanks.' Phoebe forced the smile past ten seconds. 'You didn't do me a lot of favours with Georgette, Fliss, and I don't fancy another hot date with your brother and an *Aladdin* video. He's honestly not my type.'

Fliss looked uncomfortable at the memory. 'What . . .' her mouth suddenly spread into a smile as wide as the rim of her glass '. . . about Saskia's sweet revenge?' she pointed out excitedly. 'Now there's a distraction as welcome as a streaker on a wet day at Twicks.'

'Not a great idea.' Phoebe rubbed her eyes tiredly, 'I have a vague suspicion that my rusty seduction technique would leave Felix colder than a Siberian nudist.'

'Who's Felix?'

'Felix Sylvian,' Phoebe explained impatiently, remembering too late that she was supposed to be keeping him a secret. 'You won't have heard of him.'

Fliss whooped in excited recognition. 'Heard of him! I've met him. Well, swooned in the same room he was in – and, not only that, but I'm wildly, wildly in love with his brother, Mungo. Ohmygod! Felix the hormone-wrecker. *He's* Saskia's ex?'

'Er – yes, sort of.' Phoebe didn't like the glint in Fliss's eye. She looked as if Phoebe had just told her chocolate had no calories and was good for the skin.

'Oh, Phoebe, this is brilliant, mate!'

'I'd hardly call – '

'I mean,' Fliss threw back the dregs of her wine, staining her tea dress with red spatters, 'you set out to seduce Felix Sylvian and I can pursue Mungo into the bargain. We can do it together – have a time limit and everything. Wouldn't that be great? Mungo is beautiful, Phoebes mate.' Fliss's huge eyes suddenly filled with tears and dropped to gaze into her wine. 'I mean, the others didn't take to him much – Stan hated him, I reckon. But I think he's just jealous really. Mungo's simply the loveliest thing I've ever, ever seen. And – I know this sounds grossly egotistical and I could be wrong – I think he quite fancied me.'

Oh God, Phoebe thought silently. Fliss got terrible, painful crushes quite regularly, always on beautiful no-hopers, always a prelude to getting appallingly hurt. And Stan, whom she'd once nick-named the Sniper because he was such a shrewd character assassin, had undoubtedly awarded Mungo with a well-deserved nil points for piss-artistic merit.

'Promise you'll phone Saskia tonight?'

'Okay.'

'Oh, by the way – what are you doing on August Bank Holiday?' Fliss started groping in her wine-splattered bag.

'Bank Holiday? It's only just July.' Phoebe, who always had problems getting to grips with the concept of tomorrow, watched her in bewilderment. When drunk Fliss could change topics faster than Magnus Magnusson during the Mastermind general knowledge round.

'Good, so you've nothing planned.' Fliss, upside down, was turfing receipts out of her bag, her purple scarf unravelling on to the floor.

'Well, I've an eleven o'clock, a lunch, and a couple of possible windows pencilled in. Why?'

'I thought I might organise a murder mystery house party.' Drawing out her battered fake Filofax, Fliss resurfaced.

'A what?'

'Hire a house somewhere – up north maybe – insist on twenties dress, give everyone shifty characters to turn up as, and select one person to be murderer. The rest is improvised mayhem. Then we zap the lights at midnight and the deed is done. It can't fail.'

'Sounds great.' Phoebe smiled weakly, wondering whether her parents would welcome a surprise visit to Hong Kong instead.

'Good, so you're a definite too.' Fliss opened her Filofax and dived back down to her bag for a pen, her scarf finally floating to the floor.

'How many people are coming so far?'

'Just you.' Straightening up, Fliss wrote *Phoebes def* on to a piece of bright green paper. 'And Stan. But I was thinking . . .' Pushing hair away from her smiling pink face, she looked at Phoebe euphorically.

'Thinking?'

'That August Bank Holiday could be our deadline.' She bit her plump pink lip with bursting eagerness.

'For what?'

'Felix and Mungo, mate – you dump, I hump.' Laughing at her unexpected brilliance, she polished off her wine.

She glanced at her watch. 'Bugger, I've got to go, mate. I was meant to meet Iain outside the Swiss Centre ten minutes ago. Look, can you do me a massive favour and take the car back to the flat?'

'Georgette's Merc?' Phoebe balked.

'Yeah.' Fliss was gathering up her bag. 'It's a dream to drive – I should think. Here's the keys. One of them's the alarm and immobiliser. Bugger, I've forgotten which. Never mind, you'll find it. I'll see you back at the flat. C'ya.'

And in a flurry of red corkscrews, flowery cotton and clattering clog-espadrilles, she bounded out, leaving Phoebe mouthing obscenities as though giving furious dictation to a lip-reader. Nudged by the breeze from the door, Fliss's headscarf coiled its way around her ankle.

It suddenly occurred to Phoebe that the reason for their drinks meeting had not even been mentioned until ten seconds ago. Iain.

She drained the last inch of her Coke, her guts churning in consternation. She was worried about Fliss who, like an old Hornby train set, continually threatened to go off the rails. Although chums for years, it wasn't until she started living with her irascible, energetic, red-haired friend that Phoebe realised quite how unbalanced Fliss really was beneath the practical, down-to-earth façade.

Added to this, Phoebe's fears for Saskia and the rest of the Seatons gave her the feeling that emotional burdens were beginning to weigh down upon her damp shoulders like lead pads in a jacket. Yet jobless, heart-broken and single herself, she felt both lonely and vulnerable and, for the first time since returning from New Zealand, realised how insulated from responsibility she'd been there. She was racked by a stagnant, indolent feeling of doubt and indecision which made her incapable of saying yes to Saskia's plan or no to Fliss's. She couldn't even make up her mind whether to go home.

12

From Wednesday through to the following weekend, storms rumbled in and out of London almost as regularly as the Boeings soaring to and from Heathrow. Commuters would set out to work in bright sunshine, filing into their local tubes with jackets tossed over briefcases and shirt sleeves rolled up against the sizzling, bleached morning light. Several stops later, their intricately folded *Times* tucked under humid armpits, they would emerge from their work tubes, hunching shoulders and turning up collars against another stinging deluge as they ran the short, wet sprint to their offices, or alternatively hovered inside the entrances of tube stations staring glumly out at the stair rods ricocheting off glossy, streaming pavements like a pane of obscured glass between them and their destinations.

Friday morning started with a crowd of moist, muggy black clouds pressing down on to the tower block rooftops of the City, and a distant splutter of thunder travelled in from Essex like a packed Liverpool Street train.

Across the river, Portia woke nearly suffocating under a fathom deep Peter Jones duvet which was covered in black and white stripes like an enlarged supermarket price strip. Peeking out she saw she was in Piers's open plan warehouse flat, the stretching floors all around her dotted with huge, fleshy, prickly cacti in terracotta tubs which jutted up at six-foot intervals like fat, unshaven legs. Beyond a black leather dentist's chair and an exercise rig that looked as if it would give even

Frank Bruno a hard time, was a window the size of the Leicester
Square Cannon's number one screen. Through it Tower Bridge,
like a majestic Meccano gatehouse letting in the grey pitted
tarmac of the Thames, was iced with the hundreds and thou-
sands of rush hour traffic. A huge clock with a black and white
picture of Bilko marking the hours with his revolving cigar said
it was past eight.

Portia got up and groggily located the bathroom, having first
walked into a built-in wardrobe the size of a garage. She still
couldn't navigate her way around Piers's vast, Zen-like flat; as
soon as she had learnt to place a landmark, he rearranged the
sparse, symmetrical furniture and she was lost again.

Squeezing Euthymol on to a chrome-handled toothbrush,
Portia cleaned her teeth noisily over the grey marble basin.

Even the toiletries were co-ordinating black and white, sitting
in von Trappian rows on the black glass shelf. Portia rearranged
them to look more lived in. One whole half of the room was a
vast shower, tiled in tiny chrome mirrors. Until this morning,
she had always sloped home for a long bath, never quite able to
shake off a sense of one-night-stand guilt. But today Portia was
privately celebrating three stopover dates and the fact that last
night, for the first time in three whole lays, Piers hadn't
accidentally called her Topaz. A very minor celebration, she
realised; but these days – as she found the length of relationships shortening in almost direct inverse proportion to her
lengthening teeth – it was a minor breakthrough.

Unable to resist, she turned on the shower's steaming
whiplash jet of water.

As she circled luxuriously under its searing spray her long,
lean body danced back at her on three sides, slowly disappearing
under the gathering droplets and steam. The shimmering
reflection of her wet, golden brown skin – like russet satin –
made her stop and stare. Then she gasped in horror; black,
sooty rivulets were coursing like diluted ink down her face. She
looked like Munch's *The Scream*.

Portia was still at the paranoid stage in their relationship
where she left the slap on at night, sleeping with her face to the

ceiling like a corpse in order not to smear foundation on the pillows, although the earlier sex would have undoubtedly dispersed most of it on Piers or just sweated it off. Under the pelting shower, her cheeks were now streaked with kohl and mascara like a miner emerging at the pit head into a rainstorm. She hastily grabbed a white soap bar from a symmetrical pyramid on a chrome dish and washed her face.

It made no difference, she realised in amazement. The soap was totally useless – it wouldn't even lather.

Portia dipped away from the jetting water and blinked at the perfectly rectangular cake with sodden eyes. Laughing, she stripped off the shrink-wrapping and started again, breathing in the delicious scent of squeaky cleanness that Piers radiated when he slipped from his clothes each night in the same way most men oozed stale sweat and wild garlic sexuality. She rubbed the soap up her throat, sliding it over the bumps of her trachea and closing her eyes in delight.

After drying herself on the fluffiest of glacier white towels and liberally spraying on Topaz's Panthère, which she could never afford herself and made her head float deliriously away from her shoulders, she wandered naked back into the main room in search of a cigarette.

There were several chrome and marble ashtrays littered on the ankle-high, tennis court-sized coffee tables – all filled with unbent matchbooks from the most expensive and fashionable restaurants in London, but not a cigarette in sight.

Helping herself to a mint imperial from a giant onyx bowl she went back to the bed to look at Piers.

From one end of the crumpled zebra crossing duvet poked a hairy, muscular leg, from the other thick tufts of dark red hair the colour of wet iron rust. Very carefully, Portia lifted back the cover and found his sleeping, angular face pressed to the striped pillow, with long auburn lashes drooping almost to the sprinkling of cayenne freckles that seemed out of place on such a noble nose. Lying on his front, his magnificent, rangy body was stretched out like a slain big cat in front of a baronial Scottish fireplace.

Portia reached out to touch one of the russet moles in the small of his back and then stopped, frozen like a fugitive hearing a snapping twig as he moved.

Still asleep, but aware of the sudden cool, Piers gave a deep, languid sigh and shifted on to his back, his splendid morning glory slipping from the hollow of his pelvis to plumb as he rolled over.

Portia smiled and wondered whether to wake him with breakfast in bed al fellatio. But she'd only just cleaned her teeth, so instead she stooped and dropped the lightest of kisses on the narrow, silvery-red scar that ran for two finger-widths across his stomach. He'd told her that it was from an appendix operation in his teens, but she knew that it was far too high up, and too recent-looking. She'd seen only one like it before, on her father. His was from a perforated ulcer which had almost killed him in the late eighties.

Gently dropping the duvet again, she wandered back into the gargantuan wardrobe she'd stumbled across earlier. There were rows and rows of almost identical dark grey suits dripping with exquisitely cut éclat, the tailor's chalk still puffing from the collars of a few as she stroked the rows of left arms with delight. Hundreds of cloned white shirts were stacked in regulation piles of ten – making it look more like a well-organised office stationery cupboard than a wardrobe. At one end, like a giant cardboard breeze-block wall, was a stack of shoe boxes, nearly all of which had 'Man's Brogue, size nine' stamped on the side. Portia pulled on one of the duplicate white shirts. It was feather weight silk and slid over her scented body like a whisper.

Walking back past the Sleeping Beauty, she began searching the flat for her clothes. They were remarkably spread out – and one of her favourite Louis-heeled boots seemed to have disappeared completely.

Portia tried to avoid being stabbed in the bum by a cactus as she pulled on her suede jeans and tied the white silk shirt under her bust. She then wandered to the seven-foot fridge in the red-brick open plan kitchen. All that there was inside were two cases of Evian, a half-empty jar of sun-dried tomatoes, two bottles of

Purdey's and a very musty melon. Portia binned the melon and then loaded up a glass with ice from the slot in the door, helping herself to some Purdey's.

'Good morning.'

She swung around and smiled at Piers. He was wearing an emerald green towelling robe so fluffy it looked in need of mowing. His emotionless face, still creased from sleep, read like an unfilled dot to dot page of freckles. Join them together and I might be able to read him, Portia mused.

'Hi.' She nervously tucked her wet hair behind her ears and meandered towards him, her movements deliberately as lithe and lazy as possible to drum up confidence. Piers met her full-on with broad, assured hands and lips that pressed themselves straight to hers as accurately and confidently as an archer's arrow into an apple.

Unlike most of her previous lovers, his mouth tasted sweet and moreish in the morning, not stale and dehydrated. Russet stubble grazed her chin and a magnificent erection pressed tightly against her belly through the mossy robe as Piers linked his long, pale fingers around the nape of her neck and drew her up on to the balls of her feet and deeper into the kiss.

Piers' red eyelashes were stroking her cheek as lightly as cobwebs as his tongue dived further to trace the light ridges at the top of her mouth. Despite a pulse pounding between her legs like a metronome on allegro, Portia resisted an urge to undo the perfect towelling reef knot in front of her: sober sex combined with her hangover wouldn't get beyond the blurb of the *Kama Sutra*. She was currently only feeling up to the dismissionary position.

But Piers' fingers were creeping through the front of her shirt and very slowly drawing delicate, deliberate zeros around her nipples which plink-plink fizzed towards tranquillising her hangover far more effectively than two Alka Seltzers.

'I like this shirt,' he murmured, suddenly fingering her silk collar instead.

Flustered, Portia pulled away and watched his face. He could be extremely possessive about his belongings, as she'd learned to her cost when she'd walked off with his silver Mappin and Webb pen on Wednesday and he'd embarrassingly called her at home to ask if she'd seen it. But his bottle green eyes were just looking genuinely amused.

'I wanted to slip away in something more comfortable.' She smiled awkwardly.

'You're not going before breakfast?'

'I think I should.' Portia feigned off-handedess as she pulled away from his grip to gather up her clothes. 'For one, I don't really fancy anything as healthy as Purdey's with this hangover; for two, you said last night that your wife was coming back.'

'God, yes,' Piers muttered, 'so she is.' He scratched his head so that his red hair stood up in a big bouffant like a West Coast surf chick's, yet still he looked ludicrously handsome. 'So she bloody is.'

He leant towards her and started to kiss her neck, his tongue working like an oiled masseur's fingers on her taut muscles, his hands creeping round her hips towards the seat of her suede jeans. He smelt of fabric-conditioned towels, clean sheets and dirty sex; it was as heady a mix as lemon barley water with a massive shot of tequila. Hopelessly excited, Portia pulled away and moved over to an old parking meter with a policeman's helmet on it, anxious for distraction.

'Did you steal these for a prank when you were a student?'

'No.' Piers was watching her impassively. 'I didn't go to college.'

'Oh.' Spinning the helmet on its mercenary metal pivot, Portia wandered over to the American phone booth that was bolted to the wall and picked up the receiver.

'Does this thing work?'

'Yes, of course.'

'Can I use it?'

'Sure.'

Who could she phone? she thought frantically. God, why was she always trying to do posey things to impress him and then losing impetus at the final moment?

'Can we meet on Monday?' Piers asked as she hooked the

receiver over her shoulder and gnawed at a speculative nail, which split right off in delight when he spoke.

She spat it out. 'No – I'm busy. How do you make this thing work?'

'There are some quarters on top. How about Thursday for lunch?'

Portia stabbed out a telephone number. 'I'll have to check my diary first. I'll call you.'

'Make it to the office, Topa— I mean, Portia. My wife might pick up the phone here.' He didn't look remotely apologetic or embarrassed by the slip.

Bristling with indignation, she improvised quickly.

'Hi, darling, it's me,' she said huskily as her own answer-machine purred at her. 'Yes, I know – ages. I've been desperately busy. That's what I hoped you'd say, darling. No, it's fine. I had a last minute cancellation, so I'm totally free.' She flicked a wicked glance at Piers who was hovering by the parking meter pretending not to listen in. 'Okay, Sid's at eight – I'm looking forward to it. Ciao, baby.'

'Who was that?' Piers asked frostily as Portia gathered up her bag after dropping the receiver.

'My mother.' She kissed him on the nose. 'I'll call about Wednesday.'

'Thursday,' Piers's dry voice followed her out. 'But I have a feeling there's a lunch pencilled in my diary . . .'

Topaz Fox listened to a storm cracking distant whips of thunder as she lounged back in Felix's bath, her slender arms draped over the enamel edges, terminating in a glass of Buck's Fizz on the left and a Marlboro Light on the right. She stared glumly at ten coral-painted toe-nails peeking through the fast-dispersing Floris froth at the far end like crocuses in melting spring snow, and swigged the last pithy inch of orange before ramming the smeary flute into a pile of crumpled towels. A swollen copy of *The Birthday Party* toppled from the top.

Topaz picked it up and examined it with distaste. At the moment Felix was very into Pinter of whom she knew nothing.

She was trying to steer him towards Albee, as she'd studied *Zoo* in high school, but he was stubbornly ignoring her recommendation. No bad thing, Topaz reflected, as she'd missed most of her American Literature classes to sneak off to cheerleader practice and meet up with her then boyfriend, a true blue-eyed Ivy League quarter-back who'd ended up doing time for date raping an eighth grader. It was a period in her life she seldom chose to mull over.

'Felix!' She tilted her head towards the half-open door. 'You coming in here? The water's getting cold.'

There was no answer. A muffled beat was throbbing out of a distant bedroom with a deep baritone wailing 'Soul Man!' in a completely different key to Sam and Dave.

Dylan was clearly up, Topaz reflected sourly. His unending good humour, slightly vacuous naïveté and ubiquitous presence irritated her, but Felix doted on his soppy friend so much she was forced to jolly him along and flatter him between sly kicks like a rather stinky pet dog.

'Felix!'

Topaz waited and then sighed with impatient relief as she heard bare feet slapping the floorboards of the hallway in the direction of the bathroom. At last.

She curled one foot over another and flexed her knee so that one slim thigh rose from the frosted water in a glistening acute angle. Flicking her ash over the rim of the bath, she then draped both forearms against the tiles on the walls behind her so that her small, neat breasts jutted from her chest like two raindrops poised on a smooth ash twig, the nipples as dark and appetising as milk chocolate buttons.

The effect was totally wasted on Dylan, who lurched into the bathroom and buried his stubbly face under the gushing cold tap of the basin, his tangled hair flattening to his white forehead.

'Do you mind?' Topaz snapped, disappearing to the chin under the sparse bubbles with a tidal wave of slopping bath water.

'Not at all,' he grinned as his hungover red eyes surfaced from their rinse, blinked several times, and took in the Degas-like scene. 'You carry on, darling. Do you want some toast and Marmite?'

'Get outta here!' Topaz yelled furiously, throwing Pinter at him with frightening accuracy.

'You should pause and count ten beats first – it's in the stage directions.' Still grinning amiably, Dylan loped off.

'Venus is rising to the bait in there,' he murmured as he wandered into the messy mews kitchen to plunder the bread bin. 'I think she's waiting for you to soap her back-stroke.'

'Shit, is she still here?' Felix groaned through a mouthful of bacon sandwich, his eyes not surfacing from Jack Tinker in the *Daily Mail.* 'I thought she'd pushed off while I was out.'

Shrugging without comment, Dylan flicked on the halogen hob and, removing Felix's crusty pan from the cluttered sink, put it on the glowing ring where it hissed furiously and shot water bubbles out across the work-top. Humming 'Soul Man' again, he started lobbing in the remains of the bacon, two eggs and doorstep slices of bread.

Dylan had long ago realised that his flat-mate was incommunicado before midday. On a particularly bad day, he would creep around like a Gregorian monk, resorting to flash cards if he wanted to know where Felix had left the milk. Felix was abysmally tetchy first thing in the morning and as opinionated as a *Sun* columnist. Unshaven and swigging back more tea than the PG Tips chimps, he would prowl around deliberately biting heads off anyone within range like a rabid, rebellious older chimp with the munchies.

Dylan scraped the remains of a pack of butter into the frying pan.

'I thought you were trying to shift some weight.' Felix threw away the last half of his sandwich and stood up.

'I am,' Dylan nodded, slinging in two tomatoes and a herbed sausage. 'I'm so fucking hungover I'll chuck this lot up faster than Princess Di with a Big Mac.'

'That's sick, Dyldo,' Felix snapped, wandering through to the bathroom.

Topaz was crouching over the basin wearing his striped cotton bathrobe. She had his old school tie – which normally acted as the belt – knotted around her head to scrape back her white-blonde hair as she carefully cleaned each tooth in turn with the same exacting care as a Tiffany jeweller polishing twenty-carat diamonds for the display cabinet.

Felix watched her impatiently. The annoying thing about bedding models – and he had parted several pairs of $5,000-a-day thighs in his time – was that the morning after lasted almost through until the next night before again by the time they'd applied every skin tonic, plucked every emerging hair and demanded that a specific brand of bottled water be fetched from the nearest spring. Since the androgynous cross-dressing cult, Felix had also found they made off with half the contents of his wardrobe.

'Are you going to be long? Only we're going out.'

'I can't,' Topaz spoke with her mouth half-open and her chin tilted up to stop any Pearl Drops escaping, 'I've got to get back to Piers. I told him my flight gets in Saturday at eight. You know how exacting he is; if I'm not there by nine, he'll call Heathrow and kick up a smell.'

'A stink.' Felix flashed a smile. 'Actually, I meant Dylan and I are going out.'

'Oh.' Topaz started spitting and rinsing. 'Well, give me some keys and I'll lock up.'

'I haven't got a spare set,' Felix improvised quickly. The last thing he wanted was Topaz letting herself in like a cat-feeding neighbour to snoop whenever she had no work on. 'Come on, darling, get a move on.'

'Okay, okay!' Topaz pushed past him and flapped back to the bedroom. 'Christ, your pad's a pit, Felix. Why don't you ever clean up?'

'The char refuses to come any more. Anyway, she frightened Dyldo – looks like his mother apparently.' Felix kicked a couple of pairs of boxers out of the way and lounged in the door waiting for Topaz to dress.

She might be hell to listen to for forty-eight hours, he

reflected, but he had to concede that she was superbly put together. He supposed it was like owning a vintage Ferrari – hell to drive to the office if one had tinnitus, but a definite smirk-spreader on swinging into the office car park each morning and fucking off one's workmates. It stood to reason that someone like Piers Fox, whose car, flat and office were all immensely beautiful but utterly impractical, would have a wife to match.

Felix would never have bedded Topaz at all had it not been for her dogged persistence over the past month. He and Dylan had nick-named her Toe-past-the-door as she had the pushy resilience of a duster and teatowel salesman, cramming messages on the answerphone until it packed up completely. On Piers's instruction, he'd acted as her walker once or twice. But when the press had started slavering at their heels for a close-up of a close-up, Piers had moved Topaz to a very thick ex-guards officer who fancied horses more than humans. Topaz, however, fancied Felix more than horses, other humans and, for a short while, her husband.

She possessed an awesome blue-eyed all American confidence which had never once been dented by rejection or doubt. Just as Mommy had told her she was beautiful in her teens, so scores of fashion pixies minced along on her Joseph shirt tails now, gushing their approval. She knew that her looks were her best commodity and made no attempts at intellectualising herself by wearing tortoiseshell specs to shoots and pretending to read Will Self on red-eye flights. Her feminine, slightly vapid self-assurance was refreshing in an industry manned by skeletal, androgynous would-be aesthetes with razor-hacked hair and old-man clothes, narrowing their eyes through a cloud of Disque Bleu smoke as they ranted on a coke bender about Robert Altman films, writing a novel about modelling, and how much Madonna wanted to fuck them.

Felix was aware that he was screwing dangerously close to home with his agent's wife, but Piers hadn't got him any work yet, so Felix felt vindicated. And Topaz was delightfully, kinkily easy to lay compared to his current on-off-grab-a-tissue French girlfriend, Belle, who was seldom in the same time zone these days and preferred phone sex to coital as it was safer and saved time. As Belle spoke no English, and Felix's school French was lousy, she more often laughed at 'I want your pretty mouth to eat my courgette' than got off on it.

Topaz had turned up last week when Felix had been sleeping off a very raucous party.

Faxing her husband that she would be back from America on Saturday, she had in fact flown back midweek and arrived upon Felix's doorstep, yawning with jet lag. 'You didn't return my calls, so I bought you a mobile phone,' she'd said, smiling sleepily and handing him a tiny piece of Japanese technology the size of a fag packet. Felix hadn't liked to admit that he was off phones at the moment, but, taking in the sleepy, sexy yellow eyes and endless legs, he'd politely invited her in for a drink to thank her. Within five minutes she was lying on the floor shrieking with laughter as he poured the vodka and pomelo juice she'd asked for over her naked body and sucked it off with a straw. It had left her skin looking like a piece of poppable packing plastic, but the red blotches left on her chest and neck came from quite another source – the most delightful shuddering of orgasms.

'Piers never makes me come,' she'd confessed much later that night. Her strange yellow eyes, liquid with tears, had gleamed in the dark.

Felix, who'd been considering how to chuck her out the next morning, had put her in the crook of his arm and kissed her face reassuringly. He felt no great affection for her, but her unexpected honesty was gentle and vulnerable. And she screwed like a cat on heat.

'Come here,' he growled as Topaz wriggled into a white skinny rib t-shirt, her lower half still naked – blonde, delicate and creamy as undyed raw silk.

'No, Felix,' she dismissed him impatiently from inside the shirt, 'Piers'll jump right on me when I get back – I don't wanna reek of sex.'

'Tell him you need a shower after the red eye.' Felix slipped his hand between her legs. 'Say you're totally bushed.' To demonstrate, his fingers slid through the soft blonde hair as though stroking a cat's ears and then lifted her labia lips as skilfully as a chef parting layers of filo pastry.

'Get offa me!' Laughing between squeals, Topaz wriggled away and searched the jumbled pile of clothes on the floor for her shorts.

Felix sat on the bed and tucked a long brown leg into the crook of his elbow, chewing his thumb in irritation.

'Don't sulk, baby.' Topaz was picking up clothes and hurling them over her shoulder in her search.

Pausing between identical white t-shirts, she looked up at him and her breath caught slightly in her throat. He was really unspeakably good-looking; unfairly so with his head lowered like a drooping narcissus towards the floor so that tousled hair the colour of Caribbean sand tickled his sculpted, sun-reddened cheeks and the end of his straight nose where his nostrils had flared from commas to full stops in annoyance.

It wasn't just the flawless, golden, Armani looks which fascinated Topaz – they were as ubiquitous as cigarettes and bottles of mineral water in the fashion industry. Felix had an extra angle, like the most precious of diamonds, that unique cut which made him brighter and more desirable than all the others. He had so much presence, it lit up rooms like a torch, hushing voices and drawing eyes, and then lingered on like an echo after he'd left. He just didn't care – Piers called it the fuck-off factor; one minute Felix was all deferential upper-class politeness, superb manners and gentle self-deprecating good humour; the next he was tearing people to shreds with that bitchy, drawling, lazy voice, his utter rudeness and scorching sarcasm precluding anything but astonished humiliation. His was a heady, sexy and dangerous mix as addictive as Russian Roulette. He could also, Topaz reflected, just be a moody SOB.

'I'm not sulking, and don't fucking call me baby.' Felix was obviously smarting.

'Oh – is diddums feewing a widdle negwected, huh?' Topaz thrust out her plump bottom lip as she baby-talked him.

Felix shuddered in repulsion. Perhaps he didn't feel so sorry for her, he mulled.

Topaz had cocked her head now and, lip still plumped like a fish's, was curling her fine blonde eyebrows towards one another in mock-sympathy. Very slowly she straightened up and threw her cream shorts down where she'd found them.

'Would diddums wike a widdle pussy to stwoke?' she asked, walking towards him until her crotch was level with his face and just inches away.

Felix, his expression completely indifferent, didn't move an inch.

Topaz stretched out a slim, pale hand and curled her middle finger through his cool, slithering hair, the other hand lifting her ribbed t-shirt with the mawkish innocence of a child.

'You can play with me, baby,' she purred. 'I'm your new toy.'

'Can I take you back to Harrods and trade you in for a Nintendo then?'

'Don't mob me up, Felix.' Topaz moved closer, resting her knees against the edge of the bed.

Felix's cool blue eyes were laughing at her as she pulled the school tie from around her hair and slipped it over his head.

'Pretend you're a little kid,' she breathed, bending over him and talking into his hair. 'Just in high school and lost as a pup weaned away from its mom.'

Felix rolled his blue eyes and laughed, but Topaz carried on, knowing her story would excite him.

'You're wandering around those long, dark, squeaky corridors totally forlorn. All your little friends are in another class and there's no one around to ask where you should be. The bell rang minutes ago and you know you're gonna be in real trouble soon.' She brushed his nose very lightly with the skin of her stomach.

'Then you see a senior girl on corridor duty – a monitor – she's swinging a locker door and dressed kinda slutty. You stop and stare at her and she notices you. "Kid!" she yells at you, "Come over here."'

Topaz flicked her tongue against the tip of Felix's ear. 'So you go over and hang your head. You can smell her body – it's hot and unwashed and smells of cheap scent. You tell her you don't know where you should be.'

She slipped her hand down to Felix's throat and started to tighten his old tie. 'She grabs your chin and pulls it up pretty roughly. She's laughing at you, chewing on her peppermint gum so that you can see her lips all fleshy and wet and her teeth real white. "Sure," she says, "I can tell you where you're supposed to be. But it'll cost you. You've gotta do something for me first."'

'What?' Felix's rich, throaty voice was hard to read. It could have been excited or just faintly amused.

'The monitor comes right up to you,' Topaz went on breathlessly, 'and as she moves you see her stockings are real holey and that her skirt barely covers her black cotton panties. Her shirt's buttoned up wrong and some of them are missing so you can see a strappy little bra with the ribbons coming undone and the corner of a tiny pink nipple. She's sixteen or so and you're just a little kid – you only come up to her ribs. You can hear the classes going on in the rooms of the corridor now – kids swearing the Allegiance just metres away. She grabs your ear and pushes you down hard on her plastic monitor's chair. It's real cold and your little swollen balls are so fucking excited you squirm in pain.'

Topaz's finger gripped a blond lock and pulled Felix's head back so that he was forced to look up at her, his face still totally visored, his blue eyes calm and unblinking. She hooked one long leg up on to the bed beside him.

'"You wanna know where your class is, kid? You don't want me to report you, do you? I can get you in real deep shit."'

Felix said nothing.

'Then she licks her lips real slow and stands right up against you so your little button nose is pressed to the tops of her legs where her stockings are slipping down her thighs. She bends down real close and whispers in your ear, "You're gonna lap cream, little pussy cat, or I'll get your butt kicked real hard. Lick me out or I fucking scream right now."'

Felix was staring up at her, his body as still, taut and poised as a cat just yards from a chaffinch. There was something frightening in the cold, unresponsive clarity of his blue gaze and Topaz suddenly realised it wasn't lust. It wasn't even anger. It was something close to pain.

Then, as urgently as an untwisting coil, he sprang forward and grabbed her hips, gripping both her buttocks so tightly in his fingers that she shrieked.

For a second, he buried his face in her warm, damp pubic hair, his eyes clamped tightly shut like a small boy trying not to cry. Then, standing up so quickly that Topaz lost her balance, he pushed violently past her.

'I'm going to watch TV,' he spat over his shoulder as he almost sprinted from the room.

Topaz rubbed her mouth in astonishment and pulled down her t-shirt, wondering whether to follow him and bawl him out. She'd been fooling around for his sake; he was the one who'd been feeling horny and Felix loved fantasies, they'd been acting them out between spliffs and giggling fits all week. She couldn't understand his sudden change of attitude.

But something in his blizzard-like exit made her sit down on the edge of the bed and gnaw at a cuticle instead. Felix, although drop-dead glorious in most respects, was distinctly screwy. Part of her reason for pursuing such a hopelessly fickle lay was because she'd been toying with the idea of getting pregnant by him instead of Piers – she was secretly terrified a legitimate Fox junior would be ginger, which wouldn't be at all chic. Her early return from the States this week had been a scouting session, exacerbated by Piers's reacting so unenthusiastically to her baby suggestion the morning she left for New Orleans.

Now she'd changed her mind. It was all very well having a ravishing kid, but if it was as fucked up as Felix Sylvian, it would end up strapped to a leather couch discussing its dreams in an institution. And sex with Felix frightened almost as much as it excited her; he was always so detached and expected her to work too hard. Besides, Piers's hair was more titian than ginger. And there was always Daniel Galvin.

*   *   *

Topaz watched her reflection split in two and slide sideways as the lift opened on the top floor. Mustering a rather guilty smile, she swanned into the flat and paused as she saw Piers's t-shirted back hunched over his laptop by the vast window, his hair shot almost scarlet in a shaft of light which was piercing through the heavy thunderclouds over Shadwell. By the knotted, hunched shoulders that were rising almost to his ears with tension, Topaz could tell he was in stress overload.

'Hi, honey.' She dropped her bags where she stood and wound her way over to him, noticing en route that the sofas had been moved along with his beloved Wurlitzer and the modern sculpture of a knobbly stone nude which was, as she continually pointed out, uglier than both his ex-wives giving birth. Although now she was planning to give birth herself, she was trying to make the odd flattering comment about it.

'Good flight?' Piers barely looked up as she kissed him hello.

'Great.' She stretched her arms over her head and spun around to rest her bottom on the table, still waiting for Piers to finish his sentence and pounce on her as always; he got incredibly randy in her absence, requiring at least two hours full-throttle love-making the moment she got back, only asking about her trip when he finally rolled back on to the pillows and reached for a tissue. Once or twice, on returning from an exhausting shoot in another time-zone, Topaz had booked into the Hyde Park Hotel so that she could get a decent night's sleep before the protracted bed-bounceathon ahead. Capable of going on for longer than most CDs (Topaz knew, because she tried to memorise the lyrics during their lovemaking), Piers approached sex rather like a conductor leading his orchestra through Ravel's 'Bolero' with a stabbing baton, priding himself on his ability to sustain a perfect rhythm and eye-contact throughout.

As he was clearly writing a sentence longer than the Koran, Topaz wandered through to the kitchen to fetch a bottle of water.

'Piers, why are you doing the washing?' she called incredulously, noticing that the state-of-the-art Zanussi they never used was chucking something striped around in a gallon of froth.

'Huh?'

'Washing, Piers.' Topaz meandered back through, almost shinning herself on a coffee table which had also been moved. That was another odd thing – Piers generally rearranged furniture when he'd clinched a big deal. 'Did the laundry service screw up again?'

'Economy.' He was whizzing his mouse about like a boy on the final level of Super Mario. 'We're monumentally over-drawn, as you well know.'

Clearly no clinching deal, Topaz realised. He must be acting crabbily because he was so stressed.

'I bought you a present, honey.'

'Oh, yes?' Piers stood up to gather in a spewing fax.

Topaz was scrabbling in her bags.

Piers read the three-page fax and balked. He re-read the fax and still balked. He read the signature and crumpled the sheets of paper into a tight ball which he threw at the basketball net fixed to the wall beside his blackwood table. It fell cleanly through, landing with a satisfying crack in the metal waste bin beneath. He found he suddenly couldn't stop smiling.

'Here.' Topaz handed him a pile of videos. 'The top one is about relaxation for conceptual sex so that the sperm max-imises its potency. The second is a kinda modern fathering approach to pregnancy, like how to talk to the bump and recite intellectual shit to it. And these two are general baby stuff – you know, when they teethe and how to detect illnesses. It's even got a little baby aerobics session you can do along with them. Isn't that dinky?' She pointed at a picture of two grinning first-time parents, both with Big Hair and identical romper suits, holding up a small fat baby with no hair and a matching suit. Both parents were kicking out their legs like chorus girls.

Piers nodded, flicking through them without really taking them in. Casting them to one side, he gathered Topaz into his arms and kissed her long, hard and very sexily on the mouth.

'Welcome back, darling.' He started to help her wriggle out of the skinny rib top. 'Christ, I've missed you.'

'I missed you too, baby.' Topaz pressed her length against him, realising how much she meant it.

Remembering the bed needed making up, he led her to the six-man, black leather sofa which had once graced the reception of his City office. There, he stripped her off with one hand while the other explored her long, narrow body rather perfunctorily, like a Customs official after a passenger's bleeped through the metal-detector.

As Topaz's yellow eyes narrowed, Piers wished she'd occasionally show a bit more initiative. Last night, he'd watched Portia pull away from him and slowly undress, with seductive confidence, to reveal a t-backed boot-lace g-string and tiny, cutaway bra top which jacked up her small, ice-cream-cone breasts into seductively jutting curves. Piers hadn't just been turned on by the school-boy fantasy, garage-calendar smuttiness; he'd got a tremendous sexual kick out of the fact that Portia had dressed up for him in the first place.

But beneath his wife's linen shorts, he merely found a pair of ultra-trendy and off-puttingly crumpled women's boxer shorts and, higher up, a skinny-rib vest which reminded him of the armpit-stained ones he'd once worn beneath his polyester shirts at his Catholic primary school.

Topaz closed her eyes with languorous delight, knowing she was safe with Piers. He wouldn't suddenly leap up as Felix had and produce a tub of crème fraîche, tie her up to the shower rail or demand she contort herself like a gymnast in order to make her come more strongly. Although the end result had often been devastating, Felix made sex feel like an all-night circus workshop. Piers, if less satisfying, was powerful, self-seeking and gloriously predictable.

A few minutes later, he got up and, leaving her with a kiss which put her lungs on to reserve, wandered through to the bedroom, only to re-emerge seconds later.

Topaz, glazing over with the sort of soporific lust she always felt with Piers – lazy, detached, passive – wondered why he had changed his mind so suddenly over the baby idea. She was two days away from her period and, according to the book she'd read while flying back from the States, unlikely to conceive. But as she felt him slide back on top of her, his hard hip bone against her pelvis and his mouth tracing the bony hollows of her chest, she shivered with an excitement she'd never encountered. Then she shuddered with almost equal revulsion.

'Piers, what is that on your cock?' she yelped, wriggling away.

'A condom,' he explained. 'And spermicide.'

'A what?' Topaz was furious. 'Why're you using a fucking condom, Piers? I thought we were trying for a baby.'

Seeing her venomous gaze – and the proximity of his very heavy marble statue – Piers cringed slightly and decided to lie.

'A rash,' he said without thinking, and then winced as Topaz leapt away from his shrinking erection, inadvertently kicking it quite hard.

'A rash?' she repeated in a flat, cold little voice. 'On your cock?'

Piers nodded.

'And where exactly did you get that?' The voice was still the same tone, but two octaves higher.

'My underpants.' He swallowed in appalled horror at the mortifying self-debasement of his own lie. 'I'm allergic to my new underpants.'

Topaz looked at him for a long time, her amber eyes disbelieving. Then she started to laugh. She shrieked with such mirth that she fell off the leather sofa and lay on the floor, her long, slender legs kicking the air in delight.

'You know what, Piers honey?' She turned her head up to him, cheeks streaked with tears of delight. 'I don't even care if that's a lie. I love you so much for it.'

Piers forced a wan smile and excused himself to the bathroom, where he peeled the offending rubber off and dropped it into the chrome Conran pedal bin. It had been a cheap shot, he realised. He really had to get hold of a good vasectomy clinic soon.

He sat down on the loo, wiping his hands with a pile of bog roll, thought about the fax and grinned. Portia had sent him the dirtiest message he'd read since a friend had lent him the

Marquis de Sade at school. For that he was livid – he'd thought she was more discreet. But the ensuing tip more than made up for it. It was a scoop of extraordinary dimensions, and he doubted any of his compatriots were on to it yet.

For Portia had scribbled that a friend who worked for Strassi, the huge American jeans manufacturers, had just let drop the most fascinating piece of office gossip currently ruminating around their UK headquarters. According to the vox pop, Strassi were looping up with the film company MPM to sponsor one of the highest budget Hollywood films ever. The project was totally under wraps, but was said to have a shit-hot script, vast marquee value and more spin than a mall of laundrettes. It was to be the biggest product placement campaign ever.

At first, a straightforward jeans ad would be launched slowly and strategically with the central star appearing in a series of glossy TV and movie theatre thirty-second teasers, press ads and billboards. There would be no promotional tour, interviews or mention of the film. Then the TV and cinema ads would switch to longer, more esoteric bites which started to tell a story – compelling, sexy and moreish, with a heart-throb star so spellbinding that viewers would sit up night and day hoping to catch the next one. At a strategically chosen time news of the film would blow, with press given EPKs, brochures, and hype as high as the Empire State. The last series of ads released would clearly link into the film and be so slick, stylish and extravagant that the star would become legendary before the film was even launched.

It was all about media hype and marketing, hardly at all about creating a good film, but the idea still made Piers's blood run three degrees warmer with excitement.

The rumour was that the producers were currently out shopping for stars without divulging a word about the nature of the project. They were looking at the really big guns and at up-and-coming big names like Depp, Reeves and Slater. But they were also preparing to give a brief to all relevant big-shot agents in a couple of months, outlining their requirements in the hope of scooping a total newcomer who was completely right for the product and quality enough to cope with the phenomenal pressure of being made into an overnight star. The fee for the central star alone was rumoured to be two commas plus.

Piers knew this was way out of his depth. Had he been running alongside his compatriots, he'd be trampled in the stampede. He was too new at the game, had no big stars and was too lacking in the bed-fellow contacts and back-handed venal knowledge he needed to be top of the call sheet for producers. But he was graced with one massive advantage this time. News of the project was not going to be released – even confidentially – beyond the boardroom for at least six weeks. He had a head start, and knew exactly whose headstrong butt he was going to kick into shape first.

Wrapping a towel around himself, he paced back out into the flat and tracked Topaz down by the bed where she was throwing clothes from her suit carrier on to a checked Conran sofa, which was her version of unpacking.

'D'you know if Felix Sylvian ever did any jeans modelling?' he asked rather less casually than he'd have wished.

Topaz jumped nervously and a silk shirt overshot the sofa by miles, landing on a four-foot cactus with chubby, pointed leaves serrated like hunting knives.

'Who?' she said rather foolishly.

'Felix,' Piers snapped, totally preoccupied with his own express train of thought.

'Oh, him. No, I'm not sure.' Topaz was gulping out the words like trapped air bubbles. 'Why d'you ask, honey?'

'No reason – just thinking about some potential work.' Piers moved away with his finger pressed to his nose. Still wearing the towel, he sat back down in front of his computer and tapped into a couple of files. 'Could you do me a favour, Topaz?' he asked over his freckled shoulder. 'Call Felix and ask him over here to dinner on Monday?'

'I'm busy Monday,' she croaked.

'Shit – I'd forgotten about that German contract.' Piers was looking at something on his screen. 'What?'

'I'm busy Monday.' She crept towards him. 'Can't you take him out to dinner?'

'No.' Piers was too distracted to look round and see her pinched, terrified face. 'Actually I'm meeting Bateman then anyway – tell Felix Tuesday.'

'I'm kinda busy all week.' Topaz swallowed. 'I can get some stuff in for you to heat up, though.'

Piers scratched his chin abstractedly and then looked up at her, something clearly occurring to him as his eyes glittered like dark green stained glass suddenly caught with sunlight streaming through it.

Seeing his face register its rather sinister, visored look, Topaz backed away slightly. She hoped he wasn't going to ask her what she was going to be busy doing. She had a feeling that this week she'd be catching up on all the films she'd been meaning to see – sitting alone in a Curzon with a Diet Coke and a pervert on each side. But Piers merely smiled rather vaguely and nodded.

'Okay, I understand.' He was sounding uncharacteristically benign. Had Topaz not been so relieved, she would have suspected his calculating mind of being at its most cunning. 'Just call Felix and tell him that Tuesday or Friday are best.'

As his wife left a very garbled, gulping message with Felix's answering service, Piers reflected with relief that if he said nothing to Topaz about the Strassi project, she wouldn't be able to put herself forward as a candidate for any female interest. Her being out of the way when he gave Felix the merest sliver of a hint would be no bad thing either. And her being out for most nights this week would also give him the opportunity to take Portia out and thank her for the tip. The thought made him feel unexpectedly excited, as though two warm hands had just crept on to his shoulders and were massaging away the tight knots which herded like clinging barnacles under his skin.

Going out on the prowl with Felix usually gave Dylan the same feeling of invisibility he'd experienced on the odd occasions he'd accompanied his parents anywhere as a small child. With guests as affluent and politically influential as Nigel and Lydia

Abbott, consorts were unlikely to drop their simpering smiles towards the small, scruffy urchin with the dribbly nose lurking at knee level. Often, they failed to notice Dylan's presence at all. Even Nigel and Lydia were apt to forget their son was with them. Several times in his early youth, Dylan had been left playing in his own private world beneath a food-laden table in a swish Surrey house or draughty Chelsea terrace belonging to one of his parents' cronies, while Nigel and Lydia drove home discussing how dreadful the party had been.

At eight, he'd been packed off to boarding school and later, when he became what his mother termed 'problematic', the Abbotts had invested in a live-in au pair instead of the day-time nannies they had once used, thus removing any remote chance that they'd have to take Dylan anywhere with them.

Just as women with abusive fathers often go on to marry abusive men, Dylan occasionally wondered if he'd chosen Felix as a friend because his attitude was similar to that of his parents. Felix could be extremely detached, almost embarrassed by him socially. But, in that curious volte-face manner he possessed, he could also be the greatest company, confidante and companion; ferociously loyal when called upon, a superb agony aunt, and extremely generous with money. Most of all, he really believed in Dylan's talent and spent endless evenings coaxing, bullying and bribing him to work on a book instead of going out to get hammered. Sometimes, when they were out, Felix introduced Dylan as 'a writer' and made up loads of lies about his non-existent published works which gave him a tremendous kick.

Tonight was one such night, but it didn't lessen Dylan's feeling of invisibility. For he had realised a long time ago that when he was with Felix, absolutely no one took any notice of him. He was like a policeman acting as a human shield to a crowd of eager fans at a rock gig; even when he was nose-to-nose with someone, they were still looking at Felix.

He noticed it again when he paid for the drinks in the O Bar in Soho. The barmaid – far too sparky-eyed to be anything other than an out-of-work actress with resumés and ten-by-eights hidden behind the bar – gazed past Dylan's ear and over the shaven head of a nearby gay as far as Felix, who was trying to light a cigarette with a duff lighter. By the time Dylan struggled back with the two bottles of beer – one fashionable, the other cheap – Felix had been given three matchbooks, two of which had girls' phone numbers written in them.

'This place is fucking dead.' He squinted against the first cloud of Chesterfield smoke and tossed the spent match on top of two rejected matchbooks in the ashtray.

'It's early.' Dylan swigged back half a bottle in one gulp and nicked a cigarette. 'And I really have to go after this beer.'

'Phone in sick.'

'Yeah, and who am I supposed to call? I'm the manager.'

'Pete.' Felix looked up as two girls walked in, clomping past on ultra-fashionable espadrille clogs.

'He's in the Cayman Islands.'

'So – reverse the charges.'

Dylan stared at the revolving ceiling fan in exasperation.

But, bored and restless as a child on Christmas Eve, Felix was watching the girls at the bar now. One was totally stunning – tall, skinny and dressed in an elongated see-through white cheese-cloth shirt over an A-line crotch-length mini, she could have stalked straight off a Pam Hogg catwalk. Scraping a thin hand through razor-cut plum-red hair, she glanced over her shoulder at Felix, her mouth curling into a smirking smile as readable as a big green GO sign.

Felix's eyes slipped away to her friend. Tiny, pinch-faced, with a beer-glass figure and hyper-fashionable stringy hair which just looked unfashionably greasy above her scowling face, she was totally swamped by a coarse linen coat-dress and crocheted thigh-high socks which were straining over the top few inches of white, cellulite-dimpled thigh. Tip-toeing to be seen over the bar, she paid for the drinks and turned to her tall friend with a glass of wine. The friend spoke with barely a flicker of her lips and slid her eyes towards Felix.

When the short girl looked at him, he beamed her the biggest smile he possessed. The effect was so devastating that the girl started to cough mid-swig and wine spurted out of her nose.

Felix laughed.

'Stop it,' Dylan hissed.

'What?' Not looking at him, Felix shot the girl another smile – warm, apologetic and kindly.

Blinking nervously, she looked over each shoulder like a criminal on the run to check that he wasn't smiling at someone else. Then, realising his eyes were locked on only her, she stared back at him in delighted, terrified awe, a frightened little smile now twitching at her own lips which were dry with fading lipstick. Beside her, the skinny friend gawped at Felix in disbelief, her hand clamped around a glass which she was holding at forty-five degrees without realising, so that red wine was pouring unnoticed down her shirt like blood. Then, narrowing her eyes at her quivering friend, she slouched back against the bar in sky-high dudgeon.

'Cut it out, Felix,' Dylan watched the small girl, gaining in confidence, hold Felix's eyes for slightly longer each time.

Sighing, he looked away and grinned at his friend. 'C'mon, Dyldo, it's just for a laugh.'

'I know,' Dylan sighed. 'But I don't find it even faintly amusing any more.'

'Well, I do,' Felix looked back to the girl and this time, unsmiling, trailed his eyes very slowly down the length of her body, which didn't take long as she was just a matchstick taller than five foot.

Gulping, she threw back the dregs of her drink and then groped for a cigarette with shaking hands.

Still watching her, Felix fingered the matchbook and smirked.

'That's it,' Dylan sighed irritably, 'I'm off.' Downing the last of his beer as he stood up, he grabbed his jacket and stalked off before Felix had even looked up.

'Hey, Dyldo!' Felix called, leaning right back on his chair as he craned to see where he'd gone.

'Er, excuse me?'

'Yes?' Snapping crabbily, Felix looked up to see the earlier object of his attentions trembling with nerves as she stood over his table with an unlit cigarette.

'Er,' she coughed, her eyes so stretched with fear and desire that the dark brown corneas were swimming in acres of white, 'I wondered if you had a light?'

She had a soft, sweet Yorkshire accent. Close up, she was quite pretty, Felix noticed, with big, gentle eyes, plump lips and a little button nose like a teddy bear's. Hidden in the unflattering clothes was a curvy, puppy-fatted body that would probably have peach-smooth skin and delightful little curves and folds like a chubby baby.

'No, sorry.' Felix looked up at her, his face now a shuttered mask of indifference.

'Oh.' She looked utterly mortified as she tried not to glance at the matchbook.

Dropping her eyes to the floor, she fled back to her friend who had just noticed the wine stain and was shrieking with horror. Their fashion status in the cliquey bar totally shattered, they grabbed their outsized duffle bags and stomped out with as much dignity as they could muster.

Felix slouched back in his chair and sulkily drained his beer bottle. There was no satisfaction in playing the game without an audience. Instead, he ordered another beer and wandered over to the bar to talk to the waitress.

For the next two hours, he attracted attention like a sleek, friendly spaniel tied to a railing, incongruous for being pretty, desirable and alone. Brooding and abstracted, Felix allowed himself to be chatted up and bought drinks by the little clusters of both sexes who gravitated towards him like walkers to a bluebell wood in May. Yet he was as well mannered as an over-disciplined public schoolboy; laughing at jokes, nodding raptly as he listened to self-opinionated monologues, promising to call their scribbled phone numbers and politely declining offers to move on to parties, films, restaurants or clubs. It was how he always behaved when he couldn't be bothered, slipping almost unconsciously back into the manners which had been drummed into him over and over again by banshee nannies as a child, then queer masters and bullying sixth-formers as a boarder, and finally his drunken, power-crazy father as a young adult.

Making his way home after midnight, Felix was so drunk that he got on a bus to Hampstead by mistake. He'd started to feel nauseous. After lighting a fag the wrong end and smoking it without realising, he walked down Haverstock Hill towards Chalk Farm to try and sober up, ending up just minutes from Dylan's bar in Belsize Park.

The busy little bar had extended licensing hours and, immensely popular, was packed with hot bodies. Feeling sicker than ever, Felix fought his way through and helped himself to a sextuple scotch.

'Can you help out?' Dylan yelled, feeding two glasses from optics simultaneously as he watched the progress of an unattended pint of Guinness spilling over underneath the taps.

'Three double vodkas!' cried a girl, leaning so far over the bar that her lips were practically pressed against Felix's.

Ignoring her, he threw back the scotch and helped himself to another before lurching over to the phone.

Having borrowed ten pound coins from a group of girls nearby, he fed them in and bashed out numbers as though trying to stab a hole through the dial.

The pips took ages to clear. Felix squinted, woozily guessing it must be teatime in LA.

Finally a voice answered, deeper than a bass saxophone, sexy and rasping.

'Hi, Philoman – Philomeesh – Philo – fuck! Yeah?'

Felix closed his eyes so tightly that he could hear the blood pumping through his ears. She was already so drunk she couldn't pronounce her own name.

Having kicked out the last straggler, Dylan gathered the final cluster of glasses into the dishwasher and started flipping off lights. As he passed Felix, slumped in a corner with his head in his hands, hair clutched like last straws in his white-knuckled fingers, the picture of an impossibly tortured poet, Dylan sat on a chair opposite and nicked a fag. He'd seen it before; Felix on self-destruct was about as ugly and pointless as it got.

'You called her again, didn't you?' He emptied the ashtray into a metal bucket before lighting up.

'The bitch,' Felix muttered into his clenching hands.

'Why d'you do it?' Dylan's voice was deliberately practical and phlegmatic.

Gnawing on a thumb-nail, Felix looked up through his tousled fringe.

'Because I have to,' he said simply. His Spode blue eyes had dulled to bloodshot pools of unhappiness.

Like windows on a lost soul, thought Dylan sadly.

13

Phoebe reluctantly spent the first fortnight of July job-searching, attempting to trace Saskia, who had apparently left Deayton, and trying not to contact Dan. One bright spot in the month was that Milly discovered the demolition of their Wandsworth squat had been delayed due to council fund-cuts, so she and Goat moved back in, taking most of Phoebe's clothes, Fliss's tape collection and the Breville toasted sandwich maker with them (no bad thing, Fliss pointed out, as it had been without a fuse for eighteen months). They returned sporadically to watch television, raid the fridge and make long-distance phone calls, dropping off a four-pack of cider in thanks, which they themselves inevitably consumed on their next visit.

Phoebe got a temporary cash-in-hand job waitressing at the same bar Fliss occasionally worked in: an ultra-trendy cellar conversion in Soho called Bar Barella, which served Japanese beer so cold that the bottles stuck to the drinkers' hands and gave them chilblains. But no one who valued the kudos of being seen in the latest watering hole hotly tipped by *Time Out* cared, and the cellars became a deafening, sweaty mass of shoving, crushed fashion victims by nine each night. Among them were Fliss's artist friends, who were all regulars. With Phoebe working behind the bar, other old mates began rolling up too, and the Bar Barella soon resembled the sitting room at the Islington flat during a particularly raucous party.

'You're going to have to get yourself a proper job, you know,'

Fliss told Phoebe as they collapsed back into the flat in the small hours after a Saturday night shift together.

'I am looking,' she pointed out grumpily, heading through to the kitchen. 'So far my temp agency's offered me two days filing in Hounslow and one morning licking envelopes in the City. And my CV is being "kept on file" in more East End offices than Ronnie Kray's criminal record.'

Fliss sidled up to the fridge to guard her last Mars Bar from Phoebe's attack of munchies.

'You could do more than glancing through yesterday's *Standard* which Iain's left behind, and asking a few mates if they've heard of anything,' she said bluntly. 'Didn't Georgette give you a few numbers to try?'

'Okay, okay.' Phoebe settled for a toffee yoghurt and went in search of a spoon. 'You're going off Iain, aren't you?'

'Stan's looking for a nude model, if you need any more cash.' Fliss ignored the question, proving Phoebe had hit a new bruise with classic tact.

'Thanks, but I *was* aiming a little higher than lying around in the buff for a fiver an hour.' Phoebe rinsed a soup spoon under the tap.

'You might be able to push him to six quid.'

'Ha ha.' Phoebe headed back towards the sitting room.

'And Phoebe . . .' Fliss was marking her like a Cup Final defender now.

'Yeah?' She tried to dodge towards her bedroom, but Fliss headed her off then cornered her on the sofa.

'Try Saskia again tomorrow,' Fliss ordered, kicking off her wedge-heeled sling-backs, 'or I'll invite your sister for Sunday lunch. Every frigging day.'

Phoebe rolled her eyes, suddenly going off the toffee yoghurt.

'And you're right,' Fliss picked it up and started spooning it into her mouth like a diabetic with a biscuit an hour past mealtime, 'I *am* going off Iain. What do you recommend? He's so bloody keen; wants to move in here and redecorate in ancient Peruvian colours which symbolise fertility and the phallus in simpatico. I've stalled him. Said we were pretty keen on the seventies George and Mildred look. Phoebe, I don't know what to do!'

'Dump him.' Phoebe gave her a hug and then went to bed, for once grateful for her single status.

The next morning, when Phoebe called the Seatons, it was Gin who picked up the phone, her voice taut with worry. Forced to speak to Phoebe, she said in frosty tones that Saskia was apparently staying with her sister Sukey in Battersea but since she hadn't seen fit to call home, they knew very little else.

But when Phoebe phoned Sukey's flat, her haw-haughty barrister boyfriend, Guy, told her they hadn't heard from Saskia or the rest of the family in weeks. The same was true of the eldest Seaton sister, the conceited Zoe, who treated Phoebe's call with much the same desperation to get her off the line as she would have had Phoebe been trying to sell plastic lattice replacement windows for her Buckinghamshire manor house. Phoebe tried Portia's number several times, but she had her answermachine switched on continually.

Phoebe spent the afternoon mindlessly watching the East-Enders omnibus and then sat through the whole of *Gone With The Wind* for the first time, weeping buckets and smudgily covering the chipped red varnish on her toenails with an ancient shocking pink which Fliss had spent the previous winter using to stymie ladders in her tights.

Several hours later, Fliss arrived back at the flat, very drunk, with Iain in tow. Talking loudly about some missing garibaldi biscuits, she crashed excitedly into Phoebe's bedroom.

'Felix was in Bar Barella tonight!'

Surfacing from canyons of deep sleep, Phoebe blinked into her pillow with swollen eyelids and then winced as a sharp crick sawed through the tendons in her neck. 'You what?'

'The shit-and-run artist himself; rolled up with half a dozen mates in tow – including Sel – and nearly caused a bloody fight.' Fliss was bouncing around in the rectangle of light from the doorway, her shock of hair almost on end. 'I tried to call you, but the fucking manager was breathing down my neck all night. Christ, it would have been such a perfect opportunity to hit on him.'

'What?' Phoebe wriggled groggily up the bed until she was sitting on her pillows, her sheet clutched to her chest in a vague attempt at modesty. She rubbed her stiff neck and tried to force her eyelids to open beyond her pupils.

Flicking on the light, Fliss reeled into the room and crashed down on the bed, almost jettisoning Phoebe completely out of it. Iain, his hair flopping on to his nose, pitched sideways, tripped over an open laundry bag and then followed Fliss, cramming Phoebe up against her pink Dralon headboard as he dive-bombed the six square inches of free space.

'This is cosy,' he hiccuped mildly and then, closing his unripe conker eyes, appeared to lose consciousness.

'He and Sel came in around ten with this rowdy gang of lads.' Fliss leaned down and grabbed Phoebe's old glass of wine. 'They were all steaming, totally boxed.' She polished off the wine and groped in her bag for a Marlboro.

'This is Felix Sylvian you're talking about?' Phoebe was still surfacing from sleep, like a deep-sea diver adjusting to a decompression chamber.

'Yes, yes,' Fliss snapped impatiently. 'And Sel, and a gang of friends that looked like they should be lounging about in the Gods' common room in *Another Country*.'

'Weren't there any girls with them?' Phoebe's foot was going to sleep under the weight of Iain's comatose head.

'There soon bloody were.' Fliss rolled her eyes towards the ceiling. 'I've never seen anything like it. They were all over them – well, over Felix mostly. Not physically mind, but lurking nearby with unlit fags, empty glasses and winning smiles. You know those stunning GFY chicks who stub their Gauloise ends out on the walls and spend half the night in the bog straightening their waxed centre partings?'

'*They* were all over him?' Phoebe gasped.

She and Fliss had nick-named the girls GFY (Go Fuck Yourselves) because they had more attitude than Madonna on a parochial New England chat show. They were all exquisite-looking, like glossy shop mannequins, and checked their reflections regularly in the mirror behind the bar to prove the fact.

But if any unsuspecting man tried to pick one of them up, they shot him a narrowed, sliding gaze of complete, derisive indifference and virtually kneed him in the balls with the instant, drop-dead retort. 'I take it your girlfriend's having her ear tagged?' was a favourite.

'One of them was in tears at the end of the night because he told her that if she stood any closer she'd give him friction burns, and that she looked like Janice Joplin after the autopsy. Afterwards, Sel tried to chat her up and she threw a vodka and cranberry juice in his face. That's five quid a throw, too.'

'And Felix?' Phoebe was trying frantically to wriggle her buzzing foot from underneath Iain's lolling head. 'Did he hit on anyone?'

'That's the weirdest thing.' Fliss elbowed Iain awake. 'See if there's any drink around, duck,' she told him. 'And fetch us an ashtray. Felix,' Fliss gazed at Phoebe intently, 'picked on this girl so ugly, you'd never believe. Battersea Dogs' Home would have put her down long before her seven days were up.'

'Fliss!' Phoebe howled in shock, watching Iain reel around the room in search of the door.

'Okay, I know that's mean, but Christ, you should have seen her – thirteen stone of unsqueezed pus, unwashed peroxide hair and smudged blue eye-liner. She was sitting between these two really pretty mates – both were being chatted up by lads. All of them were completely ignoring her, like she was a beermat. So there she was, trapped in the middle, staring at her empty Budweiser bottle, chewing her stubby nails, shooting evils at her mates and trying not to cry. Every so often she glanced up at Felix; not because I reckon she rated herself in the running, just 'cos he's so fucking gorgeous everyone stares. Christ, you've only seen the pics, Phoebe, but in the flesh he's seriously lush.'

Iain, who was feeling his way along a wall now, tripped noisily over Phoebe's piles of books that were still waiting for the shelves Fliss had promised to build.

'Then, the weirdest thing happened – door's to your right, chuck,' Fliss called out helpfully dragging on her fag. 'I was gabbing with Sel and he says, "Watch this." All these really beautiful fash vics were lurking around Felix, hanging off his every slurred word. His mates were pranking about trying to keep him entertained. And he brushes them all off, like beggars in a Moroccan market, and heads straight for the Gooseberry's table.'

'The girl with the pretty mates?'

'That's right.' Fliss flicked an inch of ash into the empty garibaldi packet. 'And he hits on her. Like nothing you've ever seen. He just steps up on to her table with his great long legs, sending drinks flying, and hops down beside her on the bench, introducing himself. Within ten minutes, Gooseberry's face is heating the entire bar and Felix practically has his tongue through the sleeper in her ear.'

'Christ!'

'You can tell she thinks she's dreaming,' Fliss went on. 'I mean, she keeps looking around at her mates, whose eyes are out on stalks. And Felix – who's pretty cross-eyed himself by this stage – is acting like Peter Sellers with Sophia Loren. He keeps getting his cronies to bring drinks over and is telling her how beautiful she is, cracking jokes, touching her face, wiping her mascara stains and feeding her beer from his own bottle with his lips still attached to it. The whole bar is trying not to gawp. Thanks, love.'

Iain had staggered back into Phoebe's bedroom with the flat's huge pub ashtray, a plastic half bottle of duty free brandy they used for cooking, and three mugs, still dripping from a recent rinse. He flumped back down on to Phoebe's foot so heavily she heard her ankle crack ominously.

'Did they leave together?' she asked incredulously, blinking away tears of pain. 'Felix and this girl?'

'Christ, no.' Fliss glugged some brandy from the bottle neck and handed it to Phoebe. 'I haven't got to the best bit yet.'

She passed the bottle straight to Iain, but he was crouched on top of her foot, too intently ripping Marlboros apart and sticking king-sized Rizlas together to notice.

'An hour or so later, Felix and this girl are up at the bar.' Fliss wiped her mouth. 'He's introducing her to his mates and she's lapping it up, loving the fact that her girlfriends are still back at the table looking like they've swallowed the entire gooseberry bush complete with bird droppings. Felix's mates are so fucking nice to her, it just doesn't ring true. I mean, they've been bitching her up all night – I heard them while I was working, particularly Sel – then suddenly, they're all over her like the Ugly Sisters with the slipper.'

'That's when I arrived,' Iain announced, not looking up from his concentrated task of holding a lighter up to a tiny lump of brown fudge and crumbling its heated end into the Rizla jigsaw. 'He introduced me to her too. And asked me to a party in Clapham next Friday. Excellent bloke.'

'One of Felix's mates,' Fliss continued with a sarcastic roll of her eyes, 'I didn't catch his name – he was pretty short and dull, looked like Will Carling – chatted me up a bit, actually. He was the only one not playing along. He practically ignored fat Mother-of-all Gooseberries and kept hissing at Felix to cut it out.'

'I can guess who he was,' Phoebe said, thinking back to the kind, panting Rottweiler outside the Kensington wine bar.

'Then Felix starts shrieking with laughter and – '

'Snogs the girl's gob off.' Iain grinned at the memory, licking his Rizla gum with glee.

'Yeah, he just grabs both her red cheeks in his hands, presses his great, long body to her little fat one, and starts kissing her in front of everyone.' Fliss stretched her eyes. 'I mean, we're talking serious necking here, he was making me excited just watching. Gooseberry's practically floored with lust and her mates are turning as green as the soles of Nick Faldo's feet.'

'Phoebe?'

'Huh?' She looked away from Fliss to see Iain proffering a soggy-ended, crumpled spliff, bent almost at right-angles in the middle like a boomerang.

'No thanks, Iain.' She smiled and turned back to Fliss. 'And?'

'And then,' Fliss took the hissing paper boomerang and inhaled deeply, 'and then he lets her go, rests his elbows back on the bar, grins like a Cheshire cat on E and tells her to piss off.'

'What?'

'Just like that. "Piss off, you sad bitch, you've had your Scooby snack," I think he said, and he and his mates start howling with laughter.' Fliss took another drag and held it in so that her voice croaked out on an artificial vibrato. 'The poor cow bolts off to the bogs in tears and Felix watches her, clashing beer bottles with his shrieking cronies, virtually in tears of laughter. A second later they're doling him out tenners.'

'It had all been a bet?' Phoebe gasped

'Definitely.' Fliss finally let her lungs collapse as though released from a corset.

'Shit.'

'Ten minutes later,' Iain took up the story as he repossessed the spliff, his voice ringing with admiration, 'this Felix guy was hit on by a girl that looked like a teenage Michelle Pfeiffer fresh from reading *My Secret Garden*. We're talking fit. She was all over him, practically straddling him against the bar. He just laughed and lapped it up. I mean, they were practically screwing. She was absolutely gorgeous.' His reddening eyes misted over and he flopped back on to the bed, staring through his reefer smoke to the ceiling in delighted, unfocused recollection.

Fliss plucked away the burning spliff and narrowed her eyes furiously. 'She had fat thighs and VPL,' she dismissed tetchily. 'Anyway, her pre-pubescent boyfriend rolls up and starts trying to pick a fight. Felix just beams a polite smile, drops her like a dead cat and he and his mates shoot off, still howling with laughter. And they didn't pay their fucking bill. But Sel said he'd phone next week.' She beamed happily, hugging the prospect to her like a warm kitten.

Phoebe let this sink in for a few seconds. 'And Gooseberry?'

'I found her when we were shutting up, still in the bogs.' Fliss shrugged. 'She looked like all her relatives had just been wiped out in a car accident.'

'Oh, the poor, poor darling,' Phoebe sighed.

'Fucking ugly, though,' Iain burped, almost asleep, then started giggling to himself.

'Let him crash out here,' Fliss whispered pleadingly. 'Please, Phoebe? I can't face him tonight.'

'Fuck off, Fliss!' she hissed. 'Put him on the sofa.'

'You know how dangerous that is,' Fliss raised her eyebrows, 'he might suffocate.'

They both looked at one another for a few seconds in silence.

Taking a final swig of brandy, Fliss threw the spliff pip into an empty mug and pulled Iain's dangling arm over her shoulder.

'C'mon, sunshine.' She started to take his weight with a groan. 'Let's get you settled in the lovely, squishy sofa.' Raising a farewell eyebrow at Phoebe, she heaved him out of the room, clicking off the light switch with her freckled nose as she passed it.

Phoebe watched the headlights of cars in the road below sweeping across the ceiling, feeling like a prisoner of war trying to time the passing search-lamp before his plotted escape. The room stank of cigarettes, dope and spilled brandy. She closed her eyes and tried to concentrate on fluffy four-legged furries leaping over stiles, but sheep reminded her too painfully of the tedium of New Zealand and her desperation for Dan and for another letter from Saskia.

Snapping her eyes open, she listened to a Saab car alarm going off below and imagined Felix Sylvian lounging around his father's trashed mews house, crowing over the hysterical time he'd had in Bar Barella tonight. An evening of pranks which had probably wrecked one girl's confidence for years.

Phoebe felt as though someone were sand-papering her skin with sulphuric acid. Her loathing was so intense, she wanted to get dressed, find his house and spray-paint 'My Balls Haven't Dropped Yet' on the garage door.

Taking an overwrought gamble, she extracted her address book from the pile of letters, half-finished novels and the Felix file by her bed.

Picking up the phone, she dialled Portia's number. Her ancient digital clock, which had several verticals missing, was winking two in the morning. Hearing the digits pipping, Phoebe debated whether to slam the phone down.

Thank God. As she had predicted, Portia's machine picked up after two rings and purred cryptically about not being able to 'get to the phone right now'. For the first time, Phoebe listened through to the beep.

'Portia, it's Phoebe Fredericks. This is a call for Saskia actually – I hope you're in touch with her at the moment? Listen, if you see her can you pass on a message. Can you tell her that I'll do it? I know that's pretty obscure, but I think she'll understand. Thanks a lot. I hope you're well. Bye.'

Flopping back on to the bed, Phoebe clenched her eyes shut and wished, not for the first time, that there was a way of deleting answerphone messages after you'd left them.

The next morning, Phoebe dejectedly worked her way through a vast mug of black coffee and a pile of standard rejection letters from the glossy media companies she'd ambitiously fired her CV off to. Flipping past several bills, she came across an envelope which made her ribs seem to compress and interlock with excitement.

Phoebe Fredericks had been written in small, spiky handwriting that brought memories of florists' cards and scribbled pillow notes flooding happily in front of her eyes, along with the inevitable tears. Underneath, her Islington address had been added in blue fountain pen by an unfamiliar round, schoolgirl's hand.

Inside was a short note written on a *Satellite Newspapers* compliment slip.

> *Phoebe,*
> *   Please get in touch; no longer own Barb. flat. Office number best. Direct line written above (not Tues). Meet up for lunch whenever you want. LFTHFY*
> *D.*

There were no kisses, no endearments, no clichéd quotes. Phoebe, who'd once received a fizzling punch in the groin from

Dan's directness, his abbreviated urgency and lack of pseudo-romance, howled aloud and scanned the words for hidden subtext. She sniffed the compliment slip for traces of his aftershave, scoured it for tell-tale teardrop smudges, and tried to think of an alternative mnemonic for LFTHFY other than 'looking forward to hearing from you'; Longing For The Happy Freddy Yesterdays? Lusting For Thy Hot Fanny Y-fronts (did he know about her trendy new underwear)? Love Forever, Truly, Honestly For You?

Bouncing around the flat with growing excitement, she held the slip up to the light in case a more verbose, sentimental version had been written first and rejected, leaving its impression dented into the final draft, but the only words carved invisibly on the slip were those of her address, added later by the anonymous hand.

The phone rang. Chewing on a nail, Phoebe picked it up, still staring at the compliment slip.

'Hello.'

'Freddy?'

'Saskia!' Phoebe sat down heavily on the sofa, her legs shooting into the air.

'No, Freddy darling. It's Portia. How are you?'

'Oh, Portia, hi – yes, I'm fine.' Phoebe tried to hide the thumping disappointment in her voice. All the Seaton girls sounded so alike. 'You got my message then?'

'Message? When?'

'Last night. I left it on your machine.' Phoebe traced the capital *D* on the note with her finger.

'I haven't been home yet,' Portia laughed. 'What did you say?'

'It was actually for Saskia. I was wondering if – '

'I haven't seen her for ages. Isn't she supposed to be with you?'

'First I've heard of it.'

'I'm sure that's what Mummy said.' Portia's voice was fading into sporadic fizzles. Phoebe guessed she was on a mobile phone. 'Look, darling, I'm dashing to a meeting, but I wanted to pin you down and ask you to drinks this Friday.'

'Drinks?'

'Yes, don't sound so horrified. Just a few friends. Can you make it?'

'Well, yes, I – '

'Great. Make it sevenish. You know where the flat is, don't you? Ciao.' There was a curt beep.

Phoebe stared at the silent receiver and wondered if hanging up on someone was embedded in the Seaton chromosomes along with acres of blonde hair and a propensity for calling people 'darling' like a thirties Noël Coward heroine.

Still welded into the sofa, she gazed back at the numbers written by hand on the slip, and felt her fingers slipping involuntarily towards the phone again. They crept around it in a do-si-do, one finger threaded in and out of the knotted curly flex then traced the buttons like a child with a fuzzy-felt letter.

Snatching her hand away, she decided to go out and buy herself the largest bar of chocolate she could find, far away from those eleven tempting digits.

Forced by the total lack of food in the fridge to replenish supplies, Phoebe spent an hour trailing round her local Europa. When she got back to the flat, the muffled grunts, groans and creaks that were being emitted from Fliss's room led her to the conclusion that her flat-mate had now forgiven Iain for his brewer's droop, disloyalty and badly rolled three-skinner the night before.

Phoebe peered at the answermachine in case Saskia had rung, but it was unplugged for the iron again, so not even working.

Extracting Fliss's coffee-stained Corona typewriter from behind one of the smoked-glass sliding cupboard doors in the landlord's treasured 1973 teak sideboard, she went through to her own room and dispiritedly typed a few more application letters, crossing out the jobs she had circled in yesterday's *Standard* as she signed each 'yours faithfully'.

Fliss emerged just as Phoebe was peering at an advert for an assistant in a theatrical agency in an attempt to read the address that she had obliterated with her red circle.

'Hi – just came back for a spot of lunch,' Fliss poked a hot, pink face around the door to Phoebe's bedroom, clearly en route to the shower. 'Iain's here.'

Phoebe watched her curiously. 'Are you all right Fliss?'

'Sure fine – feel dead good, in fact,' Fliss insisted, beaming with far too much sincerity.

'Okay, what is it?' Phoebe pulled a knee up to her chin and looked at her in mock menace.

'I don't know what – '

'Look, Fliss, you might be able to pull the wool over everyone else's eyes more often than a jumper shop assistant, but I can always tell when you're about to lie – you look far too honest. Just save yourself the effort and spit it right out.'

'It's Saskia,' Fliss hung her freckled head.

'What about her?' Phoebe said anxiously. 'Has she rung? Is she okay?'

'Well yes, sort of – there was a message on the machine earlier. She said she was staying in London and left a number – oh, Phoebe I feel awful.'

'What is it?' Phoebe jumped up excitedly. 'I'll listen to it – or did you write it down? I thought the machine was switched off just now.'

'It is – I was trying to cover up.' Fliss trailed Phoebe through to the sitting room. 'You see, Iain wanted to call the speaking cricket result line and he sort of pressed the wrong button.'

'He what?'

'Recorded the results at Headingley over the whole tape, in fact. I'm sorry.'

'And you didn't get Saskia's number?'

Backing nervously towards the bathroom, Fliss shook her head.

'Was it a London one?'

'Not sure,' Fliss shrugged, cowering behind the door now, 'we were sort of snogging when it was playing. England are one hundred and thirty-three for four, though.' The bathroom door clicked shut abruptly.

Groaning, Phoebe sagged back against the ironing board and almost scalded her elbow skin off as it brushed against the iron.

'Hi, Phoebe – sorry about wiping the message from your friend. Has Fliss explained?' Iain wandered through to the sitting room wearing a revolting pair of snakes and ladders boxer shorts and carrying a crumpled shirt. He had very fluffy, skinny legs, Phoebe noticed irritably.

'Yes,' she muttered through gritted teeth.

'Good, good, all sorted then, silly old me, huh?' Iain grinned, rubbing his tortoisehell hair in very Merchant Ivory fashion and pulling an apologetic pout. 'Has that iron heated up yet?'

'I think so.' Grabbing the starch spray from the board and marching up to him, Phoebe pulled out the elastic waist of his boxer shorts and squirted a liberal amount inside. 'Because, I always believe in striking while the iron's hot, don't you?'

14

O n the day of her drinks party, Portia left a message on
Phoebe's machine.

'Darling, it looks as though I'm going to be tied up till late –
can you do me a massive favour and lurk in the flat from about
seven doing a bit of pouring in case I'm not there when people
turn up? I've left the keys with Miranda in the flat below and
told her to expect you – there's some nibbles in the fridge – oh,
and keep Groucho's snout away from them, he's a greedy
bugger. Thank you so much, Freddy. I'll see you later. Ciao.'

Portia then dialled straight through to Piers's mobile.

'Can you talk?'

'No.' he cleared his throat uneasily.

'At home?'

'Yup.'

'Topaz there?'

'Absolutely.' He was at his most truculently professional.

'Still on for tonight?'

'Indeed so. Felix is definitely coming, so we'll check up on his
availability for the project and on any outstanding contracts
which he might breach – he can be a shifty little sod. He's
bringing some friends, but it can't be helped.'

'I'll get rid of them all before they're halfway down their post-
prandial fags.' Portia dropped her voice to barely more than a
breath. 'I won't be able to eat at all; the only thing I want to taste
in my mouth tonight is you.'

'No, I'm afraid Topaz won't be able to make it – she's going to stay with a friend in Amsterdam for the weekend. Yes, I know, it's irritating, but she arranged it weeks ago apparently.'

'And then I'll run my tongue around your delicious balls and up that long, long, strong cock. I can't wait to taste every delectable inch, to feel those steel girder legs of yours around me and for you to be inside me so deep and so fast that – '

'That's right.' Piers's voice was thick with lust. 'Yolande Richt. Yeah, I'll pass on your regards, Angus. And you. What?'

'– come so hard you'll think your tired, sated, shuddering body will never, ever recover. So I'll rub you all over, massage every aching muscle and tight, angry sinew, until you're bobbing on a sea of complete physical pleasure.'

'Right, I'll make a note of that. Thanks, Angus.'

Portia replaced the phone with satisfaction and gazed across her messy cubicle office, past the dying flowers, spewing in-tray, Post-it sticker-laden computer monitor and over to the far wall where fifty or so framed covers of *Élan* matrixed the wall like a thickened glass ceiling. From one, pouting like a sulky brat, decked in gold Versace and over-exposed so that only her huge yellow eyes, pert little nose and vast, swollen mouth showed in the flawless white face, was Topaz Fox. To add character to that smooth, mindless mask, Portia had recently uncapped a marker pen and added a pair of Joe Ninety specs, a Salvador Dali moustache and several big zits.

Portia flipped idly through some features ideas for the winter issue put together by Polly, her assistant, who was in the office fractionally more often than her boss.

Supermodels and their Ski Chalets, she read with a wrinkled nose. *Models that Marry into the Aristocracy*; *The Importance of Being Jasmin Aldworth*; *Life After Twenty-Five for The Supermodel*; *Model Debs*.

Binning the lot, Portia wrote a huge note to Polly: NO MODELS, DOGS OR IRISH. Then added, AND GET RID OF THOSE DEAD FLOWERS. HOPE BALI WAS FUN – ED. MEETING, FORTNIGHT TUES.

Marginally happier, she dialled through to Seaton

International's Sloane Street head office where her younger sister Sukey, who worked in the family business, would just have come out of the Friday three o'clock sales meeting.

'It's about Saskia.' Portia lit a cigarette and crouched behind her desk. The open-plan team office was fearsomely anti smoking and pro bottled water – one was often used to extinguish the other, and as Portia was wearing her Helen Storey suit today in anticipation of seeing Piers, she had no desire to be squirted with Badoit.

She listened to her sister's stern, abrupt voice, modelled she suspected on Princess Anne and the Radio 4 Shipping Forecast, hampered by a weak 'r' which made her sound like a feminine Jonathan Ross.

'– in the desk to the right, Camilla,' Sukey fog-horned before dropping her voice to a more intimate hand-held Klaxon for her sister's benefit. 'Saskia? She's at Grampy's – no, top drawer, Camilla. Vincent Square is SW1, for fuck's sake – driving him up the wall apparently.' Sukey was speaking into the phone between instructions to some poor, down-trodden minion.

'I know.' Portia ducked lower as the new fashion editor – a life-time member of ASH, who now booked only non-smoking models (reducing her choice to about three), stalked past clutching a pile of newly biked photographers' portfolios. 'Look, Sukey, she looks bloody awful. I want you to have a word or something.'

'We've all had words with her, Portia,' Sukey snapped impatiently. 'Short of – oh, just stick it on my desk, Luke – short of booking her into a fat farm, which none of us can afford to do, I can't – two minutes, James – I can't see a way of helping her.'

'Can't you have her to stay?' Portia tapped her ash into a desk drawer. 'Grampy just feeds her acres of Welsh Rarebit and vats of port to stop her talking about Felix.'

'No way!' Sukey protested. 'Guy's started staying weeknights with me now – one sniff of Saskia's snack-pile and he'd be straight back to Fitzrovia. One minute, James, promise. Why can't you have her?'

'Same reason as you.' Portia stubbed out her cigarette against the side of her metal office chair.

'Who is it?' Sukey was only mildly interested.

'Old flame – sinfully rich, half-Greek, very discreet, you've never met him,' Portia lied.

'Not looking for a seven-figure house in Cadogan Square, is he?'

'Nope.'

'Shit! We're in serious trouble, Portia. Daddy's trying to sell the International arm before the bank forecloses next month. Be right there, James.'

'Really?' Portia was looking at her watch. 'Look, Sukey, I have to go, I'm hosting a party tonight. At least speak to Saskia.'

'God, but that means I have to listen to Grampy boasting for yonks about hunting, fishing and shooting his mouth off at the bloody club first.'

'Just call him during Top Of The Pops or something and press the phone's mute button – that's what I always do. And tell Saskia that Oprah Winfrey's diet is brilliant. Ciao.'

Getting Portia's message after a back-breaking shift with lunch-time drinkers at Bar Barella, Phoebe dropped the phone into the cradle and chewed a thumbnail angrily. The last thing she wanted to do tonight was act as waitress to Portia's gruesome media friends as they washed down sun dried tomatoes, basil pâté and melba toast with New World wine whilst rushing out sporadically to silence their car alarms or call their answerma-chines from their mobiles.

What she really wanted to do was to meet up with Saskia and see how she was. But, grumpily conceding that she couldn't wriggle out of it, Phoebe washed her short hair, which had now inadvertently grown out into the shaggy razor-cut currently in vogue, and raided Fliss's wardrobe.

As it was the end of the month and all their bills were turning redder than ankles in a heatwave, nothing unworn immediately presented itself. But, because she was slightly intimidated by the prospect of the night ahead, Phoebe wanted to don an outfit which changed her mood and allowed her to assume a fresh personality, like slipping into the skin of one of Portia's friends – a black sheep in Naomi Wolfe's clothing.

In the end, she resorted to the black Gaultier dress again with her super-trendy white fish-net shirt underneath and Fliss's fuck-me-pumps strapped to her feet. She topped it all with her floor-length button-through silk coat-dress left totally open to reveal glints of leg. But, as she wandered into the bathroom for a final teeth-brushing, Phoebe caught a glint of thigh as white and stubbly as an unripe strawberry in the unfortunately placed mirror above the loo. Realising her legs hadn't seen the sun or a razor in over a fortnight, she scraped a Bic over them and slapped on some fake tan in the hope that it would take by the time she got to Portia's flat.

It did. But not just on her legs. Having forgotten to read the instructions in her haste, Phoebe watched in horror as her unrinsed hands turned from ivory to darkest toasted tan during her tube ride.

By the time she'd changed on to the Piccadilly line, they were already café au lait. Whizzing through Green Park, she noticed in amazement that the percentage of lait had been considerably reduced. At Knightsbridge, they deepened to a blotchy café avec off lait, and, as she stepped on to the District line at Earl's Court, Phoebe almost screamed as she glanced down and saw two wrinkly, weathered Mediterranean hands gripping her bag. Realising they were her own – the fake orangey-brown brought out so many love-lines that a palmist could have written her racy biography – she slumped into a seat beside a whiffy drunk and wondered where one could buy gloves in Fulham at seven in the evening. A pair of yellow rubber Marigolds from the local Spar, although great to get a grip on a bottle with, would probably not go unnoticed.

Portia's flat was in one of the many leafy avenues which criss-crossed between the two main Fulham roads like neat lace-work. Outside, a snatching wind was rattling and creaking the plane trees like old ships' masts and bringing down wrinkly unripe little apples from the ferociously pruned trees in tiny paved front gardens. To the west, a butter-yellow sun flashed on and off like a smuggler's torch between dashing, rain-heavy clouds.

Phoebe noticed a huge pile of post for Saskia's sister which hadn't been collected from the scuffed tallboy in the gloomy hall. Gathering it up, she bounded up two flights to collect the keys.

Miranda – the key-holder in the flat below Portia – tried very hard not to look at Phoebe's chromatically challenged paws, mainly because she was too preoccupied gawping at her outfit, but she let herself down at the last minute as she wavered, her jangling bundle of Yales hovering an inch above Phoebe's stained palm.

'That isn't infectious, is it?' she asked rather archly. 'Only, I have small children.'

'No,' Phoebe smiled weakly, 'it's from my job.'

'Oh, yes?'

'I process nuclear waste – they glow in the dark too, which is quite handy when I'm trying to fit my front door key in the lock late at night.'

Miranda leapt away and bolted behind her door before Phoebe could explain the real reason for having mitts which looked as though she'd been doing a hand-stand in a tub of molasses.

Expecting to be faced with the sort of clutter which had once spilled from Portia's room in Deayton Manor Farm like a slow-moving nick-nack neap tide, Phoebe was surprised to find the bright little flat as tidy, gleaming and regulated as a guardsman's wardrobe the day before a parade. Decorated in whites and creams, the furniture was minimalistic and uncluttered, the polished floors dotted with thick, pale woven rugs, and the few pictures in broad, stripped wood frames which were hanging on the pale walls were extremely good, well-chosen originals; Phoebe recognised at least one emerging Glasgow artist and a couple of Stan's more mainstream contemporaries amongst the signatures.

Even the cat matched the decor, she noticed, as Groucho, a

very fat white mog, came strutting up to her on delicate tip-toes, his tail curled into a question mark, purr and miaow mixing greedily as he wound his way around her ankles and head-butted her calves.

For a moment, Phoebe rather ungenerously wondered whether the flat was rented out fully furnished, or whether Portia was house-sitting for a friend. It seemed such an incongruous place for Portia, who collected obsessively – anything from rocking horses to cow creamers, back copies of *Harpers & Queen* to antique china dolls. Yet here there was nothing that was not merely practical or in the best, most nominally discreet taste. She seemed to have re-invented herself.

Without the whipping wind, it was startlingly muggy inside. Phoebe's skin, moist, pore-blocked and oiled by the fake tan, immediately started to glisten with sweat. Groucho's fur was already sticking to her tangerine legs.

Rushing straight into the bathroom, she wore down half a cake of Floris soap in her attempt to lighten her hands but, although one fluffy white towel ended up revoltingly streaked, her paws remained obstinately orange. And they smelled, too, Phoebe noticed; a foul chemical stench floated around her like a midge cloud, however much of Portia's Chloë she squirted on. In combination, the stench was even worse, like a flower garden suddenly coated in organic liquid fertiliser.

Despite the breeze outside, Phoebe spent ten minutes battling with painted-over window locks and threw open every sash she was strong enough to heave up. Realising it was already well past seven, she wandered through to the kitchen to put out a few snacks, switching on the extractor fan as she passed it.

Groucho, perched Sphinx-like on a work-top, watched her impassively, narrowing his green eyes as she passed.

The fridge was crammed with a case of vintage Taittinger, six punnets of fleshy red strawberries, two cartons of duck eggs, several fat packets of smoked salmon and a vat of double cream.

Groucho was off the work-top in suicide-quick time and wriggling through her legs with a series of plaintive, throaty miaows.

'Nibbles,' Phoebe said rather weakly, wondering if she was supposed to do Portia a 'massive favour' by whipping up feather-light scrambled eggs and then doing something creative with the strawberries.

The most creative thing Phoebe could think of right now was to eat them, so she demolished half a punnet and, smacking her red-stained lips, felt far better. Groucho, tucking into several ounces of smoked salmon on the floor, seemed quite perky too. After helping herself to a couple of glasses of champagne and flipping through Portia's very arty but nonetheless hysterically explicit *Kama Sutra*, Phoebe was feeling ecstatic, if bored. She snooped in Portia's wardrobe and gazed in rapture at the rows of delectable clothes, all this season's, all wrapped in their own protective zip-up bags like deep-frozen, laboratory-stored bodies in a Clive Barker novel. She was just debating whether or not to hop into the sumptuous little white bathroom for a shower when the buzzer went.

'Hello,' she breathed in what she hoped was a suitably gushy and 'media' way.

'Hi,' crackled a voice, distorted by the traffic outside. 'It's me.'

Whoever 'me' was obviously assumed he was talking to Portia.

Deciding it would be anti-social to keep 'me' dangling outside while she explained Portia's absence through the squawkbox, Phoebe buzzed him in and dashed through to the kitchen to rinse her glass and stash the champagne in the fridge so that he didn't realise what a thieving soak she was.

'Come on in,' she called over her shoulder as she heard a rap on the door, 'it's open. I'm afraid Portia's tied up for a – '

Phoebe froze in the doorway, her voice trailing away into a strangled croak like a chewed tape.

His jacket was already slung over a cream sofa-arm and he was standing with his back to her, straightening his hair in a vast gilt-framed mirror, his pink and white striped shirt-sleeves rolled up to the elbows. His forearms and the smooth back of his neck between the bristly, clipped hair and his shirt collar were tanned the colour of Armagnac, his bitter-chocolate hair clean, dark and glossy as a well-thumbed bronze.

Only Dan has a bottom that beautiful, Phoebe thought as a great air-bubble of delight caught like a marble in her throat. In the mirror, their eyes locked and she found herself trembling with ridiculous knock-kneed, stomach-twisting happiness.

'Hello,' she croaked.

Dan blinked slowly. 'Hello.' His soft, deep voice could have melted the polar icecap.

Then, as he dropped his gaze for a split-second and glanced at her over his shoulder, Phoebe saw two huge, speckled grey eyes blink in apprehension before the boyish grin stretched across his face and he walked towards her, arms outstretched.

Groucho, who had been slinking forwards for an ankle head-butt, shrieked furiously as his tail was trapped under a Chelsea boot. Fluffing out as though tumble-dried, he hissed his way behind the sofa.

'We seem to be on the same party circuit.' Phoebe swallowed down the leaping ebullience in her voice and backed away slightly, tucking her hands behind her back. 'Portia's due back any time.'

'No, she's not.' Dan was keeping pace.

'And there are other people turning up any minute,' she gulped, reversing towards the fridge. 'I'll fix you a drink before the rush, shall I?' Her heel slipped on Groucho's rejected bits of smoked salmon and she almost went over.

'No one else is coming.' Dan watched her cannon into the fridge with amusement.

'What?' Phoebe looked up at him furiously.

'No one else is coming,' he repeated, reaching out and covering her hand to hold the fridge door shut as she scrabbled blindly to open it. 'I have a confession to make, actually.'

'Go to church then.' Phoebe was swinging from the fridge rather unsteadily, thrown off-balance by Dan's warm hand pinning hers to a fridge magnet.

'When you didn't call,' Dan dropped on to his haunches beside her so that his iron grey eyes were on a level with hers, so close that their eye-lashes almost tangled, 'I asked Portia to do me a favour and set us up. I'm sorry, Phoebe.'

Phoebe opened her mouth, then closed it. A fridge-magnet clattered on to the marble floor as Dan took her hand and held it between his like a fragile, broken-winged bird. Then, dropping his head, he stooped to kiss it.

'Christ, what happened?' He held out one of her dyed mitts as though the fragile bird was suddenly crawling with maggots. 'They look – and smell – awful. Are you ill?'

Phoebe snatched her hand away, still far too angry at his subterfuge to care about her fake-tanning disaster.

'You mean,' she stalked to the opposite side of the kitchen before turning to face him, which, because the kitchen was the size of a cupboard, meant that they were still just a foot apart, 'that this was all a set up – tonight's drinks party, me coming early, Portia being tied up? Just so that you could see me?' She was furiously trying to hide how elated she felt.

Dan nodded sheepishly, straightening up. 'I'm sorry, Phoebe, but it was the only way I could think of to see you. Portia wouldn't actually give me your address or number – I've never even met her, just spoken to her over the phone. My friend Susie put us in touch and Portia forwarded that note to you. She only agreed to help tonight because she wanted to get me off her back. Apparently I filled her answermachine up so that she missed a key call from Argentina.'

'But,' Phoebe chewed her lip to hide a smile, 'I only got your note the day Portia invited me here.'

'I gather she's been a bit distracted lately.' Dan smiled thoughtfully.

They ended up sitting opposite one another on matching ivory sofas, knees rammed into opposite ledges of a squat, reconditioned pine coffee table on which several thick art books were stacked at very exact angles to one another, forming a spiral. Glancing around awkwardly as she avoided Dan's eyes, Phoebe decided the place looked as though the Through the Keyhole team were about to arrive, or as if Portia expected a 'surprise' early-morning visit from Keith Chegwin and a microphone. From behind Dan's sofa came the occasional little angry growl as Groucho still sulked about his squished tail.

'What *is* that?' Dan was still staring at her hands.

Phoebe hastily put down her glass of champagne and sat on them. 'Fake tan,' she muttered, deciding against the nuclear waste line. It wasn't one of her best.

'Why,' Dan tried not to laugh as he looked back up to her face with crinkling, amused eyes, 'were you trying to make your hands look tanned?'

'I put it on my legs.' She scuffed one of Fliss's fuck-me-pumps against the table leg – they were beginning to pinch like man-traps. 'I just forgot to rinse my hands afterwards.'

Dan was gazing at her legs now. 'They don't look as bad.' His eyes dwelled pleasurably upon one very long, slim thigh which had turned an attractively cinnamon-toasted golden brown.

'Thanks.' Phoebe hooked a bit of coat-dress over one knee, feeling stupidly demure. 'How's work?' She was trying to steer him safely to a conversational harbour in which they could bob between inane subjects while her churning, sea-sick thoughts had time to settle. But Dan had clearly dropped anchor already.

'Fine.' He grinned boyishly and let his eyes roam kneewards again. 'I think I can see a streak.'

'Where?' Phoebe followed his gaze.

'Just above your right knee – I'm not quite sure – just lift that silk thing a bit.'

Pursing her lips, Phoebe shot him a suspicious look. He was smiling far too innocently; like an indulgent old vicar in a christening line-up, benign face belying the fact that he'd just groped a choir-boy. She knew she should really stand up and walk out right now, but her orange hands were creeping towards the hem of her coat-dress with mischievous reckless-ness.

She stared straight into Dan's roan eyes and saw them crinkle in the corners as of old, certain of his ability to attract. The charming, child-like innocence, the wide-eyed delight, easy-going modesty and playful, laughing games were really the slyly concealed homing weapons of a caddish, old-fashioned rogue.

The grin had curled up in lop-sided enjoyment of the sport now, his eyes still gazing into hers, refusing to drop.

He might not recognise the specific elements of his technique, Phoebe mused, but he still used them to such devastating effect that he collected the highest quota of office Valentine cards in the Satellite building each year and caused more London crushes than a rush-hour tube, seemingly unaware of the over-dressed, short-skirted, sweet-scented women who punctuated his working day with offers of lunch, requests for advice and suggestions of 'quick drinks' after work. Phoebe knew he'd had a very short, fiery marriage before Mitzi and that history suggested he grew bored, frustrated and sulky much as a child did.

Seeing through his charm didn't make her immune to it, but it gave her a fighting chance to defend herself. Like a burns victim watching sparks dancing above a beautiful, destructive bonfire, she was totally entranced, yet absolutely terrified of feeling the pain again.

Lifting her chin with a defiant smile, Phoebe decided to walk out on him later. It would have far more impact than sloping off now.

'Is it streaked here?' she asked in a husky whisper, pulling the hem of her dress slightly away from her thigh.

'Can't really tell.' Dan leaned back against his jacket on the sofa and, pressing a finger to his smiling mouth, cocked his head slightly to one side. 'Lift it a bit higher.'

Phoebe did as she was told. 'Can you see anything now?'

Dan shook his head. 'Uncross your legs.'

She stretched one long leg out in front of her and then tucked it back against her chest, surreptitiously wriggling her pinched toes. Fliss's shoes were killing her now.

'Anything?'

'There's something on your left leg.' Dan's eyes played between hers like a schoolboy dancing the reflection of a watch-face on a pretty teacher.

'Really?' Phoebe didn't move. Cramp was starting to grip at her toe like a dropped blacksmith's anvil.

'I think it's a streak.'

'Oh, yes?'

'Here, let me see.' Dan leaned forward across the table and brushed the backs of his fingers along the inside of her thigh, sending leaping electric currents rattling through Phoebe's nerve endings like hailstones on hot skin.

He pulled her leg out towards him and rested the crippling shoe on his knee.

'Yes, here it is – a funny little streak. Looks like a birth mark.' He ran a slow, deliberate hand up the inside of Phoebe's left leg until he reached a tiny crown-shaped patch discolouring the soft, pale skin on the inside of her thigh. Circling it with his thumb, Dan looked up at her face triumphantly.

'It *is* a birthmark.' Phoebe snatched her leg away grumpily. He'd once taken great pleasure in kissing it, she remembered indignantly.

'So it is.' Dan watched as, unable to bear the pain a moment longer, she began unstrapping the long leather coils around her ankles.

'Let me do that for you,' he laughed, holding out his hands.

'Sod off.' Phoebe tugged at a stubborn buckle. 'I'm not stripping off from unbridled lust – my bloody feet are killing me.'

Shrugging, Dan wandered back through to the kitchen to refill his glass. Phoebe – already tight from her earlier pilfering – hadn't touched hers. She wished she hadn't knocked back quite so much. Although deliciously light-headed, she felt distinctly rebellious.

Sensing the coast was clear, Groucho crept out from behind the sofa, shot the kitchen a dirty look, and tip-toed huffily over to Phoebe's sofa where he pounced heavily onto the arm, kneaded madly and then settled into his narrow-eyed Sphinx pose once more.

Her feet released from their bondage, Phoebe sagged back against the sofa and stroked him, listening as Dan switched off the vent in the kitchen and pulled down the windows before carefully locking them. A loud, hollow pop followed as he opened another bottle of champagne and then, instead of dumping it back in the fridge as she had slobbishly done, he emptied a couple of ice trays into a wine-cooler.

Bloody pedant, she thought sulkily. Unromantic, forgetful, calculating bloody pedant.

She tucked her feet and hands underneath herself, so that she was folded up like a sleeping bat, and glared at him. Beside her, Groucho did the same.

A rattling summer shower outside was dimming the flat to half-light, enclosing them in one fading patch of light which was fighting to filter through the net curtains.

But as Dan came back into the room and leant towards her, his breath touching her throat with its warmth, Phoebe's stomach squirmed with such excitement that it let out an unfeminine series of groans.

'How's Mitzi?' she asked suddenly.

Dan's hand, which had reached the tiny hairs on her thigh, went into reverse as fast as a cornered getaway car.

'Fine,' he swallowed, backing off. 'In New York on business. She thought you were charming.'

'How nice.' Phoebe remembered that Mitzi had thought she was some sort of simpleton. 'I'll put her down as a referee on my CV.'

'Why did you bolt off so suddenly that night? Tony said you'd got some disaster in London.' He was edging forwards again now, the fingers of one hand having slithered back undetected gently to pleat the black silk of her coat-dress.

'Saskia threw me out,' Phoebe explained, defensively crossing her arms in front of her like a rugby player in a team shot, 'after she saw us together in the kitchen. I don't want to talk about it. Do you love Mitzi?'

Dan, who'd been admiring the jacked-up cleavage in the Gaultier dress, looked up at her sharply. 'What?'

'Do you love her? Not just chained affection – I mean real heart-stopping, breathing together, trusting, loyal love?'

'I don't know,' he hedged, not looking her in the eyes. 'It's much more complicated, and that's one hell of a generalisation about love. Why do you want to know all this?'

Phoebe shrugged. 'We spent so much time together, exchanging platitudes and witty anecdotes like shared cigarettes before, after and during sex, and I never once dared to ask you about your wife – what she did, what she looked like, how you met her. It's like asking to be tortured by the thorns of a dozen red roses.'

'I don't like talking about it much either,' Dan muttered, sitting down and looking hugely uncomfortable.

'I wanted to know so much more about you,' she went on, deriving a strange, masochistic pleasure from the pain her words wrought, a vindication for her guilt. She was acutely aware that each sentence was blasting a nail the size of a harpoon in the coffin lid of their frivolous, fragile, superficial relationship. 'I wanted to know how you felt about me, how you filled evenings when we weren't together, what you dreamed, what your childhood was like . . . but I was too much of a pleasure-seeking coward, terrified that the answers weren't what I wanted them to be, frightened that my nicely rounded, touched-up, hawked-about picture would be forced into sharp focus.' She suddenly realised she was leaning so close to him that they were practically Eskimo-kissing.

'You were everything to me, Phoebe,' he protested, already dredging up the platitudes. His hand reached to cup her cheek.

'But, you see, I can ask anything now.' She ignored him, ducking away. 'And there's a lot to get through.'

'Why?' Dan looked appalled at the prospect of being pinned on the psychiatrist's chair all evening instead of romping around on it.

'Because,' she dropped her voice to a caressing whisper, 'after tonight, I don't want to see you again.'

'What?'

Phoebe stood up and wandered over to the window, where a rain-damp net curtain was being whipped against several very small cacti. That was another odd thing, she mused, Portia wasn't someone she'd put down as a cactus lover. She reached out with a finger and touched the sharp little bristles on one, not yet mature enough to prick through flesh. It reminded her of Dan's morning stubble which had once left her red-faced for hours.

God, this was hurting. She wasn't even at all sure she wanted to go through with it. He had looked as though she were pulling his finger nails out with acid-coated tweezers.

Turning back to Dan, who was still frozen on the sofa, blinking at her in confusion, she summoned her nerve and smiled apologetically. But smiling pushed the tears glazing her eyes into tiny droplets which gathered in the outer corners, threatening to spill over and give the game away. Phoebe hastily turned her head and stared fixedly at a glass vase of unopened lilies on a twisting wrought-iron table, stretching their long buds from slim green necks like pterodactyls.

'C'mon, Dan.' She tried to sound as cheerful and pragmatic as possible but, like reading a psalm at a funeral service, her real voice kept breaking through. 'It's not as though this relationship is alive any more. It's been over a year and we've both had a chance to breathe separately, to move on. I think it's far better to stop anything happening again, don't you?'

Not giving him a chance to answer, she grabbed her champagne and, downing half of it, carried on: 'But, as I was saying, I think there's a lot we should lay bare, don't you? Well, perhaps not, being a pretty reticent sort of chap and all that – '

Aware that she was rattling, Phoebe shut up for a moment and polished off the champagne dregs in her glass. As Dan didn't offer to fill the silent gap with a handy clichéd truism about refilling her glass, she stumbled on.

'Yes, there's a lot I have to ask you.' She was hopping around in search of visual distraction now, fingering a pot plant here, a picture frame there. Damn Portia for having such a minimalist flat, she thought irritably.

'Have you met someone new, Phoebe?'

'What?' She glared at him, furious that he'd got in there first.

'You're in love with someone else, aren't you?'

'I – er – ' Oh, the sweet temptation to lie. Phoebe, battling with her conscience, busily straightened the pile of books on the coffee table.

'Is it this Stan boy?'

'Who?' Phoebe creased her forehead in bewilderment. He sounded as if he was referring to a character from Steptoe and Son.

'Stan MacGillivray. The artist.' Dan made 'artist' sound like 'sheep-molester'. 'You were seeing him before you went to New Zealand, weren't you? I went through seven different kinds of hell trying not to warn him off.'

'You knew about Stan?'

'Of course I did. Look, Phoebe, this is all too much for me – '

'Before I went to New Zealand?' Having destroyed a lily, she moved on to straighten another spirit-level-straight picture frame.

'Yes, yes.' Dan was standing up and reaching for his jacket. 'I don't think I want to hammer all this out now.' He sighed miserably. 'I didn't realise you felt like this at all. Phoebe, stop pushing that damned picture about and look at me.'

Doing as she was told, she saw his eyes were swimming with distress.

She held her breath, pinning air in her lungs along with the barely controlled urge to reach out and hold him, laughing and crying with relief into his warm, creased pink striped shirt as she suggested they put on the Cat Stevens, uncork the champagne and curl up like randy hibernating dormice in a hot, fuddled fug of lust.

Instead she stared at him, her face so contorted with rigid self-control that muscles were twitching and hammering around every feature.

'Phoebe,' Dan breathed, his voice cracking with emotion like static on an old 78 record, 'who is it? Christ, I know that's a bitch of a question!' He hung his head and snatched a breath. 'But I have to know – even if it's only a name. I have to know.'

She blinked, her face reddening and cramping as she found she now couldn't breathe. The flat had grown so dark that Dan was almost a shadowed silhouette, only his dark hair and the whites of his sad eyes gleaming in the half-light. God, how she longed to fold herself around him like a warm blanket.

'Who?' he repeated, almost whispering. 'I just want a name. Something to latch on to and hate.'

'Felix,' she croaked, hardly believing the word she could hear echoing in her ears like a hiss. 'Felix Sylvian.'

Flecked eyes searing into hers, Dan carried on staring as though she hadn't spoken.

'You wouldn't have heard of him.' Phoebe's voice was arch with falsity. 'Different generation.' She was digging spears into her heart with her own cruelty.

As Dan turned to walk out, she almost broke down. When, head still hanging like a dying, petal-scattering rose, he reached out to open the door, she opened her mouth to cry out in apology, but the first hoarse croak of desperation was drowned out by the front door-buzzer.

'Christ!' Dan froze by the door.

'I'll get rid of them – it's probably a salesman.'

'At this time of night?'

Phoebe picked up the entryphone. 'Yes?'

'It's me.'

This time, she couldn't mistake the voice. Saskia had such a distinctive tone – light, clear and with perfect diction – that she could have put a handkerchief over the pavement mike and spoken in Serbo-Croat and Phoebe would still have recognised her.

'Freddy – that is you, isn't it?'

'Yes,' she managed to rasp.

'Well, bloody let me in then. I've walked all the way from Putney in the rain.'

Phoebe looked at Dan and mouthed, 'It's Saskia.'

Hovering in the door, he shrugged, not seeming to care.

'Freddy, it's the button in the middle of the phone – just push it,' Saskia was saying.

Dan was backing out of the door now, slipping away into the gloomy depths of the landing like an oil painting disappearing under a layer of grime.

'Wait!' Phoebe wailed.

'What?' Saskia was yelling over the traffic.

'I love you.' Dan suddenly looked back and stared her straight in the eyes, his own gleaming with despair.

'What?' Phoebe whispered.

'I said, it's the button just by the – '

'I love you,' Dan murmured, walking towards her again. 'Truly. I haven't stopped loving you for one moment since we were apart. God knows how many times in the past year I picked up the phone to book a flight to New Zealand and then chickened out of it, or started a letter I flunked posting, convinced you'd tell me to piss off. I guess I was right, wasn't I? I wanted to live with you, Phoebe, to be with you. I'm falling apart over this. I swear to God I love you.'

'Freddy, are you deliberately fucking me off or what?' Saskia howled down the phone, which was still pressed to Phoebe's ear.

Dan had moved so close now that they were inches apart, the ends of his fingers lightly tracing the taut knuckles of Phoebe's free hand, the warm silk of his loosened tie brushing her sweating cleavage like a feather as he bent down, clean, dark hair tickling her chin, and reached an almost humble hand up to touch her cheek.

Ducking away, Phoebe sagged back against the wall and closed her eyes in turmoil.

'Saskia?' she managed to breathe out in a strangled sigh.

'Just buzz me in, Freddy.' Saskia sounded livid.

'Saskia, I – ' Phoebe gasped as Dan's hand slithered down from her cheek, slipped like a dropped pearl the length of her throat and, skimming lightly over the dress, slid to the inside of her thigh.

Before she could catch a quickened breath, his mouth had landed hard against hers and the entryphone holster was rammed into her back as she was pressed to the wall like a piece of Blu-tack.

'Ouch!' she howled, her mouth full of champagne-flavoured tongue. Furious, she tried to expel it, but Dan had hooked two firm hands behind each thigh and, the next moment, Phoebe travelled six inches up the wall, her mouth disengaged from Dan's by levitation alone.

'Does Felix do this to you?' Dan breathed into her collar bone, his teeth gripping it for a second like a spare rib.

Phoebe tried to kick him, but her legs were wrapped around him to support herself. Instead she bit him hard on the ear.

Shying away, he laughed and traced the other collar bone with his tongue.

Shivering with repressed lust which was coiling tightly like an overwound spring in her pelvis, Phoebe realised that he was excited by the thought of someone else making love to her.

'Felix likes playing games,' she whispered into the ear she'd bitten.

Dan slid her away from the phone cradle and on to a light switch, illuminating the room with sudden 100-watt intensity as she crashed against it. Hardly seeming to notice, he crossed his wrists beneath her and then started to slide his thumbs between her legs, hooking them in the hollow at the tops of her thighs.

'Am I a better fuck?' he hissed.

'Much.' Phoebe could feel herself slipping back down the wall again and was almost winded as Dan flattened against her and then hooked her back up.

The intercom phone was smacking against the skirting board beneath them now, but Phoebe barely noticed, her pelvis squirming with sudden, fizzing pulses of excitement as she felt Dan's chest pressed into her ribcage as though crammed by a jostling crowd and she was forced to keep balance by clutching at his hips with the inside of her thighs. Her mouth was full of his hair now. Lifting her chin, she shuddered with delight as Dan's tongue lapped the hollow of her throat and then very slowly flickered up towards her chin. Then, as she felt his teeth nibbling at the sinews in her neck as lightly as bursting bubbles in a scented bath, she dropped her head and ran her tongue around his ear and into the delicious hollow which tasted of shampoo and warm, salty skin.

Tangled like children in a mock-fight, they pitched away

from the wall and, laughing, kissing and tussling, moved in a slow, staggering dance of popping buttons, jumbled limbs and scrambled, dropping clothes until they half fell, half sank on to a muffin-coloured rag-rug beneath the widest window.

Phoebe, her coat-dress somewhere near the door, her fish-net shirt entwined like a twisted stocking around her body as Dan fought to remove it from beneath the corseted dress, suddenly remembered Saskia at the door and bleated with horror.

'Did that hurt?' Dan's mouth was nuzzling in the crook of her arm.

'What on earth are you doing, Freddy?' cried a voice at the turn of the stair, panting heavily as Saskia undertook the last flight.

The door was still ajar from Dan's near-exit earlier. A faint tang of Marlboro Light was already wafting into the room.

'Fuck!'

Thinking on her back, Phoebe rolled away from Dan and leapt up like a stunt-fighter, straightening the tangled shirt and dashing across the room to kick her coat-dress under the coffee table.

'Hide!' she hissed over her shoulder to Dan who, tumbled on to his side, was rubbing his knee angrily.

'What?'

'Hide – it's Saskia. She'll go ballistic if she sees you.' Phoebe hastily tucked a champagne flute behind a cream cushion.

This was enough for Dan who, gathering his jacket and tie, bolted to the nearest door.

Wrenching it open, he leapt back in terror as a tidal wave of debris spilled out.

Like a packed Transit van crashing at a car boot sale, the results of Portia's years of obsessive collecting were revealed in all their gaudy glory. The walk-in cupboard, crammed to bulging capacity with old magazines, chintzy cushions, antique dolls, teddy bears, ornaments, dried flowers and all manner of collectables, was suddenly intent on spewing out all its contents as violently as a schoolgirl bringing back a bottle of Vermouth at her first unsupervised party.

'Shit!' He frantically tried to gather a few things up and clamber into the cupboard.

'Where's Portia?' Saskia was on the last few stairs now, pausing as the unmistakable click of a lighter and suck on a filter preluded a throaty exhalation of a fresh Marlboro Light.

'Leave it!' Phoebe hissed, watching in despair as Dan tried hopelessly to shut himself in the cupboard with the door jammed against a stuffed Liberty frog and several back copies of *Élan*. 'Dive behind the sofa.'

Doing as he was told, he disappeared at exactly the same moment as Saskia appeared through the door in a cloud of cigarette smoke.

From behind Dan's sofa came a furious series of hisses and growls as Groucho was ejected at speed, fluffed up as though wearing a fake-fur muffler.

As Phoebe turned around, assuming an innocent welcoming smile, she spotted Dan's silk tie poking out from beneath the coffee table. Beaming at Saskia, she kept one eye squinting tie-wards and bounded forwards with a deft side-kick to hide it.

'Hi, Saskia! You look well!' Phoebe spoke in high little squeaks as the pain from accidentally shinning the coffee table rattled through to her nerve-endings. Wiping tears of agony from her eyes, she kissed Saskia on both cold cheeks. They seemed remarkably clammy and far apart.

Backing off slightly, Phoebe took in two reddened eyes glaring at her as though she were a mistress at a family wedding, and blinked in horror. Letting her gaze register on Saskia properly for the first time, she realised 'well' was perhaps an unfortunate choice of word. Well-endowed, well-padded or Robert Maxwell, maybe, but Saskia was clearly not looking well.

She must have put on another stone since Phoebe had last seen her. Even in the semi-gloom of the flat she looked appalling. Her dull black hair, sodden with rain, clung to her pale face like a shredded nun's wimple. She was wearing an ancient cream mackintosh, stained dirty grey from the deluge outside. Her bulging bust and stomach clad in a grubby white t-shirt were bursting out between the buttons like rising dough.

Saying nothing, Saskia walked purposefully over to the largest of the cream sofas – behind which Dan was still cowering – and heaved herself down. There was a slight crunch as a champagne flute was decimated under her descending rear, but she didn't appear to notice. Groucho was still lurking nearby, hissing sporadically in the direction of Dan's hideaway.

Phoebe hopped after her, her heart leaping around like an excitable grasshopper in Doc Martens, terrified that Saskia would smell Dan's aftershave or spot the tip of the silk tie which was still poking out from beneath the coffee table.

'Why are you limping?' Saskia watched her with narrowed eyes.

'Bumped my leg.' Phoebe chewed her lip and perched on the arm of the sofa from where she could just see the top of Dan's ducked head. 'I was – er – doing step exercises.'

'In here?' Saskia was looking around. 'Christ! Where's all Portia's stuff? Has she been burgled?'

'Over there.' Phoebe nodded towards the spewing cupboard.

'Why d'you put it all in there?' Saskia gazed at her in amazement, realising that she was looking decidedly shifty. 'Have you got one of those obsessive tidiness syndromes or something?'

'No, no.' Phoebe, who had just noticed one of Dan's boots poking out from the end of the sofa, leapt up and started dead-heading a bowl of white roses so that she could kick it out of sight. 'I just opened the cupboard to look for an – um – for an aerobics step and everything fell out on me.' As she kicked the boot, Dan – who was attached to the other end of it – snatched his leg away.

Phoebe wrestled with a tough rose-head to distract from the action, ignoring Dan's frantic hand-signals from behind the sofa.

'Freddy, what are you doing?'

'What?' Phoebe looked down. 'Oh, I just thought they looked a bit past their best, that's all. Thought I'd neaten them up a bit.'

'They're silk,' Saskia pointed out flatly.

'Oh, yes.' Phoebe laughed nervously and kicked Dan again

because he was gripping on to her ankle and trying to mouth something.

Saskia gave her an odd look, which became even more puzzled as Phoebe hastily pretended to be doing a few aerobic leg swings.

'What are you doing here anyway?' Saskia watched as Phoebe started to roll her shoulders in their sockets and tried out a couple of pliés. 'Isn't Portia here?'

'Er – no.' Phoebe did a squat-stretch.

'So why are you here?'

'Good question.' Phoebe smiled blithely, trying frantically to think of a reason. She felt quite ridiculously guilty and nervous, like a fifth-former caught with a Jeff Stryker video, a bottle of Malibu and a courgette under her dormitory bed. 'I'm house-sitting!' she improvised with relief.

'I see,' Saskia plainly didn't. 'And since when did Portia need a house-sitter? Especially one that does step-aerobics without a step?'

'Yes, well, I couldn't find the step so I just imagined it.'

'Did you make him join in too?'

'Who?' Phoebe gulped, almost blacking out.

'The fattest cat in Fulham.' Saskia was looking at Groucho, who was huddled grumpily in the corner, still fluffed like an electrocuted Persian, eyes boggling with fury. 'If I go on a diet, that mog's coming to Weightwatchers with me. I'm certain Portia stays thin by feeding it all the food she denies herself. Typical of her, really, hiring a personal trainer for her cat.'

Desperate to get off the topic of her fictitious exercise routine, Phoebe offered Saskia a drink.

'Just fill the washing-up bowl and bring it through,' she called out as Phoebe slid past Dan's spinning eyes and hairline-nudging brows. 'And wash your hands – they're filthy brown.'

Phoebe threw away half a bottle of flat champagne with the insouciance only pure panic inspires, and, battling with the foil of another, tried hard to formulate a plan.

By the time two glasses were frothing over and a shiny pink pile of smoked salmon was overlapping a white plate, she was still no further on from the vague plan of escaping via the metal staircase which led off the tiny plant tub-sized balcony.

As she wandered back through to Saskia, the dreaded happened.

'I hired an actress to get back at Felix,' she said in the artificially flat voice of someone poised on the ledge of Abyss Hysteria.

'Oh, yes?' Phoebe yelped, backing into the kitchen again in total terror.

I told Dan I was in love with Felix, she remembered in total horror.

'Christ, oh Christ, oh God, oh Lord, I wish I was a goddamn Christian,' she muttered under her breath as her eyes darted around hopelessly.

Phoebe was so desperate to help Saskia, to know all that had happened, talk her through it, mop tears and bolster her shattered confidence. Yet with Dan's ears pressed to the sofa, she knew this would be as suicidal as wearing a Manchester United strip in a bull ring. She dithered in consternation.

'Freddy?' Saskia called out, her voice leaping through two octaves like Sarah Brightman speared with electrodes.

'Er – come through here,' Phoebe ad-libbed desperately.

'Why?' Saskia looked round.

Phoebe gasped. Saskia's chin and Dan's hair were inches apart as Saskia gaped at her over the sofa back. They looked like Scooby and Shaggy peeking around a corner to see if the Ghoul of the Cagoule had gone.

'I – er – '

Beneath Saskia's sad, drooping lips, Dan was mouthing: 'Get rid of her,' frantically.

'Don't you give a fuck about Felix, Fred?' Saskia snarled.

Phoebe looked at Dan. He was sitting slumped against the sofa, his legs tucked into his chest like a boy hiding from assembly, torn between fury and earwigging, voyeuristic humiliation.

'Of course I do,' she muttered numbly.

Dan's eyes widened.

'Just come and talk through here,' she carried on, her voice hoarse with sadness. 'I want to try on some of your sister's clothes.'

'What?'

'For Felix.' Phoebe swallowed what felt like an unhusked conker.

'You mean – ' Saskia's tear-swollen eyes widened with excitement.

But Phoebe, battling tears, had scuttled through the narrow passageway to Portia's bedroom.

Saskia was so distracted by anticipation that she didn't even notice that what tripped her up on the way to her sister's bedroom was Dan's foot.

When Phoebe went back through to the kitchen ten minutes later, Dan had gone. Any traces that he had ever been there in the first place had been eradicated. Not even the faintest tang of his aftershave lingered. Only Groucho, his eyes gleaming with mirth as he sprawled belly-up on the sofa, bore any sign of Dan's earlier presence. Attached to one flexed claw was a shred of torn trouser leg.

15

'I must go soon or I'll miss the last tube.'

'We'll meet this weekend to work out a proper strategy.' Saskia bounded after Phoebe as she wandered into the kitchen to rinse her glass. 'I can't bear another Juliet disaster happening again. She was so bloody stupid.'

'I'm hardly likely to do what Juliet did,' Phoebe snapped irritably, batting Groucho away. 'I can't think of anyone I'm less likely to fall for than Felix. I'd rather don a Chelsea strip and bonk David Mellor.'

Saskia was ecstatic. At last, something was about to happen. And Phoebe was being surprisingly tractable. Not once in the past two hours had she raised an objection to Saskia's suggestions. Even when, hitting her second bottle of champagne and polishing off the strawberries, she had hinted that Phoebe should dye her hair, buy a Wonderbra and work out a little, Phoebe didn't snap back with the obvious: why, when she was so unhappy with herself, didn't she work out a little too?

It was a question that the curt, abrupt Sukey Seaton had asked her younger sister on the phone earlier that evening, politely enquiring after their grandfather's health and then bowling in with a suggestion that Saskia join her for an early-morning swim at Battersea Health Club one day that week. Saskia had snarled back that she was far too busy. She couldn't even bear to talk about her weight at the moment. She knew she was a wreck, loathed herself for it, and spent sleepless, tear-wracked nights plotting starvation diets and crazy exercise schemes that she hadn't the will-power to start. She longed more than anything to act positively, but the moment someone tried to be helpful she bit their head off, hurt and defensive, and then raided the fridge to cheer herself up.

Phoebe, however, barely seemed to have noticed Saskia's appearance. Saskia guessed that her old school-friend's subdued mood was the result of some brimming unhappiness, and kept meaning to ask her about it. But somehow there was so much to discuss over the Felix plan that she forgot.

In the past month, she had given up totally on Phoebe taking up the Felix challenge and had enlisted the help of Juliet, an old drama school associate. Juliet, the daughter of a well-known RSC director, was an exquisitely pretty actress with minimal talent but terrific gall and just the right sense of mischief. She was also 'between projects' – as she had been more or less since leaving LADA – and therefore more than willing to flex her method muscles. Saskia didn't particularly like her, and was not surprised when Juliet had asked for payment. But when Juliet successfully ingratiated herself with Felix's cronies within days and was clearly attracting a certain amount of attention from Little Shit himself, Saskia had obliged, warning her under no circumstances to say how she felt for him, do anything schmaltzy for him or sleep with him.

Then, days later, Juliet had rolled up on Grampy's Putney doorstep in floods of tears. Between sobs and swigs of twenty-year-old malt, she confessed that after doing his washing, cleaning the mews and cooking a fiendishly expensive dinner that night, she had slept with Felix and, true to form, he'd calmly thrown her out afterwards. Reading between the fault lines of a disastrous union, Saskia guessed that the real spur for Felix's venom was Juliet's refusal to introduce him to her father.

What hurt Saskia more than anything as she'd mopped tears and listened to Juliet's moanologue ranting, was that Juliet had fallen so badly for Felix she seemed to have forgotten everything Saskia had told her about what a louse he was, or why she'd met him in the first place. Instead, she'd described his exquisite attentions and mesmerising love-making with the self-absorption of the heart-broken, and had dug the last spears of humiliation into Saskia's tattered self-confidence, like a cat's claws through silk.

In the next batch of Sunday papers, a glossy photograph appeared in two of the tabloid magazine's shot-slots, hastily syndicated by *Paris Match*. In it, Felix was snapped with a half-naked woman at an orgiastic private party in Les Bains Douche. His hair, longer than Saskia remembered it and even blonder as a result of lounging in the sun, was brushing against his companion's half-naked chest as she pressed her lips against his tanned neck. No one could mistake the huge, flashing black eyes, the broad sensual mouth and the curving, dark-nippled olive breasts: La Belle Delauney. *Is Felix Going To Ring His Belle*? ran one headline in a gossip column, quoting rumours that he had asked his infamously temperamental French lover to marry him.

Saskia followed Phoebe through to the sitting room where she was hovering uncertainly, shooting the sofa odd, regretful looks.

'Are you okay, Freddy?' she asked, noticing Phoebe chewing on a quivering lip.

Phoebe, suddenly desperate for comfort about Dan, looked up at her, bright green eyes swimming with tears. She was so close to blurting everything to Saskia that she took a deep breath ready to wail her tale.

'Er – could you not chew your nails like that?' Saskia smiled apologetically. 'Only Felix loathes bitten-down nails. I mean, really loathes.'

Phoebe blinked furiously. And then, letting her breath out with a moan, whipped her hand away from her teeth and rubbed her eyes with her palms, determined not to crack. Two days away from her period and burnt out from working all week at the Bar Barella covering shifts for holidaying staff, she was feeling very over-emotional. She wanted to weep and wail and gnash her teeth over Dan, and instead she'd listened to Saskia talk about nothing but Felix, Juliet and Isabel for four hours. Normally she had the self-control to cope. Tonight, she didn't.

The phone rang and Saskia raced to intercept it before the machine did, still not out of the habits of the recently dumped, leaping on every call like the mother of a kidnapped child.

'Hello – hello? I said HELLO. Oh, fuck off then, you sad old freak!' She slammed it down furiously.

Ten seconds later it rang again. Again the caller didn't speak.

'My sister always encourages heavy breathers – keeps them panting away for hours.' Saskia sank down beside Phoebe after she'd hung up again. 'I guess it spices up the old dear's non-existent love life.'

Despite a night as muggy as the inside of a protest marcher's Doc Marten, Phoebe was shivering. It must have been Dan calling, she reasoned. To see if the coast was clear. She was fighting a desperate urge to boot Saskia out on to the fire escape and hug the phone.

'Well, it looks like you've missed your tube – you'll never get a connection now.' Glancing at her watch, Saskia sounded cheered by the thought.

'If I get to Charing Cross, I can hop on the night bus.' Phoebe reached for Fliss's shoes, anxious to escape Saskia's clamouring, obsessive clinginess.

'Rubbish – that's far too complicated, Freddy,' Saskia bleated desperately. 'Let's fling down some more poo and eat something while I fill you in on more details about the enemy. I'll make scrambled eggs – it's good for you, Freddy. Build your tits up for Felix. Oh, you're going to be just brilliant, I know it. I'll love you forever for this. You're saving my life.'

Phoebe let herself be crushed in Saskia's arms. As she laughed and cried simultaneously on to the silk coat-dress like a hostage victim released after months of captivity, Phoebe had a horrible feeling she might be doing just that.

Saskia started opening a totally empty diary with clumsy fingers in anticipation of their next 'Felix' meeting, anxiously trying to conceal the blank pages from Phoebe as she uncapped the pen from the leather loop. Suddenly Phoebe's heart felt as large as a lung, cramming her chest with painful, winding compassion.

I always lose the pen by the middle of January, she thought emotionally. Oh, poor, poor Saskia.

Phoebe realised that she had been selfish and utterly contemptible, barely listening to a word Saskia had said, because she was so preoccupied with those few moments she'd had with Dan. Yet Felix had almost killed Saskia with his bloodless contempt, and she, Phoebe, was the only piece of driftwood that Saskia could cling to in an increasingly fierce, squally ocean of unhappiness and self-destruction.

'I'll help you,' she promised, reaching out to touch the stringy hair. 'I promise I will.'

Frantically flipping through her diary to stop herself crying, Saskia nodded.

They arranged to meet again on Sunday. On Saturday Phoebe had agreed to work a double shift in the Bar Barella, taking over Fliss's lunchtime slot while her flattie took Iain to the Lakes for the weekend to have a 'talk'.

'I'll make lots and lots of notes, I promise.' Saskia hugged her at the door, her voice quivering with emotion and gratitude. 'You take care – and read that file I gave you again tonight. We must think you up a false name. How d'you fancy Frances?'

Right now, Phoebe thought miserably as she wandered outside and straight into a heavy shower, I only fancy Dan.

Exhausted by the three in the morning session, Phoebe wanted to let herself in to the flat and go straight to bed for a couple of hours. But as she tottered bleary-eyed along Douglas Street, splashing through puddles she was too lazy to steer around and ricocheting off lamp-posts, she groped for her keys and found that they were missing.

'Oh, God, please, no!' she whimpered, digging through her bucket bag.

But even with the bag upturned and the contents strewn around the doorstep in front of the house, Phoebe failed to locate them amongst the furry Tampax, ancient chewing gum strips, overheated Biros and pavement flyers. She must have left them in the flat and then locked herself out, something she'd done at least once a week since moving in. So far she'd got away with it each time, relying on being let in by a tutting, sanctimonious Fliss, dangling Phoebe's forgotten keys under her nose. Today she wouldn't be so lucky. Fliss had said she and Iain were going to set out for the Lakes – travelling in style in Georgette's car, no doubt – straight after her shift at Bar Barella the night before.

There was no way Phoebe could get in without a locksmith. And that would cost all her bill money.

She slumped down on to the step for a few seconds to gather her thoughts and the contents of her bag, battling hard not to break down in tears as she fought nervous exhaustion and the last of the caffeine-induced shakes. If only their seventies fanatic landlord wasn't on his yearly constitutional to Ibiza, she could phone him and beg to be let in. She racked her brains.

In the end Phoebe's brightest idea was to try the doorbell – there was just the faintest chance that Fliss had come down with Red 'flu or something, she reasoned.

Finally conceding defeat, Phoebe was just moving away from the door when the entry buzzer suddenly returned fire, droning out its long, rattling ingress without the precursory muffled voice from the squawk box.

With a split-second double-take, she lunged towards it and just made it through in time, falling on top of two final demands on the fluffy brown hall carpet. Bounding upstairs, she thanked every saint she could remember. The door ahead of her was ajar, and Phoebe sighed with relief. Fliss had hopefully crawled back to bed with Iain and his repulsive Fred Flintstone boxer shorts, which had been the focus of much sniggering kitchen laughter over the past fortnight.

Clutching the final demands to her chest, Phoebe staggered into the flat, kissing the door as she passed it and rolling her eyes when she spotted her keys on the teak nestle table. Then she stopped in her tracks.

Fliss's bedroom door was wide open, as were her curtains,

her wardrobe and the copy of *Oranges Are Not the Only Fruit* beside the bed. Early-morning light was streaming on to a duvet which looked as though it had been used by a couple of Dirt Devils for a randy game of hide and seek. It had looked just like that when Phoebe left the flat yesterday.

She felt the few regrowing hairs on the back of her neck spring up like a prodded hedgehog's spines.

Something odd was going on, she realised, and if she weren't so tired, she might stand less chance of getting bludgeoned to death by a lock-picking, door-buzzing Islington pervert on the rampage.

She squinted across to the kitchen and then around the sitting room, but there was absolutely no sign of life.

Picking up one size ten Nike of Iain's, Phoebe held it aloft and burst through her door.

Dan was lying on her bed, his long fingers curling behind his neck, elbows jabbing out at acute angles, body stretched in a long, lazy line from his tanned neck to his red-socked feet which were dangling over the end of her bed, showing a lot of tanned, cat-scratched hairy ankle. His smile was as big and playful as the fluffiest Harrods teddy bear on the fourth floor.

'How did you get in?' Phoebe asked, dropping Iain's trainer which was wafting a cheesy aroma around her.

'I took your keys from your bag.' Dan's smile grew even wider. 'Your address was in there, on your credit card bill – which is overdue incidentally. I was terrified your flatmate would think I was a burglar.'

'She's not here,' Phoebe said, as if Dan hadn't already guessed.

'I fathomed that after four hours or so.' Dan sat up, hooking his arms over his knees. A narrow pool of light turned his espresso coffee hair a deep, tawny gold and spilled on to his shoulders like ceremonial military epaulettes.

Chewing her lip as she let the sight of him in her messy room, on top of her worst duvet cover and beside a bra she'd owned since her schooldays, sink in, Phoebe didn't notice the Felix file spewing pages from its hastily hidden position under the bed.

'You're wearing the socks I gave you!' she gasped in delight.

'I'm trying to win you back with my devastating socks appeal,' Dan joked nervously, leaning back against the pillows again. 'Come here.'

Phoebe dithered for a second, wishing there were a way she could remove her teen bra from the bed just in case he hadn't noticed it. But she was too distracted by the sudden, unexpected uncoiling of that sexy spring which had wound in on itself all night to dwell on the dilemma for long. Something about the incongruity of Dan in her dusty, sun-streaked room was an absurd turn-on; this powerful, urbane man who made and broke fortunes, who was known and feared throughout Europe and could halt a spiralling career with just one phone call, was sprawled out on her frayed Habitat duvet cover, his grey eyes sparkling with anticipation, body as warm and welcoming as a long, hot bath.

Smiling back, she unhurriedly unclipped her tiny, seed-pearl earrings and rubbed her lobes, revelling in fizzing, revitalising lust drowning out weariness like a tingling, pummelling essential oil massage.

'I meant it, by the way,' Dan said quietly, watching her.

'Meant what?' Phoebe dropped the earrings onto her dusty desk and moved towards him.

Biting his lip with white teeth, he caught the hem of her skirt between his fingers. 'That I still love you,' he whispered.

Phoebe had never seen him look so awkward or fazed. Creasing her forehead, she fought hard to hide her jubilation. Never once in all their time together before her escape to New Zealand had Dan admitted he loved her. All the alternative euphemisms had been liberally applied – 'I adore you' and 'I'm very fond of you' were favourites, along with 'I don't know what I'd do without you', but 'love' had always proved as hard for Dan to say as Llanfairpwllgwyngyllgogerychwyrndrobwllllantysiliogogogoch.

'Phoebe?'

'Yes?'

'Do you still want me around? I mean, I know there's this boy in your life now, but I thought – '

'Dan,' Phoebe butted in, 'what religion is the Pope?'

He looked up, the grin suddenly creasing his cheeks again. 'Come here.'

Whooping with delight, Phoebe vaulted forwards and landed plumb on top of the greying 34AA bra.

It wasn't the most sophisticated of seductions but Dan seemed delighted, pulling her into a frantic teeth-nose-and-tongue-kiss, so long and luscious that she almost needed another one to bring her round again.

'God, you smell delicious.' He nuzzled into her neck like a hungry cat as he cast aside clothing with an abandoned disregard for buttons, poppers and zip fasteners.

At least the fake tan pong had faded, she realised with relief as she heard the unmistakable Velcro grate of ripping silk.

Then, with a heart free-falling like a parachutist with lead boots, she suddenly remembered that she was no longer on the Pill and that any condoms she had buried in a forgotten bath bag would be almost as far past their sell-by date as a tub of houmus in a Bethnal Green corner shop.

Dropping a long kiss on to Dan's popper-rummaging hand, she backed away. 'I – er – I don't think I've got – oh, yes! Come to think of it, hang on a tic.'

Scrambling out of bed, she hobbled on Fliss's crippling shoes into the bathroom to raid the cabinet. True to form her pragmatic flatmate had a selection of contraceptives as wide and comprehensive as a Boots warehouse. Selecting a conservative-looking condom – she doubted Dan would relish the prospect of seven inches of yellow, banana-flavoured rubber stretched over his manhood – Phoebe rearranged her few remaining clothes in the mirror so that she looked slightly less like a kinky farmer's scarecrow, then wandered back through to the bedroom where Dan was gamely trying to hide mild irritation behind a bemused, tight-curling mouth and seductively beetling eyebrows.

Coughing with embarrassment, aware that were she a really practised seductress she should offer to roll it on with her mouth, Phoebe held out the little gift like a vicar with a communion wafer.

'Christ, I haven't used one of these in years.' Dan hooked himself up on to one elbow and examined the foil package.

'You once told me you quite fancied getting into rubber.' Phoebe perched awkwardly beside him dressed in just her fishnet shirt, knickers and Fliss's shoes.

'Not quite what I had in mind.' Dan glanced up at her with a slight smile and then trailed his roan gaze down her body with the slow, sideways sweeps resting at last on her feet, where he watched her curling her fingers around the fragile straps of the bed-me shoes.

His eyes wrinkled at the corners with appreciation and he covered her fingers with a warm hand.

'Leave them on,' he murmured, tracing a finger up the length of her leg. 'They're quite appealing.'

Phoebe's feet twitched in their compressed little prisons at the thought of flailing around still trapped for the duration of what was undoubtedly destined to be a long-haul trip to nirvana. But she was rendered incapable of objection as Dan's fingers slid into the hollow of her thigh, beneath her knickers, and traced their way through her soft, springy pubic hair like grass snakes before starting to circle with delicious delicacy.

Biting her bottom lip, Phoebe closed her eyes and half gasping, half laughing with happiness, tumbled on top of him.

'I've missed you so much,' she breathed joyfully, covering his lovely, warm neck with short, sharp kisses as she undid his buttons with infinitely more deft skill and respect for his Turnbull and Asser than he'd shown for her Gaultier. Then Dan's fingers burrowed deeper and she bit a button right off, squealing with pleasure.

'You've found my on-button,' Dan laughed, tracing his wet finger across her navel and up to a tight, nerve-skipping nipple.

'I just,' she started kissing her way down his chest, 'can't resist that old socks appeal.' Phoebe winced into his stomach, aware that she was sounding like an italicised sentence from Satellite's flagship tabloid *The News*.

'Very old.' Dan, seemingly not bothered, was pulling the shirt up over her head as she moved downwards to kiss his belly button.

'Very socksy, though.'

Phoebe unthreaded a leather belt as soft as a pony's muzzle and coaxed his trouser buttons undone, helped on the other side by a huge, eager erection bursting to be liberated.

As she pulled his trousers down his thighs, it sprang enthusiastically through the gap in his boxer shorts. Looking up, Phoebe slid her teeth over her bottom lip and held her breath.

'Where did you get those?'

'What?' Dan looked down in alarm, his cock already starting to wilt slightly.

'Those cheesy pants.' Phoebe, trying not to laugh, was devoid of a more delicate vocabulary.

'Oh – er, birthday present, I think.' Dan wrinkled his brow. 'Don't you like them?' He admired his Fred Flintstone boxer shorts and the erection bounced back up to perpendicular again.

Phoebe wrinkled her nose.

'Torch them,' she suggested helpfully, then carried on pulling his trousers down, dextrously swiping off the red socks in the process.

16

'What time is it?'
'Mmmm?'

Phoebe stretched across Dan's hot, downy chest to look at the ancient digital clock.

'Shit!'

She scrambled over him and picked the clock up, rattling it hard.

The lights flickered, but it still said the same time.

'Shit, shit, shit, SHIT!'

Groggy with half-sleep, bow-legged from the first sex she'd had in a year and fighting a body which was certain that it was the middle of the night, Phoebe reeled on the spot for a few seconds.

'What's up?' Dan was looking up at her drowsily, roan eyes half-closed.

'I should have been at work half an hour ago.' Gnawing her lip, she gazed around for a towel.

'Phone in sick.' Dan reached out and, sliding a hand around one buttock, started to draw her back into bed.

Tempted, Phoebe let herself be steered, shuffling forwards. She was suddenly swamped with the morning-after gauche shyness she'd only ever encountered on the occasions she slept with someone for the first time.

'Have you been working out?' she asked, noticing the first traces of a six-pack set of muscles quilting his stomach. 'You look great.'

He shrugged. 'I've had a lot of free evenings.'

Letting his fingers curl up to her coccyx, Phoebe moved until her knees were pressed against the side of her bed. Then one foot came into contact with something lukewarm and squelchy.

'Ugh!' She leapt back. 'Oh, Christ, Dan – you could have aimed it at the bin – I'm going to have a shower.'

Racing back into her bedroom a few minutes later, she found him still stretched out and now almost asleep, squinting at her through a veil of eyelashes, his chin sprinkled with black pepper stubble.

Still dripping from the shower, she climbed on to the bed and, straddling his hips, gave him a long, toothpaste-flavoured goodbye kiss.

'I'll call later,' he murmured, tracing a sleepy hand up to her nipple.

'Sure.' Phoebe tried hard to believe him. 'The number's on the phone in the sitting room – help yourself to breakfast.'

'There's no food in the house,' Dan muttered, eyes closed now as he drifted off to sleep. 'I discovered that when I was waiting for you last night.'

'You weren't going to cook for me?' she asked in delight.

'No, I was fam—' The word slid into the murmuring heavy breathing of the fast asleep.

Fighting a screaming urge to plump down beside him and conk out like a fused light, Phoebe swung her legs back on to the crusty carpet and, gazing down, scanned it for some clothes.

Battling through London in full summer-tourist swing, Phoebe could hardly stay awake, could hardly walk, and had such appalling stubble rash that she looked as though she was growing a spotty red beard.

Having showered and dressed in one minute flat, she was wearing an oddball selection of clothes – her fashion sense dictated by what was on the floor beside her at the time. Sadly this had been her rattiest pair of black denim shorts and an ancient paint-stained green t-shirt with *Chris de Burgh UK Tour, 1985* emblazoned on the front, which Fliss had bought in with a job-lot at a jumble sale. Far too distracted to notice it when she dressed, Phoebe had read the logo in horror when she saw its reverse image in the opposite window on the tube. Combined with flat hair, fake-tanned hands and a pair of frayed, greying trainers, the overall effect was one up from Cardboard City, one down from New Age traveller. Even her trendy dark glasses failed to improve the disaster. She just looked like a hungover tramp with a glass eye.

When she wandered bow-legged into Bar Barella twenty minutes later, the rest of the staff didn't recognise her. They gave her the beady-eyed side-glances of waiters unwilling to serve such a gross customer – it was bad for corporate image in a bar where potential clients checked out the fashion-status before they read the restaurant board.

When Phoebe walked stiffly towards the door marked *Private* to dump her bag, a hand was thrust out to stop her progress.

'I'm afraid that's a restricted – Christ!'

It was Tom, a gay actor who worked in the bar during the day and had Peter Cushing side-burns because he was currently spending every evening playing Edgar Linton in a profit-share production of *Wuthering Heights* on the Fringe. He stared at Phoebe in total amazement, his forehead corrugated with astonished furrows as his eyes narrowed on the t-shirt slogan.

'Phoebe baby, what's happened? Did someone burn all your clothes? You borrowed those, right?'

'No.' She edged past him.

'Have you had a burglary?' he squealed excitedly.

'Worse.' Phoebe threw her bag on to a peg and donned a Bar Barella apron which obliterated the shorts but still allowed Chris's gig guide to loom large.

'You've had a flood and all your gorgeous clothes were ruined?' Tom wailed in horror.

'I had sex, Tom,' Phoebe said to shut him up, smiling wearily and ramming a pen behind her ear before she wandered towards the bar to collect her pad.

Tom shrieked with delight. 'That is so, so divine, Phoebe baby, I love it!' He followed her to the bar, ignoring several frantic excuse me's from tables as he passed them. 'I mean, I've heard of losing all control during orgasm, but all dress sense . . . Wow! That is *so* kinky.'

By the time Selwyn Wolfe walked into Bar Barella, Phoebe had been serving for five solid hours and was so exhausted she was pulling customers pints of trendy Japanese lager whilst perched on a bar stool. Every so often she would lose focus as she drifted into dreamily mulling over the glorious two hours with Dan, a soppy grin gluing her lips to her stubble-rashed cheeks, lager pouring over her hands. The rest of the Bar Barella staff – primed with the gossip by Tom and shooting her indulgent, knowing smiles – had generously taken on her tables and posted her behind the bar to save her aching legs; she was now walking like a jockey after riding the Grand National bareback.

When she saw Selwyn, Phoebe and the stool shuffled very hastily in the opposite direction. With him was a short, haughty Hooray with slicked-back brown hair and a mobile phone lifting one side of his linen jacket like a false breast, and a very blond, utterly beautiful youth who looked as though he and his clothes had just climbed out of a hot tumble dryer – all red cheeks, creased shirt and uncombed white-blond hair.

Selwyn – Italianate, long-limbed and extremely dishy – paused for a few seconds at the door until he was certain of an audience of admiring eyes. Then he wandered lazily towards the bar, wearing a black silk shirt, cream chinos and a dashing smile, fully aware that he was as devilish as Mephistopheles, more Armani than Emporio, and as raven-haired as the Tower of London's oldest feathered residents.

Phoebe was supposed to be serving behind the bar, but remained glued to her stool, cowering over the glass-washing machine in the hope that one of the other Bar Barella boys would rescue her and ask Selwyn what he wanted. This didn't mean cowering for long. Tom practically flattened everything in his path to get at him first.

While Tom was mincing around with a bottle of vodka, flashily juggling it and spinning it around his arms like a drum majorette's baton, Phoebe sloped to the farthest end of the bar and poured herself yet another industrial strength coffee. She was weak with anxiety, certain that Selwyn would recognise her or – much worse – Felix would turn up at any second. If he did then Saskia's entire plan would undoubtedly be decimated unless Phoebe improvised fast.

As she edged her way towards the cloakroom, she could hear Selwyn's portly friend hooting with very smug laughter, soon joined by a louder, raucous cackle. Peeping over her shoulder, Phoebe saw the cackler – the pretty blond boy – winking at a very pink Tom as he took a Bloody Mary from him. He looked incredibly familiar, Phoebe realised, wondering if she'd met him at one of Fliss's parties.

She glanced across at Fliss's brother and hastily ducked her head as she realised he was admiring her rear in its shredded shorts and apron strings. Thankfully he didn't seem to recognise her – it had been over eighteen months since she'd last seen him and, as his memory was as holey as an old exhaust pipe from all the alcohol and drugs he knocked back, she was hoping he wouldn't remember her too vividly. Admittedly, he had once stuck his tongue down her cleavage at a New Year's Eve party, but she'd had shoulder-length hair then and he'd passed out ten minutes later.

She crept quickly into the cloakroom and searched through her bag. All she could find were her dark glasses, an outsized spotty hanky she used for her hay-fevered sinuses, and a very garish pink lipstick freebie from Lancôme. Phoebe winced; this was going to hurt.

Before donning the specs, she wrapped the hanky around her head like an out-dated acid house addict and painted her lips. The effect was extraordinarily unflattering. The lipstick made her skin appear sallow and yellow, the scarf gave her a certain Long John Silver androgyny, and she'd forgotten quite how beaky the glasses made her nose look.

When she re-emerged, Tom dropped three Budweiser bottles in shock.

'Have you ever thought about celibacy?' he asked, trying not to giggle.

Phoebe stalked back to the bar and lurked malevolently. Three students from the nearby art school wandered in, took one look at her and turned on their clog-espadrille heels.

'I quite fancy going to Café Bohème,' one said hastily, shooting Phoebe a frightened backward glance.

'Yes, it's far too crowded in here,' gulped another, pulling her ultra-cool seventies flower pot hat further down over her razor cut and shuddering.

Phoebe banged a few glasses about angrily. Selwyn and his cronies weren't looking as though they were keen to pounce upon the only free table. Instead they leaned on the bar, draining Bloody Marys faster than Lawrence of Arabia's lemonade. Every so often they looked at Phoebe and cracked up with giggles. She grumpily emptied their ashtray and handed it back sopping wet so that their fags would go out if they rested them there.

'Three more red ones, darling.' Selwyn suddenly leaned across to her. His Mancunian accent, carefully roughed round the edges despite three years at Oxford to go with the angry young man image, was as hoarse and sexy as ever. In the past, Phoebe had admired his ability to sound constantly as though he was recovering from a heavy bout of laryngitis and had just smoked his first Marlboro in weeks. Tonight, for the first time, she realised that he sounded just like Phyllis from Coronation Street.

'I am being sooorry.' Phoebe leaned away from the cloud of Polo aftershave that accompanied him. 'I am jooost here from Sveeden and I am not speeeking the British very good. Whaaat is a reeed one, ya?'

Selwyn's friends were weeping with laughter.

Tom, who had just sashayed up with one empty glass as an excuse to gawp at Selwyn's blond friend, looked at Phoebe instead and dropped his jaw in astonishment.

'Three Bloody Marys, darling. Do you know how to make them?' Selwyn flashed his very white teeth with a twinkle of very white eye. His nostrils were red and flaky from snorting up so much coke, she noticed with revulsion.

'Yeeees, I dooo.' Phoebe was aware that she was sounding frighteningly like the chef from the Muppets.

'What part of Sweden are you from?' He dropped his voice huskily so that it was lower than an idling Ferrari engine.

Stifling a gulp, Phoebe smiled blithely as she jabbed the vodka optic, frantically trying to remember somewhere in Sweden. She'd given up geography at thirteen.

'Er – Stockhoooolm.' She disappeared beneath the bar to fetch the tomato juice.

Dropping down too as he fetched a pile of matchbooks, Tom coughed loudly, rolling his eyes at her.

'How delightful.' Selwyn watched her bottom rise up as she bent to grab the Tabasco from the bottom shelf and dropped his voice to a growl. '*Ta med mig hem, så ska vi ha det trevligt.*'

Phoebe stared fixedly at a row of Dos Equis. How dare he speak Swedish? she thought furiously. Fliss once told me he failed his French O level because he fancied the examiner and pretended he didn't know the difference between aural and oral.

'Mmm,' she eventually murmured in what she hoped was a very Swedish, completely ambiguous way.

When she straightened up, Selwyn was nibbling a beer nut and grinning wolfishly. 'Might I ask you a question?'

'Yeeees?' Phoebe chewed her pink lips and got a mouthful of gluey perfumed gunk.

'Is – er,' Selwyn's gaze traced up and down her body as if she were a Damien Hirst sheep preserved in formaldehyde, his eyes lingering thoughtfully on her t-shirt logo, 'is what you're wearing fashionable in Sweden?'

The blond youth creased up with tearful delight at this, and the porky mobile-phone wielder, getting the joke after the short, open-mouthed delay of the erstwhile common entrance failure, fell off his bar stool in a fit of giggles.

'Nooo,' Phoebe shook the pepper pot over each glass for a good ten seconds, 'it is the cloothes of my chooorch, the Temple oof the Sacred Lady in Red. If you wooont, you can come to our bible meeting in Kilbooorn. Excuse me.' And she stomped off to serve another customer.

Felix rolled up an hour later, almost silencing the bar as he wandered in, blue eyes raking the room from behind a pair of circular, blue-tinted sunglasses which would have looked ludicrously camp on anyone less staggeringly good-looking.

Phoebe could tell he'd arrived even before she looked up from trying to solve the last two clues in *The Times* crossword. The setting was too perfect for him to miss the opportunity to make an entrance; the bar had lulled to a busy hum, Peggy Lee was murmuring Fever from a throbbing stereo, the sun was filtering through the high arched windows, highlighting rising smoke and settling dust. Even the espresso machine had entered the most sensual phase of its cycle – the long, mournful hiss that produced a haze of thin, trailing steam and precursed a bubbling putter.

Phoebe kicked it grumpily and it let out a series of scatological-sounding spurts.

Beside her, she heard a sigh as deep and delighted as a stray St Bernard puppy finding he's been adopted by a butcher.

Looking up, she noticed Tom gazing dreamily in the direction of the spiral staircase that led down from the street, the tea-towel in his hand polishing a wine glass with such vigour that the stem broke away from the bowl.

'That,' he sighed even more deeply, 'is just *so* exquisite.'

Phoebe bit her lip and got another mouthful of pink gunk. Watching Felix move across the room, she started to realise the utter impossibility of her task.

Heads didn't just turn as he passed, they practically swivelled back on themselves like owls', chairs creaked like chirruping crickets as they were angled back on to two legs, drinks lingered inches from open mouths and fingers raked back hair to allow widened eyes to get a better look. Phoebe doubted that the Queen Mother would have got more attention if she'd just walked in and asked for a pint of Guinness.

She felt a hand prod her in the ribs as Tom whizzed irritably past, summoned away from his chance to serve Felix by the flailing arms and loud 'garçon'-ing of a drunken Channel 4 executive.

'Excuse me, could I have a pint of Guinness, please?' The voice was as soft and polite as a children's TV presenter's.

'What?' Phoebe looked up from *The Times* in surprise.

'I'd like a pint of Guinness,' Felix smiled, not gracing her extraordinary outfit with even the most perfunctory of amused glances.

'Oh, yes, right,' Phoebe muttered. Then, suddenly remembering she was supposed to be Swedish, added, 'I will get it fooor youuuu.'

Felix's blond eyebrow lifted slightly at this, but he was too busy being greeted by his friends to comment.

'What are you doing out of school, little snake?' He cuffed the blond boy around the head.

'Ha, ha.' The blond kissed him on both cheeks, making Tom sigh even louder as he whisked back behind the bar for an invoiced receipt. 'I bumped into Sel in Broadwick Street and he said you might be in here later. I need a favour.'

'Queens,' Tom muttered smugly into Phoebe's ear as Felix and the blond went into a huddle.

'I somehow doubt it.' Phoebe gave Felix's Guinness a massive cottage-loaf head to guarantee he'd get a frothy moustache, and then rammed the drink on the bar between them.

'Thanks.' He looked up and smiled at her.

God, it was a ravishing smile. Phoebe narrowed her eyes and twitched her bright pink mouth in a half-grin, half-grimace.

'Ah – the Swedish evangelist.' The blond youth followed Felix's gaze and giggled. 'So will you do it?'

'No fucking way, Mungo,' he replied calmly. Disconcertingly, he was still staring straight at Phoebe.

Backing away, she pushed her dark glasses further on to her nose and twitched her pink lips a bit more.

'Look, you wouldn't get caught or anything.' Mungo waggled his empty glass at Phoebe with raised white-blond eyebrows. 'Just make it a double vod this time, Ulrika. Honestly, Felix, it's quite safe.'

'Smiiiirnoff?' she asked. 'Or Absoluuut?'

'Shut up, darling.' Mungo waved her away and turned to look earnestly at Felix. 'I mean, you're always going there.'

'Forget it, little brother.' Felix extracted a bent cigarette from a soft-pack and started tapping it on the bar, his eyes still watching Phoebe as she poured Mungo the revolting bar-sponsored vodka instead of anything decent. Then she selected a handful of the most slushy ice and a piece of lime that had four pips and fluff on it before throwing them in.

When Phoebe turned back, she beamed at him malevolently and dumped the drink in front of Mungo.

Of course, Felix and Mungo were brothers, she remembered as she hastily retreated to her coffee and *The Times*. That's why he looked so familiar – he possessed a lot of the attributes that made Felix so delicious-looking, but not in quite the same sublime balance. His hair was paler and thinner, his nose longer and his eyes closer together. Had he worn Felix's dark glasses, he would undoubtedly have looked extremely camp. In fact, he was doing pretty well without them.

This, she realised sadly, was the object of Fliss's desire.

Ignoring some incoming shop assistants slapping down crisp tenners hot from the hole-in-the-wall, she chewed the end of her pen and stared murderously at the paper, filling in the penultimate clue and trying not to listen to Felix's soft, languid voice as it answered Selwyn's demands about 'what that criminal, Piers Fox wants'.

Soon the conversation drifted on to journalism as Selwyn, unable to keep the focus of attention away from himself for more than a few minutes, described the celebrity profile he was working on for one of the Sunday supplements.

'The fat old soak gave me tea with sour milk, forgot my name and tried to get me into bed. The house stank of cat's piss and all the mirrors were coated with rust because she can't bear to look at her wrinkles.'

'How revolting,' Mungo shuddered.

'Good fuck though.'

Suddenly Phoebe was aware of someone sharing her space.

The faintest trace of a slightly peppery aftershave and Chesterfield cigarettes hit her nostrils like wood smoke and the warmth of another body made the air beside her close.

'Permeate,' suggested a soft half-whisper.

'You what?' Looking up, Phoebe almost fell off her stool in her haste to back off.

Felix, staring at *The Times* thoughtfully, didn't look up.

'Permeate,' he repeated, "imbued with constant nourishment" – perm-e-ate – it fits.'

'Sooory?' Phoebe had her back pressed against the glass-washing machine in order to keep her face in the shadows.

'For someone who can hardly speak English, you do pretty well with the prize crossword,' Felix laughed amiably.

'OUCH-FUCK!' Suddenly realising that the bare backs of her legs were pressed against the burning metal of the glass-washer, Phoebe leapt forwards, grabbed *The Times* and fanned her scalded thighs as she hopped frantically from foot to foot.

'Not a bad command of bad language, either.'

Shooting him a dirty look, she hobbled with an even more awkward walk to serve the tenner-proffering masses. By the time she returned to her coffee, Felix and *The Times* had disappeared.

'Thieving snake,' Phoebe muttered, nabbing a deserted *Express* and turning to her horoscope, which announced that she should pay more attention to her finances and consider getting around to those long-awaited DIY jobs while things on the romantic front were so quiet.

'You lucky, lucky darling – pandering to their every whim,' Tom sighed, shimmying past as he removed his apron and headed to the cloakroom at the end of his shift.

'Who?' Phoebe was reading Dan's horoscope now – a depressing spiel about cutting away dead wood and reassessing close associates.

'I saw the prettiest one chatting you up.' Tom winked, nudging his eyes towards Felix and his cronies who were now causing mayhem at the fag machine. 'Think – they might stay till closing!' He clasped his hands together and gazed at her in delight. 'Meanwhile, I've got to go to a basement theatre the size of a pygmy's boudoir and pretend to fancy Cathy like mad – a girl with Dolly Parton tits, a ghastly home perm and a passion for ten-pin bowling.' He grimaced at Phoebe and skipped off.

When he re-emerged from the cloakroom wearing his black D. H. Lawrence hat and an absurd flowered velvet jacket, Phoebe was still lurking at the end of the bar, scratching underneath her handkerchief headscarf with a chewed Biro.

'Do yourself a favour, darling,' Tom whispered in her ear as he shuffled past, 'dump the headscarf and the bins – that divine, divine creature's been staring at you non-stop for the past quarter of an hour. You lucky minx. Can I borrow that t-shirt tomorrow? C'ya.'

Looking up, Phoebe noticed that Felix was still shooting her long, thoughtful glances. She ignored him. There was no way she was going to let him play his pick-up-and-drop game with her, incognito or not.

Keeping up the Swedish accent was murder – especially when two genuine Swedes wandered in later and asked her if she was a Geordie right in front of Selwyn. But by the end of the evening, Phoebe felt she had pretty much mastered it. Even after Felix and his cronies, giving up on getting any sport out of her, had moved on to another bar, The Dog House, Phoebe found herself asking what customers 'woooonted'. In fact, the only problem seemed to be shaking it off. She thanked the Underground guard at Islington tube in her Swedish accent, and then found herself asking 'Hooow moouuuch?' when she bought some bread and biscuits in her local Europa.

In the flat she searched around for signs of Dan, but once again every last hair, smell and bed-crease had been eradicated. He was the Mary Poppins of adultery.

Sagging down on the bed with her mouth full of pippy raspberry jam, she buried her face in the pillow that had hugged Dan's stubbly chin and closed her eyes, relishing the prospect of the hours and hours of sleep ahead of her.

Then one lolling foot scuffed against something scratchy and, bending lethargically down to move it, her fingers closed around the spewing Felix file.

Phoebe groaned. She'd promised Saskia she'd go through it that night. She stifled a yawn and picked it up, glancing at her ancient digital clock. It was almost one.

Chewing down the last of her sandwich with a swig of tea, Phoebe started to flip through the file.

At three o'clock that morning, the light in her bedroom finally went off.

17

Phoebe slept through until three in the afternoon, only crawling out of bed because the phone was ringing on and on, the answering machine having been unplugged for Fliss's ironing yesterday and then never reconnected.

But when Phoebe lifted the receiver with a sleep-lagged arm and yawned a lethargic 'hello', the connection was abruptly broken.

Shrugging, she pottered tiredly into the bathroom for a shower. Her mental clock felt completely confused, as though she had crossed several time-zones in the Tardis and then taken twenty-four hours to get through customs. Blinking soap from her eyes and cursing the flat's boiler, which changed temperature more often than a child with meningitis, she abstractedly washed her hair with Fliss's ultra-precious cellulite thigh cream, lathered her freshly shaven armpits with pine kernel conditioner and tried to exfoliate her face with Factor 15 sunblock.

'Get a grip, child,' she muttered under her breath as she caught sight of her sleepy reflection squeezing spot cream on to her toothbrush.

With the dental tape rammed between two molars, Phoebe suddenly gleaned enough waking cognisance to realise that the dropped call must have been Dan. He'd probably been trying to contact her all yesterday when the machine was off. Today he must have sloped away from honking Mitzi for a few minutes after his Sunday lunch, only to find his call unanswered. Tap still running and dental floss swinging from her mouth like unsucked spaghetti, Phoebe dashed out of the bathroom.

Back in the sitting room, she stood in the buff staring at the phone and willing it to ring again. She picked it up and checked that the dialling tone was there before carefully replacing the receiver so that all the coils in the flex were untangled, just in case a twist would block incoming sound waves like a bent hose-pipe did water.

With the walkabout phone from beside her bed close by at all times and watched as anxiously as a newborn baby, Phoebe dragged on a strappy sundress missing a button and a pair of frayed espadrilles. The day was sticky and close again, an unpleasant sauna of sweat-eeking moistness, hazy sun and rampant flies. The bin in the kitchen was already on the turn and a Galia melon Phoebe had splashed out on two days ago was a wrinkled sphere of mush as soft as a deflated football.

She took the portable phone with her as she trogged downstairs to throw the rubbish into the crawling, reeking, wasp-infested refuse bin. She had clambered back up the three flights of stairs before she realised she'd thrown the phone away too.

Three wasp-stings and much throat retching and squirming later, she extracted a phone coated with tea-bag stains, melon juice and cigarette ash. With her body now running with sweat and the backs of her knees glueing together with damp slaps on every stair, she puffed her way back into the flat.

The entryphone was buzzing furiously.

'Where were you? I was beginning to think you were out,' rasped a voice.

It was Milly.

Sighing, Phoebe buzzed her in and turned away to clean the pongy phone, but the buzzer went again.

'Yes?'

'Come down here and help me carry this stuff up,' her sister demanded.

'What stuff?'

'Saskia's. Goat and I overtook her in the Dormy. The poor

old darling was staggering here from the tube. She's just gone to get some fags.'

Gritting her teeth, Phoebe blasted some more deodorant down the cleavage of her dress before thumping downstairs again.

Outside, Goat and Milly were leaning against the Dormobile surrounded by grip-bags and suit carriers. Both were enviably prison cell pale and swathed in black, their eyes hidden behind John Lennon specs, hair buried in a baseball cap and felt flowerpot cloche respectively. The only colour between them came from the copious plaited pieces of embroidery thread laced around their wrists, throats, rats' tails and ankles. Phoebe, remembering that they made these 'friendship bracelets' for each other when they had argued, deduced the relationship had hit one of its legendary bad patches.

'Have you washed your hair in Lenor or something?' Milly croaked breathily as they heaved piles of zip-bags upstairs. 'It looks wicked.'

'Cellulite cream,' Phoebe muttered.

'Christ!' Milly whistled in awe. 'I mean, I know you're vain, sis, but aren't you getting a bit paranoid here?'

Ignoring her, Phoebe groaned the last few steps into the flat, buckling under the weight of a vast cardboard box.

'What is all this stuff?' she gasped, collapsing on the sofa and landing on a broken spring so that she was tipped sideways at a rakish angle.

'Dunno,' Milly said helpfully, throwing down a battered leather suitcase and heading straight for the fridge.

Goat made a deep, rumbling noise which could have been an attempt at speech, or just a vigorous clearing of phlegm, before he flicked on the television and slouched down beside Phoebe, pitching her into an even more acute angle as another spring twanged loudly. Opposite them, Desmond Morris loomed cheerfully with a furry microphone, furry knitted tie and furry llama.

'Is Saskia moving in then?' Milly yelled from the kitchen, where she was busily squishing the last of the cream cheese along with several cherry tomatoes and fat slices of brown-flecked avocado into some ancient pitta bread.

'Christ, I hope not – Fliss will go herballistic,' Phoebe groaned, poking cautiously into a nearby suit carrier.

The contents were not encouraging. Several large t-shirts, peeled back, revealed a size sixteen blazer and an XL jogging suit.

'Don't you mean ballistic?' Milly wandered back through, dropping tomato pips everywhere. 'There you go, lover.' She handed a pitta bread sandwich to Goat who, admiring Desmond patting a yak, grunted his thanks.

'We brought you some scrumpy.' Milly settled on a sag bag and kicked off some very hot-smelling canvas plimsolls. 'But Goat started it on the way here and spilled most of it when I had to do a U-ey on Pentonville Road. We saved what we could.'

'Thanks.' Phoebe leaned back against an embroidered cushion that was spewing its foam stuffing and closed her eyes.

The telephone rang, the one by the sofa sounding discordant and out of sync so close to the walkabout that Phoebe had recently rescued from the refuse. A split-second later, the entryphone in the hall buzzed.

'I'll get this – you answer the door.' Milly stretched towards the sitting-room telephone.

'No, I'll get it!' Phoebe pounced on the walkabout one. 'Ugh!' Slimy with melon juice, it slithered out of her grip.

In the hall, the entryphone buzzed again. Milly was picking up the ringing telephone beside the sofa now.

'Get the door, I'll answer that!' Phoebe lunged forwards to grab the receiver from her sister.

'Don't be stupid, I've already picked it up.' Milly held on tight, as stubborn as a huffy Taurean mule.

'Give it here, Milly!' Phoebe tugged at the flex.

'No!' She tugged back, trying to lift the receiver to her ear. In the hallway, the door buzzer was going continually now.

'Give!'

'No!'

Milly was far stronger than her sister as a result of moving the

contents of her home from van to van so often. Giving a
decisive last tug, she got the phone up to her mouth.

'Hi, this is Phoebe Fredericks's private fetish line. Ten quid
for fervent panting, twenty for a fake orgasm and thirty for a
racing tip – we take Visa, Amex, Switch and Luncheon Vou-
chers. Please state your choice and then repeat the number
twice, not forgetting the expiry date.' She winked at Phoebe and
then listened intently to the receiver. 'How extraordinary,
they've rung off.'

Saskia, panting up the final flight of stairs a few minutes later,
looked far from grateful to see Milly and Goat still in situ. She
slumped down on to a rickety director's chair ungratefully,
barely nodding a 'hello' to Phoebe.

'Any chance of a drink, sis?' Milly asked cheerfully.

Taking a sharp, hiccupy breath, Saskia shot Phoebe a get-rid-
of-them look.

Gritting her teeth so hard that she could taste the fragments
of her fillings, Phoebe filled a bag with food, added the four-
pack of Woodpecker's Extra Strength Cider that her sister had
left on the last visit, bunged in a couple of her favourite skirts
and threw them out.

The moment she turned back, Saskia burst into tears. After a
few minutes of gasping, spluttering, mopping a dribbling nose
with a hastily snatched piece of kitchen roll that Phoebe handed
her and coughing bronchially, she managed to sob and cough,
'I'm okay.'

'I – er – I saw Felix yesterday.' Phoebe perched beside her,
prepared for another floodgate burst of waterworks. 'He was in
Bar Barella.'

Saskia became very still. 'Did he see you?' she whispered.

'Sort of.' Phoebe reflected on the headscarf and dark glasses
disaster. 'But I disguised myself pretty well.'

Saskia was gnawing at her bottom lip so viciously that it
reddened dramatically. 'Who was he with?'

'His brother – Mungo, is it? – and a couple of friends. Fliss's
brother Selwyn was among them.'

'Selwyn is Fliss's brother?' Saskia croaked anxiously.

'Yes, didn't you know?'

Saskia shook her head, her movements strangely frozen and automatic.

'And, er,' she croaked, her throat as infested with frogs as a garden pond in a heatwave, 'how did he look?'

Phoebe hesitated. Saskia was torturing herself here, and she had no desire to twist salted knives.

'Okay.' She shrugged. 'A bit thin and seedy maybe.'

Still barely moving, Saskia chewed her lip harder and nodded very slightly.

'He wasn't with a girl?' Her voice was getting quieter and quieter.

Phoebe shook her head.

Pressing her thumbs into tightly creased eyes, Saskia stretched out her legs and rested two very scuffed sandals on a cardboard box.

'I still love him, Freddy,' she breathed, her voice barely audible, 'I still love him so much.'

'I know.' Phoebe hugged her.

For the first time, Saskia accepted the gesture gratefully, clutching on to Phoebe and sobbing quietly into her flimsy dress so that she could feel the wet of her tears against her collar bone. When Saskia spoke, her words were almost completely muffled.

'I don't want you to really hurt him, you know?' she mumbled. 'I just want you to shake him up a bit.'

Staring fixedly ahead, Phoebe secretly expected that her ability to hurt Felix was going to be far, far less than Saskia hoped for, but she knew she had to keep her doubts concealed while Saskia was so emotionally fragile.

'He'll be fine. Rattled and humiliated, yes, but it would take a lot more than what we're planning to cause lasting damage,' she assured her. 'He'll probably just realise how perfect you were – are – and what a bastard he's been.'

Or just completely ignore me from the start so that the entire thing backfires, she thought privately.

'Do you really think that?' Saskia looked up, her tearful face desperate for reassurance.

Phoebe stroked her damp hair back from her face and nodded, hating herself for her cowardice.

'So, do you think he'll have me back eventually?'

Phoebe held back an angry scream that he didn't bloody deserve her. 'You might not want him back by then,' she said carefully.

'I want him back now! Can't you see that?' Saskia pulled away violently and struggled up from the sofa. 'Christ, Phoebe, isn't it obvious I'd take him back tonight, today, this minute if he asked?' She groped for another cigarette.

Phoebe straightened up and watched her jabbing hands snapping two cigarettes in their haste before shakily lighting up.

'Then I think,' Phoebe started hesitantly, anxious not to snap Saskia's nerves which were as tight as the highest string on a harp, 'we're going about this the wrong way.'

'Yes, how?' Saskia snapped, hardly seeming to care.

Phoebe bit her lip and changed her mind. She'd been about to back out, to tell Saskia that it was she who really needed changing, not Felix. She'd been on the verge of spewing out some well-used psychological platitudes like 'you'll never stop loving him unless you learn to love yourself again' and 'revenge may be sweet but the aftertaste is twice as bitter'. But who was she to preach, she realised, when she found it so utterly impossible to see Dan with anything other than rose-tinted prescription spectacles for the blindly smitten?

'Perhaps,' she tried an oblique approach instead, 'it should be you that takes Felix to task, not me.'

'Oh, yes, sure!' Saskia hissed, shambling over to the window, her voice wobbling with such emotion that she sounded as though she was sitting on a revving tractor. 'Great idea – just look at me, Freddy. Don't be fucking thick. I'm sorry.' She rubbed her forehead tetchily much as her mother did when forced to climb down. 'It's just that I'm so revolting right now, I know for definite he'd not touch me except in one of his sick games.' She threw her cigarette away impatiently and went in search of another. 'Besides, I'm simply not strong enough to do it at the moment.'

She looked up, her face a clown's mask of unhappiness. 'Let's face it, I'm totally fucked up about it. Whereas you are completely objective.'

'Not quite.' Phoebe bit at a nail. 'I hate him for what he did to you.'

Saskia shrugged. 'That's why you're going to teach him a lesson – not me. But first – don't bite your nails, Freddy – first, I've got to teach you some tricks about how to win Little Shit.' She nodded towards the bags and boxes that were littering the floor.

'So what is all this stuff?' Phoebe noticed that what looked like an ostrich feather was brushing Saskia's heat-swollen ankle.

'I borrowed a job lot from Portia,' she explained, 'the rest is a lot of old stuff I can't get into any more – nothing too distinctive, of course, in case Felix recognises it – and some attic fodder Gramps found in Bowscombe before he moved out.'

'Do they know about all this then?' Phoebe asked awkwardly. 'Portia and your grandfather?'

'Christ, no! Portia would be horrified, and Gramps would get out his blunderbuss if he heard the full Felix saga.'

'And – er – I mean, do you want to stay here while we're plotting and whatnot?'

Saskia shook her head, 'Thanks, but I'm going to stay at Portia's while she's away – in fact I've just been there, collecting the keys and dumping my stuff.'

'Away?'

'America, I think.' Saskia delved into a suit carrier at random and produced a fresh packet of Marlboro Lights. 'The old bag called to apologise this afternoon – we had a bit of a strained call yesterday,' she explained. 'She'll be away for at least a fortnight, so what I thought we'd do is use her flat as Frances's base for the first few hot dates, and then perhaps have her move around a bit to add to the mystery.'

'Who's Frances?'

'You, you dope!' Saskia lit up and then winced as she caught sight of the suit carrier Phoebe had examined earlier. 'Shit, that's one of mine. I meant to leave it in Fulham. Frances Courtault, I thought. Sophisticated without being jumped-up. Now,' she dug into a broken-strapped Vuitton satchel, 'I booked you into the hairdresser's tomorrow – ten o'clock, The Studio on Southampton Street.'

'My hair?' Phoebe clutched what there was of it nervously – but it was revoltingly sticky and lifeless from being washed with cellulite cream, so she slurped some tea to bolster her resolve instead. You agreed to this, she told herself firmly.

'There's a really big private PR party at The Nero Club on Wednesday night,' Saskia went on, 'to celebrate the wrap-cum-launch of a new Channel 4 late-night prog called Showdown – a real fash-trash, dirty gossip hour – and it'll be rentaceleb, count the models big time.' She rolled her eyes slightly. 'Felix is bound to be there – I'll call his agent tomorrow, pretending to be the Channel 4 press office, just to check. If so, then it's the ideal launch for the Frances attack. We'll get you in – Portia's got a press invite she can't use so I just need to get the guest list doctored. Once there, you circulate Cinderella style until Felix can't help but notice you, bewitch him, and then leave early.'

'Slinging a size seven clog over my shoulder as I leap in a cab?'

'You're going by tube,' Saskia smiled balefully, 'the budget doesn't stretch that far.'

'What have you washed this in, sweetypie – the loo?'

The Studio's top stylist, Lou, held up a limp strand of growing-out razor cut and raised a very plucked, very arched eyebrow at Phoebe over her left shoulder.

'Close.' She was staring anxiously at the rows of glossy pics girthing The Studio – endless twelve by tens of stunning models with nothing but a scattering of stubble between their scalp and the open air. Her recent dine-off-it experience of hairdressers looked likely to be bettered in the next half hour.

'Black, you said?' Lou hitched up the other eyebrow.

'Huh?' Phoebe's scruffily plucked brows shot up too, so that she and Lou were staring at one another like a pair of Parisian mime artists.

'Yes, sweetypie – it's in the book. Black, short, shocking.'

'Did I really say that?' Phoebe gulped, starting to panic. She could feel her chest palpitate in the first stages of hyperventilation, felt each hair on her head trying to hide in its follicle and was sure she could see her eggshell-pale reflection opposite disappearing into a telescopic-mirror tunnel in the reflected screen of sweat on her forehead. As far as she was concerned, the only difference between a hairdresser and a dentist was the mask.

'I've got "jet black pudding basin" pencilled in the book.' Lou pursed his lips and cocked his head. 'Not the kindest cut on the face, but with your cheekbones and that long neck, you might carry it off in a cute way. We'll see – I just love a challenge.'

Phoebe flashed a weak smile and decided that she was going to throttle Saskia.

'Christ, you look stunning!' Saskia gaped over the top of *Vogue*, her blue eyes wide in amazement as she watched Phoebe emerge over an hour later.

Face still flushed from the hairdryer, Phoebe reached up to ruffle the unfamiliar sleek black tresses on her head but her hand was swatted firmly away by Lou who was stalking her as far as the reception desk, eager for his tip.

'Isn't she beautiful?' He nodded at Saskia, hastily averting his eyes from her own unruly black mop which was already showing a streak of pale root at the parting. 'I wasn't sure we could carry it off, but we're looking quite sensational, aren't we, sweetypie?'

'Sure are, honeybunny hotty-botty pusscat.' Phoebe gave Lou a wry smile and then looked over his shoulder at her reflection in one of the baroque mirrors which seemed to make the entrance walls of The Studio lean inwards.

It was certainly striking. Very, very striking, Phoebe reflected. A short, glossy bob skirted her ears and forehead in a neat pudding bowl curtain. It continued at the same shorn length around the back of her head, the hair below and at the nape of her neck clipped to nothing more than bristle. And it was so shiny and black that she could almost see her shocked face in its reflection on the mirror.

'You'll need the back cut and dyed each fortnight – the rest every four weeks or so, sweetie—er, Phoebe.' Lou had a final self-indulgent stroke of his handiwork before waltzing around the desk to make up her bill.

'Stunning,' Saskia repeated, standing up and walking round Phoebe like a Japanese tourist circumnavigating Eros.

'Christ!' Phoebe stared at the bill. 'Shouldn't the decimal point be one digit to the left? Delilah gave better value than this.' Her Visa would snap under the strain.

Lou winced, clearly deeply offended by having cut the hair – however beautifully – of a prole. His other clients would never dream of even glancing at the bill, let alone questioning it before they tossed their burnished Amexes across the counter and then dug into quilted purses for a spare twenty-pound cash tip.

'I'm paying for this,' Saskia bustled in quickly.

'Don't be daft, Sasky.' Phoebe wondered if she could get away with dating a cheque 1985, or whether they'd notice it. 'It's my hair.'

'And it's my revenge.'

To the accompaniment of Lou's arched eyebrows, Saskia butted Phoebe away and dug out her own credit card.

Having trawled around South Molton and Bond Streets filling carrier bags at an alarming rate, Phoebe and Saskia knocked back a juice and a gin and tonic respectively before parting company.

'I'll pay!' Saskia insisted, grabbing the saucered bill before Phoebe even noticed it.

As they were walking out on to Davies Street, Phoebe pinned Saskia down beside the Vivienne Westwood shop and started delving in her bag for Georgette Gregory's number.

'Saskia, I know you'll get daft and proud if I bring up the subject of money,' she gabbled quickly, terrified of upsetting her, 'but I am worried about it and – no, don't argue – and I promised I'd pass this on to you anyway. She's a party organiser – you might have heard of her? Fliss works there a couple of days a week, but she's looking for a permanent PA. She's gorgeous, she's off-the-wall, and she might also be able to help with this Felix thing.'

Phoebe swallowed. Why did I say that? she thought in horror.

Saskia, who had just been looking as though a hand-bagging session was imminent, suddenly assumed the expression of a pools winner.

'Thanks,' she gulped gratefully. 'I mean really – she'll be able to help?'

'Well, it's more if you want a job, really – she pays extremely well.'

'Yes, well,' Saskia stuffed the number in a pocket hurriedly and dropped her gaze, 'I'm – er – I'm not that sure I'm up to working right now. I mean, typing's beyond me and I can't stand my own company at the moment, let alone work for someone else's. But thanks, Freddy, I mean it. Not just for this – for everything. For being here. I'm so grateful.'

Blushing furiously, she kissed Phoebe on both cheeks and scuttled off, the denim of her jeans making scratchy swishing noises as her thighs rubbed together.

Watching her disappear into Grosvenor Square, Phoebe closed her eyes and leaned against a scalding railing, hot as a branding iron from the sun. She was now so deeply regretting her decision to go ahead with this that she could barely admit it to herself, aware that it was far too late to back out.

Slinging a Brown's bag over her shoulder, she headed up Duke Street.

It was almost as though her shadow was Saskia, seeping into the gaps between the paving stones, dancing around corners, scaling walls and hunting her everywhere. In her duffle bag was a pair of contact lenses as unnaturally purply blue as the ink of a schoolgirl's love-letter to Take That.

Pausing by a lamp-post plastered with bill-flyers, Phoebe fought a very childish, extremely hormonal urge to burst into tears. She'd suddenly remembered that her period was due on Wednesday.

She was acutely aware that a degree of selfishness was making her doubt her decision; she was terrified that she'd fail, and frightened of being humiliated, convinced that Felix could hurt her more than she could ever try to hurt him. But above all, Phoebe was almost certain that Saskia would wind up the most devastated and tormented of any of them.

Phoebe was vaguely aware of some extra attention on the way back to Islington, but was too preoccupied with worrying about Saskia really to notice. A man on the bus sat so close that his hairy leg gave her calf friction burns. Three builders practically swung monkey-style from some scaffolding and a crew-cut woman in dungarees left her cash in the Abbeylink in order to race after Phoebe and ask if she'd dropped her free copy of *Midweek*, which she hadn't.

Fluffing up the pudding bowl, Phoebe hoped she wasn't looking too Jamie Lee Curtis.

Every so often, she caught sight of a strange-looking woman with a scrawny neck, mad, staring eyes and a very stern haircut glaring at her from shop windows. Fearing a crazed lesbian stalker, Phoebe raced towards Douglas Street. It wasn't until the woman glared menacingly at her out of the window of the Dôme on Upper Street that Phoebe realised she was stalking herself.

Back at the flat, Fliss had clearly done a whistle-stop before shooting out again; her whites were gurgling in the washing machine, a lump of souvenir Kendal Mint Cake had been tossed on Phoebe's bed, and there was a very rude note on the fridge about 'naffing salad thieves'.

Fliss had spent most of the previous Thursday night reciting a devastatingly moving, compassionate 'You're a nice bloke but I'm dumping you' speech in anticipation of her weekend away with Iain. It was therefore slightly disturbing, Phoebe reflected, that Iain's kitbag was once more nestling by its usual skirting and his much-ridiculed navy blue Barbour was yet again hooked over the landlord's black ash-effect 007 hat stand. Even more worrying was the enormous basket of flowers which had been left to droop on the kitchen table. The display was almost as large as the fridge and considerably sweeter-smelling. They were all, Phoebe noticed jealously, red. Every last bloom – banked as tightly together as the serried bunches under canvas outside posh tube stations anticipating rush hour adulterers – was as red as Georgette Gregory's office reception.

Iain was clearly pulling the stops out, Phoebe mused. It was no wonder the Final Chuck had been aborted. Even she, pragmatic, hay-fevered, unromantic Phoebe, might get a bit wistful and Jane Seymour over a stack of petals that sumptuous. Iain and Fliss were probably at Highbury Town Hall getting the marriage licence right now. Then it would be off to Burnley and Bungalow Wolfe, where they would break the happy news, remind Pa and Ma W that it was their duty to cough up for caterers, pour over the Portmeirion catalogue for the wedding list choices and agonise over which family brats were aesthetic and well-behaved enough for pages and bridesmaids. 'Don't worry,' Iain would ooze, 'I can liaise with the florist, it's a penchant of mine.'

'Ostentatious prick,' Phoebe muttered in her old-single-hag-with-a-gingerbread-cottage voice. 'I'm not being another bloody bridesmaid again. This chick is traipsing up that aisle as a maid of honour six months pregnant, with a barn conversion in Wiltshire, flat in Chelsea Harbour and top exec job in marketing.' She fingered a blood-red rose so intently that it snapped off. 'And Dan gazing at me lovingly from a nearby pew,' she added as an afterthought.

18

Piers was such a punctilious adulterer that he not only booked himself and Portia on to completely different plane seats, he booked them on different cross-Atlantic flights, with different airlines. This wasn't just because Portia – a nervous flyer – required an aisle seat where she could wear her life-jacket close to the emergency exit in the chain-smoking section, whereas Piers liked a First-Class, smoke-free window. Piers was going to extremes of subterfuge because he suspected that Portia's discretion was as unreliable as that of a double-crossing Mafia priest taking confession.

Piers relaxed back against several United cushions and rotated his ankles to prevent swelling. Lined up in front of him were three one-litre bottles of mineral water, half a dozen bananas, a gel-pack eye mask and the entire spectrum of the daily newspapers from England and the major US States. A seasoned traveller, he had long since settled into his ideal red-eye survival recovery routine.

Donning the mask as the overhead signs went out and the seat belts started clanking open, he briefly contemplated the complexities of his last-minute decision to bring Portia with him. It was a foolish spur-of-the-moment suggestion which he'd made, quite uncharacteristically, when she was leaving the flat on Sunday morning. As ever, Piers had been allowing plenty of time for his scrupulous clue-expunging tidy up before Topaz's return from her weekend away, yet he resented Portia's early departure and had asked her to join him on his American trip more from thinking aloud than genuinely voicing a desire.

'I can't leave work,' she'd replied in her classic, cut-glass, abrupt way.

If there was one thing that really turned Piers on to Portia it was her complete cool; she would treat the most diabolical of situations with the abrupt, impatient pragmatism of a clipped-speech fifties film heroine. 'A severed leg – how ghastly. I'll call you a blood wagon. Gin and tonic while you're waiting?'

'You hardly ever go into the *Élan* building,' Piers had pointed out as he'd watched her dress from his vantage point between two pillows.

'I do a lot of work from home, you know that.' Portia had hooked a leg up on the bed to roll up a very sheer stocking. 'And the Winter issue editorial deadlines are coming up.' She snapped a suspender clip shut.

Piers loved the pose, aware that she was doing it for him. Topaz – on the few occasions she wore stockings for fashion-victim purposes – hoicked them up with the grace of a school-kid dragging up loose socks; Portia fingered hers with caressing care, stroking out wrinkles as though running her hands along a marble statue. Her legs were a good six inches shorter than Topaz's and far knobblier, but Piers was growing increasingly obsessed by them.

'Then work from the States.' He had stretched out and run a thumb up the back of one stockinged thigh. 'You can fax or modem any work straight to the London office.'

'Thanks, but I don't really fancy sitting around in hotel bars waiting for you to come out of meetings.' She whisked away to collect her face creams.

Later that day she'd called curtly, confusingly, to change her mind and accept, not even thinking to use his mobile line. Topaz had picked up the phone in the flat and yelled out that Cher was on the phone feeling 'real sorry for herself' – Portia's accent had mercifully foxed her totally as she had the sort of breathy, upper-class voice that meant she pronounced her own name 'Poor Cher'.

It was at that point that Piers had realised the foolishness of suggesting off-the-cuff that Portia come along on his Strassi fact-finding tour. After the call, he'd been forced to make up a lot of balls about Cher casting around for alternative representation. Thankfully, Topaz had got bored halfway through his spiel and changed the subject to babies. For the first time in weeks, he had embraced the topic enthusiastically. Topaz was now so well read on fertility she could bore for America, England and the UN on conception, the menstrual cycle and XX chromosomes.

Piers swigged some more mineral water and extracted the phone from his seat's arm rest to ring through and check that his and Portia's suites were, as they'd promised, on different floors, in different buildings.

Portia waited nervously behind two very calorifically challenged Americans at the First Class check-in, hopping her weight from one brand new, unfamiliar Blahnik sling-back to the other. Because she'd bought them in the July sales they were half a size too small and the wrong colour, but it didn't matter as she was planning to take them off on the plane and ease them off in the cab – then the moment she was ensconced in Piers's suite she would drape them over a squishy sofa for a few seconds before kicking them off once more.

'This isn't a First Class ticket, madam,' the check-in clerk announced sniffily.

'What?' Portia looked up from heaving her almost-matching luggage on to the conveyer belt scales. 'Don't tell me it's bloody Club?'

'No, madam.' The clerk pulled her chin back into her fake-tanned bronze neck and smirked malevolently. 'This is an Economy ticket. If madam would care to remove her baggage, she can queue to check in over there.' She nodded towards a long, spiralling queue which was stretching out from a BA desk in a messy tangled line of young families off to Disneyland, shiny-suited salesmen excitedly off to Mid-West conferences, and loud Americans off to tell Mom and Dad how 'cute' and 'claustrophobic' England is.

Hissing through her teeth, Portia dragged her bags back on to her kamikaze trolley and stalked over to the Smoking Area – a sad, cordoned-off room full of nicotine-stained Dralon chairs, coughing travellers and shiny silver ashtrays. Working her way through a vast vodka and cranberry juice and half a packet of extra-low fags – it took so long to get a kick out of them – Portia left it until the very last minute to check in. Her flight was already being called, so she was whisked through in super-quick time and upgraded to Club as there were no Economy seats left.

'Does madam mind a smoking aisle seat?' the clerk asked nastily. 'It's all we have left.'

'Oh, I'll just have to cope,' Portia beamed back, positively floating on vodka and the prospect of monopolising Piers's bed for two whole weeks.

Twelve hours on a bucket-flight via Seattle almost put her off Piers entirely, however. Had it not been for a very dishy Research Fellow flying West Coast on the cheap too, she reflected, she might have cashed in her return for a U-turn. But Herbie from the Gonner Institute in San Antonio was so flatteringly keen, gibbering with nerves as he chatted her up and spilling his drinks everywhere Leonard Rossiter-style as he furtively attempted to stroke her knee, that Portia perked up considerably, even when she had to mop a large vodka martini off her chiffon trousers. Fresh from a cheering snog in the loo – did that qualify for L-plates in the Mile High Club, she wondered? – and a very furtive grope on descent, Portia wandered towards arrivals feeling more jet-shagged than lagged and quite prepared to coast through a few of Piers's frosty fronts.

In The Factory, as she called her and Piers's apartment, Topaz lounged on the squeaky leather sofa and waited for the varnish on her toes to dry, carefully adjusting the sculptured wedge around them so that they were evenly separated like fingers clamped in foam rubber knuckle dusters. Leaning back against a hand-woven, tribal-blessed ethnic cushion cover, she pressed one of the phone's presets.

'Anything for Wednesday yet, babe?' she asked Nadine, the top booker at her modelling agency, Shots. They had long since dispensed with the kiss-blowing, how-are-yous that preceded even the most professional of calls in their industry. They liked each other too much to bother. It generally ran that the more a booker loathed their models, the sweeter and gushier he or she was to them.

'Uh . . .' Nadine was clearly spinning the revolving filing system which reared out of the communal office like a giant mill cog with details of models and bookings flapping and clacking in hinged ranks. 'Nope. There was a chance of some last-minute catalogue stuff in Morocco – Chesca Uni fell asleep on a Riviera roof terrace and is currently looking like something Princess Di shakes hands with when she needs good PR – but it might stretch to two days so we wouldn't be able to get you back for the Hulberry job in time. They want you near Loch Hourn at six on Thursday morning. Lester's flying up with you the night before.'

'Can't you cancel that, hon, and I'll do Morocco instead?'

'For seven grand less? No way, babe.'

'Pleeeease?' Topaz begged.

'I've booked Silka, she's already in Tangiers doing handstands on camels for Krizia. You got something you want to avoid on Wednesday?'

'The Showdown launch.'

'Christ – thanks, yes. I need to confirm that. You get paid an appearance fee, you know. And I have it on good authority that none of the Storm girls and boys are getting more than a free drink. Have fun. Speak soon.'

And she hung up.

Bracing herself, Topaz rang Felix.

'Yeah?' a voice yawned after about thirty rings.

'Dylan, is Felix there?'

'Hang on, darling, I'll ask.'

She could hear voices muttering in the background and

caught indistinct snatches of sentences – 'didn't you ask?' – '. . . American, I think.' – 'Could it be Mum?' – 'No, sounded sober.'

Finally Felix picked up the receiver. 'Hi.'

'It's Topaz,' she said curtly. 'Piers asked me to call – he wants you to walk me on Wednesday. The Showdown party – you can get in on my invite, Piers has okayed it with the publicity guys.'

'Is he with you? I need a word.'

Topaz twisted her lips into a tight coil of fury, resenting Felix's casual monotone, as offhand as a glove in a heatwave.

'He's in LA – so can you do it?'

'Is he chasing my jeans ad?'

'Well, he's gotta real busy schedule on, but I guess he'll look up some players if he's got enough time left.' Topaz wanted to irritate him, furious that she'd heard nothing about a US jeans ad. 'So, I'll get the car to pick you up Wednesday night then, huh?'

'Wednesday?'

'The Showdown wrap, Felix – it's plus guest, so Piers wants you to get a bit of coverage by walking me there.'

'Oh, no, forget it. Belle's over – she's a live guest on the show that night so I'm going with her. At least, I think that's what she said – she speaks French so bloody fast, she could be going on Des O'Connor or something. You okay?'

'Uh?' Topaz was completely taken aback by his cheerful enquiry. 'Fine,' she spluttered eventually.

'Great. Bye.' He rang off.

Topaz ate half a grapefruit, a fat-free yoghurt and one square of slimmer's chocolate on a cheer-up binge.

Feeling fat and sick, she snatched up the phone as soon as it rang, battling the unpleasant hope that it was Felix.

'Hi, Tops, it's Gabby.'

Topaz tried not to curl her lip. Gabby was Piers's bouncy, efficient Sloane Ranger PA. She looked like an overweight Peke and sounded permanently as though she'd just bounded up several flights of stairs, but was efficient, enthusiastic and resilient enough to have lasted longer than any of Piers's other secretaries who usually pushed off after six months of crying in the loos, leaving several dead busy lizzies and a badly typed three-page resignation letter which Piers never read. Gabby, who just laughed when Piers called her a 'thick cow' and would even tidy the office and water the plants during the Four Minute Warning, had lasted nearly a year.

'Just calling to let you know that the Channel 4 peeps have buzzed me to say Feely's got his own invite now, so he can go to the Wednesday night bash separately. Piers gave me a list of clients he wants to get in, so I'm putting Frank Grogan's name down as your guest instead, okay?'

Topaz shuddered. Frank was a revolting bi-sexual comedian fighting to get his career back on the rails after a panned solo television series and some ill-timed Fairy ads which had coincided with being Outed in the gay press. He was so immoral that, if pushed, Topaz reckoned he'd sleep with a close relative rather than hold his own for a single night. On each meeting she'd struggled to extract his tongue from one or other of her upper orifices.

'Do you reckon Feely would rather take Imogen Blake or Fanii Hubert?' Gabby debated breathily.

'Oh, Fanii's much more likely to get snapped, I'd suggest her.' Topaz grinned to herself. Fanii was a six-foot Australian ex-model-cum-actress-cum-pop-star phenomenon who was great for gossip columnists as she was liable to beat up whoever she was with. Nicknamed Pale Grace because she promoted herself as a white Grace Jones, she was as frightening a potential date as Lucrezia Borgia with PMS. She was also so thick that she'd once been quoted in a phone interview saying she preferred condoms to The Pill when asked whether she believed in the immaculate conception.

'Wilco,' Gabby giggled.

'What?' Topaz curled her lips even more.

'I said "wilco" – it means, I will.'

Topaz raised her eyes to the tiny, precision-accurate spotlights which Piers had dotted at very regular intervals across the acres of high mezzanine ceiling. The English sometimes totally floored her with their daft little vernacular abbreviations – telly, pressy, comfy, honey-bunny wunny. And, of them all, Gabby appeared to have taken a degree, a masters, a PhD and several evening classes in dividing two nations by a common language.

'Bye bye then, Tops.' Gabby was still mid-gush. Even her name was abbreviated with a 'y'. Topaz wondered if she closed her desky when she finished worky, then caught the tubey, visited the shoppies and then troggied back to her housey in Greenwich.

'Bysey wysey, Gabby baby,' she said sweetly, and bashed the phone's off button so violently that it got stuck.

Fliss spent all of Monday in Camden Lock with Stan, who had agreed to dig out his box brownie and take some snaps of her sculptures to add to her portfolio. As a result of a very flattering piece in the *Evening Standard*'s Rising Star section, she had the slimmest chance of securing one of the best commercial venues for sculpture, The Gillam Gallery, for her autumn exhibition and was due to meet its director next week to show off her work in progress. The only problem was that work was currently progressing at the speed of a dead snail that's been superglued to a patio.

Stan, grumpy, jealous and hungover, was at his most blunt, assuming his surly pastiche-Cockney drawl to irritate her.

'There's nuffink much here, is there, girl?' he grumbled, lifting up the odd piece of damp hessian to reveal another untouched lump of clay. 'I mean, we've hardly seen you in here for weeks. Been finking of offering your space out to tender. Thought you'd snuffed it or summink.'

'I've been frigging busy.' Fliss guiltily poked around in her cupboard for a white background cloth. 'I'm holding down two naffing jobs, remember, mate?' She was retaliating with the full clogs-and-pigeons Lancashire monty.

'Yeah, sure, I know you're starving,' he sneered. 'After all, that Merc must cost a bob or two in petrol. Nice motor.' He watched as she threw the contents of the cupboard over her shoulder in her search for the backcloth.

'It's Georgette's!' Fliss was feeling so tetchy with him that, under normal circumstances, she would have thumped him, something she took quite regular pleasure in doing. But today she needed him to play Lord Snowdon with her chubby creations, so merely explained yet again that Georgette had lent her the car while Honk was being mended – an undertaking which had lost her the Merc for weeks on end.

'Daft cow must be bloody batty.' Stan shrugged thoughtfully and located his bottle of vodka which he unscrewed whilst watching Fliss flap around with yards of muslin, her red hair escaping in corkscrews like the spewing contents of a zapped android's innards.

Scattered around her were various items covered in clay dust which she kept in the studio. Her smoking gear – an antique Middle Eastern bong and Zippo lighter – her ancient Walkman which chewed up more tapes than an MoD scrambler, several eighties Gothic tapes and dozens of slim paperback novels skirted her feet.

Stan stooped down and picked up a book. Scratching clay off the spine, wet sand hair falling into his eyes, he scoffed in astonishment. Picking another from the floor, he started to cackle.

'You still read this crap?' He looked up at her in amazement.

Taking in what he was clutching, Fliss turned pink and then thrust out her chin rebelliously. A lie was on the tip of her tongue, but she guessed Stan wouldn't hack it; he was the only person she lost eye contact with when she lied.

'So what if I do?'

'I mean, Mills and Boon?' He made the two words sound like 'Brady and Hindley'. Two blond eyebrows were tying themselves in Boy Scouts' advanced exam knots in the centre of his forehead. 'And Red Rose is even more slushy, isn't it?' He held out the second book, gazing at its cover. 'I mean, who, when she's at home, is Henrietta Holt? A twenty-stone housewife from Walsall, I'll bet, desperate to make a fast buck. *Three Little Words* – don't tell me! – fucking awful tripe.'

'I like them.' Fliss turned back to the muslin, her face burning. 'They're better than you think – funny, romantic, happy, escapist; like watching a dead good soap. Borrow one if you like. Might learn something.'

'Have to learn to read adverbiage first.' Stan tossed the book away with a very superior flick of his long, thin wrist.

'You can always trace the words with your fingers till you pick up speed.'

Stan watched her sulkily as she flapped out the muslin like a nurse with a sheet, and then started folding it up to hide the stains and fag burns. He leaned back against a long trestle mixing table and swigged his vodka with narrowed eyes.

'You chucked him, then?' he asked suddenly.

'Who?' Fliss feigned calm fascination with a tea stain.

'The pin-head who wears his old school scarf out clubbing and thinks getting stoned's somethink to do with corporal punishment.'

'If you're referring to Iain, then – er – we've reached an amicable agreement.'

'You haven't dumped him,' Stan sighed.

'Well, not exactly.' Fliss swallowed uncomfortably. 'We're just moving more towards an open relationship, that's all.'

Stan whistled, and then grinned disbelievingly. 'You? In an open relationship? Ker-ist! I thought I'd see Babs Cartland in a clinch with Roy Chubby Brown first. You're joking, arencha?'

Fliss smiled weakly, and she hoped enigmatically, back.

She was currently facing up to a very embarrassing predicament. Having told everyone from Phoebe, to Stan, to Georgette, the Bar Barella boys and her own mother that she was desperate to dump dull Iain, she was starting to fancy him again. In fact, after an ecstatic weekend bonking, drinking, walking, eating and bonking again in the Lakes, she fancied him rotten and developed a disturbingly fizzy pelvis every time she thought about him.

The only problem was that Iain was now such a big joke amongst her friends that she was loath to tell them of her weekend-by-the-sea change. Instead she was resorting to her favoured escape tactic of lying through her teeth.

'Ask him round to dinner at my flat next week, if you want,'

Stan suddenly offered. 'Bring Phoebes, too – and her mate Saskia, if you like, seeing as she's part of the package. I might find a mate to set her up wiv.'

Fliss stared at him in stupefaction for a moment, torn between expressing horror at the potential humiliation of such an encounter, or at the more pressing threat of Stan's culinary expertise – a minefield of possible encounters with copious quantities of toilet roll, Andrews salts and cramps.

'You're – er – going to cook us a meal then?' she asked in a croaking whisper of fear.

'Yeah, I fought I might.'

'Ker-ist.' Fliss grinned at him. 'I can't – er – wait. But I'll only come on condition that you're nice to Iain.'

'Sure.' Stan shrugged.

Fliss didn't like the evil little glint in his narrowed grey eyes.

Clicking the red door behind her and heading for the lift, Saskia clenched her eyes tightly shut for a split second of rare delight before impatiently elbowing her way through the sliding silver doors.

Georgette Gregory was, she reflected, simply divine. She had practically offered Saskia a job on the phone and had only really called her into the office, Saskia suspected, to get the gossip which Phoebe had already – slightly disloyally, Saskia mused – hinted at.

Saskia usually hated telling people about Felix, but Georgette was different. Saskia had noticed from the moment she first spoke to her; Georgette had just the right mix of sympathy and screamingly funny come-backs to make a listener of the rare sort that cheers one up.

'The little sod sounds like he needs putting over a knee and smacking thoroughly,' she'd gasped.

Saskia had shaken her head with a sad laugh. 'No, he'd enjoy that.'

'What about being strapped into leather-weave sandals and corduroy trousers and being made to go on a New Man self-improvement birthing weekend in Wales?'

Saskia's mouth had curled into a rare smile. 'Now that's more like it.'

'Can you type?' Georgette had suddenly asked.

Saskia had picked up on Georgette's tendency to flit from topic to topic like a television channel-hopper. Thankfully, she found it more amusing than irritating.

'Not really,' she confessed, 'just two-fingered with lashings of Tippex.'

'Good – then you'll produce letters just like mine, so none of my grumpy old regulars will cotton on to the fact that I'm not writing to them personally. Knightsbridge housewives can be frightful old bags about dealing with just their "dear chum" Georgette. Stupid cows! If they weren't paying me exorbitant amounts to circulate the canapés, I'd piss in their soup. So do you ever see Felix now? Have you got your own back?'

'Um.' Saskia had wavered for a moment and taken the plunge, explaining the whole Phoebe revenge plan.

'Oh, how utterly wonderful,' Georgette had breathed excitedly afterwards.

Now Saskia felt totally purged and far more confident in her plan.

In her handbag, she had three weeks' worth of slimming tablets prescribed by a Harley Street friend of Portia's. Somehow, she didn't think she'd need them any more.

Georgette pressed the Memory #2 key on her phone.

'Susie Middleton, hello.'

'Susie, darling, it's me.'

'Goggy!'

'Please don't call me that, darling. I'm an ancient crone these days and far too regal.' Georgette rammed her tongue in her cheek.

'What d'you want, wicked step-mother?' Susie laughed delightedly. 'You haven't called me in ages, you old bag. How are you?'

'Better for a face-peel and several weeks without your father in a girls-only health spa,' Georgette confessed happily.

'Oh, God,' Susie sighed. 'Who is it now?'

'His secretary,' Georgette admitted with an apologetic intake of breath.

'Not again?' Susie gasped, disbelievingly.

'Give him credit, darling – he's had at least two actresses, an air hostess and a countess-by-marriage in between. Even David Mellor isn't that original.'

'Does she look like Mummy too?' Susie's other line was ringing, but she quickly silenced it.

''Fraid so, darling. Don't they all? Except me.'

'Oh, poor Goggy, are you terribly upset?'

'No – no, darling. I mean, yes, admittedly I want to strangle the big, stupid rogue more than the usual once a day, but that isn't why I called. In fact, I'm a vindictive old bitch for blurting. I called for quite another reason. You know that embarrassingly slim-line gold thing he gave me for my birthday?'

'The Merc?' Susie laughed.

'Hairdresser's car, yes. And he knows how much I hate driving. Well, listen to this – I mean, I planned it for weeks before doing it.'

'Not one of your tests, Goggy?'

'Yup. I gave the gold monster to my daft, half-there secretary to look after. Told her she could – hang on, my other line's flashing. There! Lost in the switchboard – told her she could run me around in it and then keep it overnight in whatever revolting part of London she lives – Kentish Town or Muswell Hill or somewhere awful like that.'

'Goggy!'

'I know, darling, but I'm knocking on, so I can be as bloody snobbish as I like and blame it on reading too much Nancy Mitford in my youth.'

'You only read Nancy Mitford now.'

'Do you want me to carry on with this particular recollection, or do you want me to tell you why I really called?' Georgette muttered impatiently. 'Because I'm knocking on and I might forget both if you keep diverting me.'

'Carry on with the story.' Susie was diverting another in-coming call. 'You gave the Merc – I simply cannot *believe* you would have the nerve to do this, Goggy – you gave the Merc to your secretary to maintain and – '

'And then I casually mentioned it to your father over his first Macallan of the day. Last Thursday morning, I think it was. About ten to eight.'

'You didn't? What did he say?'

'"Good idea, dear. I'll be going to the club again tomorrow night. Don't wait up."'

'Oh, God, he is smitten,' Susie groaned.

'Don't worry, darling – I've met her. Brain like a starving Somalian's rice-bowl.'

Susie winced, diverting yet another call. 'So why did you call, Goggy darling?'

'Ah – yes. Is it my imagination, or do you talk about gorgeous Jocelyn Sylvian rather too often?'

'I know him, yes.' Susie was instantly cagey.

'Well, forgive me if this is a bit of a family saga, but his son – '

'Felix?'

'That's the one – you represent him, don't you, darling? And keep a protective eye on him for Pa Sylvian if I'm not mistaken. Well, Felix and Tony Seaton's daughter – '

'Goggy, I know all this,' Susie sighed. 'Felix was engaged to Saskia, and it all fell through at the very last minute – largely due to Felix going as ballistic on Saskia as his father went on me.'

'Ah.' Georgette played out her pause. 'But you don't know what Saskia is planning now.'

'Saskia? What?'

'Have you heard of a Phoebe Fredericks?'

'Name's vaguely familiar. Should I have?'

'You soon will. Within a couple of weeks, Felix will be talking about no one else. Listen, I've just done something rather reckless which I hope is going to prove a huge source of insider gossip to you, darling . . .'

The moment Felix wandered in the door, Dylan started going through the long-winded file-closing routine that precursed switching off his computer.

''Lo.' Felix grabbed a nectarine out of the bowl of fruit that Dylan used to gnaw during writer's block in order to cut down on the amount he smoked.

Felix, trying to read over his friend's shoulder, was foiled as the screen blinked with static and then went blank.

'Why d'you always do that?' he wailed in frustration. 'You never let me read a bloody word you've written.'

'Oh, I'm sure you'd find it far too trite and formula for your tastes,' Dylan grinned amiably.

'Rubbish. I'll read anything, you know that.' Felix followed him through to the sitting room and flopped on the sofa, his nectarine-juiced hand already reaching for the television re-mote. 'I don't think you write at all.'

'Oh, no?'

'No,' Felix flipped on Blockbusters. 'I think you pretend you're an aspiring writer as a sort of seduction accessory; like wearing glasses. You think it makes you appear to have more depth.'

'Hasn't worked very well, then, has it?' Dylan laughed, rubbing his shaggy brown hair so that it stood up on end.

'You should try printing the thing out and reading it aloud at parties. How long is it? Must be massive, you've been working on it for years.'

'Well, I do a lot of re-writing,' Dylan hedged.

What Felix didn't know, he thought, was that his flat-mate was already a published author, with several titles to his nom de plume. And, if his success carried on at the same rate, Dylan had calculated that in less than six months, he could give up bar management altogether.

19

By Wednesday, Phoebe had done more last-minute crib-sheet revision than she'd ever attempted for GCSEs, A levels or her finals. She was also far, far more frightened.

A night working at Bar Barella on Tuesday bolstered her confidence somewhat. The boys were wildly flattering about the new haircut and Tom, rolling up late with lots of cheek-kissing cronies from his show, had whooped, slapped his hands together in mock-prayer and fallen very hammily to his knees.

'Lord be thanked!' he howled in a Southern US drawl. 'Your child, Phoebe Fredericks, didn't have sex today, your Holy Snow-white Beardedness. May you keep her pure and babe-like through sordid temptation and sweaty, snoggy moments of lasciviousness.'

That night, Phoebe glowed with incredulous joy as tenners were handed over to pay for drinks complete with scribbled phone-numbers, and she was cornered again and again to be asked about the state of her social life over the next week.

Ironic then, she countered, that she couldn't reach the only person she really wanted to see this week. Dan was always 'in court' or 'in a meeting' when she called, and there was no question of trying him at home in case Mitzi answered, torturing Phoebe's guilty, black-spotted soul with a jolly, honking 'Hullo'.

Added to this, Saskia wasn't helping much. Her mood swings were more unpredictable than a method actor understudying the entire cast of *Hamlet*, and her revenge tragedy was rapidly turning into a French farce. Buoyed up by Georgette's job offer and avenger's enthusiasm, she momentarily lifted from her emotional swamp when she arrived at the flat on Wednesday morning to select an outfit for Phoebe's first night, and endeavour to find her a 'walker' to arrive with.

'Get your kit off,' she giggled as she bustled in and started attacking all the suit carriers. 'But pour me a vast glass of something intoxicating first.'

To begin with, she threw clothes at Phoebe and made her meander across the sitting room as she made up a mock-fifties fashion show spiel.

'And here we see Phoebe, wearing a floor-length oyster silk slash-sided robe of exquisite tailoring. To complement this, she has on unmatching wrinkled bed socks and the more discerning amongst you will spot that those toes poking out are painted with a delightful salmon pink from a late-eighties Rimmel nail polish collection, slightly chipped for the *très à la mode* distressed look.'

But within half an hour of watching Phoebe parade around in a variety of outfits, she plunged back into a mood so black that she suddenly grabbed the phone and dialled Felix's number. Disguising her voice, she left a long, screaming, Banshee wail on his mobile phone answering service before slamming the receiver down and running off to sob in Phoebe's bathroom for over an hour, refusing to unlock the door.

At which point Fliss walked in and politely enquired whether the boiler was playing up again.

'Sometimes when you run a bath, the thing sounds like a soul in torment,' she moaned, throwing down several bags of Waitrose shopping.

'That *is* a soul in torment,' Phoebe explained, starting to pick through the bags hopefully. 'Are we having another party?'

'Er – no.' Fliss batted Phoebe's fingers away. 'I'm just having a mate round for dinner tonight, that's all – while you're at the party, like.'

'Who?' Phoebe watched a poached salmon terrine and a vast tub of ice-cream being rammed guiltily into the fridge. 'A man?'

'No, no.' Fliss looked shifty. 'Just Claudia.'

'Hmmm.' Phoebe nicked one of the dozens of ripe cherries from a paper bag and went back to try and deal with Saskia.

'Oh, Phoebe – Stan'll go with you tonight,' Fliss called over her shoulder, trying to hide two bottles of excellent Chablis in the rear of the fridge. 'I saw him earlier at the studio and he reckoned it'll be fun. Tell Saskia to give him a call if she still needs someone – oh, and we're invited to dinner at his place on Friday. Saskia too.'

'Stan's cooking?' Phoebe balked.

Fliss grinned, 'Exactly. But I thought ahead. Look.'

Digging into a Waitrose bag, she extracted a family-sized pack of Rennies and a jar of bile beans and waggled them triumphantly.

When Phoebe related the news through the bathroom door, Saskia deigned to come out, head hanging, and muttered a muted apology before handing Phoebe a bottle of nail varnish remover and scuttling into Phoebe's bedroom to call Stan in private. Ten minutes later, strangely heady, she scuttled out and demanded that they re-start the fashion show.

Which was why Phoebe found herself staring at a stranger in Fliss's full-length mirror on Wednesday evening. Gaping back was a tall, slender, raven-haired raver with purple pansy-like eyes. Swathed in a crotch-length white bias-cut silk dress, she bore no resemblance to the headscarfed Swedish weirdo Felix had hit upon a few days earlier. The only similarity was a gnawed-at pink mouth, hunched shoulders holding up bootlace straps and knees which were knocking together so violently that they could have started a Boy Scout's camp fire. In just a few days, Saskia had re-painted her. It was an entirely temporary, skin-deep beauty, but Phoebe still caught her breath.

Over her bare shoulder, Stan was also admiring the overall effect – his, not hers.

'These cacks are well smart.' He rebuckled his belt and hip-nudged Phoebe out of the way so that he could get a view of his rear. 'Where d'you get them, Saskia?'

'They're Iain's.' Fliss was perching awkwardly on her bed, watching the proceedings. 'His one and only pair of Armanis, so if you stain them, mate, I'm frigging dead.'

'It must be love.' Stan cocked a sarcastic sandy eyebrow at his reflection, seemingly talking to himself. 'Should I put my hair in a pony tail, d'you reckon?'

'NO!' came the gasp from Saskia, Phoebe and Fliss in unison.

'I don't know.' Milly, lounging against an off-white self-assembly B & Q vanity unit, looked quite keen on the idea. 'Show off your beautiful bone structure. What d'you reckon, Goat?'

From their different parts of the room, Goat and Phoebe grunted. Phoebe was slightly irked – okay, totally miffed, she privately admitted – that Stan hadn't so much as passed comment on her outfit. She might not fancy him any more – found the accent and the big honk a decided turn-off, in fact – but no one likes an ex rolling up and failing to clock the sexiest look one's ever donned. Particularly when one's sister is positively salivating at said ex's every move and complimenting him right down to his visible nose hair. Phoebe had taken great pains to cultivate Stan as a friend since her return – on which, she recalled moodily, he had called her up for a date – but right now she felt like cultivating him and her sister as big-nosed wax effigies.

'I don't know why you turned up, Mill,' she grumbled, teetering on unfamiliar and tight shoes towards the kitchen to top up her angostura bitters and tonic to which, since it was currently very in vogue, she was trying to acclimatise herself. 'I feel like I'm under a microscope with everyone gawping.'

Milly and Goat – loving a spectacle – had rolled up with two litres of Merrydown and their own unique blend of fashion advice between swigs and giggles. Clapping eyes on Phoebe's metamorphosed state, Goat had gone strangely silent and had, for the first time in known history, parted his matted white-blond fringe to get a better look. Underneath, his eyes were strangely disappointing. Phoebe had expected narrowed pale mad ones to match the sharpened teeth and scrawny, kick-boxer's body. Instead they were huge and blue, kind as a Friesian cow's and totally devoid of intelligence.

Since arriving, Milly had done nothing but scoff at the way Phoebe looked. 'I've seen hair like that before. Where was it? Something on daytime TV, I think – got it! It was Monkee, d'you remember?' She only paused from pouting derision to flirt with Stan whom she clearly thought far superior in the looks ranks to her Japanese warrior sister.

'You're bound to be picked up,' she told him in her deepest, huskiest growl. 'Might even get spotted and propelled to stardom.'

'Sure.' He fingered the collar of his pin-cord silk shirt and grimaced at his reflection. His hair, freshly washed for once, gleamed in long, tawny waves like a sixties pop idol. 'The only place I reckon I'll get propelled tonight is the door, crashing this flash do with those dodgy invites.'

'They're not dodgy,' Saskia muttered from the corner of the room, 'I had them changed to Frances's name.'

'Who's Frances?' Stan looked nonplussed. 'I fought I was going with Phoebe?'

'You've got to call her Frances tonight.' A cigarette glowed fitfully in the dark corner. 'I explained that.' Saskia sounded ratty and impatient.

'Yeah, but I still don't understand what's going on here,' Stan sighed, rubbing his forehead and walking towards her. 'I mean, I know Phoebes is going there done up like a lapdog's dinner to pretend to be someone else, but I fought . . .'

'It's complicated,' Saskia snapped and sidled out of the room.

Stan turned back to the others, raising his eyes to the polystyrene-tiled ceiling.

It was the first time he'd seen Saskia since their brief fling the year before, and he'd been really looking forward to it. True, she looked a bit of a mess, which Fliss had already warned him to expect. And, yes, she looked more death-like than even Stan – whose imagination enjoyed skirting around the more extreme, seedy and unappetising elements of the human condition – had ever expected. What was worse, however, was that all the life, the energy and the wild-child wilfulness that first attracted him seemed to have seeped out of her, leaving only a moribund, cowering husk. She hadn't looked him in the eye once since he'd arrived, even when she'd muttered a compliment about the sexy final effect of his preparations. Stan felt deflated and down as a result. He wanted to go and get hammered with his mates at the ICA tonight as he'd originally planned, not accompany Phoebe to some poncey media do like a stick with a cocked arm.

'She's nervous,' Fliss explained feebly.

'Why?' Stan moaned. 'It's not as if she's even coming tonight. I haven't a fucking clue what's going on here. Is she trying to get Phoebe into acting or summink?'

Three loyally blank, secretive faces stared silently back at him. Well, two faces and a nose poking out of a large, shaggy white hairdo into which a cider bottle neck was inserted at regular intervals.

'Suit yourselves.' He shrugged and wandered off to the loo.

20

The Nero Club's smoky windows, discreet chrome sign and huge, stern, suited commissionaires – bouncers to non-members – faced out on to the heart of Soho where girly peep shows were shoulder-to-shoulder with haute trash fashion shops, gay bars, and some of the trendiest, most exclusive and most over-priced clubs in mediaville. Of them all, The Nero Club had a reputation for being so selective and so over-priced that it was practically a pastiche of others around it, private drinking holes which were the school common rooms of the fickle, refuse-to-grow-up gossip-column fodder who populated them. The Nero Club was a catch-phrase for cynics who joked about celebspotting, designer-labelling and wannabe sycophancy in the media. That didn't stop people weeping when they were black-balled from its cliquey membership list, bribing associates who were members to sign them in, and bragging about their attendance for weeks afterwards. The Nero Club was so exclusive, it made Bar Barella seem like McDonald's.

'We'll never fucking get in,' Stan hissed to Phoebe, as he swung Georgette's Merc up on to a nearby pavement and cut the engine.

'Won't we be clamped here?' She flipped down the visor to check her lipstick.

'Not in the time it takes us to be turned away from the door, we won't,' Stan muttered, hopping out. He was incredibly nervous because Saskia had begged him to drive even though he was disqualified. Consequently he had jumped every red light and taken several one-way streets the wrong way.

As Phoebe waited for him to whisk around the boot and open the passenger door for her, she mentally ran through her elegant exit routine – one hand out to take his, knees together, swivel on the seat and rise up in one smooth, fluid movement to pose for the cameras.

A minute or so later, Stan banged irritably on the driver's window and pressed his nose against it.

'What's keeping you, girl?' he called, steaming the glass up then turning to redo his hair in the wing mirror.

Phoebe squinted out of the windscreen and noticed that the two Nero Club doormen – both of whom looked as though they could lift the combined weight of the cast of La Bohème, starring Pavarotti – were watching them with mild, retarded interest.

Determined not to attract attention, Phoebe slipped from the car as lithely as possible and trotted around to Stan. Grabbing him by the hand – slightly clammy, she noted – she dragged him towards the imposing duo and the smoked glass swing door, said to be harder to pass than a gallstone.

Several paparazzi lurking nearby eyed Phoebe with vague interest, but didn't adjust their apertures in her honour, despite Stan's rather trite attempt to shield their faces as he rushed her past.

'Steady,' Phoebe hissed into his ear as they hurtled towards the swing doors, 'these shoes go airborne at five miles an hour.' The last thing she wanted was to appear on the other side of those hallowed doors in a horizontal position, several inches above the ground as she flew into The Nero Club and straight on to Felix's loafers.

But she needn't have worried, for once they had passed through the doors – remarkably easily, with a twitch of the invite from a quaking Stan – they found themselves in a large, deserted reception area with so much marble that a chisel-wielding fifteenth-century sculptor would have demanded squatters' rights and got cracking.

Stan, however – a deconstructionalist from the Goldsmith's school of abstruse conceptualism – clocked it with a withering shudder.

'Looks like a fucking mausoleum in here, girl,' he muttered, peering over a receptionist's desk so high that interviewees for a prospective post there would have to be over six foot or very good at balancing on boxes; even the little electric spot-light sconces were set so high it would take a crane to change a lightbulb.

Phoebe, listening to a low burble and a rhythmic thumping from yet more smoked glass doors on the left, ignored him and wandered closer.

'It must be through here.' She nodded towards her own reflection in the doors. 'We'd better go through.'

Stan dragged his eyes away from the guest-list, which lay unattended on the desk and read like the cast from a Ken Branagh spectacular.

Phoebe swallowed, suddenly terrified and in desperate need of reassurance. 'Er – do I look all right?'

She winced at herself. Why dig now for that compliment that had eluded her earlier? Stan, given his predisposition for obdurate sarcasm, would almost certainly slam her down and wreck her confidence at the vital moment.

But, quite uncharacteristically, he up-and-downed her for a full ten seconds with appreciative pale grey eyes before letting out a low whistle and nodding until his hair swept across his face like a theatre's velvet drapes.

'You'll do,' he said bluntly.

'Christ, we could have flashed a bus pass and got in.'

'Wait for the long arm of the doorman,' Stan muttered darkly. 'Any second now, we'll feel a walking stick handle around our snowy-whites and get dragged out like a duff act in a talent contest.'

As he followed Phoebe through a party crowd so loud, cackling and resonant that he expected his ears to be pierced from lobe to tip like a King's Road punk, he vaguely took in a small host of familiar faces eyeing each other jealously, a far larger host of unfamiliar faces staring at him in the hope that *he* was a familiar face, and a party host gawping at him in case he was a gate-crasher. 'Spot on, mate!' he wanted to yell. But, by and large, he remained preoccupied – as he had been since about six o'clock that evening – with stealing covert glances at Phoebe's rear view.

When he'd dated her, Stan recalled, she had been something of an enigma, so fiercely independent that the thrill-of-the-chase had turned into the thrill of the I-need-my-own-space; yet she had snatched his calls on the first ring, stressed his name lovingly – if wrongly – all the time ('Dan' had been an obvious and regular slip) and burst into angry tears twice when he'd said – in vino veritas – that she deserved far better than him. Then he had sensed a girl who waited hopefully by the phone, and was disappointed when it was him calling. Stan was somewhat in awe of Phoebe – totally in awe tonight, in fact – but found her thoroughly over-the-top at the same time. While she was in New Zealand, he'd discovered that she'd had a long fling with an older, married lawyer – whom Fliss and now he referred to pleasurably as The Corps – and had become even more intimidated by her.

As Phoebe wound her way towards the bar with admirable confidence, through a throng of appreciative sideways, backwards and downwards glances and whispering about her identity, he was so busy watching two perfectly tanned buttocks dipping in and out of a white silk hem with no apparent knicker-support, that he didn't notice the suspicious host closing fast.

Just as he was about to hit upon a convenient bowl of lime-marinated pistachios while Phoebe ordered a brace of doubles, Stan's Armani shoulder was enclosed in a very tight grip.

'Hi – I'm Malcolm,' gushed an oozingly camp, speed-enhanced voice.

'I know,' Stan managed to murmur, trying unsuccessfully to lose the shoulder-grip. Getting eye contact was even harder as the host's beady gaze was about a foot lower than his and buried beneath a Nicky Clarke thatch of peppery hair.

Malcolm twitched a few facial muscles in what was obviously an attempt at a smile and eyed Stan's lengthy physique with a window-shopper's practised once-over. 'And you're . . .'

'I'm with her!'

Losing his cool totally under the gaze of such an overt seeker of young flesh, Stan jabbed a paint-stained thumb at Phoebe and then groped in his borrowed pocket to retrieve the named invite, which he thrust under Malcolm's nose so hastily it practically wedged itself up one nostril like a coke-sniffer's fifty-pound note.

'Ah.' Malcolm smiled benignly and batted the invitation away, gliding his omnipotent gaze Phoebewards. 'I see.' The comment was loaded with interest.

Stan gulped, suddenly realising that he'd forgotten Phoebe's assumed name.

But Malcolm merely nodded thoughtfully and placed an appreciative finger on a smiling mouth as he watched Phoebe for a few moments before drifting away to welcome Mariella Frostrup and a couple of alternative comedians.

Sagging back against a trellis with relief, Stan eyed the room nervously, watching a slight disturbance that was being kicked up in a far corner. Hemmed in by the padded linen shoulders of a crowd of amused onlookers, journos and photographers, a couple appeared to be having a full dress row. A woman whom Stan couldn't see, but guessed to be American from the shrieking insults seeping out of the muffled, peopled sound-proofing, was screaming self-righteously at someone she claimed was a 'perverted, low-down, shrink-dick, toupee-wearing, bony-arsed louse'.

Stan could only see the top of the louse's head, and had to disagree with the toupee bit – this man was thinning all right, he noted, but there was no apparent fun-fur covering his receding widow's peak, just a small crocheted cap of the sort favoured by eighties one-hit-wonder pop stars who spent all their money on Gaultier, Greenpeace donations and a house in Tuscany, and having lost their riches, worked for environmental causes and lived in Clapham.

Trying to recall this man's hit, Stan suddenly remembered where he'd seen him before. This time last year, on one of their first dates, Stan and Phoebe had caught his very blue, very drunken stand-up act at a comedy benefit evening, and had been chatted up by him in the bar afterwards. He'd offered them dinner at The Ivy if they'd both have sex with him – simultaneously and, Stan suspected, during the course of the meal; which course hardly mattered as they'd turned him down flat.

Frank Grogan, Stan remembered. He'd finally thrown up in Phoebe's handbag and been carried off to his dressing room by two barmen.

Right now he looked to be in imminent danger of suffering a similar fate, although the handbag was attached to another woman. The unknown source of the insults was wielding a padded Chanel sak-on-a-chain which was sporadically flying up and down to be followed a split second later by a loud howl as it made contact with varied parts of Frank's anatomy.

As Phoebe weaved back from the bar carrying two glasses and scanning the room with her eyes, Stan nodded in the direction of the commotion.

'Recognise him?'

She jumped in fright and just missed dousing her white dress as she swung around to look. Her beautifully painted, wide-eyed face seemed to fill out with relief as she took in Frank's handbag dodging antics.

'Oh, yes, the vomit comic. He seems to be taking all the punch-lines tonight,' she sighed, setting her drink to one side without even sipping it, and glancing nervously towards the door again.

Saskia's plan that she arrive so late she'd make a stunning entrance had been marred by one slight oversight, she reflected sourly. Saskia had failed to take into consideration that a press launch party like this really only consisted of grand entrances and exits; the focus was almost entirely concentrated around the swings of the door, and with such a bunch of publicityseekers, the door was swinging open with increasingly loud creaks and shrieks the later it got. The only chic time to turn up was first thing the next morning. In celebrity terms, she and Stan were the equivalent of the party guest who arrives clutching a bottle of Blue Nun and a packet of twiglets while their hosts are still in the bath. Felix, she reflected, was almost certainly still in the bath, probably soaping between La Belle Delauney's crimson-painted toes, breaking off occasionally to sip freezer-chilled vodka.

Stan had returned to gazing at the side-show, which had abated enough for the snappers to get bored and drift towards the door-swinging action again. But Stan was no longer taking in the direct hits; as the spectators moved aside, he started gaping at the punch-thrower herself.

It was Topaz Fox and, far from having a full-dress fight, she appeared to have been having a near-nude one. She was wearing the slinkiest dress he had ever seen, although dress was perhaps an over-statement for the five or six small triangles of metallic-rust cloth and the criss-crossing lengths of curtain cord which were wrapped around her lithe, creamy torso and hips.

'That,' he cleared his throat emotionally, 'is a better-looking bird than Elizabeth Siddall.' His voice died away into a speech-less croak.

Hearing a compliment which for Stan was the equivalent of the Pope demoting God to second favourite, Phoebe took a look.

'Christ!' she muttered, taking in an overall effect only slightly less dramatic than the before and after shots of Michael Jackson's plastic surgery.

The androgynous kid whom Phoebe had seen slouching in men's underpants and pouting out of a bill board a few weeks earlier wasn't the same girl as the one here tonight. At least, Phoebe was having trouble getting her head around the fact that it *was* the same girl. She thought she herself had undergone a pretty radical re-invention, but compared to this chameleon amongst babes, she'd done little more than get a haircut and slap on a bit of eyeliner.

The white-blonde hair was slicked back into a Roman plait so tightly that Topaz's vast amber eyes were narrowed like a cat's under the pressure, and her slanting Slavic cheekbones jutted out of her face like two ping-pong balls. The famous pouting lips looked as though they'd just been stung by a bee-swarm and the long, long body was propped up on heels so high that a Yorkshire terrier could have walked beneath them with several inches clearance.

Most extraordinary of all, however, was The Dress. At her most critical and jealous, Phoebe decided it was something of a cross between a bikini and a hammock. But it was nonetheless stunning. Anyone with an ounce of fat on them would be left looking like a trussed beef joint, or as though they'd just been the victim of a four-hour bondage session that went wrong, but on Topaz, with her whip-crack body and elongated lines, it looked as though it had been painted on.

'She looks okay,' Phoebe conceded grumpily.

'Now that,' said Stan, groping with difficulty for the art of speech, 'is major league.'

Phoebe was forced to agree, self-confidence draining rapidly away.

But, as she looked towards her escape route, a thick screen of French cigarette smoke wafted through it along with a similarly dense cloud of black hair, Amerige and minders. Flash lights were going off so thick and fast that it was as though someone had erected a strobe over the doorway. Suddenly the volume of chatter in the room seemed to crank up several notches, as did the temperature, the oxygen-consumption, and Phoebe's heart-beat.

With a slash of sulky red mouth parting on cue to show a crescent of slightly uneven white teeth which seemed to out-flash the photographers, La Belle Delauney arrived. What's more, she was wearing a black chainmail tunic which possessed only fractionally more fabric than Topaz's Versace.

The mild interest that Phoebe had been attracting transferred itself immediately to La Belle, as did most of that directed at Topaz.

Frank Grogan did a spectacularly clichéd Carry On double-take and lurched forwards to get a better look, unaware of the fact that Topaz's sak-on-a-chain was still attached to one of the tassles on his suede jacket, leaving them linked like pooch and owner. Only Stan remained loyally gazing at Topaz, his lightly stubbled jaw dropping in hypnotised wonder as he drank in the hay-net dress.

Lurking in a position where she was part-obscured by a pillar, Phoebe stared fixedly over Isabelle's shoulder, frantically trying to keep her stomach from squirming its way out of the back door as she waited for her first glimpse of Felix.

It didn't come. La Belle was with five butch minders who were prowling around their charges like starving Dobermanns who know their owner has a stash of Bonios in his pocket. But their owner wasn't La Belle; the beefy boys belonged to her companion, and when Phoebe caught a glimpse of him – dwarfed by the combined height around him despite being balanced on five inches of Cuban heel – she held her breath. For it was the very small, excessively famous, exquisitely formed pop legend whose latest triple-platinum album Phoebe had been tapping her toes to while she shaved her legs earlier.

Nick-named The Phallus of Pop because of his raunchy, overtly erotic dancetracks and his fabled trouser-fly proportions, this little man was the living, breathing embodiment of the journalist's dream meal ticket. An interview with him was harder to achieve than the Holy Grail. He might only reach up to La Belle's armpit, but in terms of publicity he was a front-page splash as opposed to her left-hand page eight filler. The Phallus was hardly ever seen out in public, and whenever he was, he was accompanied by the most beautiful women in the world – rumour had it that a well-known Greek playboy had offered him seven figures for his phone book.

The Showdown press officers were going into overdrive, delighted with this last-minute crowd-puller. One went into a frenzy of coat-taking welcome; the other went dashing straight into a dark corner where she whipped a mobile phone out of her handbag and started tapping out the numbers of all the most exclusive media clubs where invited guests would currently be sprawling on leather chairs in a self-congratulatory 'I won't turn up to another rent-a-celeb bash as long as I'm getting eight percent return on my millions' fashion. The moment they heard about His Petit Sexiness's presence, they'd dig out their invites and burn the rubber of their Lobb & Co brogues as they lurched drunkenly along to The Nero Club. The coverage in the papers and glossies would be as legendary as the time Madonna – in England for the Wembley gig of her World Tour – popped into Tramps for a quiet drink on the same night it was hosting Ross Benson's annual fancy dress knees-up. Or so the story went . . .

'Christ, I didn't even know he was in the country, did you?' a voice rumbled at the exact same time as a hand slithered up one of Phoebe's buttocks and twanged her g-string.

It was an approach that was one step up in the food chain from the schoolboy snapping the teen bra, one step down from the male white rhino clambering unceremoniously on to the back of the female white rhino once a decade. It could only be Frank Grogan.

She jumped away and looked angrily into two dissipated brown eyes so bloodshot that the corneas seemed to be osmosing into the whites.

'We've met,' he breathed, slithering the bloodshot gaze over her body with heavy-lidded absorption. It was a little like being crawled over by giant snails dipped in cod liver oil.

Unable to deny it, but not sure whether this was – as she suspected – a wildly corny line rather than a genuine desire to reminisce, she debated snapping 'Yes, you offered to have sex with my boyfriend and me, said you had some great coke in a pill box in your underpants and then threw up all over my tube pass, house keys and Filofax', but decided against it; she hated confessing she had once owned something as completely eighties as a Filofax.

Instead, she shrugged and looked back at The Phallus, who was strutting as fast as his Cuban heels would carry him towards the darkest corner of the club, flocked by his minders, the Showdown press agents, the paparazzi and what appeared to be his lawyer. He paused momentarily to up-and-down Topaz – there was no time for courtship subtlety in his multi-million dollar roadshow – gave her a smile so charming that she almost burst out of her Versace hammock, and then sashayed into his corner where he went into a huddle with his entourage.

Belle, meanwhile, headed straight for the bar. Ignoring the serried rows of champagne flutes lined up in front of her, she demanded a bottle of tequila and started lighting one Gauloise from the butt of another.

Admiring her cool tremendously – who else dumped The Phallus at the door? – Phoebe scrutinised her in wonder. She was far older than Phoebe had imagined, possibly ten or twelve years added to Felix's twenty-six. Yet her searing eyes, been-around gaze and sassy siren's sang-froid far out-stripped the shallow appeal of the rest of the young flesh on display around her. The chain mail dress was sensational – out-classing Topaz's by a mile of subtle, intermeshed fine black wire. Compared to Topaz's elongated ironing board physique, Belle was all gleaming slopes, curves and shadows. Phoebe watched the way the barman quivered in reverence before the curling red lips and stormy black gaze. To have the chutzpah to blow out Felix was ballsy enough; not to stick to The Phallus like gum in a Doc Marten sole rut was history being made. Phoebe wanted to shake her by the hand, but was too afraid of the two-inch red fingernails.

Suddenly La Belle squinted up through the smoke-screen she was generating and caught Phoebe watching her.

She shrank back slightly, so intimidated that she found she couldn't shake off the eye contact. Belle glared at her sulkily and then seemed to change her mind, smiling briefly instead. It was a smile of such sensual, oozing warmth that Phoebe found herself glowing back, suddenly buoyed and cheered. She didn't just feel she'd squeezed blood from a stone, she felt as though she'd drawn Excalibur from it as well. Shaking Frank off, she decided it was time she mingled.

Isabelle Delauney was, in fact, in a foul, black industrial

depression. She'd spent all day filming a lot of ridiculous schmaltz for the debut show, involving riding round on an open double-decker in constant drizzle wearing nothing but a basque and a mackintosh, accompanied by the most objectionable shaven-headed Scouse 'yoof' presenter she had ever encountered, and no interpreter. Then she'd been forced to indulge the unprofessional Sapporo-swigging Showdown team by recording several ten-second show trailer plugs written out for her on an idiot board in indecipherable capitals: 'Slow down for the low down with the slippery-smooth, hipply groove Showdown' had played havoc with her pidgin English. She had then returned to her hotel to find a last-minute message from Felix saying he'd been pressured into walking someone else to the party, and would arrive separately.

Knowing Felix, Belle realised that he'd left it until the last possible moment on purpose. He'd clearly never intended to take her, but was such a spoiled brat that he was deliberately trying to screw up any publicity she was jostling for her latest film, *La Grande Fumée du Sud*. When he was feeling spiteful, Felix was capable of turning milk sour in a Rumanian orphanage.

Belle had gone on to throw such a three-dimensional, threescore, three-ply-soaking tantrum that her agent had pulled the longest string amongst her latest group of beaux, and enlisted the help of The Phallus of Pop himself.

Languishing in Paris and playing a few underground gigs in between conducting a very heated love affair with a fresh-from-the-cradle French starlet, he had been summoned across the Channel as a one-knight-stand in shining lurex armour. His arrival with Belle had been purely for the cameras and, far from dumping him at the door, she had merely released him from his duties for a couple of hours. They had once luxuriated in a very short, high octane, low morals liaison which had thankfully escaped the press's attention, and which meant he still held her in high enough esteem to do this favour.

'Hello, sexy lady,' crooned a slurred voice as a hand slithered up one buttock and groped for a g-string. There wasn't one. The hand groped around some more just to check, grazing one buttock with a cheap pinky ring as it delved further.

'*Va t'en, muzzerfuckeur!*' Belle snapped, grabbing her tequila bottle and smoothly crowning the groper as she turned to a beckoning Showdown producer who'd rustled her up a group of sponsors to woo.

Unnoticed by the shrieking, babbling throng, Frank Grogan slithered on to a bar stool, rubbed his receding hairline and slumped against the bar, his crocheted hat landing neatly in a bowl of lime-soaked pistachios.

Phoebe had been cornered by Malcolm, the show's executive producer and prowling party host.

A very dapper little man who would have looked like an accountant were it not for the ageing media hippy accessories of side-burns and thatched peppery hair curling over the collar, he was also highly inquisitive in an off-hand, smile-flashing way. He had sidled up to Phoebe with a lot of cuff-pulling and room-scanning, introduced himself in the manner of the professional social engineer, alternated between burrowing eye-contact and glances over her shoulder, and then proceeded to grill her like Lady Bracknell interviewing a maid.

Having passed herself off vaguely as a 'freelance feature writer', Phoebe was now having some difficulty keeping the vagueness going.

'So who have you worked for recently?' Malcolm twinkled.

'Er – yes,' she gulped. 'Well, I've been in New Zealand for a year, working on projects out there, but my portfolio's doing the rounds right now. Should be with *The Sunday Times* today.'

Did feature writers have portfolios? she wondered. And why had she added the bit about *The Sunday Times*? Fliss, the queen of liars, had emphatically told her to keep any fictitious biographical stuff very brief, simple and ambiguous.

'I'd like to have a look at it,' Malcolm murmured, helping himself to a lengthy peep at Phoebe's cleavage which required him to hoick himself up on to tip-toes and look very hard indeed.

'You what?' she yelped, not used to such brazenness.

'Your portfolio,' Malcolm laughed, looking up merrily. 'Who's got it at Wapping? Mike Friel?'

'Er – I can't remember off-hand.' Phoebe tried to shrug casually, but her shoulders were already welded to her ears with tension.

'Well, I'll call him in the morning and get him to bike it to my office. Here's my card – call me. Do you have one of yours with you?'

Phoebe swallowed, aware that her eyelids had stretched to such nervous limits that she was going unflatteringly cross-eyed.

'A card?' she mumbled stupidly. 'Er, no – I mean, they're at home. In my Filofax.' She winced.

'No problem.' Malcolm whipped a pen out of his inside pocket – conspicuously flashing the YSL label sewed to his suit lining – and flicked up the nib. 'Fire away.'

Phoebe repeated her number in a monotone, in such a state of nerves that she quite forgot to do her usual trick of changing the last digit.

'And that's your home number, right?' Malcolm's eyes were burrowing again.

Thankfully at that moment the commotion at the door went back into overdrive as Felix arrived with Fanii Hubert.

Phoebe allowed herself a split-second to take in the height, the gleam of blond hair, the staggering faces and absurdly scruffy outfits of both new arrivals before backing away from Malcolm, smiling apologetically and crossing the room according to plan, straight towards Felix, who had been trapped by the revolting Scouse presenter for a word-to-camera. Beside him, Fanii was slouching broodily against a pillar, all sulky, lynx-eyed liability in a belligerently ripped denim crotch-skirt and child-size lollipop t-shirt.

Trying not to bite her lip, Phoebe walked very slowly and very deliberately towards them, as nervous as a model on her first haute couture catwalk, only just stopping herself from closing her eyes and counting out her measured, leisurely steps one . . . two . . . one . . . two . . .

As she drew level with the little group at the door, she looked straight ahead and passed within inches of Felix's nose, the corners of her eyes watering madly as she strained to catch any reaction. Then, realising she could watch the action in a smoky mirror opposite, she saw that Felix was indeed looking across at her, his beautiful face totally inexpressive. But instead of glancing away again, he carried on looking, ignoring the waggling microphone in front of him.

Bingo! Phoebe almost cartwheeled with relief. Contact made as per instructions.

Not allowing her face to flicker, she did exactly as she'd been told and turned as though drawn by his gaze. Locking into those cruel, true blue eyes, she stared him out for a count of five before flashing the briefest of hardcore smiles and wandering away, aware that his eyes were following her every wobbly step. Far from feeling elated, the incident made her feel sick with nerves. Particularly as she was supposed to weave her way up to Stan at this point and he appeared to have sloped off to the loo.

She paused undecided by the bar, eyeing the gloomier corners of the room in case Stan was lurking in one. From the darkest corner of all a momentary torch-like smile beamed out of a beautifully chiselled, subtly lifted face as The Phallus of Pop eyed her through his coterie.

Utterly taken aback with a great, surging whoosh of flattered euphoria, Phoebe sank back on to a bar stool. She simply couldn't risk drinking, she realised. Instead she leaned across and caught the eye of a towel-flapping waiter who was himself gawping at La Belle and her orbiting group of admirers in the middle of the room.

'Could I have a coffee?'

'A coffee?' he repeated as though she had just requested distilled musk of antelope scrotum on the rocks with a twist.

'Please.'

As he minced sulkily off to switch on the espresso machine, Phoebe noticed that Felix and Fanii were being rewarded with a couple of drinks at the opposite end of the bar now, attended to by an increasingly stressed publicity girl. Fanii was clearly intent on sticking to Felix as though trussed in a three-long-legged race, while Felix was louchely trying to catch Belle's eye. His blue gaze admired the black dress, seemed to creep an inch at a time down and up the brown legs, and then finally came to rest on two black eyes scowling furiously in his direction.

His covering fire came in the form of Frank Grogan who, conscious again and fresh from washing pistachio nuts out of what was left of his hair in the loos, lurched up to Fanii for a fumble under her skirt, clearly his equivalent of 'You forgot to tell me your name in my dreams last night'.

Far from taking a swipe at him, she gave him the benefit of her lingering, catatonic gaze which clearly terrified Frank – who was under the misapprehension that it was the result of requited desire and not merely acute stupidity.

This gave Felix the opportunity he needed to slope away to Belle.

Phoebe watched in amazement as, without greeting or endearment, he grabbed the tequila bottle from her and took a deep swig before planting a long, wet, and not at all tender kiss on her sulky red mouth.

Pulling away, Belle spat a few furious words at him and tugged angrily at her cigarette. Felix laughed amiably and borrowed it for a puff. While the little group around them gaped in delight, Belle, still hissing insults, slid a red-nailed hand around his neck and pulled him back into a kiss even more aggressive, animal and unfriendly than the first. Then a long red nail traced its way from the dip of Felix's collar bone, up the sinews of his neck and slid its way under his ear where it was jabbed very sharply into the soft skin just below his jaw.

He let out an angry howl and leapt away.

Smiling broadly, Belle blew him another kiss and turned on her pin-prick heels to Malcolm who had lined up a group of jibbering VIPs and was drooling voyeuristically nearby.

Wiping his mouth and then touching his neck tentatively, Felix turned his gaze back towards the bar and straight at Phoebe's front row observation of him.

Caught off-guard, she elected against looking away and

instead brazened it out with what she hoped was a knowing half-smile.

Standing stranded in the middle of the room, Felix looked at her for a few silent, speculative seconds and then smiled broadly and devastatingly, with a self-deprecating shrug of those wide shoulders swathed in white cotton jersey and a knotted cream jumper.

Phoebe tried not to panic as she smiled back. This was still according to plan, she realised. Now all she had to do was make another swift getaway before he could home in.

He was wandering idly towards her now, so Phoebe grabbed her bag and tried for a casual I'm-just-scanning-the-room smile this time. Where the hell was Stan? she wondered. Surely he couldn't *still* be in the loo?

'Your coffee, madam.'

She was stopped in her tracks by the almost flooring odour of pungent, hot coffee as the grouchy waiter thrust a tiny cup under her nose.

'Er – thanks. I don't actually think . . .'

'Hello,' purred a voice as deep and playful as a lion pup's.

Too late. Felix was already occupying the adjacent bar stool, rolling the tequila bottle between his palms as he smiled across at her.

It was a smile of such total, fearless honesty and old-fashioned British charm that Phoebe started to realise quite how perfect his seduction technique was. Matched with those desperately unfair good looks, drawling, honey-soaked voice and long, languid body, it made him the sort of man mothers, daughters, grandmothers and vicars all fell unquestioningly in love with.

'I'm Felix,' he purred on, still grinning between winces as he brushed the tender patch on his throat with his fingers.

Sipping her coffee to give herself time, Phoebe practically burned her top lip off. In theory, she wasn't supposed to talk to him tonight, but she guessed a bit of idle banter would look far better than running off and leaving a full cup of coffee and a lukewarm bar stool.

'You seem to be bleeding, Felix,' she said eventually, her voice somewhere close to her sister's in its imitation of Barry White in a neck-lock.

It wasn't her best in terms of drop-dead witty one-liners.

'Am I?' Seemingly unbothered by bloodshed, Felix didn't take his glittering eyes from hers. 'Where?' He leant towards her so that she could show him, a dangling sleeve of his knotted jumper brushing her bare arm, his breath touching her face like warm velvet.

A combination of heat from the coffee and a sudden, unexpected sexual frisson made Phoebe's pores prickle.

'On your neck,' she croaked, not moving an inch.

The grin broadening into a smile, eyes still locked onto hers like a Mig's guns on an Iraqi F111, Felix stretched his brown neck. 'Here?'

Deciding that her next move could look more revolting than sexy, but electing to risk it anyway, Phoebe took a plump white serviette from the bar and touched it with her tongue before gently dabbing the blood-reddened graze under his jaw. It was a bit bloody mumsy, too, she realised in horror as she was doing it. Brushing closer to him than was necessary, she leaned her other hand on his denim knee to keep her balance and added a few light little wrist touches to his ear plus a deliberately accidental stroke of her knuckles across his Adam's apple to try and spice things up a little.

The move practically bowled her over with excitement – the knee was wonderfully sinewy and he smelled divine – but she had no idea if he was reacting to plan or just gagging at the mollycoddling babe who was leaning heavily on him and swabbing his blood with her gobbed-on hanky.

As she leant back in the stool, Phoebe realised her gamble was paying off. Felix remained with his head cocked, eyes mischievous, smile playful, looking enchanted and dangerously seductive.

'What's your name?'

'Frances,' she remembered with a cringe, and paused. What the hell was her second name again? 'Frances Courtier,' she finished, knowing she was slightly wrong somewhere.

'Courtier?' Felix looked at her again.

'Er – yes.' Phoebe swallowed. 'My ancestors were courtiers in the reign of – er Charles II – no, Charles I, that's right. When his head hit the basket, my family were relegated to commoners by Cromwell and simply known as Mr and Mrs Courtier. Lots of Royalists were given similar surnames.'

She stopped, panting with the exertion of such a detailed and, she felt, spellbinding lie. If Fliss had been present, she would undoubtedly have wept at such amateurish antics, but Phoebe felt she'd done pretty well.

Felix was looking highly amused.

'I had no idea old Cromwell was so revolutionary.' He shook his head. 'Extraordinary.' He smiled across at her happily, blue eyes brimming with interest.

Then it happened. That sticky, quivering moment where any vestige of conversation is rendered impossible as a great yawning pause stretches out between two people whose eyes are hopelessly locked in one another's gaze. The pause becomes an aching, tension-loaded silence and then the silence becomes a desperately embarrassing, thoroughly enjoyable suspension of all around as hormones, pheromones, moisture and adrenalin drench two mutually attracted bodies.

Phoebe struggled valiantly to come up with an escape hatch, but some invisible harpy appeared to be stapling her legs and behind to the bar stool. As her eyes continued their sparkling and excited entanglement with Felix's, her mind raced in terror.

This wasn't in the plan, she realised, madly groping around for some improvised inspiration. Take control, she told herself frantically.

The pause was now so pregnant that its waters should have been breaking at any second, but still it stretched on as Felix's blue gaze ate up Phoebe's equally willing purple one, pulse points fizzed, hearts crashed around frantically and groins ached with anticipation.

Do it now, she told herself. Do something to get out of this *now*. He dumped Saskia. He's a shit. You HAVE to do this. Three . . . two . . . one . . .

Nothing. She did nothing. Except – was it her imagination, or was her left hand creeping towards his, itself inching towards hers? And had their knees been touching like that – tight, hot and pressing hard – a few seconds ago? Surely not?

Okay, we'll try this one more time – God, he's pretty – ONE more, one LAST – time. Three . . . two . . . one . . .

Dragging her eyes away with immense difficulty, she put down her coffee cup – thank God it didn't clatter – and stood up on slightly shaky legs.

Before Felix could move, she leant forward, kissed him very slowly on the mouth then walked away without a backward glance. Even when her hand groped behind her back and tugged her hem out of her g-string where it had got rucked up, she carried on staring ahead, face burning with mortification.

As soon as she was out of Felix's sight, she bolted to the loos.

When she closed her eyes and took some deep breaths, the image of him still played like a glossy advert in on her brain's mental bill board. Felix had been all lounging, casual lethargy in a white t-shirt, caramel coloured jeans and a very old cream school cricket sweater knotted around his neck. In the same way that Topaz, Belle and ultimately she herself were conspicuous by their attempts to out-tart everyone else, Felix stood out because he hadn't bothered; those were doubtless the clothes he'd worn all day and it was clear from the admiring glances he'd been drawing from jealous arrivistes nearby that there were several women here tonight who would go to great lengths to get him out of them.

Saskia may have dressed her up to compete on a physical level with these people – just – she reflected, but she suddenly doubted her ability to flaunt an iota of their get-lost attitude and carpet-brushing balls. The last few minutes had knocked years off her shelf-life as she'd realised she was going to have to make a lot of this up as she went along – Saskia's plotting and planning could only get her so far, but most of the time, Phoebe realised, she would be floundering alone trying to bewitch Felix with a combination of lies, eyes and guise.

'Oh God,' she muttered as she locked herself in a cubicle, 'please let me get this right.'

She was still totally sober, ridiculously nervous, but clear-headed and in control. A quick check in the mirror as she came out confirmed that she still looked reasonably okay, if pale. She ran a shaking comb through her glossy pudding basin bob, squirted on some more Ysatis scent – Felix's favourite – dropped some eye-soothers into her unnaturally purple peepers and reapplied the crimson lipstick. If only Saskia were hiding in here to issue last-minute instructions, she thought miserably.

A gaggle of models burst into the loos just as she was killing time trying to drag her tits up into some sort of gravity-defying cleavage arrangement. Having disposed of their companions, they were clearly desperate for a bitch.

'Seen Topaz – looks gorgeous, doesn't she?' one gushed in a gasping falsetto, pulling up her skirt to reveal nothing but a tiny, rounded bottom and neatly trimmed ginger fluff, before heading straight into a cubicle to take a pee without shutting the door, so that she could carry on gossiping.

'Stunning,' another replied breathily, heading for the mirror, fag hanging from a divinely droopy pink mouth. 'It's such a shame she's got a couple of zits on her back – did you notice? Quite ruins ze look of zat Versace.'

'Poor darling, didn't Linda wear it in the show?' A third model scrabbled in her bag for a compact. 'I think she has the legs for it, really – Topaz's are gorgeous but just a bit too twiggy.'

'True.' The pink-lipped model – a statuesque Eastern European – hopped up beside the basins and stroked her own long legs which she stretched out in front of her and examined minutely. 'And I sink Piers iz straying a bit. He's not here, huh?' She looked straight at Phoebe, her pretty face questioning.

Realising she was being included, Phoebe made a non-committal murmuring noise and rammed her comb back into the minute designer bag Saskia had lent her, planning to go and execute phase two before she lost her nerve.

'Felix is here, though,' the girl in the cubicle gushed dreamily as she pulled hunks of loo roll and threw them at her friends. 'D'you think he's dumped Belle for Fanii? Topaz will freak. Belle's not a threat, she just fucks him – Fanii's knocking on; she needs a few lover-and-home spreads in *Hello!* Rumour has it she's so desperate for publicity, she's going to do *Playboy* again.' She stood up and flushed.

'No!' shrieked the girl with the compact. 'How truly sad. I wonder what Felix sees in her? I mean Jasmin was so gorgeous – if a bit fucked up and bony-arsed – and he dumped her for that Sloaney dog – Sally, was it?'

'Saskia, I think, honey. Then he booted her out for Bucket-bitch Belle – who ain't gonna be pleased.' Ginger Pubes walked back through and lit a fag without washing her hands. 'And now Fanii Hubert . . . has he got lousy taste! All the time he's fucking around with Topaz as well. She says he screws like a gigolo.'

'He'd be fuckeeng around viz you if you had your way, baby!' shrieked the Eastern European. 'And vash your hands, you dirty beetch.'

Ginger Pubes stuck out her tongue and they all fell about at their witty repartee.

Phoebe, hovering by the basins, decided to wash her own hands as an excuse to linger and listen.

'Didn't we do Donna Karan together last year?' asked the dyed-blonde, razorcut model, watching Phoebe over her compact. Not waiting for an answer, she flicked the mirror back to reveal two neat lines of white powder. 'Coke, honey?'

Completely ruffled, Phoebe turned the taps on so strongly that she blasted the front of her dress with a jet of frothy water. 'Shit!'

Scrabbling to turn them off, she knocked into the soap-squirter and splatted the drenched white fabric with a green trail of what looked like an alien's bogey. Jumping away, she knocked into Ginger Pubes's cigarette and looked down in horror at a massive grey ash-stain.

'Shit!'

'Oh, you poor honey!'

Suddenly she was surrounded by beautiful, anxious, vacuous faces offering helpful advice.

'Stick it under the hand-dryer.'

'Rub it with a towel.'

'Flap it around.'

'Take eet off.'

'Yeah – Helki's right. Take it off.'

Phoebe looked at them in horror. 'Are you suggesting I go back out in my knickers?'

'No, babe,' Ginger Fluff giggled delightedly, 'just whip it off and give it here. We'll get it dry.'

'She's right.' The compact girl looked at her sincerely as she snuffled up her white powder and snapped the little gold clam shut with a delighted shudder.

Phoebe looked at herself in the mirror and realised she had little choice. Soaking wet, the front of her dress was looking a dirty grey, crumpled, revoltingly stained, and see-through. She had no desire to repeat the 'sad bint' look that had so delighted Felix in the Kensington wine bar. This called for desperate measures.

Dragging it off over her head, she handed it to Helki, then tried to cover as much of herself up as she could manage.

None of the girls seemed to care about her nudity as they fell on the dress like old ladies on a baby, carefully rinsing away the soap and ash before flattening it out and positioning it under the hand-dryer.

Realising they spent much of their lives stripping off and dressing up again, Phoebe relaxed and sagged back against a mirror, letting the glass cool her tense, knotted shoulder muscles.

A moment later, Belle Delauney stomped into the loos in the inevitable cloud of French tobacco smoke. Barely glancing at the nude girl by the sinks or the laundry coven around the hand-dryer, she slammed her way into a cubicle.

'Sulky!' Ginger Fluff giggled in an undertone to titters from her friend.

A moment later they were giggling even more, collapsing on

to each other in a heap of angular, bony limbs, muffled guffaws and tearful high jinks like schoolgirls who've just hung the dykey lacrosse goalkeeper's 38DD bra on matron's door knob.

'Er, honey, I think there's been a bit of an accident,' spluttered Compact, giggling so much that tears were streaking her run-proof eyeliner.

Phoebe watched in total disbelief as they held up a crumpled white dress which now had a large scorch-marked hole burnt through the front of the featherweight fabric. Then they themselves crumpled with it – toppling on to the floor into a shrieking, weeping heap of mirth, their six-inch ultra-trendy clog espadrilles waggling dangerously close to faces that were due to pout across *Harpers* double-page spreads in the coming months.

Burying her head in her hands, Phoebe groaned in despair. She was trapped stark naked in a loo with a gaggle of six-foot, hammered morons and nothing but a shredded piece of silk which resembled a very dodgy fake of the Turin Shroud to go and charm Felix in. And there wasn't even a window to crawl out of.

At that moment Belle burst out of her cubicle and stormed up to the mirror, black eyes burning into her own reflection. They then slid very slowly sideways and took in Phoebe and the Three Witches. Widening slightly, they looked momentarily fascinated before sliding away again to have their mascara calmly reapplied.

Phoebe debated whether to burst into tears, pretend to drop down in a dead faint or throw a raging tantrum before running through the party-of-the-month wearing nothing but a g-string and a manic smile.

She'd just decided that bursting into tears was perhaps preferable on a scale of one to ten years in clink wearing a long-sleeved jacket that tied at the back, when Belle swung round to her.

'You need 'elp?' she asked in a thick French accent, her voice gruff and unfriendly.

Tears still welling, Phoebe nodded. Rather obvious, that one, she reflected. Use your bonce, Belle – no wonder Saskia had complained that the only reason Felix didn't chuck her was because the language barrier prevented him rumbling how thick she was.

Belle heaved an irritated sigh, glanced witheringly at the cackling contingent around the hand-dryer, and then back to Phoebe.

'*Attends ici!*' she ordered, banging out through the doors.

In despair, Phoebe locked herself in a cubicle and shivered miserably; on top of everything else, she realised as she huddled on the loo seat, she was in serious danger of developing triple pneumonia, and her period was starting.

Finally, a sharp series of bangs and some incomprehensible French summoned her out. The models had thankfully cackled off to spread the news yet further, leaving her dress in a soggy heap on the floor along with their fag butts. Standing squarely on top of the lot, Belle was waiting with a scowl, a large cream jumper and the bottle of tequila.

With a shudder, Phoebe recognised the jumper; it was an old cricketing one – stretched almost to knee length, hand-washed and loved for over a decade, she surmised. Moments earlier, it had been wrapped around Felix's neck. The neck she had been groping rather inexpertly with a damp napkin.

Taking charge, Belle pulled it over her head for her like a nanny, folded the sleeves over until her hands poked out and gave the hem a few sharp tugs so that it stretched to a decent length. This done, she silently unscrewed the lid of the tequila bottle and thrust it under Phoebe's reddened nose.

No longer caring if she passed out blind drunk, she took a huge swig, winced, coughed and started to feel fractionally warmer. The jumper was vast and scratchy and smelled of an unfamiliar perfume. Then Phoebe realised it was her own – Ysatis, plastered on in regular squirts since six o'clock that evening.

'Thank you so much.' She smiled at Belle gratefully. 'You saved my life.'

Shrugging, Belle offered her a second swig, lit another fag and banged her way back out of the loos again.

Phoebe looked at her reflection. The jumper was shapeless and the same colour as her pasty face – undoubtedly divine when encasing the broad shoulders and quilted stomach of Felix Sylvian, but swamping her narrow frame, it looked like something she slept in during December. The low V-collar plunged far beyond the cleavage she had been trying to find earlier, and the purple and green stripes around it matched her eyes.

'Wha?' In horror, Phoebe leaned forwards and peeked at herself.

It was true, one tinted contact lens must have popped out while she was snivelling, leaving her revoltingly mismatched, like a low-budget extra from *Star Wars*.

Her face was red from crying, her make-up everywhere. In despair, Phoebe washed the lot off and sank to her hands and knees to snuffle about on the floor for the missing lens.

After several women had trooped for a toilet stop and got an eyeful of bottom rearing out of an ancient cricketing sweater, Phoebe gave up the hunt and straightened up. A slight crunching sensation around the knee area made her look down and, peeking closer, sigh despairingly. Drying in crusty pieces on her left knee cap was one purple lens which she must have knelt on as she sank down to search for it earlier. She picked off the pieces and took a bolstering breath. The tequila still left the faintest tingle of bravery prickling at her veins so she splashed her face with cold water, slicked the pudding bowl away from her forehead and stomped back out to the party.

Her reception beat any that had gone before at the far more salubrious doors opposite: the dramatic hush and frenzied, pointing banter that followed surpassed even The Phallus himself for focus-pulling power. She could almost hear the patter of tiny column inches being filled up by small-hours typewriters.

Phoebe had chosen her moment perfectly. The party was at the climactic full-swing point dreamt of by the most daring of late-entrance queens, and her choice of entrance door was even more original than most.

The gathered crowd seemed to consist of short, fat powerful

corporate men; short, thin, hedonistic media men; short, stringy ageing celebrity men; one or two glossy hunks with IQs that matched their penis measurements; several Nicole Farhi-draped media witches trying inconspicuously to dab mascara from their crow's feet as they networked; the odd female 'personality' digging into the buffet and scratching a midge bite on a hairy leg with her fork; and endless leggy, giggling models chain-smoking and clutching their litre bottles of mineral water in one hand, their pencil case-sized designer handbags in the other.

Almost all of them were looking at Phoebe.

Stan was nowhere to be seen.

She tried to shuffle sideways along a wall and attract as little attention as possible, except from Stan whom she hoped to locate and hiss at, indicating a swift exit was required.

But, bored and in need of distraction, people were anxiously pressing forwards to angle for an introduction to the weirdo loo-freak that everyone was talking about. Phoebe recognised several faces in the approaching crowd of fascinated stalkers: the giggling models, Malcolm the creepy producer, and – horrors! – Belle and Felix. Outpacing them all, a couple of photographers loped up, demanded a smile and then asked her name for their notes.

'Phoebe Fredericks,' she said absently, realising too late that she'd been introducing herself as Frances Courtault/Courtier/ Caught-out all evening. She wondered if it would be too far-fetched to pretend to be someone else – minus the dress and make-up, she had to be pretty unrecognisable.

The models were crowding around her lovingly now, swinging thin arms around her shoulders and pouting as the photographers snapped off the rest of their reels.

'Are you okay, honey?' asked Ginger Pubes, cocking a caring heart-shaped face and shooting up a questioning wire-thin eyebrow.

'Yes, thanks.' Phoebe smiled gratefully.

'That looks neat.' Compact – whose pupils were like pin-pricks now – took in the cricket sweater. 'Really cute. Good thinking to wash the make-up off too – well wise to go for the little girl wearing Daddy's sweater look. It's so in. I think I'll buy one.'

'Are you doing Paris thees year?' asked Helki, brushing Phoebe's bob into shape again.

'Not to my knowledge, no.'

'Oh, well, I guess we'll meet in New York again, then. Ciao, baby.'

They drifted off to regather their very small, very rich and very ugly partners, who to a man looked like sugar daddies wearing their own Pringle sweaters under shiny leather blousons.

'Am I imagining it, or are you the same girl I met earlier?' Malcolm's merry eyes twinkled up at her as he homed in.

'Er – sorry?' Phoebe hoicked up the V-line which was plunging navelwards.

'No, no – my mistake.' He examined her pale, scrubbed face with its piggy red eyes from washing off a ton of muck with green squirty soap. His smile suddenly turned from seductive to sickly. 'You are?'

Phoebe glanced away nervously to see Belle and Felix lurking nearby, clearly arguing in the stiff-jawed, eyes-out-front way of those not wishing to be overheard. The tequila bottle – now almost empty – was swinging dangerously close to Felix's cranium, she noticed.

'Phoebe Fredericks,' she muttered.

'What?' Malcolm barked, leaning closer so that she could smell both deodorant and Clorets losing the fight. There was no oozing chumminess now, just abrupt enquiry.

'Phoebe Fredericks,' she mumbled, averting her face and noticing Fanii Hubert pressing her long, thin groin into the paunch of one of the short, fat corporate men nearby as she writhed and ground her hips to the latest grunge-techno jazz band.

'Speak up, darling.' Malcolm cocked a couple of furry eyebrows menacingly so that they looked like jumping caterpillars. 'There's no need to be shy. Phoebe what – Hendrix?'

'Fredericks.' She shook off his beady gaze and glanced across at Belle just in time to cop a very furtive ten denier knee jabbing up into Felix's balls.

Leaving him reeling, the fuming actress hissed, '*C'est fini – absolument fini. Pas jamais!*' and whisked off towards The Phallus's inner court, still in attendance in the far corner of the room. Passing Phoebe, she paused and kissed her firmly on both cheeks.

'*L'avez s'il vous voulez,*' she whispered, '*mais faîtes attention!*'

As she swayed off, Malcolm was momentarily transfixed by her swinging hips and big, satisfied smile – not the flashing false one laid on for the cameras earlier; a wide, cheesy, delighted one which transformed her sulky face completely.

The distraction, however, was short-lived.

'Did you say PHOEBE FREDERICKS?' he yelled, snapping Phoebe's attention back to him.

Realising Felix had stopped bending over tearfully and was bravely straightening up nearby, his watering blue eyes watching her sceptically, she tried to look cheerfully non-committal.

'Are you on the guest list?' Malcolm suddenly wiped off the sickly sheep's smile and assumed a wolfish, withering grimace. 'I must say, I can't recall the name.'

'Er – yes – well . . .' Phoebe gulped, desperately looking around for Stan.

'You *are* on the list?' Malcolm demanded abruptly.

'Well, yes – that is no, not exactly.' Phoebe's eyes were raking the room now, burrowing into groups, straining to see around corners, peering through pot plants, tables and Showdown promotional material. Stan was nowhere to be seen.

'Look, dear, either you are or you aren't,' Malcolm sniffed, glancing around for one of the security staff. 'This is a private party, you know.'

Phoebe suddenly realised that the reason he was being so utterly unpleasant was because she was no longer the siren in the sexy white dress; she was a dowdy, slightly odd-looking individual in a cricketing sweater. No matter that there were a dozen or so of these already peopling the party – they were

male, famous, members of the Lord's Taverners and good for a
quote. She was female and anonymous, and by the rules of the
Horseferry Road house of glass publicity machine, she was as
unwanted as Fred Flintstone's cricket ball. The siren in the dress
could potentially get a job with Malcolm on the back of batting
her 2,000-calorie mascara and twinkling a false little laugh at his
jokes, the loo-freak in the jumper could have the Nobel Prize
for Media Communication Skills and she'd still be treated with
the respect of a mongrel scratching a flea at Crufts.

'I think you'd better leave without too much fuss, don't you?'
Malcolm muttered in an undertone, the rictus smile forced back
in place. He took her upper arm in a tight grip and started to
steer her towards the door. 'And don't ask anyone for their
autographs.'

'Now hang on!' Phoebe dug in her heels and swung round to
face him, her fury firing on all four cylinders and a couple of
swigs of tequila. 'Don't you dare be so fucking rude to me, you
under-developed, middle-aged, pot-bellied toad!'

Oops, she realised in horror. Why did she always do this?

There was an instant lull in the immediate vicinity as the
comment sank in and was spread in a giggling repeated whisper
around the room. In the ensuing hush, Malcolm turned as red
as a squeezed thumb.

Phoebe pulled her arm out of his grip and dragged up the
shoulder of her borrowed jumper which had slipped off to
reveal most of one brown nipple.

'Get out!' he muttered in a voice so murderous that Phoebe
balked. Suddenly something snapped with the echoing velocity
of Robbie Coltrane on bungee elastic.

'I've watched you trying to clamber into the knickers of most
of the women here tonight,' she fumed on regardless, 'although
Christ knows why you didn't bring your step-ladder with you, it
would make life so much easier. Well, if you think that by
pressing your moist, pudgy little body against some girl's knees
you're turning her on to anything more than the opportunity to
use your sad old ego and tug your wrinkled little cock like a
doorbell to further her career, you're desperately misguided.'

'Now look here!' Malcolm puffed, looking closer to a by-pass than Swindon.

Realising she had a delighted, cheering audience – including the roving film crew, several photographers, the Scouse reporter and the giggling models – Phoebe gallantly pressed on to entertain them.

'Men like you should stick to fingering their daughter's friends' underwear and driving slowly alongside steamed-up parked cars late at night. And remember, sad old gits like you are only as old as the combined age of your last three lovers, so you could knock a few years off yours tomorrow by cruising a few playgrounds and putting your name down for the 1997 intake at Downe House!'

'I'm so sorry,' apologised a smooth, drawling voice, as diplomatic as David Owen's in Sarajevo. 'Is she blowing her lid again? Really, darling, I've told you not to pick on under-developed, middle-aged, pot-bellied toads. They get terribly upset.'

Before she could take in what was happening, Phoebe found another – far tighter – grip encircling her upper arm and dragging her away from her theatre-in-the-round audience.

'You wha?'

She swung around angrily to see two now familiar glinting blue eyes positively brimming over with mirth.

'I'll take her off to cool down, shall I?' Felix told an astounded Malcolm, who was still puffing away like a menopausal bull frog. 'And incidentally, she *is* invited. She's with me – don't you recognise her? You should. Her name's over the doors of a top notch theatre not one minute from here, and under the bill board ads for a first-run film absolutely everywhere at the moment.'

Thus saying, he whisked Phoebe through the glass doors before anyone could even begin to speculate which theatre, which film, where, and how come she looked like she'd just crawled out of her lover's bed and donned his jumper to stagger to the kettle. Although, they reasoned, if she was here with Felix, perhaps she had . . .

*   *   *

'What the fuck did you do that for?'

'Because you were making a fool of yourself,' he said, calmly steering her through Soho and into a nearby bar, heaving with pre-club gays sweating it out in PVC and trash-fash. 'What do you want to drink?' he yelled over the din as he pulled her too far into the heaving mass to allow easy escape.

'I wouldn't drink with you if you were a camel in a desert with the only full hump for two hundred leagues,' she yelled back.

Perhaps that was taking too much control, she reflected a split-second later. But she hardly cared, she was so incensed.

'White wine?'

'Fuck off.'

'Spritzer then?'

'Fuck off.'

'In that case, I'd like my jumper back, please.'

'Fuck off.' This was said with far less conviction.

'Right now. Here. Take it off and give it back, then I'll push off.' Felix laughed, not moving but clearly seconds away from swiping the only cable-knitted wool that stood between her and flashing through Soho in her g-string.

Phoebe looked at him grumpily. God, he was loving this, those sexy, alert cobalt eyes gleaming like a Persian cat's when sitting on a shredded shrew.

Suddenly, Phoebe suspected that he knew the whole scam – that she was the girl in the white dress earlier, the Swedish weirdo in Bar Barella, the sad bint in the Kensington wine bar, the old school-friend of Saskia who was trying to exact revenge.

'Mineral water,' she acquiesced, resentfully plumping down at a recently vacated, dimly lit table to cut down on the odd looks she was getting.

Felix was an age at the bar during which time Phoebe considered and rejected all manner of escapes. She should hoof it to the nearest tube. Yet, her conscience argued, now that she was alone with him – except for a hundred or so fascinated queens – she had the ideal chance to observe her prey in disguise. Then again, she mulled, *was* she in disguise?

He hadn't seemed to recognise her, she reflected, watching his caramel denim bottom being studied by several excited gays at the bar. But what had Belle said to excuse her sudden removal of his jumper before her abrupt dumping scene? 'There's a weeping black-bobbed girl whose white dress has been frazzled in the bog, *chérie* – can I borrow this?' Was her English that good? Surely, though, he was too fazed by said latter abrupt dumping scene to draw parallels between the slicked-back, scrubbed loo-freak in his jumper and the glossily-bobbed, painted creature who'd pounced on him with a tissue earlier.

By the time Phoebe had finally elected to stay put and assume yet another I'm-a-weirdo-laugh-at-me pose, she'd left it too late to abscond with the jumper anyway.

Felix had now secured a couple of drinks – both of which looked suspiciously like neat tequilas doused in lime and salt – and was lounging at the bar, grinning at her until she was forced to pull the jumper down, her smile up and stalk over to him.

'Feel calmer?' he asked politely as she wriggled in between two gays in PVC trousers who were closing fast on him. Both gave her very dirty looks and turned, ballroom-dancer fashion, on their heels so that she was rammed against Felix so tightly she had to lean back to stop him swallowing her nose.

She backed away far too fast, so that she head-butted a nearby clipped skull and got stuck to a sweaty back.

'Here's your mineral water,' Felix laughed.

Ignoring him, Phoebe took the proffered drink and swigged a sip which made her gag.

'Bottled at source from Chernobyl, I take it?' she coughed, her eyes streaming. Thank God she didn't have on any eye make-up to smudge. But still, she had no idea how to play this. Should she be trying to win his confidence? Ask if he was upset about Belle's leg-up?

Felix grinned good-humouredly.

'As you wouldn't sip from my hump, I reckoned you'd have to resort to sucking cactus juice,' he murmured. 'We've met, yeah?'

Phoebe shrugged, stalling as she wondered just how much

he'd guessed and whether it would be worth risking an accent –
Swedish excepted.

Knocking back his drink in one and signalling for another,
Felix didn't seem remotely fazed by her reticence. 'You can't go
back in there now, you realise that, don't you?'

'Why ever not?' Giving up on the accent idea, she settled for a
slightly croakier version of her own voice.

'Because Malcolm Hutchinson is *the* independent producer
of the moment – name the best of current comedy and light
entertainment on Beeb Two or Channel Four and he's behind
it.' Felix moved forwards slightly, adding in an amused undertone, 'I hope you weren't looking for a job?'

Was it her imagination or was he up to his old seduce-a sad-
bint tricks? she wondered. Pick on the loo-freak and have a
laugh; roll up, roll up.

'I don't need a job.' She thrust her chin out, inwardly
churning over the fact that she'd given Malcolm her number
and all that balls about a portfolio.

'Oh – right.' Still grinning, Felix signalled for another couple
of drinks.

Still only one sip into her first, Phoebe ignored all Saskia's
tosh about keeping up with Felix's phenomenal alcohol intake
and put hers down.

God, she felt unsettled, she realised. As the heat from his legs
started burning into hers, she shuddered afresh with the discomfort of wearing nothing but his jumper and her knickers.
She hoped the white dress hadn't been too expensive.

'D'you want to come back with me?' he suddenly asked.

Phoebe stalled. Surely he couldn't be that direct? But his eyes
were on her lips. He *could* be that direct, she realised. The shit.

'To the party?' She swallowed.

'No.'

The word was growled so throatily that, despite herself,
Phoebe squirmed with the potential once-off lust of the situation. Behind her, PVC trousers was sighing sadly at the scenario
he was frantically earwigging. *Such* a waste, he seemed to be
insinuating with every heartfelt exhalation.

Felix wasn't giving an inch – in fact he'd gained by several. Without making a single gesture of a pass, he was making contact with most of his cricket jumper now, and with quite a lot of what was below it.

'I'll get us a cab, shall I?' he breathed.

Phoebe looked at him. This was the closest he'd got to victory yet, she realised. The audience was there, the scene was set – despite herself, she was almost floored with indecision and recklessness. One breath of the word 'yes' and Felix could perform his favourite trick and turn the tables faster than a dodgy casino, laughing in her face and telling her she'd had her 'Scooby Snack' and should go home to a Prince CD, copy of *For Women* and her Power Shower nozzle.

'No,' she said firmly.

'I'm sorry?' He dropped his head closer to hers, looking cheerfully hard-of-hearing. Blond hairs were brushing her neck now, warm breaths stroking the arch of her shouder and neck

'I don't want a cab, thanks.' Phoebe side-stepped, neatly extricating herself from the Felix-and-gay sandwich, inadvertently springing them together like a mouse-trap. 'I'm off home. Thanks for the drink – I'm afraid I didn't catch your name?' She bravely thrust her outstretched hand into the trap.

'Felix,' he said numbly, shaking it.

'Well, thanks a lot for the drink, Felix.' She smiled merrily. 'I'm Freda Loufreik. Ciao.'

And she weaved off into Beak Street as fast as three inches of stacked leather would carry her.

Outside, Phoebe side-stepped the throngs of Soho clubbers, pubbers and scrubbers, and, having put as much distance between herself and Felix as her burning feet would allow, leaned against the glass windows of a nearby post production house, pressing her scalding cheek against its cool, smeary sanctuary and breathing in the stench of discarded fast food wrappings which littered the pavement below.

She wasn't quite sure if that last action had been totally wise. In fact, playing it back through her head, she realised she'd

probably blown her cover as surely as a bird watcher in a day-
glo orange kagool bursting out of a hide and shrieking: 'Look! A
rare spotting of the shy Greater-spotted Neazel-wader with
feather-mange and an unusual genetic webbed-claw mutation!'
But he'd totally rug-pulled her. The seductive, genuinely keen
Felix of earlier that night and the playful, teasing rogue who
chatted up the ugliest girl at a party were almost impossible to
differentiate. He was as difficult to read as *The Canterbury Tales*
in Chaucer's original handwriting.

Trying to figure out what she was going to tell Saskia about
tonight – picturing her brimming, hopeful face tomorrow
morning – Phoebe clenched her eyes shut tighter and groaned.

'Here's my number,' growled a deep, husky voice tinged with
nectar-sweet irony. 'Call me when I can have my jumper back.'

Spinning around, she bashed foreheads with the louse himself and then pressed herself back against the window like a
mugging victim as he waved a piece of paper in front of her nose

How dare he? she thought fretfully. I'm totally unprepared,
off-guard and feeling gooily reflective. How dare he bulldoze in
like an obsessive sweater-stalker demanding to know the future
whereabouts of his poxy jumper? Is he that attached to the hairy
old thing? And what am I called again? Frances? Phoebe? Freda?

'Oh – thanks,' she muttered rather lamely.

Felix was looking strangely uncomfortable, as though he half
wanted to run away himself.

'Right. Well, let me know when you've finished with it.' He
cleared his throat.

'I will,' Phoebe promised, looking at the piece of paper with
its carefully rounded digits. She double-took, surprised by the
neat handwriting. 'Thanks for the loan.'

He hovered around a little longer, digging his hands into the
pockets of his jeans – no mean feat as they were pretty snug-
fitting – and watching her through his hair. The pose was too
deliberate to impress Phoebe – very poised, filmic and pretty.

Why wouldn't he go away? she wondered. Did he want to tag
the damn jumper like a sheep's ear? Sew in a name-tape? What?

Felix was shifting round in front of her now, his shadow –

between her and a street light – alternately swamping her in darkness and blinding her with neon light.

'It suits you,' he breathed, leaning forward so that she was suddenly in shadow, her face tickled by clean blond hair. 'You look great. It's much better than the white nightie thing you were wearing earlier.'

She leant away from his Wash and Go-ed tresses and looked up into his face, biting her lip to stop herself smiling. Of course he'd know that she was the girl in the white dress, she realised. Long distance lorry drivers provided enough information for criminals' identikit pictures on the basis of driving at seventy miles per hour along the A1 six months before Crimewatch and spotting a shifty-looking character in a hooded anorak in a lay-by. Recognising a scrubbed siren who'd swabbed one's neck wound and was now dressed in one's own sweater was a cinch.

Suddenly she felt as though she was in full slap, the white nightie thing and half a bottle of Ysatis again, Saskia's repeated instructions clear in her head as though relayed via a hidden wire.

Stretching up, Phoebe ran her right hand around to the back of his t-shirt neck, curling her thumb inside it, and leant up on her toes so far that she could feel her stomach muscles stretch against his as she kissed him very lightly on the bony arch of both cheeks and then very softly on his blinking eyelids before turning on her uncomfortable heels and heading towards Leicester Square.

That's more like it, she thought with relief. Saskia will be proud – I've got the number, I've pecked the bony bits, and I've left the boy intrigued. I just have to wash the jumper without shrinking it and get the image together again and we're all set.

Trotting happily past the Three Greyhounds, she was almost brought down as someone gripped the hem of her – Felix's – sweater, dragging it back like Charlie Chaplin's braces.

'Wait!'

Phoebe spun around and found herself pressed against a lot of denim and cotton jersey, the cricket sweater twisted up her body like a skater's tu-tu.

Terrified, she tried to wriggle away and succeeded in backing off about two inches before Felix hauled her to an abrupt halt-and-reverse.

'Will you lay off?' Phoebe snapped, realising she would now have to think up a third last-liner. Really, this was too much. She was reasonably good at dramatic exits, but this was getting close to Turandot flinging herself off the battlements only to find that the stage crew had replaced the air cushion with a trampoline.

'What are you doing tomorrow?' he asked, freeing her.

'I haven't decided,' Phoebe hedged, totally floored.

'Do you want to go for tea?'

'Tea?'

'Yes – it's an infusion of leaves from an Asian shrub. Quite popular around here.' Felix was gaining the initiative again.

So that was it, Phoebe realised. *He* wanted to make the Big Exit. What an old drama queen.

'Sounds faintly familiar.' She played for time. 'Do you need me around to drink it?'

'It might help.'

'What time?'

'Four, Pat Val's, Knightsbridge. D'you know it?'

'Let me see – Knightsbridge . . .' Phoebe sighed witheringly, aware that he was extracting more piss than a urologist, 'Isn't that West? Somewhere near Slough?'

'And will you bring my jumper with you?'

'What?'

'My jumper – I'm rather fond of it; Pa wore it before me. It's taken countless wickets and hit at least twenty sixes.'

Phoebe flipped. Was the jumper freak hitting again? Did he think she was going to nick the disgusting thing? It scratched, itched and reeked of Ysatis for Chrissake.

'Well, don't panic, Felix,' she said soothingly – as a matron to a toddler rid of its snot-stained, much-fondled comforter, 'it hasn't bowled this maiden over. In fact she's heading for the club-house right now to unbuckle her pads.'

Not really thinking what she was doing, she dragged the controversial jumper up over her head and handed it back to him.

'Shit!'

Felix gripped it – and her – as though clutching a grip bag full of heroin thrust at him by an anonymous student as he passed through the green channel out of Bangkok airport, desperate to cover it up.

Aware of a blastingly cold breeze, Phoebe was wondering in a panic what exactly she'd done, when she spotted her original date exiting the Three Greyhounds where he'd been hiding with a pint.

'Stan!' she yelled, knowing he didn't want to hear this.

Sensibly, Stan ignored her.

'Stan!' Phoebe yelled again, aware that she was at the point where she no longer had pride. Felix was now gripping her like a copy of the *Satanic Verses* in deepest Iran. She was wearing nothing but a g-string in Soho. People were starting to jeer. She was desperate.

Thankfully, Stan rolled his eyes sideways and moved swiftly forwards.

'All right, girl?' he asked; an obvious Stan understatement.

'Of course I'm not all right!' Phoebe growled, pulling away from Felix – who was starting to enjoy this, she suspected – and facing up to Stan. 'Can you lend me your shirt or something?'

Taking in her state of undress, Stan had never stripped off quicker.

Felix couldn't stop laughing now.

'Thanks,' Phoebe ignored him and buttoned up a pin-chord silk shirt which thankfully was longer than her dress earlier. She then waved Stan's nervously proffered jacket back at him. 'Wear it – you'll look lovely and sexy with nothing underneath. I'm sorry about this. Ciao.'

Waving at him, and shooting an evil glance at Felix, who was now laughing so much that his beloved cricket sweater was in threat of being drenched in tears, she hared for the tube.

'You're fucking screwed up, you know that!' Felix shouted delightedly after her. 'A sad fucking bint!'

'See you tomorrow!' she yelled back. 'Tea for two-faced liars.'

21

Twenty minutes into America's Top Ten and sobbing wildly over the latest Michael Bolton lurve ballad, Saskia knew she was in for a sleepless night. It was only just past one and she was already two-thirds of the way through a bottle of Tanqueray gin, a box of Kleenex and forty Marlboro Lights.

She blinked yet more scalding salt water from her eyes and looked woozily around her sister's Fulham flat. It was a tip. When Portia came back, Saskia realised, she would flip.

Detritus from a week's bingeing, dieting, drinking, exercising, video-watching and sobbing lay everywhere. The skirting boards had been replaced by an even rim of pushed-back take-away bags and cartons, the coffee table was crammed with plates acting as ashtrays, bowls acting as ashtrays, video shells acting as ashtrays, and open copies of the *Rosemary Conley Hip and Thigh Diet* complete with wrinkled sob stains, snotty glued-on tissues and textured take-away splashes.

Groucho, propped precariously on a wine-stained sofa arm munching three-day-old chicken satay and flicking a white tail, had put on about two pounds. Saskia, folded up on the floor with her sister's thigh-firmer and stomach cramps, had lost nothing but yet more self-esteem.

She hardly cared. Despite feeling closer to suicide than she had on the night her first pony had twisted its gut with colic and been destroyed, she had a weird, semi-masochistic feeling of euphoria. She had taken six slimming tablets today and eaten nothing more than an apple and two muesli bars. Added to which, she had taken the stairs on the Underground two at a time on her way to Phoebe's flat earlier, had done a three-up, two-down on Portia's staircase and had just executed ten sit-ups to the new Janet Jackson hit.

Squinting across at the gin on the table, she vaguely tried to work out how many calories were in a bottle, but gave up. After all, the tonic had been slimline.

Instead, she stared at the phone again. God, she wished Phoebe would call. Her tummy was being chewed into a long, frayed string – and not just by hunger. Her acidic, empty guts were really churning from a fear and excitement that blended bile with adrenalin in equal, near lethal, proportions.

Phoebe let herself into the flat and wearily dropped the shoes she had carried upstairs on to the pile of unforwarded mail. Ignoring the message indicator flashing light on the answerphone as she passed it in the hall, she noticed that Fliss's light was still glaring despite her obvious absence, and paused momentarily to switch it off. Speculating on where her flatmate had got to, she plodded into the bathroom for the most abbreviated of ablutions.

She was just taking the brief sit-down opportunity of a pee simultaneously to clean her teeth and remove her knickers from her ankles with some wriggling high-kicks when someone wandered into the bathroom, swinging a set of car keys menacingly.

'Hi.'

Phoebe almost fell off the loo in fright as she whimpered with a mixture of first-reaction terror and then total mortification. But she was still mid flow and had never carried out all the pelvic floor exercises that glossy magazines promised would improve one's sex life, so was forced to stay put, perching like a stubborn child playing musical chairs.

'You're late,' the voice said smoothly. 'Your dinner's on the credit card.'

It was Dan, looking tired and tetchy. Great charcoal bags

underlay his narrowed eyes and a sprinkling of stubble had darkened his chin like the shadowed side of the moon. He propped one wide shoulder against a tiled wall and rubbed his hair so that it stood up on one side.

'Piss off!' Phoebe wailed, more angrily than she'd intended.

Looking even more outraged, Dan skedaddled so quickly that his keys flew into the basin with a plop, landing in six inches of scummy lukewarm water and rinse-off cleanser.

Two minutes later, suitably composed and wrapped in the only towel she could find in the bathroom – a ratty pink one belonging to Fliss that was stained with henna and stank of Boots aromatherapy revitalising shower gel – Phoebe stalked back out clutching a dripping BMW keyring.

She found Dan propped uncomfortably on the wooden sofa arm like a colonel on a shooting stick, having rejected the bottom-clamping cushions in the middle in case he needed to make a quick getaway.

'What are you doing here?' she asked bluntly.

'I came to borrow a cup of sugar, what do you think?' he snapped.

Phoebe bit her lip and stepped carefully towards him to avoid the tangled mess of clothes, art pads, CD cases and newspapers on the floor.

The lights in the sitting room were still switched off, so apart from a harsh shard of light angling out of the bathroom which lit his feet, he was in darkness.

Phoebe thrust the keys in the general direction she assumed his face to be.

'Yours,' she muttered.

In the gloom, a hand moved to take them.

She snatched them back.

'You can give me the ones to this place first,' she whispered.

'What?'

'The ones you've had cut.'

'What?'

'The ones you obviously had cut when you "borrowed" my keys last Friday.' Phoebe backed off slightly, suddenly uncertain that she was justified in her fury. 'How else did you get in here tonight?'

In the darkness she could hear Dan breathing out a huffy sigh. 'The door was open.'

'That's so lame I can hear it limping. We never leave the door open – the bloke downstairs would kill to sniff Fliss's knickers.'

'Is he blond with a squint? I met him on my way in.'

'What?'

'Joke.'

Anxious to break the crackling, angry static in the air, Dan rose so that she could suddenly feel the heat of his breath on her cheek.

'Was it really open?' Phoebe asked sheepishly.

'Yup.'

'Christ!' She rubbed her eyes with her finger and thumb.

'I had to see you.' His mouth, confused by the dark, made contact with Phoebe's knuckle. 'I was missing you so much, I started trying to look up your name in the phone directory just to comfort myself.'

Pulling her hand gently away, she sighed, swamped by exhaustion and the last fragments of churning embarrassment.

'We're ex-directory,' she muttered. 'And I've missed you too.'

'You sound so sincere,' he mocked.

'I'm sorry.' Phoebe moved across to the light switch and shouldered it, still staring towards him.

Suddenly illuminated, the big, crinkly smile wavered uncertainly. He was in his post-work casuals – all soft denim, cashmere, and crumpled, freshly laundered cotton. She wanted to leap right on him and bury her face in warm, Dan-smelling fabric but determinedly stopped herself acting on impulse for once and remained leaning against the switch, the plastic moulding digging into her bare shoulder. She felt too exhausted for five-act sex and still too uncertain of him to ask just to be held; he looked shattered and nervy, not the warm, open-armed mixture of smiles, hugs and screaming full-throttle lust she had put on a pedestal in New Zealand.

Phoebe was still trying to align the rose-tinted mental photo

album she had hawked around for a year and the reality she had
so briefly and transiently rekindled since returning to England.
It was easy to recapture lust and sex, she reflected, but trust and
intimacy needed far longer. She wasn't even sure they'd had
them in the first place.

Dan, meanwhile, was staring at her as though she had
sprouted a second head.

'Your hair,' he finally managed to splutter.

'Yup,' Phoebe said tiredly. 'Grows out of my scalp at the rate
of half an inch a month. Washed daily. Now black.'

His smile was suddenly as creased as his green cotton grandad shirt.

'I like it.' He moved towards her cautiously. 'It's stunning.
Makes you look like Louise Brooks.'

He stopped about a yard from her and continued staring, a
finger pressed to his grinning mouth.

Unable to bear the scrutiny, Phoebe heaved herself away
from the wall and headed across to the balcony windows,
tightening the towel around her.

Sometimes, perhaps unintentionally, he could make her feel
like a cut-out doll. Tonight, despite an overwhelming urge to
bury herself in his comforting, crumpled bulk, she was too tired
and traumatised to humour him, too aware that it was *he* who
sought the comforting – ego, vanity, power, mid-life-crisis virility
– and she who merely acquired indirect solace through giving it.

Dragging back the windows, she ignored the goose bumps
popping up like nettle rash on her skin as she turned her face to
the biting breeze and searched for a star in the shot-silk navy
sky, glowing with orange from London's combined street lights.

She was just about to wish on a star that Dan would stay – but
would also drop off on the sofa and let her have a churning
night's sleep to sort herself out before any rumpy-pumpy –
when she felt a sharp pain searing through one palm and,
looking down, realised that his keys were still clasped in her
hand.

Dan was hovering just inside the doors, glancing awkwardly
around him.

'Christ, this place is a flea pit.'

'Thanks!'

'No – I mean, it's just too squalid for you to live in. The cheap furniture, the damp, the awful wallpaper. Couldn't you do any better?'

'Not for the money, no.' Phoebe pulled at a frayed piece of towel. 'Anyway, I quite like its trashiness. It has a certain appeal.'

'Come inside,' he coaxed. 'I have to get back soon. Mitzi will be calling the police. I only popped out for five minutes.'

'I see.'

There was a lull as he swallowed noisily and awkwardly behind her.

Phoebe watched the illuminated curtains of the flats opposite with their tiny slits of inviting bright light enticing binocular-wielding voyeurs to prop themselves against their balcony rails with a Thermos and a sandwich box.

'Er – can I have my car keys then?' he wavered.

Phoebe wanted to scream: 'WIMP!' at the top of her voice and throw a punch. Instead, hardly pausing to think, she threw his car keys. High up into the night air they flew, in a perfect arc, glinting in the light of the flat until they dropped into the garden without so much as a satisfying rustle of bushes as they landed in total silence.

Which pretty much matched the sound level up above as Dan took in the action with remarkable, frozen calm.

Turning back, Phoebe broke the monastic hush by slamming the balcony doors shut and stomping inside.

'You can fucking fetch them,' she hissed, passing him with a swish of flapping towel and a waft of revitalising aromatherapy shower gel. 'I'm off to bed.'

'Phoebe, I – '

'And don't try to clamber in with me,' she added angrily over her shoulder. 'I've got my period, cystitis, a headache, I'm knackered. And, besides, I just don't fancy you tonight!'

After she had banged the bedroom door, Dan wavered in the flat for a few moments, totally panic-stricken. He could hardly phone Mitzi and ask her to drive over with the spare keys, he realised, but stood equally little chance of finding them outside in the dark.

More worrying still was Phoebe's behaviour. He knew she could be fiery and irascible – downright ratty at times. She flew off the handle more times than a fly on a doorknob and loved nothing more than a sexy play-fight, but tonight was different.

He hovered by her door and considered tapping on it, but couldn't drum up the nerve. Instead, he plodded to the answerphone and malevolently removed the tape before burying it in the kitchen bin by way of cheap revenge. Having listened to all the messages from Saskia as they came in that night, he had no idea what was going on, but was pretty certain that it involved Phoebe and this Felix character she had mentioned.

Dan prided himself on his lack of jealousy and petty resentment. Whilst loathing the hanging-loose ex-hippy types amongst his social circle who condoned open relationships and discussed their affairs in between toting opinions about politics, Andrew Neil and the Booker shortlist at dinner parties, he liked to think that his blind eye was discretionary and liberal when it came to his lovers. Yet right now he felt as though he'd been poked in it. He was murderous with envy of this unknown Felix and the obvious fascination he exerted over Phoebe, her friends and her answerphone. He had even located a note from him in the kitchen earlier, signed simply 'F'. It had been a boring little flimsy about some missing salad, but Dan had torn it up with loathing and scoured the rest of the flat for further evidence. There were definite signs of his presence: a Barbour on the coat stand – a hooray London Sloane? Dan had wondered – a pair of boxers tucked down the side of the sofa, a kit bag full of sports gear by the skirting board.

Dan hid the tape under an empty cream cheese tub and chewed his lip.

Unable to help himself, he once again crept towards Phoebe's door and hesitated, craning his head forward to listen for signs of movement, a rustle of dropped towel, a swish of drawn-back bedclothes.

He cowered back on his heels as the door was snatched open and Phoebe's arm shot out.

Expecting it to smack him across the cheek, Dan flinched. But the arm merely curled its way around his waist and pulled him inside.

'Would you mind awfully,' Phoebe pressed her nose to his throat and breathed into his collar bone, 'just holding me for a few minutes? And then,' she drew her mouth up to his with a series of feather light kisses on his chin, 'I'll help you find your car keys. Sorry.'

'Me too,' Dan breathed, flicking his tongue very lightly into her mouth before drawing her tightly towards him so that her face was tucked into his cashmere shoulder.

Smiling into her glossy black hair, he felt quite victorious that he had just emptied the sludgy cold water from Phoebe's washing up bowl into the kit bag full of sports gear he had found in the flat. This Felix character, he reflected, was about to hear the final wolf whistle – from the man who was planning to blow his new house down.

22

With the aid of Fliss's rape alarm torch and with very dirty knees, Dan and Phoebe located the BMW car keys in a freshly dug border, flattening several lush bedding plants lovingly put there by the pensioner in the basement.

'I guess that provides my excuse,' he grinned, brushing damp earth from his trouser legs as he straightened up. 'Flat tyre, having popped out for some fags.'

'You don't smoke.' Phoebe followed him through the hall to the front door.

'Actually, I do.' Dan shrugged sheepishly. 'I started again last year – after, well, after you left, really.'

'Not much then, surely? I mean, you never smoke in front of me.'

'Twenty a day – and no, I don't, because I know you don't like it.'

Phoebe raised her eyebrow thoughtfully. 'I shouldn't worry. Fliss usually has about three on the go in various rooms of the flat. I'm used to it – and you never smell smoky.'

'Mitzi bought me a new aftershave to hide the pong.' Dan thrust his neck under her nose. 'Bloody disgusting stuff – get a whiff.'

He needn't have bothered; Phoebe had already adopted the new smell as part of him – had only this week trailed around Dickins and Jones' perfume hall in an attempt to locate it for a reassuring, indulgent whiff – and had been beginning to grow rather fond of its cloying muskiness. She'd even spent a lot of Saturday night with her nose pressed to her sheets trying to recapture it.

Now she suddenly decided she didn't like it at all and wrinkled her nose.

'Who's Fliss?' Dan turned to look at her.

'My flatmate. Surely I've told you about her? She lives here too.'

Dan shrugged. 'Maybe – before New Zealand. I forget.' He brushed her bob back from her eyes and smiled. 'God, you're so beautiful, Phoebe.'

They were at the door now and he gathered her into his arms for a long, indulgent kiss.

Luxuriating in the fizzing effect of his touch, Phoebe kissed him back, but her heart was pounding an unhappy funeral march in her ears. Again the distance between them was hitting home, prickling her skin like sharp, blistering wasp stings.

It was such a petty thing not to know that he'd started smoking again, and yet to Phoebe it was a measure of their shallow bond. She should be flattered that he didn't smoke in front of her. Instead she felt ludicrously betrayed, as though again she was only seeing part of a picture, cut across by scissors to hide the other people in it.

In most relationships, she found the drip-drip water torture of gathering information exciting – their birthplace, childhood, star sign, ex-lovers, family, politics, passions. The slowly gleaned learning curve ran hand-in-hand with the sexual and emotional ones for satisfaction. Yet with Dan, whom she had known so little of for so long, each new piece of information merely made her feel insecure, confirmed the tiny cluster of facts she based her love for him on. *And* he didn't know who Fliss was, Phoebe stewed – Fliss was so much a part of Phoebe's life it was like not knowing her birthday.

Closing her lips like a startled clam, she drew back from the kiss and blurted, 'When's my birthday, Dan?'

He looked slightly bemused, but didn't hesitate. 'The twelfth of August. Why?'

'No reason.' Flustered, Phoebe felt her face redden. 'I'd just forgotten.'

Dan laughed. 'Rubbish! Look, that's pretty soon, isn't it?'

She nodded. 'A couple of weeks.'

'Okay, I'll think of something.'

'What?'

'Something special for you.'

Her cheeks coloured even more to an unflattering crimson. 'Oh no! I hope you don't think I was digging for a present. No, no! It wasn't like that at all. I was just – well – just testing really to see – '

Gently muttering, 'Shut up,' he put his finger up to her mouth and kissed her on the forehead. 'I love you for it. We'll go away for a couple of days.' He grinned, suddenly inspired. 'Christ, yes! That would be a great tonic. I'll call you soon, I promise.'

And, parting her lips with another long, honeyed kiss, he swept off, keys jingling and front door swinging.

At that moment the timer light in the hallway clicked off, plunging Phoebe into darkness.

Licking her lips and tasting the last traces of Dan's mouth, she stood in silence for a few minutes, her face still flaming, her stomach churning, a pulse thrumming in her temples like a frenzied insect. She had walked right into it, she realised, asked for it even, meal ticket thrust out like singing tramp with a hat. She'd just displayed the hackneyed behaviour of the spoiled, pot-hunting mistress anxious to be a trophy wife, begging weekends, diamond earrings, credit cards and a flat in Little Venice. And, worse still, Dan seemed to relish the prospect.

Watching the Daybreak TV weathergirl waggling her manicured nails over a cold front, Saskia decided she ought to sober up.

By the time she'd clambered in and out of the shower and started knocking back a three-teaspoon mug of black coffee, the male presenter was perched on a pastel sofa, wiping sweat from his moustache and puffing out his Jacquard Pringle jumper with flushed excitement as he questioned the studio guest.

Saskia sank on to her own littered sofa in fascination and watched Isabelle Delauney pouting her red-slash lips at him, angry black eyes rolling tiredly. Swathed in black leather and as pale as the presenter was fake tanned, she looked monstrously hung-over but fabulously carnal.

'I do not understand zis question?' she growled in her husky Disque Bleu voice, hating being interviewed in English and therefore determined to make Pringle jumper squirm.

'Rumour has it that you are engaged to England's handsome blond hero, Felix Sylvian, Belle,' oozed Pringle man, his football commentator's voice making Felix sound like a sports star. 'Is this true?'

'No, I am not engaged to Felix.' The red slash curled wickedly. 'If I get engaged to every man I fuck, I have more rings that Tiffany's, *non*?'

The camera cut to Pringle man wiping his moustache and frantically waggling his script, and then the Daybreak TV logo was flashed on screen with its jingly bit of Musak accompanying it. Seconds later they were into a commercial break.

Saskia was aware of a burning sensation coursing across her chest. For a split-second she thought she was suffering a heart attack but, looking down, realised she was covered with dripping black coffee.

Because he had to be on top of potential libel suits – his own company's and those of other papers – before they even bubbled in the imagination of the litigators, Dan took delivery of all the main papers at his Barnes home before five in the morning and, rising at about half-past each weekday, would spend over an hour scouring them whilst listening to London Newstalk and knocking back very sweet tea. He kept the sugar hidden in his golf club bag in the back lobby because Mitzi, who strongly disapproved of anything that tasted good on the grounds that it was undoubtedly a toxin and therefore thickened either arteries or waists, had banished everything sweet bar Hermesetas and honey from the house.

This morning Dan didn't even get around to fishing the PG

Tips bag (another thing Mitzi frowned upon) from his mug. Flicking through the papers as he waited for the kettle to boil, he felt like Columbo lifting back a murder victim's coat to reveal a dropped earring. He then took precisely ten minutes speed-reading through the whole pile before showering, dressing and dashing for his car to head east.

Banished to the guest room last night by a livid Mitzi, he'd taken his Prozac and lain awake for the remaining early hours thinking his way through the Phoebe situation until he felt sharply focused and optimistic. He was now pretty certain that he knew who 'Felix' was. No wonder Phoebe had looked pole-axed the previous night.

As soon as he was sitting behind his desk, listening to the contract cleaners vacuuming the boardroom at the far end of the corridor, he propped the phone receiver against his ear with his elbow and fished out his portable razor from the bottom drawer. Firing it up, he listened to the phone in the cuttings office ring on and on. They should be in scouring the rivals by now. He had a fairly shrewd idea that they were in fact bunched in the smoking room with pilfered filter coffee reading one another's horoscopes out of every single paper, as they did for the first half hour of every morning. Normally he would storm downstairs and haul the manager out for a roasting, but this morning his attention was too centred on the task ahead to warrant the distraction.

'Blast them!' he muttered, slamming the receiver down and starting to shave around the nub of his chin. Chewing his bottom lip to draw the skin tightly back, he hit upon an idea.

With his free hand he struck the E-mail command up on his computer and one-finger typed a message through to the cuttings department requesting all the clips they could find on Felix Sylvian. Then he typed another to an old mate who was a staff reporter on the *News* and owed him several bottles of Johnnie Walker for off-the-record back-chat that had been swiftly turned into italicised quotes from 'an insider'.

Greg, he typed. *Felix Sylvian – model/actor/slacker. Know anything you can't substantiate?*

*   *   *

'Phoebe?'

'Mmm?'

'Is your phone okay? It sounds really muffled.'

'Hang on, I'm under the duvet.' She let out a shuddering yawn. 'Is this better?'

'Yes. It's Saskia.'

'Oh, Christ – yes, hi – I was hoping you'd call.' Phoebe blinked herself awake and clambered up the pillows to prop her head against the wall. 'The thing is – '

'Can we meet for lunch?' The question was snapped in such a demanding tone that it was rendered more or less rhetorical.

'What?' Phoebe yawned again. 'Oh, lunch – yes, I suppose so. When?'

'Half an hour. Mad Dogs and Englishmen – it's near Georgette's office. Do you know it?'

'No.' Phoebe squinted at her watch. It was almost midday. She'd had three hours' sleep, and had missed signing on yet again. She really had to get her time-clock sorted out soon – she was moving from nocturnal to hibernating.

Saskia very curtly gave her instructions and then rang off before Phoebe could utter another word.

She was just staggering into the bathroom to clean her teeth when the phone rang again.

'Look,' Fliss whispered urgently as soon as Phoebe had picked it up, 'it's me – Saskia's just gone to the loo so I've got to be quick. Brace yourself for a grilling – oh, and listen, buy the *Sun*, the *Mirror*, the *News* and a *Standard* if you can get one before you go to lunch. Bye, mate.'

By twelve-thirty, it would have taken an industrial load of Mr Sheen to wipe away the smile slicked across Dan's face. He finished a very instructive call to his old friend Susie Middleton, with the usual oblique reference to the dinner he was always promising but had yet to provide, and then dialled straight through to Phoebe's flat.

No one answered. Dan glanced at his watch while he waited and then started shrugging himself one-handed into his jacket in preparation for racing off to his pub lunch with Greg as soon as he'd finished the call. Still the line repeated its short, trilling rings.

Dan hung on, certain that her machine would switch itself on after twenty rings or so.

Then he closed his eyes and groaned as he remembered throwing the tape away.

Three-quarters of an hour later, Phoebe crept into Mad Dogs and Englishmen, cowering behind the assorted papers which she was clutching to her chest as she slid her dark glasses down her nose to peep furtively over them for Saskia.

By some horrific coincidence, it was the same bar where she had made her accidental foray into the men's loo a few weeks earlier and overheard Felix and his friend. Even the barman on shift today was the same, beaming at her knowingly as he plunged a corkscrew into a bottle of house red.

Phoebe stepped behind a pillar and peeked around it.

'I'm here,' muttered a voice immediately behind her.

Saskia was sitting at the table that Phoebe had her bottom pressed against, looking sullen and ghostly behind equally black sunglasses.

'Hi.' Phoebe sank gratefully down opposite her.

'I see you've got the papers,' Saskia grunted, watching her squirm uncomfortably in her seat. 'You look dreadful.'

'Likewise,' Phoebe hissed. 'Who said revenge was a dish best eaten cold?'

Ignoring her, Saskia reached out for the *Evening Standard*, flicked calmly to page eight and began to read.

'"*Bar Nero was teeming with celebrities last night for the launch of . . . blah . . . blah . . .*" here we are: "*Chief amongst the drama was the unexpected arrival of pop legend, The Phallus. Recently photographed in Paris with sultry starlet, Lili Etoile, the petit pop icon instead chose last night to accompany French actress Isabelle Delauney, who is to appear on Friday night's debut show. Delauney, 39*" – God, I didn't know she was that old – "*until last night linked to London male model, Felix Sylvian, refused to comment on rumours that the couple's fiery relationship is now dramatically off, despite recent speculation that they were to marry. But Sylvian, 26, who arrived independently last night with leggy, tempestuous model, Fanii Hubert, 23, was only too happy to confirm the split.*

' "'Belle is a very maternal woman – she is looking for someone closer to her age who shares her breeding instincts.'

' "Asked whether he was now with Ms Hubert, Sylvian – who has a reputation for dating difficult women – refused to comment beyond, 'Let's just say I like women who enjoy giving men a good dressing down. And I almost lost more than my heart tonight.' Pictured right, Sylvian later went on to illustrate his words." '

Voice rasping with bitterness, Saskia thrust the article under Phoebe's nose.

'I've seen it,' she muttered.

'Well, look at it again!' Saskia howled. 'What did you do all fucking night? Drink free champagne, chat up Jonathan Ross and do a bit of star-spotting with Stan?'

Swallowing, Phoebe looked again at the photograph of The Phallus watching in delighted amazement through several millimetres of darkened Perspex and a couple of minders' armpits as Felix – all delightful, rumpled sex-appeal with no shirt on, his jeans belt undone and his long-sleeved t-shirt wrapped around Fanii Hubert's neck – pressed his long, lean body against hers and indulged in a very deep-throat kiss.

'No, I know exactly what you were doing.' Saskia started to unfold the *News* with shaking hands. 'Here – "Unknown Beauty to Slam Top TV Exec in Front of Millions" – there's a piece in the television preview, telling viewers to watch out for your little party pooper act on Friday night as Malcolm Hutchinson has decided to air it in the Showdown party footage just to prove what a swinging, democratic guy he is. They'll cut the footage to make you look like an example of Care in the Community at its most dangerous, by the way.

'What were you doing last night, Phoebe?' she snarled. 'Tell me if my eyes are going, but you appear to be wearing a pretty revolting cricketing sweater in this picture. Did you even *see* Felix last night, or were you too busy beating up producers and borrowing clothes from passing sixteen-stone spin bowlers? Did you try and get off with Ian Botham? Is that it?'

'Look, Saskia, I don't think – '

Phoebe paused as the waiter, smile still beaming, whisked up with a twirling note-pad and a knowing wink.

'Think fucking what?' Saskia wailed, shocking the other lunchers in the bar to a fascinated hush.

Phoebe gulped and smiled at the waiter apologetically.

'Er – two white wines and two omelette baps,' she spluttered, anxious to get him away.

The waiter chuckled delightedly and whisked off.

'Think fucking *what*?' Saskia repeated. She had demolished the carnation-in-a-Perrier-bottle with shaking fingers and was moving on to the paper napkins.

'Look, I don't think it's as bad as all that. Let me explain. The thing is, I progressed pretty well last night and I'm not sure,' Phoebe rubbed her forehead anxiously, 'but that quote of Felix's in the *Standard* might just be a cryptic reference to it. He wants to meet me for tea today.'

'He what?'

The waiter, creeping up with two vast white wines, slowed down even more and tried to linger.

Despite Saskia's high-rise eyebrows and fly-catching mouth, Phoebe fell silent until he'd dumped the glasses and huffed off. Then she took a deep breath.

'Let me explain . . .'

For the ensuing twenty minutes, Phoebe couldn't tell whether Saskia left her omelette bap untouched because she was excited, or upset, or whether it was just because, as she herself discovered, it was the most revolting mess of egg and starch she had experienced since boarding school eggy bread. But half an hour later, her bap still as round as Silbury Hill, Saskia was staring at Phoebe in a furious combination of relief and shuddering jealousy.

'But you can't go to Pat Val's dressed like that!' she wailed, taking in Phoebe's shapeless black dress.

'Well, I rather thought it might be a good idea to stand him up,' Phoebe muttered lamely. Strangely, with all that had happened with Dan in between, it hadn't occurred to her that she would actually have to go through with it and meet Felix.

'Don't be mad!' Saskia was suddenly animated and excited, her blue eyes rolling and expressive, her face alive, her hands waving about like a conductor in the allegro movement of a Vivaldi concerto. 'It's far, far too early days to stand him up – anyway, he'll probably do that to you. But, just in case he doesn't, you must be there. Look, you're going to have to come back to the office to smarten yourself up. Christ, I hope Georgette is there.'

'Georgette?' Phoebe said weakly.

'Yes, yes.' Saskia was impatiently digging in her handbag for the money to pay for lunch. 'She knows all about it. God, I must have a pee!' She gazed around for a sign to the lavatories.

'Downstairs on the right – I mean left,' Phoebe said vaguely. 'Georgette knows about the revenge thing?'

But Saskia had thundered off, sweeping carnations-in-a-bottle off almost every table in her wake with her swinging handbag.

Back at the office, Georgette was flapping about in white silk palazzo pants, spouting grumpily about women who wore last season's Jaeger twin-sets ('Definite summer sale rail,' she sniffed) and who pressed a sherry on one before eleven – ('honestly, darlings, you know I can't face anything but vodka before yardarm').

Seeing Saskia, she waved her in without pausing for breath.

'She had every bloody *House and Garden* since decimalisation in chronological order on her shiny repro coffee table, can you believe it? The stupid cow made me so late I could only have the quickest of mineral waters with my girlfriends at Daph's. I'm honestly, honestly spitting.'

Grumbling that the woman had finally announced – 'with

frightful vowel sounds, I might add' – that she was going to shop around for more party planner quotes – 'as though I'm a bloody builder about to stick a jacuzzi and sauna on her revolting pink gin palace!' – Georgette was only too happy for a distraction.

'Bring her in!' she screeched at Saskia, who had left Phoebe hovering in the crimson lobby.

'Darling, darling Phoebe!' She greeted her by depositing a smear of red Lancôme on each cheek then took her under her scented silk wing. 'Of course we can give you a quick makeover – what fun! Now pop through there and strip off and I'll raid what clothes I keep here for something suitable. The girls can make merry with my tart sack. Fliss! Stop being all boring. Quit typing that letter, grab my muck bucket from the bathroom and get cracking on Phoebe. Saskia darling, come and give me some advice. Oh – fix us all a vast vod and something first, will you? Look in the fridge, there's bound to be something fizzy to top the glasses up with.'

'You all right?' Fliss deposited a vanity case the size of Phoebe's largest suitcase on to the butter-yellow sofa.

'Not really.' She shook her head. 'Can you believe I'm going through with this? I mean, I explained how awful it was when I left Felix in Cambridge Circus last night, but she's convinced he might turn up today. I don't think this is very good therapy for her at all – she's coming unscrewed.'

'And you're so very hunky-dory?' Fliss drew her freckled chin back sarcastically.

'That's different,' Phoebe muttered, unsnapping the make-up case.

'Sure, Phoebes,' Fliss sighed, dropping a kiss into her hair and rubbing her shoulders comfortingly. 'Every time you look at me, I see one of those Walt Disney cartoon characters whose eyes suddenly turn into the symbols of a fruit machine when they hit upon an idea. And yours just say "Dan".'

Phoebe smiled unhappily and held up an eyeliner. 'Well, you'd better paint "Felix" in then.'

*   *   *

'You all right?' Georgette looked at Saskia sternly as she unzipped plastic dust covers on clothes.

Saskia nodded fervently, ice rattling like maracas in the tumblers she was holding.

'Sure?'

'Absolutely!' Her artificially high voice crackled with tension. 'It really seems to be working out as I planned.'

Georgette lapsed into silence for a few moments and then sucked in a cautious breath.

'Sometimes,' she started reluctantly, 'having an idea and acting it out are two very different things, darling – I think this yellow's rather smashing – and the latter can be far more painful – or the green? What I mean is, if you feel at all doubtful, you'd be far better to stop things now, at an early stage, rather than them get out of hand and make you even more unhappy. Do you understand?'

Saskia smiled at her bravely, understanding totally.

'The green,' she said firmly.

Across the road from Harrods, Phoebe hovered nervously, pulling a ridiculously short bottle green skirt down as yet another passing car beeped enthusiastically at her. Because Georgette was so tiny and wore everything on the cusp of too tight, Phoebe barely fitted into her clothes and they were cut far, far too short for her gangly frame. The skirt was secured by three safety pins and a staple at the back; the jacket arms were practically three-quarter length. By contrast, the vast, long-cuffed white shirt had a bulldog clip hidden in the back to pull it into a seductive shape beneath the jacket. She was under strict instructions not to remove the jacket under any circumstances.

'But I'll fry!' she had wailed.

'Then do it,' Georgette had insisted firmly, pins in her mouth like a dresser just before a catwalk show. 'You're frying in the face of fashion, darling.'

Please don't turn up, Felix, Phoebe prayed as she killed time in Boots. The only subject I can talk about today is Daniel Neasham. Hardly seductive.

Getting engrossed in the record section as she tried to find every single album Dan had ever played for her, Phoebe killed rather too much time and raced into Pat Val's twenty minutes late.

Felix wasn't there.

Rammed into a tiny corner that had clearly been designated as the spot for sad, unwanted singles, she ploughed her way unenthusiastically through a lemon tea and a muffin, acutely aware that the rest of the clientele was scrutinising her very dressy, very solitary and highly uncomfortable presence with interest.

A quarter of an hour later, Felix still hadn't turned up.

How dare he blow me out? Phoebe thought furiously. God, I must be ugly. I'm obviously as sexually attractive as a Latvian shot-putter on steroids. Even Felix Sylvian doesn't fancy me enough to roll up for tea, and he picks on the ugliest girls in bars. Dan has probably gone right off me in the cold light of day too.

Snorkelling up the last of her tea in double-quick time and revolting her audience, Phoebe threw down her money and left in a huff.

She couldn't face going back to Georgette's office to admit defeat – they were all no doubt currently engrossed in specu- lation as to what was happening between her and Felix. Phoebe suddenly had an instinctive feeling that he was in fact lounging around a vast king-sized love trampoline with Fanii's long, painted toes in his mouth, having forgotten all about tea with the loo-freak flasher with attitude from last night.

She plodded past Harrods in a daze, wondering what Dan was doing. She tried to visualise his office – undoubtedly sumptuous, air-conditioned and crammed with squishy cream sofas, wrought-iron sculptures and vast, deconstructionialist oil paintings framed in heavy stripped wood. She had a quick fantasy that she was sauntering in dressed very tackily in nothing but a floor-length Cossack coat, clutching a bottle of chilled Krug and a Harrods bag of moreish pre-carnal goodies.

The fantasy was somewhat quashed as Phoebe told herself that she couldn't afford a bottle of Black Tower right now, let alone Krug, but she indulged herself for a few minutes more by slipping into Harvey Nichols and floating up the several escalators to the fifth floor, day-dreaming that she was there to buy their erotic eats.

In the food hall, she guiltily realised that she should give Georgette something to say thank you for the loan of the clothes and pointed out the glistening bowl of foie gras to the assistant at the delicatessen counter, meanly narrowing her finger and thumb to a pinched point when she copped the price. She was just lingering covetously over a vast basket of quails' eggs when she felt a warm hand lightly touch her arm.

'So you shop here too – how horribly pretentious of you,'

Phoebe looked up to see Felix smiling down at her with the charm of Lancelot requesting her hanky before the joust. The intensity of the blue gaze shot her a few paces in reverse.

'Just a few bits and pieces,' she smiled back, 'for tea really.' Her Dan fantasy shattered, she battled to stop her lips trembling tearfully.

Felix cocked an angled eyebrow. 'Foie gras for tea?'

He sounded conceited and snobbish, Phoebe mused, like her mother snapping 'Milk in second!' to her father.

'Yes – why not?' she challenged, snatching her basket to her stomach and stalking towards the nearest set of shelving.

Felix followed her. 'You look delicious.'

Aware that the safety pins were digging in, Phoebe stared fixedly at the shelves in front of her. Then she swallowed as she realised that she was now opposite a load of very off-the-wall condiments and pickles. Felix was still right behind her. What the hell. Undaunted, she tossed some artichoke hearts in olive oil and a small jar of courgette chutney into her basket before stalking off to grab some strawberries, a tub of cream, a quarter of brie and a bottle of Australian wine called Crocodile's Breath Creek which seemed fitting. Finally, she located some muffins and a tin of Darjeeling.

'Look, you don't have to be so fucking uptight, you know,'

Felix muttered in a low voice, lifting the hair above her left ear with his breath and practically shooting her into a display of potted anchovies.

'I'm sorry.' Phoebe quailed away, still battling not to descend into ridiculous, weepy misery over Dan. She had to be charming, coy and captivating, she told herself. Think seduction, think enchantment, think balls.

But when she looked up at him with what had started as a beguiling, apologetic smile, it started to wobble dramatically.

Not saying a word, Felix took her by the upper arm and steered her into the wine section, cornering her in a quiet alcove beside rare Far Eastern reds.

'What's the matter?' His voice was as soft and coaxing as a nudge from the Andrex puppy.

'Nothing.' Phoebe shrugged, shook her head, tried for the beguiling smile once more and failed miserably.

'Okay, okay – look, I realise we hardly know one another, so I can quite see why you don't want to dump anything on me.' He dropped his gaze to her basket. 'But I'm glad we bumped into one another again.'

Blinking the salt from her eyes, Phoebe squinted up at his face. She couldn't tell whether he'd turned up at Pat Val's or not and had an odd feeling that it would be against the game-plan to seem so insecure as to ask. He was in the area, true, but that meant nothing. Knightsbridge was part of his very confined London play pen. Felix and his cronies were as plentiful as black cabs in this area, and probably as easy to pick up.

'Look, I don't think I caught your name last night?' she said, wondering if that was a bit fuck-off even by Saskia's play-it-cool standards.

It clearly was. Felix carried on staring into her basket, a slight smile playing on his cruel, kissable mouth, hair slipping forward so that it tangled with his eyelashes. He fiddled with the loose cellophane on the Darjeeling, not looking up.

'Yes, you did,' he finally murmured, the smile widening slightly. 'You caught my name as often as a commuters' bus last night.'

'Did I?' Phoebe threw a question back, stalling for time as she frantically tried to work out what Saskia would want her to do.

'And I caught all of yours.' Felix finally looked up, eyes playing between hers as though choosing which one he preferred. 'Frances, Phoebe, Freda Loo-Freika.' He smiled so widely that his eyes creased into bright blue triangles. 'Now I like that last one best. Was it your mother or your father's choice? Don't tell me – a mad, Abba fan granny?'

'Well, at least Mummy fought her down from Bjorn,' Phoebe smiled weakly.

Laughing, Felix bit his bottom lip with very straight white teeth. 'You are deliciously, delightfully cookie. In fact,' he cocked his head and watched her for a few moments, 'you are just basically delicious. Please may I eat you, Freda Loo-Freika?'

Not sure if he was being cute or downright blue, Phoebe thoughtfully studied a bottle of Tanzanian Shiraz, wondering whether Saskia would condone her boffing him over the head with it for added spice.

A warm hand creeping around her waist towards the safety pins and a breathy murmur of, 'Come back with me and fuck,' told her that blue was his preferred colour choice.

Nearby, a Knightsbridge housewife eyed them suspiciously over her Cutler and Gross shades.

As Felix's surreptitious exploration of her waist inched within a nail's flick of the safety pins, Phoebe pulled away in the nick of time and caught his hand, staring into two blue-chip eyes as cool as iced curaçao. The contrast with the warm, dry hand now lacing through hers and paddling between her fingers couldn't be greater.

'I've actually just had tea,' she muttered. 'And I never let anyone eat me between meals.'

Tightening his grip on her hand and twisting it until her wrist was weakened, Felix pulled Phoebe towards him until their hips connected. 'I thought you were just shopping for tea?' he breathed, his mouth an inch from hers.

Bugger! Phoebe glanced into her basket in horror. So she had been.

'We delicious cookies have to keep our sugar levels up,' she explained feebly. 'I guess I'm just a prick teas.'

Wrestling her hand from his, she stalked back to the fruit counter and bunged half a pound of cherries, a wrinkled yellow exotic number and a water melon into her basket. She was just toying thoughtfully with the courgettes when she realised that Felix had followed her and was breathing very softly down her neck, having selected a bottle of champagne from the fridge. It was only when she moved meaningfully on to the cucumbers and he remained panting against her top three vertebrae that it occurred to Phoebe that he might be trying to filch a sly gawp at her – or rather Georgette's – jacket label. The shallow fink!

'It's Top Shop,' she muttered darkly, sweeping across to squeeze a couple of aubergines.

'What?' Felix looked dumbfounded, falling in beside her to play with a patti pan, tossing it between his hands like a cricket ball, champagne tucked under his arm.

Okay, perhaps he wasn't trying to cop the Bella Freud, Phoebe realised guiltily. She hurriedly moved off to the pre-made soups fridge.

Tracking her like a defender marking Ryan Giggs, he didn't pass comment until he was queuing up behind her at the counter.

'Actually, I got bored waiting for you at Pat Val's so I pushed off. I loathe unpunctuality,' he murmured, looking around politely as though anxious not to inflict a mere domestic argument upon other shoppers.

'And I loathe punctuality,' Phoebe muttered back, frantically trying to calculate the value of goods in her basket and work out if she had enough to cover it. Nowhere near, she decided. 'It's so reactionary.'

'So are muffins,' Felix pointed out as she heaved her basket on to the counter.

'Are you saying my muffins are reactionary?' Phoebe turned

on him, instantly seeing her escape route and embracing it with a virago's gusto.

'Well, they're hardly subversive.' Felix drew back in amusement.

Suddenly, Phoebe realised how smart he looked – he was wearing a suspiciously new-looking cream silk jumper and baggy linen trousers of the sort that could only be worn once before gathering stains like an Aquavac filter; his hair was as squeaky clean as the Pope's driving licence, and he smelled delicious – all soap, toothpaste and subtle aftershave.

So he had made a real effort for her, she mused – he had turned up on time and dressed up to boot. The seduction according to Felix Sylvian had begun just as Saskia had predicted. Now she was going to blow it to save herself the shame of being caught short at the check-out.

'I suppose you think strawberries and cream are reactionary too, do you?' she asked sweetly, aware that her goods were now being passed through the till and loaded into a smart paper bag with double-quick efficiency.

'Of course they are,' Felix grinned.

'Good.' Phoebe licked her lips nervously, her eyes searching surreptitiously for a security guard. 'Then I suggest you compose yourself to reactionary to this.'

Piercing the foil of the cream with a new acrylic fingernail, Phoebe had been about to slop it into Felix's face followed by cramming a strawberry into his mouth, but at the last minute she stopped, realising that to play the embittered, screw-loose shrew would kill off Saskia's plan. She might need an escape right now but, hate Felix as she did, she had to be more subtle.

She looked down at the cream pot thoughtfully and then, cocking her head, smiled up at him.

To the astonishment of the till girl, she licked her finger and took a strawberry from its plastic punnet by the stalk. Dipping it slowly into the cream she popped it gently into his mouth and smiled. Then, helping herself to a second strawberry, she shot him a wink.

'Lovely having tea with you.'

Wandering idly towards the escalator, she glided down it until she was just out of view before legging it down the others as though she had half a shelf-worth of their best Beluga Caviar thrust up her knickers. Miraculously no one shot her so much as a suspicious glance. Phoebe half-considered lifting a couple of DKNY outfits while she was about it, but decided not to push her luck.

Outside, she leaned against a wall and closed her eyes, waiting for her breaths to last longer than her heartbeats.

Reliving the moment like an action replay of a home goal, she started to colour with embarrassment. How truly, truly awful, she realised. She had behaved appallingly; Saskia would climb the walls with despair. But Phoebe found it almost impossible to hide how much she hated him.

'Your shopping, madam,' panted an out-of-breath voice, high with nerves.

Phoebe snapped her eyes open to see one of the assistants from the food hall beaming across at her as she thrust out a paper carrier bag.

'Oh – thank you.' Phoebe reddened even more. 'But, you see, I haven't paid for it. The fact is I can't – '

'The gentleman paid,' the girl said quickly. 'He insisted. If you'll excuse me, I must get back.' Dashing away, she looked over her shoulder, blushing furiously. 'He's really gorgeous. You're so lucky.' And, lovingly fingering the tenner in her pocket, she raced back into the store.

Phoebe sagged against the wall and blinked in bewilderment. Then she glanced in the bag and saw that the cream and strawberries had been replaced with fresh cartons and that Felix's bottle of champagne was in there too. Written on the label of the muffins was a number and a hastily jotted note in that round, clear hand.

Please call – I sense a chemical reactionary. Felix Sylvian.

'Strike two,' Phoebe muttered in delight and wandered in the direction of Georgette's office, thoughtfully breaking into the strawberries.

23

'Okay, leave it until Sunday and then call him,' Saskia told Phoebe, gnawing at a reddened cuticle.

'Surely Friday will do?' Georgette cut short her phone call to butt in over her shoulder.

'Saturday,' Fliss compromised, tucking into her third strawberry as she perched on her boss's desk.

'Oh, do it now, darling, so we can all listen!' Georgette spun around on her chair excitedly. 'You can do it on the tranny phone so we can all hear – pass me a strawb, Fliss – and Saskia can give hand signals, can't you, darling?'

'Sunday!' she insisted, her knuckles as pale as her bleach-soaked dishcloth face.

Georgette and Fliss looked grumpily indignant at missing out on the fun.

Relieved, Phoebe went through to the yellow sitting room and started laboriously to undo the safety pins securing the back of her borrowed green skirt.

Saskia trailed her wanly.

'Can I look at those muffins again?'

'Sure,' Phoebe smiled, 'over there, in the bag on the floor.'

Saskia rummaged in the bag and drew them out.

While Phoebe changed back into mourning, Saskia read those few short words as though they were the final clue to the priceless Masquerade hare. Then, unable to stop herself despite three slimming tablets washed down with two bottles of

Evian, she broke into the cellophane wrapping and wolfed two in short succession before sinking down on the canary yellow sofa and bursting into tears.

'Oh, Freddy,' she whispered between hacking sobs as Phoebe frantically wriggled into her dress before rushing over to comfort her, 'please make this work.'

'Of course I will,' she soothed, trying desperately to reassure herself as well as Saskia.

Later Georgette called Susie from her husband's car-phone. Sir Dennis Middleton was too busy taking a very hushed, abbreviated call on his mobile phone beside her to notice.

'Listen, I have to be quick. Latest development, darling. Felix has taken the bait and by all appearances is keen as spiked punch.'

'Oh God, I hoped he'd not fall for it. What's she like?'

'Bright, funny, opinionated – bit odd-looking, but striking. Big nose. Very dare-devil. Almost fits into my clothes, the lucky thing. Wish I still did.'

'Felix'll get frightened off,' Susie sighed. 'He likes easy targets.'

'I hope you're right, darling. She's certainly not at all interested in him, just acting as though she is.'

'I know,' Susie muttered. 'She's involved with a friend of mine.'

'But you said you didn't know her?'

'I don't – but I heard the name again recently and realised who she was. From what I hear, she's far more dangerous than we thought. Doubly so because she's so madly in love with someone else. I'd hoped so much that Felix wouldn't find her attractive. You say she has a big nose?'

'She's not one of your models, darling,' Georgette pointed out kindly. 'She's allowed to have uneven facial features and still be considered attractive. She's bright as a Chanel button and has great style. Very fashionable. Not too keen on going through with this whole business either, I'd say. So, shall I still help the girls and earwig like mad?'

'For now,' Susie agreed. 'I'm almost beginning to think that if this thing works it'll do Felix good.'

'What fun! Must go, darling. Old fart to right hanging up. I'll let you know latest as soon as I catch on.'

On Thursday afternoon, Piers Fox's cuttings service in the UK faxed through all the relevant coverage that his clients had provoked at the Bar Nero party. Piers slept very soundly that night.

He was particularly delighted with the coverage Felix had attracted at the Showdown party, apparently outshining even The Phallus as the daring darling of the paparazzi. Felix had thrust his clean, pink tongue out to the press in quite the most delightfully headline-making way, and he'd given Fanii terrific coverage to boot. What a pro!

'Marvellous!' Piers said for the third time as he re-read them in the back of a cab on Friday morning. He was on his way to meet the Second Assistant to the Deputy Vice Director in Charge of Project Co-ordination for the Strassi PR campaign. The meeting had taken him three days to set up and he was determined to ride it with his punchiest pitch.

With the help of a hotel room phone bill that read like the hotel's phone number, Piers was rapidly getting to know the Strassi philosophy. They wanted a sexy, rogueish, likable party animal with intellectual edge who shagged, surfed and read Sartre in his Strassi jeans. Felix could have been born in a pair of Strassi's.

Piers tucked the cuttings in with Felix's model composite, assorted photographs, resumé and showreel. He felt supremely confident today, helped by the one-hour isolation tank session he had just enjoyed in his suite followed by a breakfast of blanched papaya slices on nut-free muesli with skimmed soya milk, ugli fruit juice and caffeine free tea made with filtered spring water. All this, succeeded by the arrival of Portia wearing nothing at all beneath her long jacket dress, to give him a kiss for luck just below his belt, gave Piers the sense that today was going to knock the required digit off his overdraft – and add several zeros to his credit on a separate account.

*　　　*　　　*

'Have a nice day, ma'am. Missing you already. I'll be seeing you in my dreams tonight. Byeee!'

'Oh, piss off.'

Portia stomped out of the hotel restaurant and eenie-mee-nied on her freshly manicured fingers to decide whether a second afternoon lounging beside the pool with the sales reps' wives from Arkansas was preferable to going down-town for yet another prowl around the department stores, boutiques, beauticians and pet astrologers.

Deciding she could face neither, Portia returned to her room – a mean, poky attic with sub-zero air conditioning and a jet shower that removed a layer of skin with every wash – and lay back on her bed cradling the phone on her stomach and wondering who to call. It would be ten at night in the UK.

She dialled through to the Fulham flat and then listened sulkily to her own answerphone message until the beep went.

'Hi, Saskia – s'me. Where are you? Just called to check all's okay. Don't forget to feed my cacti.'

Replacing the receiver, she decided to go and have her crystals analysed uptown before meeting Piers after his meeting.

That night, wanting to work on some papers for the second Strassi meeting he had scheduled, Piers booted her out of his hotel room like a call girl who'd served her purpose. Spitting venom and red pubic hairs from her mouth, Portia found herself back in her room, pressing her chin to the phone receiver as she wondered whether to try Saskia again or just dial straight through to the Samaritans.

She counted forward in her head to work out the time in the UK. Seven in the morning. Christ! She felt exhausted just thinking about it.

Closing her eyes, she smiled dozily. There was only one person she knew who was super-efficient enough to get up and jog before her children woke up demanding breakfast. And happily it was one of the few people she'd told that she was accompanying Piers to the States.

'Susie Middleton,' panted a voice fresh from four miles around Totteridge with weights strapped to her shapely ankles.

'Suse – s'me. Cheer me up.'

'How is it?'

'Oh, Suse, he's *awful*. I don't know what to do.'

'Come home.' Even at seven in the morning, puffing from her jog, Susie was practical and blunt as an Agatha Christie murder weapon.

'I can't,' Portia sighed. 'The magazine's set me up with a load of celebrity interviews while I'm out here – I've got Goldie Hawn tomorrow morning, Nicholson as a possible later, then a load of European beef-cake action adventure thickies next week. Basically, if someone's plugging something here, I'm opening my note pad, arms and legs for them. I HATE America, Suse.'

'No, you don't, you just hate LA. It never changes,' Susie laughed. 'And what's wrong with Piers? Last week you thought he was a better lay than the golden egg.'

'He's a prig, he's mean, he's paranoid, he's sexually prudish – and he always orders the daftest, healthiest thing on the menu in duplicate. I had the runs all last night from ocean-soaked mollusc purée on seaweed lasagne with sun-dried mango sauce and rich, jellied spinach glaze.'

'Ugh!'

'And, God, Suse, is he *married*.'

'Well, that was part of the package, darling.' Susie dropped her voice in stern admonition, suddenly unsympathetic.

'I know, I know – and I accept that, truly I do. But need he be quite so married when he's in a different continent to his wife? We're booked into separate hotels, for Christ's sake. And he won't take me anywhere decent for fear of being recognised. He's worse here than he was in England. Every time I touch him, he all but gets out a duster to remove the fingerprints.'

Susie sighed and dropped the phone to her throat as she yelled out a demand that The Big Breakfast be silenced.

'Look, darling, he's just getting safety conscious. They all do it – after the pursuit and the stolen afternoons, they take stock and take fright. Soon afterwards they start to pay hotel bills with cash, enrol in evening classes as alibis and introduce you to associates you bump into in restaurants as their PA to cover

their tracks. I bet you anything, he's off-setting you against tax.
And remember, Topaz is far better known over there than she is
here.'

Portia chewed her lip. 'That's another thing. He's not very
popular here, darling. Mr Topaz Fox gets slightly worse seats in
restaurants than Michael Winner.'

Susie laughed.

'So what's happening with you?' Portia decided she was sated
with bitching about Piers – enough, in fact, to quite fancy him
again.

'Oh, the usual.' Susie was clearly looking at her watch.
'Although I had a fascinating call yesterday, actually. Do you
remember my mentioning Dan Neasham? I tried to set you up
with him?'

'Of course. He who has very hush-hush meetings with my
little sister's friend at my flat. I've even forwarded post for
him.'

'Of *course*, you fixed them up, didn't you? He begged us both,
I'd quite forgotten. God, that's even more intriguing.'

'Why?'

'Well, he is dying to know all about Felix.'

'*The* Felix? Mr slippery Sylvian?'

'Yup – gagging, my dear. Of course he tried not to let
anything slip, but I get the *distinct* impression that your sister's
little friend . . . what's she called?'

'Freddy.'

'Freddy? I thought it was Phoebe something? Anyway, I get
the impression that she's enmeshed with Felix right now and
Dan is wildly – '

'But that's impossible!'

'What?'

'Saskia's told her everything about the Felix fiasco – Mummy
and I had our ears pressed to the walls all weekend to try and
listen in. There's no way Phoebe would mess with Felix,
unless . . .'

'Unless what?'

'Oh, nothing. I just can't see it, Suse – Dan must be wrong.'

'Well, maybe.' Susie sounded doubtful. 'So you haven't heard anything? Saskia hasn't mentioned Phoebe and Felix?'

'Not at all.' Portia stroked her legs to check for stubble patches. 'Susie, do you know something you're not telling me?'

'Wish I did, darling,' she said smoothly. 'Oh – more news. Not good, though. The Neashams have put in an offer for your parents' house.'

'Deayton?'

'Yup. I'm sorry, darling.'

'I'm not.' Portia twisted the counterpane in her fingers. 'Daddy's so belly up his arse is collecting barnacles. If he accepts, it might just save them. What am I going to do about Piers, Suse? Should I ditch him or persevere and try to get my rent paid?'

'Portia!'

'Look, darling, if I'm going to be a mistress, I'm getting the full monty – rings on my fingers and bells on my sucked toes. Not to mention a flashy little Audi like Di's and a couple of Versace frocks a year. If my heart's going to bleed, the least I can do is make his pocket do the same.'

'No, no, no, no!' Gin screamed, frightening the dogs under the table with a scuttle of claws on tiles – apart from Tebbit who started yapping madly and springing up into the air from all fours like a cat jumping on an open Aga hot plate.

'If you're going to get hysterical on me, then we'll discuss it this evening.' Tony didn't lift his eyes from the *Daily Telegraph* as he plunged his knife into the coarse cut Oxford marmalade. 'And turn that bloody wailing woman off.'

'I am not hysterical, Tonic.' Gin gave Tebbit a sharp kick and then whipped him up into her arms to apologise, ignoring Tony's request for her to silence Radio 3. 'I just cannot believe you would drop this bombshell on me without at least a shot across my bows by way of warning. I can't even take it in, let alone get hysterical. God, I only wish you had a sense of humour, then I could ask if this was a sick joke.'

'Of course it's not a bloody joke, Gin.' Tony started calmly spreading his toast. 'Good God, it's been glaringly obvious to everyone else for weeks – I've already written Reg a couple of work references, for Christ's sake.'

'You've *what*?' Gin went very still as Tebbit squirmed for release.

'You're the only person who's been too damn blinkered to let herself see the brutal facts,' Tony ploughed on with all the vitriol of one who's hidden the truth for too long. 'If we don't sell this house right now, the damned place'll be taken off our hands by the bank anyway. We have no bloody option.'

'Surely it can't be taken away, Tonic?' Gin's voice was reduced to a low, husky whisper of fear. 'You paid off the mortgage with what was left after your pa's death duties.'

'It's now part of the security on the company's loan, you stupid woman!'

'Christ! What loan?'

'If you took any interest in the state of the business then perhaps you'd damn well know!' He turned to the sports section and scanned the cricket column.

'If you bothered to come home occasionally to tell me about the state of the company, then perhaps I would know, yes.' Dropping Tebbit on to the quarry tiles, Gin reached across and switched off the radio, fighting to keep calm. 'Now let's be sensible about this and discuss the options properly, Tonic. What can we do to save this house? Can you sell off part of Seaton's?'

'As I said, there are no options, Gin,' he muttered dismissively.

Clutching on to the kitchen surface for support, she started to shake. 'You can't do this to me, Tony,' she whispered hoarsely. 'We *must* discuss it.'

'There's nothing to discuss.' He sighed, looking up at her over his reading glasses, suddenly so sad that he seemed to leave his face sagging towards his paper in a losing battle against gravity, like a bloodhound. 'If we don't get half a million by the end of September then we're washed up. Property isn't an investment any more, Gin – it's a debt.' He forced a rueful smile. 'And we can always buy back. The Neashams are the sort of couple who change their house as often as their cars.'

'The Neashams?' Gin's voice shook in the same tremolo as the soprano she had just switched off. 'The Neashams? The couple who came to dinner? You're selling this place to them?'

Tony nodded, turning to the Obituaries column.

Gin mindlessly started to clear breakfast, even tidying away the half-eaten piece of toast Tony was clutching and distributing it equally amongst the dogs' bowls.

'But,' she started with a catch in her voice that made it rasp like a saw hitting a nail, 'they're so bloody, rottenly, bloody young!'

Stifling her tears just long enough to escape from his sight to the cellar stairs off the back lobby, Gin started to cry, comforted by five eager snouts licking her streaming cheeks.

Mitzi was so annoyed with Dan's secretary claiming he was busy on both occasions she called, that she sent him a couple of faxes.

The first was a brief note telling him that, after his twenty-four hours' grace, Tony Seaton had accepted their ridiculously low offer – admittedly one that Dan knew nothing about, as she had made it herself, but she knew he'd be pleased anyway. The second fax was a copy of his Diners Card statement with the restaurant entries underlined meaningfully.

Of course Mitzi knew that he was up to whoever-she-was again – Mitzi had never bothered to find out the name, and simply thought of Dan's fluffy flingette as Miss Tress because she had once found an extremely blurred photograph, hidden in his tennis shoe box, of something very young with a long, scraggy neck and more tousled brown mop than face.

Mitzi didn't mind the affair much – Dan was superbly guilty, relatively discreet, and it let her off his demands for weekday sex. What bothered her was that he was so downright *thick* about it. To use a Visa would go unnoticed, so would his business Mastercard or Amex. But to use his Diners Card – which he never, never used except in dire emergencies on overseas trips when he needed to book into a Hilton – was pure, transparent stupidity. It was obvious that anything which appeared on that statement would glow luminous, but this seemed to bypass him. The fact that he apparently thought he was deceiving Mitzi by charging his extra-marital shagging expenses to it depressed her far more deeply than the adultery itself. He was so hopelessly gauche.

Worse than all had been the excuse of the flat tyre last night – about as original as claiming to have left one's homework on the bus. Mitzi hadn't even bothered to check for the perfect spare wheel that was no doubt still bolted under the boot of the BMW. Dan's cutesy little smile had said it all. Besides, he couldn't change the wheel of his computer mouse, let alone a car. His folded pyjamas had been waiting for him on the pillow of the spare bed.

Had she not been so infatuated with someone else, Mitzi suspected that her itchy-skinned derisive irritation at her husband would be angry, sobbing, car-crash grief. But right now, she merely found him irksomely pitiable and felt her own discreet infidelity rather pleasantly vindicated in the light of his smutty, banal behaviour.

Susie Middleton walked into the office determined to exert motherly control, only to find that *Woman's World* had last-minute cancelled one of her top girls for their November cover, that the new receptionist had accidentally diverted all her calls into the mobile messaging service which she never used and had lost the pin code for, and that the coffee she'd spilled on her computer earlier had now rendered it clinically dead. Worst of all, the money plant cutting she had been lovingly nurturing in the kitchen had been chucked in the bin as someone had used its milk bottle incubator to water their dratted busy lizzie.

Her office was full of the publicity team waiting for the weekly meeting.

By four o'clock, she was howling with frustration. Gossip now had it that two of her highest-earning female models – including the cancelled *Woman's World* covergirl – had just signed a contract with a top American publisher to collaborate on a book which promised to blow the lid off the fashion industry. Both girls were top-league models who had survived the drug-supported anorexia of grunge to re-invent themselves in the mid-nineties but were getting bored and stroppy and complacent; one was losing jobs through weight-gain, the other had such a publicity-crazy, kiss-and-tell lesbian lover that she was getting increasingly difficult to place beyond *The Face* and *ID*. They both resented having to do the rounds again with their portfolios instead of just calling up for automatic daily work as they once had, and were clearly seeking the gratification of a fat cheque for doing no more than gossiping to an editor with a Dictaphone over a couple of uneaten lunches at The Ivy.

Immensely irritated, Susie fired them both from the agency with curt faxes and then squared up to a barrage of complaints from her booking staff who now faced a week of late nights fighting to resecure the girls' contracted work with other agency models. In retrospect, Susie realised her move had been ill judged; it would just add fuel to the girls' vitriol when mentioning the Elect Agency to their ghost-writer.

Added to which, Felix was still stalling on the German perfume ad campaign, evasively mentioning various vague projects concerning Piers which he couldn't put a date to because, he claimed, his wily agent had gone 'Stateside without leaving a fucking number, Suse'. Knowing precisely where Piers was and that his fucking number was that of a different hotel to his business number, Susie was doubly furious when Piers refused to take or return her calls. Even Portia, nose-to-nose with Goldie Hawn in the back of a Cadillac, was unavailable.

Susie gnawed a glossy lip in angst and called Felix again. She had dialled the number so many times that day that her fingers moved across the phone as swiftly as a child playing 'chopsticks' on a pianoforte.

'What are you doing next week then?'

'Next week? Not sure.'

'Please, please, do the Deus Chrissy shots for me – it's Paris, not hard work, lots of time off and freebies. You can even take a friend.'

Felix laughed. 'They want me that much, huh? Boy, am I flattered.'

In fact, as Susie well knew, Deus's advertising agency had long been threatening to get a new face for the campaign altogether, although Felix's recent publicity had made them stall slightly. In many ways it would suit her better if they were to take on one of her other boys, but right now she had a feeling she had to get Felix out of the way for a while.

The girlish revenge plot was worrying but, aided by her potty step-mother and her confidence in Felix's shallow inability to commit, Susie hadn't been unduly worried by it until now. She'd thought of the whole, silly girlish game as more a fun distraction for Georgette than a serious threat. But, as Susie had recently discovered, it was Phoebe Fredericks who was trying to seduce Felix. And Daniel Neasham was moulding Phoebe as a potential long-term mistress.

Dan Neasham's involvement in the Felix plot was dangerous, she realised. If Dan moved in on Felix, the likelihood was that Susie's golden boy would have his career curtailed as fast as a prize boxer popping his hand into a fish talk to stroke a pirhana. It was said that the Libel Detector sniffed a flower for one of only two reasons – he wanted to raise it for profit or raze it for profit; he simply wouldn't waste the time to savour the smell alone.

Susie wasn't totally sure what Dan was up to, and longed not to care – if Felix was heading for a fall, she reasoned, then he'd had it coming for longer than a drunken fashion critic on Vivienne Westwood platforms. But while he was still on her books, and still the favourite for the Deus campaign – which was worth almost half a million Deutschmarks – then she felt she should protect him. Added to which, she realised that Felix, for all his lackadaisical arrogance, was far more vulnerable than he appeared. Susie knew enough of his terrible, neglected childhood to see that Felix possessed a terrifying number of hang-ups, and a remarkably low opinion of himself. She hated the thought of how much this schoolgirl plot could potentially back-fire and destroy his fragile pride.

'Will you do it for me, Felix?' Susie tried to keep the imploring note out of her voice, but it still dragged her words into hearty, anxious coercion, like a head girl coaxing the school swot into appearing on Blockbusters. 'Huge, chummy meal if you do – and I'll release you from that bubble-gum mag pullout calendar.'

He sighed. 'I can take a friend, huh?'

'Sure. Is it your new girlfriend?'

'What new girlfriend?' he laughed.

'I've heard rumours.'

'Where from?'

'Confidential sources.'

'Pul-ease. You sound like a DI on *The Bill*. What sources?'

Knowing Felix so well, Susie realised that she wasn't going to get anywhere on this one. He'd just throw questions back at her until she was screaming for mercy.

'So you want a second ticket to Paris?'

'I can have one even if it's not for a confidentially saucy girlfriend?'

'Yup – but if it's for Dylan then please try to stop him from trashing anywhere, getting barred everywhere and phoning the other models in the small hours saying he's lonely.'

'Sure.'

'So you'll do it?'

'I guess so – I could use the cash. I bought a lot of groceries yesterday.'

'Thank you, thank you, thank you, darling – eat nothing but proteins this weekend, and don't get your hair cut, they want to do it for you.' Susie yelped happily to herself and cut him off before he could change his mind, dialling straight through to the German ad agency.

'He'll do it,' she breathed happily, and waited for the whoops of delight to subside at the other end. 'But I'm afraid it's going to have to be next week after all. And there are a couple of conditions attached . . .'

24

Phoebe had to pull out of Stan's dinner party at the last minute. Dan called her that afternoon, saying Mitzi was having dinner with clients so why didn't they have a night in together? He promised to arrive by eight but by the time the flat's buzzer went, Phoebe had more or less given up hope. She had almost paced the carpet bald between Fliss's bedroom and the phone as she'd alternately checked her reflection and then waited, like a teenager on a first date, certain that Dan was going to call at the eleventh hour and cancel.

She'd left half-drunk cups of tea all over the flat until she had run out of mugs and moved on to cans of Diet Coke; she'd watched ten minutes of *The Bill*, five of *Brookside* and almost half an hour of a new Ruth Rendell before giving up on each in turn, unable to concentrate. Her teeth were so clean they squeaked whenever she ran her dry, nervous tongue over them; she reeked of Ysatis (the only perfume she had at the moment) and her body was so hairless she kept slipping off the furniture.

The buzzer practically sent her orbiting around the light fittings as she double-checked the neatness of the flat and the straightness of her underwear. She raced into the bathroom to squirt some toothpaste into her mouth, then frantically rinsed its mint green coating from her teeth. Next she dashed into her bedroom and checked that all ratty underwear, trash fiction, fun-fur cuddly toys and mouldy apple cores were firmly out of sight before racing through to Fliss's room for one final head-to-foot check in the mirror.

She was going for the white trash tacky touch tonight. Greeting Dan in nothing but a slither of opaque silk slip, stockings and the strappy heels that she and Fliss had jointly bought for purely in-house seduction purposes was not her most original move and she rather despised herself for doing it, but there was no denying that she felt absurdly sexy. If she was going to be a mistress, she mused, she might as well do it with big hair, and big attitude.

'Hello,' she rasped into the doorphone in her huskiest purr.

'Cab for Fredericks,' announced a jolly Indian voice.

'What? I didn't order a cab.'

'Instructions of Mr Neasham. He is saying to pick you up here.'

'Oh, right. I mean, oh, Christ! – I mean – just hang on, will you? What car are you in?'

'Nissan Bluebird – metallic grey, B registration.'

'I know, two hundred thousand on the clock and a bobbly wooden cover on the driver's seat.'

'Huh?'

'I'll be five minutes.'

Phoebe felt like a birthday toddler as she raced around blowing out candles. The only decent dress that she and Fliss liked at the moment was currently wrapped around her flat-mate in much the same way as said flat-mate was undoubtedly wrapped around Iain. Phoebe bellowed in frenzied despair as she hurriedly deposited the contents of both wardrobes on to both beds in turn and found nothing suitable except the newly dry-cleaned Gaultier number which she couldn't possibly wear a third time running.

Her five minutes was already up and she had done nothing. She had no idea where her keys, her purse or her condoms were. She had no emergency overnight kit handy, no pockets to ram her tube pass in, and her toothbrush had lost most of its bristles from all the frantic chewing on it she had done earlier.

'Damn! Bugger! Bum!' she wailed as she wriggled into a long

brown crocheted dress that showed every underwear line and had an unravelling hem, but was at least figure-hugging and gave the odd tantalising hint of sheeny skin.

The cab driver was leaning on the buzzer again, so Phoebe grabbed her keys and what she took to be her purse before bolting from the flat.

The taxi dropped her outside a long, railed garden leading to a leafy Highgate terrace. The fading light was taking out the last warm gold of the sunset to a sensual twilight of purples and pinks, as though a Greater Power had hit the dimmer switches and cranked up the Mantovani ready for the seduction scene. Only the Mantovani was being played out with birdsong; in the sloping, narrow side street it was as though they had left London behind and parked in an aviary twittering with feathered friends indulging in pillow talk before putting on their one-wing eye-masks.

'Which number?' Phoebe asked in confusion as she was faced with several wrought-iron gates.

But the cab driver had accelerated off, grateful to make his escape from the girl in the kinky dress who had insisted on sitting in the front seat, had dragged his rear-view mirror around so that she could gawp at her own reflection throughout the journey and had then demanded that they stop at the late-night chemist in Crouch End. At that point she'd realised that she'd brought out her flat-mate's pencil case instead of her purse and, with red-faced apologies, had borrowed a fiver to buy some condoms and a toothbrush.

'It's an account cab,' the taxi driver had explained patiently as she'd tried to write him an IOU on his *A to Z* with one of Fliss's many soft pencils. 'Mr Neasham, he is paying.'

Abandoned on the pavement, Phoebe was faced with a dilemma. A row of identical, elegant red-brick houses seemed to be on fire in front of her as their huge sash windows reflected the deep red sunset. As usual in times of deliberation when in love, she set herself a bet. If I get the house right first time then Dan and I are going to last forever, she decided, walking up the path to the left and then doing an abrupt U-turn as she saw the

Save the Whale, Vote Glenda and *Nukes Make us Puke* window stickers. She opted instead for a path on the right where several understated hessian blinds covered the lower windows and white-painted Victorian shutters had been drawn across several of the upper floor ones.

Now there were three bells to chose from, she realised anxiously, selecting the top one. There was no answer, so she tried each of the others in turn. Nothing. Damn! She'd lost her bet with herself. She and Dan would probably last for another half hour, tops. He had called her out to dump her, she decided. And she hadn't even got her cab fare home.

She was just backing away from the house when the front door swung open and he bounded down the steps towards her.

'No entryphone yet!' he panted, striding forward to hug her. 'Christ, I'm glad you came.'

Drawing away from a luscious tooth-nose-and-talk kiss, Phoebe cupped his smiling face in her hands and pressed her nose to his enquiringly. 'Dan, what are we doing here? I thought you were coming round to my flat.'

'That's right.' Dan laughed and took her hand in his before turning back towards the house. 'Come and look – it's only just been converted. You'll love it!'

Inside, it was clear that no one was living in the house, and that its most recent occupants had been builders. The halls were crammed with folded dust-sheets, paint-coated buckets, boxes of light bulbs, stacks of old free papers and uncollected post. The whole place reeked of fresh paint and new carpets.

Still towing Phoebe behind him, Dan sprung up the un-carpeted stairs two at a time until they were on the second floor. A very glossy white door with a shiny new brass '3' screwed to it was half-open ahead of them.

He nudged it open with his foot and then spun round to grab Phoebe beneath the knees and around the shoulders as he hauled her up into an untidy newlyweds' lift.

'Dan, what are you doing – ouch!'

Unfortunately the door swung back just as he was lurching through with his load, catching Phoebe on the knees. Her crocheted dress, caught on the top bolt, was unravelling faster than knitting pounced on by a kitten.

'Sorry.' Less than a foot into the flat, he buckled and dropped her so abruptly that she landed in a leggy sprawl, bumping her coccyx so hard on the bare polished floorboards that her eyes streamed.

'So what so you think?' He dropped to his haunches beside her and wiped a tear from one of her mint green eyes.

Blinking, Phoebe looked around her and shrugged. 'Lovely – very Zen.'

It was really just one huge, high room, split in half by a wide, panelled folding door. Glacier white walls seemed to stretch up forever from a lustrous, polished wooden floor to sculptured plaster cornices, broken only by huge, tall windows on the left which, despite the dusky meanness of the light outside, still allowed the room to appear blanched with bright, cool airiness. All Phoebe could see by way of furniture was a large checked Chesterfield still in its bubble wrap and, through the folding doors, a very gothic wrought-iron bed with its plastic-wrapped mattress leaning against it, the delivery note flapping in a draught from an unknown source.

'A friend owns the building,' Dan grinned, striding across to a door in the panelling on the right. 'There's a spanking new little kitchen through here,' he poked his head into it as though to check it hadn't disappeared, 'and a huge bathroom just off the bedroom. Isn't it terrific?'

'Lovely.' Phoebe rubbed her numb bum as she scrambled up. 'So is this going to be your London base once you move to Berkshire or wherever?'

Dan looked at her over his shoulder and twisted his mouth in the cutest of horny smiles. 'That's what I'm hoping.'

He was taking control again. Suddenly his mood was upbeat, his sense of purpose re-established and, although it gave him a raunchy edge which Phoebe couldn't help being turned on by, she was not at all sure she was happy with such a dramatic shift in power. This was the old, pre-New Zealand Dan – assured of his ability to attract, utterly domineering in his single-minded determination to seduce her, and very, very sexy.

Phoebe longed to talk things out and find her feet in the shifting sands of their relationship but, unbalanced and bowled over by his change of attitude, she inevitably found herself on her back. There was no time to strip the plastic from the new bed; Dan stripped her instead, urgently and excitedly, and took her on the cool, waxy floor. She shuddered with pure self-indulgence as Dan ran his tongue in a delicious figure of eight over her buttocks before digging its wetness into the hollow at the base of her spine. Then, lapping like a child with a lolly, he slowly climbed up the bumps of her vertebrae and buried his face in the back of her neck, coating it with long, breathy kisses.

Stretched out on the cool floorboards on her stomach, her arms reaching out in front of her, Phoebe wriggled with delight when he nibbled the short bristles at the nape of her neck, using his tongue to lift them and his teeth to grip them until she was squealing aloud with giggling, happy relish.

His right hand was creeping in soft finger-steps over her ear and across her cheek while his left slid between her buttocks and, hitching her bottom upwards, burrowed blissfully.

Phoebe stretched an arm behind her neck and touched his hair before tracing her nails as far as she could reach to his right shoulder, feeling the bump of the little mole there. Dan's fingers were cupping her chin now, drawing her head back towards his nipping, licking kisses, bringing her straining, arched neck to the soft edge of pain. Digging her nails into his shoulder, Phoebe fought his grip and dipped her face until she could draw his fingers into her mouth, sucking them in until she had enveloped three in a damp, warm embrace of tongue, lips and fleshy inner skin. She tried hard not to notice that they tasted of cheese and onion crisps.

'God!' she groaned, tightening her grip on his shoulder as the fingers between her legs slipped inside her and curled around to cup her cervix in a tight, nudging arc. 'Oh, that feels so good.' She dropped her forehead to the floor and chewed her lip with pleasure.

'How good?' Dan started to press his warm weight on to her back.

'Oh so, so good,' Phoebe moaned as the fingers curled into a taut grip. 'Please don't stop.'

'Do you want me to fuck you?' he breathed into her ear.

'Mmm.' Closing her eyes, she squirmed delightedly as the fingers inside her tightened their curling grip.

'Do you really?'

'Yes.' Phoebe opened one eye and peered at a skirting board with an inaudible, discontented sigh. She knew exactly what was coming next.

'Then say it.' Dan started to slip his fingers from inside her. Involuntarily, Phoebe tried to grip them in, hitching her pelvis up further until she felt the tight bulge of his erection jabbing between the cheeks of her rear.

'I want you to fuck me, Dan,' she whispered, the feeling of sexy déjà vu as familiar as watching *Basic Instinct* for the third time.

'Yes?' Biting her shoulder blade, Dan lifted his weight away from her, letting cold air creep between their bodies to tickle the tiny hairs on Phoebe's spine, chilling her hot, moist skin.

'Yes,' she hissed urgently, pressing herself up against him.

'What?' His hand started to slide away from between her legs.

'Yes!'

'Tell me.' Suddenly, Dan slid his damp fingers through her pubic hair and rubbed his thumb in a light, repetitive motion.

'I want you inside me, Dan,' she gasped, knowing her lines by rote, saying them because she didn't want him to stop what he was doing with his fingers. 'I want your cock – all of it. I want it to fuck me so badly. Please, please, Dan.'

'You're a greedy little whore, aren't you?'

'Yes.' Phoebe winced. Why did he always say that?

'A randy whore with her skinny white thighs spread and her hot little cunt aching for it. You can't wait to be full of cock, can you?'

Phoebe wished she had the guts to swing around and tell him to his red, excited face that she really hated it when he said that.

Tracing the hollow of her back with his teeth, Dan shifted his weight on to his knees as he slipped both hands to her buttocks, pulling her up in front of him.

Phoebe's nails scratched the shiny floor polish like a cat's claws as Dan took the end of his prick with his fingers and coaxed it between her buttocks before thrusting his full weight behind hard, straight muscle, plunging into her with such velocity that they both moved forwards across the slippery floorboards.

'Ohmygod,' Phoebe gasped, wrapping her arms around her head and pressing her cheek to the floor to pin herself down.

Now this, she realised with shuddering delight, was when she could really start enjoying herself. Dan had hips on elastic.

Driving his cock into her with such force that it punched the base of her uterus with each thrust, he stroked his hands around her waist then slipped them up to her nipples, circling with his fingers. Biting hard into the flesh of her shoulder blades, he thumbed her nipples roughly, the lunging rhythmic movement of his hips pushing the thumbs off-centre with every drive.

Not enjoying herself at all, Phoebe bit her lip and lifted her face from the floor.

'You're hurting me, Dan,' she whispered.

'Okay, okay – sorry.'

Covering her back with apologetic kisses, he slowed right down until she gasped with delight at every smooth, caressing lunge, her back arching to meet it.

But within seconds, Dan was speeding up like a racing driver first off the grid again, dropping and pushing upwards then grinding and circling, then dipping right out and pausing for seconds until Phoebe was pulling splinters up from the floor and into her nails without feeling them in her desperation to have him inside her again.

He came, as ever, with a deep, delighted grunt which Phoebe had fought for almost two years not to think of as a sign of porcine pleasure akin to locating a truffle the size of a house brick.

Carefully extracting himself and rolling on to his back to

remove the condom, Dan let out a satisfied, slightly idolatrous sigh and muttered a very rare post-coital, 'I love you.'

Gently feeling the tight, abrasive stinging left by the condom on her damp inner skin with her fingers, Phoebe rolled her head until her cheek was resting against the hot, damp hairs of his chest and kissed them with her breath.

'And I love the way you do that,' she lied, tracing the bumps of his fluctuating ribs with the nub of her chin.

'Really?' Dan grinned that wide, heart-stopping smile as he craned his head over his shoulder to look at her.

'Really.' Phoebe dropped her eyes.

She knew for definite that a year ago she would have told him the truth. Now she was too unsure of him, too lacking in confidence to be honest. The realisation left her hollow with self-hatred and sexual frustration.

They were re-enacting familiar, routine fucks, she realised sadly, with even less emotional connection than there had been a year earlier. And of them all, that one – the whore-wheel-barrow-shuffle – was about her least favourite. Not so unstimulating that she would make Dan stop – sometimes, in fact, she found the 'yes-please-fuck-me-now' extremely arousing, and she knew that he loved it more, perhaps, than any other. But there was an unpleasantness to the way the scenario repeated itself that made her uncomfortable. It was stock sex, part of a timetable – predictable, repetitive, lacking in emotion and attachment. She hated not being able to see his face, being passive and submissive like a coy geisha girl. It was, she realised, the ultimate mistress fuck. The mistress one mistrusted.

Twenty minutes later Phoebe was sitting naked in the high-ceilinged, draughty flat, clutching two sets of keys.

Outside she could hear Dan's car revving up excitedly and engineering its way out of a parking space to race back to Barnes before Mitzi returned from her corporate achievement dinner.

She tucked her knees so tightly into her chin that her nipples, still excited from his earlier attentions, stung under the pressure. Burying her wet eyes against her kneecaps, she threw the keys across the room.

She didn't want – didn't need – a lonely, cavernous flat rented for her by a man who could walk in at any time, whether she was bingeing her way through a family pack of digestives and watching *Neighbours* with a mud mask on, or lounging naked on a twisted wrought-iron bed watching nothing but his approaching hard on. What she really wanted was for that man to be sitting with her right now, letting her stroke and touch him and slowly, coaxingly, extract his shadowed side like pearls from a stubborn oyster.

Instead he'd muttered, 'Traffic can be murder around the South Circular at this time of night,' before heading off to wash her off his skin in the bathroom and then drop a kiss on to her head, the keys into her hands, and the latch into its socket as he slipped away, leaving her with nothing to hug but an unravelling dress and her flat-mate's pencil case.

25

Listening to the touch-tones bleeping through, Phoebe realised that Felix's phone number was remarkably tuneful.

Typical! she thought irritably. He would have a number that sounds like a bloody concerto.

The line rang for a long, long time at the other end before it was picked up.

Phoebe could hear a man and a woman arguing in the background, but no one spoke into the receiver.

'Hello?' she tried to make herself heard.

The arguing continued – the woman shrieking, obviously closer to the mouthpiece, probably holding it. The man's voice was muffled by her outraged screams.

'. . . coming to you if you think you're going to get away with this, you sick son of a bitch!'

'Bitch is too good a word for my fucking mother, darling.'

'Don't smart arse me, Felix, you louse. I want a shitting explanation!'

'And there was me thinking you'd called round for a cup of tea with my bible-reading group – just let me take the call, darling, and we'll swap gossip then.'

'Rack off! You're not taking this call until you tell me what the fuck is – '

'Give me the phone, Fanii!'

Phoebe diplomatically hung up.

'So what happened. Did you get the machine or what?'

Saskia, who had been hovering by the door to listen in, pounced on her excitedly.

'Nope.' Phoebe reached for her tea. 'He was preoccupied. I think Fanii Hubert had popped in for a social dirty phone call. I'm glad I wasn't his granny ringing.'

'Shit!' Saskia bit her lip, eyes narrowing. 'I told you she'd try and muscle in on him after that public exhibition. She was always trying to get off with him when we were going out together, the scrawny cow. Were they in bed or something? Don't tell me they were in bed?'

'No, I somehow don't think Felix was laying on the red carpet for her,' Phoebe assured her. 'I'll try again in an hour or so.'

'Do you want to watch the Showdown vid again while we're waiting? You seemed to spend most of your time with your head in a cushion when we watched it this morning.'

Phoebe winced. 'Not particularly. I have to do my ironing. There's *Fatal Attraction* somewhere in that pile of videos if you want to pick up some tips.'

'Ha bloody ha.'

The next time Phoebe called, Felix was in the shower washing off the remnants of one of Dylan's ageing pizza take-outs which Fanii had hurled at him.

Dylan was working at the bar and the answermachine was still broken, so Felix raced to collect the call before whoever it was rang off, hoping that it was Piers with some more news from LA.

'Hi.' He hooked the body of the phone under his fingers and held it away from himself so that he didn't drip on it.

'Hi.' Phoebe swallowed to try and stop herself sounding like a Clanger. 'This is Frances.'

'Who?'

Phoebe clenched her teeth slightly, aware that Saskia was now so close she could probably catch every word.

'Thank you for doing my shopping.' She dropped her voice to more of a Soup Dragon pitch.

'Oh – hi! Yes, I remember. Hang on a minute, darling, I just have to fetch a towel. I'm starting to steam here.' The phone clunked as it was put down on a hard surface.

Phoebe covered the mouthpiece and rolled her eyes at Saskia.

'What's he doing?' she whispered urgently.

'Fetching a towel.'

'Try and arrange to go out tonight.'

'Tonight? Isn't that a bit previous? I mean – '

'Hi, sorry about that. How are you?' Felix was back, purring into the phone like a tickled tiger cub.

'Fine.' Phoebe tried to avoid catching sight of Saskia still mouthing furiously. 'Look, I'm about to go out, but I just wanted to get in contact to thank you for picking up my food bill. Can I post you a cheque or something?'

'No.'

'Oh – right. Well – thanks a lot.'

'But you can give one to me in person,' he laughed.

'Oh, I see.' Phoebe was practically falling off the bed under the weight of Saskia leaning against her to earwig.

'Basically,' Felix carried on lazily, 'I'm going away for a few days next week so if you post it, it won't get here in time. You'll have to bring it round.'

'Oh, I'm sorry,' Phoebe wriggled away from Saskia, 'I had no idea you needed the money so much – you really shouldn't have paid for my stuff.'

Reaching out to grip Phoebe's arm, Saskia gawped questioningly at her and shook her head.

'I don't need the money,' Felix said simply. 'I just want it. Where are you going now? I'm in Notting Hill – can you drop it off en route?'

Saskia nodded frantically at her.

'Not really. I'm heading to Camden, then Highgate.'

Eyebrows shooting up in horror, Saskia muffled a howl.

'Why d'you need to go there?' Felix's voice was teasing and languid, as though not particularly interested.

'I don't need to, I just want to.' Phoebe matched his tone with a sly wink at Saskia who buried her head in a pillow and groaned.

'Oh, right. Well, I guess I'll see you around then.' Felix sounded miffed.

Phoebe closed her eyes. She'd blown it. Saskia's fingers were stapled so tightly to her arm that she could almost feel the bones bruising.

'I guess so,' she murmured, crossing her fingers and praying. 'Around six-thirty?'

There was a long pause.

'Where?' he finally said, his voice warm with smiles.

This time two sets of lungs let out relieved sighs at the other end.

'Do you know Café Delancey in Camden?'

'See you there.' He abruptly rung off.

Phoebe lay back on the bed and wiped her sticky forehead. Leaving Saskia with instructions for Fliss to lurk incognito in Café Delancey in case of problems, Phoebe began a frantic assault on her wardrobe.

Felix, the self-proclaimed upholder of punctuality, was even later rolling up than Phoebe. He wandered into Café Delancey at seven, wearing extremely frayed jeans and a tatty, oversized Guernsey, clearly having made the minimum of effort for her this time. His hair was clean but uncombed and he looked monumentally hung-over, bruised blue eyes riddled with bloodshot lacework, dark blond stubble peppering his chin.

Sensing she had some catching up to do on the allure front, Phoebe stretched back in her chair and beamed out her slinkiest, most vivacious smile as he approached her table.

Felix's return-fire smile was far less full-on. He sank down on the seat opposite without a greeting and irritably batted away the menu that an eager waiter was waggling in front of him.

'I'll have a bottle of red,' he snapped.

'Would you care to look at the wine list, sir?' the waiter offered helpfully.

'No.' Felix didn't so much as look at him. 'Any old shit'll do. Now buzz off and take that laminated thing out of my face.'

Once the waiter had gone, Felix grappled with a cigarette and, breaking it with quick-fingered impatience, sagged back in his chair and squinted at Phoebe.

'Hello.' She dropped her voice as low as it would go and gave him her best bedroom smile.

He didn't answer, his face totally unfriendly. Instead he stared at her in silence for a full half-minute.

Deciding not to rise to the bated breath bait, Phoebe let the smile play on her lips and settled for staring him out. His eyes really were bloodshot, she noticed. And one was being lifted with a tired, tense little tick which seemed to rattle up from his clenched, quilted jaw. Whilst still undeniably, cruelly beautiful, he looked a total wreck. This wasn't the purring, teasing charmer she had envisaged lounging in nothing but a fluffy towel at the other end of the phone earlier.

'Fuck, it's hot in here,' he finally muttered, stripping off the Guernsey to reveal an inside-out grey t-shirt which looked suspiciously as though it had once been white. 'Did you bring the cheque?'

Phoebe was fast rejecting the idea of a spirited game of footsie under the table, and also deeply regretted wasting the sexy grey tunic on him. The dress – which she had hoped to wear if, God willing, Dan wanted to meet her next week – would be forever ruined under this critical, sulky scrutiny.

Saying nothing, she stretched down to her bag. She and Saskia had earlier dashed around Islington to find a hole in the wall with some cash left in it. Inside her purse was two hundred pounds in crisp, pungent twenties. There was no way she could write him a cheque, they'd realised – it would instantly give away the fact that she was Phoebe R. S. Fredericks, with a Barclay's bank account still based in Exeter, where she'd opened it as a student.

'How much do I owe you?'

'About a hundred.' He was trying for another cigarette, flicking his lighter with an angry thumb and shooting up nothing but sparks.

Phoebe shuffled out the notes and dropped them in front of him. Then, picking up a matchbook from the ashtray, she calmly peeled a stalk off and lit it, holding the flame out for him.

Looking up, Felix gazed straight through the flickering, spitting little flame at her face, his mouth twisting into an unfriendly half-smile.

Then, dropping his lighter, he gripped her hand in his tight, warm fist and pulled it towards his face to light the cigarette. Not letting go, he clasped the hand with his fingers and ran his thumb up the length of hers.

The match flame was lapping at the tips of her acrylic nails now, its heat starting to sting the ends of her fingers.

'That's hurting,' Phoebe warned in a low whisper.

'I know.' Felix's thumb was still pressed against hers – he must have been feeling the biting hot flame too, but didn't seem to notice.

'For Christ's sake!' Phoebe leant across to blow it out but, from nowhere, Felix's other hand shot up to her face and his fingers pressed themselves to her lips so tightly he could have counted the bumps of her front teeth through them.

Still gripping her hand in his other fist like a horseshoe in a farrier's vice, he steered the stinging, guttering match down to the notes fanning out on the plate in front of him.

Phoebe tried to mumble 'No!' but merely ended up wetting Felix's fingers with a damp mumble. His grip was remarkably strong – she could see the veins popping out on the muscles of his lower arm and his sinews straining like cables as he fought against her wriggling hand.

Smiling widely now, he held the last few seconds of dying flame under the corner of one twenty-pound note and it took immediately. The match died in their reddened, blistered fingers as he kept his grip on her wrist and watched the new pale blue flames start to lap into yellowing peaks as they spread across the Queen's face in a quick, even tide. Within seconds, all the notes were aflame.

Smoke was beginning to seep up from their table now. The waiter, sidling back with an extremely expensive bottle of red wine, took one look at the little inferno and grabbed the water jug from the couple on the next table. The next moment Felix, Phoebe, and their table were doused in cold water, ice cubes and the odd lemon slice.

Her mouth released from Felix's grip, Phoebe spluttered a hasty, gibbering apology to the waiter and started to mop her lap with a soggy napkin. Her face was scalding with embarrassment under the delighted gaze of most of Café Delancey's amazed clientele.

'Could we change tables?' Felix asked calmly. Seemingly unmoved by the incident, he looked up at the waiter enquiringly.

'What?' Phoebe gaped across at him.

'What?' the waiter almost dropped thirty pounds' worth of well-breathed wine.

'Now, if you don't mind,' Felix snapped. 'Over there will do.' He nodded towards a table in a dusky alcove lit by a guttering candle. 'Okay with you? Come on, darling.' Clutching Phoebe's hand far more gently this time, he steered her towards the other table, dropping ice cubes in her wake.

'But, sir?' the waiter was holding up the damp dog ends of the burnt money.

Ignoring him, Felix pushed Phoebe down in a corner chair and scraped the one beside it around until it pinned her in before sliding on top of it, his knees crammed against hers. Then he removed the plastic 'Reserved' sign from the table and tossed it over his shoulder.

Phoebe leant back against the chair as far as she could and tried to control the white-hot, raw fury that was currently causing her every nerve end to prickle with barbed spikes. Control never being one of her greatest skills, she curbed it for about three seconds before letting rip.

'That,' she hissed furiously, 'was the stupidest, most spoilt, childish and pointless piece of ignorant exhibitionism I have ever seen!'

Felix stared at her with rapt absorption, his bloodshot blue eyes dipping between her mouth and her eyes.

'I cannot *believe* someone would behave with such self-ishness,' she snarled, 'such total disregard for the value of that money to someone else. Its value to people who, unlike you, aren't privileged enough to have their freshly powdered bums wiped with velvet by toady sycophants every time they take a dump. It might amaze you to learn that most people haven't been handed life on a banqueting plate by being acutely stupid, but genetically pretty enough to pout in front of a camera for corrupt amounts of money, gifts and free fucks!'

His bloodshot eyes still slithering up and down her face, Felix let out a delighted laugh.

Ignoring him, Phoebe ground her teeth and played out the last of her rush of rage.

'Rather than ponce around like a faggot aesthete showing off to me,' she blazed on, 'you could have pocketed that money and handed it to the next homeless person you saw, to Battersea Dogs' Home, to anyone in fact. Okay, it might not have been quite so fuck-off cool, quite so anti-materialistic machismo heroic, but it would have been a damn sight more bloody fair.'

Played out, she sagged back against her chair and glared at him, ramming her knees even tighter against his in the hope that she'd make his kneecaps crunch, although she only succeeded in practically decimating her own.

'That,' Felix licked his smiling lips, danced his tired blue eyes between hers for a moment longer, and then leant back into his chair, 'was wonderful. I've got a fucking hard on so tight it's killing me.'

'You *what?*' Phoebe wailed in horror.

At that moment the waiter tip-toed up and nervously dithered with the neglected red wine, clearly plucking up courage to dribble a half-inch into Felix's glass for him to taste.

All polite, deferential English charm now, Felix turned and looked up at the cowering little man, smiling widely. He sniffed the wine with a verbose rush of flattering, grateful adjectives and then apologised profusely about his 'little bonfire earlier', insisting that they add the cost for any damages on to his bill.

As the waiter melted gratefully away, Felix lit another Chesterfield in the candle flame and looked up at Phoebe through sooty lashes, his big blue eyes apologetic.

'I'm sorry, I'm in a shitty mood.' He straightened up and rested his elbows on the table so that the smouldering cigarette smoked in the six inches between their faces.

'Oh, really?' Phoebe leaned away until the back of her head made audible contact with the wall. 'That's reassuring – I just thought you were a shit.'

'And I think you're a total bitch.' Felix tugged dispassionately on the cigarette and narrowed his eyes. 'But you excite the fuck out of me.'

'Thank you so much.'

'My pleasure.' Felix's smile stretched up from his mouth to his eyes, creasing his cheeks and wrinkling his forehead as he poured her a glass of wine.

It was a devastating, practised, totally seductive smile. If he were the raunchy hero of a strip cartoon, he wouldn't have needed a thought bubble; the big cheesy grin said it all. 'Bed – you – me – hours.' Phoebe guessed he had laid women on the strength of his smile alone. She longed to remove every one of his straight, white teeth and make Saskia a necklace from them.

'Do I excite you?' he murmured, narrowing his blue eyes at her through the smoke in a close-up straight out of a Fabio soft porn movie.

The vain little spic! thought Phoebe furiously.

'Yes,' she murmured back. Excite me to violence, definitely. Make my flaps wobble – nope.

Phoebe wondered whether this was her cue to leave. Just as she was deciding it was and surreptitiously groping for her bag beneath the table, Felix butted in with a comment that made her clutch the thick, sturdy table leg for support.

'Will you come to Paris with me next week?'

She tightened her grip on the soft cloth wrapped around the chunky table leg. Now this was classic Felix, she realised excitedly. She and Saskia had never dreamed he would play one of his favourite up-the-sleeve cards so soon. The offer of a holiday. It was part of the standard Sylvian routine.

Whilst outwardly flicking him an enigmatic smile that would have wiped the inferior one from the Mona Lisa's face, inwardly she was on full red-alert panic.

What should she say? The 'must check my diary first' line? The 'I've got a power lunch with Lynne Franks I can't cancel' one? The 'what shall I pack' one? What? Saskia hadn't dared to brief her for this yet.

'I can't,' she finally managed to croak lamely. Thankfully, it came out as a husky, esoteric purr of off-hand disappointment.

'Why?' Felix looked furiously sulky at the prospect of being turned down.

Phoebe suddenly remembered Saskia's earlier dressing down and improvised hastily.

'Because I'm going away on business.'

'Oh.' Felix had dropped his gaze and was flicking his ash tetchily.

'To Paris,' she added smoothly.

Felix looked up and stared at her. Then he grinned like the Cheshire cat that's just done a double-backed somersault with piked entry into the cream.

'When are you flying out?'

Phoebe balked, wondering how long it took to book shuttle tickets to Paris. What if there were none available? How on earth were they going to fund this? She had a feeling that Saskia would go ballistic if she claimed overseas travel as part of her expenses.

'I'll have to check my diary,' she coasted, still tightly clutching the table leg to earth her nerves. 'I think the company's stuck me on standby – they've got so tight-arse recession conscious these days. I have a feeling they want me out there by Wednesday.' Wednesday was a safe bet, she concluded – bang in the middle of the week, allowing her two days to do a stopover in India and develop bubonic plague.

'Fly out with me,' he offered. 'I've got a spare ticket for the sycophantic bottom wiper of my choice. How's your right-hand swipe?'

Phoebe grinned. 'Honey, I'd wipe the floor with you first.'

Felix cupped his chin in one palm, the burning cigarette between his fingers making his right eye water. With his left hand, he reached out and touched Phoebe's cheek very lightly.

'You can let go of my leg now if you want,' he breathed. 'But please don't.'

'What?'

Biting her lip, Phoebe extracted her face from his fingers and glanced down at her own hand. It was gripping on to Felix's leg

– the mistaken sturdy warm table leg that had supported her through the last few minutes' lies. Her acrylic nails were digging into the damask-soft denim covering his shin bone.

Phoebe didn't let go. Instead, she looked back up into Felix's face and matched his amused smile as she very slowly furrowed her nails from shin to thigh bone and then around to trace the line of dipped muscle from thigh to hip. He was so beautifully proportioned, it was like groping Michelangelo's David. She found herself wondering if he was similarly poorly endowed in the fig leaf region, and had to swig some red wine to stop herself laughing at him. He was so gloriously placid about being felt and fondled, she noticed – like a sickly child enjoying the attentions of a GP, utterly accustomed to it. She wondered just what she had to do to arouse him, to make him squirm with first-night, free-fall excitement.

For the first time in this ridiculous challenge, Phoebe was beginning to enjoy herself. She had lied so much now that she was beyond caring. Instead, she was riding on a tide of adrenalin, two-faced cheek and exhilarated daring.

'Would you like to play a game?' Felix asked suddenly, stubbing out his half-smoked cigarette and reaching into his jeans back pocket.

Shrugging, Phoebe laughed and nodded. Releasing his hip, she refilled Felix's drained glass and then took another tentative sip at her own, aware that red wine had the same effect on her as hash cakes had on a toddlers' tea party.

Felix was spinning a fifty pence coin between two fingers of his right hand now, watching her guardedly through those thick, curling lashes.

'Am I supposed to have a bet?' She reached for her purse.

'No.' Felix lazily tossed the coin in the air and snatched it back into his fist. 'Heads or tails?' He pressed his hands on top of one another, the coin trapped between them.

'Tails.'

Palm still pressed to knuckles, he shifted forwards until his face was so close to hers, she had to fight not to go cross-eyed.

'Okay.' His words breathed hot air on to Phoebe's lips. 'Tails you kiss me first; heads I kiss you.' He lifted his right hand and dropped his eyes.

Following his gaze, Phoebe was briefly aware of a glint of Elizabeth II's miniaturised profile before she was gathered into one of the most erotic kisses she had ever experienced.

Warm hands slipped around her throat and jawbone as two soft lips and a stubbled chin traced the length of her face from the hollow of her neck to her hairline. Then she caught two blue eyes staring steadily into hers for a split-second before Felix angled his face to one side and pulled her lips on to his. The kiss started hot and slow, turned fast and greedy, ate her in on a hungry binge and then delicately, deliberately tasted every inch of her mouth with Epicurean indulgence, oblivious of a delighted, excited audience.

Despite herself, involuntary sexual excitement kick-boxed Phoebe's groin. Within seconds her fingers were curling back around his frayed denim hips and her legs inching either side of his soft denim knees. Faced with such bodily mutiny, she elected to kiss him back as though an Olympic Gold medal for technical merit, artistic impression and bare-faced tongue-in-his-cheek depended upon it.

Coming up for air, they drew back, unwillingly parting hot, fizzing mouths. Fingers of their right hands stabbing through one another's, they glued eyes, panting, laughing and pressing foreheads together.

'Ch-rist,' Felix whistled, stroking his nose to either side of hers and then plunging back into her mouth with a jabbing tongue, like a Labrador puppy seeing the sea for the first time and thirstily trying to drink it all at once.

As the tongue probed and stabbed deeper, marked and caressed by Phoebe's, the fingers of Felix's right hand suddenly closed over her knuckles, starting to fight in a clumsy, tangled arm wrestle. Phoebe fought back, but was far less brawny and lost within seconds, the back of her hand crashing into the ash tray. A moment later, the kiss was veering towards gnawing, biting violence and Felix's left hand was creeping between her legs. Then, drawing back and breathing on to her cheek for a moment, he slowly and deliberately indulged her in the most gentle, languid and lazy of Sunday morning, breakfast-in-bed kisses.

All the time, she kept her eyes firmly open. All the time, Felix returned her gaze.

It was the oddest, closest feeling of cerebral connection Phoebe had had with him all evening. She almost felt that he knew precisely who she was and what she was doing, and what's more didn't care.

Well, I care, she thought furiously. I care that he almost killed Saskia, I care that he thinks I'm such a pushover, I care that I'm effectively prostituting myself for the second time this weekend and, oh Christ, I care that this is such a fucking turn on I'm not going to sleep for days thinking about it!

'I hate you,' she hissed into his open, lapping mouth.

'I hate you too,' he breathed back, gripping her tongue between his teeth and rolling his own around the tip until, gasping, she pinched the skin on his thigh between her fingers as tightly as a mouse-trap to make him stop.

At the same moment as Felix's fingers were digging into the soft flesh of Phoebe's inner thighs and his tongue was probing her mouth, Fliss was ordering a large bourbon and Coke from a waiter without once glancing up at his beaming, tip-seeking face.

'Jack Daniels or Wild Turkey?'

'Hmm?' She wasn't listening.

The waiter followed her gaze. Just watching them was turning him on. They were the most highly charged, the rudest and most insufferable couple he had ever encountered – and as a result he was as green as the empty bottles he regularly spirited away from tables.

'Disgusting isn't it?' he sniffed.

Fliss shook her head abstractedly. 'Nope,' she sighed. 'Every-one's loving it.'

Except Phoebe, she added silently as she saw her flat-mate finally pull away from Felix's divine, moreish, greedy mouth and take a deliberately slow swig of red wine to recover, her faux purple eyes rolling.

Looking up, she caught Fliss watching her and rolled them even more, to Felix's bemusement, before excusing herself, wriggling past Felix as he scraped back his chair, and bolting to the loos.

Waiting until her drink was plonked with flourish in front of her, Fliss followed.

The loos were unisex – set off a thin lobby with green louvred doors that allowed a good eight inches gawping space top and bottom; not ideal for furtive tactic-swapping.

'Shit, Phoebe, your stubble rash looks like Clive Sinclair's beard!'

'He wants me to go to France with him next week.'

'He doesn't? Ace, mate! You're in!'

'What do I say?'

'Yes, of course, you daft cow. Saskia'll be made up.'

'Did you catch the back-row, front-seat-tickets snog?'

'And some! Christ, Phoebes, is he as good as he looks?'

'He's a conniving, low-down, immoral little bastard, Fliss. What do you think?'

'That good?'

'Look, I don't know how to play this. He's asked for my number – Saskia wants me to give him Portia's, but she gets back from the States in a couple of days. Should I give him ours?'

Fliss wrinkled her freckled nose. 'With all the people who hang around? What if Stan or Claudia or your sister or someone picks it up and he asks for Frances?'

Phoebe nodded and bit her lip. 'Okay, I'll think of something.'

'Here, let me splat some of my compact on that rash.'

'Thanks.' Phoebe thrust out her burning chin. 'Look, Fliss there's something else.'

'What? He doesn't want you to go back with him tonight?'

'No, not that. I think he's really, seriously fucked off about something.'

'Huh?' Fliss dabbed the end of Phoebe's nose with Christian Dior.

'When he turned up tonight, he was so strung out, he

twanged when he sat down. I thought he was hung over, but I don't know – I think he might have been crying, Fliss. There's something weird going on and I'm dying to know what.'

'Ask him, then.'

'No way. You know what Saskia says: dig under his surface and you pull out your own plug.'

With a final flick of powdery sponge on Phoebe's chin, Fliss shrugged. 'I've never known a man who doesn't enjoy boring for England, Scotland and Wales on his personal problems.'

'I'm not sure.' Phoebe looked in the mirror and balked at her new chalk-white beard. 'I think it might just shoot us two giant twenty-league footsteps back.'

'S'your choice, Phoebes.' Fliss shrugged, redoing her own lipstick. 'But if it was me and I'd just used his epiglottis as a punch-bag with my tongue, I'd ask him.'

'Oh, and what should I say I do? He needs to know because I – er – I said something about going to Paris anyway on business.'

'Media consultant,' Fliss answered without hesitation, looking in the mirror and rubbing her lips together. 'Always works. Just be really, really vague.'

'What's a media consultant?'

'God knows but it never fails for me. You'd better get back. You're doing great. Don't forget the Saskia Seaton byword.' She gave Phoebe a final brushing down, like a ringside trainer psyching her boxer up as the fifteenth round bell went.

'What?' Phoebe was fighting a sudden urge to suggest that she and Fliss crawl out through a back window.

'Gogettimbabe.'

Phoebe slipped back into her seat with a big smile on her face and a small lump of panic wriggling like a gremlin fed after midnight in her innards.

Felix, having polished off the last of the bottle, was gazing at her barely touched glass of red wine with blue-eyed longing, bony fingers drumming the table, black mood firmly back in place.

Hoping Saskia would forgive her for her alcoholic intolerance, Phoebe pushed the wine towards him and started to gather up her bag.

'You're not going?' he asked, for a brief moment looking almost forlorn as he parted the rim of Phoebe's glass from his lips and stared across at her.

'Soon, yes.' She tightened the drawstring on her duffle bag and let it drop to her feet again. 'But first I want to know what's under your skin.'

'What?' He narrowed his eyes.

'You were pretty insufferable when you first got here tonight.'

A snatched hand irritably ploughed through clean, tangled blond hair as Felix shrugged dismissively.

'Was I?' He threw back the question. 'Why didn't you walk out, then?'

'I almost did – but I guess I must like getting my fingers burnt.' Phoebe flicked her index finger back and forth through the candle flame, too quickly for it to hurt. 'Just call this a hot date.'

Felix watched its progress, a hypnotic smile stretching across his face.

'Do you think I'm dangerous then?'

Phoebe shrugged, knowing he'd love it if she said yes, but hating him too much to give him the satisfaction.

'I know you're very pissed off about something.'

'Really?' Sliding his eyes away, Felix feigned complete boredom.

'What is it?'

'Nothing.' He reached for another cigarette.

'Okay,' Phoebe sighed, diving for her bag and carelessly brushing her forearm along the angled calf that was pressed to her leg like a splint. It gave her the same feeling as stroking a sleeping setter with its freckled stomach laid out – heartbreakingly pretty but utterly devoted to itself, so used to the attention that it barely stirred.

Dragging the strap of her bag over her shoulder, she stood up as straight as she could behind the constricting lip of the table.

'Hang on, I need your number.' Felix barred her way with his arm.

Phoebe hovered. 'Tell me why you arrived looking like the ghost-writer at Naomi Campbell's feast tonight then?'

Blue eyes boring defensively into hers, Felix scowled. Then he forced a very weak, deferential smile and, dropping his gaze, fiddled uncomfortably with the matchbook in front of him.

'Sit down,' he muttered.

Phoebe was on her chair faster than a child playing musical bumps.

'I'm not going to tell you,' he said quietly. 'But thank you for asking.'

'Bullshit.' She stood up again.

Felix's arm still firmly barred her exit. Phoebe pushed against it like a desperate, ticketless fan at a Cup Final turnstile.

'I – I – oh, for fuck's sake, sit down, Phoebe!'

She sat down. Then she almost bit her bottom lip off as she realised what he'd just called her.

Felix was pulling off matches and carefully laying them out in front of him in a little stick pile.

'I looked in your purse,' he said in a low voice. 'Why did you lie to me, Phoebe Fredericks?'

'Multiple personality,' she gulped.

'Crap.' One match was laid carefully on another.

'Compulsive pseudonym dropper?'

'Sure.' He ripped another wooden strip from the book.

'Okay, so I guess I'm just as evasive as you are.'

Match clutched in his fingers like a cigarette, Felix looked up at her thoughtfully.

'I like your face.'

'What?'

'I like your face. It's not beautiful, but it has the most incredible attraction. Do yourself a favour and bin those coloured lenses, though. I much preferred the green one you flashed on Wednesday.'

Phoebe was lost for words, her flesh crawling with mortification, certain that he'd completely rumbled her, that he recalled

Saskia mentioning 'Freddy Fredericks' who was going to be their bridesmaid, or had seen an envelope addressed to her lying around his mews when Saskia lived there. That was why he'd been seething with barely controlled fury tonight, she guessed. He must have suspected a silly, girly revenge plot all along. And still he'd snogged her, the louse! She braced herself for a tirade of vindictive fury. Instead, what he said next practically made her swallow her well-kissed tongue.

'I was fucked off when I arrived here because my mother called this evening. It's why I was late.'

Phoebe blinked in amazement. 'Your mother?'

'Yes.'

Felix lapsed into silence as he concentrated on latticing matches on top of one another.

'And what did your mother say that made you so upset?' Phoebe fought to sound normal under such an unexpected change of tack.

Felix spluttered a derisive half-laugh and glared up at her, a match snapping in his fingers.

'You could try sounding a little less like a shrink,' he hissed. 'You wanted me to tell you. I'm gaining no particular therapy from this. She's a bitch, that's all. She's a bitch and she fucked me off. Now can we change the subject?'

He put his fist to his mouth and chewed the index finger irritably. Phoebe had a feeling that he'd upturn the table if she asked any more questions.

'Okay, I'll give you my number.' She extracted her diary from her bag and dithered. In the end she furtively looked up and then copied down the number of the contentious new Highgate flat, ripping out the page and handing it over before she could dwell on the consequences.

'I'm in the middle of moving, so I won't be on this number long but it'll have to do,' she explained. She'd spotted a complicated-looking answerphone in the flat and was planning to rush around there later and tape some sort of vague, ambiguous message.

'Right.' Felix looked at it, his hand shaking slightly. He was still as tense as a wound coil, unable to focus on any one object for more than a split second or to keep still. 'I'll call you later.'

'Later?'

'Later tonight – to let you know the time of the flight,' he snapped tetchily. 'It's tomorrow afternoon sometime.'

'Tomorrow? I – er – in that case, I don't think I can come along with you.' Phoebe's head spun with thoughts of getting hold of Dan, trying to sort out the flat fiasco, changing her shifts at Bar Barella, plotting with Saskia.

'Yes, you can.'

'I'm needed at work.'

'Rubbish. They're getting you to Paris for nothing, put up in a five-star hotel, fed, chaperoned. I'll even fuck you as part of the freebie package as well if you like.'

Phoebe blinked. The sulky spoilt brat who had stormed up to her table an hour earlier was back with a vengeance. She couldn't handle sixty minutes with him, let alone several days in Paris. Sorry, Saskia.

Saying nothing, she stood up and forced her way past him. As she headed determinedly to the door, she caught sight of Fliss being chatted up by a couple of hippy-chic Camden lads.

Outside, she looked back through the windows to see Felix still sitting at the table, his blond hair flopping over his hands as he buried his head in them.

Phoebe crossed the road and looked back one more time. He was ordering another bottle of wine. Looking over his shoulder as the waiter backed away, he stared straight at a table where two girls were surreptitiously watching him and giggling – one tall and pretty, the other skinny, short and plain. As Phoebe slipped away to the tube, Felix was beaming his big, bedroom smile at the latter.

The Highgate flat was cold and unfriendly, the overhead lights far too bright, the smell of paint asphyxiating. There wasn't so much as a tea bag in the new, empty white kitchen units. Plastic rawl plugs still littered the stripped wood worktops and a newly delivered microwave sat in its cardboard box in the centre of the green-tiled floor like an improvised table. Phoebe sat on it and chewed around her nails for a few minutes before raising the energy to fathom out the phone.

Before taping a message, she called Saskia at Portia's flat. Saskia was on the line within a ring.

'You're back early. How did it go?' she panted.

'He wants me to go to Paris with him tomorrow.'

There was a long silence. Eventually, Phoebe could hear Saskia lighting up a Marlboro Light and inhaling deeply.

'And what did you say?' she whispered as she exhaled.

'I'm not exactly sure how we left it,' Phoebe sighed, giving Saskia a brief précis of the evening, carefully toning down the length, height and weight of the kiss. Instead, she focused on his ridiculous mummy's-boy sulks, hoping Saskia would start to see a little of his shallowness.

But she was merely furious.

'Why the hell did you ask him about his mother, Freddy?' she hissed frostily afterwards. 'Didn't I tell you to lay off ever mentioning his family?'

'I thought you meant his father and that little brat of a brother. Anyway, how was I meant to know he was in a bad mood because his bloody mother had called? Christ! I get grumpy when my mother yaks on for hours about my failure to get married and have her grandchildren, but I don't torch a pile of dosh on dates afterwards.'

'Felix's mother is different,' Saskia sighed. 'As far as I'm aware this must be the first time she's voluntarily got in contact since the cheque for his final term's school fees bounced.'

'Is she a bit of a cow then?'

'Felix's mother is Philomena Rialto, Freddy.'

'Who?' Phoebe stifled a laugh. The name was ludicrously camp.

'Hollywood C-list alcoholic – dries out occasionally to show *Hello!* around her fur-lined Malibu house or to film another corny Euro-trash mini-series, from which she usually gets fired. Most of the time she's playing tinker tailor with her pills and signing divorce papers that have Chivas Regal rings dried on to them.'

Phoebe exhumed a vague memory from her distant, beer-soaked phase of watching late-night television as a student.

'Wasn't she the one in all those seventies Hammer House of Horror movies?' she giggled. 'Stretching her eyes, batting her false eyelashes and screaming her lungs inside out as Oliver Reed approached her with a ketchup-smeared meat cleaver in one hand and the head of Ian Ogilvy in the other?'

'That's her.' Saskia was clearly bristling at Phoebe's amusement. 'She was a really big star then – incredibly beautiful, a bit Bardotesque.'

'Did lots of chat shows in the eighties, plugging exercise videos and beauty-tip books?'

'Yup. She'd fly over to England, stay in the Ritz and get her PA to fire off a postcard to Felix's school, telling him to watch her on whatever show she was on. Then she'd fly back to the States without once visiting him. Not even ringing. Dylan told me. Mungo lived with her for a bit when she first left Jocelyn and moved to Hollywood, but Felix never even had an invitation.'

'But she must be far too young to be Felix's mother. Anyway, I thought she was found dead in Englebert Humperdinck's heart-shaped swimming pool years ago.'

'There was a lot of scandal when she took an overdose after marriage six or seven broke down and her ex got to keep the Shi'tzu in the settlement, but she survived it,' Saskia explained. 'She's been leaving her toothbrushes at re-hab centres and her resumé with producers ever since. Mungo says the only scripts she ever gets sent are so well thumbed by the countless other actresses that have rejected them, the words have practically rubbed off. She does a daytime soap now – reading her lines off idiot boards because she's always too pissed to remember them.'

'Why didn't you put any of this in the file, Saskia?'

'Because Felix didn't volunteer any of it. Dylan told me bits, Mungo quite a lot, and I looked the rest up.' Saskia paused for a moment, audibly sucking on her fag. 'He hates talking about it, loathes even the mention of her name. One of her old films came on television once when we were couching out at the mews, and the cronies and I were all laughing at it. Felix flipped – I mean, totally ballistic. We only just stopped him trashing the place.'

Phoebe rubbed her forehead. 'I'm sorry, Saskia. I had no idea. What do you think I should do? Call him and apologise?'

'Christ, no. I think,' Saskia sighed, 'that you'd better get over here quick and hope he rings.'

'I – er – ' Phoebe bit her lip, '– I gave him another number.'

'Whose? Not your flat? I thought we'd agreed here.'

'A friend is away and I've got the keys to her place,' Phoebe lied. 'So I'll just doctor her answerphone.' She winced, wondering when was the last time she'd told the truth.

'How long is she away?'

'Who?'

'Your friend.'

'Oh, ages I think. That is – '

'And is her place decent? I mean, better than your place?'

Phoebe looked around at the empty, heartless flat. 'It's okay, I guess.'

'Good, then we'll use that as Frances's base for now. Actually it works out brilliantly as Portia's due back any day now. You'd better give me the address and number.'

'Saskia, I really don't think – '

'It's not Finchley or anywhere awful, is it?'

'No. Look, Saskia – '

'Great. I'll just grab a pen. Okay, fire away.'

Reluctantly, Phoebe passed on the information, wondering how the hell she was going to wriggle out of the hole she was digging herself into faster than a bionic mole.

'Okay – where are you now? Islington, yes? You go round to your friend's place straight away, sit tight and hope he calls tonight. Ring me as soon as he does, or if he doesn't ring by tomorrow morning, we'll think up something desperate. I'm sure he will. I know Felix. Once he decides you're going somewhere with him, you go. He'll be all oozing, playful, apologetic charm again, you wait.'

The speeding, stressed, hyperbolic Saskia was back. The one

who filled the air with rattling, excited words as she plotted and planned and schemed and remembered.

Phoebe sighed.

'Listen, I'm really not sure about this.' She bit her lip, remembering Felix's parting comment. 'It's a hugely compromising situation to be in if I want to keep control of this thing – I mean, we'll probably be in the same hotel room, plus he'll be paying for everything.'

'So? Milk him.'

'It's not that simple. I mean, we're hardly likely to be booked into twin beds. He's more or less made it clear that he's expecting me to sleep with him if I go. And there's no bloody way I'm – '

'For Christ's sake, Freddy!' Saskia wailed. 'Don't fucking give me this! You wouldn't do it, would you? You wouldn't spit in my face like that, surely? I can't *believe* you're thinking of sleeping with him.' Her paranoid screech was so loud that the phone crackled with interference.

'No, no! Of course I don't want to bloody sleep with him!' Phoebe howled indignantly. 'I didn't say that. I said that I think it'll be really, really awkward trying to fight him off if I go to Paris.'

'Don't flatter yourself,' Saskia snapped bitterly, eaten up with such jealous demons she was rendered illogical. 'You've started to fancy him, haven't you? I knew it was bound to fucking happen, guessed you didn't like me enough to follow this through, but I was so bloody desperate. Christ!'

Phoebe could understand Saskia's demented jealousy, but that made it no less difficult to counter.

'Look, I think I'd better just say I can't go to Paris if he calls – arrange to meet him when he gets back,' she said quietly, immensely relieved.

'No!' Saskia wailed almost hysterically. 'He won't take that. He'll bug you and bug you to go, and if you don't he'll get into an awful black gloom and not call again, I know him. Oh God!'

Phoebe could hear her beginning to sob.

'Okay, okay – look, calm down, Saskia. I'll think of something, I promise.'

'Just say yes – please, Freddy, just say you'll go,' Saskia hiccuped in a tearful voice and rang off.

Forgetting about the message she was supposed to be concocting for the phone, Phoebe leapt up and paced the flat for ten minutes like a loon in a padded cell. Still almost foaming at the mouth, she glared at the new sofa and kicked it hard.

'Ouch!' she wailed, reeling back, her toes throbbing. 'Bloody, buggery thing!'

Howling with frustration, she ripped the bubble plastic from the hated checked Chesterfield and then jumped up and down on the discarded wrapping, popping madly, to vent her rage. Then she ran through to the bedroom and did exactly the same to the mattress until, soaked in sweat and totally out of breath, she dive-bombed the sofa and slid halfway across the shiny, polished floor on its newly freed casters.

Phoebe buried her face in the cool, new-smelling upholstery and groaned. What would she tell Dan if she went away this week? And what the hell was she going to do about this flat?

She looked up, hating the place with its high, cold white walls, polished school floors and bland, Ikea-clean newness. She loved places and people who were weathered and tatty and lived in, who wore their history well. This place's past had been smothered in new emulsion; its chapters taken away in a Pickford's van.

Phoebe tried to envisage it full of her junk and, more importantly, full of Dan's lovely warm presence. But it was like imagining the wrinkled bundle of wriggling pink limbs in an incubator as a pensioner, it seemed so far into the future.

Instead she closed her eyes and wondered how she could politely return his gift without hurting Dan's feelings. Half an hour later, she had almost perfected her gentle-but-firm approach. She was just testing out a few tender, loving, reproachful one-liners to her reflection in the tall windows when the phone rang.

'It's Felix,' muttered a voice almost drowned by background noise. He was clearly still in Café Delancey.

'Hi.' Phoebe braced herself for the oozing charm Saskia had warned about.

'Why did you walk out?' He sounded miserable as hell and very drunk.

'I don't like being told what to do.'

'What?' He was clearly fighting to hear over the bustle of the bar.

'I'm sorry.' Phoebe started to peel a warning sticker off the phone. 'I guess I like dramatic exits – I'm an exit-sensualist.'

Felix hardly seemed to be listening. 'Can I come round to your flat?'

There was no oozing charm, no caressing apology in his voice. He just sounded vulnerable, sad and smashed.

'No,' she sighed.

'Where do you live?'

'You can't come here, Felix.'

'Yes, I know, I know – you said.' He was rambling drunkenly now. 'I just want to be able to picture you in your little bit of London, lying in your big, lonely bed without me.'

'Isli—Highgate,' Phoebe corrected herself just in time. 'I live in Highgate.'

'Highgate,' Felix repeated, his voice almost drowned by the din behind him. 'How fucking right on of you. Do you have recycled bin liners, Greenpeace fridge magnets and boxes of old *Guardian*s waiting to be taken in the 2CV to the paper bank?'

'No. Tell me, do you have a secret darker side or are you always this syrupy?'

'Huh? Shit – hang on.'

There was a pause as Felix fed more money into the phone, audibly dropping most of it on the floor.

'Still there?'

'No.'

'Look, I'm sorry I pissed you about tonight,' he said urgently. 'Shit, I'm in such a lousy fucking mood. I'm not usually like this. I'm usually much nicer.'

'Really?' Phoebe's voice rippled with sarcasm.

'It's just that I had a shit-awful conversation with my mother earlier. I told you, didn't I?'

She blinked in amazement.

'Er – yes.'

'I'll tell you more about it tomorrow.'

'What?'

'In Paris. Listen I called Dyl—I mean, I called my flat-mate and he's looked at the tickets. The flight's at one-thirty. I thought we could – shit, hang on, this thing wants more money and I've only got coppers – '

As he spilled yet more coins on the floor, Phoebe raked the white ceiling with her eyes for some sort of inspiration.

'Hi.' Felix was back. 'This is my last five pence. I thought we could meet in that revolting coffee place in Terminal One, d'you know it? It has round table things and looks out over the concourse. Foul.'

'Felix, I'm not coming to – '

'About midday, yes? I'll have to phone and get the tickets put in your name. What's your surname again? Fredericks?'

'Yes. Look, Felix, I can't – '

'Shit, that's my money gone. I'll see you there. Bring your – ' And his voice was cut off.

Howling, Phoebe dashed across to the flattened bubble plastic and located the last few unpopped cellophane blisters to attack with her feet.

The phone rang again.

Please let it be Felix with a newly discovered pound coin, she prayed. Then I can tell him it's off.

'Hi.' the voice was as warm and husky as a tumble-dried mohair sweater.

It was Dan.

'I'm glad you're there. Christ, I miss you. Mitzi's in the bath,' he whispered.

'Oh, Dan, I wish you were here.' Phoebe was close to tears.

'I wish I was too, darling. How's moving in going? Are you settled?'

'Not totally.' She stretched across and splatted a final plastic air bubble.

'I'll try to come round on Tuesday evening.'

'Dan, I'm not sure but I might be going to Par—'

'What, darling?' he shouted away from the receiver, voice clearly not directed at her. There was a pause and the phone was muffled.

Phoebe could just make out Dan shouting: 'What, now?' followed by another pause, and then, 'Of course, straight away,' before the phone was pressed to his mouth again.

'I must go. Love you. Don't bother calling the office – I'm in court all week. See you Tuesday.'

'Dan, I'm going to be . . .' Phoebe stopped, aware that she was talking to a dialling tone. 'Fuck!'

She took a deep breath and dialled Portia's flat, but the line was busy.

To the accompaniment of bleeps and cursed oaths, she spent five minutes recording her cryptic answering machine message and then tried Saskia again. Still engaged.

Unable to bear sitting in the cavernous, unfriendly flat a moment longer, Phoebe collected up her bag, keys and the phone's tone pad, and looked around the sparse, shiny floors for what she hoped was the last time. As she walked to the door, she caught sight of the crumpled hunk of loo roll wrapped around Friday night's condom, still nestling by a skirting board.

She flicked off the light-switch with such a furious punch of her fist that the brass casing came away from the wall.

Felix reeled back into the mews just after midnight.

Upstairs, Otis Redding was 'Sitting on the Dock of the Bay' very loudly, and Dylan, dressed in a stripy dressing gown, his hair on end, was sitting on the sofa reading a Jilly Cooper novel and eating an Indian takeaway.

Felix kicked off his shoes. 'I'm afraid Paris is off, Dyldo.'

'I kind of guessed.' He nodded towards the tickets he'd dug out earlier, still spread out by the phone. 'Who is she?'

'I'm not quite sure.' Felix grinned over his shoulder. 'But she's gorgeous.'

'Hmm.' Dylan had heard it before.

He was quite accustomed to Felix offering him free foreign jaunts, only to renege at the last minute. Dylan was usually more surprised if he got to go, having to rinse boxer shorts at the last minute and cram t-shirts into his kit bag before racing to Heathrow. Tonight's predictable – if unusually last-minute – development was probably a good thing, he reflected. Having arranged a week's holiday cover at the bar, he now had the time to slob around the flat uninterrupted and to try to finish off his latest book.

'She's gorgeous,' Felix repeated drunkenly, gazing up at the ceiling and joining in with 'Try a Little Tenderness' in his very deep, excruciatingly flat singing voice.

Dylan looked at him sharply. Felix was drumming the beat with long index fingers on his angled, ratty denim knees and twitching his scuffed Timberland boots in time. One arm stretched up to his hair and he rested his smiling face in the crook of it. He was looking as scruffy as an Irish navvy tonight, and as high and lit up as the Statue of Liberty torch.

Like translating Racine with nothing but a Berlitz phrase book for help, Dylan had slowly learnt to read Felix's strange, contradictory signals over the years as a means to self-preservation and occasional damsel-in-distress rescue. When Felix dressed up for a girl, she was an itch he wanted to scratch as quickly and self-indulgently as possible; when he set out to meet her looking as though he'd just been released from three years' captivity in Beirut, the itch had wriggled under his skin.

Oh Christ, Dylan thought miserably, please don't let it be another Saskia.

The doorbell buzzed.

'Who the – ?'

'That'll be Mungo.' Felix yawned. 'He called this afternoon – he's been chucked out of his flat again so I said he could crash here for a bit. Let him in, would you, Dyldo?'

Glaring at Felix, he heaved himself up.

26

W ith lots of tearful kisses and a plea that she call to report back every day, Saskia saw Phoebe off from the Islington flat at eleven. She then dashed back into the house and raided every drawer and cupboard for clues.

What she found gave her immense solace. Phoebe was clearly still totally infatuated with Daniel Neasham; there was no way she was going to fall in love with Felix. Although scrupulously discreet, Phoebe had hoarded what little mementoes of Dan she had like a squirrel's nuts in a barren year. Under the bed was a photograph cut out of a tabloid. In it, Dan – looking pretty dishy, Saskia noticed resentfully – was batting away photographers as he stormed up the steps of the Old Bailey to defend a libel suit brought by a leading soap actor whom the *News* had accused of cottaging in Harrods loos. Buried beneath the lining paper in her tights drawer were a couple of curt scribbled notes of no great romantic content, both on Satellite Newspaper compliment slips; there were several bad attempts at sketches of him in a cheap A4 pad, more bald notes in an old shoebox and a lone cufflink which Saskia assumed was Dan's nestled in Phoebe's messy jewellery box. The only sign of Felix in the room was the file Saskia had given her weeks before, firmly buried beneath a *Company*, an old *Evening Standard* and a letter from Vicky, Phoebe's New Zealand-based sister-in-law.

Noticing an article in *Company* about women who got back with their exes, Saskia settled down on Phoebe's bed and started leafing through it.

The phone made her quail beside its unanswered monotone, certain that the caller could see her skulking there. Then, graced with a new tape, the machine picked it up.

'Fliss, it's me,' Phoebe panted after the tone. 'There's a letter I left on the sideboard. Could you post it – like now? I'm really sorry, and yes, I know who it's addressed to, but please bung it through the red mouth and I'll love you forever and have your babies if you ever prove infertile. If you don't – post the letter, I mean, not prove infertile – I'll tell Iain you call his dick "The Lip-synch Plunger". Oh Christ, I hope he's not listening to this. I made that up, Iain – honest – to make Fliss squirm. I mean, laugh. It's a total lie. Bugger, my money's run ou—'

Saskia grabbed the letter from the sideboard and steamed it open, scalding her fingers and almost blowing up the near-empty kettle in her haste.

> *Dan,*
> *In Paris to rescue a friend – I'll explain when I get back.*
> *I love you. We must talk.*
> *P.*

Saskia tried to slip the note back into the envelope without the fold crumpling, but it ripped as she crammed it in. Pulling it out again, she dropped ash on it.

'Fuck!'

When she finally tucked it in, the flap of the envelope refused to seal again and then glued itself in corrugated creases, clearly tampered with. Despairing, she crammed it into the overspilling bin, erased the phone message and let herself out of the flat.

Phoebe deliberately missed the Paris flight.

Running up the escalator from the tube just before midday and dashing towards the only café she could see, she caught sight of a glint of blond hair and a tanned hand stirring a double espresso, and froze, totally unable to go through with it. He was chattering into a mobile phone and looking revoltingly smug and beautiful, extracting admiring glances from the other occupants at the café and clearly loving it.

Phoebe hid behind a glass display cabinet crammed with plastic Beefeater dolls and souvenir spoons. She couldn't even face a flight sitting beside Felix, let alone several days. Why was she doing it? she wondered wretchedly. Surely Saskia wasn't worth this? How on earth could her going to Paris help? Although she supposed she could try to elbow Felix off the top of the Eiffel Tower.

With a stuffed travel bag weighing down her shoulders, Phoebe spent the following hour creeping around Terminal One in a state of frantic indecision, every now and again creeping towards the café to check that Felix was still there. He stuck it out for two more coffees and a cover-to-cover perusal of *GQ* before the smug grin started to slip towards the grainy froth at the bottom of his tiny coffee cup.

Flicking through the corn plasters display for cover in a chemist opposite, Phoebe realised that she absolutely had to go through with it.

Five more minutes of freedom and then I'll waft up with lots of oozing girly apologies and a great big kiss, she thought resignedly, and bought herself some breath freshener mints. 'Hot and cold,' Saskia had said. 'Keep him guessing, never let him feel sure he's hooked you, but make him certain he attracts you. Be so unpredictable that he could almost be wooing identical twins. And never, ever try to find out what makes him tick, or do anything girly and giving for him.'

Remembering Saskia's warning, Phoebe threw the breath fresheners in a bin and slipped into the loos to apply a lot of very red, very staining lipstick which, after even the briefest of pecks, would leave Felix looking like a toddler who'd been sucking the strawberry jam centres out of doughnuts.

Just before one o'clock, she emerged and, chin up, meandered unhurriedly towards his table. Two seconds later she'd stopped in her tracks and dived for cover once more.

Mungo was there with him.

Alarmingly, Felix's brattish, white-blond brother had just rolled up and was raking another high stool to the table to join him for a coffee, cackling delightedly over something. Felix, fiddling with what appeared to be his passport, still looked boot-faced.

Blue eyes reduced to narrow slits of tiredness, Mungo Sylvian was looking unspeakably scruffy in a way that only the truly beautiful, idle and rich can achieve. Despite the shredded jeans, faded t-shirt, creased baseball cap and grubby, unlaced trainers, he still had the air of someone who was more accustomed to signing Coutts cheques than signing on. Compared to Felix's sleek, groomed beauty, he looked like the rebellious pedigree puppy who's just gone walkabout in a slurry pit.

Lurking in a nearby Knickerbox, Phoebe scratched her head in bewilderment. Surely Mungo wasn't supposed to be going with them? Now that she simply couldn't tolerate; Mungo was poisonous.

The next minute, Felix stood up and wandered into the chemist next door to Phoebe's lacy hiding place. Waiting until he'd walked behind a display of sunglasses, she fled, not noticing Mungo watching her with amusement over the rim of his coffee cup.

Cowering in W. H. Smith's ten minutes later, having speed-read as far as Chapter Eight of the latest John Grisham, Phoebe heard the last call for flight AF564 to Paris and practically shut her nose in the book as a hand gripped her shoulder.

'Are you going to buy that, madam, or memorise it?' asked a polite attendant.

'Oh – er – no.' Phoebe handed it to her, glancing around nervously. 'Thanks, it's really too American.'

She bolted towards Tie Rack and made it to the cover of a display of silk shirts just in time to see Felix heading for passport control, head swinging round as he searched the departures terminal for her. Mungo wasn't with him. Loping towards Tie Rack en route, Felix seemed to look straight into her silky lair, his eyes forlorn. Amazingly he didn't spot her loitering next to a medium-sized spotty red shirt. Phoebe wondered if he was too vain to wear glasses.

She started to shake.

'You should go,' she told herself out loud. 'You MUST go, for Saskia.'

As Felix drew level, she almost jumped out in front of him, suitcase swinging, silk shirts flying, but stopped herself, still dithering hopelessly.

'Oh, God,' she muttered under her breath as he slowly turned the corner towards Passport Control, eyes still raking the terminus.

They were calling the Paris flight again, this time asking for several passengers by name, 'Phoebe Fredericks' included. Seeing an enthusiastic Tie Rack assistant closing fast, she dashed in the opposite direction to Felix, past several snack shops, and then dived into the terminal pub.

She was leaning against the bar for support when someone walked in and went flying over her abandoned travel bag.

'Oh, God, I'm sorry!' She tried not to laugh as she helped the sprawling man up. He had totally, irrevocably split his ancient jeans – several inches of pink and white striped boxer shorts were now showing through his rear seam like a waning moon.

'No, my fault, darling,' he laughed. 'Dying for a bloody drink. Gosh.' He looked at her and smiled delightedly. 'Can I buy you one too?'

Phoebe bit her lip with horror. It was Felix's revolting brother Mungo, white-blond hair tucked into faded baseball cap, pale blue eyes gleaming like wet woad.

He was grinning at her appreciatively, relishing the crotch-length ultra-fashionable pinafore dress and knee-high laced boots worn in Felix's honour.

'No, thanks.' Phoebe shook her head at his offer of a drink. 'I'm meeting someone.'

'Then wait with me,' Mungo ordered, leaning across the bar, boxer shorts flashing like mad.

'No, really, I – '

'Shut up, I insist,' he drawled irritably. 'Don't get all coy and girly. Believe me, I don't want to get into your knickers. What d'you want?'

Phoebe sighed. There was something so insistent and auto-cratic in his snapping, staccato voice that she felt he would cause a scene if she refused.

'In that case,' she smiled stiffly, 'I think you'd better sit down and I'll get the drinks. You might not want to get into my knickers, but you're almost out of yours.' She nodded towards his rear.

Mungo followed her gaze and shrieked with laughter. Grinning from ear to ear without the slightest show of embarrassment, he wandered deeper into the bar and found them a small table beside a gaggle of lads in football shirts getting tanked in anticipation of their flight to Alicante. Waiting for the drinks, he eyed them all thoughtfully, rejected each as a spotty lout, and watched Phoebe instead. She was gloriously scrawny and androgynous, he noted, with legs to die for.

'You look familiar.' He scrutinised her as she eventually rolled up with a bottle of lager and a Coke.

'Yes?' Phoebe swallowed.

'Can't place you, though. It'll come to me – thanks.' He took a large swig of lager. 'I needed this. Had to dash here at the last minute. My bloody brother got me out of bed – he'd forgotten his passport.'

'Really?'

'Yup,' Mungo sighed, offering her a Camel. 'And I'm afraid it looks like his airhead girlfriend forgot him, poor chap. She was supposed to be going to Paris with him, but she didn't turn up, stupid cow.'

'His girlfriend?' Phoebe almost bit the end off her bottle.

Mungo nodded, sliding back in his chair until he was almost horizontal with slouching laziness. 'Never met her myself, but I think Felix – that's my brother – is pretty keen. She's bound to be a frightful scrubber – all his lovers are.' He flashed his white teeth nastily. 'I'm Mungo by the way, Mungo Sylvian.'

He thrust out a hand knuckles-up as though she was supposed to kiss his signet ring.

'Freddy.' Phoebe shook it. 'So was your brother really spitting? That his girlfriend didn't turn up?'

Mungo shrugged. 'More depressed really. I think he's quite into her – probably because he hasn't got into her yet.' He narrowed his blue eyes and watched Phoebe closely, bored of talking about his brother. 'So where are you flying, Freddy?' He pronounced the name with sickly emphasis, mocking its boarding-school, jolly old lacrosse-pitch winsomeness. 'Where's Freddy flying?'

Phoebe jumped nervously and dropped his gaze. About to say 'Amsterdam', she noticed that Saskia had scribbled 'Paris' on her baggage label.

'Er – Paris, too, actually,' she muttered uncomfortably.

'Really. How extraordinary.' Mungo grinned and then looked at her in horror. 'Hey, you're not on the one-thirty flight? Shouldn't you be boarding now?'

'No, I'm on a later one. Like I said, I'm waiting for someone.'

'Which flight?' his tone was suspiciously chilly.

'Er – two o'clock.'

Mungo squinted up at the television screen showing flight times. 'There isn't one.'

'Isn't there? Oh, I must have got the wrong time.'

'Why don't I believe you?' He rubbed the rim of his lager bottle against his lower lip and watched her intently.

Phoebe squirmed. He possessed such an evil series of facial expressions, he could have earned millions in Quentin Tarantino movies, she realised. Whilst Felix irritated her enormously, Mungo frightened her. She would never dare to exact any sort of revenge on him.

'Who are you meeting?' he persisted.

'Look, I have to go.' Phoebe made to stand up, but Mungo lashed out an arm and pinned her down again.

'What about your friend?' he hissed. 'Won't he miss you if you're not here?'

'I've changed my mind,' Phoebe sighed, fed up with lying. 'I'm a lousy flyer, and my French is appalling. I think I might go to Brighton by bus instead.'

Mungo didn't laugh. He was watching her even more closely now, as though she was an unknown virus wriggling under a microscope's glass slide.

'Are you supposed to be going with Felix?' he asked slowly. 'You're the fucking girlfriend, aren't you?'

Phoebe shrugged. It no longer seemed to matter. She'd

missed the flight, let Saskia down and failed in her task before even writing her name on the top right-hand side of her exam paper. She was secretly relieved. Now she could sort out the flat fiasco, find a job to pay her rent and try to get Saskia straightened out far, far away from Felix.

'Shit!' Mungo leapt up so quickly that he knocked into their table and both bottles went flying. 'We have to get you on that flight!'

'I'm not going!' Phoebe protested, staying put despite the fact that half a bottle of Coke was dripping onto her lap.

'You bloody well are!' Gathering up her bag and gripping her arm as tightly as a climbing rope, Mungo dragged her out of the bar, oblivious of the whoops of derision from the Alicante lads who had spotted his stripy underwear poking out of his split trousers.

Spitting and hissing like an enraged goose, Phoebe had little choice but to allow Mungo to drag her to check in. He was very strong, extremely determined, and her boots were far too unstable to run away on. Besides, she realised, he could only force her as far as Passport Control before letting her go. All Phoebe had to do was acquiesce until then, and simply not get on the flight.

'My brother left tickets here for this girl.' Mungo pushed Phoebe to the front of a grumbling queue waiting to check in for the next flight. 'She's booked on to the one-thirty to Paris.'

The check-in clerk looked up in horror.

'I'm afraid it's too late, sir. I think – '

'Rubbish!' Mungo snarled. 'Just phone through and tell the gate she's on her way.'

The girl bristled. 'I'm afraid I can't do – '

'Crap!' Mungo started rummaging through Phoebe's bag for her passport. 'I've caught flights late loads of fucking times. They always hang on. Just – here we are – just ring through now and give her a boarding pass.' He opened the passport. 'It's – er – Phoebe Fredericks. You'll have the tickets back there somewhere. God, what an awful photograph – were you going cold turkey here or something?' He looked up at Phoebe and then narrowed his eyes at the check-in clerk. 'Fucking hurry up, then.'

'The flight's already taxiing, sir,' the girl said calmly, not taking the proffered passport.

'Then put her on the next one,' he said simply, utterly cocksure.

'It's fully booked.'

'Like piss it is.' Mungo gripped Phoebe tighter as she tried to wriggle away.

With the rude, expectant arrogance of an unpopular minor Royal, Mungo snapped, stropped, shouted and ordered in his curt, superior, public school drawl until he secured Phoebe a window seat on the next flight, up-graded to Executive Class in order to fit her in. He then remained glued to her side for the following forty minutes before allowing her through Passport Control.

Phoebe felt like a hostage being frog-marched with a gun pressed to her back, hidden from public view by a folded mackintosh. She could have thumped him and run, but there was something truly intimidating about Mungo's ruthless, snobbish dominion. Phoebe had a feeling that if she punched him, he'd punch her right back with twice the strength. His attention was totally focused on getting what he – and his disconsolate elder brother – wanted.

Phoebe was beginning to wonder if arrogant bloody-mindedness ran in the family.

Gripping her like a child's battered teddy, he'd towed her with him to phone Susie Middleton, finding out which hotel Felix was staying at – he was just as rude to her, Phoebe noticed – and had even refused to allow Phoebe to go to the loo.

'Why are you doing this?' she asked him in astonishment.

Ignoring her, he pressed her boarding pass and passport into her hands.

'I'll be waiting here,' he warned with an unpleasant smile as he left her just before the Departures crossover point. 'If you miss this one, I'll simply put you on the next. And for God's sake, tell Felix you missed the flight by accident.'

Phoebe stared at him in appalled awe.

Suddenly the pretty Lochinvar face was wreathed in smiles as charming as a mumsy headmistress welcoming a new girl on the first day of term.

'You really fancy my brother, don't you, darling?'

'No,' she answered honestly.

'Meaning you've never met anyone you were more attracted to in your life.'

Phoebe sighed, amazed at the family's complete conceit.

'Absolutely,' she lied.

'Look, darling, there's nothing to be frightened of,' he soothed. 'I know my brother's an intimidating prospect, but he really does fancy you too. And beneath that slithery-catch arrogance, he's as soft as dough. Don't fuck this up. Now push off.'

He gave her a kiss on the forehead and then shoved her towards the waiting passport officials.

Watching her file through to the departure lounge, Mungo turned his baseball cap back to front in triumph and reached back to tuck his boxers into the split seam a little more.

Felix had chosen well this time, he reflected happily. This one was stunning, bright, selfish and headstrong. Mungo hoped his brother really screwed her up.

Generally, Mungo remained fairly ambivalent to his brother's control freak love-life. But sometimes it was such fun to see him teach a really jumped-up cow a lesson. Oscar Wilde might have felt that women becoming like their mothers was their tragedy, but in Felix's case the real tragedy was when women became like *his* mother.

And Phoebe Fredericks, Mungo mused, already was.

Contrary as ever, he decided he rather liked her.

'Fliss?'

'Phoebe! Where are you, mate? In Paris?'

'Yes.' Phoebe's voice crackled on a lousy phone line.

'How's it going? Is he madly in love with you?'

'Fliss, I can't find Felix. I had to catch a later flight – I'll explain later. He's not at the hotel he's supposed to be at. They say the booking was cancelled. I don't know what to do.'

'Christ! I suppose you'd better book in there and wait – hope
he turns up.'

'It's way too expensive. One night would use up all my
money.'

'Have you called Saskia?'

'She's not in.'

'Shit! Well try and book in somewhere cheaper – youth hostel
or something – and let me know where you are. I'll try and get
in contact with Saskia. She'll think of something.'

'Thanks, Fliss. Oh God, my money's running out. Did you
post that letter?'

'What letter?'

But they'd been cut off.

After hours searching, Phoebe finally found a room in a tiny
hotel off Rue Montmartre. It was seedy, in desperate need of
restoration and crawling with low life. Her room was at the top
of five narrow, creaking staircases, thinly covered with a worn,
wrinkled carpet that looked as though it had claimed countless
lives. The hotel was ludicrously named the Hôtel Dom Perignon, which Phoebe immediately abbreviated to Hôtel Dump.

Her room was just large enough to house a double bed swathed
in stained candlewick, a rickety, woodwormed, fag-burnt desk
and a lop-sided wardrobe with no hangers, its door swinging from
the hinges and a dead mouse nestling in one of its dustier corners.
The euphemistically named '*ensuite douche*' had no lightbulb,
toilet roll, towel or basin plug, was festooned with lacy damp
mould cultures and crawling with small, scuttling cockroaches.

Back downstairs, the runny-nosed Patron just about held
back the massive, snarling Alsatian which guarded the bar long
enough to explain that Phoebe was expected to pay up-front for
the room daily.

It was past eleven by now and at least the room was
ridiculously cheap. Phoebe sighed, backed away from the
Alsatian's gnashing teeth and agreed. In the bar behind her,
half a dozen drooling octogenarians dragged their eyes away
from the thirty-inch screen that was showing boxing, stopped

sipping their cognacs or puffing their cigars and peered at Phoebe excitedly.

'*Vous restez ici ce soir, oui?*' one croaked.

'Sorry! English!' Phoebe gasped in what she hoped was an intensely stupid, British way and took possession of a key which was attached to a half-sized, empty Dom Perignon bottle to prevent the clientele walking off with it.

The Alsatian sank its yellow teeth into her travel bag as she tried to get upstairs again, and had to be kicked in the ribs by the Patron – to much tubercular cheering from the octogenarians – before it would let go.

In her room, she moved the bed in order to open the window and throw the dead mouse out. Then she tried to use the phone to contact Fliss, but found herself on a crossed line with a strange, wheezing Frenchman who appeared to be putting on a bet.

Aware that she hadn't eaten since breakfast, Phoebe visited a nearby late-night *supermarché* and stocked up on dry toast, jam, Camembert and insect killer before spending her first night in France behind a triple-locked door, snivelling, nibbling and splatting cockroaches in between trying the crossed line again without success. For entertainment, she listened to the woman in the next room give the worst rendition of the *When Harry Met Sally* faked orgasm she had ever heard, over and over and over again.

The next day she woke feeling far more optimistic and determined to find Felix. Mungo had let it slip that his brother was in France on a modelling job for a German cologne Christmas commercial. Phoebe was certain it wouldn't take long to track him down – after all, a large ensemble of models, photographer, assistants and ad men shooting a campaign which involved fake snow in late-July could hardly be inconspicuous.

Paying for another night in her room in advance and just dodging the tooth-dripping, ferocious advances of the Patron's Alsatian, Phoebe headed off to buy a guide book, map and dictionary and to fathom out a few appropriate questions over breakfast in a cheap café.

She hadn't anticipated searching streets eight-deep with tourists, however. Paris in midsummer was crawling with them and almost devoid of Parisians, who had sensibly decamped to cooler climes. Sightseers sweltered under sunhats and over ice-creams. The ultra-cool, fashionable image one associated with the bustling Paris pavement traffic had been seasonally adjusted into a clashing clamour of Hawaiian shirts, buff safari casuals, sloganed t-shirts and sunburnt flesh, as Americans, Japanese and European tourists staggered between shadowed café bars weighed down with photographic equipment, fat tourist guides and fast-food.

Every pavement was an obstacle course of cluttered tables, hot plastic chairs, even hotter metal ones, portrait artists surrounded by big-eyed, flattering sketches of bug-eyed, sulky children, street entertainers surrounded by open violin cases, restaurant boards, wandering vendors and fathers trying to take a snap of their fidgeting broods before anyone walked in front of their camera lenses.

It took Phoebe three-quarters of an hour to struggle from the café she had breakfasted in to the nearest Métro station. There, she bought a massive bunch of *billets* and, clacking through the turnstile, headed off to find Felix.

That night, she trailed back to her Hôtel Dump room in despair. On landing three, she noticed that the Alsatian had done a very neat bagel-shaped poo – so perfect, she almost picked it up, thinking it a plastic joke one. The smell just warned her off in time.

Back in her room, her neighbour was already coming to an unconvincing, twenty-decibel climax. Whoever had booked into the room upstairs appeared to be opening and shutting their window about six times a minute, as though to have a heated lip-reading argument with someone in a window across the street.

Phoebe dug into her dry toast supply and unscrewed the cap of her cheap plastic-bottled red plonk. She felt worn out, sweaty, and very, very alone.

She had just packed into one day a sight-seeing schedule that even the most ambitious Japanese tourist would allow a week for. But Phoebe hadn't been looking at the architecture, the paintings, the landmarks or the history. She had just been looking for Felix and, God, she resented him for it.

Tomorrow, she was planning to stick to the Seine and the Iles, possibly fitting in the Premier Arondissement if she had time. On Thursday, she might hit Versailles or perhaps the Bastille, she decided. If she hadn't found Felix by Friday, she was trading in her return ticket for an earlier flight and throwing in the towel quicker than an exhibitionist at a Turkish Baths.

On Thursday night, she finally got through to Saskia.

'You mean you're not even with him?'

'No, I'm bloody not,' Phoebe yelled over the traffic as she called from a pay phone on Boulevard de Sebastapol. 'I said, I haven't found him or his sodding shoot. I'm utterly, utterly fed up and broke. And I've got a cold.'

'Shit, Phoebe, you're so fucking useless at this!' Saskia sounded close to tears.

'Tell me about it. You asked me to do it. You're not the one who has to sleep coated in stinky insect repellent to ward off the roaches, or who has blisters on every toe from walking around asking people if they've seen a group of models on a shoot. D'you know how many fashion shoots go on here on any one day? Hundreds. I keep bumping into Kate Moss and asking her if she's seen Felix before I get dragged away by a heavy. They think I'm a stalker.'

'Try one of the night-clubs,' Saskia suggested tersely. 'Les Bains Douche. Head there after one in the morning and really dress up. I know it's thought of as so naff it's practically the Parisian Stringfellow's, but the fash gang still go there. Go tonight, Phoebe.'

'I'll never get in on my own.'

'Please,' Saskia begged, tears rising. 'Don't fuck this up again.'

Les Bains was perhaps more famous for being hard to get into than for anything else. The club was housed in a converted

Turkish baths on rue de Bourg-l'Abbé which had once pur-
portedly made even Proust sweat. Teeming with media, fashion,
film and celebrity peeps, it was a place to see, be seen, and be in
the happening scene.

The groups of potential clubbers – high-fash, high-heeled
and generally high – which Phoebe queued up behind outside
Les Bains Douche ascended the hallowed steps and were peered
at around the obscured-glass door by Marilyn, the infamous,
bra-cup challenged door-keeper: harder to get past, it was
reported, than a sulky gay bouncer guarding Take That's
dressing room. Groups of clubbers were curtly turned away
as not beautiful enough. They stumbled off with a mixture of
embarrassed giggles and mortified grimaces.

Lurking in her position next in the queue, Phoebe fought
down the rainforest-fat butterflies which were sado-masochis-
tically flagellating one another in her stomach, and straightened
her ridiculous outfit with trembling fingers. She was aware that
she was taking a huge gamble. She would either be humiliated
or revered, she realised. There was simply no way she could be
ignored, but she'd had no choice. Destined to arrive alone and
unknown, she'd realised she had to dress up to the last of her
nine lives.

As she mounted the steps towards Marilyn's cloud of cigarette smoke and Arpège, she shrugged off her coat and tried to
still her pounding heart.

With barely a flick of her perfectly plucked blonde eyebrow,
Marilyn raised her manicured claw and silently waved her in,
whisking her straight past the cash desk before returning to
scented sentry duty.

Totally overcome with delight, Phoebe tried to go back to
pay, fishing in her purse with embarrassment.

'How much?' she asked the porcelain-pale girl at the desk.
The girl looked straight through her and then turned to
accept several two-hundred franc notes from some very loud,
very bombed, and very beautiful new arrivals.

Phoebe dithered indecisively.

'*Libre, d'accord, bébé?*' a slurred voice whispered in her ear.

Phoebe turned sharply to find herself looking into two of the most beautifully painted grey eyes she'd ever encountered. Both pupils were sliding towards one another in a slightly slewed, cross-eyed attempt to focus, but they were undeniably very well framed. This girl must have a make-up kit that resembles Michelangelo's palette to create a look like that, Phoebe mused admiringly.

'No, Leo actually,' she muttered in confusion.

'*Che*?' The girl pouted her blood-red lips and tilted her beautiful head quizzically, snaky black curls rippling on to burnished shoulders as her head started to loll drunkenly and then corrected itself.

Phoebe was starting to make the queue buckle, partly because she was getting in the way but mostly because people were turning back to stare at her outfit, holding everything up.

'I'm not a Libra, I'm a Leo.' Phoebe swallowed, suddenly aware that she was making a gross gaffe but her nerve had been too thrown by the excitement of getting in to act rationally.

The snaky-haired girl merely giggled delightedly and kissed the air beside both Phoebe's cheeks, anxious not to smudge that perfectly applied Mac lipstick.

'Eet hes delightful,' she purred in a Chianti-soaked, velvety Italian accent. 'No, no – I say, she let people een *libre* – free, s'English, no? Peoples – get in free who are *belissi* – no, beautiful, you understand?'

'Christ.' Phoebe guessed her gamble had worked.

She wanted to drop on her knees and do a Wayne's World 'I am not worthy' salute. She had never seen so many stunning, flawless people confined in one small space – it was like wandering into *Logan's Run*; no one was over thirty, overweight or remotely imperfect. Imperfection simply wasn't tolerated here. Phoebe had a sudden vision of a very trendy Hitler Youth beach party.

'You join me and friends for drink, yes?' The grey-eyed girl smiled woozily, nodding towards a small staircase ahead of them which appeared to lead up to a restaurant bar. To the left of it another, dingier staircase dropped to light-stabbed shadows where, Phoebe assumed, the club proper started. 'I'm Mia.'

'I'm Phoebe. And, thanks.' She grinned. 'I'd better dump this first.' She held up her coat.

Mia shrugged, kissed the air beside Phoebe's ears again and, lurching slightly on her fashionable strappy, cork-heeled stilettos, drifted off.

Phoebe couldn't believe it. She was in for free. She pressed behind a toast-rack model in her anxiety to get to the bustling coat-check on her right – items thrust forwards inside-out, she noticed, so that their labels could be clocked by the rest of the queue – and dump the leather coat before Marilyn could change her mind.

The outfit must be working, she realised. Inspired improvisation, Phoebe babes.

Passing the windows of a particularly avant garde haute couture designer on rue du Faubourg Saint Honoré earlier that day, she had paused to scoff at an especially revolting example of fashion at its most self-loving, self-loathing and twisted. A nasty, mangled piece of badly dyed candlewick hacked into a baby doll dress was trapped on a six-foot, size six mannequin beneath what appeared to be a black M & S sports bra. It had taken Phoebe less than ten minutes to emulate the look with the aid of the nail-scissor-hacked Hôtel Dump bed-spread and her own Sloggi sports bra. Matched with the knee-high laced boots, the slicked bob and eyes painted into kohled caverns, Phoebe was, she felt, looking about as bad as she ever had, but admittedly more fashionable than ever. And in this particular club, that was what counted.

Two days spent unable to afford to eat more than dry toast and sweaty Camembert had also lifted her ribs and cheekbones almost through her skin, adding to her free-pass appeal. Whilst still looking like a salt-beef fattened new arrival at Belsen amidst so much sunken, long-starved flesh, she was now thin enough to appear ill, defeminised, gaunt, and consequently highly acceptable.

Please let Felix be here tonight, she prayed, handing over her coat – label facing in – before heading up the steps to the dingy, trompe-l'oeil bar.

'Ahh – ere she ees!' Mia was reeling around the upstairs bar with a vodka in each small paw, her eyes still crossing, but she managed to wave at Phoebe, dripping a lot of Smirnoff down her metallic satin shift dress.

'Hi.' Phoebe headed towards her and then stopped in her tracks as she recognised an angry blue gaze behind Mia, shooting out from beneath an equally angry, totally unfamiliar hair cut.

'Phoebe, meet my friends!' Mia staggered forwards and dragged her against the wet shift dress as she steered her over to the bar on the left. 'First, the most beautifool and talented. Felixir, thees ees Phoebe. *Bellissima, si*?'

'Hello, Felix,' Phoebe said in a low voice, sliding on to a spare stool to stop her legs going from under her. 'I've been looking for you everywhere, but it's no wonder I didn't spot you.'

'I dyed in my sleep,' he muttered, staring evilly at her and snatching up a matchbook to paw in predictably sulky fashion.

Pausing to gaze around the cracking turquoise and blue murals of fat, towel-swathed cherubs on the walls, Phoebe tried not to laugh, both from delight at her luck and amazed, hyena mirth at his appearance.

Felix was now a red-head. But not of Fliss's deep auburn, autumn bracken quality. Felix had been turned ginger by an unknown, plastic-gloved hand – bright, ugly, carroty ginger. And not only that, but the lustrous, floppy forelock had been hacked into the latest, high-fash razor cut. His Cambridge blue eyes were glaring out beneath a stubble of red spikes with murderous disdain.

The Deus ad boys had exacted their revenge for his insufferable delaying, date-changing and deal-dodging. They might have shot themselves in the foot by doing it, but they had also shot themselves a lot of excellent footage for the product, plus teaching a very stroppy English model a lesson in Germanic ire into the £5,000 a day bargain. The red-headed Felix image was just right: fiery, masculine, furious, feral, libidinous, and very, very dangerous.

Only Felix could still look beautiful against such crippling odds, Phoebe reflected sourly. But he did – angry, frustrated, itchy-skinned, and yet still infuriatingly handsome. The red hair contrasted ridiculously well with his tawny, golden skin, seemed to intensify the blue of his eyes, turning them almost aquamarine, and emphasising the sooty, almost girlish, lashes.

He's probably still wearing make-up from the shoot, she decided bitchily and examined the lashes jealously. Months of slapping on 2000-calorie mascara would never make hers as long.

She wished she had the nerve to break that Roman-road straight nose or black those heart-stopping, cliché Californian blue eyes. But now was not the time, she realised – handed an opportunity like this on a plate, one didn't fantasise one was in a Greek restaurant; one grabbed it with both hot hands. She couldn't believe her luck.

'You know eeech ozer!' Mia was screeching delightedly, raking back her glossy black snakes and wrinkling her forehead in amazement as an entire vodka and ice spilled down her back unnoticed.

'Not in the biblical sense,' Felix drawled, glaring at Phoebe as though she'd just crawled out from under a reeking corpse. 'Just in the bitch from hell one.'

'*Che?*' Mia giggled, looking around her other friends in confusion.

'What Felix is trying to say,' Phoebe said smoothly, 'is that we go to bible reading classes together. I take along the Hobnobs and Felix brings the photo of Mary Whitehouse.' She smiled widely at him.

It was one of his own recent put-downs. Felix had no idea how she'd got it, but was irksomely impressed all the same. If only his hair didn't look so ghastly, he thought bitterly, wishing they had mirrors behind the bar that he could gawp at it in. The only reason he'd come out tonight was because he wanted to force the Deus hospitality team to fork out for as many two-hundred-franc-a-throw tequilas as he could wangle from the bastards. Red hair would grow out; he could always wear a hat. The chilblains from lying outside La Défense in nothing but silk undies for two days, clutching an oversized bottle of Deus above the half a ton of melting cubed ice that formed his 'water bed', would take weeks to stop throbbing. Phoebe, meanwhile, appeared to have just stumbled off a catwalk, green eyes gleaming deliciously, sexy lips curving themselves into the most graceful of apologetic smiles. She was looking ridiculously, revoltingly, fash-vic, but had the sassy sensuality to carry it off. Felix had the feeling she could have got into Les Bains tonight wearing a shell suit.

'I'm so glad we bumped into each other,' she purred as she slid up to him. 'I'm afraid I missed the flight.'

'So I gathered.' Felix looked right past her, feigning total uninterest.

'I met up with your brother and he helped me get on another, but I couldn't contact you once I got here.'

'No, well, you wouldn't.'

'Oh?'

Felix suddenly looked into her eyes incredulously.

'You mean Mungo got you on to a plane?'

'Yes – he sort of took over.' Phoebe took advantage of his eye contact to lean closer, sealing their conversation off from Mia and the rest of the entourage, anxious to make up for lost time. 'He was extremely helpful, in fact.'

'Really? How sweet of him,' Felix muttered ironically. 'He used to be a boy scout – always comes in handy, although he only joined because he fancied a cub called Rufus. Tell me, is that dress Dolce and Gabbana or did you make it out of your bed-spread?'

'You weren't at the hotel number Mungo gave me,' Phoebe ploughed on, determinedly refusing to rise but dropping her voice instead. 'So I rather gave up.'

'I'm staying with Mia.'

Phoebe deliberately didn't react. 'And, yes, I made it out of a bed-spread.'

Pressing herself over Phoebe's shoulder in a waft of very

sweet scent, Mia was making an inane, gushing comment now, in such a hotchpotch of bombed French, Italian and English it was impossible to translate. She was clearly trying to introduce a few more of her assembled group of friends into this exclusive little conversation.

Felix ignored her. Feeling rotten but thinking determinedly about Saskia and The Task, Phoebe more or less managed to ignore her too, although she was acutely aware that a trickle of icy vodka was meandering between her vertebrae.

Lighting a Chesterfield, Felix was staring at Phoebe thoughtfully, head cocked.

She stared at the ginger spikes abstractedly.

Tonight, Felix Sylvian, she decided, you are going to fall in love with the reinvented, tailor-made-for-brats Phoebe Fredericks.

'So, are you going to apologise?' He flicked off his lighter and gazed at it sulkily.

'No.'

Not looking up, he grinned. 'Okay.'

'How's the shoot going?' Phoebe was aware that Mia was now regarding her in far from friendly fashion, grey eyes uncrossing to glare at her, snaky hair flicking like a horse's tail trying to rid a rump of a hornet. The words 'Medusa' and 'vodka-pickled' sprang to mind, she mused in Angus Deayton mode. The rest of the haute couture coterie were also earwigging frantically.

'It's done. This is our wrap party.' Felix shrugged, not wanting to talk about the ice-cube fiasco of the previous few days. 'How's your work?'

'I've just started,' she replied easily. 'It was delayed a couple of days.'

'What is it exactly that you do?'

Failing to drum up Fliss's pre-prepared answer, Phoebe smiled vaguely and turned abruptly to Mia, who was grinding a swizzle stick between her teeth.

'I hear you live in Paris?'

'*Si*,' she hissed, grey eyes narrowing into little dartboards of expertly applied matt shadow.

'That must be lovely. How long have you lived here?'

'One year – on the Rive Gauche.' Mia pitched left but righted herself in time. 'I haff tiny, tiny apartment.'

'And you're putting Felix up?' Phoebe smiled. 'Gosh, it must be cramped.'

'*Si* – ees cramping my style.' Mia looked at Felix with a tearful hiccup. 'But now the shoot over, 'e move out. Tonight. Excuse, please.' She flounced off to the loo, ricocheting off bony shoulders and bar stools en route.

Biting her lip guiltily, Phoebe watched her leave and then surveyed the rest of the assorted Deus team – mostly German fashion industry gays and nervy American models. They all appeared to be going through a protracted, half-hour rigmarole of ordering drinks.

'What specific brands of eau minerale do you have?'

'That's *three* cubes of ice – *not* crushed – and *one* slice lime, understand?'

'Cranberry juice *sans sucre, oui? Compris?*'

'No, no – *not* Badoit, honey. Don't you have Perrier or Evian?'

'Vat exact proof is your vodka?'

'Can I have a cappuccino viz plenty of froth?'

Phoebe looked back at Felix and gestured towards the bar-man-harassing retinue. 'Are you going to introduce me?'

'Nope.' He took a drag of his cigarette.

I asked for that, she reflected. She was beginning to wonder if she should soften the queen bitch act a bit or a lot. Whichever way, drastic action was clearly called for – she guessed from his sapphire-eyed and steely-cool reaction that she was playing this all wrong.

'Because,' Felix went on, moving closer to her and dropping his voice, 'basically I can't remember half of their fucking names. Their combined IQ is probably lower than their combined weight. Christ, I hate modelling.'

'Pounds or kilograms?'

'Huh?' Felix was rubbing his eyes tiredly.

'Their combined weight?'

'Stones,' he muttered rattily. 'No – tonnes. Fuck, I don't care.'

He yawned widely. Phoebe suddenly noticed two or three fillings buried in those whiter-than-Colgate teeth amidst pinker-than-candyfloss gums.

'Are you sleeping with Mia?' she asked before she could stop herself.

Blinking away fatigue, Felix grinned. 'Does that upset you?'

Phoebe played her eyes back with full Katharine Hepburn ice-chip intensity.

'Yes.'

'Good.' He ran his knuckles very lightly along the length of her arm, tilting his head as he watched their progress. 'Well, I've slept with her three times,' he traced the knuckles over the bumps of her collar bone, 'but I haven't screwed her once.'

'Sure,' Phoebe grinned.

'I told her I had my period.'

'That's convincing.'

'She cancelled my hotel so I had no choice but to stay with her.' Felix moved closer so that their hips connected. 'She's the PA on the whole project. She books, cooks, hooks up, and as she would say "fooks" up. She's sweet, but takes three hours with the aid of a map to solve a dot to dot. I guess getting me into her bed was the most calculating thing she's done since her Maths GCSE.'

'In my experience, that's exactly what most men would love to fook.' Phoebe winced as his cigarette smoke snaked up into her nose. 'And Italians don't take GCSEs, Felix.'

'Well, I don't fancy her anyway,' he snapped irritably, pressing his knuckles up the soft flesh of her throat and forcing her chin up.

'No?' Phoebe's chin was so high she was looking at him through her lower lashes now.

'No.' He flicked his tongue across her upper lip. 'I fancy you.'

'Actually, I failed my maths GCSE. Twice.'

'Who are you here with?' he breathed, rubbing the tip of his nose from her chin to her ear.

'I'm alone.'

'Bollocks. No one gets in here alone.'

'Don't they?'

Felix drew back his chin and burst out laughing, blue eyes sparkling with mirth. 'You just don't give a fuck, do you?'

'Depends if you ask or not.' Phoebe dropped a kiss on his knuckles and turned away.

'Dance?'

Wolfie, the German photographer, was flashing his gold fillings at her suggestively, and turning his heavy-lidded, faded blue eyes towards the stairs.

Uncertain, Phoebe looked back at Felix and saw Mia – back from the loos with her angry grey eyes painted even more outlandishly and the snaky curls teased out so wildly that they were threatening the light fittings – weaving her way up to him and curling herself around him like a fast-closing swamp fog. Barely hesitating, Felix buried his hands in Medusa curls and, still gazing at Phoebe, drew the pursed, dried-blood red lips towards his, into a very long, very aggressive kiss.

It was the sort of trick Phoebe had once played at fifteenth birthday parties when pissed on Southern Comfort. What a complete wally, she thought crabbily, surprised at how incensed it made her.

'Thanks.' She followed Wolfie.

Downstairs, Les Bains was a watery, steamy mix of columns laced with foliage, bluey-green tromp l'oeil walls, dimly lit recesses, an even more dimly lit bar, and yet more beautiful people. The main dance floor was incredibly small. Surrounded by columns and foliage, it formed a light-dappled fairy grotto in the centre of the room. On it, Versace, Westwood, Chanel and Gaultier wriggled and jiggled on coathanger-flat bodies, bony hips sparked off one another, and glossy streams of hair whipped around like snapping, wind-tugged flags.

Phoebe tucked her bed-spread tighter into her sports bra and hoped it would take the strain. Tutting loudly, Wolfie untucked it again, clearly hoping it wouldn't.

He danced incredibly badly. Embarrassingly so, with legs and arms shooting out at random and with no apparent regard for the thudding, sexy beat of the high-energy version of 'Rhythm of the Night' pulsating from the multi-stacked speakers. Phoebe kept trying to lose him on the packed, ivy-strewn dance-floor, but he was tagging her as though she was a scrum-half clutching an oval-shaped ball, waggling his long legs and grinning enthusiastically.

Thankfully, the standard of dancing in the club was so poor that Wolfie's gyrating epileptic fit seemed to go unnoticed. Phoebe marvelled at how badly all these beautiful people moved; they looked so glorious in the saturated, blue-green stabbing light and yet they had no idea what to do when given a loud noise repeated at regular intervals.

Phoebe – a clubber since her sneak-past-the-bouncer teens – felt out of place amidst such blatant beat-ignoring. She tried valiantly to copy the trendy, rebellious vogue style that was clearly now too fashionable even to listen to the music, but she couldn't help herself. She found herself being utterly square and gyrating her hips to the addictive, compulsive beat, stabbing her arms in time and twisting her body to match.

Before 'Rhythm of the Night' was halfway through, Wolfie was so sweaty that he clearly felt the need to retire to the shadowed bar recess on one side of the small dance floor and order himself a litre of mineral water.

Seeing her excuse to escape, Phoebe darted behind a group of ignoring-the-rhythm beautiful people and thrashed around with such absorbed, sensual rhythm-respect that Wolfie fled to a dingy bar stool, swabbing his forehead with a crumpled silk handkerchief.

Once she'd lost him, Phoebe blinkered herself into a purging dance, concentrating on shaking off all the frustrations and blister-bursting street walking of the past few days. She knew that she should go and find Felix again, but allowed herself a couple of tracks to imagine that she was with Dan who – admittedly a lousy, elbow-flapping, duck-impersonating dancer – took immense satisfaction from watching her.

Seconds into a Euro-beat version of 'One Night in Heaven', a pair of very high, narrow hip bones started jabbing into her buttocks – not to the beat – and two clammy little claws headed straight for her nipples, missing by inches.

Looking over her shoulder, Phoebe was amazed to see a stunning, sloe-eyed blonde girl mauling her from behind.

'Állo, je suis Yolande.' The girl popped out a pink tongue and curled it towards Phoebe's ear.

'Are you?' she gulped, smiling politely and shying away.

Trying the M-People side-slide, she leapt right and tried to dodge the gyrating grope by dancing into a group of very self-absorbed fashion victims. Yolande's hips, however, were very persistent, although her tongue lost its grip.

Phoebe was rather lost for what to do. She had once gone to Hollywood Babylon with some gay friends and been chased around by a Harley Davidson biker-dyke, but that had been easier to laugh off. Being very polite and English, she realised that the odd 'I'm afraid this isn't really my scene' muttered over her shoulder wasn't going to work.

She decided just to dance like hell and completely ignore the unwanted blonde's attentions.

They were well into the bum-stabbing middle-eight drum section before Yolande was forcibly detached and a voice breathed something into Phoebe's ear from quite a different direction.

'You turn me on so much,' whispered a luscious combination of peppery aftershave and rising, earthy libido. 'Dance with me and then take me back with you.'

The moment his warm hips connected with hers and started to circle to the beat, Phoebe realised with relieved delight that Felix really could dance. He wasn't a limb-waggling exhibitionist, or a beat-ignoring fashion victim. He moved with silky-smooth fluidity, his body flowing against and with hers with familiar ease.

Phoebe gave as good as she got. Shifting and spinning with the thudding beat, they danced in grinding, swaying unison in that strange clubbers' dance which allows two complete strangers to touch bodies like lovers, to mingle breath and sweat, without being able to talk to one another except in monosyllabic yells over the deafening, pulsating beat.

'One Night in Heaven' thudded and mingled its way into a starlet-sung, Euro-trash version of 'Fever'.

The music was kitsch and camp, yet ludicrously sexy, with a panting babe gasping and breathily murmuring for all it was worth the up-tempo version of the classic, sensual jazz song.

Phoebe knew she could turn someone on when she danced – it was a skill she had worked on from teenage parties, through university student union discos to London clubs. She got so absorbed in the song that she did it inadvertently. The more sensuous the music, the better she moved.

What she didn't usually count on was dancing with someone who could do exactly the same thing back to her. Felix's pelvis was rotating against hers in alarming simpatico, his hands slipping over the outside of her upper thighs beneath the bed-spread, just as hers were creeping round the tight muscles of his through his peach-skin jeans.

With sudden roughness, the fingers of his left hand wound themselves through hers and pulled her hand down to the soft base of her stomach, twisting her around and dragging her body into his until she could only move as he moved, could feel the friction of his hips against the base of her spine and the harsh heat of his breath slamming with each beat against the back of her damp neck.

The sweat was starting to trickle down Phoebe's back now and her heart was hammering even faster than the high-energy beat. She fought hard to think about dull, routine things like her overdue bills, her Job Start interview, her parents – no, better not think about them, given the circumstances – Sainsbury's, Marks and Spencer, garden centres, Pebble Mill at One, Sons and Daughters, Richard Clayderman, Ken Barlow . . .

'What are you thinking about?' Felix breathed into her ear.

What deeply sensual, esoteric, Felix-alluring thought would Saskia recommend? Phoebe wondered.

'Guess,' she murmured.

'What?' he yelled over the beat.

That rather lost the edge.

Phoebe struggled to spin around and gripped his jeans belt with her fingers.

'Guess,' she breathed into his mouth.

'Fucking me,' he murmured back.

Phoebe smiled. Ten out of ten for conceit. At least the beat between her legs started to fade fast.

'No.'

'Kissing me.' Felix leant closer into her mouth, his tongue starting to dart.

'No.' Phoebe leant away and eyed him lazily. He was just where she wanted him.

'What then?' he snapped grumpily.

'I was thinking of teaching you a lesson.'

He cocked his head in amusement. 'What sort of a lesson?'

She slipped her hands around his neck and, leaning against him, raised herself on to tiptoes so that the length of her body slid against his as she stretched to whisper in his ear: 'One you will, never, ever forget, Felix. I'll get my coat and meet you outside.' She turned and walked away, her face burning, heart hammering.

Grabbing her stuff from the cloakroom, she dashed past Marilyn and down the steps to the pavement, pressing her face against the cool leather of her coat to compose herself.

She knew that it was going unbelievably well, could tell he was getting keener by the second, but still had to fight an urge to run away again.

It wasn't that she didn't feel she could do it now, or that she felt the revenge idea was any more immoral and twisted than the sick little games Felix himself played with women. Someone had to be the one to administer the massive dose of his own medicine. What made her want to flee was the awful, appalling realisation that, hate Felix though she did, he was starting to turn her on more than she dared admit even to herself.

27

They ended up in an all night café bar on the corner of rue Saint Denis and a tiny side street. The small, neon-lit bar was practically deserted apart from the odd working girl taking her coffee break, and pimp licking a nicotine-stained thumb as he flicked through a pile of crumpled five-hundred franc notes. The place was so seedy it would have been rejected as a location for an art house B-movie on the grounds that it was too much of a dive to be believable. It made Hôtel Dump seem like Le Raphael by comparison. The steamed-up windows were cross-hatched with protective metal rods and every mirror behind the bar was veined and starred with cracks.

The assorted pimps and prostitutes barely looked up as she and Felix wandered in, clearly assuming they were two of the same. Phoebe clutched the candlewick bed-spread around her and felt ludicrously affronted; the outfit had, after all, duped the cliquiest club in Paris into thinking it was a designer made-to-measure. Then again, she reasoned, the blurred boundary between high fashion and on-the-street poverty was currently as obscure as that between Evian and tap water to her un-discerning palate.

Felix, still mildly tight, like a puppy who's guzzled grandma's box of liqueurs at Christmas, was clutching a bottle of hundred-pound tequila which he'd bought at Les Bains Douche, and gripping on to Phoebe's lower back with almost equal veneration.

'You'd better stash that away in here.' She nodded towards the bottle and pulled it beneath her leather coat just in time as a pock-faced barman who looked like a Moors Murderer lumbered up, hissing through a mouth which had a massive slash-scar across it like a hare lip.

'*Deux tequila et deux cafés, 'plaît,*' Felix hiccuped, sliding into a chair by a window.

Phoebe slipped in opposite him.

Watching her as she moved, Felix slowly lit a Chesterfield and then squinted out of the window where a couple of hookers were opening their coats to the few cars that whistled past, revealing tacky nylon g-strings, chain waist-necklaces, lacy-topped stockings and assorted open-cup bras.

'So, you missed the plane?' he asked, turning to her.

'No,' Phoebe leaned back as the Moors Murderer dumped their drinks on the table with burn-scarred hands.

'What then?' Felix snapped.

Listening to the barman snap his knuckles as he loped off, Phoebe hid her indecision by shrugging, and watched as one of the girls outside was chatted up by a wiry little man with the pale blue hood of his anorak pulled up. He must be a Brit, she decided. No Parisian – even the sort that paid for sex – would be seen dead in a cagoule.

'What then?' Felix persisted.

Phoebe looked into his eyes – even when tight, they were oh-so-very blue, critical and alert. She suddenly wished she didn't have to lie quite so much to do this.

'I nearly flunked out,' she admitted, realising that the truth could, in fact, be her ally this time. 'Your pushy little brother practically kicked me on to the next flight.' She took a gulp of coffee and looked straight at him, determined to play the game like a poker pro with a minimalist smile on a rigor mortis face.

Pulling at his cigarette, Felix blinked with miffed self-mockery. 'Why?'

'Because he somehow guessed who I was and – '

'No, why did you nearly flunk it?'

Not losing straight blue eye-contact, he leaned across and,

blowing the smoke from his cigarette to one side, positioned his mouth inches from hers. He was playing with her again now, highly amused and delighted at her unexpected show of vulnerability.

'Because I wasn't sure I fancied you that much,' Phoebe shrugged calmly, sinking back on her chair and watching the prostitute bartering with Mr Anorak.

Felix scowled and stared into his coffee.

Plagued by demons, she counted to ten.

'I've changed my mind.' She slid one foot against his and applied pressure as hard as a finger to a gushing artery.

Felix looked up, blue eyes gleaming like panda car lights. 'Yes?'

'Yes.' Phoebe rolled the nub of her ankle bone around his. 'You mean you – '

Phoebe smiled. 'For now,' she slid the other foot forwards, 'I think you're so sexy I could eat all those four letter words I hissed at your brother, and swallow the exclamation marks.' She slipped her leg along his calf until her boots gave way to bare skin. 'By the way, thank you for the ticket.'

'Wow!' Felix breathed, grinning so broadly that his blue eyes creased like rumpled button holes on an Oxford stripe shirt.

Phoebe smirked, certain she was getting there, playing it to order as smoothly as a violinist in an Italian restaurant bowing Corelli during the spaghetti vongole.

'You *can* do it.' Felix dipped one long finger into his coffee and made a print on the plastic tablecloth.

'What?' Phoebe was losing him, and her edge, fast.

'You can say thank you,' he raised the cup to his lips. 'How utterly extraordinary.'

Hark who speaks, Phoebe thought irritably as she beamed out a magnanimous smile.

'Is that what you like?' she cocked her head in a way she hadn't employed since her teens. 'Feminine gratitude? Little flowery cards and butterfly butt kisses for your generous freebies?'

Felix narrowed his eyes. 'It's only fucking polite,' he said huffily. 'After all, I did pay for you to be here.'

'Did you?'

'Yes I fucking did,' Felix scowled into his coffee. 'The least you could do is be grateful. Let's face it, Phoebe, you turned up four days late.'

Little git, Phoebe thought angrily. It was Deus who paid for any old stooge you chose to be here.

'Oh thank you, Felix,' she breathed very quietly. 'Thank you, thank you, thank you,' she started to raise her voice to a husky whisper. 'Oh, thank you, thank you, thank you, Felix,' she croaked, growing increasingly Meg Ryan-ordering-salad-on-the-side orgasmic. 'Thank you so, so, so much. Oh – God,' she gasped, 'thank you, thank you. Thank – oh thank – oh, oh – thank you!'

'Shut up,' Felix muttered, eyeing a jealous hooker apologetically.

'No, I can't.' Phoebe was enjoying her audience now, as several of the pimps turned to watch, bloodshot eyes flashing up franc signs. 'I am just so grateful, I can't express it. I'm so indebted to you,' she shuddered ecstatically, leaning forwards until her face was as close to his as a pensioner with her *Daily Mail*. 'I want to be your slave, your whore, your lover, your servant, your stooge, your velvety-bottom wiper, Felix. Tell me what you want me to do to show my gratitude.'

Felix grinned. 'I want you to shut up.'

Dropping her eyes with a sideways smile at the gawping Moors Murderer barman, Phoebe sank back into her chair and took a swig of coffee. On the juke-box, Serge Gainsbourg was plinky-plinking his way through 'Chez les Yé-Yé'. One of the pimps, clearly as high as the topmost Eiffel Tower girder, paused mid-chat on his mobile phone and started reedily singing along.

Phoebe watched him for a few seconds. When she looked to Felix for a reaction, he was still staring straight at her.

'Okay, I get your point,' he shrugged.

'Huh?'

'I pushed a free flight at you,' he drew another cigarette from his packet. 'So why the hell are you here?'

'Like I say, your brother frog marched me on a plane.' Phoebe polished off her coffee. 'And I've got business meetings here.'

'What is it exactly that you do?' Felix polished off his coffee too, running a healthy pink tongue across his lips.

Still uninspired, Phoebe smiled abstractedly and looked back out of the window. Anorak and the hooker had vanished.

'God, why do you have to be so fucking enigmatic, Phoebe Fredericks?' He sighed impatiently. 'Look, it's okay. I've kind of guessed you're living with somebody in London; it's not a problem.' He was shifting uncomfortably as he followed her gaze through the barred windows.

'What?' she babbled, frantically back-tracking.

'The man who answered your phone. He sounded pretty pissed off.'

'When?' Phoebe stared at him, for a moment nonplussed then suddenly felt as chilly as Captain Oates when he'd been gone too long.

'When you didn't turn up, I confess, I called your number. Tuesday, I think it was. We all got pissed the first night, was that Monday? I forget. Whenever. A guy answered. Voice like a World Service continuity announcer.'

'Oh, that'll be Iain,' Phoebe sighed with relief. 'My flat-mate's boyf—' She froze, remembering her Cinderella's Freudian slipper escape tactics that night in Camden. 'What number did you call?'

'What d'you mean, what number?' Felix looked at her as though she was a numerically dyslexic half-wit. 'Your flat. Highgate. Your number, Phoebe.'

'Highgate?' she whispered numbly, reality finally stinging home like a boundary six cracking on to the forehead of a front row Lord's spectator. Felix had tried to get hold of her on Tuesday evening; Dan had said that he was going to visit the flat then.

Oh God, oh God. Dan must have picked up the call, she

realised in total despair. He must have answered within one loud, unfamiliar buzzing jingle of the new phone, thinking it was her ringing to explain why she wasn't there, why the place was as barren as a post-holocaust showroom.

She could picture him sitting in the bleak, pale empty flat with just several piles of popped packing plastic and a very vague answerphone message for lack-of-company, waiting hopelessly for her arrival, leaping on the call like a teenager on the Valentine's Day post. He'd have brought a showered, expectant, gorgeous, kiss-hungry body. Oh, God. Oh, Dan.

Why the hell had she given Felix that number? One glass of wine over a flickering candle in Camden and her senses had been as addled as a lap top with floppy disc virus.

'So that was your flatmate's boyfriend, then?' Felix was pursuing the line of questioning as hopefully as a policeman with a ready-penned confession.

Still deadened with misery, Phoebe shrugged dumbly. Dropping her head as she tried for a more specific nod, she caught sight of the two small, untasted glasses of tequila, and wondered whether they would dull the pain.

Opposite her, Felix followed her gaze and his revoltingly even features brightened as though spotting an air vent in a gas chamber.

'I tell you what,' he leaned forward, long legs suddenly slipping around hers until their knees were overlapping like stuck keys on a typewriter, 'we'll play a little drinking game I know.'

'Sure,' Phoebe said vaguely, still thinking about Dan. What would he have thought when he heard Felix's indolent, sulky voice asking if she was there? She was desperate to know exactly what Felix had said to him.

'We down these tequilas in one,' his eyes were sparkling with such relish that they illuminated his lashes into spangled fibre-optics, 'and then we ask each other anything we like. Anything.'

'Mmm.' Phoebe wondered if Dan remembered her trite lie about having a new lover called Felix on the night they had kissed and then missed in Portia's flat. Had Felix mentioned his name when he'd called? Had he said she was supposed to be with him in Paris?

'You can start.' Felix pushed the drink towards her. 'Down it.'

'What?' Phoebe looked up.

'Down it!'

Shrugging, she looked longingly at the clear little anaesthetic for a brief second, downed it and then almost threw up.

Felix leant his elbows on the table and plugged his chin into his palms.

'Where do you live?'

Phoebe stared at him in confusion. 'Isli—er, Highgate,' she corrected herself, far too late.

'You did exactly that to me the first time I asked you.' He bit one of his little fingers thoughtfully. 'Now tell me the truth, you little liar. Where *do* you live?'

'I'm in the middle of moving.'

'Where to?'

'Islington,' Phoebe shrugged, conceding defeat. 'Douglas Street.'

'What number?'

'You said one question each,' she hissed, suddenly imagining him dropping in on the seventies tack palace whilst she was swigging a cider on the sofa with Milly, Goat, Saskia and Fliss during an episode of *Home and Away*.

'It's an extended question,' he said smoothly. 'What number?'

'Three-seven-two,' she mumbled.

'Try again.' Felix smiled amiably.

'Twenty-seven C,' Phoebe snapped.

'Better.' He ran his tongue over his little finger and then reached down for the second glass of tequila. 'Okay.' He threw it back without a wince. 'Your turn.'

Phoebe wondered where she would be best to pitch this. One thing was certain, she remembered – his mother was off limits. Knowing so much about him already, it was difficult not to ask an obviously leading question.

She could feel him tightening the pressure of his ankles against hers.

Phoebe thought madly. God, the tequila was already taking hold, she realised. She could almost feel it swirling around her veins. Why did alcohol have such a disastrous effect on her? Most people felt less demented on grade A narcotics.

Think Phoebe, *think*. What was that video she and Fliss had giggled over the other day? *Four Weddings and a Funeral?* Yes, yes – now, what was it Hugh Grant had stutteringly asked Andi McDowell?

'How many lovers have you had?' She cupped her chin in her hands, mocking Felix, desperately relieved that she'd thought of something.

'Christ, you go straight for the jugular, don't you?' He paused to think. 'Nine.'

That's less than me! she realised with disbelieving amusement.

'You're lying. Name them. Now. Without thinking – and this is an extended question too.'

Felix didn't miss a beat. 'Rebecca – she was my first girlfriend; she had massive chain mail braces on her teeth and we could only ever do it in her parents' pony trailer. Then Gina – that wasn't much more than a one night stand really. Dallas – I know, ridiculous name – I met her when I was having a year out in Australia. She was one frightening woman. Then there was Jasmin, a crazy but beautiful model. I lived with her for a bit. After that was a Sloaney girl called Saskia – I lived with her too, actually, then Belle who's French and even more violent than Dallas was. There were Janey and Juliet – but they're hardly worth mentioning. Finally, I had a completely misjudged one-week stand with a sweet, brainless American called Topaz. Now I'm a six-inch single waiting to be played.' He flashed his big, come-on smile.

Phoebe groaned.

She was still convinced he was lying. The blue gaze was too direct, too heartfelt. It reminded her of Fliss's. Besides, Saskia was always saying how many lovers he'd had – and that he'd broken each one after he'd finished with her, like a vodka-swigging Cossack throwing his empty glasses in a fireplace.

'What about Mia?'

'I told you, I didn't fuck her,' he said, waving the barman over and pushing the tequila glasses at him. 'She wanted me to, but I didn't. I've stopped screwing women who treat sex as an aerobics work-out crossed with a glossy magazine compatibility questionnaire, and ask you your star sign before they ask your name the next morning. I finally learnt that lesson from Topaz – the morning afters lasted longer than the night befores.'

Remembering just how evil he'd been to Saskia on one particular morning after, Phoebe wanted to thump him. Biting her lip hard to channel her anger, she watched as the barman came lumbering back with a bottle of Jose Cuervos clenched in one gnarled red hand. He started to execute a complicated, showy bit of drink-pouring involving a lot of twirling around and hissing through his scarred hare lip as he winked at Phoebe.

Suddenly seeing how ludicrous the situation was, she tried not to laugh.

Felix didn't take his eyes off her.

'What is it?' he asked as the second round of tequilas were thrown down in front of him like grenades with their swizzle stick pins removed.

'Is that my next question?' Phoebe looked at her drink and wondered if it was possible to tuck a full glass of tequila into one's cheek like a patient with a pill in a mental asylum, spitting it out when the nurse wasn't looking. Somehow she doubted that gobbing a glass of tequila into one of the nearby plastic pot-plants would go unnoticed. Even if it by-passed Felix, then the Moors Murderer was bound to cop it and slap her around a bit.

'No, it's just your attitude sometimes – the way you look at me.' He scratched his red hair uneasily.

'The way I look at you?' Phoebe knew exactly what he meant, but tried hard to act totally nonplussed. 'What, like this?'

She blinked and, very slowly, slipped forward on her elbows, shooting him a look she generally reserved for bedding Dan when he was feeling sulky. It was a complete killer. But Phoebe was unprepared for the sexual kick it gave her to watch Felix's pupils widen as though the lights had suddenly been dimmed.

'No, no – it's not that look.' He shifted so that his ankles were pressed to hers like manacles. 'Down it then.' He nodded towards the tequila glass, anxious to disengage his eyes from hers and wrestle back possession of the balls in this particular power game.

Wincing, she tried not to let the clear liquid make contact with any of her taste buds as she knocked it back. Even so, she shivered involuntarily as it seemed to draw blisters from the soft skin of her oesophagus as it slid churning gutwards.

'Do you do that when you come?' Felix laughed. 'Shiver like that. It's adorable. And no, that's not your question; it's just something I can't wait to find out.' His voice chafed in the back of his throat, it was so husky with insinuation.

Phoebe shuddered as the tequila's aftertaste soaked up saliva like talcum powder on frothy bath bubbles.

'Where did you go to school and were you happy there?' he asked.

She resisted a temptation to sneer at him slightly. Old school ties in both senses of the words might mean a lot to him, but the only thing she did with hers now was to wrap it around the shoe box that contained the assorted teenage photographs – most of Saskia and clique sneering in various sports teams – which she was always intending to stick in an album.

Suddenly, she realised his potential track. He was testing out a theory. He must have guessed she was at the same school as Saskia.

'Saint – er – Melissa's,' she improvised quickly. 'Near Ruislip. And, yes, I was very happy. Wonderfully jolly days.' Was that going a bit too far? she wondered, feeling the tequila race to her head and soak up most of her wits.

Felix's tongue was so far in his cheek that it was practically out of his ear. 'Will I have to repeat questions all night, Phoebe?' he asked, highly amused. 'Now what school did you really go to? As far as I remember, Melissa was never canonised.'

'Highstead Hall.' She squirmed in her seat, watching both his faces for a reaction. Why hadn't she said Blewbury Comprehensive or something? 'And no, I wasn't happy. I was picked on and unpopular and scrawny and my tits didn't grow until the sixth form. The girls hated me and the mistresses fancied me. I was miserable as hell and lousy at sport.'

Felix looked at her in silence for a long time. Phoebe couldn't read his expression at all – was it mockery or pity or empathy? She had no idea. He threw back his second tequila without comment.

Phoebe was starting to feel decidedly tight.

'Who do you live with in London?' she asked safely.

'A guy called Dylan.' Felix grinned, suddenly realising he was on easier ground. 'We've known each other since we were kids and I worship the ground he staggers around on. He's the only genuinely good, honest, perennially funny person I know. He's a stubborn, infuriating shit, but I love him.'

'More than your brother?' Phoebe asked mindlessly, and then suddenly remembered that family was off limits. Licking her tequila-numbed lips, she braced herself for a tirade.

'Probably,' he replied flatly. 'And that's cheating – it's definitely not an extended question.' He looked up for the Moors Murderer to ask for another round.

Feeling woozier by the second, Phoebe blinked to stop the room joggling about. She watched a police car sliding up to the one girl who was still doing trade outside. The police car split into two and both halves started do-si-doing before her eyes.

'Go on then,' Felix laughed.

'Uh?' Phoebe looked back at the table to see two more glasses of fermented cactus juice already kissing rims in front of her.

With the same expression cramping her features that she had once pulled when downing cough medicine to order, she reluctantly knocked back her third tequila and immediately realised her mistake. It thumped her in the chest with a forty-percent-proof punch and eked into her veins like an anaesthetic. She could almost hear the voice counting down beside the operating table starting to fade away.

'Tell me about your parents.'

Phoebe briefly registered that this was unfair – after all, she wasn't allowed to ask him about his – before gazing into her glass, glazing over and starting to waffle.

'Father – Ralph – is an industrial architect – works mostly abroad. His wife, Poppy, begrudgingly moves around with him as it saves her having to be a mother to my sister and me.' She bit her thumb nail and then, realising it was acrylic and loose, carefully released her grip. 'Both are fifty-something, staunchly middle-class. Pa's a guilty liberal; Ma's an out-and-out social mountaineer with more chips on her shoulder than a battered plaice. I've barely seen either of them since I was a teenager. In fact, I tend to think of my friend's mother as more of a . . .' She stopped short, colour splashing her cheeks like spilled cochineal as she realised she had been about to mention Gin Seaton.

Felix tried to catch her eye and failed. 'As more of a what?' he persisted.

Phoebe stared into his brimming glass.

'Your turn,' she muttered as thoughts of Gin drew up hidden emotional detritus in the quagmire of pity, guilt and affection. Poor Gin, Phoebe thought wretchedly, remembering how upset she had been at her disastrous dinner party.

Felix stalled pensively before downing his clear, bitter truth drug.

Determined to get all thoughts of Gin out of her mind, Phoebe searched around for a distraction. Her eyes settled on something red and fluffy.

As the tequila started to grip her by the ticklish parts, she was suddenly fighting the urge to drift in and out of drunken giggles. She now found Felix's carroty hair ludicrous and was trying hard not to stare at it in case she slid off her chair as she tittered.

'Phoebe, look at me,' he breathed.

She bit her lip, trying hard not to think about the ginger shag pile on his handsome head.

'Phoebe – '

'Have you ever been in love with any of your partners?' she butted in, trying to keep the giggling catch from her voice.

Felix shrugged. 'Depends how you interpret love.'

'Don't shirk.' Phoebe tried to look him in the eye without

catching a glimpse of the short red fringe. 'If you have to define
it then you've never felt it.'

Tilting his shoulders at an evasive angle, Felix looked away
and beckoned the loitering barman over.

'Then you're right,' he muttered in an undertone as he
beamed at the approaching murderer. 'I guess I've never really
been in love.'

Phoebe gaped at him suspiciously. Something about his set
jaw and darting, narrowed eyes told her she'd hit a nerve as raw
as one recently lacerated by root canal work.

At the same moment as she realised she was cracking through
Felix's shell, Phoebe also realised she couldn't drink another
tequila without passing out.

The barman was closing fast.

'Actually, I don't think I – ' she started apologetically.

'*L'addition, s'il vous plaît.*' Felix looked up at the looming six-
foot figure who nodded curtly and drew a pen from behind
what appeared to be half a tattered ear.

Phoebe sighed with relief. Felix was pulling rolled notes from
his jeans pocket to pay the bill. A pimp at a nearby table eyed
him suspiciously.

Outside, the city smelled as warm and sickly as a baby which
needed to be changed. The few cars whistling along rue Saint
Denis belonged to night-clubbers intent on racing home, and
only the most hardened of hookers still loitered in doorways,
hide-all coats shuttered tightly around their jazzy underwear in
the absence of trade.

Phoebe reeled off to the left, Felix to the right.

As she tottered carefully in what she hoped was the direction
of Hôtel Dump, Phoebe jumbled her leather coat buttons into
the wrong holes and listened to Felix cursing as he executed a
U-turn behind her. She avoided crashing into a lamp post and
carefully stepped around a refuse bin before she heard his
footsteps.

Phoebe had just passed a sulky-looking black girl wrapped in
pink fake fur and a rope-thick ankle chain when Felix drew
level. Sliding a long arm round her neck like a shepherd's crook,

he pulled Phoebe into a damp, reeking doorway and kissed her thoroughly.

Revolted and excited in equal measure, she squirmed away, 'This place stinks of sex.'

Felix kept gripping on to her neck, his mouth still pressed to hers. 'And we don't?' He pushed her back against a wall, leaning into her like a closing door. 'Face it, Phoebe, our minds have been fucking all night.'

The tequila triggered its alert again. Before she could take a grip on herself, Phoebe burst out laughing.

'What now?' Felix leaned back, affronted. 'What is it?'

Still laughing until tears began to seep, Phoebe pulled away and started weaving along the street. 'Our minds have been fucking all night . . .' she giggled, wiping her eyes. 'Our heads . . . where on earth did you get that, Felix? Don't tell me – the latest Sharon Stone movie? No?' She reeled back around to face him and noticed that he was still standing in the shadows of the door. 'No, you're right, too much dialogue. Perhaps it . . .' Her voice petered out as she realised that the situation wasn't remotely funny.

The tequila had taken its toll, she realised with plummeting heart. She had drunkenly disobeyed orders and made fun of him. Saskia had warned her against mobbing Felix up, but she'd forgotten in her bombed amusement. This dishy, cliché-spouting red-head was, in fact, the same dishy, acid-mouthed blond whom she was supposed to be teaching a lesson, not poking fun at from the back of the class.

Felix's tall silhouette had gone ominously still.

Phoebe stood wavering on the pavement, suddenly feeling far more sober.

'What is it with you?' he whispered from the gloom, his voice hissing like a slow puncture. 'You lie to me, you chase me, you ignore me, you kiss me like your lungs don't work, you stand me up, you're all over me. What the fuck are you playing at, Phoebe?'

She bit her lip. Think about it, Felix, she wanted to scream. It's as clear as the out-of-joint *nez* on your *visage*. You've done just that to women all your life. And you've done it to more than just nine. Far, far more.

He loomed out of the shadows and stood opposite her.

'I really, really fancy you.' His voice was slurring slightly. 'Shit – sorry, okay, fancy is such a ghastly fucking word but basically I'm saying I – hell, you know what I mean.'

'No, I don't.' Phoebe stood her ground, hardly believing that the type-cast arrogant mould was finally starting to develop a hairline crack.

'Okay, I'll sum it up, you bloody-minded cow.' He grinned grudgingly. 'You're bright, you're very, *very* sexy, and you're fucking opinionated.' He dropped a gruff laugh into his shoulder as he gave his cheek a nervous scratch on his coat collar. 'And I don't think I've wanted to follow someone around so much since I was a kid with a crush on the Dutch au pair. But if you think I'm some sort of shit-head cliché – and, let's face it, you've been acting like my lies are undone all night – then you'd better say so now, because if you just want to mob me up, I'll push off without another word.'

'Of course you're a cliché,' Phoebe murmured truthfully, trying hard to sound sober and indifferent. 'You're a howling cliché, Felix. You're blond, blue-eyed, tall, and ridiculously good-looking. You're clearly far too clever, too well educated, well brought up and quite probably too well hung for your own too-good-to-be-true good!' She took a deep breath to maintain enough tequila-slammered dignity to finish.

'Yes,' she breathed out more soberly, crossing her fingers behind her back as she geared up for her own untruths, 'you're a total cliché, Felix. You're delicious, fanciable, totally compulsive – and you're right, your lies positively gape open.'

His hazy blue gaze swivelled up from her ankles to her crossing eyes, entranced.

'And if you don't realise all this then, yes, you're a complete shit head too,' she finished with an effort.

'I see.' Felix dug his hands in his pockets and stared at her through the gloom. 'So you quite fancy me too, then?'

Phoebe laughed and crossed her fingers more tightly behind her back.

'Yes.' She shrugged, wondering why her fingers were suddenly uncrossing to straighten her bed-spread dress. 'I quite fancy you too.'

Biting his bottom lip as he smiled, Felix looked up at the sky. 'And now we've done the mutual admiration bit, can we make up?'

'Don't you mean make out?'

'Yes.'

Phoebe didn't move.

Nor did Felix.

'Come here,' she muttered, not certain that she was up to walking in a straight line.

'No, you come here.'

Still neither of them moved.

'Where's your hotel?'

'I don't think you should come back with me, Felix.'

'Where is it, Phoebe?' he sighed, finally moving forwards and slipping a smooth, sliding fingertip around her right ear.

She leaned away. 'It's a complete dump, and I really, really don't want you to see it.'

Felix grinned. 'I like dumps – they rather excite me. Why d'you think I just took you to that bar?'

'This dump wouldn't excite you,' Phoebe assured him, starting to feel more in control. 'And, besides, I have to work in the morning. I really need to go to bed. What time is it?'

'Four in the morning. Not worth going to bed. Let's slam a few more tequilas and tell a few more stories.' He slipped his arm easily around her shoulders and pulled her into him. 'Now where is this hotel, Phoebe? And don't fucking lie this time.'

His reaction to the room was predictable. He was at first silently appalled; then, hooting with seedy, tat-seeking relish, became quite excited; finally, hearing the fake orgasm scream queen still gasping to one of her regular, shrieking crescendos next door, he became hysterical with laughter. At that point he spotted the partial-absence of a bed-spread.

'You really did make it!' he cackled delightedly, pointing at her ultra-trendy dress. 'I don't fucking believe it. Christ, you're so gorgeous!'

'It got me into Les Bains.' Phoebe perched on the desk and glared at him, wishing he'd go away.

When he wouldn't stop laughing, she grabbed her cotton dressing gown and, stomping into the blackened bathroom, took off the ridiculous candlewick get-up.

Re-emerging after a good five minutes sulking, she felt more composed and ready to play mind-games. She had triple-knotted her dressing-gown cord – an improvised chastity belt – and now doubted that she would ever get out of the cotton robe again, let alone allow Felix in. Beneath it, she was still firmly encased in her sports bra, knickers and a fresh layer of deodorant. It wasn't exactly chainmail armour, but Phoebe felt it was also far enough from *les vêtements d'amour* to protect her from any sudden pounce Felix might be gearing up for. She'd also kept her boots on in case she was required to make a run for it.

She found him sitting on her bed with his long legs thrusting out towards the smelly pillow, swigging tequila and reading her copy of *Skinny Legs and All*.

'Get on the bed,' he ordered.

Phoebe hopped on to the desk.

'Okay.' Felix shrugged, watching her thoughtfully. 'There's really no need to be so up-tight, you know.'

'I know.' Phoebe crossed her legs under her and stared at him calmly. 'It's a personal choice. I like being up-tight.'

'Me too. If I'm up, I like it to be tight. And if I'm going down, I like to feel something even tighter.'

'Quite.' Phoebe wasn't sure she was following this. Was he talking about being drunk? 'The tighter the better,' she agreed, flashing a humouring smile. 'And I'm feeling pretty tight already.'

'Are you?' Felix grinned, reaching across to start to unlace her boots.

Phoebe was beginning to register that they were at unfortunate cross purposes. She nodded vaguely.

'Then, boy, I can't wait to feel you feeling tight,' Felix slurred, blinking drunkenly as he tried to focus on the lace-holes. 'I want to feel you up-tight right the way up your tight . . .'

'Then you'd better get a grip on yourself, Felix,' she snapped. 'Because, believe me, the only thing you'll be feeling tonight is yourself.'

He howled with laughter. Dropping his red head on to her feet until he was practically biting the toe off one unlaced boot, he guffawed with childish glee.

'I'm far too polite to feel myself in front of *such* a lady.'

Light was creeping over the elegant, balconied buildings opposite now and stealing through the grubby window in cold blue shafts. Illuminated by its pale, indistinct streaks, the room looked grottier than ever. Peeling, damp walls seemed to be sagging into the mildewed skirting boards, faded curtains drooped towards the dusty floorboards and the scorch-stained bulbs in the wall lights spilled weak pools of yellow light on to balding flock wallpaper.

The contrast between Felix and his surroundings was as acute as an orchid placed in a vase of dandelions. Lounging on the huge bed with his sprawling, racehorse legs stretched out so that he could tap at the brass bedhead with his suede toe, and his flat stomach twisted so that one muscled shoulder dug into the soft mattress like a stone sculpture sinking into a muddy garden, he could have been snapped there and then for an erotic Athena poster. Phoebe suspected that, framed and sepia-stained, it would be the sort of moody, schmoozy shot that every shared girly student flat would have propped up on their mantelpieces between the yucca plant and the Nancy Friday paperbacks.

Why then, she wondered, did she want to wring his wide, brown neck?

'Now tell me about your childhood, Phoebe Fredericks.' He had repossessed the tequila bottle and, propping his chin on the rim, was watching her meditatively. 'Zero through to – let's say, eighteen. Fire away.'

'That's not fair!' she howled. 'You sound like Anna Pasternak pinning down James Hewitt.'

'Seeing as I'm not allowed to open your legs,' he shrugged, 'I'm opening the questions up.' He dropped his face until he was kissing the rim of the tequila bottle, blue eyes expectant.

Phoebe took a deep breath. How on earth was she going to précis her ingenue infancy without mentioning Saskia? she wondered.

Somehow she did it; by condensing her childhood into about thirty seconds and missing out at least a decade of it, she avoided the S word totally. In fact, she had avoided most of the S words in the English language because she was now slurring her words as badly as a fetishist with a pierced tongue.

Quick-firing questions like quiz-hosts, they then moved on to pet hates, to pet likes, to pets they had loved, through losing their virginity, finding their independence, mislaying their direction in life. Phoebe started taking smaller and smaller sips from the bottle until she was only letting the tiniest dribble of tequila through her lips with each question.

Outside, the pale, early-morning sun started to wink up above the Parisian rooftops.

Wiping tequila from their mouths and giggling a lot, Phoebe and Felix confessed what made them laugh and cry, admitted their most embarrassing memories, biggest mistakes and saddest crushes; confided their worst moments and owned up to tears, tantrums and torn heartstrings.

'I had a dog once,' Phoebe found herself saying, just as her sixth tequila was stripping her of the ability to focus, 'called Rabbit. She was a fat, spoilt, grumpy Jack Russell bitch with capital-A attitude and a roaming wall eye, but she had a cuddlesome butt and loved me slavishly like nothing else ever has.' She blinked hard to tuck back a couple of hot, wet displays of emotion that were threatening to trickle over her lower lids. What had started as an attempt to make Felix laugh was starting to hurt more than she had ever imagined.

'Yes?' He sat up on the bed.

'She was killed – horribly.' Phoebe stared fixedly at a wall light. 'It was when I was about eight. My parents were living in Wimbledon. Rabbit used to escape from the garden and take late-night wanders on the common – she was a terrible tart.' She lapsed into silence as the wall light started to split and rotate like a kaleidoscope in front of her swimming eyes.

'And?' Felix reached out to tug gently at the hem of her robe.

Phoebe flinched away, terrified of bursting into tears. She determinedly cleared her throat and blurted the rest of her story in a harsh, defensive monotone.

'Some kids burned her alive one night,' she muttered quickly. 'Tied her to a tree, drenched her in lighter fluid – they'd been sniffing it apparently – and torched her. Whoever found her traced us by her identity tag and delivered her in a plastic bag the next morning. My mother just threw her in the bin. She refused to talk about it at all. Daddy said she was upset, but I think she was just embarrassed about it.' She dug a fake finger nail into her palm until the skin started to pucker and smart.

'And you?' Felix had gone very still, like a wild cat watching a limping fawn and suddenly taking pity. 'What did you do?'

'What I was told to do.' Phoebe shrugged numbly. 'Didn't mention it again, cried myself to sleep at night quietly enough for them to snore undisturbed next door, and pretended to love the fat, thick Labrador puppy that my parents wrapped up in a ribbon-coated cardboard box the following week. I seem to recall I spent ages making some kiddish little memorial bed to Rabbit in the garden and then practically camped beside it, but my mother cottoned on after about a fortnight and got the gardener to plant an azalea over it. We didn't eat rabbit stew for months afterwards just in case I threw another tantrum.' She smiled with a lop-sided attempt at self-mockery, realising that the story probably came across as rather ludicrous and babyish after all these years, even though she'd never been able to see the funny side.

Felix didn't smile back. Watching her, he buried his cheek in the crook of his arm and started to stretch out a hand before stopping himself.

'I wish I could hug you,' he muttered. 'But you won't fucking let me, will you?'

Suddenly wanting to be hugged very badly indeed, Phoebe

thrust the half-empty bottle at him and forced her tequila-steeped conscience to focus hard on Saskia's current torture, not her own childhood one.

When Felix staggered off to the loo, she shot across the room and, clumsy in her haste, extracted her bottle of Volvic from amongst her small stash of provisions. Glancing over her shoulder to check that Felix was still firmly ensconced in the bathroom, she tipped over half of what was left of the tequila into the condom-littered window box and then topped up the bottle with mineral water.

The resultant brew was far more palatable and, although her head still spun like a child reeling from its first trip to the fair, Phoebe found she was no longer rendered ever closer to a stomach pump with each swig.

The next few inches of doctored tequila extracted safer secrets – favourite songs, years and films. It was as easy as playing sacred purple pillow: a daft, drunken, post-Student-Union-disco coffee-and-Hobnobs truth game that Phoebe and her new friends had invented during fresher week at university. These were safe, giggly, hiccupy-drunk subjects that could be broached without thought or pain, as simple to drum out as answers to a market research questionnaire. It was almost as though Felix was deliberately easing off the pressure. Had Phoebe not been so certain of his manipulative, libertine cruelty, she would have believed that he was.

She was taking less and less tequila into her mouth with each round, but still her senses started to see, hear, smell, feel and taste nothing but Jose Cuervos. She was rapidly approaching the giggle-throw-up-and-collapse phase of inebriation.

When Felix started to talk about being bullied at school, she couldn't even remember asking him the question that had led to it.

'I was groped daily from eight to fifteen, until I finally shot up beyond six foot and started to fight back.' He was talking into the mattress as he spoke, not looking at Phoebe. 'The only reason I wasn't buggered like the other pretty fags – mostly camp choir boy poofs whom I couldn't bring myself to side with

– was because my elder brother, Jimmy, was there – captain of everything bar industry – and was so well loved that any move made on me was sixty laps of the field during CCF from him. He knew what was going on but he was far too fucking image-conscious to really acknowledge it – just did the minimum of damage limitation to stop me getting thoroughly fucked up, without losing his kudos-cool in the common room.

'I wasn't a fairy-voiced little sop,' Felix was talking so quietly now that his voice, muffled by the sheets, could have been coming from the next room, 'so I didn't belong to that hardened, ostracised little gang with their Oscar Wilde wit and stifled-tears-to-mummy phonecalls at weekends, but Jimmy practically bracketed me with them because I was always talked about just as much – I was either hated or lusted after, and basically such a fucking study-time joke that he found me acutely embarrassing. It took us whole holidays before we could look at one another and then, first day of term, I was a freaky little stranger again.

'What he could never forgive was the fact that I was deliberately crap at sport. I just couldn't ever see the point of hitting, grabbing or kicking a spherical object with such demented hatred.' Felix twisted his face sideways until, flushed with the heat of being pressed to the sheets, it angled itself towards Phoebe.

'I was nick-named Bum-licks Felix because I was bright and therefore unlucky enough to collect a few of the academic prizes everyone avoided and coveted.' He groped for his cigarette packet. 'And then when I fucked up my exams on purpose in an attempt to be liked, they called me Feel-tits and spread a rumour that I failed my GCEs because I was wanking off nightly into a black market 1985 copy of *Big Tits* while everyone else was copying their Roosevelt New Plan acronyms inside their shirt cuffs.'

'And were you?' Phoebe was still consciously trying to avoid S words, aware that she was now so drunk she was hissing sibilants like Sid the Snake spitting tobacco as she slurred her way through the smallest of sentences. She shook her head hard, desperate to sober up.

'Was I what?' Felix picked at the laddered sheet with twitchy self-absorption.

'Wanking into your crusty copy of *Big Tits*?' Phoebe made a slobbery meal of the last plural but it passed unnoticed.

'Yes.' He started to laugh. 'Okay, I was. The night before my Latin 'O' level I was banging a Kleenex and repeating *amo-amas-amat* over and over in an attempt to hold myself back for Gigi, the 44D busty babe from Balham.'

Letting a giggle grip, Phoebe almost fell off the desk.

'About a week later,' Felix cackled on, 'I was beaten up so badly after deliberately fucking up a cricket match with Gordonstoun that I had to be taken to casualty. The masters still think I threw myself down a staircase like Princess Diana in a fit of LBW guilt. Truth is, the team captain broke three of my ribs with a bat that had been signed by Gatting.'

Phoebe had stopped giggling. 'You didn't tell anyone?'

'Not a soul.' Felix shook his head. 'I was too bloody proud. I just became even more disruptive and difficult until, at seventeen, I was expelled for sneaking back from crashing the local Comp's school disco with some poor burgundy-haired little slag I wanted to bury my virginity into. Ironically, I became a school cult hero after that.' He grinned sheepishly.

And so they talked until seven in the morning. They talked until aching white light was streaming through the window like a pub's neons just before midnight; until bustling, clanking noises rattled up from the street below. They talked until the sun loomed up above the roofs opposite and sand-blasted the dust from the surfaces in the seedy, smoke-kissed room, spilling on to the creased white sheets, on to Felix's garish red hair and Phoebe's small collection of food nestling on the chair beside her. They talked until Felix was hoarse and sated; until Phoebe, despite the watered tequila, was practically dead with delirious alcohol poisoning.

Just after seven, the occupant of the room upstairs started to flap his wardrobe doors open with a vengeance, as though fanning a flushed body blush. Seconds later, the thin, flock-papered left wall of Phoebe's seedy room began to reverberate with the first few gasps of an unconvincing neighbourly climax.

Felix and Phoebe were weeping with laughter.

The tequila bottle was now sitting beside Phoebe on the desk with half an inch in the bottom. Felix – who had been responsible for draining more or less three-quarters of it – bit the bed sheets with mirth and slid his eyes from its neck to Phoebe and back.

Clutching her cramping, giggling stomach, she was fighting to remember her identity. So far she felt she had behaved with as much dignity as a completely, utterly slewed avenger could.

In the last two hours, she had striven to swallow before speaking and not slur her words; she had asked some extremely poignant, Saskia-relevant questions – although admittedly she could remember none of the answers; she had answered all of Felix's increasingly kinky questions truthfully and without, she was sure, mentioning Saskia once – although she wasn't totally sure what she *had* mentioned. She had only accidentally flashed her underwear out of her tightly tied dressing gown once – maybe twice – during her many, many trips to fall around in the darkened loo.

Phoebe had in fact, she mused woozily, acted entirely upon instructions tonight. She felt she had fooled Felix pretty convincingly; she could pace Oliver Reed in an elbow-bending match. Boy, could she drink a lot without feeling in the slightest bit affected. Felix must think, she resolved with a grinning hiccup aimed in his general direction, that I'm more or less sober.

Sinking his left cheek into a crumpled bolster on the messy bed, he smiled back, long lashes drooping. He clearly didn't appreciate the extent of Phoebe's near-coma drunkenness. With an indulgent, sleepy groan, he stretched out for the tequila bottle, missed a few times, and finally got a grip.

'You ask the last question.' He drained the last few dregs, worm and all.

As she tried to pin his swirling image down, Phoebe wondered if she was up to speech. It was a dilemma she had faced over the last six or seven questions and yet, when almost at the point of defeat, words had gushed from her dehydrated lips like a self-absorbed celebrity on the Radio 4's Psychiatrist's Couch.

'Tell me,' she started, pausing as she admired the clarity of pronunciation of her first two words. God, what was she going to say?

'Tell me,' she began again. Perfect once more. Well done, Phoebe. Completely amazing. Shall we try that again, or go to sleep on a good one?

'What?' Felix was stroking her leg.

God, that felt good.

'Tell me,' she closed her eyes, no longer worrying about her diction, 'about your parents.'

Somewhere in the deepest recesses of her brain, where there was still a partially pickled corner of cognisant logic, alarm bells clanged.

The stroking stopped.

Felix lay back on the bed and stared at the ceiling.

'Christ, there are fucking roaches in here, Phoebe!' he snapped.

She moaned her agreement, descending fast into the refuge of nauseous torpor.

'Do you think you could love me?' Felix asked the ceiling in a muted whisper.

With an abrupt halt of her giddy plunge towards sleep, she snapped her eyes open and, totally incapable of focusing on the dancing room, moaned again in what she hoped was a vague way.

He fell silent again.

Relieved, Phoebe was just drifting off to an uncomfortable, desk top drunken sleep when he spoke again.

'My father – Jocelyn – is a writer,' he started quietly. 'He's been married three – no, four – times. He's living with his latest blonde bint, but they're not married – at least I haven't got the photocopied announcement letter if they are. Basically, I think the old shit's finally running scared of alimony.'

Half listening, Phoebe cranked her eyes open again and fought to stay awake.

'He decamped to the Barbados house in the late seventies,' Felix continued bitterly, emotion and tequila excess pushing tears towards his angrily blinking lashes, 'because he resented paying two nines in the pound to the taxman in England. Ironic thing is, he's now practically forking that out to his ex-fucking wives.' He rolled over to bury his face in the sheets. 'Literally ex-fucking. When they stop straddling his fat, drunken paunch, he kicks them out.

'From birth to seven, all I saw of him was when whichever sadistic blonde nanny he was screwing brought Jimmy, me and Mungo down to kiss him goodnight. By seven or eight, I had a Muppet-chef Baltic accent and was wetting my fitted plastic sheet like a pierced motel water bed every night.

'Pa did a sharp bunk around then,' he went on. 'Pretty soon after that, my mother did too.'

'Your mother?' Phoebe asked, too drunk to care that she was dicing, cubing and square-rooting with death.

Shifting yet further away from her, he ignored the question.

'At eight, I was shoved off to boarding school,' he muttered. 'Told you about that. Holidayed with potty grannies or some benevolent fucking schoolfriends from then on, and saw Father once every two or three years when he was in England promoting a book, or when he got a streak of conscience – usually when he'd just married some young tart who wanted to meet us – and invited us over to Barbados.'

Phoebe's heart was weeping for Felix, yet it was all she could do to focus on him without her pupils running towards one another like lovers in a beach.

She closed her eyes and wretchedly tried to imagine what it had been like. A few seconds later, she was asleep. Ten minutes later, she was wide awake again, aware that in her boozy, woozy stupor, she had missed something very, very important.

'. . . then married a man young enough to be my fag at school,' Felix was saying, his eyes once again on the ceiling. 'Okay, that's an exaggeration, but the great, thick lump was six months older than Jimmy is, and so stupid he read one of my father's books with his finger tracing every word. Pa only writes little, easy, double-syllables because it mean he fulfils his 100,000 word contracts sooner. And all the time, this thicko's mouth is moving very, very slowly – Mungo saw him.'

He was slipping a white knuckle between his teeth now. 'It took him six months to finish *Without Contempt*, which is about as long as the marriage lasted. Then she married some film producer, which lasted until her contract with his flop of a box-office crash ended.'

He winced, digging his nails into the unnatural red hair like cat's claws through feathers.

'Now,' he hissed, 'she's linking ringed fingers up with some multi-married, multi-personality, multi-millionaire who's so old he's hooked to a drip with his lawyer and a priest panting at his side. And you know the ironic fucking thing? Mungo's seen him and reckons Mummy really loves the little corpse.'

He finally swivelled his tortured blue gaze towards Phoebe's tearful green one.

'She probably does love him,' he whispered. 'She probably bloody does. She loves every-fucking-one.'

Phoebe knew she shouldn't say it. She knew she shouldn't. But she did.

'Everyone except you?'

Springing from the bed like a punch-drunk boxer, Felix was wrapped around her in seconds.

Terrified he was going to hit her, Phoebe slid away from him in a terrified spasm, but Felix just gripped tighter, his fingers clinging on to her back with nails digging as though he was gripping on to a window ledge hundreds of feet above a street.

Phoebe was drunkenly, jumpily, aware that her cotton robe was gaping widely around its taut waist-rope now, but Felix didn't seem to care or notice. He buried his face tightly against the skin of her chest and muttered, 'I'm sorry, I'm sorry, I'm sorry,' over and over again until he had pacified her into a mistrustful, muscle-clenched stillness.

'You're right.' He pulled his head up and pressed his stubbly, drink-stale chin and mouth to hers. 'You're right.'

Clamping her lips shut, Phoebe watched with wide, barely

focused gaze as his screwed-up eyes loosened for a fraction of a second and then snapped open to look at her. Dark blue with anguish, they were also swimming with tears.

A moment later, he had pulled himself up and staggered into the bathroom.

Phoebe stayed sitting on the desk, fighting nausea, panic and pity. She wanted – perhaps childishly, certainly drunkenly – to run away and dive down a hole like a snoozy, woozy hare stunned by passing headlights. But she was too drunk to move, and she had nowhere to go.

'I didn't ask for this, Saskia,' she whispered quietly. 'I didn't ask to pity him.'

When Felix emerged again, he was completely composed, if very drunk, and acting as though the previous few minutes hadn't happened.

He calmly wandered back into the room and looked around, rubbing his short, angry red hair with self-absorbed, self-conscious cool. Then, not quite catching her eye, he helped Phoebe up and placed her carefully on the foot of the bed.

Uncomplaining because she was now too close to comatose indifference to throw a punch, she lolled tiredly, frantically resisting the pull of gravity.

Felix sagely kept his distance as he sank on to the pillows at the opposite end of the bed, long legs flung out widely like a sleeping calf, and reached for the empty tequila bottle.

Head drooping, Phoebe fought to turn the three images of him that she could see into one.

'One last game. We spin the bottle,' he said slowly. 'On the desk.' He stretched an arm towards her, fingers stopping just short of her knee to pleat the worn, bobbly sheet. 'And whoever the neck lands nearest has to make the first move.'

Drifting in and out of consciousness, she had missed most of this.

'The first what?' she more or less managed to slur.

'Makes the first move,' he repeated, placing the bottle side-ways on the desk.

Phoebe just about managed to keep her eyes open as he gave the fat, square bottle a decisive push.

It circled lumpenly on the spot.

Phoebe squinted at it. If it lands on Felix, she realised, he's going to commit the closest thing to necrophilia since Heathcliff groped Cathy's hand through the casement window.

The bottle shunted leisurely round, seeming about to halt at any moment, yet still rotating by its weighty, brick-like momentum.

It finally rattled and clacked its way to a stop, almost teetering over the lip of the desk.

The neck was directly opposite Phoebe.

Biting his lip, Felix lay back on the pillows and looked at her down the length of his body.

'It's your move,' he breathed.

Phoebe closed one eye and looked at him. Five gorgeous, piccy-friendly ginger Felixes. She closed the other eye and, fighting sleep, craned open the first. Four photogenic, auburn-headed Felixes. Marginally better. She closed both eyes. One Felix pulled into sharp, unblemished close-up in her head. No red hair at all. Blond and beautiful and arrogant; Saskia-dumping and hated. Perfect.

'Phoebe!' he snapped impatiently.

She forced her eyes open.

Christ! He was everywhere! Too many Felixes to count. Whirling around her like endless bubbles blown through a plastic hoop, his hair very, very red, his eyes very, very blue and highly expectant. She'd never pin one down long enough to make a vengeful, calculated move, she realised. She'd better just smile inanely.

'Come here, you sexy thing,' he growled hoarsely.

Phoebe still smiled inanely.

Felix shot her an odd look. 'Come here,' he repeated.

Which one was the real him? Phoebe wondered vaguely. She'd never find the real one at this low heart-rate. There were at least seven or eight Felixes in the general region of the bed, towards which her lurching body was groggily aiming.

Too desperate for horizontal posture to care, she crawled up the bed, mustering control.

This was not, she recognised woozily, quite how Saskia had planned it. And, boy, was this bed lumpy. She looked down and noticed that she was perched on a pair of thighs. Blinking to stop the thighs splitting and multiplying before her eyes, she looked up again.

Felix was watching her indulgently as she climbed laboriously up his glorious body, his eyes half-closed like a lion king basking beside a watering hole as his top lioness indulgently licked his ears.

Biting her lip with concentration, Phoebe made it to pillow level and, immensely grateful to get so far without blacking out, kissed him hard on the mouth.

He groaned with pleasure as her tongue briefly dipped to meet his like a taper to a dynamite fuse. Then it slipped away.

Smiling sleepily as she fell into a drunken dream of Dan–Felix–Dan kissing her body between life-confessions, Phoebe flumped back on to the smelly pillows and, sighing contentedly, passed out.

'Phoebe?' Felix mumbled. '*Phoebe?*'

'Go to sleep, Dan,' she murmured, kissing his top rib in her sleep.

She was having a terrific dream. When he licked her lips, she licked his back. When he scratched her back, she stabbed his lips with her tongue. When he slipped his hand between her legs, she slipped into long-awaited unconsciousness.

28

'God, I am *so* pissed off!' Portia burst back into her Fulham flat, buckling under the weight of her cases and duty free bags. 'Saskia, where are you? Christ! The flight was a nightmare. I was stuck right in front of the film screen and next to the most revolting, shifty little toddler on this earth – *Saskia*! – and when the little geek threw up on take-off, right on to my Donna Karan trousers, his fuck-thick mother flatly refused to pay for the cleaning bill. Said I should use Persil like everyone . . . Saskia, what *have* you done to my flat?'

'Just tidied it.' She finally emerged from the kitchen wearing yellow Marigolds and a weak smile. Shooting past her ankles, Groucho stormed up to his mistress with a grumbling purr, demanding food, attention and his pulse points paddled.

Pulling her keys from the door, Portia stared around the spotless sitting room. 'But it's so – empty!'

'It's how you left it.' Saskia shrugged.

'Did I?' Portia blinked at her sparse, minimalist, pale flat. 'Oh, piss off, Groucho.' She waggled a tan boot at her demanding and, she noted, incredibly fat cat. 'Have you been over-feeding him?' She peered at Saskia critically. 'And I'm certain I didn't leave this place looking quite so barren. Are you sure you haven't been pawning stuff?'

'Of course you left it like this.' Saskia sank wearily down on to a squishy ivory sofa. 'I think I remembered to do everything you asked. I fed the cacti Baby Bio twice a week, I fed Groucho boiled salmon when he drew blood, I tidied all your post into the top drawer and threw the freebie mags out and dusted away every speck that landed anywhere. Welcome back.'

'Thanks.' Portia smiled distractedly, carelessly dropping all her bags on to the carpet and stepping over the straps. 'Are you okay?' She suddenly peered at her sister more closely. 'You look a bit wan, Sasky.'

'I'm fine,' Saskia snapped, half listening as The Archers theme-tune was replaced by the Shipping Forecast on the crackling kitchen radio. Lunchtime. Her stomach was cramping and growling with hunger.

'Okay – don't bite my head off for showing a little sisterly concern.' Portia dropped her jacket on the floor too. 'I must say you seem to have lost some weight, which is no bad thing.' She started to wander towards the huge walk-in cupboard. 'Did you go to that clinic I suggested?'

'Yes,' Saskia sighed, fighting hard not to think about food. 'Are you feeling jet-lagged?'

'Not in the slightest.' Portia looked thoughtfully around her clean, pale, featureless flat. 'After the puking brat incident, I listened to a re-birthing therapy CD on my Discman for the entire flight. I bought it in California – it's quite the best giggle I've had in ages.'

Saskia was hardly listening. 'Do you really think I've lost weight?'

'Bags.' Portia nodded distractedly. 'I said you look great, didn't I? Now let's see . . .' She pulled the cupboard door open and backed away as the piles of stacked, hidden nick-nacks started to tumble out.

'What are you doing?' Saskia gasped.

'I'm going to put all this stuff back out.' Portia started to gather up a few rag dolls. 'Now do me a favour, Sasky, and dump those bloody cacti in a bin bag, would you?'

Saskia wearily did as she was told. Having eaten nothing for almost three days, she was feeling faint, sick and lethargic. She wasn't really bothered that the hours and hours of tidying and cleaning she had done throughout the night were apparently wasted on Portia, who now seemed intent on messing the place up again. At least cleaning burned up calories and took her mind off Phoebe and Felix in Paris, she reflected, as she did a couple of listless pliés whilst searching the kitchen cupboards.

'Are there any urgent messages?' Portia was throwing stacks of magazines on to the small linen-covered sofa.

'Nothing desperate. I've listed them all.' Saskia trailed back from the kitchen with a bin bag. 'Your editorial meeting on Monday's been changed to nine-thirty, and someone called Thor called to say he can't make it tomorrow.'

'My personal fitness instructor.' Portia threw several painted boxes on to the sofa too.

'And I didn't know you were friends with Daniel Neasham,' Saskia said casually as she shook the bin bag open.

'Dan? I've spoken to him once or twice on the phone, but we've never met, why?'

Saskia stopped in her tracks and looked at her disbelievingly.

'He called five or six times this week – machine messages mostly. Sounded really snappy, and flatly refused to say what it was about.'

'How intriguing.' Portia scratched her chin with a silk carnation and grinned mischievously.

Watching her sister's coy reaction, Saskia wondered if Dan was currently pursuing her. She truly hoped not; Phoebe would be crucified. Over the past few days, Saskia had begun to cling to the thought of Phoebe's adoring infatuation with Dan like a little, over-inflated life-raft in her choppy, squally, sea-sick swell of over-imaginative jealousy.

'He's supposed to be ravishing,' Portia mused dreamily.

'He's bought Deayton, you know,' Saskia hissed, hating her sister's rushing, gushing smugness. 'I'm going down there tomorrow to stay for a few days and help Mummy pack up stuff. She and Daddy are moving out by the Bank Holiday. They've bought that ghastly little farm house at the end of the lane.'

'I know.' Portia was backing out of the cupboard with a column of trashy paperback novels stacked under her chin. 'Isn't it all happening horribly, horribly fast? I wanted to go down and have a last shufti before they go, but I'm going to be simply bogged down with work this fortnight. Shit!' She looked up as the phone started to shrill expectantly from a tidy desk.

It would be Piers, she realised, calling to check that she had got back all right. His voice thick with lust, he'd want her to purr smuttily at him, tell him she missed him and then turn him on with a fashion-show description of what she assumed he'd like to think she was wearing. She suddenly felt swamped with jet-lag and snatched the receiver off the hook.

'Portia Hamilton.'

'Portia, this is Daniel Neasham speaking. I must apologise for bothering you.'

'That's quite all right.' She found herself dropping her voice, partly through tiredness but mostly through unabashed calculation. He really did have the sexiest phone manner, she realised. 'What can I do for you?'

'Well, this is really rather embarrassing.' Dan cleared his throat and continued in his soft, smoky voice, 'But I'm rather desperate and you were so wonderfully helpful before. I'm trying to trace Phoebe Fredericks again. I've left messages everywhere but she appears to have vanished. She's not at – er – her flat. I know I'm clutching at straws like a coke addict, but I wondered if you – '

'Phoebe?' Portia sighed with mild, irritated disappointment. Then, mustering her husky, smoothly professional purr again, she coiled her finger through the phone flex and cocked her head. 'Well, I've literally just tumbled off a plane from the States, Dan, but – hold on a sec. I might just . . .' She covered the receiver and turned to her sister.

'Saskia,' she whispered urgently, 'do you know where Freddy is this week?'

Her face crumpled like a crisp packet on fire, and she burst into racking tears.

'She's in Paris,' she sobbed noisily.

'Paris?' Portia clutched the receiver tightly, afraid that Dan would overhear the grief-stricken Chekovian weeping in the background.

'Yes,' Saskia wailed, clenching her eyes tightly shut. 'With Felix.'

Portia's eyes were spinning like saucers. Phoebe Fredericks, she decided bitterly, deserved to rotate in hell on a basted spit for this, the disloyal little minx! And she certainly didn't merit a gorgeous Greek god cocktail like Dan Neasham growling sexily into half the phones of London trying to chase her.

'Get some loo roll to soak those tears up, darling,' she coaxed her sister gently, wanting her out of the room. 'We'll have a chat as soon as I can get rid of him.' She waggled the phone and raised her eyebrows.

As soon as Saskia had shuffled, sobbing, into the bathroom, Portia uncovered the receiver and swallowed several times before speaking slowly and deeply into it.

'Er, Dan,' she started cautiously, her voice steeped with pain-killing empathy. 'I'm not quite sure how to break this, or whether I really should . . .'

29

When Phoebe woke up Felix appeared to have gone. He'd left his crumpled linen jacket and a soft pack of Chesterfields, but a quick, blinding squint round the room told her that all other traces had been removed. Even the tequila bottle was missing. She sank back on to the thinning, sweat-swamped sheet with immense relief, waiting for the pounding in her head to subside.

She was still shaking all over, but far more focused and conscious of light, smell, heat, touch and sound. She was therefore sharply aware that the curtains were gaping open, the room stank of Felix's cigarettes, sun was baking her like a sand-sunk mollusc and her waist was being cut in two by her dressing-gown belt. She was also aware that the Patron was banging on the door like a 1950s Brighton landlady intent on investigating a rhythmic squeak of bedsprings.

Phoebe groped for her watch on the bedside table. She then groped for her watch on the floor beside the bed. With a swill of bile into her upturned mouth, she gave up.

Sweeping back her damp hair as she sank on to the pillows, she almost took one eyebrow off with her watch winder and realised she was still wearing it. She pressed its cool, thrumming face to one eyeball and opened the lid cautiously.

It was three o'clock in the afternoon.

Shit!

She staggered over to the door and wrenched it open.

The Patron's Alsatian, held in check by a tightly constricted choke chain and a lot of very blue French verbiage, just stopped short of eating Phoebe with an inch of snarling, tripe-smelling breath separating them.

She crouched behind the door like an extra playing the criminal's wife in *The Bill* and peered around it unwelcomingly.

'*Vous n'avez pas payées pour votre chambre aujourd'hui!*' hissed the Patron, his breath similar to that of his dog, although his teeth were admittedly not so straight and clean.

Phoebe blinked vaguely and managed to croak a '*Que est-ce que c'est?*' in an appalling, hungover accent.

'Huh?' The Patron loosened his grip on the choke chain slightly and Tripe-breath lunged forwards like a Sumo wrestler tripping over his big toe.

Phoebe backed further away from the growling pong and flashed a nervous smile.

Behind her, she was suddenly aware of a vague swishing noise.

'*Vous devez me payer, mam'selle!*'

'Pay-yey?' Phoebe repeated nervously, wondering if he was some sort of New Age religious fanatic intent on making her chant a mantra. 'Yes, yes – of course. Pay-yey, pay-yey, pay-yey!' she added in a hopeful little chant before slamming the door shut and gluing her cold, wet forehead to it as she leant against the peeling gloss paint for scratchy support.

Seconds later her head was reverberating as the door was once again subjected to a thudding similar to that of Roger Taylor's snare drum skin during the last few rifts of 'Bohemian Rhapsody'.

Phoebe quailed away, certain that the Patron *avec* Alsatian was about to burst through the rattling door panel with an axe, shrieking, 'Wendy, I'm home!'

The swishing, hissing noise behind her was growing stronger. In fact it now sounded as though an oil geyser was spurting merrily from her blackened bathroom.

'*Mam'selle!*' screamed the Patron, clearly stripping his hotel paintwork with his knuckles, feet and breath on the other side of the door. A scrabble of unclipped dog claws scraped rabidly lower down the thin plywood rectangle.

As Phoebe reversed sharply towards the bathroom, the watery, swishing noise behind her increased dramatically and, tripping over a tequila bottle which was being used to jam it ajar and let in light, she found herself backing straight through the unlocked door into a cloud of steam and then up against a very wet, very lean body.

'I think he wants you to pay for the room,' Felix laughed, inserting a towel between them with leisurely ease.

Phoebe sprang away as though jabbed in the back with a droplet-soaked, pheromone-doused Ann Summers willy soap.

'I thought you'd gone!' she yelped, bouncing back towards the hammered-on main door.

'Give me five minutes and I'll be out of here if that's what you want.' Felix shrugged, turning away as he wrapped Phoebe's one and only decrepit, fraying blue towel around his dripping, tanned hips and propped the door open with one water-crinkled heel to clean his teeth with her toothbrush.

His tinted hair, after a vigorous shampooing, had faded from first-class stamp red to a more muted strawberry blond. On anyone else, it would have looked ludicrously effete, but on Felix, it just served to offset his golden, tawny masculinity.

Deliberately thinking how pseudo pin-up-gorgeous he was compared to Dan's stubbly, garlic-smelling, real-life machismo, Phoebe very reluctantly dropped her eyes and stomped shakily through to the crumpled bed to search for her purse and fork out the tripe-defumigating money.

The lock was shaking in its well-scraped metal casing as she carefully drew it back the fraction of an inch required to thrust her last few francs – including loose change and fifty centimes stolen from Felix's linen jacket – through the gap. Then, with all her shaking weight pressed to the door, she slammed it shut with her bottom and, listening to Felix noisily cleaning his teeth in front of her as the Patron shuffled away behind. She scuttled over to the bed to throw on some hastily extracted clothes. In her panic, she was forced to hack through her triple-knotted cotton robe belt with nail scissors before she finally freed herself enough to plunge head first into something else.

By the time Felix wandered into the room dressed in just his shower-damp peachskin jeans, mopping his minty mouth with the fraying towel, Phoebe had dived into a long bias-cut black dress and an inside-out skinny rib t-shirt. Avoiding his gaze, she dug around in her bag for some knickers.

'You look gorgeous.' Felix ground to a halt in front of her and, spitting out frayed blue towel fragments, smiled broadly.

Phoebe wished he wasn't quite so physically flawless. It made looking at him far too moreish. She searched hard for an imperfection – a few white-tipped spots, a strawberry birthmark, an appendix scar. But apart from the odd, tiny mole on his sleek, tawny skin, there wasn't so much as a pimple.

Felix clearly took her close scrutiny to mean she wanted to see more. He reached for his fly like Rob Lowe acting the lazy lothario in a Brat Pack movie.

'What are you doing?' Going sharply into reverse, Phoebe felt her backbone cool itself against the smudged window pane.

Felix's smile was such a delicious, roguish come-on that Phoebe had to remind herself to keep breathing. She watched in alarm as he started unbuttoning his flies.

'Well, that's a tough one.' He laughed. 'Let's see – I'll give you three guesses.'

'I thought you'd only just put those on,' she bleated.

'I'm leading by example.' Felix scratched his damp chest and then pushed his jeans over his hips. 'Now take your clothes off.'

'What?' Phoebe's hot little vertebrae were climbing the window pane in damp suction pads of excitement.

'Take everything off, very, very slowly – and then get into the bed.' Felix dropped his trousers at military-medical speed.

'Nice legs,' Phoebe croaked, determinedly not adding 'all three of them'. She was frantically trying not to stare at his erection. It was Italian peppermill huge, World Trade Centre straight and steel girder harder. Simply magnificent.

Saskia hadn't been lying when she'd said it practically reached up to his belly button. Phoebe suspected you could hit a home run from it. Looking quickly away, she purposefully stared at the smoke-stained print of the Eiffel Tower above the bed, but that was too much of a pointing phallic reminder so she peered with winsome fascination at the light switch.

'Take your clothes off, Phoebe,' Felix laughed. 'I feel a complete prat standing here in the buff. Now, come here.'

'Tempting offer but I think I'll pass,' she said carefully, battling not to add an 'out' after 'pass'. Her heart was racing so quickly now that she felt as though she'd been inhaling poppers under a towel, her pulses thrumming as if attached to electrodes. How dare he have this effect on me? she stewed.

'Do you want me to undress you?' he asked softly.

He was treating her like a gauche virgin now, Phoebe realised angrily. Although, come to think of it, she was feeling and behaving rather like one. All this predatory wolf licking his lips behaviour from Felix was alien to her. She was more of a Snow White.

She pressed herself slightly harder to the window, and wondered what Saskia would recommend her to do right now. Trying to hide was clearly out.

Felix took a deep breath.

'Phoebe, I love you.'

'You what?' She stared at him in amazement, not trusting her ears.

'I love you.' He slid his blue gaze from the rumpled bed to her with startling sincerity.

'You hardly know me,' she croaked in total bewilderment.

'Okay, I *think* I love you then.'

'You can't possibly.' Phoebe gulped. 'You said I was a complete bitch.'

'Well, perhaps I think I *could* love you,' he sighed, looking slightly indignant.

'In that case, I suggest you make up your mind before suddenly announcing it to me whilst standing in the nude with a hard on. A girl could draw the wrong conclusion here.'

'Look, Phoebe, do you mind not arguing right now?' he snapped. 'Only this wasn't quite the reaction I was anticipating.'

'You were thinking more along the Phoebe-throws-her-clothes-off-in-gratitude-and-leaps-under-the-duvet line, were you?'

Felix glared at her, pepper mill shrinking fast until it was more like a shaker from a suburban table-top cruet.

'I don't know.' He rubbed his forehead. 'I just know that I want to love you really badly, Phoebe, and I also wish you'd stop staring at me as though I'm a crazed pervert that's just wandered in from rue Montmartre. I just wish I knew what the hell you wanted.'

'I – er – well, I quite fancy a pizza,' she joked lamely, still finding Felix's sudden declaration impossible to digest.

'Oh, for Christ's sake!' For a moment he looked as though he was going to walk out. Then he seemed to remember he was naked and snatched a brief, irate breath before spinning back to face her, opening his mouth to yell something. He stopped himself as he caught sight of her excited expression.

Phoebe was smiling widely. She had just spotted the smallest, sweetest, most unexpected imperfection on one of those clichéd, peach-like buttocks. She wanted to whoop with joy.

'Is that a tattoo?' she blinked, indicating for him to turn around again.

'Yes.' Felix didn't budge.

'What's it of?'

Hot with irritated embarrassment, he dropped his gaze. 'Er, Snoopy.'

'Snoopy?' Phoebe tried not to laugh, delighted by his un-coolness.

'I know, I know – I was seventeen and very drunk. I was going to have Woodstock put on the other buttock, but thankfully I threw up before the guy got round to it.'

'I love it,' Phoebe laughed.

'Sure.' Felix ruffled his hair angrily and started to look around for his clothes.

'It's the one thing about you that isn't perfect,' she marvelled.

'What?' Felix looked up sharply.

Phoebe quailed slightly under his direct, cool blue stare. It was very difficult to talk to someone sensibly when one was fully clothed, and they were so gloriously naked.

'It's just – well, a bit seedy really, isn't it?' she said, without thinking.

Felix tilted his head and gazed at her. 'You don't think it's cute, or sweet, or dinky or sexy then?'

'Er – no,' Phoebe apologised, and then suddenly realised that she should perhaps have lied.

Saskia was always banging on about Felix's ego needing more massages than Atlas's shoulders, she remembered. In fact, thinking back to the Felix file, she distinctly recalled there being a little note about not laughing at his Snoopy under any circumstances. Reading it, Phoebe had envisaged a sad, stuffed bit of fluff that he kept on his pillow. At the time she had found the notion of the bastard from hell being attached to a cuddly toy laughable. Now, realising her gaffe, she bit her lip.

She then watched in amazement as Felix straightened up and beamed out that irresistible, roguish, come-on smile once more.

'You don't know what that means to me.'

'What? Me not liking your tattoo?' Phoebe was slightly perplexed.

'Come here,' he grinned. 'I promise I won't do a thing you don't want me to. I just want to touch skin.'

'No.' Phoebe stayed glued to the window like a CND sticker. Sorry, Felix, but you're forbidden territory, darling, she thought firmly. Saskia has put you strictly off limits.

'Come here, ' he coaxed, leaning an elbow against the wall. 'Don't tell me you don't want to.'

'Double mozzarella and plenty of pepperoni,' she bleated.

'What?' Felix looked baffled.

'On my pizza.' Phoebe realised that the joke was indeed rather back-dated to fall back on and felt her face pinken slightly with shame. God, she was feeling so horny now that even her sense of humour had let her down.

Then it hit her like a ton of breeze blocks. She did want to do as he told her. She wanted to get into bed with him, to slither all over that beautiful sculptured body, to feel him slipping between her legs just as he'd slipped into her head. She didn't think she had wanted anything quite so much in her life; not the Sindy doll's house at five, the roller skates at ten, Simon le Bon at fifteen, or Keanu Reeves at twenty. God, she wanted him.

It's just lust, she told herself firmly. You're missing Dan.

She was almost shattering glass now in her attempt to push herself and her thoughts as far from his wanton, wanting body as possible.

Felix sucked his bottom lip beneath those straight upper teeth and looked away.

'It's not that I don't want to,' Phoebe muttered in total confusion, trying hard to think about Saskia and not herself. 'It's just that I won't. I can't just screw around like you. And I don't want to be a one night stand-in for the next female challenge that comes along.'

'Oh, well, that makes everything clear as sticking mud, doesn't it?' Felix snapped sarcastically. 'What the fuck are you talking about, Phoebe? Doesn't all the stuff we talked about last night mean anything to you? I haven't told anyone some of the things I told you.'

Phoebe rubbed her forehead despairingly. Yes, it means a lot to me, she realised silently. What little I can remember of it has totally changed the way I think about you. But I'm not allowed to tell you that, because I know you'd use that fact; you'd abuse and manipulate the power it would give you to twist me into your standard game-plan. And you're the one who's supposed to be the losing team in this particular love match. I promised Saskia. And anyway, I love Dan, she added almost as an afterthought.

His shoulders hunched, Felix was almost pleading: 'I thought we'd started to get into each other's heads. I thought – think, that is I – I want you to love me, Phoebe Fredericks. You said last night that you could fall in love with me.'

'Well, I can't do it to order,' she snapped back, defensive because she was so guilty and frustrated she felt as though she'd been marinated in itching powder.

She'd suddenly realised that this was exactly where Saskia

wanted him. Somehow, against all odds, she had succeeded in getting to the big breakthrough point.

Why then, she wondered, was she feeling so hellish about it that she was fighting an urge to confess all?

This was the first stage in the Felix infatuation syndrome – declaring sudden, unexpected love. The next phase was Felix showering her with presents and kisses, wanting to see her every moment of the day, driving her to delirious new heights sexually, moving her into the mews and whisking her off to glamorous foreign locations – sometimes just to have breakfast in bed before rushing back to England. Then came the popping of the question and champagne corks simultaneously. Finally came The Dump – poisonous, vindictive and merciless in its execution.

Of all the stages, Saskia had told her, this first burst of adoring puppy love was when Felix was at his keenest and most vulnerable. At her fingertips, Phoebe realised, was Saskia's elusive chance to get even, to take Felix Sylvian down by more pegs than the entire Romany population sold in a year.

'So you didn't mean it then? Were you just humouring me when you said it?' he was asking, still disturbingly naked.

'Said what?' Phoebe looked up, not quite catching his eyes, almost certain he could read her thoughts as easily as a hypnotist with his patient in a deep trance.

'That you could love me?' Felix's voice was defensive and arrogant now – no trace of the breathy, purring come-on remained.

'No.' Phoebe involuntarily stared at his chest and noticed, for the first time, the little moles that dotted from one nipple to his navel in an off-centre 'S' across a stomach so wash board flat she could have tested a spirit level on it.

'Well, thanks for the fucking honesty!' Felix turned away and searched around for something to destroy, Snoopy clenched into a very skinny beagle indeed in his fury.

He picked up her purse from the bed and threw it against the far wall, where it split open like a confetti-filled balloon bomb and dropped to the floor, spewing out a cloud of old receipts, Métro tickets, loose change and chewing gum wrappers.

'Felix, I – '

'Christ, to think I trusted you with all my emotional shit!' He rubbed his face in his hands.

'Felix, will you bloody listen?' She gritted her teeth. 'I'm saying that no, I wasn't just humouring you last night.'

'You weren't?' he whispered sulkily, not looking round. Snoopy was gaining weight fast.

'I meant what I said,' she sighed, unwillingly noticing two little moles in the small of his back too, just above the cleft of his round, untanned buttocks. She wasn't sure exactly what she *had* said last night, but she was certain that, as drunk as she'd been then, she would almost definitely have been completely incapable of lying.

'So you could fall in love with me?' he muttered in barely more than a whisper. 'Even if I didn't have famous parents? Or didn't look the way I do?'

Phoebe pressed her cheek to the smeared, sun-warmed glass of the window. She hadn't felt less like answering a question in her life. Not even the one that her headmistress had posed about whether she was the saboteur who had dropped seventy Tampaxes into the school's indoor pool twenty minutes before the PTA swimming gala. She watched a bald man cross the street below, admiring the way the light caught his pate.

'Well, if you looked like Tony Blackburn, I might have second thoughts . . .'

'Phoebe!'

'Okay, okay. Yes, I could fall in love with you,' she said quickly. 'But I don't think you really know me, and I certainly don't believe that what you're feeling right now is love. You see, I haven't been entirely honest with you. I . . .' She stopped herself, pressing a white-knuckled finger to the condensation that her breath had made on the window.

'Oh, right. Yes, I see.' Felix breathed in, turning to glare at her over his shoulder. 'So all that shitty tears and tantrums angst last night was just a self-indulgent little ego trip was it? More of your crazy lies?'

Phoebe swallowed nervously and watched a man struggling to open a window opposite theirs. What tears and tantrums? she wondered, scouring her paltry, fragmented recollections of the night before. Had they been hers or Felix's? She couldn't possibly, possibly tell him how little she remembered of the previous night, she realised. All she could pull into focus was the odd cringing recollection of herself talking about Rabbit the Jack Russell and her penchant for the early hits of Abba. There were also vague, uncomfortable, unhappy images of Felix's grotesque, self-seeking parents, his stiff-upper-chip-on-the-shoulder brother, bullied schooldays, slavish, resentful adoration of Dylan, and complete lack of morality or self-respect. But these recollections were so abstract and vague that she could have dreamed them or been told them by Saskia. She could barely remember a word either of them had uttered between tequila-swigs last night.

'I just feel a bit rough this morning, that's all,' she mumbled hopelessly, still totally unable to look him in the eye. 'Touch of 'flu coming on, I think. I guess that's why I was a bit spacey last night.' She drew a wide 'S' in the breathy mist on the window.

'Do you ever tell the truth, Phoebe?'

She pulled her eyes away from the street below and stared at a vast cobweb angled like a flying buttress by the skirting board. She shrugged. 'Until I met you, yes.'

Felix gazed at her for a long time, during which Phoebe's eyes climbed the flock wallpaper maze in tortuous scrutiny, traced their way around the dusty plaster cornice and trailed along the ceiling.

Finally, saying nothing, he stooped to the floor and gathered up his jeans.

As Phoebe stared numbly upwards, he remained crouched by the carpet, scooping up part of the spilled contents of her purse.

Trying to gather herself together, Phoebe noticed a huge brown damp patch on the ceiling and focused tightly on it. She knew that if Felix had asked her what she'd meant about not being entirely honest with him, she probably would have told him the whole sordid plot to dupe him. Instead, he'd reacted with his predictably sulky, childish anger. She could feel new-found resolve tightening the sinews in her neck. She mustn't let this chance slip, she told herself. Saskia would never forgive her. Felix was a spoilt brat, she reminded herself. She mustn't, mustn't fall under his spell as all the others had. If she did, he would break her.

Very slowly, she straightened up and crept silently across the room towards him. He was still squatting by the bed, his jeans unbuckled, looking at a piece of paper which was hidden from her view behind his knee. Phoebe hoped it wasn't an itemised chemist's receipt for Tampax, KY Jelly and Dio-calm or some such image-shattering item.

As she drew close enough to reach out and trace her nails across the sculptured muscle and bone on his hunched shoulders, she noticed what it was that Felix was looking at. Her hand froze in mid-air as though she'd suddenly been eyed up by Medusa.

'Who's this?' Felix held up the torn, tear-stained and battered photograph of Dan which had crossed continents with her, spent every night under her pillow for almost a year, and been kissed so many times that its subject's mouth was wrinkled like an over-bathed finger.

Looking at the photograph, Phoebe's voice shrank to a non-existent pip of misery. She'd stolen it from Dan's Barbican flat ages ago, and treasured it like Gollum's ring ever since. In it, Dan – holding a tennis racket across his chest like Clapton with his guitar – grinned sweatily into the camera. It wasn't a particularly flattering shot – in fact, she noticed afresh, Dan really did look like a bit of a nerd in it. But Phoebe knew it so intimately, it was more familiar than the back of her own hand which she'd scoured far less often. She knew just how one of Dan's black eyebrows arched slightly higher than the other, how his teeth appeared ridiculously white in the overexposed light and his hair gleamed like jet, how his eyes crinkled into amused little lines and one ear looked as though it had a distant tree growing out of it.

'Is this your father?' Felix asked in a distrustful undertone.

'No.' Phoebe sank heavily on to the bed. 'He's an ex-lover.'

'How ex, exactly?'

Phoebe thought about Dan and her tear ducts started hotting up. It was such a mess, she remembered as she thought back to their last disastrous union. The flat, the half-affair, his total, subjugated terror of Mitzi. And now Felix.

'Not very ex,' she admitted in a shaky voice. 'But not particularly current either.'

Felix had gone very still. 'He's got a great smile.'

'Yes,' Phoebe croaked, barely trusting her voice.

As Felix held the photo up to the light and squinted at it, she noticed that the nails clutched around its battered edge were chewed almost to non-existence.

'He's the guy you live with, isn't he?' He turned to watch her.

Phoebe shook her head. 'No, I don't live with him.'

'But he answered the phone in Highgate this week, right?'

'Yes.'

'And are you in love with him?' he asked quietly.

Phoebe found she couldn't answer.

'Now, I want you to tell me why you're mucking around with me when you're not very ex is still on the scene?' he demanded, blue eyes mere slits of suspicion.

She muttered something vague about a temporary trial separation.

'How temporary?' he persisted gripping her arm.

'Well, permanently temporary really.' It was Phoebe's turn to hang her head. 'He's just slightly married.'

Felix released his grip on her wrist as though she was a vampire suddenly decomposing in the first rays of daylight.

'You're someone's mistress?'

'Not exactly – well, not any more.' She bristled at his icy, censorious tone.

'Has this guy got kids?' The question was as sharp as a gunshot in a hall of mirrors.

'No.'

Felix shrugged and scratched his blond stubble angrily with bitten nails.

'My father was always having affairs,' he muttered. 'It totally fucked my mother up. She was a bit of a wild child media star and they crucified her when they found out that my father – the hero of the strait-laced, literati Establishment – was poking everything he could ply with enough booze.'

'Dan's not like that!' Phoebe hissed.

'Dan, is it?' Felix spat the name like an oath, but his train of thought was too runaway to focus on the name for long. 'For a long time my parents were the beloved in-love luvvies that *Sun*-readers loved to love-hate – the dah-ling, mismatched couple of the British press. Ma was England's favourite upper class tart; Pa was their favourite stiff-upper-lip tartar. When some little slut did a kiss-and-sell on him in a Sunday rag, then legions of others followed the following week, my mother took Mungo out of prep school and pissed off to America to build a reputation as a wrinkled mini-series cleavage who'd screw husbands, wives and maids to get kicks. If she's not in *National Enquirer* one week, she takes an overdose.'

Phoebe swallowed and let this sink in.

'If Pa's in *Hello!* draped over a new wife on a leopardskin sofa the next week, she takes another overdose and marries her minder for a double-page spread,' he went on with an angry, mocking laugh.

'Felix . . .'

'She actually doesn't marry that often – I'm exaggerating.' He buried his face in his hands. 'I mean, she usually lays off laying teenagers when there's an RSVP bash in the month. And her latest husband is so old he's incapable of being laid out in anything other than a coffin. My father says she's given up sex because she's discovered that liposuction is better for trimming the thighs.' He rubbed his hands through his spiky hair and pressed his face into the crook of his elbow.

'Felix,' Phoebe started cautiously, 'I'd give anything to take this pain away. But it's not your fault. And it's not mine.'

Eyes blinking furiously, he looked up at her, tight white knuckles pressed into his hair.

'And,' Phoebe took a deep, wavering breath, 'until you see

that, I can't see you loving me, yourself, or anyone else for that – '

Before she could say another word, he had launched himself across the floor and, clutching her like a life buoy in a whirlpool, buried his face in her stomach. 'Let him go.'

Closing her eyes to blank out an image of letting Dan go, Phoebe mindlessly stroked Felix's head and dropped a kiss into the shampoo-smelling hair. She could feel his eyes blinking against the thin fabric of her dress.

Felix clung on even tighter.

'Don't go away from me,' he mumbled into her belly button. 'I need you now. I want you in my life.'

Looking down at his beautiful, forlorn head, she gently rubbed the back of his neck and felt the great knots of tension that had gathered his muscles into taut, tangled clusters.

'I love you.' His muffled voice was hot against her stomach.

'No, you don't.' Phoebe sighed sadly. 'You want – you need to be loved, Felix. But you've got to learn what it is first.' She winced at the melodramatic truism.

He hardly seemed to be listening.

'I do love you.' He pressed his face tighter into her dress. 'You understand. Or did you make up all that stuff about your parents never being around when you were a kid too?'

'No, I didn't make it up.' Phoebe eased some of the tight tangles of muscle from the top of Felix's spine. 'But I had none of your demons to deal with, Felix. I was just a typical kid with expatriate parents – shunted around friends and relatives or jabbed in the arse with immunisation shots and bunged on a long haul flight every holiday. And I think I reacted the opposite way to you. I hated commitment. If a friend got too clingy, I dumped them. I guess that's why I hang on to Dan. I know he's never going to get too close.'

'But I'm the same,' Felix muttered, whispering so quietly that Phoebe had to lean down to hear him. 'I always shit on people who get too close to me.'

She froze, realising what he was saying.

'I think I deliberately let down the people who need me,' he went on, twisting his face sideways and staring at the wall, the side of his face pressed to her thigh so hard that she could feel his cheekbone jabbing into her flesh like a tight stocking top. 'I don't know why I do it – I mean, I've thought about it a lot.'

He took an unsteady breath and rubbed his eyelids with his thumb and forefinger. 'I suppose something unconscious in me figures that it always happened to me, so why the fuck shouldn't it happen to them? No one should rely on someone so much that their life revolves around them.'

Running a wary hand through her hair, Phoebe let this sink in for a moment or two.

'So why do you demand love so much, Felix?' she asked quietly. 'Why? When you know that, as soon as you've got it, you're going to destroy it?'

He went very still, his voice almost a breath. 'Because one day, I might just – believe in it. Oh, I don't fucking know, Phoebe! I always throw myself in there with such bloody hope and come out feeling like Faustus given that last twenty-four hours he begged for and never got. I've treated people who've loved me appallingly. But, I just have this feeling, this awful, cynical notion . . .' His voice petered out.

'What?' Phoebe couldn't stop a cold note of anger stealing through her voice.

Felix twisted his head around to look up at her. His eyes were tortured.

'Anyone who has ever said they love me – with the possible exception of Dylan and my insufferable grandmother – has become so fucking supplicatory and clinging that I end up despising them.' He paused, clearly striving to make sense to himself as well as her. 'It's like they lose their identity and adopt mine just to please me. I'm probably not making sense here, but I've stared at women I thought I loved and suddenly realised I'm looking at a mirror. There's nothing worse than hearing "I agree" after everything you fucking say and then realising that person's lying just because they love you. You stop believing in them.'

'And meanwhile, you're justified in crashing around destroying other people's lives, right?' Phoebe bit back her anger. 'You're planning just to carry on trying out people's love for size until you "believe in them"?'

God! She'd almost fallen for it, she realised. One minute, he had been practically sobbing into her lap about his forlorn childhood, and Phoebe's heart had bled as though skewered: she couldn't believe he could be so manipulative.

In the bathroom she threw cold water over her flushed face. As she straightened up and looked at the very faint, dim reflection of her pale, dehydrated features in the mirror, she pressed her nose to the cool glass and crossed her eyes at her own, gullible stupidity.

'Game on,' she muttered quietly.

30

Fliss was resentfully covering one of Phoebe's shifts at Bar Barella when Mungo Sylvian walked in.

She was not looking her best. She'd been slaving at the studio all the previous night, working with Georgette all day – admittedly not hard, having made numerous ratty personal calls to Iain before sloping out to pretend to be Phoebe and sign on for her. Fliss had then dashed straight to the bar to pick up the busy after-office shift just as her energy levels were finally giving up. She felt as stale and sweaty as the last cheese sandwich wilting in a cafeteria's glass case.

Mungo, by contrast, had spent all day sleeping off a hangover and had only crawled out of his duvet three hours earlier. He was showered, scented, laundered, and had just visited his hairdresser courtesy of Felix's credit card. He looked staggering.

'Huge, huge Bloody Mary, darling.' He smiled over a crisp fiver, not recognising her at all.

Diving beneath the bar for the Tabasco, Fliss hastily removed the tatty baseball cap which was crammed over her red mane and wiped the mascara smudges from under her eyes. As she stretched across for the Worcester sauce, she hoicked up her cycling shorts and gave her armpits a furtive sniff. Thankfully Lady Mitchum was fighting off any trace of paranoid pong.

When she re-emerged, she mustered what she hoped was a rumpled, sexy smile and peered at him through her lashes over the pepper grinder.

'It's Mungo, isn't it?' she croaked.

'Yup.' He was gazing around the bar's tables distractedly. 'Oh – there he is. Bring it over, will you, darling?'

And, without looking back at her, he wandered off.

Fliss bristled, but it didn't stop her peering longingly at his retreating bum as he headed over to a dark corner. Now that was a truly great-shaped rear end, she marvelled dreamily as she watched the frayed jeans sink themselves on to a stool at one of the farthest tables.

When she took Mungo's lovingly prepared Bloody Mary over to him, she found him sitting with a dark, stocky, faintly familiar-looking figure. Mungo's scruffy companion had a mop of loose brown curls in dire need of a cut and blow dry and possessed a big, chummy grin and huge, trust-me chocolate eyes. Fliss had seen him in the bar several times.

She carefully placed the Bloody Mary on a little paper coaster, lowering her profile until it was level with Mungo's nose so that he couldn't fail to notice her. It took her a lot of nerve to do it, and when he finally spoke, her heart was pounding in her ears almost too loudly for her to hear.

'Don't we know each other?' he murmured with only the faintest trace of interest.

'Mmm, I think so.' Fliss tried to sound nonchalant, but her voice had shot from smoky alto to castrato soprano. 'I'm Selwyn Wolfe's sister. I think you've been to a couple of my parties.'

Mungo grinned. 'So I have. Fran, isn't it?'

'Fliss,' she beamed, delighted that he'd got so close.

'Of course – Fliss.' Mungo stood up and politely kissed her on both cheeks. 'The terrific cook, I remember. How the devil are you? You look gorgeous as ever. Join us for a drink. This is Dylan Abbott – he works in a bar too. Well, runs it actually. Dylan, this is Fran Wolfe.'

'Hi, Fliss.' Dylan smiled up at her, not for the first time admiring the shock of red hair and the big blue eyes. 'Actually, we've met. I've – er – I've been to one of your parties too.'

But Fliss had already dashed back to the bar to grab herself a drink and take Mungo up on his offer before he had a chance to forget about it. So that must be *the* Dylan – Felix's flat-mate – she thought as she hauled open the fridge. He was a bit of a nondescript stooge, really, she reflected sadly. Poor bloke.

She raced back to their table so quickly that she spilled frothy Coke all over her Bar Barella apron, but Mungo was too busy looking at his reflection in the mirror behind his companion's head to notice. Dylan did, and smiled sympathetically.

'D'you want a napkin to mop that up?' he asked as she plumped down on the closest chair to Mungo.

Hugely embarrassed at her display of nerves, Fliss ignored him.

'So, Fliss,' Mungo hoicked a long, tattered denim leg up on to the edge of his seat and rested an unfairly chiselled chin on the frayed knee, 'are you planning any more parties?' He dragged his eyes away from the mirror and looked at her from beneath drooping lids.

'Well,' Fliss gulped, wondering if she dared mention the murder mystery weekend so soon, 'we were thinking of doing something around Bank Holiday.'

She was fighting hard not to reach out and brush away a very clean strand of hair that was tickling Mungo's charcoal eyelashes.

'August Bank Holiday, huh?' He smiled sleepily.

'Mmm.' Fliss chewed her lip and realised this was perhaps going to be her only chance to invite him along.

Stealing one of Mungo's cigarettes – which he had in fact stolen from Dylan – she explained about the murder mystery house party with as many exaggerated Flissisms as she could possibly embellish it with. In fact, when she made what was rapidly becoming a bit of a non-event sound like an invitation to a Balmoral shooting party, she wondered if perhaps she had gone too far.

'It sounds wonderful,' Mungo laughed, looking at himself in the mirror again. 'But then again, you always do have terrific bashes.'

I'd stare at myself if I was that beautiful, Fliss thought headily.

'There are simply loads of people coming,' she went on, lying through her teeth now. 'We've hired this massive place in – er –

Hampshire, I think it is.' She hadn't actually hired anywhere, although she had a copy of *The Lady* in her duffle bag with a few numbers circled. 'And we're all planning to dress up twenties style and camp it up from Friday until Monday – endless booze, grub, dope and sun.'

'Camping it up, huh?' Mungo grinned at Dylan and winked. 'Sounds just up my street.'

Dylan was looking worried but, as Fliss had barely noticed him, she failed to pick up on his discomfort.

She bit her lip, summoning her nerve. Then, realising that she had her teeth clenched on to an emerging cold sore, released it and fought not to probe the stinging little spot with her fingers.

'You'd be welcome to come along if you're free?' She smiled, hoping she didn't sound quite as keen as she thought she did. 'I mean, both of you, of course,' she added politely, although she privately thought that Dylan came across as a wetter blanket than the one Stan had used to extinguish the barbecue at the last party.

'I'll certainly let you know.' Mungo reached forwards to touch Fliss's cheek.

For a moment she froze with delight, thinking he was about to stroke it or some such delectable, unexpected show of affection. But he merely extracted the pen that was tucked behind her ear and flipped over the soggy paper coaster.

'You'd better give me your number.' He uncapped the pen with his teeth. 'I'll call you later this week to let you know.'

Fliss was so excited that she forgot her own telephone number and had to repeat it twice to get it right.

Hauled back to work by the manager, who was having a nervous breakdown behind the ten-deep bar, she gave everyone double measures of all the wrong drinks and chewed her cold sore with distracted happiness.

'Why do you encourage her like that?' Dylan drained his Sol bottle and nicked back his cigarettes to light one up.

'Sweet, isn't she?' Mungo watched her curly red head bobbing around behind the crowd at the bar.

'Far too sweet to waste a honking great crush on a lost cause like you,' Dylan shrugged.

'Yeah, she has got me pretty bad, hasn't she?' Mungo smirked. 'But I've got rather a soft spot for her too – you know me and red-heads. I thought I might develop her as a fag hag.'

'You're not planning to go to this murder thing, are you?'

'I might.' Mungo shrugged. 'Sounds fun – and she's got some terrific friends. You went to one of her parties, you must remember?'

'Yes,' Dylan looked up at the bar sadly. He remembered it perfectly. He had talked to a very drunk, very funny northern red-head for over half an hour when they'd both been trapped on an extremely uncomfortable sofa; the same red-head who had just made it thumb-nail-pulling and in-your-face clear that she had totally forgotten the incident. Dylan, who had given her his number at the time, had prowled around the phone for a week afterwards before giving up hope.

He'd seen her in Bar Barella quite a lot recently, and had made the odd half-hearted attempt to engage her in conversation again, but it was like trying to engage an ancient Moke in first gear – one rammed in a hopeful, punchy thrust only to find it had popped back out again and stalled within seconds.

Phoebe was plotting another dramatic exit.

Realising that she should leave Felix feeling high, slightly uncertain and very hooked, she had reluctantly agreed to go to Mia's flat with him to collect his bags while she thought up something good. Unfortunately, she hadn't counted on giggling with him quite so much. So much, in fact, that her only dramatic exit so far had been from Hôtel Dump earlier when, pursued by the unleashed Alsatian, she and Felix had tumbled hastily through the door and crashed on to the sticky, sun-soaked asphalt of rue Montmartre.

'It's a *ménage à* tar.' He had kissed her on her grazes afterwards.

They were now sitting in a very classy bistro just around the corner from Mia's tiny fifth-floor apartment, waiting for two

Ricards to appear. Beside them, a couple of morose-looking crayfish were avoiding one another in a bubbling glass tank.

'The one on the left looks like my publicity agent.' Felix watched them closely as he attacked the basket of bread like a rationed wartime child handed its first banana.

Propping her feet up on Felix's battered leather suit carrier, Phoebe stared out of the window at the cluster of little antique shops opposite the bar which sold everything from ornate gilt frames to religious icons to chipped Lalique vases. She adored the Left Bank because it was so eclectic; off-beat haute couture salons nestled beside bustling student cafés which in turn clattered between avant garde commercial galleries. And of all the tiny, twisting, romantic streets, Felix had located one for their anisette which would make a film location-seeker dollar green with envy.

'I thought you were supposed to be working today?' He was watching her though the usual haze of Chesterfield smoke. His blue eyes didn't blink.

Phoebe, her own eyes smarting, stared at him, for a moment, nonplussed.

'You said you had meetings today,' he reminded her.

So I did, she remembered in a panic.

'I cancelled them,' she lied clumsily – fingers across mouth, eyes not quite catching his.

'What exactly is it that you do?'

It was the question she had dreaded all week, and she still hadn't thought up a convincing answer. She stared at the crayfish in hope of inspiration, but decided that 'marine biologist' would be a bit hard to substantiate.

Thankfully the Ricards arrived just as she was toying between actress and media consultant, knowing that he would rumble her posturing about either.

Felix watered down both their drinks from the chunky 52 bottle, watching them turn from pale brown to translucent milky white before he looked up at her and narrowed his eyes again.

'So what d'you do for a living, Phoebe?'

'I don't want to talk about it.'

Felix sighed and stared at the ceiling. 'Matilda, she told the most terrible lies . . .'

'Okay, okay,' Phoebe blurted. 'I admit it – I fibbed again. I said I had work in Paris when I didn't at all. I just didn't want to feel quite so compromised by you as I do right now. And I was sacked from my job – honestly – although it was weeks ago now. I was awful at it, hated it, was worth more than its shitty commission, pension and company share scheme. I do bum-pinching work in a bar now and dream a lot. Satisfied?'

She took a huge swig of her pastis, aware that she was letting far too much out of the bag, like a Scottish piper with a hacking cough.

Felix dropped his gaze level with hers and stubbed out his cigarette long before the glowing end had reached the filter.

'I love you.' He stretched across to deposit a sweet, slow kiss on each of her cheeks, her forehead and then her mouth.

'No, you don't.' Phoebe moved her face to one side so that his tongue slipped on to her cheek, terrified by the sudden, over-whelming urge to kiss him back.

Felix pulled away.

Feeling wretched, Phoebe looked listlessly at the delicious, pong-filled menu and wished she could hit McDonald's for a quick fix. But that, according to the Felix file, would be far too oikish and plebian for his quixotic tastes. She would no doubt shortly be expected to make steamy eye-contact as she let half a dozen oysters slither down her throat washed along their way by well-chilled Pouilly Fumé and Felix's tongue.

'Are you hungry?' He was scrutinising his own menu.

Phoebe looked across at his concentrated, down-cast expression and fought an urge to stretch out a hand and touch those glossy, red-tinged spikes of hair.

'Famished,' she mumbled, her hungover stomach curdling as, hastily looking down again, she read a description of the hot chèvre salad with crushed garlic and soured cream topping.

Felix threw his menu into the fish-tank, shooting the cray-fish into the gravel like braking tyres.

'I'm bored of Paris,' he announced suddenly. 'Let's fly back. I want to have a fry up in a greasy spoon and go clubbing in London.'

Phoebe burst out laughing. 'Egg, chips, sausage, tomatoes . . .'

'Bacon, black pudding, mushrooms.' Felix started grinning too.

'Fried bread, baked beans, ketchup . . .'

'Mushy peas, bubble and squeak, fried eggs.'

'I said eggs.'

'Did you?'

'Yup.'

'Well, we'll have double eggs then. Sunny side up. Swimming in fat.' He was stretching across the table again.

'Yum.' Phoebe took another gulp of her pastis to keep him away from her lips. 'Back-stroke or crawl?'

'Breast stroke.'

'With arm-bands and flippers, I take it?'

'A must, I'd say.' His lips made contact with her nose. 'And buttered toast on the side.'

'And mugs of tea.' Phoebe tried and failed to close her mouth as his tongue stroked the soft inner flesh of her lips.

'And Danish pastries with glâcé cherries the size of ping pong balls.' He slipped his lips to her ear.

'And then a vast dose of Andrew's.'

Felix's lips were back on her mouth. Why, oh why, oh why was kissing him so delicious? Phoebe wondered guiltily.

For a moment he pulled away and, stroking her damp mouth with his thumb, gazed into her eyes, fingers suddenly tangling with hers.

'Promise you won't ever lie to me again?' he breathed.

Phoebe swallowed, totally unable to lose eye contact, and finding it impossible to cross her fingers behind her back as they were laced through his.

'I promise,' she whispered.

'You took these when she was asleep?' Dylan asked quietly, looking at the glossy little photographs.

'Couldn't resist it,' Mungo shrugged, eyeing a particularly

unflattering one of Fliss, in her bra and knickers, stretched out like a corpse on a Habitat duvet, a can of Crucial Brew spilling on to her wrinkled storm grey bra and freckled spare tyre. 'Doesn't she look darling?'

Saying nothing, Dylan gathered all the photographs together and, very slowly, ripped them into small, mosaiced squares.

'Why the fuck did you do that?'

'Where are the negatives?' he howled so violently that Mungo covered his head as though under Iraqi fire.

'In the wallet,' he said grumpily, too frightened of Dylan's rare, unexpected fury to lie.

Extracting the negatives, Dylan took his lighter to them and shrivelled the thin plastic strip within seconds.

'God, you must fancy her,' Mungo giggled, watching his set face in amazement.

'No,' Dylan sighed, looking up at him and dropping the smouldering, foul-smelling plastic remains into the ashtray, 'I just despise your pulchritude, turpitude and shitty little ways. If this weren't your father's house, I'd boot you out today.'

Mungo was grinning sweetly, not one word having hit home.

'What does pulki – pul – what did that mean exactly?'

'It mean's you're a hopeless little fuck-wit,' Dylan hissed.

'But I've read all your books.' Mungo suddenly stretched his eyes in camp mock-idolatry.

'What?' Dylan was instantly defensive.

'*Hearts in Twain* and *Three Little Words* were my favourites.'

'How the hell do you know about that?' Dylan stiffened.

'I've a friend who works at Red Rose – she told me that one of their biggest new authors was a chap.' Mungo giggled with assumed theatricality at the memory. '*Imagine* my surprise when she told me that Henrietta Holt was in fact one Dylan Abbott of West London – oh, she thinks you're a pub landlord by the way. I did nothing to dispel the rumour.'

At the airport, Phoebe sloped away while Felix was trying to get them on to a standby flight, and changed the last of her English money in order to buy Fliss and Saskia some duty free.

Finding herself in possession of a lot of small change, she couldn't resist pausing by the phones and digging her touch tone answerphone pad from her bag.

Her breathy, cryptic message was still gushing forth from the Highgate machine. She cut it short with a couple of trill tones and listened with a dead-weight heart as Dan left a series of increasingly frantic demands that she call him. The next message made her catch her breath in surprise.

'Phoebe, this is Felix. Look, I'm drunk. I phoned a couple of hours ago and some chap answered – he wouldn't say who he was, but he knew me and was bloody rude, in fact. He thinks you're here. Shit, I hate these machines. Where are you? I'm staying in a squalid little flat in Paris . . . hang on, I've got the number here somewhere. Will you at least call me – damn, it's definitely here somewhere. Oh – here it is . . .'

Phoebe gnawed her cuticles. Felix must have got that bit about Dan knowing him wrong, she realised. Dan thought she was in Paris to rescue 'a friend'. He couldn't possibly know that she was here with Felix, unless someone had told him. Then, with her heart plummeting like a lift with its cables cut, she remembered that Fliss had denied all knowledge of her last-minute, scribbled letter to Dan.

She closed her eyes as she realised how fragile her alibi had been; Paris – city of romance; 'a friend' – how equivocal could one get?; plus the 'my new lover, Felix' bull she'd fed him all those weeks ago when it hadn't mattered. Dan had put one city and two lies together and made an eternal triangle.

The final message on the tape made her blood drop in temperature like an unlucky, red hot horse-shoe plunged into a bucket of cold water.

'It's me again.' Dan's voice was harsh with pent-up irritation. 'We need to talk. I'm tied up all weekend, but I'll be round here on Monday straight after work. For Christ's sake be here – and tell Felix your friend never to call this number again. I hope you had a fucking awful time in Paris, you bi—'

31

'There's a terrific greasy spoon in Notting Hill called Spike's Café,' Felix announced, hanging out of the doors of the tube as it waited at Earl's Court. 'I'll meet you there around nine. Don't be late – I'll only wait five minutes this time, I mean it.'

'But it's already half seven.'

'Just walk out of the tube and turn right – you can't miss it.' Leaning out and glancing along the platform to check that there were still plenty of people trying to get on, he hopped back into the carriage and kissed Phoebe hard on the mouth. 'And dress up – Spike likes classy women. He'll give you extra beans if you're lucky.'

He turned to hop out of the doors before once more spinning back to face her.

'I'm so pleased I met you.' He stood in the centre of the carriage, grinning goofily. Even when wearing a liberal, smeared coating of her lipstick, he was ridiculously handsome.

Phoebe laughed. 'The doors are closing, Felix.'

'Shit!' He leapt out just in time, dropping his bags on the platform.

As the train moved off, Phoebe craned around and saw him, blond and beautiful, shrugging his palms up to heaven and laughing delightedly.

Phoebe sank back in her seat and ignored a crowd of teenage girls opposite who were shooting her furtive looks from behind their *Just Seventeen*s and tittering excitedly. Then, catching her reflection in the window above their heads, she realised that Felix had just kissed her ultra trendy crimson lipstick right the way up her nose. Instead of wiping it away, she found herself grinning goofily too.

The smile was wiped off Phoebe's face as soon as she arrived back at Douglas Street. As she galloped up the stairs, desperate to remove her killer boots, she slowed to a shuffling step-at-a-time earwig as she heard the unmistakable sound of her flat-mate trying to dump a man in her own inimitable style.

Rounding the last bend of stairs, she caught the odd word – 'sorry' being chief amongst them, closely followed by 'terrific', 'fanciable', 'gorgeous', 'good-looking' and 'you'.

Phoebe wavered outside the door and sighed miserably as she caught the tail end of a classic Fliss line. 'You're one of the most desirable men I've ever met in my life.'

Fliss's method of giving the elbow was to be so flattering first that she buttered the blow with more Anchor than was ever used in *Last Tango in Paris*. She would then generally bottle out of administering the blow at all.

Holding her breath and waiting for the timed landing light to click off, Phoebe slipped her key into the lock with quiet, tip-toe dread. She made it into the hall unnoticed and, standing on top of her credit card bills in the gloom, clicked the door silently shut and peered at the unbridgeable gap between the flat door and her bedroom, wardrobe, mirror and the opportunity to remove her boots.

Pacing around like an actress trying out her lines in every voice within her range, Fliss was looking shattered, and was indeed in the middle of one of her many recent attempts to dump Iain gently.

Looking very confused, he was perched on the most split of the flat's Dralon sag bags, spilling little polystyrene hailstones with every shift of his clenched buttocks. The curtains of his floppy tortoiseshell hair were firmly drawn across his eyes, but his mouth was a tense line of much-chewed worry and a muscle was sledge-hammering his cheek. In front of him, Fliss was prowling around on the fluffy Argos mat, her heels crunching on the salt which had been poured on so many red wine stains that it had formed a thick, pink crystalline crust.

'And it's not that I don't fancy you,' she was saying anxiously. 'You're a seriously fanciable lad. Or that I've gone off you – well, not much, anyway. I mean, not at all. No. It's just that we don't really have a lot in common, do we? What I mean – oh, Phoebe, you're back!' She grinned gratefully as her flat-mate stumbled in, desperate to prise off the boots which were now causing too much pain for silence.

'So I am,' she agreed, pausing for the briefest of seconds to beam encouragement at Fliss before heading hastily through to her bedroom.

'Cup of tea, mate?' Fliss yelled through to her, desperate to keep up contact, thus avoiding any immediate return to Iain and The Dump.

'Only if you're making it.' Phoebe was frantically unlacing. 'I have to go out again in a sec.'

'How was Paris?'

'I forgot to ask it. It looked quite well, though.' Phoebe gasped with relief as her feet were freed.

Released from her boots, she stripped off and wrapped herself in a towel.

As she wandered back out of her room to dash into the shower, she noticed that Fliss and Iain were paralysed in exactly the same position she had just left them, as though freeze-framed on video. Both were staring at her as an excuse not to look at one another.

'I'm having a shower,' she explained nervously.

'There are loads of messages for you,' Fliss gulped, nodding towards a peeling scabies layer of Post-it stickers on the wall above the phone. 'I started a league table between Saskia and Dan. Saskia's ahead by one message and a dropped call, I think.'

'I'll ring her in a minute.' Phoebe was retreating speedily into the bathroom.

'She's at her parents.' Fliss, suddenly animated, pursued her.

'Said for you to go down there this weekend if you were back in time.'

'Oh, right.' Phoebe had made it on to the bath mat. 'I'll be out soon.'

'Just let me come in for a piddle,' Fliss insisted, bouncing through the door before Phoebe could stop her and slamming it with a hasty backwards kick.

'What about Iain?' Phoebe whispered urgently, nodding towards the sitting room.

'He'll just have to cross his legs,' she muttered. 'I need to gab with you for a sec.'

'I see.' Phoebe braced herself for a rush of questions about Felix and Paris. But Fliss's dilemma was far more pressing.

Plunging a freckled hand into her red curls, she rolled her eyes and whispered, 'I don't think he's taking this very well. He came round with a takeaway and the latest Schwarzenegger video, and I just snapped and decided to finish with him. But I've mucked it up.'

'You sounded as though you were doing pretty well to me just now,' Phoebe reassured her.

'He hasn't spoken or budged for over half an hour.' Fliss pulled down the loo seat and perched on it. 'From the second I broached the subject, he clammed up and just stared at me with those sad chihuahua eyes. I've been talking crap for the last ten minutes just to fill the air.'

'He hasn't said a word?'

'Well, he mumbled something about the Chinese food going cold just as I was telling him what a great boyfriend he'd make someone else. Oh God, Phoebes, I feel so mean.'

'But you don't want to go out with him any more, do you?' She sighed.

'I don't think so.' Fliss looked up at her, blue eyes blinking uncertainly.

'Then you're doing the right thing.' Phoebe dropped on to her haunches and reached out to tidy Fliss's electric-shock hair. 'You're being brave and honest and kind. It's much better to let him know now – quietly and painfully. Far worse after you've snogged someone else because you're so unhappy, or not returned his calls for days, or – '

'Sounds like you and Dan,' Fliss muttered tetchily.

Phoebe blinked at her, feeling the cold, wet trace of Judas's kiss on her cheek.

They both froze as there was a loud thump from the other side of the wall.

'I think you'd better go back out there.' Phoebe nudged Fliss's shoulder, not looking her in the eye.

'I can't,' she gulped.

Phoebe leant back against the bath and sighed.

'You go,' Fliss begged.

'Me?'

'Yes. You can be nice to him, make him feel better about himself. You're good at that.'

'I don't think that's a very good idea, Fliss,' Phoebe muttered, selfishly thinking about the minutes that were slipping away from her Felix preparation time.

There was another thump from the sitting room.

Fliss stiffened. 'God! You don't think he's trying to do something silly do you?'

Phoebe gasped, 'You mean, top himself?'

'Yes.' Fliss craned to listen.

It had gone ominously silent.

'Please go out there,' Fliss entreated, close to tears. 'Please, Phoebe – I just can't face it.'

'Coward.' Phoebe gave her a big hug and tightened her towel before venturing back out, hoping there wasn't going to be any blood on show.

'It's all right, Fliss,' she yelled a few seconds later. 'He's gone.'

'He can't have!' Fliss raced out to scour each room of the flat.

'He's taken his kit bag,' she noticed with a catch in her throat. 'And he's made off with the chicken chow-mein – the bastard.'

'He's left his Barbour.' Phoebe nodded towards the hat stand.

Fliss wandered across to the waxy blue coat and, unhooking

it, gathered it into her arms. Burying her face in the checked lining, she burst into tears.

By the time she had mopped up Fliss's wet eyes and nose, made her laugh at a few feeble jokes and settled her down in front of Brookside with a pot of tea and a new packet of chocolate digestives, Phoebe was running disastrously late. She had no time to phone Saskia.

Instead, she showered in seconds and, dripping everywhere, climbed straight into a very sexy metallic body-suit, which she had never worn because it was a bit too tight, and black suede jeans. Grabbing her snakeskin boots and an assortment of make-up, she kissed Fliss on the head and reluctantly left her sobbing as Barry Grant told Ron Dixon that his rent was due.

Phoebe pulled on her boots as she tripped down the stairs and, racing towards the tube, stuffed the make-up into the pocket of her jacket.

Before she had even made it out of Douglas Street, she realised that the body-suit had been a bad choice. Because it was too short for her torso, the crotch poppers undid themselves within a few long strides. Phoebe darted behind a car and undid her jeans belt to reach in and re-pop them. She was then forced to dash towards Angel with tiny little steps, as though her laces were tied together.

As she ran past the pay-phones she did a U-turn, almost floored a child on a skateboard, and, dithering for a few uncertain moments, dashed into a call box.

After trying to ram a one franc coin into the slot, Phoebe finally got lucky with a twenty-pence piece. She guessed it must be almost nine already.

The phone rang for a long time before anyone picked it up.

'Hello,' purred a sugary male voice, almost drowned out by the throb of 'Light My Fire'.

'Er – is Felix still there?'

'What?'

'Is Felix there?' Phoebe yelled over the din.

'He's in the bath, darling,' the voice oozed.

Phoebe sighed with relief. It must be earlier than she'd imagined.

She listened as the voice yelled for the music to be hushed. The Doors were cranked down enough for Phoebe to register a lot of talking and whooping in the background. Someone was demanding another beer in a very loud voice.

'Can you tell Felix that Phoebe might be a bit late?' She watched her digits plunge into single figures on the pay-phone's LCD.

'Habit of yours, is it?' the voice hissed. 'Don't tell me, you're waiting in a bar across the street and you're going to stay there and watch Felix being stood up?'

'Hello, Mungo,' she sighed.

'Hello, Phoebe,' laughed Mungo. 'Look, just come round here for a drink. I'll go out and get some wine.'

'Well, I . . .' It was the last thing Phoebe wanted to do.

'I'll tell Felix to hang on until you arrive,' he went on insistently. 'He's been hogging you far too much. The boys all want to meet you.'

There was even more laughter in the background.

'It's number three Albany Mews. See you later.' He rang off.

Phoebe applied her war paint with shaking hands and, leaping off the tube at Notting Hill with just one eye done, was forced to finish off the other in the mirror of the photo-booth. It seemed essential that Felix's friends approve of and accept her. That way, her eventual public revenge would be all the more humiliating for him.

Why they would accept her any more with a second coat of More Than Mascara was a debatable point, but she was far too nervous to dwell on it.

Albany Mews was tucked away behind a grandiose, ivy-clad arch and vast black, glossy wrought-iron gates that were open just wide enough to allow a Bentley to scrape through with a millimetre to spare on either side of its wing mirrors. Phoebe finally found it hidden discreetly on the left hand side of one of the smaller side streets leading from the Bayswater Road to Westbourne Grove.

Felix's red-brick mews cottage was towards the end of the cobbled side-street, with glossy British Racing Green garage doors dominating its lower half and matching window boxes stapled across its upper floor, overflowing with variegated ivy and dead fern. Compared to the lush, multicoloured flora packed sumptuously into the boxes of both neighbouring cottages, Felix's looked as though someone had been harassing him with a Paraquat hate campaign. Playing sentry to the doorstep, three bottles of gold top milk, a carton of orange juice and a red Express Dairy bill were waiting to be taken in.

Phoebe checked her reflection in a car window and straightened her hair before rattling the brass knocker on the lustrous green door. When it was finally wrenched open, the noise that boomed out of the mews threatened to split her eardrums. She was almost knocked backwards with the thudding, thrashing wail of Meatloaf revving his Harley Sportster.

A very drunk, red-eyed lad opened the door. Phoebe immediately recognised him as one of Felix's cronies who had been in Bar Barella on the night she had pretended to be Swedish. He was overweight in ego and body with slicked-back hair and a very wet-lipped grin.

'Hi, I'm a friend of Felix's.' Phoebe backed away from the beer fumes. This was a man who applied deodorant to the armpits of his shirts only after three days' hard wear, she surmised.

'I don't care who you are, darling,' he hiccuped, widening the door to reveal a set of scuffed wooden stairs. 'Just come in.'

This place must once have been stunning, Phoebe realised as she followed the portly, Chino-straining bottom upstairs. The carpets, interior decoration and furniture were all of sublime quality if very stained, grubby and tatty. This paintwork wasn't just slapped over with a sponge roller and a five-litre bargain bucket of B & Q's cheapest off-white emulsion as her flat's was; it was stippled and rag-rolled and speckled and dragged in the most exquisite shades of egg-shell glaze. The paintings were sombre and masculine and absolutely not her taste, but they were thick with knifed oil and clearly worthy of two porters and a hushed silence at Sotheby's. Even the wrought-iron sofa in the kitchen at the top of the stairs had a thick scattering of worn, genuine William Morris cushions dotting its cream seat pads.

She followed Big Bum through to a very messy sitting room hung with yet more luxurious paintings. It was so thick with cigarette and dope smoke that a dry ice machine could have been pumping whiffy mist out from behind one of the oak box settees. A vast hi-tech television in the corner was showing MTV with the sound turned down; Beavis and Butt Head were cackling on a cartoon sofa. Draped across the various real sofas and rugs in front of the huge screen was an assortment of pretty men and one or two even prettier women.

Felix was nowhere to be seen.

The only familiar faces that Phoebe could pick out in the half-light were those of Mungo and Selwyn, both of whom were practically crossing their red eyes with bombed, giggling euphoria. Suddenly Soft Cell replaced Meatloaf as Marc Almond started moaning his way mournfully through 'Tainted Love'.

'Freddy!' Mungo leapt up and, gripping her face with his hands, twisted her head like a shi'atsu masseur, planting a kiss on both her cheeks. 'I must say you're looking fer-ighteningly good. Let me introduce you to everyone.'

There followed a list of Jamies, Johnnies, Saras, Claras, Mileses, Gileses, Pollys, Mollys, Ferguses, Anguses and Magnuses which Phoebe couldn't hope to catch as Mungo's pointing finger jiggled drunkenly around the room. Selwyn was stretched out on a very cracked leather sofa, with his long legs draped over the prettiest of the girls.

'Hi, Phoebe, darling, you're looking very Sci Fi.' Phoebe smiled back weakly, wondering where Felix was.

Big Bum – the chunky Hooray who had showed her in – appeared to be called 'Abers'.

'I'm really called Angus,' he explained, his big, square face turning red.

'But everyone calls him Abers – Aberdeen Angus – because

he's built like a bull, hung like a bull and talks nothing but bull,' Selwyn cackled.

'Let me fix you a drink, Freddy,' offered Abers, scooting back into the kitchen before she could ask for something soft.

'Come and sit your delicious bony arse down here, Freddy.' Mungo plumped back onto a very frayed striped sofa and patted the six or seven inches of space left between himself and the arm.

Phoebe reluctantly perched there. Balanced precariously on one buttock, she distinctly felt one of the crotch poppers on her silver teddy give way once more.

'Where's Felix?' she asked, shifting her weight to curb the popping tide.

'Not sure. I love your jeans.' Mungo gave them an admiring stroke and then suddenly started wailing along as The Cure launched into 'Friday, I'm In Love' on the stereo. The next moment he was crashing his arm against the sofa-back in time to the beat.

Phoebe jumped forwards in alarm and felt another crotch press-stud pop, plucking a couple of pubic hairs as it went. Her eyes started to smart with pain. She wished Felix would wander in and rescue her.

Instead, Abers waddled back into the room, a Marlboro smouldering between his plump, wet lips and a clutch of brimming glasses gathered into his beer gut. He held one in front of Phoebe which she managed to grab a split-second before it spilled on to her jeans. It was full of frothy amber liquid which looked like Goat's home-made cider. It tasted, however, like distilled toxic waste.

'What *is* this?' one of the Miles/Giles men asked haughtily, his mouth puckering like a popped balloon as he took a swig.

'Gin and ginger beer – very trendy,' Abers guffawed, holding a glass out to one of the giggling girls. 'Get your suck buttons out and you can have a glass too, Lucy,' he ordered with a lot of laddish shoulder-swaggering.

Lucy – a blonde Sloane with slipping mascara and a skirt that was shorter than her hair – shrieked with even more laughter and started groping around to undo her Wonderbra.

The room was suddenly filled with a rowdy slow-clap, and

Lucy, shrieking with even more laughter, flashed a very pink nipple for a split-second before collapsing with embarrassed giggles on one of the Jamie/Johnny shoulders and taking her victory glass of yellow froth.

Feeling horribly alienated from the sort of activity that required a lovely, unknowing sparsity of brain-cells, Phoebe put her revolting drink on a very ring-stained, very, very rare ormolu gueridon which Tony Seaton would have sold his major body organs for. She then made her excuses and headed off to locate a bathroom in order to re-pop her teddy.

On her way she searched forlornly for Felix, rather jumpy at the prospect of bursting into a darkened room to find him shooting up drugs, or straddling a Polly/Molly, or even just hiding from her. The degenerate, debauched atmosphere that made the mews resemble a public school dormitory during an end-of-term gang-bang was putting her on edge. She wished she'd had time to call Saskia.

In the end, the only person that Phoebe burst in on was a delectably fragile girl trying to glue a false eyelash back on with spit as she peered into the smudgy mirror of a very dirty luxury bathroom.

'Come in!' she said in a slurred SW1 voice as Phoebe tried to back out unnoticed. 'Did they pick you up too?'

'I'm sorry?' Phoebe looked around the room, breathing in the combined smells of toothpaste, loo bleach and Felix's peppery aftershave.

'They found us in a wine bar off the Old Brompton Road,' the girl giggled, delving into her 30AA Ultrabra and extracting a lipstick from the little pouch that was supposed to hold the uplifting pads. 'Aren't they divine? Fourth of June swoons, most of them. Are you coming to Iceni later too? I say, you don't belong to one of them, do you?'

Phoebe shook her head, and fought hard not to try and work out which toothbrush belonged to Felix. She felt ludicrously like an undergraduate peering around the inner sanctum digs of the third-year Theology heart-throb she had a crush on. Any minute now she'd be sniffing the towels.

Instead, she extracted her own lipstick from her jacket and, locating another splash-stained mirror, started the reapplication ritual to be companiable.

'I'm Clara.'

'Phoebe.'

'What a sumptuous name.' The saccharine was as over-applied as the mascara. 'I'm an actress.'

'I'm unemployable.'

Clara giggled awkwardly and admired her tiny, sylph-like reflection from every conceivable angle, including bending right over to see if her knickers showed. When they didn't, she rolled the waistband of her velvet mini-skirt over a few times.

'Have you seen the other one that lives here yet?' she asked, ripping off a piece of Andrex to blot her lips with.

'Which one?'

'Not the dark chap who went off to get the drinks – actually, my friend Issy rather likes him.' Clara giggled again, sounding more and more like Bonnie Langford. 'No, I mean the absolute honey-hunk whose picture's up on the wall in the bedroom next door. The one from the yoghurt ad on TV. Talk about a babe-magnet.'

'Who?' Phoebe knew exactly who she meant.

'Here – blot your snoggers on this, and I'll show you.' Clara passed Phoebe a fresh hunk of loo roll and steered her into the next room. Because she was so petite, it was like having one's arm taken by a precocious toddler.

The bedroom was in the sort of mess that only a very dedicated subscriber to Chaos Theory could create. It just had to be Felix's. The smell of aftershave was even more intense, mixed with stale Chesterfields and clean washing. The last of the evening's light crept in from a vast set of arched French windows which appeared to lead on to a small roof terrace, illuminating the jumble and litter cluttered everywhere. More than anything else, books dominated the room – hundreds of them, and none on shelves. They toppled in great spiralling piles across the floor, were propped in tower blocks against the whitewashed walls, or lay – open, broken-spined and well thumbed – wherever Felix appeared to have been reading them: on the bed, on the wicker chair by the windows or on the floor.

His flight bags and duty free had been thrown on the huge, cluttered bed and were topped with the clothes he had travelled in. Next to them lay a damp towelling bathrobe and a can of deodorant, all signs of a hasty wash and change.

'Here.' Clara pointed to the far wall, and tripped over the *Collected Works of W. H. Auden* as she towed Phoebe closer.

She had been expecting one of Felix's glossy modelling shots to be pointed out to her – and to think him extremely vain for having such a thing in his bedroom. Instead, she found herself looking at a mosaic of family photographs pressed into a clip frame. She had possessed just the same type of thing at university, cramming in more and more shots until only small, cubist angles of each face were visible.

Felix's was far more sparse than hers had been. There were some exquisite childhood snaps of the Sylvian boys looking the perfect advertisement children, pressed between two adoring, famous parents; by far the largest picture was one of Mungo, looking incredibly mischievous in a Pony Club tie with his nose pressed to a furry Shetland muzzle. Dominating the centre of the frame were a couple of publicity shots of Felix's parents. These were surrounded by photographs of various small boys Phoebe didn't recognise, although one scruffy little urchin could have been Dylan, and lots of snaps of dogs through the ages. Crammed next to a picture of a gaggle of teenagers with their tongues poking out was a shot of a beautiful, ivy-clad country house, and beside that was one of a couple of stern-looking older women who could be either grandparents or nannies.

Then Phoebe spotted a photograph which tore at her heart like a flexed claw.

'There, that's him,' Clara sighed dreamily. 'Abers said that this guy actually lives here, can you believe it?' She was pointing out a glossy, recent shot of Felix with a cognac tan, his blond hair sun-streaked and his blue eyes squinting uncomfortably against the sun as he stood beneath a palm tree with his arm around his ageing, raffish father. 'I think he's an actor. Knowing our luck, he's away on location, or gay, or married – or all three!' She went off into peals of high-pitched laughter.

Trying to laugh along, Phoebe looked at it briefly before returning her attention to the photograph that had knocked the air from her lungs like a kick from a mule.

She had seen it before, had held it in her hands whilst sitting in Gin Seaton's kitchen just a few weeks earlier. No one could mistake the girl with the biggest, happiest smile in the world. It was the shot of Felix and Saskia, hot and excited from dancing as they posed outside a marquee at the charity benefit party last year. And Felix had it clipped into a frame alongside the most important people in his life.

'D'you know her?' Clara followed Phoebe's gaze.

'I – er – I think I went to school with her.' Phoebe was finding it hard to speak.

'I suppose she's the competition.' Clara sighed. 'God, I wish she were just slightly less of a babe.'

I should be elated, Phoebe realised. When – if – she reported this back to Saskia, it would cheer her up more than a Prozac sandwich. But instead she felt as though a couple of her limbs had been lopped off.

Groping her way over to the bed, she sat down heavily on Felix's duty free cigarettes and buried her head between her knees. She was feeling distinctly nauseous – a mixture of in-flight food and gin and ginger beer was rinsing her stomach in acid bile until it blistered. I can't feel jealous, she told herself in disbelief. I can't – I mustn't – feel jealous of Saskia. Felix crucified her for loving him too much; he twisted her neck as indifferently as a gamekeeper with a pheasant. And I feel jealous.

'I say, are you all right?' Clara tried to hide an embarrassed giggle without much success.

'Fine,' Phoebe croaked into her suede knees. Her silver body chose this moment to loosen control of its poppers entirely and she felt them give way, suddenly aerating her crotch.

'You go back,' she muttered, 'I'll be through in a couple of seconds. Period pains.'

'Oh, right – poor you.' Clara sounded relieved. 'See you in a minute then.'

'Clara!' Phoebe looked up, suddenly realising that something wasn't making sense.

'Yup?' She spun around and hovered reluctantly in the door, tugging at one of the fashionable plaits which served to make her look even younger.

'You haven't seen Feli— seen this guy all evening?' Phoebe pointed at the clip frame.

'If only,' she sighed.

'When exactly did you get here?'

'Oh? – about eight-thirtyish.' She shrugged, looking suspicious. 'Why?'

'Just wondered.' Phoebe shook her head vaguely, anger grinding like chili pepper into her guts.

Seeing her murderous expression, Clara melted away.

Phoebe looked for her watch and remembered that it was still in her flat. It must be after ten, she realised. There was no way Felix would still be waiting for her at the greasy spoon. She wanted to throttle Mungo. In fact, standing up and delving into her jeans for her teddy poppers, she decided she was going to throttle him here and now. She looked around for something suitable to do it with. A dressing gown cord? A tie?

Ah, yes! Her eyes narrowed as they hit upon a leather belt lying on the floor. As she bent down to retrieve it, her poppers went once more. Straightening up with the start of an angry howl, she suddenly paused, her ears on elastic.

Above the din of Billy Idol screaming 'White Wedding' in the next room, Phoebe could just hear someone banging the front door and clomping loudly up the stairs. She held her breath in hopeful anticipation. Then she heard the clomper yelling cheerfully that he'd walked most of the length of Notting Hill to find a working cash machine before going to the off-licence.

The voice wasn't Felix's.

Battling disappointment, her anger discharging in a puff of despair, Phoebe caught sight of the clip frame again and paused to re-examine it, unable to drag herself away.

Felix's parents fascinated her. She knew them to be monsters, and yet, with the blithe, much-practised smiles of media celebrities, each appeared the epitome of adoring parenthood. Jocelyn was gorgeous, the sort of man Phoebe's mother would swoon over. He had just the right mix of urbane sophistication and dissipated sex appeal – his blond hair always immaculately stroked back from his straight tanned forehead, his blue, crinkling eyes twinkling with dissolute, bad-boy mischief. He also looked frighteningly intelligent.

The shot of Philomena was from the seventies when she was at the height of her fame, posing on a woven rug wearing an amazing cheesecloth cat-suit with flares as wide as parachutes and with a lot of glossy brown cleavage plunging between open ribbon ties. She was undeniably beautiful, possessing a secret, faraway smile which made her appear both passive and carnal. Softened by a Vaseline-smeared lens, her smooth, line-free face was dominated by huge, watery turquoise eyes and a mouth as soft and plump as the centre of a guava. The famous tousled ash-blonde mane rippled like a glacier down her back and fell in carefully teased icicle tendrils across her face, tickling the button nose.

'Don't try to find hidden depths in that beautiful creature,' said a gentle voice immediately behind Phoebe. 'She's as shallow as a puddle.'

Phoebe spun around and practically bashed noses with someone. Backing away, she saw that he was wearing a Dennis the Menace jumper and a pair of scruffy black cords that made Iain's beige ones seem positively hip by comparison. His wavy brown hair was on end and he had his odd socks on inside out.

He grinned amiably. 'I don't think we've met – I'm Dylan. Don't tell me – you're a friend of Lucy's. I must say she seems to know the most extraordinarily good-looking people.'

'Not exactly.' Phoebe guiltily held the belt behind her back. 'I'm a foe of Mungo's.'

'What?' Dylan laughed.

'I'm Phoebe.'

The smile dropped from Dylan's face as though wiped away by a sudden, paralysing stroke.

'Felix's Phoebe?'

'I suppose you could put it that way.' She swallowed.

'What are you doing here?' He put up a hand to ruffle his hair in agitation. 'Is Felix around, is that it? He brought you back with him?'

Gritting her teeth, she told him what Mungo had said on the phone.

'The trouble is, I don't have a clue where he is now,' she explained. 'I was about to go and find this Spike Café place to look for him.'

'God, he won't still be there. I walked part of the way with him over an hour ago.'

'I could kill Mungo,' Phoebe hissed, and then smiled apologetically at Dylan. 'Sorry. I'm sure he's lovely under the spoiled brat façade.'

'No, he isn't.' Dylan shrugged. 'Fucked-up childhood makes for a screwed-up adult hoodlum, as they say in the States,' he put on a New York drawl.

'Yes?' Phoebe stared at him.

'Not for me to say, though,' he added hastily, grinning noncommittally. 'He's extremely bright. It's pretty tough living in your brother's shadow – he just adores winding Felix up. Look, you'd better stay here and have another drink. I've a pretty good idea where Felix will have got to.'

One look at the Bacchic play-pen that had amassed in the dim sitting room, and Phoebe went swiftly into reverse. A raucous game of cards was in progress, involving drinking inches of vodka straight down with every round; someone had put on a very trashy blue video which no one apart from Abers was watching; Clara was sitting on Selwyn's knee now, chatting to her friend whom Selwyn was in turn draped over. Mungo was busy making a bong out of two plastic Coke bottles and some kitchen foil.

'Come back here, Freddy!' he howled as he caught sight of her backing away. 'The boys are all dying to chat you up, dress you down and cage you over.'

Phoebe caught up with Dylan at the front door. 'I'm coming with you.'

'I don't know if that's a very wise idea. Felix's favourite pub is a complete shit-hole.'

Ignoring the warning, Phoebe plodded alongside Dylan as he headed for deepest Notting Hill. He walked remarkably slowly considering the urgency of his mission, Phoebe decided. He clearly had one, ambling pace which he doggedly wouldn't alter, however hurried or late he was.

'Have a good time in Paris?' he asked politely.

'Mmm.' Phoebe wasn't sure how much to give away. 'Have you known Felix long?' she asked, already familiar with the answer.

'Years. We were at school together from about fifteen. Then university.' He squinted up at the last traces of red in the sky. 'It'll be hot again tomorrow. Did you and Felix do much talking in Paris?'

'Lots.' Phoebe was glad that they were walking slowly. Her unpopped teddy was beginning to ride up inside her jeans. 'So you and Felix went to school together?'

'Yup.'

'That was after he was expelled from Marlborough?'

'Yup. He tell you all this in Paris?'

'Some.'

This was hopeless, Phoebe realised. Each was far too cagey to let the other know what they were fishing for. Dylan was too fiercely loyal to say anything indiscreet about his friend and Phoebe was too uncertain of where she stood to let anything slip. Besides, Dylan was bright and shrewd enough to cotton on to the Saskia link at the slightest indiscretion. Yet, united by their quest to find Felix, Phoebe felt a strange sense of comfortable, immediate intimacy with him. With his laughing face and his gentle charm, he was very easy to like.

Dylan led her as far as a very seedy-looking backstreet pub called The Drunk Punk. They could hear the thudding beat long before they caught the glow of a light over a swinging sign, or smelled the mixture of stale smoke, beer, and what was un-mistakably the bonfire reek of dope.

'Delightful picture.' Phoebe looked up at a peeling sign which featured a leather-clad youth with a green mohican picking his pierced nose.

'It was trying to be trendy in the early eighties,' Dylan sighed. 'It's now the biggest dive in this area. Remarkable that it's still going really.' He pushed open the doors.

The place stank like the armpit of a tramp's overcoat, was as dimly lit as a post-operative cataract recovery room, and was positively shaking under the high-decibel onslaught of The Clash from the twenty or so speakers that hung from the ceilings along with smashed-out television screens, electric guitars, tattered Union Jacks and Sex Pistols memorabilia. There wasn't a horse brass in sight. Nor was there a single punk amongst the grubby, grungy clientele.

Wearing a vast Aran sweater and his most ancient pair of shredded jeans, Felix was sitting at the bar with his back to the door, chatting to a middle-aged man who had a spider's web tattoo across his face. They were openly sharing a spliff and howling with laughter.

Dylan pulled Phoebe behind a spray-painted pillar.

'Just go to the loo for five minutes, will you?' He nodded towards a sign that read 'Punks and Bints Piss Pots' with an arrow pointing to a set of stairs that led down to the cellars.

'Charming.' Phoebe winced, and glanced towards Felix and his tattooed companion again. She wondered if Felix had swapped notes about his Snoopy with him and decided not.

'No, Dylan.' She'd hit upon a vague idea. 'You go to the loo. If you hear the sound of breaking glass, then I might need rescuing.' She gave him a gentle shove towards the stairs.

Looking over his shoulder with an 'On your head be it' shrug, Dylan did as she asked.

Phoebe sidled up to the bar, close enough to hear Felix's conversation whilst keeping directly behind him so that he couldn't see her. She had a vague plan to creep up behind him and do something seductive, but couldn't as yet figure out what.

'Then they fuck you around so much, don't they?' he was drawling. 'I mean, you go out of your way to be just what they want – you buy them drinks, meals and presents. I even bought this bitch a bloody holiday. You tell them you're interested in their heads, when really it's their other empty space you want to get into.'

Spider-man howled with laughter and sucked on the spliff.

Phoebe fingered the towelling bar mat twitchily. She could tell that Felix was pretty high, and was undoubtedly putting on a loutish, bravura act for his cackling audience, but his words were nonetheless wounding. Her plot to do something seductive was rapidly revised into doing something violent.

'And they fucking blow you out, the ungrateful tarts,' he was muttering bitterly.

'Can't complain about being blown, mate,' Spider-man croaked as he held the smoke in his lungs until his eyes watered.

'I said blow you *out*, Itzy,' Felix muttered, taking the spliff. 'I offered this bitch a seat in the best bloody restaurant in London, and she doesn't fucking turn up. I tell you, if I see her again, I'll . . .'

'What?' Spider-man was on tenterhooks. 'Knock her block off? Trash her place? Newcastle Smile – what?'

'I'll –' Felix looked at the spliff and handed it back without taking a drag. 'I'll kiss her beautiful arse,' he laughed. 'Christ, I've never met anyone quite that bloody desirable or fucking infuriating. I'm going to phone her.' He started delving in the pockets of his jeans.

Phoebe shrank back behind a pile of charity pennies on the end of the bar. Violence was giving way to a ridiculous urge to hug herself.

Spider-man was looking nonplussed. 'Nrr, mate. Knock her block off. Women respect that.'

Patting him on the shoulder, Felix headed for the phone.

About to pull her jacket up over her head and duck, Phoebe was relieved to notice that the phone was at the opposite end of the bar. As Felix moved towards it, Spider-man spotted her and grinned.

'All alone, darling?' he called over to her. 'Can I buy you a drink?'

Phoebe glanced nervously towards Felix, but he had his back to the room and was already punching out a number on the pay-phone. He didn't have to look it up, she noticed with amazement.

'No, thanks.' She smiled politely and, moving past him and towards Felix, stretched back and whispered in Spider-man's multi-pierced ear, 'Watch this. I'm just going to show you what women respect.'

Phoebe crept up behind Felix just as he was leaning back against the bar, a fag hanging from his mouth, clearly listening to the ringing tones. She crossed her fingers and said a small prayer to the only saints she could bring to mind – Jude and Francis; hardly appropriate, but she hoped they were having a quiet night and fancied a fresh challenge.

'Hello, this is Phoebe's answering machine,' she breathed. 'I'm afraid I can't pick up the phone right now because I set off hours ago to meet a gorgeous guy called Felix. Then Felix's little brother told me he would be waiting for me at his house, and not the greasy spoon where we'd arranged to meet.'

Felix spun around and stared at her furiously, cigarette still burning Clint Eastwood style between his lips.

'Imagine my surprise,' Phoebe went on, trying to stop her voice shaking, 'when I got to his house and found he wasn't there. His cute little brother had played a joke on us both. But the joke's on him now. Please leave your name and number and I'll get back to you as soon as I've had my arse kissed.'

For a moment Felix looked so incensed that Phoebe geared up for a hasty exit, certain a pay-phone receiver was about to make sharp contact with her cheekbone. Then, shaking his head in wonder, he burst out laughing.

'Hi, guys.' Dylan was hovering a few feet away, clapping his palms together and rocking on his heels with embarrassment. 'No need to introduce you two, then – that's good. Drink?'

'I'll get them.' Felix bounded up to the bar and waggled a tenner.

As they were finding a table together, Dylan muttered to Phoebe in an undertone: 'I don't know what you said to him, but you're a bigger miracle worker than the guy with the beard and the sandals.' He grinned. 'I was half tempted to call out the emergency services while I was waiting down there.'

He sank back in a chair, still watching her closely. He had curry stains on his jumper, she noticed. Yet, although he was a slob, there was an intense and very likeable sincerity about him.

'So did you know Felix from Bar Barella a long time before you went to Paris?' he asked easily, as though making feather-weight small talk.

'No, I've worked there less than a month.'

'But you met there?'

'No, we met at a party.' Phoebe was growing increasingly uneasy with the line of conversation.

'Which one?'

'Showdown.'

'But I thought – '

'That he got off with Fanii Hubert that night?' Phoebe felt as though Dylan had turned an anglepoise light on her. 'He did.'

'But he spotted his ideal woman over a canapé sort-of-thing?' he grinned.

'Sort of.'

'You play the game very well,' he laughed, shaking his head to himself.

Phoebe stiffened slightly. 'What game?'

'That's what I'm wondering,' he replied slowly. 'Felix is right – you're impossible to work out. Just like him.' He gave her a meditative look, then smiled affably.

Dropping her eyes, Phoebe lapsed into another silence. At the bar, Felix was buying some dope from Spider-man.

'Can I ask you a very, very slightly personal question?' Dylan groped for a cigarette and offered her one.

'I don't smoke, thanks,' Phoebe smiled up at him. 'And you can ask what you like, although I must warn you that I'm an easy lie.'

Dylan looked unexpectedly fidgety.

'Do you know a red-headed girl who works at Bar Barella?' His tone was suddenly less assured.

'Fliss Wolfe?'

'Yup.'

'Yes, I know her. Why?' Phoebe was instantly fascinated. Despite the dim lighting, she could have sworn that Dylan was blushing like a spotty fourteen-year-old asking Kim Basinger for her autograph.

'I just wondered – I know her brother,' he muttered.

'Selwyn?' Phoebe nodded. 'He was at the mews earlier. They're very different.'

'You know her quite well then?' Dylan was trying desperately hard to sound casual, but it was as impossible as the Queen trying to sound sexy during her Christmas Speech.

Phoebe was just debating whether to tell him that Fliss lived with her, and wondering quite how she could draw him out about his real interest in her red-headed flat-mate, when Felix finally wandered over from the bar.

'I forgot to ask what anyone wanted,' he said, rolling up with three glasses and several packets of crisps. 'So I got us tequila slammers all round.'

'Great,' Phoebe and Dylan said in unison, both without conviction. They caught each other's eyes and grinned.

'So what do you think of this divine creature?' Felix asked Dylan, as he sat beside Phoebe and hooked one of his long, muscular legs over her knee. 'Isn't she just perfect?'

'Too much so.' Dylan laughed amiably, but there was a very slight catch in his voice.

After several drinks, Phoebe decided that she adored Dylan, but that he didn't trust her one bit. He was the sort of person she naturally fell into step with – they all shared a similarly childish humour, inability to shut up when they wanted to make a point, giggling sense of daring and willingness to try anything once. She knew exactly why Felix doted on him so much. Like all good comedy double-acts, they were great foils for one another; put together, they made a lethal, laughing-gas combination.

Phoebe giggled, hooted and chuckled so much that her sides ached as though she'd just done the Cindy Crawford Workout.

But despite all the self-deprecating, ironic wit and sharp, sardonic insight, Dylan was clearly as soft-centred as a strawberry cream in a chocolate box, and as winning as the kitten on the lid. Phoebe suspected he could be very easily hurt. And for all his experience of mopping up the tears of Felix's girlfriends, he seemed to have remarkably little romantic track record himself.

'He had a girlfriend called Janey at university,' Felix shrugged when Phoebe quizzed him later, after Dylan had set off for the mews. 'Real puppy-love stuff – skipping around holding hands and weekends giggling in bed. Could hardly drag himself out to play rugby or get drunk for the first few months. He adored her, but she went off to travel the world after we graduated and never came back. It really cut him up.'

'You mean, she got killed?'

'Christ, no!' Felix laughed. 'The stupid bitch married an Australian sheepshearer. Has three boys and a pet dingo now. I still don't think Dylan's got over it. He'd asked Janey to marry him endless times and she always said she'd make an honest man of him at Chelsea Reg, on their thirtieth birthday. They were born on the same day – Dylan sets a lot of store by that. But Janey decided she wanted to be a farmer's wife and made a laughing livestock out of him.'

Shared birthdays made Phoebe think painfully of Saskia. It was theirs on Sunday, she remembered with a guilty pang. She realised that she'd been giggling for almost an hour without a single thought for the real reason she was here.

Felix was tracing the neckline of her hated silver body.

'Have you ever asked anyone to marry you?' she asked jokily, praying that she didn't sound too unsubtle.

'Would you like me to?' He dropped his voice and grinned mischievously.

'No, thanks,' Phoebe leant back, realising that she must have sounded far, far too leading. 'I was just interested.'

Felix lifted his chin and brushed his bitten nails along the stubble on his neck.

'Yes, I've asked the question – I've also been engaged, in fact,' he muttered, not looking her in the eye.

'How often?'

Felix laughed. 'I get the oddest feeling that you already know.' He stared down at the table and fiddled with his empty glass. 'Has Dyldo been filling you in?'

Phoebe balked, realising that she was giving away too much of her information from Saskia.

'It was just a question.' She shrugged nonchalantly. 'I'm certain Dylan wouldn't tell me your shoe-size unless you okayed it first.'

'Okay.' Felix ran a finger around the rim of his glass. 'But who would think to ask "how many times" at that moment?' He looked at her with incredulous amusement. 'I'd ask "who to" or "when" or "what went wrong" but not "how many times".' He moved on to play with his cigarette packet, sooty lashes veiling his eyes so that she couldn't read his expression clearly.

'Well, you're not me,' Phoebe muttered sulkily, trying to dig herself out of a rapidly widening hole with a fit of mock-pique. 'Was it just the once or what?'

'Twice.' Flipping the cigarette packet over, he didn't look remotely remorseful. 'And both times for entirely the wrong reasons.'

'What was wrong about them?' Phoebe let her anger rip. 'Didn't you "believe in them"?'

'I guess I – ' He was fiddling around with his cigarette packet so much that it shot off the table. 'Oh, I don't fucking know. I don't want to talk about it.'

'I get the feeling you've never been dumped,' she said in barely more than a whisper.

Felix grinned, catching her jacket collar in his fingers. 'Is that a fact?'

'You tell me.'

He shrugged. 'No, I've never been dumped. Why – are you planning to give me the sack? Or will you wait until you can leave me standing next to Dylan in a morning suit, exchanging embarrassed platitudes with the vicar?'

Phoebe almost passed out as she absorbed the awkward, uncomfortable irony trapped in the question.

'What would you do if I did?' She tried to keep her tone as light and frothy as a soufflé, but it was sinking fast.

'Get drunk and go to live abroad probably.'

Getting her act together, Phoebe smiled teasingly. 'And, don't tell me – if I trawled up the aisle wearing several acres of raw silk and a musty old blue borrowed suspender, you'd do exactly the same thing anyway?'

Felix laughed. 'Like father, like son-of-a-bitch – although I'd want a gawp at the suspender first.' He slid his arms over her shoulders. 'Come here, you gorgeous thing.'

God, he kissed well, Phoebe realised afresh as she was almost floored by the groin-fluttering effect of Felix's lips. Kissing him back was as instinctive a reflex as flexing one's toes in a luxurious bubble bath.

'I love you,' he breathed into her mouth.

'No, you don't,' Phoebe retaliated as their tongues met once again.

Felix gripped her by the thighs and pulled her tighter to him. 'Do you want to go out clubbing with the boys, or stay in?'

Going back alone to her own flat didn't seem to be an option, she realised.

He caught her chin with his dope-smelling fingers and pulled it towards him.

'You're beautiful,' he said simply, leaning forward to kiss her again.

'No – you're beautiful,' Phoebe said honestly, suddenly not caring how corny it sounded.

God, she must get a grip on these soppy urges, she told herself firmly.

Felix ran his fingers from her chin to her hair. 'In what way?'

Conceited bugger. What did he want her to do? Give him a run down on the finer aspects of his enviable bone structure?

Then, seeing the guarded, anxious expression on his lovely face, she suddenly realised that were she to do that, she'd simply be running him down. Felix knew that he was beautiful; he was reminded of the fact daily in the same way a Pekinese was patted on the back by a doting owner and told that it was sweet. It was absolutely everything else about himself that he doubted.

She stretched forward and touched his mouth with her lips even more lightly than he had done to hers.

'You're a bright, funny, infuriating bastard,' she breathed. 'And that makes you beautiful to me.'

As she pulled away, she saw that his face was wreathed in smiles.

'I love you,' he laughed.

'No, you don't,' Phoebe grinned.

The journey that had taken Phoebe and Dylan less than five minutes earlier that night took Phoebe and Felix over half an hour as they kissed on every corner, pounced on one another in every doorway and felt each other up before crossing every road. They also pigged out on sweets from a late-night tobacconist, fell about laughing as they balanced along walls like small kids and played hop-scotch with the lines between paving stones.

It was daft, childish stuff, but Phoebe revelled in it. Dan would be far too stuffy and image conscious to kiss at every bus stop along Ladbroke Grove or to nick apples from the outside display of an all-night grocery, and too concerned about his Savile Row worsted to share a hot-dog in an each-end race.

She had always imagined Felix to be equally vain if not more so – the romantic gestures Saskia had talked about had been more of the walking hand-in-hand through St Mark's Square at midnight and staring meaningfully into one another's eyes as the bells struck all across Venice sort. This childish, giggling Felix was a revelation. This wasn't a challenge; it was heart-skipping, free-falling, breath-snatching fun.

Panting for breath as they rounded the last corner, with Albany Mews finally in sight, he pulled her down on a bench.

'They'll have gone without us!' Phoebe laughed.

'They'll wait for me – they always do,' he said with the assurance of one who knows that he's the key member of the pack.

'Always?'

'Always.' Felix pressed his nose to her neck. 'Unlike you, you old bitch.'

'I can give you a good couple of years!' She wailed, pretending to be insulted.

'I want you for a lot longer than that.' He traced his lips towards her mouth.

She just wished that kissing him wasn't such a pleasure. It would spoil her for life, and certainly tarnish the next, tongue-nose-and-talk clinch that she had with Dan.

Thinking about him made her pull away.

'What's the matter?' Felix clung on to her, burying his chin in her shoulder and looking up at her with big, imploring eyes.

There were moments, Phoebe realised, when he acted like a small child desperate not to let go of his mother's hand at the school gates. She couldn't work out whether it was because he was insecure or spoilt.

'Nothing.' She looked up at the sky and spotted The Plough – the only constellation she could identify.

Try as she might, she found she couldn't shake the image of Dan from her mind. He even loomed out of The Plough, shooting her a crinkly grin. It had been a week since she'd last seen him – that awful night in the Highgate flat. The flat she had done absolutely nothing about, just as she had done nothing about getting a job or paying her snowballing debts.

Dan would be beside himself with irritation, she realised.

Her life was in such chaos, and now she was confusing it even more by taking up Saskia's challenge, and finding it far, far harder than she had ever envisaged.

She looked down at Felix and into his smiling, expectant eyes. It terrified her that her feelings towards him were no longer cold and clinically detached. The prospect of hurting him as much as he had hurt Saskia was getting harder and harder to rationalise. No one deserved that sort of pain, she realised, not even in recompense for that they themselves had inflicted. An eye for an eye merely blinded, when what this aggressor really needed was to open those heartbreaking blue eyes and see.

Phoebe knew that those who set out to bully or abuse had almost inevitably been victims themselves. Felix's hellish childhood haunted her thoughts at the moment. She had an agonising premonition that to inflict a second burden of woe by way of revenge could completely back-fire, and render him twice as combative.

'I love you.' He slipped his hand around the back of her neck and pulled her face back down to meet his.

'No, you don't.' She closed her eyes and let him kiss her until all her churning thoughts were blanked out.

32

The music throbbed and shrieked and howled and thrummed in a monotonous, sexy pulse. Lights stabbed and jabbed frantically in time, voices whooped, sweat rose. Writhing, connected bodies were momentarily caught in a shard of saturated, coloured light and then plunged into darkness.

Phoebe couldn't help it. She was enjoying herself. Dancing with Felix was heaven. She was almost blind with perspiration, her hair soaked into rats' tails and her cropped silver teddy shining like antique pewter. She'd drained the last dregs of her little Evian bottle over her face moments ago, yet still it glowed like hot embers in a fire. Opposite her, Felix's eyes smiled into hers.

Their pelvises stapled together, they rotated them in a wide, rhythmic circle as their torsos leaned away with loose, writhing shoulders.

Tiredness totally forgotten, Phoebe pressed the insides of her elbows to her wet forehead and, draping her forearms towards the back of her neck, danced for fun.

'They're a stunning couple,' Issy yelled at Dylan from their vantage point on the balcony above the dancefloor. Given the volume level, yelling was the only form of communication feasible. And even then, it was hit and miss.

'A what?' he yelled back, pressing himself to the balcony in order to avoid her bony little hip digging yet further into his.

He looked at his watch. It was almost five in the morning. He had to work at lunchtime. The rest of the mews coterie had dispersed hours ago, staggering away to bed or to get cabs to Bar Italia in order to dissect the evening over countless espressos and Marlboros. Only Felix and Phoebe had carried on dancing, feeding from a stamina brought on by new, unchannelled lust. Right now, Dylan reflected anxiously, the unexplored unexploded potential of their relationship was electric.

He had stayed on, despite mammoth yawns and drooping eyes, to keep Issy company. She claimed to have lost her cloakroom ticket which meant she had to wait until the club closed at six to claim her jacket. Dylan was by nature generous and patient, but right now he was fighting not to hide from her. He felt rotten, but her sweet, sickly attention made him shrink like a talc-coated slug. He knew that she was coming on to him, but he was too tired and didn't fancy her enough to respond. All he wanted to do was bundle her into a cab and then walk home to crash out, alone, in his own bed.

He glanced down at the dancefloor again. Issy was right: Felix and Phoebe looked stunning together, both moving with a loose-limbed, animal lack of self-consciousness. Phoebe's silver top was riding up almost to indecency as she circled around Felix, arms high over her head.

Draining his bottle of beer, Dylan watched as Felix slid his arms over her back and pulled her into him until they were moving in lilting unison, laughing the whole time.

Dylan was frightened by the way they clicked. He knew he shouldn't get involved with Felix's love life, had told himself countless times to steer clear. And yet he had always used it as a substitute for his own lacklustre one, and had agonised as Felix made wrong move after wrong move. Now that he had made the right one, Dylan was almost more afraid.

Phoebe Fredericks, he reflected worriedly, was too good to be true.

Kissing Felix and dancing with him at the same time, Phoebe was vaguely aware of something tapping around her shoulder.

Spinning around, she found herself face-to-chest with a giant in a Westwood t-shirt and paint-stained black leather trousers. His thick mane was pulled back into a pony tail, he was wearing tiny, circular-framed dark glasses and had the first scraggy traces of a blond goatee beard bristling around his grinning mouth.

'Stan!' she gasped, releasing her grip on Felix.

'All right, girl?' He was jiggling around in front of her as he danced with a lot of jabbing elbow and creaking leather. 'Fought you'd got a double there for a minute.'

'What?' Phoebe could see his mouth moving between the stubble, but couldn't hope to hear the words above the din of the music.

She looked over her shoulder at Felix, who was wiping his face on the sleeves of his t-shirt like a tennis player and eyeing Stan suspiciously.

Phoebe smiled at him and nodded towards the dark, swampy chill-out-room where exhausted clubbers were sagging out on settees and tugging at little water bottles as they waited for the sweat to evaporate and the heart-beat to drop below three figures. Felix shrugged and, hooking his arm over her shoulder proprietorially, steered the way through the bopping masses.

They found a deserted sofa where the sound of one's own voice was almost audible.

'What are you doing here? I thought you hated clubbing?' Phoebe yelled into Stan's ear.

'Got tanked at the ICA with me mates and came here sharking,' he yelled back. 'They've all scored, but my bird was a Spanish student and pushed off to learn her verbs or summink. I couldn't understand a word of her excuse, to be honest.' He removed his dark glasses to reveal two very red, unfocused eyes. He was clearly extremely stoned.

Phoebe laughed. 'Stan, this is Felix.'

'All right, mate?' Stan thrust out his hand.

'You were at the Showdown party.' Felix took it warily. 'You gave Phoebe here the shirt off your back.'

'Didn't you get in all the papers afterwards?' Stan was slouching so much on the sofa that he practically slid off it.

Felix shrugged.

'Fought I recognised you.' Stan shot Phoebe a meaningful look and, because he was at the pitch of drunkenness that lost all aspirations to subtlety, mouthed '*the* Felix?' before pointing very obviously and then getting the giggles.

Phoebe swallowed and looked at Felix, who seemed confused.

'Shall we go?'

He nodded. 'I'll just see if Dylan wants to share a cab.' He kissed her on the cheek and walked off. Phoebe stared after him, loving the easy way he moved, the shock of hair, the way heads turned as he passed.

'That's Saskia's Felix?' Stan was still laughing. 'Didn't recognise him with the new hairdo. Bit radical innit?'

'It was for a job.' Phoebe muttered defensively, moving to the opposite end of the sofa and trying to ignore him.

'You were coming on a bit strong, on the dance floor werencha?' Stan slid closer to her.

'What?' Phoebe glared at him, aware that her face was reddening fast.

'You were snogging the gob off him, girl,' he cackled. 'Isn't that taking method acting a bit far? I's all right. She's told me all about it now. I thought you were just s'posed to lead him on a bit. I saw you dancing – you two were virtually humping.'

'Stan, will you lay off?'

'She know you're here?' He donned his dark glasses again. He clearly meant Saskia.

'I'm seeing her tomorrow.' Phoebe sighed unhappily at the thought. 'She wants me to go to Berkshire for the weekend.'

'Took her out for a drink last week. She looked awful,' he sniffed.

'You took Saskia out?' Phoebe stared at him in amazement.

'Yeah – thought she needed cheering up, but I couldn't stop her crying all night. Bit embarrassing really, considering we were in The Criterion. She said you and Fart-face were in Paris.'

'We came back tonight.' Phoebe bristled at the insult on Felix's behalf. 'Was she really upset?'

'Wretched.' Stan stood up. 'I don't know what you're playing at, girl,' he bent down so that his big nose was practically pressed to hers, 'but I fink you'd better get your act together pretty quick.'

'Shut up, Stan.' Phoebe closed her eyes.

'While that girl's dragging herself around looking like a road accident, you're looking far too fucking good,' he muttered. 'Don't tell me you're doing this from the goodness of your heart, Phoebes. You're enjoying yourself, arencha? D'you fancy him or what?'

'Oh, fuck off!' Leaping up, Phoebe ran out through the dancefloor and into the club's foyer where she crashed straight into Felix.

'Are you okay?' He caught her by the shoulders and gazed into her face.

'Fine!' she bleated in an artificially jolly voice.

'You sure?'

'Never better.' Phoebe batted his hands away from her shoulders, worried that Stan was spying on her from behind a pillar. She felt completely paranoid.

'Where's your friend?'

'In the dog house,' she hissed.

Felix raised one eyebrow. 'Look, Dylan wants to hang around here and look after some girl until her pumpkin arrives. D'you want to go?'

'Please.'

They queued for their coats in silence. Phoebe kicked at the floor with a snakeskin toe and gnawed at her bottom lip. Compared to the moist, rising heat of the club proper, the foyer was freezing. She started to shiver.

'Is he a friend of Dan's or something?' Felix muttered eventually. 'Is that why you're so upset?'

'No – he doesn't know Dan.' Phoebe dug in her pockets for her cloakroom ticket.

'What is it then?'

'Nothing.'

'You're lying, honey,' he said sarcastically. 'Phoebe, look at me, for Christ's sake.'

She took a deep breath and glanced up. He looked tired and worried, his eyes dulled by a hangover, chin dusted with stubble.

'He warned me off you,' she sighed.

'He what?' Felix laughed bitterly. 'What business is it of his?'

'It's complicated.'

'He thinks I'm a bad lot, huh?' Felix grinned. 'That I'm going to corrupt you with my wicked, playboy ways?'

'Something like that.'

They were at the front of the queue now. Phoebe handed her ticket over while Felix searched for his.

'Actually,' he extracted several crumpled tenners and a taxi receipt before he found it, 'Dylan's just had words with me too.'

'Words?'

'Said – and I quote – "That girl is dangerous."' His imitation of Dylan's low, earnest voice was spot on.

'Dylan said that?' Phoebe looked at him in astonishment as she took her jacket.

'Yup.' Felix passed his ticket over and turned back to her, his eyes playful.

'Well, it's nice to know our friends approve,' she muttered, feeling ridiculously hurt.

'Makes for fewer wedding invitations, though.' Taking her jacket, Felix wrapped it around her shoulders and pulled her closer. 'Saves on catering.'

'I thought I wasn't going to turn up.'

'I'd slip your pa fifty quid to frog-march you vicarwards.'

'That should do it.'

'Love you.' He kissed her nose.

'Don't.'

Outside the club it was light. A low, mist-hazed sun fought to clamber above the high, regal buildings that Phoebe and Felix wandered aimlessly past as they headed nowhere and talked nonsense.

'I thought we could have a female vicar, get hitched in black fishnet and dress the page boys as sex slaves just to piss off the parents.'

'We could change the vows from love, honour and obey to cheat, lie and shag around.'

'Coke can rings and a three tiered hash-cake.'

'Naturally.'

'Of course my mother will up-stage everyone with a cleavage you could lose a bridesmaid down.'

'Mine'll obscure her totally with a hat as wide as a pew and pussy cat collar to match.'

'Pa will get pissed and try to snog her.'

'So will mine.'

'Mungo will spike all the great aunts' drinks with acid and send several telegrams purporting to be from my extant wives in Tobago.'

'As will Milly. Which will probably lead to at least one fatality and a lot of custard creams with fangs trying to eat support hose.'

'I'll save myself for the wedding night, by the way.'

'I'll save myself the trouble and bonk everything I meet from now on.'

'Which is all incidental because at the time of hitching, I'll be stuck naked on the Intercity to Aberdeen with my legs in plaster, covered in lipstick kisses from the stripper my friends hired at the stag party.'

'I think we should call it off, don't you?'

'Or elope?'

'Nrr. You'd never get a ladder up to my bedroom window without being lynched by Neighbourhood Watch.'

The sun, directly ahead of them now, peered above Hyde Park, drenching the tree tops in white, gauzy light.

'I really like you.' Felix pulled her closer to him.

'I really like you too.' Phoebe tucked her face into his neck and laughed.

I'm going to sleep with him, she decided headily. I must sleep with him. I can't help myself, I want to know what it's like. Just the once.

Excitement was bubbling between her legs as Felix pulled her into the street and kissed her long and hard in front of a hooting black cab.

'Let's go riding.' He stared straight at the sun, eyes narrowed to two creases.

'Riding?' Phoebe pulled him away just before the cab revved up and raced through the spot they'd been occupying.

'You can hire horses on Rotten Row around now.' Felix stumbled over the kerb and pulled her tighter to him. 'Do you want to go?'

Phoebe yawned pointedly. 'I have to get to Paddington later.'

'You're going away this weekend?' he asked forlornly.

'Mmm – Berkshire. Long-standing arrangement.'

'Can't you make a short, lying excuse?'

'No.'

'Okay,' he conceded grumpily. 'You can go there after we've been riding.'

'Aren't you tired?'

'No.'

Perhaps I'm not going to sleep with him, Phoebe realised. She wished she didn't feel quite so disappointed.

Nearly two hours later, they were sitting at the front of the top deck of a bus heading towards Paddington, dusty boots propped up on the sill in front of them as they peered into passing windows, watching Londoners burn toast, brew tea and blink themselves awake after their Saturday morning lie-ins.

Still moodily trying to dissuade Phoebe from going to Berkshire, Felix played absentmindedly with the frayed hem of her silver top and clutched onto her knee like the safety bar of a fairground ride as they swung around corners.

'At least come back to the mews for breakfast,' he coaxed, reaching across to press his nose into the nape of her neck. 'I cook a mean Pop Tart.'

Shaking her head, Phoebe shifted away.

Now so acutely aware of every touch of his body against hers that she jumped each time he moved, she was deliberately avoiding his eyes, and trying hard to distance herself from him. She needed to detach her mind in anticipation of Saskia's interrogation, but her nerve endings were drum-skin tight with the longing to be touched more. She was finding it impossible to come down from the ebullient, head-spinning high of new-found lust and old-fashioned romance. Every time she thought that she had succeeded in popping her bubble of sexy, heady happiness, Felix simply had to touch her for it to fill with hot air and sail sky-high again.

Anxious for distraction, she craned around to watch a morning dog-walker trotting efficiently towards Hyde Park, two red setters weaving their leads into knots behind him. Seeing them enthusiastically tie their owner to a lamp post, Phoebe burst out laughing.

'I love the way you laugh,' Felix murmured, his fingers tip-toeing with Thumbelina lightness along her leg once more. 'It's gorgeously dirty.'

'Thanks.' Phoebe had a feeling she'd just been unflatteringly compared to Sid James. She twisted her legs away. Yet despite the insult, the electric currents were now shooting so high that she felt as though she was undergoing bikini line electrolysis. She crossed them grumpily and peered sideways at him.

'You know,' he was staring fixedly ahead, seemingly in a world of his own, unaware of the havoc his hand was wreaking on Phoebe's shaking thigh, 'I never had much of a childhood.'

'I guess that's why you're such a big kid now,' Phoebe sniped, and then instantly regretted it.

For a moment, Felix's face was as set and visored as Sir Lancelot squaring up for a joust.

But then he took the jibe on the chin. Turning to her, he laughed so that his lovely, wide mouth creased at the corners, furrowing grooves right the way up his cheeks to his eyes. Shrugging, he simply said, 'You could be right.'

Phoebe found her leg stretching across to nestle against his once more.

'I think you're the same.' Felix stared out of the front window again.

'A big kid?' Phoebe grinned.

He shook his head, suddenly serious. 'I think you had a shitty time as a kid. It makes you cling to driftwood in later life. I mean, we know there are solid trees on the river bank just metres away, but basically we're so bloody frightened of letting go that we carry on clinging to this lump of rotten wood, knowing all the while that we're whizzing downstream.'

Phoebe raised a dubious eyebrow.

'Are you saying I'm clinging to driftwood then?' she asked cautiously.

'Dan,' Felix started slowly, 'is your driftwood.'

'Dan?'

She swallowed, suddenly certain that she didn't want to talk about him right now. Just saying his name had broken the mood as sharply as a high note shatters glass.

'I honestly don't think that my childhood was anywhere near as hellish as yours,' she said quickly, anxious to race away from the D word.

'Maybe.' Felix retreated into a diplomatic silence, seemingly absorbed in watching the heads of commuters in the bus queue beneath them.

Just as Phoebe relaxed back into her seat, grateful for the break, he turned swiftly back to her, hand sliding higher up her thigh, blue eyes trapping hers once more.

'What are you going to do about him, Phoebe?'

Phoebe almost fell off the seat into the aisle in her desperation to break the stifling need to throw herself onto his chest and bawl her eyes out.

'Are you going to get him out of your life?' he asked nervily.

Dragging her eyes up to the *No Smoking* sign, Phoebe found that she could barely speak for the lump in her throat.

'I don't know,' she croaked. 'He might not let me; he can be extremely bloody minded and domineering.'

'Do you love him?'

Phoebe watched the '*No*' blur in front of her eyes, closely followed by '*Penalty £50*'. 'I certainly used to think so,' she muttered.

'And now?' Felix's voice was so quiet that he was almost inaudible over the rattle of the bus engine.

'I guess it's got to the point where I have to test the pain factor,' she said shakily, glancing around as an elderly lady ricocheted up the aisle and settled in the seat behind them. 'I know I detest most things about the relationship; I loathe the lying and colluding, the lack of intimacy; I hate crying over broken dates, tearing my hair out when it's a weekend and I can't call him, or hold him, or tell him when something amazing's happened. But I guess that's just the mistress's lot – crying more salt than Lot's wife ever did.'

'Then let him go,' Felix snapped tetchily. 'You can call me every bloody weekend, hold me as much as you like, tell me lots of amazing things and get as intimate as you want – in fact, please do. You don't need him now, you've got me.' Despite the light, slightly conceited tone, there was an urgent edge to his voice.

'And I thought you were frightened of commitment,' Phoebe smiled uncomfortably, aware that the woman behind them was sucking a pungent Pear Drop and listening in avidly.

'So are you,' Felix shrugged. 'But you want me more than you want Dan right now.'

His smooth arrogance, tinged with only the slightest trace of uncertainty, made Phoebe want to mob him up. Yet she found she couldn't. Instead the lump in her throat seemed to swell like rising bread dough in a hot kitchen as she realised he was spot on. Right now, she wanted him more than anything. Her pulse points were exploding like April buds, her legs were in serious need of callipers, her breath was coming out in shallow, ineffectual puffs which wouldn't blow the froth off a cappuccino in a glitzy Hollywood love-scene. This was no longer actressy artifice according to the Saskia Seaton rulebook; this was breathless, groin-thumping Fredericks desire at its most ungainly.

They passed the rest of the short journey in silence.

Felix saw her off at Paddington, kissing her thoroughly at the bus stop, beside the Casey Jones burger bar, at the ticket office, half way up the platform and then through the sliding door window of the Intercity train.

'Why d'you want to go to Berkshire anyway?' he sulkily complained again. 'I want you to come back with me for a hot bath, a huge breakfast and a long sleep.'

'I promised I'd visit this friend months ago,' Phoebe shrugged listlessly as the whistle blew, hating herself for her lies. 'She's been ill,' she added, deciding that it wasn't too much of an untruth.

'Well tell her to get well soon so that I can bloody well have you back.' Felix tried to keep pace as the train started to move off. 'I love – '

'Bye, Felix,' Phoebe began to slide up the window.

'And why haven't you got any luggage?' Felix mouthed as he stopped chasing the train and stood forlornly on the platform in its hissing wake – blond, beautiful and intensely irritated.

Good point, Phoebe realised as she weaved down the aisle and collapsed into a garish blue checked seat. Reaching for a discarded *Times*, she started to examine the crossword with half-focused eyes. After five minutes, she closed them tightly and sighed.

'I want to be in a hot bath with Felix,' she said out loud, astonishing both herself and three businessmen in pin-striped suits opposite her.

Saskia was waiting by the Golf in the car park of Hexbury station, smoking a Marlboro Light and reading a newspaper spread out on the car roof. Wearing a sweatshirt and cycling shorts, she had her black hair scraped back into a graduated plait beneath a New York Raiders baseball cap. She was also looking as though she'd shed the fat suit with the aid of a zip not a diet. Phoebe could hardly believe her eyes. The legs were almost back to their shapely, slender selves, the face almost recognisable again and close to beautiful.

Phoebe whooped in admiration. 'You look terrific,' she gasped, rushing forward to kiss her.

Saskia flinched away.

'Get in,' she hissed, nodding towards the passenger door.

'You look incredibly brown.' Phoebe swallowed anxiously, not at all sure how to cope with the frosty reception.

'Sun-bed,' Saskia climbed into the car. 'Get in then.'

Phoebe found herself sitting on a box of Clairol hair dye and two hundred Marlboro Lights.

'You dyeing again?' she asked as Saskia fired up the engine with a wail of Radio 1 from the speakers.

'No, I'm being born again blonde.' Saskia looked over her shoulder as she reversed. 'I hate black hair.'

Phoebe glanced across at her pinched, bronzed face and suddenly realised that Saskia wasn't looking quite so good after all. If she had lost weight then she had gained black rings under her eyes and sallow, lifeless skin that seemed to pucker her face like a deflating balloon.

As they spun around to career out of the car park, a copy of the *News* fluttered past the windscreen before sliding down the bonnet, part of the sports section trapped in the windscreen wiper. Saskia hit the brakes so hard that Phoebe felt like a driving test examiner tapping the windscreen with her clipboard.

'I want the Diary section from that.' Saskia leapt out of the driver's door, releasing the clutch so that the car stalled.

As Saskia scrabbled around on the tarmac in front of the Golf, Phoebe hastily pulled the hand-brake back, aware that they were on a slope. She then gave her neck a tentative prod, worried that she'd developed whiplash.

Saskia hadn't greeted her as she'd expected at all, she realised. She hadn't demanded to know the latest on the Felix situation. Phoebe flipped down the sun visor and checked that her stubble rash wasn't looking too obvious. Thankfully Felix's bristles were far less coarse than Dan's and she merely looked as though she had a healthy glow. Gibbering with guilt and terrified that Saskia could smell Felix on her, she wound down the window and clicked in her seatbelt.

When Saskia jumped back into the car, she threw a crumpled

piece of torn newsprint on to the back seat and slammed the door shut so violently that a can of de-icer shot off the dashboard caddy and onto Phoebe's lap.

'Shouldn't think you'll be in much need of that,' Saskia snarled, starting the engine again and pelting the Golf out of the car park.

'Why are you covered in dust?' she asked as they queued to get on to the Hexbury ring road, engine revving.

'I went riding this morning.' Phoebe bit her lip nervously.

'In London?'

'Hyde Park. We'd been clubbing. Seemed like a good idea at the time.'

'And you fell off?'

'Not exactly.' Phoebe fiddled with the de-icer can and tried to battle down the bubbling high of excitement as she remembered challenging Felix to a race and then, as they'd both reined to a hot, dusty halt beside the Serpentine, tumbling out of their saddles into such a laughing, play-fighting clinch that they'd ended up on the ground where they were almost trodden to death under hoof.

A tutting woman in a Hermès headscarf had reported them to the riding centre, from which they were now banned.

The latest number one romantic ballad was throbbing lovingly from Radio 1 now. Why was it that one only really listened to the lyrics and felt a buzz when one was lusting after someone? she wondered dreamily.

Then, looking across at Saskia and noticing that the set, blinking face was desperately fighting tears, she realised her friend was listening to the words too and feeling every sad, mournful declaration of love twice as sharply as she was.

Phoebe didn't utter another word until she heard the crunch of gravel under rubber tyre.

'I'm afraid the place is a shambles,' Saskia apologised as they raced along the drive. 'Tea-chests and dust sheets everywhere.'

'Oh, that's all – '

'Only your married lover bought the house this month.'

Phoebe fell silent again. God, she wished she hadn't come.

Gin and Tonic weren't there to meet them. Only the dogs spilled out of the house, tails gyrating, to greet her as she climbed from the Golf.

'Where's the Range Rover?' she looked around. 'Is Reg out gallivanting?'

'Sold.' Saskia clambered from the car and then reached in for her fags and Clairol. 'And Reg and Sheila have gone.'

'Gone?' Phoebe hung onto the car door for support.

'To somewhere near Reading, I think.'

Phoebe wanted to weep. She hadn't even had the chance to say goodbye and wish them luck.

As she walked into the house, the tight ball of emotion that was swelling in her throat threatened to explode out through her mouth in a loud, childish sob.

The busts had gone, as had the hats. Pale patches dominated the walls where paintings had recently hung; the drawers of the vast, antique Spanish sideboard were stacked up on its top, cleared of clutter. The hall had been stripped of its identity as surely as a brain-washed cult member was deprived of person-ality. Almost nothing of the Seatons' warm, loud, clannish presence remained stamped on it.

Phoebe fought a ludicrous urge to throw herself on to the dusty floor and bawl out loud. She also felt a silly, illogical need for Felix's reassuring arms around her, his strengthening kisses and daft, repetitive I love yous.

'I'm so sorry, Saskia,' she mumbled, her wet eyes scanning the bare walls.

'Of course you're fucking not.' Saskia stomped towards the faint wail of opera emitting from the distant kitchen. 'This all belongs to the tabloid fuck-monster now. You can come down for bucolic bonks when Mitzi's away.' She slammed her way through the green baize doors to the back lobby.

Phoebe hung behind and buried her face in a sympathetic Labrador pelt for a few seconds before following.

Gin was as stiff-backed, terse and unwelcoming as her daughter. She had the contents of the dresser spread out on the kitchen table and was alternately chucking things into cardboard boxes which she'd labelled 'Rubbish to stay', 'Rubbish to go' and 'Rubbish to argue about'.

She looked terrible. The blonde highlights which she'd had done during Phoebe's last stay were already sporting a streak of grey re-growth along the parting and had dried to a bleached frizz in places from hours of gardening without a sun-hat. She was wearing an ancient pair of creased cream shorts which had a grass-stained bottom, and an old checked shirt of Tony's with a tatty collar that swamped her tiny, stooping frame. Her brown legs were covered with dog-claw and bramble scratches and a chipped red toe-nail was poking out of a hole in her espadrilles.

She barely looked up from a pile of rosettes as Phoebe walked in. Tebbit rushed over, lips smacking with grinning joy, and scrabbled excitedly at her knees.

'Drink?' Saskia was rattling the kettle.

'Coffee, please.' Phoebe stifled a yawn and smiled warily at Gin. 'Hello.'

'How are you, Freddy?' The rosettes hit the 'Rubbish to go' box, their string ties draping over the cardboard rim like spaghetti.

'Fine, thanks. Very well.' Phoebe picked up Tebbit and gave him a cuddle. 'And you?'

'Don't ask stupid questions,' Gin snapped coldly, a tomato-shaped egg-timer flying into the 'Rubbish to stay' box.

'Freddy's just been to Paris, Mummy.' Saskia was scooping dessertspoons of instant coffee into three enormous mugs.

'Have you?' Gin peered at a pile of letters. 'That's nice. Did you go with a friend?'

'Sort of.' Phoebe stared at Saskia in amazement. What was she playing at? She cuddled Tebbit closer.

'That explains why your mother said you hadn't returned any of her calls.' Several letters flew towards the 'Argue' box and missed.

'Mummy?' Phoebe tensed slightly.

'Yes, she phoned yesterday.' Gin peered up over her half-moons critically. 'Sounded very chipper. She and your father had just been racing with a lot of Corporate big-wigs. I gave her our new address. She said how lucky we were not to be moving very far.'

Phoebe swallowed. 'I'm so sorry that you're losing this place,' she said cautiously. 'I know how much you love it. It must be heartbreaking.'

'It is,' Gin replied flatly, slinging out an old Summer Exhibition catalogue and several horse show schedules. 'Would you mind putting Tebbit down, Freddy? Only he has a bit of a rickety hip and isn't too fond of cuddles these days.'

Feeling like a scolded twelve-year-old, Phoebe did as she was told. She knew that Gin was picking on her because she was upset, but the sharp reprimand left her feeling even more tearful. She swallowed down the massive lump in her throat once more and blinked in horror as she noticed the pile of wedding invitations spilling out of the 'go' box.

'Can I help at all?' she asked quietly.

'No.' Gin's fingers were drumming on the table. 'Although it would make my life easier if you two girls got out from under my feet.' Her voice was shaking now as she battled tears and fury.

She hasn't once looked me in the eye, Phoebe realised wretchedly.

'We'll go in the garden.' Saskia posted a mug of coffee in front of her mother and then led the way through the kitchen door and out on to the back lawn.

Stumbling over piles of wellies beside the door as she followed, Phoebe clambered up the mossy steps and waded through the thick drought-dry grass in her snakeskin boots, thinking how trashy and London they must appear.

Saskia dropped down the steps beside some weed-infested lettuce frames and led the way towards the old hot-house that had been the scene of much childhood role play.

As she wandered inside, Phoebe vividly remembered re-enacting Charlie's Angels with the three youngest Seaton sisters years earlier. Gin had issued them all with cheap, plastic handbags that had been left over from a village jumble sale, and with cap guns and fake police badges. With these bags swinging from their shoulders, they had all raced around Deayton chasing imaginary underworld drug mobsters, pausing only occasionally to reapply their lipstick. All, that is, except Phoebe who, as the fourth member of the team, had been issued with the role of Boswell, the slow-speaking stooge. As such, she'd been permanently posted in the hot-house with an old Bakelite phone, pretending to liaise with Charlie. On the odd occasion that she'd seen any action, it had taken the form of being tied to a chair by the imaginary gangsters and left there until the Angels had solved the mystery and returned to base to find her. This was usually long after tea.

The same collection of old, woodwormed chairs were thick with cobwebs in one corner along with several deck-chairs with torn, faded canvas seats, and a rusty cast-iron table on which tens of broken flower pots were stacked like the terracotta army's mess tea cups.

The dusty windows were almost white with bleached sunlight, broken by shadowed veins from the branches of the apple trees on the lawn.

Saskia put the coffee mugs down on a rickety trestle table and perched on a window ledge.

'Do you think I've lost weight?'

'Of course you have.' Phoebe took her coffee and blew on it awkwardly. 'Lots. I can't believe you've lost so much, so fast.'

'I've done a lot of exercise – and pill-popped a bit.'

'Isn't that dangerous? I thought one was supposed to do these things gradually.'

'Well, we can't all be fucking broomsticks who can guzzle as much as we like without getting fat!' Saskia hissed. 'So what the fuck do you know about it?' She stood up and kicked a deck-chair, which toppled over in a cloud of dust.

'I didn't sleep with him, Saskia.' Phoebe finally realised what was going on.

'No?' Saskia's voice was a high, tight pip of disbelief.

'No.'

'Oh, thank you – thank you, thank you, Freddy!' Laughing

and crying at the same time with the whooshing pressure-release of relief, Saskia raced across and enveloped her in a huge, twirling hug.

Trying not to tense up, Phoebe allowed herself to be spun around in a few euphoric pirouettes.

'You can't *believe* how relieved I am!' Saskia sobbed between smiles. 'I've been going through seven kinds of hell worrying about it. Oh, God! I'm such a bitch for even thinking that you would. Will you forgive me, Freddy? Forgive a suspicious, scheming, stupid old cow?'

Phoebe shrugged and forced a smile too. 'You've been under tons of pressure – and I didn't help by not calling you enough. But I ran out of money.'

'You must tell me *all* about it. Top to snakeskin toe – I bet Felix loves those boots, doesn't he?'

'Yup.'

'Okay. Park your suede bum on something that won't wreck those lovely trousers and then tell all.' Saskia danced around the hot-house, setting up a little interview room.

Sagging down on to an upturned bucket and scratching her head, Phoebe took a huge gulp of coffee and rubbed her eyes. She was beginning to feel so fatigued that her vision was blurring. She allowed herself a few shuddering yawns and tried not to think about Felix curled up in his big, plumptuous duvet back in the mews cottage with her copy of *Skinny Legs and All* which he'd now become too engrossed in to let go.

He was probably sleeping off the excesses of the night now, she realised; his long, sooty lashes pressed to those tanned cheeks, straight nose tucked into the crook of his elbow.

Within minutes, Phoebe realised that all was the last thing Saskia in fact wanted to hear. Sitting cross-legged on an old swing-chair cushion with her chin pressed into her hands and her blue-grey eyes raking Phoebe's face like a baby transfixed by a tumble-drier, she started arguing and picking holes as though the story could be changed as she wanted it.

'He can't have said that!' she wailed. 'Felix never talks about his parents. He's ridiculously screwed up about them.'

'Maybe it's because he was drunk, I don't know.' Phoebe rubbed her forehead, feeling hopelessly disloyal to Felix all of a sudden. 'I think the fact that his mother phoned him last week probably triggered off a lot of anger too. He wanted to get it out.'

'He probably told you a pack of lies to make you feel sorry for him – that's a classic Felix tactic.'

Letting this pass, Phoebe tried to tell Saskia about him picking up on every one of her own lies, but Saskia was barely listening.

'Did he go back to his hotel that night?'

'I told you, he was staying in a flat which belonged to this girl called Mia. I think she was a stylist.' Phoebe sighed. 'But she told him to get stuffed pretty soon after I turned up.'

'So he stayed with you?'

'Yes.'

'So you *did* sleep together?'

'If me passing out drunk on the same bed as him fully clothed constitutes sleeping together then, yes. He was in the shower by the time I woke up.'

'But you said you hadn't slept with him!' Saskia ran her bitten nails back through her hair.

'I didn't sleep with him. I was unconscious with him.'

'You didn't screw?'

'Of course we bloody didn't. I couldn't have screwed in a lightbulb without electrocuting myself that night.'

'But you kissed him.'

'We'd already kissed that night in Camden,' Phoebe reminded her, trying to sound calm. 'I told you about that. I could hardly close my mouth and clench my teeth in Paris.'

'Did you enjoy it?'

'What?'

'You heard me.' Saskia looked up through her fingers. 'Did you enjoy kissing Felix?'

'If I said no, would you believe me?'

'No.' Saskia pushed the palms of her hands into her eyes. 'I'm so sorry, Phoebe. Really I am. I know I asked you to do this. I know I'm being an ungrateful bitch. But it hurts so much. It just hurts – so – much.'

'I know.' Phoebe closed her own eyes. It was hurting her too.

'He says he loves me, Saskia.' Her voice almost broke as she spoke the words.

The silence that followed stretched into taut, impenetrable minutes. Her face cramped with guilt, Phoebe watched the blurred outline of a hot air balloon through the dirty window as it travelled right the way across the horizon, hissing its gas burner sporadically. She could hear her heartbeat speeding up, could feel the sweat rising on her forehead and the tired, neuralgic little tic in her eye twitching at the lid more and more often until she was winking like a pervert in a brothel.

'I thought it was what you wanted?' she said eventually, desperate to break the hot, airless tension.

Saskia, her hands in her hair, was biting at her bare knees with her eyes scrunched tightly shut.

'I did,' she croaked in a shaky whisper.

Phoebe dropped on to her haunches beside her.

'Don't touch me!' she hissed, wrapping herself into a tight ball and flinching away.

Phoebe bit her lip. 'Do you want me to leave you alone for a bit?'

Still curled up like a battered dog, Saskia didn't answer.

'I'm sure he doesn't really mean it.' Phoebe fought to keep her voice from wobbling. 'Every time he says it to me, I tell him he doesn't and he just smiles and takes it. It's like you said about him finding it as easy to repeat as the alphabet, but not meaning – '

'Yes!' Saskia snarled.

'What?' Phoebe almost fell over backwards with the force of her venom.

'Yes, I want you to leave me alone,' Saskia mumbled tearfully into her knees. 'Just leave me alone, Freddy.'

Phoebe wandered rather aimlessly around the garden for a few minutes, trailed by one of the Labradors which was pushing a furry, damp tennis ball into her calves, anxious for a game. She was so tired and distracted that she continually tripped and stumbled over divots. At one point she wandered straight into the path of the lawn sprinkler and, for a few listless, distracted moments, assumed that it was suddenly raining.

She trailed back to the low, shady sunken terrace that ran beside the kitchen and sat on the wall, well away from the kitchen windows so that Gin wouldn't spot her moping presence. Dropping her face into her hands, she prayed that Saskia wouldn't hate her forever.

'I did as I was told,' she muttered to herself. 'I made him fall for me. I made him like me and trust me and want to bed me. I just wish I didn't feel the same fucking way about him. Oh, God!'

'Freddy?'

Phoebe almost fell off the wall as she looked up and saw Gin squinting at her over the rim of the 'Rubbish to go' box. She was clearly en route to the wheely bins, buckling under the weight of dresser detritus. She had also heard every word.

'Feel the same way about who, Freddy?' she asked rather impatiently, her sympathy not at its most attuned.

Phoebe stifled a sob.

Gin peered at her more closely. 'Are you upset about something?'

Feeling as though her heart was being chewed out from her chest, Phoebe fought an urge to run along the terrace and throw herself into the shallow, slimy silt of the swimming pool.

'Look, I'll just sling this rubbish out and then we'll have a massive, pre-lunch G and T, shall we?' Gin gave her shoulders a bolstering nudge. 'In fact, I've just dug out all the photo albums from the dresser ready to pack, so we could have a bit of a giggle over those to take our minds off things. There are loads of shots of you with braces on your teeth as you beam out that big, winning smile of yours.'

'Actually, Gin,' Phoebe sniffed apologetically, 'would you mind awfully if I had a bath? I know it's terribly rude, but – '

'Of course you can, Fred,' Gin laughed, standing up. 'In fact, by way of apology for being such an old bag, I'll even run it for you.'

'No, really.'

'I insist.' Gin stood up. 'I'll just pop upstairs. You bung that box in the bin, darling, and then fix yourself a drink to snorkel in the bath.'

With another encouraging pat on Phoebe's shoulder, she went inside, pursued by her coterie of dogs.

Phoebe's head was just sliding under the scented surface of the bath water when there was a loud banging on the door.

She woke up with such a start that most of the contents of the bath slopped out on to the wooden floor and Tony's flannel shot up into the air, landing with a plop in the scummy water. Water that was freezing, she realised. She must have cried herself to sleep.

'Phoebe, are you all right in there?' Gin shouted through the door.

'Fine!' she called back groggily, rubbing her eyes with fingers as wrinkled as raisins. 'Sorry, I fell asleep.'

'Lunch is ready whenever you are.'

'Thanks.'

Phoebe reared out of the bath and, stepping out on to the slippery, wet floor, almost went flying. She gripped the side of the bath and reached across for a towel.

Her clothes, lying in a crumpled heap beneath her, were soaking wet. As she didn't have anything to change into, she picked them up and wrung them out over the bath. The suede jeans would dry like chamois leather, she realised.

Wrapping herself in the towel, she wandered over to the mirrored cabinet and squinted at her reflection. As she'd dreaded, her eyes had puffed into two tiny slits and her nose was the only spot of colour in her white face. Even her lips appeared to have drained of blood. She supposed that was because her nose was so big, it needed a big supply to keep it glowing.

There was another knock on the door, lighter and less decisive this time.

'Freddy?'

'Saskia?' Phoebe gaped at her reflection in horror.

'Can I come in?'

Blinking hard in an attempt to open her eyes slightly wider, she slid back the lock.

A pair of equally puffy eyes peered around the door at her.

They stared at one another for a few seconds, each taking in the other's unrecognisable face.

'I think this is the point where we burst out laughing and hug one another,' Phoebe smiled weakly.

'This isn't fucking "Peter's Friends", Freddy.' Saskia pushed past her. 'There's some lunch ready downstairs. Pa has just thrown a purple fit because you're here and is sulking in front of the one-thirty at Doncaster with a scotch the size of an elephant's urine sample.'

'Because I'm here?' Phoebe closed the door and pulled her towel tighter for support. Somehow she knew what Saskia was about to say.

'The Neashams are – '

'– coming for dinner.' Phoebe closed her eyes.

'Lunch tomorrow, actually.' Saskia reached into the bathroom cabinet for some Optrex.

'I can be gone by then.'

'Just try it.' Saskia unscrewed the bottle lid. 'Ma is humming like an old kettle downstairs right now and planning a huge birthday lunch for us both. She's still blissfully unaware of any connection between her darling Freddy and the see-you-later-litigator.'

'Oh, God.' Phoebe sat down on the side of the bath.

'Are you and Dan still an item, then?' Saskia's hands were shaking as she poured Optrex into the eye-bath.

'I'm not sure.' Phoebe picked up her damp jeans. 'He's rented me a flat.'

'Really?' Saskia placed the tub over her eye and knocked her head back. 'Well you must be pretty permanent then?'

'I don't want it.'

'Oh.' dipping her head, Saskia moved on to the other eye.

'I don't even know that I want Dan any more,' Phoebe found herself suddenly confessing. 'Not the way things seem to be going, anyway. I don't want to be organised into his after-work schedule along with the gym, the club and the London dinner parties.'

'He's married and he's got a hugely stressful job, Phoebe,' Saskia said bluntly, tipping her head back. 'You can hardly expect much spontaneity. He has to slot you into his agenda like any other meeting, or he'd never have time to meet you at all.'

'Maybe it would be better if he didn't.' Phoebe could barely bring herself to say it.

'You mean you want to end it?' Saskia turned to gape at her, pinning the Optrex tub to one eye with her finger like a blue plastic pirate's patch.

'I should never have let it start up again,' she muttered. 'It was selfish and stupid of me.'

'Of Dan, you mean.' Saskia turned back to the mirror, one blue eye wide with worry. 'He's taking it too fast. You should be flattered; it shows how much he wants you.'

Phoebe gaped at her. Saskia, as far as she remembered, had been dead against Phoebe resurrecting anything with Dan in case it interfered with her plan. Now she was sounding like a dating agent with a commission target to make up.

Summoning her nerve, she realised that she would have to confess yet another unplanned twist in Saskia's carefully plotted revenge tragedy.

'And Felix knows about it,' she mumbled.

'You told Felix?' gasped Saskia.

'He found a photograph in my purse. And he spoke to Dan on the phone when he was trying to contact me from Paris.' Phoebe hung her head. 'I know I'm a fucking imbecile, but that friend's flat, I told you about . . .'

'It was the one Dan's rented for you?' Saskia finished in a horrified voice. 'Why, Freddy? Of all the stupid – '

'It was new and weird and unreal,' Phoebe tried to explain, picking up her soggy, crumpled silver top. 'I guess I wasn't taking the flat – or Felix – seriously. And I had no idea Dan would be there. It was incredibly unlucky.'

Saskia headed for the door. 'I'm going to get you some clean clothes, Freddy,' she snapped.

She was back moments later with a repulsive-looking lime green jogging suit.

Aware that it would cheer Saskia up to see her in it, Phoebe swallowed her pride and donned both parts. It transformed her into a squishy, skinned kiwi fruit.

Gin was calling them for lunch again.

'Are you coming down?' Phoebe asked Saskia as she rolled back the sleeves of the jogging suit until she found her hands.

'No, I'm not hungry,' she lied. 'I'm going to bleach my hair. Bung your wet stuff in the laundry cupboard.'

On her way back from the laundry, Phoebe found Saskia sitting at the top of the stairs, wearing a pair of plastic gloves and reading her hair-dye instructions.

'How did he react?' she looked up.

'What?'

'Felix. How did he react when he found out about Dan?'

Phoebe looked into her face and knew that she couldn't possibly tell Saskia about Felix clinging on to her and burying his face in her stomach as he blurted out the awful, agonising history of his parents' infidelities.

'He told me I was a tart, compared Dan to his philandering father and hasn't mentioned it since,' she said quickly. 'I think he assumes I'll dump Dan for him.'

'Typical Felix.'

Seeming satisfied, Saskia stood up and wandered through to the bathroom.

In the kitchen, Gin was poring over the photograph albums.

'Freddy – look, lots of pics of you and the girls. There's even one or two of me looking very Sloane Ranger before I – ' Looking up over her spectacles, Gin stared at Phoebe in amazement. 'Freddy darling, you're wearing Tonic's old jogging suit.'

For the next hour, Phoebe chomped her way through several cheese and pickle sandwiches and indulged Gin in fond reminiscences of those jolly, far-off days. While Gin flipped the stiff pages and swigged back wine, Phoebe winced at the numerous shots of herself looking like a tall, mousy ironing board alongside the slender, blonde-maned beauty of the Seaton sisters. Over and over again, she caught sight of her youthful little face beaming out a brave, false smile and was reminded of how cruel the summer holiday bullying had been.

'I'm going to throw you and Saskia a bit of a party tomorrow,' Gin said as she peered at a shot of Phoebe smiling a toothache smile on the night of her eighteenth birthday.

'That's truly lovely of you, Gin,' Phoebe swallowed anxiously.

An hour later, Saskia's hair had turned a slightly khaki fawn, but it was a vast improvement on the funereal black, and lightening her hair seemed to have lightened her mood. Smothering precious Lalique figurines in great wads of the *Daily Telegraph* and ramming them rather carelessly into a tea-chest, she talked endlessly about how Phoebe was going to chuck Felix to best effect.

'Fliss said you were thinking about doing it at her murder mystery party,' she said excitedly.

'Did she?' Phoebe mumbled.

Her stomach awash with cheese and pickle, she was starting to feel slightly queasy.

'I think it's a brilliant idea,' Saskia enthused. 'Particularly if we can get a lot of his friends to go along. You said you went out clubbing with them last night?'

'Yes, but we didn't really mix much.'

'It doesn't matter. If you get Felix to go along, they'll follow.' Saskia reached for a Staffordshire dog. 'They're like ducklings. Have you asked him?'

'Not yet, no.'

'Ask him when you see him next. Let's think. When's the Bank Holiday?'

'Fortnight.'

Phoebe was feeling sicker and sicker. She sat on a squeaky leather sofa arm and pressed the cool bronze of a galloping huntsman to her forehead.

'See him non-stop between now and then,' Saskia told her. 'It shouldn't be hard. I know Felix when he's into someone – he'll want to be with you all the time. And you'll have to find a very subtle way of mentioning that I'll be at the party.'

'What?' Phoebe almost dropped the bronze huntsman.

Saskia looked at her angrily. 'I'm not missing this,' she snapped. 'I want to see him burning in hell. I'm having a front row seat, knitting on my lap and camera in my hand.'

'I know – I know, of course,' Phoebe said weakly, bile climbing her throat. 'I just can't think how to tell him without his guessing.'

'Say I'm a friend of Fliss's. Better still, that I'm Stan's girlfriend. I'll square it with him.'

'Do I have to mention it at all?'

'He might do a runner if he turns up on Friday afternoon and comes face to face with me.' Saskia applied the *Telegraph*'s Weekend Review section to a second Staffordshire dog. 'I think he needs to be warned.'

'In which case he might not come at all,' Phoebe reasoned.

'Point taken.' Saskia flicked back her khaki hair. 'Just say you think one of his exes might be coming, but you can't remember her name.'

Phoebe felt too sick to argue. 'I don't actually think Fliss has a venue for this party,' she told Saskia, trying hard to sound disappointed.

'Yes, she has,' Saskia said smoothly.

'What?'

'I rang your flat yesterday to see if you were back. We got talking and she told me about her lack of a big, stately Agatha Christie-style pile. So I said she could use this place.'

'You what?' Phoebe gaped at her.

'The Neashams take possession on the first of September. Ma and Pa are planning to move out before Bank Holiday. It seemed ideal.' Saskia laughed. 'So I offered Fliss this place.

She was over the moon and said something about having asked Mungo already.'

'Oh, Christ.' Phoebe sagged back in to the sofa. 'But he's gay, isn't he?'

'Swings both ways, I think.' Saskia didn't quite look her in the eyes.

'Not towards Fliss.'

'Wouldn't imagine she'd be his secret fantasy, no.'

'She's Dylan's.' Phoebe decided it was time to be indiscreet.

'Dylan Abbott?' Saskia dropped a hound with a hollow clunk. 'My – I mean Felix's – Dylan?'

'I think so.' Phoebe pulled an anxious face. 'I don't think she's even really noticed him.'

Saskia came to sit beside her.

'This Bank Holiday weekend party,' she said slowly, 'is going to be a wine, dine and minefield.'

That night, despite wracking, cramping tiredness, Phoebe couldn't sleep. She wound herself into a papoose as she tossed around in her sheets and counted more sheep than a New Zealand dipper, but still she lay awake, staring at the ceiling with wide-open eyes, buzzing nerve-endings and twitching ankles.

At one in the morning, she slipped downstairs and, fighting off the attentions of several sleepy, crotch-sniffing dogs, opened the fridge.

It illuminated the sparse, packed-away kitchen with its cool, blue light. Inside tomorrow's lunch was waiting to be cooked – a huge side of pork dominated the fridge, which was devoid of plastic shelves in order to accommodate it. She ate a couple of mushrooms and a tomato from the salad tray, searching around all the time for some chocolate. There was none. Grabbing an apple and then collecting a photo album from the top of the pile on the kitchen table, she wandered through to the scruffier drawing room in order to let the dogs sleep in peace.

Settling down on an ancient, scuffed velvet chaise, she flipped open the album and almost choked on her apple.

It was full of pictures of Felix and Saskia, beaming like a

couple in a coffee commercial from every sofa, chair and garden bower in Deayton. Even the dogs sucked up to Felix, staring at him in the same adoring manner as Saskia did.

Within minutes, Phoebe was in tears. Not thinking what she was doing, she raced over to the phone by the *Country Life*s and, after a couple of wrong numbers, dialled Albany Mews.

Felix picked up the call within two rings.

'It's me,' she blurted, hopelessly tearful.

'I was hoping you'd call,' he laughed sleepily. 'How are you? How are your mysterious friends?'

'Hell,' she was trying hard not to sob.

'I miss you,' he dropped his voice to a smoky whisper. 'I've been thinking about you all fucking day. God, I wish you were here now.'

'Do you?' Phoebe gave way to a slight sob.

'Yes, I bloody do.'

She couldn't speak for relief.

'Phoebe darling, are you all right?'

'Not really,' she sobbed, suddenly finding that she couldn't hold back the tears long enough to hang up with dignity.

'Phoebe, shh. Darling – hshhh. Oh God,' he sounded incredibly worried. 'What is it, baby? Is it Dan? Don't tell me you're with that fucking – '

'No, it's not Dan,' she sobbed. 'Well not really. Yes, it bloody is. Felix, he's co-coming to lunch tomorrow. With his wife. I d-don't know what to do. I think we're washed up. I want to end it.'

Why the hell was she telling him this? she thought in horror.

Felix had gone very quiet and, for a moment, Phoebe thought that he'd hung up on her. She buried her face in a velvet sofa arm and tried not to howl.

'Phoebe?'

'You're still there!' she gasped, wiping her wet eyes and smiling with relief. The tears ebbed away as quickly as they had risen.

'Of course I bloody am,' he sighed. 'Phoebe, I can't tell you what to do, can I? I mean you know what I'm dying for you to do.'

'I know,' she hiccuped.

'It's up to you,' he took a deep, noisy breath and then released it with a lot of phone blow-back.

'I know,' she repeated, suddenly wanting to talk to him for hours. She snuggled tightly into the arm of the sofa and let the final, wracking shudder of tears course up her back-bone.

'I love you.'

'I know,' Phoebe forced herself to drop the phone back on the hook. She then pressed her wet eyes onto it.

'I thought you always said "you don't love me, Felix darling",' hissed a tearful voice. 'You fucking liar, Freddy.'

Phoebe twisted around so sharply that her neck cricked.

Standing in the doorway, shaking with fury, Saskia's silhouette was as black as Phoebe's conscience. As Saskia backed tearfully away towards the stairs, Phoebe could see the portable phone from the landing clutched in her hand and realised that she must have heard every word.

33

'Happy birthday, darling,' Gin deposited a tray of toast, orange juice and tea onto Phoebe's duvet. 'Sorry if I pong of cider – I'm not a secret swigger, I promise – I've been stuffing the pork. I've left Saskia's tray outside her door like a hotel breakfast. See if you can get her out of her ten-tog, could you, Freddy?'

'I'll try.'

'Many happy returns.'

'Thanks.'

'Oh – we've got the house-buyers coming to lunch, by the way.' She turned around in the doorway. 'The Neashams – of course, you've met them. Silly me. That's all right then. See you downstairs.'

Phoebe fed her toast to a visiting Labrador and deliberated between the enormous green jogging suit and her crispy black suede trousers which had dried to a solid crust in the airing cupboard. She didn't dare ask Saskia if she could borrow something.

Phoning Felix last night, she reflected sadly, had not been one of her greatest moves. Not only had she blown her cover wide open by showing him how vulnerable she could be, she had also managed simultaneously to kick Saskia in the teeth.

'You're dangerous, Phoebe,' she muttered to her reflection in the dressing table mirror. She was amazed to see that instead of looking haggard and puffy-eyed, her face was glowing healthily after its first decent sleep in days.

After a quick shower in her little guest bathroom, she eased herself into the suede trousers and then limbered up around her room for a few minutes in order to soften them up enough to move without watering eyes. But, even after a couple of attempts at the splits and a very wobbly set of high-kicks, she still felt as though she was wearing the lower half of a rusty suit of armour.

Still naked from the waist up, she was sitting cross-legged on the bed and painting her face with what little make-up she had with her when Saskia slammed into the room like a whirlwind in a hurry.

'Happy birthday,' she threw a pile of clothes onto the bed, not looking at Phoebe. 'If you're going to let Dan have it in the face with Attitude, you might as well do it in style. I can't fit into these any more. Have them.' She raced back out again.

'Thanks. Happy Bir—' Phoebe jumped as the door was slammed shut with a bang as loud as a gunshot.

Seconds later, Saskia had punched it open again and was peering at her through a six-inch gap.

'You are going to do it, aren't you?'

'What?' Phoebe gaped at her, an eye pencil poised in one hand.

'Do what Felix wants! Dump Dan.'

Phoebe winced as she jabbed herself in the eye with the sharpened nub of charcoal brown kohl pencil.

'Well not here and now,' she spluttered. 'Not today, no.'

'I would,' Saskia narrowed her blue eyes, her voice a hard, hushed demand. 'You want to, don't you? You said so yesterday.'

'I know I did, but – '

'Do it today then,' Saskia nodded at the clothes. 'I'll help.'

With another loud, wood-splintering bang of the door, she was gone.

Phoebe looked into her compact and found that she'd covered her face with eye-pencil in fright, so that she now resembled a Maori warrior.

*   *   *

Three quarters of an hour later, Phoebe slipped downstairs. The sense of déjà vu was now so intense that she was almost tempted to run through the recipe for guacamole in her head before popping into the study to see if Tony was waiting to warn her off once more.

Taking a deep breath and licking her lips nervously, she wandered into the drawing room.

The French windows were open, letting in a sharp breeze, a waft of slurry pit and a babble of polite conversation. Out on the higher of Deayton's two terraces, Gin, Tony and the Neashams were sipping white wine and burbling politely. Dan was bored and made no attempt to hide it. Pulling impatiently at a Silk Cut, he leaned on the terrace's cast-iron railing and squinted up at the house as though staring at an unwanted baby.

Backing away from the window slightly, Phoebe watched him.

She couldn't help herself; lust still pummelled her in the groin and total, helpless longing knocked the air from her lungs. But she was aware of a shift in mental attitude. She could stare at the wedding ring on his left hand without her eyes starting to prickle and could calmly tell herself that he was really quite short, without her conscience arguing that no, it was she who was, in fact, freakishly tall.

Suddenly his roan eyes dropped to the level of the window she was lurking behind and he stared straight at her.

Phoebe ducked away, but it was too late. Dan's crystal wine glass went crashing onto the paving stones.

Tony began the 'please don't apologise at all' platitudes long before Mitzi started apologising on behalf of her silent husband. Dan, seemingly freeze-framed, was too shocked to speak.

As she heard Gin excusing herself to fetch a cloth, Phoebe bolted across the hallway to the scruffier drawing room and pressed herself to a panelled wall away from the door, heart pounding. She could hear Dan asking directions to the lavatory now, followed by Mitzi telling him off in a loud, embarrassed honk.

'We've been around this house three times, darling – surely

you can remember where at least one loo is located? What is the matter with you today?'

The phone was still tucked in the sofa where she had left it last night, Phoebe noticed. Next to it was the fat, leather-bound photo album that she'd been unable to bring herself to look through after her disastrous call. Biting her lip, she remembered Felix's concern and worry, his complete lack of scorn when she'd started rambling on about Dan. Then she blushed as she recalled that she'd blubbed very noisily down the phone before hanging up on him.

She listened as Gin's footsteps clacked away through the baize doors. A few seconds later the court shoes were followed by the softer, heavier pad of Chelsea boots on the polished hall floor.

She pressed herself tighter to the panelling and held her breath.

'Phoebe?' a voice whispered on the other side of the door.

She could see the edge of a lock of bitter chocolate hair poking past the door.

Suddenly Gin's court shoes clacked back into earshot.

Dan leapt through the doorway and ducked out of view, his back to her.

She watched him as he listened to Gin clicking past. His hair was on end, his collar turned up by mistake, the back of his cotton jacket crumpled from sitting in a car for so long. His bum wasn't nearly as great as Felix's either, she realised.

'Hi, Dan,' she stepped forwards, instantly determined.

Dan span around and gaped at her. The delighted, crinkly smile was almost too much to bear.

'You look utterly, utterly gorgeous,' he breathed, glancing anxiously over his shoulder. 'Christ, I thought I was seeing things back there.'

His eyes slithered very slowly up and down her body.

'Close the door, Dan.' Phoebe rolled her eyes towards the hall.

Dan pushed the door to without taking his eyes from her.

Phoebe wondered if the outfit hadn't been a bit too much. She supposed a skimpy, boot-lace-strap floral dress in

translucent silk chiffon and no shoes was a bit wild-child of
nature for the commuter belt. But it certainly had Attitude –
sullen, sulky, sexy, sixties attitude. And right now she needed
every flimsy floral inch of it.

'I had no idea you'd be here,' he breathed, inching forwards.
'I've been phoning you all bloody week.'

'It was a last minute decision.' Phoebe dodged to one side. 'I
only flew back on Friday.'

Dan abruptly stopped inching.

'From Paris?' his eyes narrowed.

'Yes,' Phoebe matched his gaze. Act like a bitch from hell,
give him hell and then run like hell, she told herself firmly.

'I waited for hours on Tuesday.' He rubbed his hair tetchily.
'You could have left a fucking message to let me know that you
wouldn't be there.'

About to tell him about the unposted note, Phoebe stopped
herself and shrugged.

'The flat looked as minimalist as a naturist's wardrobe,' Dan
went on in a hushed, accusing whisper. 'I take it you haven't
moved in yet?'

'I'm not going to,' she cleared her throat.

He stared back in amazement.

They both froze as someone came thundering down the stairs
and then clattered across the hall to the main drawing room,
followed by a scrabble of pursuing dog claws on polished wood.

'It's Saskia,' Phoebe muttered. 'She's gone outside.'

Dan sighed with relief. He glanced at his watch, clearly
working out how long he could justifiably be on the loo.

'Okay, let's quickly back track a bit here,' he walked across to
the velvet settee and sat down, his voice hushed to an accusatory
whisper. 'I want to get a few things straight before we start
discussing the ethics of assured short-hold tenancies. Like what
in Christ's name you were doing in Paris with Felix Sylvian this
week?' He adopted his clipped, abrupt legal manner as he
indicated a threadbare armchair opposite him.

Phoebe didn't move.

'I must say I've been trying to justify your actions all week,'

Dan went on in a muted snarl, glancing edgily at the door. He picked up the photograph album and placed it on his lap as though holding his clutch of legal notes.

Phoebe held her breath.

'I want an exceptionally good explanation for this, Phoebe,' he flipped open the album in the same manner as a power-crazed boss rustling busily through paperwork while he reprimands an employee. 'Because I'm feeling pretty bloody wound up about it. Are you and Felix Sylvian – Shit!'

Phoebe closed her eyes.

'This is him, isn't it?' he muttered, turning stiff pages in horrified fascination.

'Yes.'

'Here – in this house. Him in this house.'

'Yes.'

Dan paused over a couple of shots, absorbing the handsome, smiling face.

'Who's the girl?' He glanced up at Phoebe and then back down at the book. 'She looks a bit like you – same hair. Christ, she's even wearing the same bloody dress in this one.'

'It's Saskia.' Phoebe couldn't bring herself to look at him.

'Saskia?' Dan laughed. 'You've got to be – ' he suddenly stared at the door in horror.

It was swinging open very, very slowly as though pushed by a tentative, tearful hand.

Dan quailed back in the sofa. Phoebe tried to make a bare-footed dash for the curtains.

With a low, nosy whine, a grey, grizzled dog snout appeared, gave a thoughtful sniff and then nosed its way into the room followed by a stout, undulating body and waggling black tail.

Just as Dan and Phoebe were breathing out, a voice honked, 'Dan? Where the bloody hell are you?'

Phoebe thanked God that she wasn't wearing shoes as she pelted silently behind the door with half a second to spare.

'What are you doing in here?' Mitzi barged in.

Trying not to breathe, Phoebe pressed herself against the wall and listened as a pair of sensible heels marched across to Dan.

'Just getting a feel for the place, darling,' he lied with surprising cool. Phoebe couldn't help admiring him. The snake.

'Hiding from Tony Seaton, you mean,' Mitzi sighed irritably. 'You could try to look just slightly interested when he talks. Are those family pics?' She had clearly clocked the album. 'Not snooping on our hosts, are we? Gosh, he's a bit of a hunk. Isn't that one of the Seaton girls with him?'

'Hullo there!' oozed an ingratiating voice from the door. 'Wondered where you'd got to, Dan. See Mitzi's run you to ground.'

Phoebe squinted through the hinged gap and spotted Tony Seaton's bulk hovering in the doorframe with a glass of wine and an oily smile.

'I must apologise – you've caught us snooping at some shots of your gorgeous family, Tony,' Mitzi said smoothly. 'There's one of you here looking very dashing in your shooting garb. Grief! Is that Camilla Parker–Bowles stalking past in the background with a couple of brace?'

Tony plodded across the room.

'It's Gin,' he guffawed.

'Don't they look similar, though?' Mitzi said sweetly. 'Same aristocratic gait.'

Silly old bitch, Phoebe smarted on Gin's behalf. Then she shrank deeper into the shadow of the door as she noticed the grey-muzzled Labrador creeping up on her, tail thumping against the panelling, brown eyes shining with eagerness.

'Is this one of your married daughters?' Mitzi was asking.

'Ahh – no,' Tony coughed uncomfortably. 'That's Saskia with her fiancé last year. I – '

'How lovely!' she gushed. 'I must say, he's a gorgeous-looking boy.'

'They're no longer together.' Tony said flatly.

Phoebe tried to bat the Labrador away, but it was snuffling ever closer, clearly dead-set on a friendly goose up the chiffon dress.

'Oh, I'm so sorry,' Mitzi was apologising.

'No need – you weren't to know. Nasty business, really. Best not talked about,' Tony forced a hearty laugh. 'Now do come through to the kitchen for a re-fill.'

'What on earth's that dog doing?' Mitzi laughed, trying to lighten the atmosphere.

Phoebe stopped breathing. The grinning Labrador rammed its snout up her dress and she held back a pained yelp as a cold wet nose made contact with her skin. The next moment a great long tongue slurped across her clenched thigh.

'Probably got a chew stuck back there,' Tony guffawed, grateful for the jokey feed. 'I'll just get – '

'I'll get it!' Dan yelped.

He dragged the Labrador away by the collar as Tony and Mitzi trooped out. When he looked up at Phoebe, he glowered at her. 'We'll talk later,' he mouthed, disappearing with the sound of scraped claws.

They ate lunch in the garden, grouped around a wide wooden table that smelled of potting compost and weedkiller. The dogs lolled nearby, stretched out like morning-after orgy-goers as they propped muzzles on one another's backs and panted, pink-tongued, in the mean shade of the branches overhead.

A sharp breeze was whipping around the side of the house, constantly threatening to snatch napkins from laps and to whip Phoebe's dress into indecency.

'I think you look gorgeous, Freddy,' Gin said over and over again.

Tony cut her short each time with an embarrassed cough.

'Try honey tea with a dash of essential oil,' Mitzi twinkled at him sympathetically. 'I swear by it whenever I have a bit of a hack.'

'Hasn't had one of those since she chatted up James Whittaker at Andrew Neil's fiftieth,' Dan muttered under his breath. 'Terrific wine, Tony – is it Chevalier-Montrachet?' He was drinking far too much of it.

'Of course it is, darling,' Mitzi hissed in an undertone. 'It says so on the label. You've just read it – I saw your mouth move.'

'It's both Freddy and Saskia's birthdays today,' Gin told Mitzi excitedly, as oblivious of any cross currents as a chain ferry. 'They've been chums since they were ankle-biters. Went through school together and still as thick as thieves.'

'Really?' Mitzi smiled politely at Saskia, who was prodding her starter tartlet with a fork like a gamekeeper flipping over a dead fox.

'We're still thick,' Saskia stared back at her earnestly. 'Although we've cut down on the shop-lifting since Phoebe was done over for that jar of cuticle cream in Superdrug.'

Mitzi almost choked on a corn salad leaf and then laughed cheerily as she finally caught the joke. She gave Phoebe a cautious look, remembering the village loon of the dinner party quick-exit routine. It had taken her a few minutes to recognise Phoebe with her glossy black bob.

'You two even seem to share hair-care tips,' she sipped her mineral water. 'Last time I saw you girls, you were dark-haired, Saskia, and Freda was blonde.'

'Mouse,' Dan hiccuped slightly.

'Sorry, darling?' Mitzi stiffened.

'Phoebe was mouse, not blonde,' he continued, reaching unsteadily for his wine. 'Or at least I think she was – you are the girl from the dinner party a few weeks ago, aren't you?' he asked Phoebe nastily. 'The one who had to go back to London half way through? Had mousy brown hair?'

There was an awkward silence broken only by the heavy-breathing sound of the dogs panting close by. Phoebe bit her lip and looked away, unable to bear Dan's humiliated, bewildered, drunken anger. Mitzi was peering at her dubiously now, a neat, unpainted fingernail pinging against the rim of her glass.

'Freddy and Saskia have known one another since birth,' Tony butted in, his chin disappearing into a Chinese fan of disapproving folds. 'They're more like sisters than friends – and they share everything. Isn't that dress one of yours, Sasky darling?'

'Not now,' Saskia said smoothly, watching as Phoebe nervily reached for her glass. 'I don't fit into it any more, so I gave it to Freddy. It looks lovely on her. Don't you think so, Dan?'

Phoebe took such a huge gulp of wine that it started streaming out of her nostrils.

'Lovely,' Dan cleared his throat and gave Phoebe the briefest of cursory smiles before squinting up at the house, as though fascinated with the guttering.

Beside him, Mitzi's glass-pinging finger nail was speeding up.

'Aren't you a bit chilly, Freda?' she asked with a curt little smile.

'No, Mizzy,' Phoebe gave a curt little smile in return as she dabbed her nose with a napkin. 'I seem to be in a patch of hot air just here.'

'More wine anyone?' Tony butted in again, looming over the table with his precious vintage and blotting out everyone's light like a huge thundercloud.

'Please,' Gin held up her glass. 'And Dan's empty too. Come on girls, drink up and tuck in. I have no idea how you youngsters survive on one lettuce leaf and a bottle of Evian a day.'

'They eat men,' Dan muttered sarcastically.

Still scrutinising the guttering, he groped for his glass and picked up Gin's by mistake, almost draining it in one.

'Quite.' Gin laughed awkwardly, too polite to ask for her drink back. 'They even share boyfriends, don't you, girls?'

Phoebe and Saskia both gawped at her in horror. Even Dan dragged his eyes away from the guttering.

'Dishy artist chap called Stan that Portia was referring to recently?' Gin raised her voice playfully, angling for a motherly dig.

Phoebe tried not to look at Dan, who was now having considerable trouble swallowing a slither of cucumber garnish.

'Phoebe passed him on when she went abroad,' Saskia explained smoothly.

'Really? Have you been away?' Mitzi clearly didn't know quite how to take Phoebe. She was torn between the village simpleton image of yore and the bitchy siren who was obviously exerting a strange fascination over her drunken, gutter-obsessed husband.

'New Zealand,' Phoebe muttered uncomfortably.

Mitzi almost puked out her undressed radicchio. Bells were starting to ring in her shrewd, sharp head like a clock shop at midday.

'She was working for her big brother, weren't you, darling?' Gin smiled encouragingly. 'Picking grapes.'

'Of wrath,' Dan added, starting to laugh to himself as he polished off Gin's wine and started on his own again.

'No, sour grapes, actually,' Phoebe stuffed a forkful of salad into her mouth. It was like eating rabbit food.

'So you two both fancied the same chap, huh?' Mitzi was peering at her with mounting mistrust.

'Mmm,' she chewed very slowly.

'Phoebe graciously let me win that time,' Saskia removed a caterpillar from Mitzi's water glass and refilled it. 'She has so many boyfriends, she has to keep notes so that she doesn't muddle them up.'

Gin laughed, 'How utterly wicked of you, darling. Still, I'm not surprised – a pretty girl like you can't be short of offers.'

Phoebe couldn't bring herself to look at Dan.

'Oh, Phoebe's notorious,' Saskia laughed. 'I'm sure she won't mind me saying that she's known as A to Z amongst her friends.'

'Why?' Mitzi asked with the same intonation as one asking why a mass-murderer was nick-named The Strangler.

'Because she's the only person any of us know who's snogged through the alphabet,' Saskia giggled. 'From Adam to Zach. She's amazing.'

'What fun,' Gin laughed delightedly. 'What about Q, Phoebe? That must have been impossibly difficult.'

'Quentin,' Phoebe croaked in a frozen voice, realising exactly what Saskia was doing and knowing that she'd been offered her ticket to freedom, albeit via rat-infested steerage. 'Nice chap.'

'And U?' Dan hiccuped angrily, pointedly pushing his glass towards Gin who was refilling her own.

'U?' Phoebe replied slowly, playing the double meaning for all it was worth and almost dying inside. 'You? Let me think – oh, yes, that was Unwin. He played rugby for Wales and kissed like a dream. But he was a bit short, boring and religious. Every time we scored, he thought he could convert me.'

Everyone except Dan laughed.

The conversation thankfully moved on to the state of English rugby.

Over coffee, Gin suddenly disappeared under the table. 'Now,' she resurfaced with two wrapped presents, 'here we are – one for each. I'm sorry yours is a bit mean, Fred, but I didn't know that you'd be here until the last minute.'

'Thank you so much, Gin.' Phoebe took the little parcel. 'You really didn't have to.'

'Just what I said!' Tony laughed rather too heartily.

While Saskia was enthusing rather automatically over a Discman and several top ten CDs, Phoebe unwrapped a chunky, heavy rectangle. Inside was a photograph of her parents looking very seventies and raising wide-rimmed glasses of champagne to whoever was pointing the camera. Between them, Phoebe was grinning goofily dressed in an Abba Fan Club t-shirt and Milly, straddling a plastic tractor, was picking her nose, her pig-tails skew-wiff. The photograph was trapped behind glass in a familiar, weighty silver frame. Phoebe winced slightly as she recognised it; it was the same one that had, until recently, contained the Felix and Saskia photograph.

'Thank you so much, Gin,' she laughed bravely, stretching across to kiss a beaming Gin on the cheek. 'It's wonderful – I'd forgotten quite how dreadful Daddy looked with those side-burns. I shall treasure this.'

'May I see?' Mitzi reached across the table and took the frame. 'Gosh, weren't you sweet, Freda? When was this taken?'

'God knows,' Gin poured herself the last of the wine. 'Late seventies I should imagine, judging from the state of that camellia in the background. I think it was seventy-eight, actually – Tony's fortieth; we had a huge party in the garden.'

'Seventy-eight?' Mitzi looked across at Dan. 'The year we met, darling.'

'Huh?' Dan, who had been staring fixedly at Phoebe, jumped nervously.

'The year we met,' Mitzi repeated tartly.

'So it was,' he smiled at her, his speckled grey eyes fighting hard not to cross. 'What a terrific, bloody fucking wonderful bloody year.' He was so drunk that the sarcasm disappeared into an inaudible series of slurred words.

There was another embarrassed hush.

'We've got my mother coming around this evening,' Mitzi explained hastily as she practically lifted Dan from his chair. 'And I haven't prised a thing from the freezer. Plus, I have to help this squiffy man recover from your glorious hospitality – I'm afraid he's rather over-indulged on the bonhomie. He's been in court all week, then dashing back to the office to sign all the next morning's editions off – terribly stressful, poor darling. Lots of late nights.' She gripped Dan's arm so tightly that he wailed.

'We quite understand,' Tony cleared his throat awkwardly.

'Thank you so much for the lovely lunch, Gin,' Mitzi quacked on, grabbing her bag from the back of her chair and hooking it over a padded silk shoulder. 'It's been a revelation.' She shot Phoebe a look of pure acid.

'We'll walk you out.' Tony rolled his rhino eyes at his wife. 'Such a shame you couldn't stay longer.'

Dan smiled a sweet, unfocused smile at Saskia and then gazed at Phoebe.

'Fascinating to meet you – again,' Dan managed to say, his eyes widening as though trying to flash up a long list of closing credits. 'Best of luck with the rest of the alphabet. Where are you up to?'

'F,' Phoebe croaked miserably.

As Gin and Tony followed them through to the house, disappearing from earshot with a series of 'it's been so nice – must do it again' burbles, Phoebe pressed her forehead to the compost-smelling table.

Saskia unplugged a Discman headphone from one ear.

'I think that just about did it,' she muttered.

'We're supposed to be meeting in the flat tomorrow night,' Phoebe remembered. 'He might want to thrash things out more there.'

'Twenty quid says he doesn't turn up.'

'I wish I could afford the bet,' Phoebe crossed her eyes into a wood-wormed turpentine stain.

As she straightened up, Saskia said the dreaded words: 'Felix will be so pleased you dumped Dan for him.'

Wet green eyes looking down at the photograph which Gin had given her, Phoebe tried and failed to say something in return.

'About last night,' Saskia toyed with her untouched glass of wine.

'I'm so – '

'Shut up!' Saskia interrupted. 'I cried for a stupid, wasted amount of time after your little chat with him.'

'I'm so sorry, Sa—'

'Shut the fuck up, will you?' she howled.

Phoebe shut up and listened as the Neashams' Range Rover sputtered into diesel-fed life and reversed with crackling, gravel-dispersing tyres across the Deayton drive.

'What I was about to say,' Saskia went on, 'was that I suddenly stopped blubbing this morning, pulled my screwed-up act together and realised how bloody close we are.' She looked up at Phoebe triumphantly. 'You've done it, Freddy. You really have.'

'What?' Phoebe closed her eyes as she heard the Range Rover accelerate away from Deayton, Van Morrison blaring, horn honking.

'Felix is totally smitten,' Saskia laughed. 'I heard it on the phone last night, Fred. He really thinks he loves you. I was so bloody shocked at first that I got stupidly jealous, but now I know why. I mean, it took me months to get as far as you've progressed in a fortnight. Knowing all that stuff I told you about him has really worked. I didn't think it would but, Christ – he's fallen for it, the egotistical little shit. All that baloney you've been feeding him about how clever he is, how handsome he is . . .'

'Saskia, I haven't been – '

'Don't argue, Freddy.' She grabbed Phoebe's hands and

squeezed them hard. 'You've done it and I'll love you forever for it. We're two weeks away from rift-off.'

Her high, bubbling enthusiasm, the messy blonde hair, earnest blue gaze and wild, warm smile, suddenly reminded Phoebe so acutely of Gin that she allowed her thumbs to lose feeling before she spoke.

'Rift-off?' she squeaked, her fingers turning white under the pressure of Saskia's grip.

'Bank Holiday,' Saskia sighed in an impatient explanation. 'The murder mystery. Here. In front of Dylan, Selwyn, Mungo – the lot. You tell him that you never loved him. That you loathe and despise him. You tell him that he revolts you.'

'I do?'

'Of course you bloody do, Freddy. What d'you think you were going to say to him? "I wuv you wots and wots?"'

'Of course not,' Phoebe muttered, her chest as hollow as a tightly stretched balloon. 'Now tell me exactly what you want me to say again?'

As she listened, appalled, to Saskia's killer drill – cruel, vindictive, childish but undeniably effective, Phoebe looked down at the photograph which Gin had given her and remembered just who had been holding the camera.

It had been Saskia herself. Minutes earlier she'd told Phoebe that she and the Seaton sisters thought she was too freakish and stupid to join their gang; that she would have to go through an initiation ceremony to prove her worth. A ceremony that she still, occasionally, had nightmares about to this day.

'You'll do it, Freddy, won't you?'

Phoebe glanced up at the excited, compelling, bright-eyed face and nodded, feeling seven again, totally overpowered and bullied into something she didn't want to do.

34

'Are you chucking Iain again, because I can come back later?'

'Don't joke about it. Come in and shut that bloody door, there's a frigging draught coming in.'

Phoebe arrived back in Islington on Sunday evening. Anxious to avoid any probing questions about Paris, or her weekend in Berkshire, she trailed straight through to the kitchen and thrust her dirty laundry into the washing machine.

'Helps if you add powder.' Fliss followed her through, scooping her house keys up from the kitchen table.

'Oh, yes.'

'Happy birthday.' Fliss pecked her on the cheek and thrust a scruffily wrapped present at her before grabbing her jacket and heading through to the sitting room again.

'Are you going out?' Phoebe's voice wobbled.

'Studio,' Fliss sighed. 'I've got to get enough work together for the Gillam.'

'You got the venue!' she gasped. 'The Gillam Gallery is going to show your stuff? Oh, that's wonderful, Fliss – I'm so chuffed for you.'

'They gave me a cancelled week.' Fliss searched for her bag, sounding ratty and exhausted rather than euphoric. 'They were going to show Sylvester Stallone's early work, but Henry Gillam said something extremely sarcastic at a party about naive art, which Brian Sewell repeated in print the next day. One of Sly's contacts must have let him know because he's pulled and Fliss is in the best commercial gallery in London for a fortnight.'

'I'm so excited for you.'

'Yeah, you sound it.' She was gathering up a pile of hard-backed sketchbooks. 'The exhibition previews on the second of September.'

'But that's just a couple of days after the party.'

'Exactly. Are you going to open that birthday present or squeeze it to death?'

Phoebe unwrapped a lovely little glazed ceramic maquette of a fat, grinning old man with a flat cap, tweeds and fishing flies pinned to his braces. 'He's gorgeous.'

'Reminds me a bit of Dan,' Fliss said coolly. 'Same generation.'

Phoebe's lips quivered tearfully, but Fliss was far too busy to notice.

'Anyway,' she shrugged herself into her jacket, 'as I've still got half a dozen figures to fire, plus this party to organise, I've just got to work through the nights.'

'Couldn't you postpone the party till after your exhibition?' Phoebe suggested hopefully.

'God, no!' Fliss headed towards the door. 'The thought of celebrating is keeping me sane – I'm planning to have all my sculptures finished and packed in their crates ready for collection before we go to Saskia's on Friday. That way I just have to roll up the following Tuesday to shout orders. At least Georgette's giving me some time off – plus helping arrange the party. In fact, the old cow is being weirdly generous – offering us loads of advice and freebies. And Steve at Bar Barella said he'd let us have a load of cheap booze, so we're definitely cooking with gas.'

I feel more like turning it on and shoving my head in the oven, Phoebe thought weakly.

'I'm thinking of junking in the job with Georgette after the Bank Holiday.' Weighed down with stuff, Fliss stooped to pick up her tube pass from the sideboard with her teeth. 'I'm just too knackered to face it, and anyway she's got Saskia now.'

'Bet you end up working twice the hours because you flunk telling her.' Phoebe trailed through to the sitting room.

'You're probably right. Oh – did Saskia tell you about us using Deayton?' Fliss was almost out of the door now, still talking with her tube pass between her teeth.

'Yes.' Phoebe sank forlornly on to the sofa arm.

'Brilliant, huh? Sounds perfect for it.' Fliss leaned back into the hall to check she hadn't forgotten anything. 'And we can trash the place before your lover boy and his wife move in.' With a rattle of slammed door, she was gone.

Phoebe pressed her knuckles into her mouth and stared at the ceiling with wet eyes.

A heap of post that had amassed for her over the past week. Along with a pile of birthday cards, there were several stock rejection letters from her job applications, a great wad of junk mail and a very shirty letter from the bank reminding her that she was extremely overdrawn.

'Ten pounds more overdrawn once they charge me for this,' she muttered, folding it into a paper hat and putting it on her head as she arranged her birthday cards on the mantelpiece.

There wasn't a card from Dan, she noticed wretchedly. Perhaps he had been planning to give it to her tomorrow night.

She stared at the phone, willing it to ring.

It didn't.

Resisting the temptation to do anything as truly pathetic as taking it off its cradle and checking the dialling tone, she crunched her way across the cluttered floor and put on her Van Morrison tape. Van, not at his most tactful, launched straight into 'Baby Please Don't Go'.

She stomped over to the cassette player and ejected him in favour of Leonard Cohen, who crooned his way straight into 'So Long, Marianne'.

'So long, Married Dan,' Phoebe started to wail along.

Leonard was quickly ejected too. She put on Fliss's favourite Suede CD, which was safe as Phoebe had never been able to understand a single word of the lyrics.

Trying not to mooch, she had a bath, taking the portable

phone with her just in case Dan called. She then draped her wet washing over the radiators, keeping the phone in constant, easy reach. Still it didn't ring. She took out the photograph that Gin had given her for her birthday and tried it out on every surface to see how it looked, finally deciding that it looked best right next to the phone. She picked the receiver up and checked the dialling tone. Twice. It purred back as cosily as a tickled cat.

Fliss's Suede CD was frisbeed across the room and replaced with The Greatest Hits of Megadeath, a touching collection that Iain had left behind.

When Saskia called just before midnight, Phoebe couldn't keep the disappointment from her voice.

'Oh, it's you.' She sank on to the floor and pulled her knees into her chin.

'Have you called Felix yet?'

'No.'

'Don't you think you should?'

'I'll do it tomorrow.'

'Well, when you do, try and sound a bit more cheerful. And don't whinge on about Dan this time.'

Phoebe swallowed down a sob.

'Saskia, there's something I forgot to mention to you,' she croaked, suddenly desperate to do something good after a weekend of inflicting nothing but pain.

'What?' Saskia's voice leapt up a few octaves.

'Felix has a photograph of you – both of you together. It's in the mews cottage. I saw it when I was talking to Dylan on Friday night.'

'Really?' She sounded hopelessly pleased. 'You're not just saying it to make me feel good?'

'It's in that big clip frame he's got.' Phoebe closed her eyes as she once again felt a stab of jealousy like a hot, salted blade through her guts.

'With the pictures of his parents and stuff?' Saskia laughed excitedly.

'Yes.'

'Oh, gosh, thank you, Phoebe.' She was almost whooping. 'Thank you so much for telling me. He must still feel something for me, don't you think? I mean, that clip frame's the only thing he'd save in a fire. Christ, I wish there was a way of you asking him – I'll try and think of something subtle. Look, I'm coming back up to London tomorrow afternoon to do some typing for Georgette. Shall I call you in the evening for an update?'

'Make it Tuesday,' she told Saskia. 'I'll call you. Where are you staying?'

'At Sukey's flat. She and Guy have gone to the Gambia for a fortnight. Mummy's praying that he doesn't pop the question when they're out there. Pa simply can't afford another wedding at the moment. Especially one that goes ahead.'

Phoebe winced.

Then a self-torturing little harpy held a gun to her back and made her ask, 'Saskia, do you still love Felix?'

She didn't reply for several seconds.

Sliding her face sideways, Phoebe picked tearfully at the plastic number label on the phone and noticed that Fliss had left a big Post-it note demanding sixty quid for the phone-bill by the end of next week.

'I haven't stopped loving Felix for a minute since I met him, Phoebe. It's like being an alcoholic – you can have drunk nothing but orange juice for years, but you'll always be an alcoholic. And I'll always love Felix. Always.'

Phoebe wiped away slow tears and tried hard not to sniff.

'I'll never, ever forget what you're doing for me, Phoebe,' Saskia went on quietly. 'He'll go on breaking hearts for kicks until he's twinkling his old blue eyes at nurses from his GTI bath chair if you don't do this. You're saving my sanity.'

'I know,' Phoebe mumbled, wishing she was more certain she wasn't sacrificing her own in the process.

Felix called her at almost half-past one in the morning, clearly having just returned from a very drunken night out. Phoebe, lying with the phone on her stomach, heard his voice and felt ludicrously cheered up.

'I can't believe you're up – I had my machine message ready,' he laughed, yelling over the boom of the Beastie Boys in the background.

'The phone woke me up,' she muttered untruthfully. 'What was your message going to be?'

Felix paused to light a cigarette. In the background, Phoebe could make out Mungo asking him if he wanted any of the Indian takeaway.

'No, bruv.' Felix did his Phil Mitchell impersonation. He was clearly incredibly tight. 'Still there, Phoebe baby?'

'No.' She wished that his voice didn't have quite such a duvet-snuggling effect.

'Okay – message, yes?'

'I'm pressing play.'

'Hi, Phoebe, it's Felix. I want my tongue inside you, I miss you – shit, this is awful! I'm too bloody pissed. I love you, but I'm hating every bloody minute of it. Call me tomorrow.'

He hung up.

Phoebe pressed her face to her pillow and found, to her amazement, that she was smiling. Why was it that one short call from Felix could make her forget about Dan and want to dance around the flat singing 'Oh, What a Beautiful Morning'?

Then she thought about Saskia and pulled her pillow over her head, groaning in despair.

The phone rang first thing the next morning. Phoebe, still bleary-eyed with sleepiness, picked it up in the sitting room.

'I'm in the car – shit, hang on.' A car horn honked in the background.

She leant against a wall for support. 'Oh, Dan I – '

'Will you come to the flat tonight? We need to talk.' He snapped.

'Dan, I'm not – '

'I'll meet you there at eight.'

They were abruptly cut off. Whether it was by Dan or an overhead bridge, Phoebe couldn't tell.

*   *   *

On Monday morning, Portia phoned her office to let them know she'd be working from home all day. She then flicked through the transcripts of her California interview tapes for about twenty minutes to appease her guilt before dancing through to her bedroom to try on endless outfits in anticipation of her lunch with Dan Neasham. She'd lived in leggings all weekend as she'd jogged, stepped and stretched any LA bulges away. Having streamlined herself to be almost slimmer than her coathangers, she couldn't wait to get to grips with a lovely, indulgent what-shall-I-wear session.

When she looked into her wardrobe, she blinked a couple of times and cleared her throat. She then calmly shut the door, swallowed, and opened it again. Then she screamed.

'My clothes! My bloody clothes have disappeared!'

She raced through to the sitting room and pounced on the phone.

Saskia had just arrived at Georgette's office and was keeping her voice hushed because her boss was on the other line.

'Ah – yes, oops.' She swallowed nervously. 'I – er – sent quite a lot of them to the dry cleaners.'

'Why? I have them dry cleaned every other wear.'

'Do you?' Saskia mumbled. 'I'm sorry, I just thought it would be a nice surprise for you when you got back from the States.'

'Well, it's not,' Portia snarled. 'Which dry cleaner are they at? I'll go round there now.'

'I'm not sure. I think I left the tickets in Deayton.'

'Well, go back there tonight and get them. I want my clothes, Saskia. I'm – I'm *naked* without my clothes.' Portia hung up.

Flipping furiously through her very limited selection of outfits, she finally settled for a subdued Nicole Farhi linen suit with a wrap-around skirt that flashed a lot of slim thigh when one crossed one's legs casually. It reminded her of the outfit Phoebe had been wearing on that wet day she'd given her a lift from Tower Bridge. Dan was bound to go for the look, Portia concluded, and anyway, it held just the right mix of busy professional and sexy, caring friend. Perfect.

She was amazed that she'd taken ten minutes to do what

normally took over an hour. Treating herself to a small, celebratory gin and low-cal tonic, she conveniently forgot that her range of choice had been reduced by a factor of ten.

Whilst Portia was being treated to lunch by Dan, Piers was power-lunching Felix today. Portia had gone to great lengths to find out which restaurant they would be in, in order that she and Dan didn't clash. Such lengths, in fact, that Piers now assumed she was desperate to see him and had grudgingly announced that he'd pop around to the Fulham flat some time that evening.

As Portia had been hoping to stretch lunch into the early evening, she was feeling very anti-Piers. But, because she was slightly frightened of him, and in a concession to his vanity, she donned her rubber Marigolds and dug through her kitchen bin in an attempt to locate the cacti she'd recklessly thrown out on Friday night.

Halfway down, wrinkling her nose against the pong, Portia uncovered some crumpled paper balls which were covered in her sister's scrawled handwriting. She turfed them out on to the kitchen surface and carried on searching for her cacti. Only two were recoverable. Both were coated with cigarette ash.

Having rinsed them under the tap and placed them back on her windowsill, Portia returned to the kitchen and carefully unfolded the paper balls.

With Groucho purring greedily at her elbow, she read and re-read the stained, smelly notes. One sentence seemed to leap out and slug her in the eye with each reading.

> *Remind Phoebe to kiss Felix's ears at every opportunity – and then, during the dump, to tell him that his ears stink of wax and that his belly button is cheesy.*

'Ears?' Portia looked at Groucho and laughed in bewilderment. 'Belly button?' She ran her eyes further down the page with amusement.

> *Marvin Gaye and Squeeze – buy tapes for Phoebe. Felix's favourite song – 'Up the Junction'.*

At the bottom of the second page, there was a far more telling line.

Essential not to let Dylan guess what is going on. Mustn't guess that Phoebe knows me at all, or he'll rumble the plot. Must say she's met me very, very recently – or never? Think of something.

'Well, little sister,' Portia whistled, 'I think I know what you're up to, you sly old bag!'

Left alone in the flat on Monday, Phoebe suddenly realised how impractical she was. She had read somewhere that spring cleaning was the ideal way to take one's mind off unhappiness. Aged aunts were always saying 'Tidy house, tidy mind', or 'Sweep, don't weep', weren't they? Looking around the flat, Phoebe realised that she had enough sweeping lined up to keep her dry-eyed for months.

Fliss, alternately buried in her sculptures, plotting the Bank Holiday murder mystery, drumming up party-goers and fending off the landlord's hysterical demands for his rent, had slacked on her usual Mary Poppins domesticity.

Things were going furry in the fridge or seeping through the wire shelves, the milk smelled like a muck spreader's boots, the carpet crunched underfoot, the windows were white-washed with smears and the washing up had started to grow enough penicillin to supply a small African aid camp. When Phoebe shoved a couple of slices of bread in the toaster, the popper glued itself down with a combination of grease and honey, and refused to pop up again. It was only when small flames started to lap out of it that she gave up digging around with a knife and chose the safer option of pulling out the plug and throwing a wet tea-towel over it. She then realised she'd used the only clean tea-towel, which considerably dampened her enthusiasm for washing up, as well as anything to dry it with.

She flicked on the radio and thought vaguely about throwing some of the rubbish out. But every song made her think of Dan and she just stood moonily in the kitchen, a bin-bag in one hand, croaking tearfully along to the lyrics for half an hour.

Switching the radio off, she tried to boil the kettle for a cup of tea and, forgetting to add water, blew that up too.

'I am NOT going to crack up,' she told herself sternly, throwing out this week's *Time Out* and a pile of Fliss's slushy novels by mistake before carefully knotting the top of the bin liner and mindlessly cramming it into the washing machine.

She flipped through some of Fliss's notes for the murder mystery and started to feel slightly sick.

Fliss was planning to hand out characters a week before the party, giving people enough time to get their costumes and motives together. Stan was destined to be Mestick, the evil butler with a sideline in blackmail; Claudia had been given Billie Havitawayday, the blues singer with a secret love-child; Fliss herself had elected to be Lady Euthanasia and had pencilled Milly in for Nymph O'Maniac the cellist.

Iain had a question mark beside his name along with a quick profile of Bart Stard – Lady E's estranged younger son, Crispin, no less – now a Hollywood matinée idol and closet queen. Phoebe suspected that Fliss's old friend Paddy, down as Bart's club-footed 'personal assistant', Quentin French-fry, would have a few objections to raise next week.

What worried Phoebe the most were the notes about Felix and his friends – all down as 'possibles – check with Phoebe'. Mungo was down, rather obviously, as Otto Licher, Lady Euthanasia's German tennis coach and sex-mad toy boy; Selwyn was her disinherited playboy gambler eldest son, Peregrine Fitzacoffin. Disturbingly, Felix was to be lined up with the role of Tess Tosterone, a bisexual ex-male stripper, and impresario of a notorious New York drinking club. Phoebe herself was a lesbian Czech poetress, Monika von Dyke.

Dylan – whom Fliss had written on her list as Duncan, Phoebe realised – was to be Ivor Grudge, the local pest-control man, called in during the party to remove an infestation of rats.

'Rats being the operative word,' Phoebe groaned. 'What are you doing here, Fliss? Cutting down on your friends?'

What she loved the most was the role allotted to Georgette who had wangled an invitation in return for helping to organise the bash. Fliss had scribbled her in as Dora Mestick, the whiskery old housekeeper and long-suffering mother of Mestick.

'She's going to be sacked for this,' Phoebe sighed, and then remembered Fliss saying that she was thinking of giving up the job anyway.

Knowing Fliss, it was just the sort of roundabout method of handing in her notice that she'd use.

'Tess Tosterone and Monika von Dyke,' she whistled as she slid her eyes down the list once more. 'What a couple. Thanks, Fliss.'

Phoebe stared blindly at the television where Judy Finnigan was smiling her warm, comforting smile and telling viewers that the diabetic toddler fact-sheet would be available to all who called a special 0891 number.

'I love Felix,' Phoebe said suddenly and unexpectedly, surprising even herself.

Judy told viewers that it would be cheaper to call after six.

'I love Felix,' Phoebe muttered again. 'Oh, shit.'

'I think Phoebe might be deliberately trying to seduce Felix Sylvian on Saskia's behalf,' Dan told Portia, leaning back to let the waiter place coffee in front of them.

Keeping her reaction deliberately low-key, Portia smiled politely up at the waiter.

Dan checked the time once more. He was very carefully glancing at his watch only when she looked away, which was less and less often as the meal progressed. Nonetheless, Portia had picked up on the Tag Heuer fetish and was drawing out what little information she had to impart to him, just to keep that lovely, crinkly face opposite hers a little longer.

'How do you mean?' she asked edgily, looking at the slimline briefcase that was resting by her slimline ankles. In it were the notes that she had found in the bin of her flat. Portia could almost smell their stale-trash presence in the tightly zipped Italian leather case. She had been glancing at it twitchily throughout lunch, but couldn't bring herself to decide whether to show them to Dan or not.

'As you said, Felix was a total bastard to your sister.' Dan put the case for the cuckolded prosecution. 'And she and Phoebe are very close, aren't they?' He looked up from stirring a huge spoonful of sugar into a very small espresso.

Trying not to sink forever into those divine, peppery grey eyes, Portia held her hand palm-down over the table and waggled it, pulling a sceptical face. She was grateful that she'd had her nails manicured in California; they glittered as pink and white as a schoolgirl's skin.

'They were never really friends, no. Saskia bullied Phoebe mercilessly at school. And anyway, Phoebe was away in New Zealand during the whole affair,' she pointed out smoothly. 'She'd never have known Felix's devious little ways. Freddy was in another hemisphere when it all happened.'

And I wish she bloody well was now, Portia thought murderously.

Although aware that Dan had asked her to lunch to talk about Phoebe, Portia wished they had at least had the briefest of rests. A quick chat about art perhaps? Or favourite holiday locations? Their backgrounds? Susie's twins? Even politics and religion would be preferable to Phoebe Fredericks and her messy love-life.

She admired Dan's wide-shouldered charcoal power suit, the broad-striped shirt, spotted Armani tie and red braces. He dressed exquisitely, she mused, wondering what he'd look like stripped of the Savile Row executive armour. The thought made her shudder deliciously.

'Freddy?' Dan was smiling thoughtfully.

'Yes, Freddy – Phoebe.' Such a lovely smile, Portia sighed.

'All you Seatons call her that. Why?'

Portia hooked a glossy blonde curl from behind her ear so that it covered one batting dove-grey eye. 'Well, Freddy for Fredericks, obviously.' She smiled warmly. 'And then later it became Freddy Krueger.'

'Nightmare on Elm Street?' He flared a shocked nostril.

Such a beautiful nostril, Portia noticed.

'Yes, it was a family joke,' she lied. 'Freddy spent a lot of

holidays with us. And she was a bit of a wound-up child –
terribly bright and clever but enormously shy. You'd never
believe it now, of course.'

'So why Freddy Krueger?'

'Well,' Portia dipped a perfect, square-tipped finger nail into
her cappuccino and then licked the cream from it with a very
pink tongue, 'I wouldn't say this if Phoebe weren't so grounded
nowadays but even she herself laughs about it. She used to, er –
have nightmares,' she improvised.

'Oh, I see. Poor darling.' Dan's eyes softened.

'And wet the bed,' Portia added quickly, caught between
feeling hellish for such lies and triumphant for such a glorious
reaction.

'Wet the bed?' The other nostril flared as Dan looked into his
coffee with nauseated speculation.

'Only for a very little while – and we were all very sympathetic,' Portia breathed caringly. 'She's much calmer now, but
I'm afraid the tag "Freddy" has rather stuck. Even her own
family use it.'

'Her brother in New Zealand, for example?' Dan fought to
get back on track, trying hard not to think about plastic
sheets.

'Dominic? Yes, I think so.' Portia unloosed another strand of
hair. 'The wine he produces is really quite palatable, although
I'm still a bit of a snob about New World wines, aren't you?'

'No. And she had no contact with Saskia when she was out
there? With Saskia and Felix?' he persisted.

Portia sighed irritably. 'Well, Saskia wrote to her I think –
told Phoebe about the engagement et al. In fact, I believe
Phoebe was going to be a bridesmaid, poor thing. The dresses
were atrocious. But she never actually got to meet Felix.'

'Which is exactly why she'd be the ideal person for Saskia to
ask to get back at him on her behalf.' Dan looked up persua-
sively. 'Felix had never met her during his relationship with
your sister.'

Portia kicked her briefcase to one side and sipped her
cappuccino. 'Do you really believe that Saskia's asking Phoebe

to methodically try and make Felix fall in love with her, just so that she can hurt him as much as he hurt her?'

'What do you think?' Dan smiled equivocally, his teeth as white as the mints in Portia's saucer.

Still staring at the teeth, she shrugged.

'It's a bit far-fetched, isn't it?' he was leading her now.

'You said it.' Inadvertently taking up the bait, Portia decided she loved the way he smiled – it was so wide, warm and welcoming, like a West Indian seascape. Piers smiled slightly less often than he moved his bowels, she thought sourly.

'So – why far-fetched?' Dan turned the question back on her with practised ease. 'The facts lead to exactly the conclusion I've been drawing.'

Portia suddenly realised what was happening.

'Not too far-fetched to imagine, perhaps,' she said swiftly. 'Just very, very difficult actually to do. Felix is too bright to fall for it.'

'Not too bright to fall for Phoebe, though?' Dan drummed his fingers on the rim of his espresso cup.

Beautiful nails, Portia noticed – large, square and even, like the tips of matchbook matches.

'You did, and I've been told you're one of the sharpest minds in corporate law – as well as the sharpest dresser,' she flattered him willingly.

Dan ducked his head with a shrugging, not totally modest, smile.

Sucker for succour, Portia realised delightedly. I'll cut through your defence, Dan Neasham, as fast as a blow-torch through ice-cream.

'We all pick the wrong horse sometimes,' she went on softly. 'And then, when it loses, we try to think up all sorts of Dick Francis-style doping and duping intrigues as an excuse, when really it just didn't run in the right direction fast enough.'

'I know. Sorry. Suspicious legal mind to blame,' he sighed, pushing his cup away and staring sadly into the flower-arrangement. 'Forget I ever suggested the idea.'

'I can understand your need to hope,' Portia said gently. 'We all carry it around with the photos and mementoes when something's over. And time is a heel, not a healer.' She caught her breath daringly. 'What you need is a new lover.'

When Phoebe phoned the mews, she found herself chatting to Dylan.

'Hi, darling. How are you? Felix said you might call, and that I was to keep you talking until we traced the number. He's having lunch with his agent.'

'Susie?'

'Piers Fox, the sly guy with the jazzy ties,' Dylan laughed. 'I can't stick him, he's like moulting hair – always plugging something. He was on the balloon game on Radio 4 once and got slung out before the thing had even taken off. Tragedy is, he's so lightweight, it wouldn't save them enough height to get over a bump in the mud.'

Phoebe guessed from his racing voice and quick-fire wit that Dylan was speeding on something. She hoped he'd be more indiscreet if high.

'Are they doing a deal?' she asked casually.

'Big bucks, my dear – all very secretive. Piers won't even tell Felix much, but I'd hazard a guess that it's in America.'

'America?' she repeated, trying to hide a sudden, squirming fear.

'Yup, big place next to Canada. Go west and you can't miss it – ouch!' he suddenly howled. 'Get off, you little bugger.'

'Are you all right?'

'Fine – ow, bloody hell.' Dylan was clearly sucking his thumb. There was a lot of yappy growling in the background.

'Have you got a dog there?' Phoebe laughed.

'Er – no,' he said quickly.

The growly yapping was followed by a couple of sharp, high-pitched barks.

'Don't tell me that's a cat with an identity crisis?'

'No – no, it's just – er – the television!' he announced with relief. 'I'll just turn the volume down – hang on.'

The yapping suddenly changed to a furious series of

indignant squeals, and Phoebe distinctly heard Dylan muttering 'Shut up, you little monster' before the squeals were silenced by the sound of a door shutting.

'There, I turned it off.' He was back. 'It was that Danny Baker pet quiz thing. What were we talking about?'

'America. Big place next to Canada.'

'Oh, yes – well, Piers has just been there so, putting two and two together and sniffing a fortune, I'd say Felix is about to get his ecologically friendly greetings rectangle.'

'His what?'

'Green card.' Dylan was speeding away. 'Piers wants to export our blond friend Stateside. Although I don't know how well Felix would react to a zip code. He's certainly not too fond of dress codes – if it says black tie on the invite, he wears an anorak to piss them off. And his zip isn't exactly famed for it's – '

'Do you think he'd have to live out there then?' Phoebe cut him short, realising that Dylan wasn't just indiscreet when high: he was a rambling, truth-drugged confessor. And right now she wasn't up to handing out Hail Marys.

'Put your rod away, honey,' he laughed. 'I haven't a clue. But the lease is up on this place next month, and Felix isn't exactly rolling in it at the moment so my guess is he'll head for the bucks as fast as a flirty doe.'

'Or head for the dough as fast as a flirty buck?'

'Yup, I guess that's more along his sexual line.'

Phoebe bit her lip.

'I'm sorry, darling – God, I'm being a bloody insensitive sod, aren't I? Look, I haven't a clue what he'll do. I don't even know if he's being offered work out there at all. Anyway, I'm sure he'd talk to you about it first.'

'It's okay, Dylan.' Phoebe bravely tried for an insouciant laugh which came out as more of a manic cackle. 'I can hardly lay claim when I haven't even laid Felix. It's not as though we're an item.'

'Aren't you?' He sounded accusing. 'You looked pretty much like one when you were dancing on Friday night. Or was that a show reel?'

'I don't think we should be having this conversation.' Phoebe was starting to feel jumpy.

'Neither do I. Sorry, darling. It's just that . . .' He coughed uncomfortably.

'What?'

There was a long pause. Phoebe was sure she could hear scrabbling and whining in the background.

'Nothing,' Dylan suddenly sighed. 'Forget I spoke. D'you have a nice weekend?'

'Lovely,' Phoebe said without conviction. They had glossed over the weather, the latest number one, today's political sleaze scandal and the likely time of Felix's return when she suddenly blurted: 'By the way, I wondered if you and Felix would like to come round for a drink tomorrow night – only Fliss and I've both got the night off.'

'Fliss?'

'Yes, the red-head who works at Bar Barella. Are you working tomorrow night?'

'No, actually I'm not.' Dylan sounded as though he was sitting on a spin dryer. He clearly was working, but had instantly decided to be violently ill. 'That sounds great. I'll get Felix to call you about it, but I can't see why not.'

Felix was all for it. Phoning Phoebe that afternoon, he was still tight from his boozy lunch, and as high as a weather balloon.

'Dyldo's mentioned Selwyn's sister a couple of times,' he laughed. 'I can't believe you live with her. Talk about small global house-warming party. You'll be telling me your other flat-mate is an ex-girlfriend of mine next!'

Phoebe found she couldn't answer.

Thankfully, he was too distracted by his lunch with Piers to notice.

'That guy is a total shit, but I love him,' he enthused. 'There's a really big deal going on in the States that I'm up for. I can't believe he's wangled it, but he has. I'll tell you all about it tomorrow night. No – in fact I can't wait that long. I'll tell you about it tonight.'

'I think I'm working,' she gulped, remembering Dan's abrupt phone call that morning.

'That's okay – I'll come to the bar. I just want to see you.'

'Please don't bother, Felix,' Phoebe improvised hastily. 'The manager is after my blood as it is, and anyway I've promised I'll go straight to Tooting to visit my sister after my shift. She's feeling a bit down.'

It was getting more and more difficult to lie to him, she realised.

'Milly, isn't it?' Felix laughed, blissfully unaware of Phoebe's discomfort. 'God, I wish I could see you tonight. Can you come round here afterwards?'

'Not really. Milly usually bangs on until the small hours. And she said she'd cook me a birthday meal.'

'Birthday? When?'

'Yesterday.'

'Why didn't you say?'

'You didn't ask.'

Felix fell quiet for a few seconds. There was the same yapping in the background that had punctuated her chat with Dylan.

'Is that a dog?'

'Radio,' he said smoothly. 'What if you're working? Won't your sister's meal go a bit cold?'

'She never eats before midnight.' Phoebe was almost pressed to the floor with the effort of lying.

'See you tomorrow then. I love you.'

Portia stared at her wardrobe doors and gritted her teeth. In front of her, Piers's very clean, very red feet were twitching delightedly at the end of his fluffy, muscular legs.

'Oh, yes – oh, great – oh, yes, baby!' he moaned, gripping her waist between his hands and speeding up.

Portia grabbed his knees to steady herself and dropped her head forwards as his hip bones plunged more violently into her buttocks.

'Put your head back,' he gasped out. 'So I can see – ah! – your hair down your – oh, baby! – back.'

Doing as she was told, Portia glared at her wardrobe doors once more. This was Piers's favourite sexual position, and her least. He got to stare at her back and, she suspected, fantasise that she was his nubile wife showing more energy and enthusiasm for sex than the usual lying back on the counterpane and opening her legs originality. Portia got to stare at the twitching red feet and worry that she had spots on her bottom.

'Oh, yes – oh, baby – oh, yes!'

Portia cocked her head and narrowed her eyes at the wardrobe, remembering that Saskia had whipped most of her clothes off to the dry cleaner for some absurd reason. The stupid girl! she stewed. She wondered if Saskia had left the green Amanda Wakely suit in there. She quite fancied wearing it tomorrow.

'Oh, Christ! Oh, yes!' Piers was punching his groin upwards with the monotonous rhythm of a housewife doing fifty buttock-firming exercises in front of Mr Motivator's breakfast TV slot. 'Oh, yes – yes – baby – yes!'

Portia fought an urge to look at her watch.

When he finally came, he pushed her off with a perfunctory, affectionate squeeze and picked up the tissue box from beside the bed, peering grumpily into its empty depths.

'Get some loo roll out of the bathroom, will you, darling?' he asked, tying a knot in the top of the condom and holding it out for her to take as well, like a child with an apple core.

'Get it yourself.' Portia reached for her dressing gown and stomped through to the kitchen to fetch herself a glass of wine. She switched on Radio 4 and forked out some food for Groucho.

Piers followed after a few minutes, wrapped in one of her pink fluffy towels, which clashed with his hair.

Lounging by the sitting-room door, he gazed around the flat for a few seconds. 'This place is a bit of a mess, isn't it?' He whistled, noticing the new nick-nacks, books and clutter. 'Is this your sister's stuff?'

'No, it's mine.' Portia wandered back through the bedroom to the bathroom, wine in hand.

'Are we going to have a shower?' he growled hornily as he followed her.

Portia turned around in the bathroom doorway, reaching for a new loo roll from one of the pine shelves and giving him a withering smile.

'No, I am. Here.' Throwing the loo roll at him, she shut the door and locked it.

Having washed himself at the kitchen sink, Piers was dressed and poking distastefully around the clutter in the sitting room when Portia re-emerged. She was still in her dressing gown, with a pink towel wound around her head and a cigarette dangling from her mouth. Piers looked up from a pile of rag-dolls, slightly appalled by her appearance. There were foundation stains on the towel, he noticed. And she had mascara smeared under her eyes.

'Are you all right?' he asked brusquely, glancing at his watch and deciding he could allow her twenty minutes chat-time.

'Mmm.' Portia sank on to the sofa and hooked her feet up on the coffee table, flexing her painted toes. 'I've had rather a successful day in fact. You?'

Giving her feet a disapproving glance, he drummed his fingers against his legs and moved away from the cigarette smoke. Groucho, stalking out of the kitchen and licking his lips, wound his way up to Piers's ankles and rubbed his salmon-stained cheek across a very expensive trouser leg. Piers gave him a sly kick.

'Topaz thinks she's pregnant,' he muttered, leaning against the mantelpiece.

'Christ!' Portia's eyebrows shot up.

'It's too early to take a test,' he went on, squinting snootily at some paperback bookspines, 'but her colonic irrigologist and her aromatherapist have both told her that they think she is. She's already hit Hamley's with my credit card.'

Portia stifled a laugh.

'It's not funny.' Piers rubbed his red hair fretfully. 'We simply can't afford for her to give up work right now, and anyway I really don't want another child.'

'Why did you marry one then?' Portia shrugged.

Piers turned to gape at her. He'd never heard her speak like this before.

'I need some support here, Portia,' he snapped tetchily.

'Try the CSA.' She tapped her ash into the pot of a cactus and hooked one slim ankle over the other. 'I hope you don't expect me to be a godmother? Only I'm lousy at remembering birthdays.'

'What is up with you tonight?' Piers watched as she pulled an old copy of *Vogue* on to her lap and started flipping through it. 'You seem to have gone on some sort of assertiveness training course. Are you still jet-lagged, is that it?'

'Nope,' Portia was peering calmly at a shot of his wife swathed in Ralph Lauren checked mohair.

Piers pushed Groucho off the sofa arm and, perching there himself, coughed awkwardly, not at all comfortable with sounding out women emotionally. Groucho, still huffy about the kick, started clawing the sofa end very noisily, which didn't help Piers's concentration.

'I know this must be difficult for you – getting back to normal after the intimacy of LA,' he said in his flat, expressionless voice. 'But I assure you that I'll make every effort to secure us – '

'LA wasn't intimate, Piers.' Portia flipped a page and came face-to-face with Topaz decked in Ralph Lauren camel coating. 'I was lucky to get scheduled into your diary before midnight. And you even wore dark glasses in bed in case room service recognised you.'

Looking at the magazine over her shoulder, he cleared his throat and tried again. 'Is it Topaz being pregnant that bothers you?'

'Nope.' Portia took a drag of her cigarette. 'I never wanted kids. I'd find it far too hard to give up smoking. And there's the back-ache, the stretch marks, broken nights, loss of sex drive, babysitters from hell, whiffy nappies . . .'

'I know, I know!' Piers stood up, horrified at the reminder of what was in store. Batting away Portia's cigarette smoke, he looked at his watch once more and sighed.

'Have you pencilled Topaz in for your nine o'clock window?' Portia looked up at him. 'You can call from here to confirm, if you like.'

'I see no point in continuing with this conversation.' He gathered his coat and keys, shooting her the sort of disparaging look he normally saved for taxi drivers who complained about their tip. 'I'll call you tomorrow and hope to find you in a more rational frame of mind.'

'Don't bother.' Portia watched him head for the door. 'I'll be tied up all day. I might be able to fit you in for the three o'clock conference call with my other lovers, though.'

'You what?' Piers turned to stare at her.

'You're no longer my heart-and-sole agent, darling.' She stubbed out her cigarette and smiled.

'You're seeing someone else?'

'No-o, not exactly,' Portia said slowly. 'But I think it only fair to warn you that I'm seeking alternative representation.'

For the first time since she had known him, Piers burst out laughing. A huge, hearty booming laugh that was quite out of character. His green eyes gleamed like wet jade with delight, his thin, patrician mouth gaped like a huge orange segment, showing all his teeth, fillings and very pink tongue. He clutched his coat to his stomach with mirth, and looked at her in amazement, his clever, calculating eyes brimming over with respect.

'You,' he fought to control the laughter until he could speak calmly again, 'can be just as cold and clinical as me, can't you? I never would have believed it.'

'Yup.' Portia scratched her chin and stared at him, slightly bewildered.

'I like that.' He nodded thoughtfully. 'By God, I really admire that.'

'Thanks.' Portia swallowed, wondering quite what she'd just done.

'Sure – go shopping for another lover if it makes you happy.' He shrugged, reaching for the door latch. 'After all, I've never been able to offer you an exclusive, have I?'

Portia smiled weakly.

'You'll still pencil me in for the odd eight o'clock window, though, won't you?' He grinned wickedly from the door, looking more like his namesake than ever.

Portia smiled with slightly more conviction. That was the first joke she had ever known him to make. Her smile turned into a big, wide grin.

'Sure.'

'I'll call you later this week. We'll have lunch.' As ever, he didn't say goodbye.

35

That night, Phoebe set off to meet Dan at the flat in plenty of time. Arriving at Highgate tube station, she wandered vaguely towards the village, trying to work out what she was going to say.

Half an hour later she was sitting on a tombstone in the cemetery, her hair dampened by drizzle, her teeth chattering from the cold. She still hadn't got beyond 'Hello, Dan' and now she was late.

An hour later she was still on her tombstone, her face in her hands, oblivious of the fact that drizzle had given way to rain. Her clothes were soaked through; the silk coat-dress was as black and shiny as PVC, her clog espadrilles were as heavy as steel-capped work boots. Late-evening dog-walkers, hoods pulled tightly over heads, shot her wary looks as they scuttled past, anxious to be home. An old lady with a creased pink brolly picked her way across a couple of graves and offered her a boiled sweet.

'Are you lost, dear?' she enquired politely, pulling her ancient Westie away from Phoebe's foot which it was trying to cock an arthritic leg over.

'Totally.' She rubbed her sodden hair.

'Where do you want to go?'

'Back by about a month,' sighed Phoebe, picking at the wet lichen on the pitted, blackened stone beneath her. 'Alternatively, New Zealand would be nice.'

The old lady hurried away.

Phoebe stayed for another half hour, watching the gun-metal grey horizon tarnish to black and the street lamps brighten like ripening oranges, knowing that she had committed the ultimate act of cowardice.

Someone had moved into the newly converted bottom flat. As Phoebe approached the red-brick house, she saw that the shutters on the ground floor windows had been opened and that a warm yellow light was glowing behind newly hung curtains which still bore indented crease-marks in the cream lining fabric. There were no lights in the second-floor flat, she noticed guiltily.

She let herself in very quietly, praying that no one leapt out to introduce themselves.

They didn't. The Panorama theme music was blaring behind the door of Flat 1, and several cardboard boxes were lined up outside, stuffed with paper packing shreds. The smell of fresh paint was stronger than ever.

She climbed the stairs. Walking into the flat almost broke her heart. The Mary Poppins of adultery had clearly been feathering his love-nest in her absence. The place was transformed.

A heavy, reclaimed wood table, several chairs and a corner cupboard filled some of the gaping floorspace in the huge room. Pictures were lined up against the walls waiting to be hung; a pile of bulging, green and white John Lewis carrier bags sat on the chintz Chesterfield and a big red rug was rolled up like a vast, uncooked sausage across the kitchen door.

He had even made up the bed, Phoebe realised, staring at the crisp white linen and fat, plumped pillows puffed out like his and hers car airbags after an emergency stop.

On the new table was a pile of free property magazines, the instructions for several electrical appliances, a copy of *Yellow Pages* and a big red envelope.

Seeing her name scrawled across it in Dan's small, spiky handwriting, Phoebe stifled a sob.

He had only given the gum a mean little dab of his tongue, so that it pulled away from the paper as though unsealed.

The birthday card was an arty Paperchase one with a textured picture of a landscape on the front, made from metal, string and sandpaper. It was very masculine and very Dan. When Phoebe opened it, a travel agency ticket wallet fell out. Stooping to retrieve it, she read the typically abbreviated message inside the card.

P

Happy Birthday

D

x

One quick kiss, no love. She sighed sadly. It summed them up.

Inside the paper wallet were two First-Class tickets to Florence. They were dated for Bank Holiday weekend.

Phoebe pushed them back inside and threw them on to the table without even a slight twinge of regret. She felt totally affronted and ludicrously angry.

Dropping the card on the floor, she gazed around the flat, at the clean white walls, the gleaming new furniture and crinkled mounds of shrink-wrapping and bubble plastic. The little light on the phone was flashing eight. She wandered across and unplugged it with a satisfyingly destructive snatch before returning to her bag to scrabble inside for a Biro.

Turning the envelope over, she scratched out her name and wrote Dan's above it. She then dropped her flat keys inside and hovered with her tongue millimetres away from the remaining gum, wondering whether she should leave a note. She sank down on to one of the chairs, stood up again to remove a row of plastic rawl plugs from beneath one buttock, and then sank down once more, anger evaporating like steam on a hot plate.

How could she possibly write down what she felt with only half a cartridge of ink between 'Dear Dan' and 'Love, Phoebe'? She wanted to write a great, tear-stained novella about how much she had once loved him, and how guilty and wretched she

was feeling to be doing this to him now. She wanted to tell him
that this was her fault, not his. That she had never really been
mistress material, had never wanted the flat, weekends in Italy,
flowers, whispered phone conversations and a gold bracelet to
cherish during lonely Christmases. She simply wasn't strong
enough, didn't have enough distractions in her life to make up
for the yawning gaps of a time-share relationship.

Phoebe was more or less in touch with all of her ex-
boyfriends. The odd call, occasional drink, Christmas and
birthday cards, and sporadic, drunken moments of rekindled
lust passed between them. Cutting all contact dead was a
terrifying prospect, but with Dan she had a feeling that it would
be the only option. He was as persistent as a salesman with a hot
lead, as resilient to blows as Lennox Lewis's punch bag, as
assiduous as a terrier that wouldn't stop gripping with its teeth
or shaking its head unless it was punched on the nose. These
were the qualities that made him superb at his job, at cruising
through life in that do-or-die-for-it maelstrom of energy that
propelled him from one victory to another. Dan barely entertained the halting, wavering uncertainty that others lost sleep
over. Phoebe had always adored his untiring, relentless opti-
mism and lack of wishy-washy moral ethics, but knew they
would simply provide her with excuse after excuse never to cut
loose. He'd hold on to her as a matter of principle.

The only way to let Dan go, she realised, was to do to him
exactly what Felix had done to Saskia and Jasmin and countless
others. To hurt him more than he was capable of hurting her.

She bent over the card and chewed the end of her pen,
reading those abbreviated, businesslike words.

P

Happy Birthday

D

x

Phoebe bit her lip and started to do a bit of doctoring, her
inky words blurring in front of her eyes.

Phoebe doesn't love you any more. She had a very

Happy Birthday, thank you. But she won't be going to Florence.

Don't call her again. Ever. She'll just hang up. She doesn't want you any more. She's

extremely happy with Felix, who screws like a steam train, doesn't snore or have bad breath, and doesn't have to run back to his wife ten minutes after he's shot his wad.

Have a nice life.

Ps Not keen on the rug.

x

Pushing the card into the red envelope along with the keys, she placed it on the table and let herself out of the flat before she had time for second thoughts.

Phoebe was woken up the next morning by the phone.

'It's your sis,' rasped Milly. 'You're going to hate me for this, but Felix-your-bum was up to his old tricks last night.'

'What?' Phoebe froze.

'Picking up a stray dog, patting it on the head and then swinging it by its wagging tail.'

Phoebe closed her eyes. 'Where?'

'Bar Barella. Pissed out of his head. He'd gone there to see you. I suppose you were with Dan?'

'No.' Phoebe leant against the kitchen door frame. 'It's over. Kaput. Finis. Final curtain with too few regrets to mention and too many tears for a packet of three-ply Kleenex to cope with.'

'Oh, Phoebe, I'm so proud of you!'

'Wish I were,' she sighed. 'Tell me about Felix.'

What she heard did nothing for her plummeting spirits. He had acted out his standard scenario. When Milly and Goat had gone into Bar Barella, Felix was already chatting up a girl who, as Milly succinctly described her, was 'uglier than Derek Jameson in drag'. Just as her eyes were lighting up with delighted, disbelieving idol-worship, he'd slapped her down as easily as a militia man taking out a kitten with a Kalashnikov.

'He was crazy, Phoebes,' Milly finished. 'I mean, Christ, he's so bloody lovely looking and clever and funny and basically to die for. But his brain's boiled.'

'It's not,' she said hotly. 'He's just incredibly insecure and unhappy.'

'You what?' Milly laughed sardonically.

'He hurts people because he's hurting so much himself,' she tried to explain. 'It's the only thing he can relate to – total, chopped-limb rejection. He's twisted, yes, and gets his kicks by kicking other people in the teeth. But he doesn't appreciate that they haven't deadened their nerve endings as he has. He's so desperate to be loved, and so certain that he won't be, he somehow tries to kill it before it dies of natural causes.'

'Phoebe,' Milly started cautiously, 'have you been eating hash cakes or dropping acid or something?'

'No.' She sighed unhappily. 'But I was thinking of making a cup of tea.'

'Phoebe, tell me you don't give a damn about Felix Sylvian and his twisted little ways?'

'I think the milk's off, though.'

'Tell me you don't love him, Phoebe?'

'I'll have to go to the corner shop and search through the cartons for something within a month of its sell-by date.'

'Phoebe, you're going to get so, so burned. He'll crush you, Big Sis.'

'I'm pretty crushed already.'

'And Saskia will die. She will simply die if you do this to her.'

Phoebe couldn't answer.

'I'm beginning to wish you'd stuck with Dan.'

'Thanks, Mill.'

Fliss had to be summoned from the Camden studio to be told about Phoebe's kamikaze drinks party that evening. She was extremely short on the phone.

'I'm busy, Phoebe,' she muttered distractedly, Jazz FM blaring in the background.

'Felix and Dylan are coming round for drinks tonight.'

'How nice,' Fliss hissed. 'If you want me to lend you twenty quid for gin and twiglets you're out of luck. And I hope you're not planning to use my bottle of cooking Fitou, because it's been open over a week.'

'I want you to be here,' she sniffed tearfully. 'Please.'

'I'm glazing all night.'

'Please, Fliss,' Phoebe sobbed. 'I need you. Why are you being so bloody?'

'If you don't know that, then you clearly haven't opened your big green eyes on those very few occasions you've been at home recently.'

'Look, I know the place is a mess and I'll tidy it up this afternoon, I promise. Just come back this evening for a couple of hours.'

'Phoebe, I don't give a fuck about the fact that I can see more of your junk than the carpet at the moment and that every time I want to get a mug for my tea, I have to go through to your frigging bedroom to find the one with the least fur growing out of it.'

'No, you don't sound like you mind,' Phoebe said in a small voice.

'Okay, it winds me up,' Fliss admitted grumpily. 'But what really makes me bloody, frigging well despair is having your left-of-Trotsky sister marching around the flat with that animated-astrakhan coat boyfriend of hers, chucking out my minced-beef, and sloping off with my clothes. Then there's the fact that I'm a one-woman receptionist for your friends' calls, chat-line for your mother, debt collectors and married lover, and counsellor for bloody Saskia! I do have a life of my own, Phoebe – albeit very dull and uneventful compared to your globe-trotting, model-seducing, whacky one.'

'It's, not exactly been fun, Fliss,' Phoebe muttered between clenched teeth as she fought tears. 'Right now I'd willingly swap.'

Desperate and beginning to panic, she played a very dirty trick.

'If you come back, you can drill Felix about Mungo.'

'I don't need to,' Fliss said in a chilly voice. 'Now, was there anything else?'

Phoebe closed her eyes and went for broke.

'Okay, here goes,' she spluttered. 'I dumped Dan last night and my sister has just told me that Felix was doing his famous kiss-and-beat-up routine in central London at about the same time because he thinks that I was in fact Dan-banging. Saskia is going to kill me for it – but only if she finds out in time to get in there before I kill myself. Dylan fancies you rotten. I, despite everything, fancy Felix rotten. And I'll burn all your sketchpads, your murder notes and your signed photograph of Sean Bean if you're not back here by eight.'

Fliss was racing up the stairs within half an hour.

She found Phoebe washing up in floods of tears.

'Is Sean still intact?' she joked uneasily as she wavered in the doorway.

A sud-covered plate smashed against the wall with remarkable force.

'Oh, Phoebes.' Fliss dashed across the room and gave her a hug. 'I'm so sorry for being a moody bitch.'

'No, I am,' she wailed guiltily. 'You've been a brick.'

'Through a window, you mean,' Fliss laughed. 'I'm just as stressed out as an old elastic band at the moment. I'll make us a cup of tea.' She took a saucepan from the drainer and, filling it with water, carried it over to the hob.

She moved the hissing pan around on the hob and hummed awkwardly. 'Does Dylan Abbott really fancy me?' she muttered, red curls falling over her red cheeks.

'Lots.'

'But he's a bit of a stooge, isn't he?'

'He's lovely,' Phoebe wailed indignantly.

'Well, then.' Fliss pulled a couple of mugs from the drainer and started flapping cupboards open as she searched for tea bags. 'We'll just have to get tarted up. Can I have the Gaultier?'

'If I can have the fuck-me-pumps.'

Straightening up, Fliss grinned, and then bit her lip worriedly.

'You don't really fancy Felix, do you? After everything he did to Saskia?'

Phoebe washed a saucer for the third time, practically removing the glazed pattern with her rubber-gloved fingers. 'No,' she lied. 'I was just trying to throw you into marching back to give me a telling off.'

'You did that all right,' Fliss laughed. 'Christ, you should have bloody heard the way Saskia's been banging on about you and him this week. She was climbing walls like a steeplejack on acid, mate. If you don't go through with this, she'll go into one and never come out.'

'Go into what?' Phoebe fished around in the soapy water for the cutlery.

'Into one – you know, a crazy bender. It's a figure of speech.'

'Oh.' Phoebe attacked a potato masher with the washing up brush. 'Well, I have a feeling that Felix is going to go into one tonight.'

Dressed in one of Portia's slinky, oyster pink slip-dresses, Phoebe was shaking so much that Fliss forced a vast brandy down her before Felix and Dylan arrived.

'Thanks for tidying up,' she said gratefully between slugs.

'Had to,' Fliss grinned. 'You're so accident-prone at the moment, you'd turn over a bumper car. Are you getting the curse?'

'No I'm just basically cursed,' Phoebe smiled, her teeth chattering with nerves. She was terrified that Felix wouldn't turn up at all, or that he would storm in and go straight into the I-wouldn't-piss-on-you-if-you-were-on-fire routine.

'Do you really think he'll try to pre-empt you? Get in there first with the big heave-ho?'

She shrugged. 'I haven't a clue what he'll do, but I have a feeling it'll be pretty messy.'

Felix rolled up on time with a huge, wrapped parcel held out like a smoking bomb in front of him. Leaving faint traces of peppery aftershave in his wake, he looked unspeakably hand-some, dressed in a beautifully cut green suit with a crumpled white silk shirt beneath and coffee-coloured braces. His hair gleamed with freshly showered cleanness, his blue eyes with sparkling malevolence.

Phoebe knew instantly that his attitude to her had totally changed. He was outwardly all polite, deferential, flop-haired English charm, but it was as though he was holding a knife behind his back waiting to pounce without warning. She could almost hear him ticking.

'Happy birthday.' He kissed her hard on the cheek and crammed the parcel into her arms. 'You look beautiful, darling. In the pink, like Babs Cartland.' Despite the big, charming smile, there was an icy edge to his voice.

'In the red, actually.' Phoebe gripped on to the parcel, which was shifting alarmingly and very damp in one corner. 'You look lovely too.'

But Felix, as jittery as a caged jaguar at feeding time, had already moved on to Fliss with his big, on-off smile. 'Hi, you must be Jess. Dylan's just getting the booze – he'll be up in a minute. Gorgeous dress.'

'Thanks. Hi.' Fliss swallowed shyly and rubbed her damp palms on the skirt of the Gaultier dress, totally floored by his pacing, unchained sex-appeal. He seemed to eat up the space with his presence like a forest fire.

He gazed restlessly around the flat. 'Very *Withnail and I.*'

'We're not very domesticated,' Fliss apologised, positively melting under the effects of a head-to-foot blush. Standing behind him as he gazed around, she looked across at Phoebe and mouthed: 'He's *so gorgeous.*'

Phoebe widened her eyes meaningfully, but Fliss was staring at Felix again, her freckled face pink with aesthetic admiration.

'I'll have to get Piers over here.' Felix raised an eyebrow at the knicker-loaded radiators. 'He'd love it.' He turned back to Phoebe, eyes drinking her in.

'Piers is your agent, yes?' She was still clutching on to the parcel.

'How clever of you to remember, darling.' He flashed that bewitching smile again, his tone utterly condescending, his gaze unfriendly.

'How did your lunch go yesterday?' Phoebe cleared her throat uncomfortably, determined not to rise.

'Oh, you know – knife, fork, plate, food. The usual,' he said lightly.

Fliss laughed, unaware that Felix's eyes were now boring into Phoebe's as though he was pointing a gun straight at her temple.

Turning back to Fliss, his gaze lit upon the split brown Dralon sag-bag. 'Tell me, is that some sort of seat, or do you have an elephant with worms?'

'Hi, everyone!' Dylan appeared through the door. 'Sorry – took ages to find an off-licence. Brought you some sham.'

He wandered in clutching two bottles of Bollinger, hair on end, collar inside out, and kissed Phoebe on both cheeks. 'Happy birthday for Sunday, darling. You haven't opened your present yet!'

Phoebe looked down at her wriggling, leaping box. She'd been holding it so tightly for support, so appalled by the change in Felix, that she'd almost forgotten about its shifting presence.

'It appears to be opening itself,' she noticed in amazement. A small, pink snout was forcing itself up through the paper. 'Hi, Fliss,' Dylan added shyly, hardly looking over his shoulder at Phoebe's flat-mate.

'Hi. Open it then, Phoebes.' Fliss was bustling about in embarrassment, shifting bowls of crisps around by a vital few inches and dashing over to the CD player to put Squeeze on as planned. She didn't once look at Dylan, acutely aware of his admiration and terrified of shattering those flattering pre-conceptions by doing something daffy.

The box was threatening to take off. Phoebe put it on the floor and the spotty pink snout abruptly disappeared with a startled, growling yelp.

'She sounds like my brother first thing in the morning,' Felix muttered, peering into Phoebe's bedroom. 'I thought you could call her Bitch, because she is one – my favourite song's playing. How sweet of you to know.'

Tensing her back at his biting sarcasm, Phoebe ripped at the hole in the paper that whatever was inside had already created itself.

As 'Up The Junction' described a love-affair in a smelly Clapham bed-sit, she flapped back the cardboard box's lids and gasped with amazement. One brown and one wall eye peered up at her cautiously. Then one brown ear and one white one cocked merrily. Several inches behind them a tiny, stumpy tail was thumping excitedly. Phoebe laughed with amazed delight and reached out a cautious hand.

As a pink tongue the size of a postage stamp lapped at her fingers, the thumping stump accelerated so much that an entire, small skewbald body started gyrating and quivering like a jelly in a Los Angeles tremor.

'What is it?' Fliss stretched over the open box.

'A puppy.' Phoebe laughed tearfully. 'A Jack Russell puppy.' She gathered the little bundle up. It was wearing a huge, pink ribbon around its neck, so large that it looked like a child with a joke bow tie.

'She's just like Rabbit.' Phoebe looked up at Felix happily, letting the puppy lap her chin and snuffle her mouth. 'Thank you. She's utterly gorgeous. Thank you so much.' She laughed as the puppy tried to nibble her nose.

For a brief moment, his steely gaze threatened to soften as he watched Phoebe burying her face in the squirming, ecstatic little bundle. But he just cocked his head and flicked a big, shallow, male model smile.

'Glad you like her,' he replied curtly. 'Now is there any chance of a bloody drink around here?'

Dylan coughed awkwardly. 'I'll open one of these.' He waggled a Bollinger bottle and escaped to the kitchen.

Phoebe put the wriggling puppy down, where it immediately squatted and peed liberally on the landlord's shag-pile before staggering behind the sofa like a driver groggily escaping from a car accident.

'Is she ill?' Phoebe crept after her worriedly.

'Car sick,' Felix muttered. 'Believe me, you'd feel like that if

Dylan had just got you from Notting Hill to Islington in twenty minutes.'

Fliss's laugh disappeared into a nervous cough as she saw his wintry expression.

'She's throwing up,' Phoebe noticed anxiously.

'I'm afraid that's Mungo's fault.' Felix was lighting a Chesterfield. 'He's been house-training her over the last couple of days. He always pukes up behind the sofa too.'

'Does he pee on the carpets as well?' Phoebe looked at him over her shoulder.

'Mmm, but he always puts the lid up.'

'I'll – er – help Dylan get some glasses!' Fliss dashed into the kitchen.

Felix and Phoebe gazed at one another in silence. 'Up the Junction' thudded its way to a halt. From behind the sofa, the sound-effects of a very small stomach regurgitating puppy food were rapidly replaced by the sound of a small, pink nose trying to inhale half a Hob-nob from beneath the shaggy rug.

'I got very pissed last night,' said Felix, his face expressionless. 'I called in to see you, but you weren't there. So I got drunk.'

'I know,' she muttered.

'You do?'

'My sister was there.'

Felix ignored that.

In the kitchen, Dylan and Fliss were trying to stretch out their small talk with Pinteresque pauses in order to avoid going back through. Dylan was lingering because he wanted to be alone with Fliss long enough to try and chat her up; Fliss was loitering because she thought Phoebe and Felix wanted to be alone together. She still hadn't looked Dylan in the eye.

The sound of Squeeze pounding through from the sitting room prevented them from hearing the sotto voce discussion by the sofa. Fliss assumed that Phoebe and Felix, from the red hot looks they had been giving one another just now, were indulging in a high-octane necking session.

'You're a sculptor, I hear?' Dylan cleared his throat noisily as he unwound the wire on the champagne cork.

'Mmm.' Fliss dived nervously into the fridge for some celery, suddenly finding that she couldn't think of a thing to say about her sculpture, a topic she normally bored for England on.

Pulling off the metal casing, he swallowed and decided to try again.

'D'you like Squeeze then?'

From inside the muffled sound-proofing of the fridge, Fliss thought he said: 'Do you want a squeeze then?'

'You've a frigging nerve!' She backed out furiously.

'I went to one of their gigs years ago,' Dylan was saying. 'With my elder brother. We – I'm sorry?'

'Nothing!' Fliss realised her mistake and, shooting across to the chopping board, began hacking away at the celery, her face burning.

Dylan watched her firm, plump bottom gyrate as, ignoring him, she cut rather chaotic crudités. He then stared at the champagne bottle rather forlornly, certain that he didn't stand a chance.

From the sitting-room speakers, Squeeze were cheerfully getting to grips with a long riff.

Phoebe was getting to grips with Felix at his most explosive.

'D'you want to know why I got pissed last night?' he whispered, shivering with animosity. 'Although I guess you already do. I'm sure little sister fully re-briefed you after your married lover de-briefed you. You're a fucking slut, Phoebe.'

'Felix, I – '

'You'd wrap those long legs around anything with a gold card, wouldn't you?'

'Now wait a – '

'Dan was very short on the phone, wasn't he?' Felix cut in, his voice barely more than a breath. 'I take it you two were humping at the time?'

'What are you talking about?' Phoebe blinked in confusion.

'Oh – didn't he say that it was me calling?' Felix cocked his head. 'I guess he was a bit distracted.'

'You called the flat last night?' she gasped. 'Dan's flat?'

'Catch up, darling.' He groped for a cigarette. 'You're not that thick. You gave me the number, remember?'

'Oh, God.' Phoebe buried her face in her hands. Felix must have called while Dan was pacing around waiting for her, and assumed that they were there together. And Dan must have pounced on the call thinking it was her.

'Oh, God. I've screwed everything up,' she moaned into her palms.

'No, Phoebe,' Felix hissed. 'You've just screwed Dan. I guess I'll have to wait another ten years and marry someone else before you want me, is that it?'

The puppy chose this point to trot out from behind the sofa, gripping the strap of an ancient Wonderbra between its little white teeth. The bra, trapped under a sofa leg, stretched out like bungee elastic.

'I want you to know,' Felix breathed, pulling Phoebe's hands away from her face and glaring at her, 'that I'm only here tonight because Dylan fancies your flatmate so fucking much that he's been pleading with me all day. I came to shut him up.'

'Felix – ' Phoebe blinked, his beautiful face swimming in front of her eyes.

'Don't you dare play that big-eyed, lost soul act on me.' He turned away. '"Dan and I are washed up, Felix." "I don't want to be a mistress, Felix." You're so two-faced, I'm surprised you can see straight!'

He gazed at the kitchen, his voice suddenly switching from steely to friendly and upbeat as he yelled through to the others: 'Any chance of that drink, Dyldo? Don't tell me the foil's foxed you again. You peel it off, mate. Think sweety wrapper.'

Phoebe sagged against the sofa, astounded that he could sound so completely cheerful. At her feet, the puppy was growling furiously and tugging at the Wonderbra.

'Think fuck off.' Laughing, Dylan loped in from the kitchen with the bottle and four glasses, followed by Fliss who was carrying a tray of nibbles and had a huge blob of blue cheese dip on her fringe as well as a celery leaf poking out of her watch strap.

'That looks glorious, darling.' Felix grinned at her and sank down on the sofa.

Fliss flushed, settling her tray on the coffee table. She found him impossibly shy-making.

Phoebe, her back to the room, carefully wiped her tears and wondered whether to run away, or stay and fight.

The next moment, Felix had reached out an arm and pulled her down on to his lap, wrapping his arms around her shoulders affectionately and propping his chin on her shoulder.

'I'm going to feed this beautiful, skinny bird up,' he laughed, reaching out for a crisp.

Phoebe, clamped in like a joey in a kangaroo pouch, wondered what the hell he was playing at.

'Have a crisp, darling,' Felix breathed in her ear, holding a tortilla chip inches from her mouth and dropping a slow kiss on her shoulder. 'I'm going to nibble you instead.'

Dylan, trying to distribute the champagne around four very mis-matched glasses, looked up from pouring and suddenly caught Phoebe's eye.

Seconds later there was an enraged yelp from below as the puppy, dripping with Bollinger, shot beneath the coffee table.

'I know you're not the biggest animal lover in the world, Dyldo,' Felix laughed, winking at Fliss, 'but isn't drowning puppies a bit macabre even by your standards?'

From then on his behaviour ran to a predictable pattern. Whenever Fliss and Dylan were in the room, he was all over Phoebe, as charming and attentive as a gigolo on a big-bucks job. Whenever they were alone, he cut her dead.

Phoebe fought her way to the opposite end of the sofa, clutched the squirming, wall-eyed puppy and fought tears.

Fliss and Dylan, far from getting on like house-mates on fire, were barely looking at one another, let alone talking, she noticed wretchedly.

'We could all tell a joke,' Dylan suggested in desperation.

'You start then.' Felix cocked his head at him, his hand stroking Phoebe's thigh with disturbing, lazily cruel expertise.

'Right – okay.' Dylan took a huge swig from his glass and

glanced nervously at Fliss, wondering just how politically incorrect and blue he could get away with being.

Sensibly, he opted to be as clean and green as Jonathon Porritt. And sadly about as funny.

'I went for a drink with some mates last night,' he started hopefully. 'And they said "Dylan, – why have you got that mushroom on your head?" And I said: "Hey – "'

'I'm a fun guy to be with!' Fliss, Felix and Phoebe finished in unison with a disappointed groan.

There was a sticky pause, momentarily broken by the puppy clambering stiffly off Phoebe's lap, stretching her pink nose towards the ceiling and kicking out her short, white back legs behind her with a contented sigh, then heading across the sofa's Berlin Wall towards Felix's lap where she curled up again and dropped off once more, her white snout buried between his green trousered knees.

Disloyal fink, Phoebe thought irritably, glaring at the tiny, sleeping skewbald curl.

Once Fliss had excused herself to the loo and then provided the alibi of a lost contact lens, she and Phoebe held an emergency meeting in the bathroom. The puppy insisted on coming too, launching itself off Felix's lap and pursuing them in a flurry of excited yapping.

'What are you doing, Phoebes?' Fliss demanded. 'Felix is crazy about you. He's all over you, and you're mooning around like a frigging zombie.'

'He's changed, Fliss.' Phoebe repaired her make-up in the mirror for something to do, her hands shaking so much that her face was under threat of looking like a Jackson Pollock painting.

'He's divine,' she sighed, hoicking up her tights with a few star-jumps. 'I mean, I know he's a monster underneath and all that, but I had no idea he'd be so funny and laid-back. God, you can see why no one ever says no.'

'That is not the Felix I was in Paris with,' Phoebe muttered, jabbing a finger towards the door. 'He's freaked. He's suddenly started playing the game by his rules, and I can't cope.'

'You bloody have to,' Fliss insisted. 'For Saskia's sake.'

Phoebe almost blinded herself with her mascara wand. She'd barely given Saskia a thought all night, she realised wretchedly.

At her feet the puppy, having peed twice on the pink bathroom carpet, was now trying to eat a cotton wool bud, holding it between her tiny, white front paws like a Gladiator with a pugil stick.

'You have to get a grip, Phoebe.' Fliss loomed beside her shoulder in the mirror and caught her eye with a persuasive, beady stare. 'His rules are there to be broken, mate. I know it must be horrible to pretend you fancy someone you don't, but you promised Saskia you'd do it. You can't give up now, just because he's doing the big seducer act on you.' She sighed slightly dreamily. 'I half wish she'd asked me to do it for her. He is such a girl's day-dream!'

'He is not.' Phoebe angrily screwed the top on her mascara.

'Get a grip then.' Fliss grabbed the mascara from her and waggled it like a sergeant major's baton before uncapping it and peering suspiciously at the colour.

'In that case,' Phoebe sighed shakily, 'help me out and try a bit harder with Dylan, Fliss. He's making a real effort to talk to you.'

'I have tried.' Peering straight ahead as she dabbed the wand end on her lashes, Fliss avoided Phoebe's gaze.

'Offering him the crisp bowl once every five minutes isn't the greatest conversation starter,' Phoebe pointed out kindly. 'He really likes you. Chat him up a bit.'

'Do I have to?' Fliss asked, muscling in on more of the mirror as she reapplied her lipstick. 'He's so boring – and he looks like Will Carling.'

Phoebe took a deep breath, realising that Dylan didn't come up to the Fliss aesthetics minimum height mark. She guessed that she'd have to be indiscreet just one more time.

'He writes those books you read with your mouth open and your hanky poised.'

'He *what*?' Fliss turned so quickly that she striped crimson lipstick across her flat-mate's nose. 'I'm sorry! Here let me get you a tissue. He what did you say?'

'He's Henrietta Holt, Fliss, Red Rose's steamiest romantic author.' Phoebe rubbed the lipstick away with her finger and found heself looking like a port-swilling pensioner. 'Felix told me in Paris.'

'Dylan is Henrietta Holt?'

'Shh!' Phoebe glanced nervously towards the door. 'Dylan doesn't realise that Felix knows, so for Christ's sake don't let on. I'm sure I shouldn't have told you.'

'I'm glad you did.' Fliss spat on to a piece of loo roll and lunged towards Phoebe's nose.

Phoebe ducked away.

'And you've got to admit he's got stunning eyes,' she tested the ground.

'Stunning,' Fliss agreed enthusiastically, dropping the tissue in the bin. 'Are you seriously okay?'

'No,' Phoebe smiled bravely. 'But I guess I'll call on hidden lack-of-reserve and fight Felix at his own game. For Saskia.'

'Calm down,' Dylan hissed at Felix as he flipped through Phoebe's mail. 'She's gorgeous, isn't she?'

'She's a cunt.'

Dylan took in a sharp breath. 'I was talking about Fliss.'

'She's a wet fart.' Felix moved on to stare at the pictures on the wall. 'And this place is a fucking pit.'

'I rather like it – it's kind of retro.'

'Kind of let go, you mean,' Felix drained his glass. 'They're a pair of total sluts.'

'So are we.'

'That's different,' Felix snapped.

'No, it's not,' Dylan sighed, glancing towards the bathroom door. 'Just bloody well calm down, will you?'

Biting his lip, he knew that he should take Felix home, should sober him up and harangue him about the way he was treating Phoebe. Instead he opened the second bottle of champagne and helped himself to some Dutch courage, deliberately not offering Felix any. He felt guilty as hell for being so selfish, but wanted to try just once more with Fliss.

Felix headed for the bottle in murderous silence.

'What d'you suppose they're doing in there?' Dylan stared at the bathroom door again.

'Drowning the puppy?' Felix swigged straight from the Bollinger bottle. 'How the fuck should I know?'

Dylan stared at him. Felix's blue eyes were sparkling with vitriol and spite. He was high on nervous energy, overdosing on adrenaline, freebasing on unhappiness, and despite the steady hands and clear gaze, he was very, very drunk. He'd been knocking back tequila since before five. Felix could hide the signs better than anyone Dylan knew, but there came a point when even he was no longer in control of what he was doing. Dylan had only seen him on this sort of bender a couple of times before.

'Don't do this, Felix,' he pleaded.

'Why not?' he demanded, raising the bottle with a big, easy smile. 'She's behaved like a fucking whore, she deserves to get treated like one. She's taking it, isn't she? I mean, forgive me for going deaf, but I haven't heard any complaints. So why not?'

'You know why not,' Dylan said quietly, feeling his knuckles whiten.

'Because you want to get your rocks off with her gingery little flat-mate?' Felix laughed. 'C'mon, she's a cheap, northern slapper.'

Dylan glanced back at the bathroom door, terrified that Fliss would overhear. He knew he had to stay calm. Rising to Felix's bait and yelling back at him was the equivalent of trying to put out a fire with paraffin.

'Because,' he muttered, almost too angry to speak, 'Phoebe's different. Which is precisely why you're being so utterly bloody insufferable right now.'

'She's a cunt.' Felix threw back another long swig of Bollinger and then spun around as the bathroom door opened.

'Phoebe, darling,' he purred, brushing past Fliss and pulling Phoebe into a practised, delicate kiss of faint-making tenderness.

Phoebe froze for a moment and then, curling her arms

around his neck and arching her body up towards him, started
to kiss him back, her eyes locked with his in an angry challenge.

Fliss tried not to watch, but voyeurism got the better of her
for a few guilty seconds. The electricity crackling between them
was phenomenal. Scuttling back towards her sag-bag, she
caught Dylan's eye and shot her red eyebrows up.

Dylan coughed and looked away, unable to watch.

'So – er,' he pushed a full glass of champagne towards Fliss,
'tell me about this murder mystery party. It sounds wonderful.'

'Actually, you might be able to help.' She looked at him with
shy excitement.

'Yes?' Dylan looked delighted.

'With the characters and motives and stuff.'

'Well, yes, if you want me to.' Dylan scratched his head,
absurdly flattered. 'But, I mean, why me?'

'Er . . .' Fliss glanced across the room at Phoebe, who seemed
to be under attack from both Felix and the puppy now. 'Phoebe
said you were a bit of a writer.'

'The blocked bit mostly.' Dylan smiled modestly. 'Okay, run
your ideas past me, but I warn you, I'll compliment every single
one.'

'You're hurting me,' Phoebe warned as Felix's teeth sank into
the soft flesh of her lips.

'I know,' he muttered.

'I was talking to the dog,' Phoebe pulled away and headed
through to the kitchen, pursued by the skewbald puppy which
was grappling with the strap ends of her fuck-me-pumps.

Following a few seconds later, Felix lounged against the
kitchen table and swigged from the Bollinger bottle, watching
her as she poured the puppy some water and milk before
delving further into the fridge for a bottle of wine, then stalking
back to the table for the corkscrew.

'Take the foil off first,' he muttered, idly watching as the wall-
eyed puppy, bored of its snack, tottered across the lino to sniff
Phoebe's duffle bag.

Ignoring him, Phoebe started plunging the metal spiral

straight through the foil and into the cork. Of course it got stuck, and she was left grappling with a little heap of shredded metal and crumbling cork.

'I'll do it,' Felix breathed into her neck, suddenly behind her. She jumped away as though stabbed in the back.

'Feel free,' she snarled. 'I'm sure you've pulled harder things.'

'You, my darling, were as easy to pull as an aged aunt's leg.'

'I wasn't pulled, I was pushed.'

He freed the cork within seconds, sliding it out with a satisfying, squealing pop.

Unable to bear the smug conceit in his face, Phoebe watched as the puppy clambered on top of her duffle bag like a toddler scaling a king-sized bed and, waggling its little white stump, curled up and conked out.

'Glass of wine, darling?' Felix smiled.

'No thanks,' Phoebe stormed back into the sitting room.

Fliss and Dylan were nose-to-nose now. Neither took any notice as Phoebe hovered nearby, willing to offer a few ropy suggestions for characters – Stu Pidbint and Sadie Stick-B'stard for starters.

Feeling excluded, she wandered over to the stereo and put Cat Stevens on. She then picked her way huffily over to the most isolated sag-bag and perched on it like a buzzard on a corpse.

Cat was crooning soothingly through Moon Shadow. Phoebe closed her eyes and wished that she could be carried away too. When she opened them again, she found herself staring straight at Felix. He was shouldering the kitchen doorframe and watching her now. Phoebe realised his expression had softened to near tenderness, his eyes no longer as cold as two Eskimo fishing circles in the flat, Arctic ice.

When the phone rang, she jumped so much that her head almost glued itself to the ceiling.

Felix, standing right over the ringing receiver, picked it up.

'Hello there,' he smiled mockingly at Phoebe and then turned away, 'you have got through to Phoebe Fredericks' boudoir,' seeing the framed photo by the phone, he bent over and peered at it as he spoke. 'I'm afraid she can't come to the phone right now, because she's coming elsewhere. Can I take a message? Hello? Hi there? How extraordinary – they've rung off.' Replacing the receiver, he squatted down to examine the photograph more closely.

'Oi, that could have been for me!' Fliss wailed. 'I'm expecting R.S.V.P.s at the mo.'

Phoebe was glaring at Felix's back with such fury that she half expected two little holes to start to smoulder in the back of that crumpled silk shirt as though burned by lasers. Gripping onto the landlord's favourite tapestry magazine stand, she struggled up from the sag-bag with some difficulty.

'How fucking dare you,' she hissed angrily, finally clambering out of the bag. 'You spoiled little shit.'

'Who dares rings,' Felix murmured, straightening up with the silver frame. 'I take it that was the Bionic Dan?' he nodded toward the phone and then looked down at the photograph. 'I must say, you were an extraordinarily freaky-looking child, Phoebe. Tell me, did you have operations to correct the ears and the squint or did they just come right themselves? And who's the moron with the side-burns? I take it the nose-picking gnome on the tractor is your sister and the Dana lookalike is – '

Too angry to speak, Phoebe threw a slap of such velocity that his eyes smarted. But the smooth smile stayed firmly in place.

'I don't know about you guys,' he laughed, 'but I rather fancy watching a video. You don't have a copy of *Love Story* by any chance?'

Somehow, in vino and in desperation, Phoebe made it through the rest of the night.

They sat through *The Big Chill* with dips on their laps and wine-glasses between their knees. Phoebe, next to Dylan on the sofa, stared fixedly at the screen as though her neck was in a surgical collar, and didn't take in a thing. Felix, lounging on the rickety papisan chair with his ankle hooked across his knee and the puppy curled up on his silk stomach, watched her throughout. Fliss and Dylan talked over most of the film's dialogue, drank too much, smoked more than a packet of cigarettes between them and discussed the murder mystery house party, taking ideas from the film and drunkenly singing along to the famous soundtrack.

As the titles slid up the screen, Dylan turned to Phoebe. 'You okay, darling?'

'Huh?' She looked at him and found that tears were sliding down her cheeks and on to her neck.

'You big wet lump,' Dylan laughed, putting a comforting arm around her shoulder and pulling her into his side. 'I hate to think what Bambi does to you.'

Phoebe pressed her cheek to his warm, deodorant-smelling cotton shirt and tried to laugh it off.

'I always cry at weddings, funerals and bank statements,' she sniffed, stealing a glance at Felix.

He was glaring jealously at Dylan.

Unaware of his anger, Dylan ruffled Phoebe's hair and kissed her on the head.

'Must have a piss.' He hauled himself out of the sofa and staggered rather unsteadily into the bathroom.

'I'll open another bottle.' Fliss scuttled through to the kitchen, as cowardly as ever.

The puppy scrabbled off Felix's lap and tottered greedily after her.

Felix glared at Phoebe.

She glared back and then, switching tactics, smiled.

Yawning widely, she stretched back on the sofa and flexed her stiff legs out in front of her, rotating her ankles.

'Cover your mouth,' Felix muttered in an undertone.

Staring at him, Phoebe raised her eyebrows mockingly and carried on yawning. 'You cover it.'

The next moment, he was across the room, his mouth landing so hard against hers that the sofa nearly fell over backwards. All the air was knocked from her chest and she battled for breath, fighting to struggle free as Felix almost kissed her lungs inside out. With the whole weight of his body pinning her down, he gripped the back of her neck to keep her mouth clasped to his. Then, shifting his hips against hers, he forced his knees between her legs.

Unable to breathe or scream, Phoebe flailed her one free lower arm, madly searching for a glass or bottle to crown him with. Instead she groped her way through the ashtray, a tub of taramasalata and the video box.

'I'm afraid it's just Sainsbury's Muscadet . . .' Fliss wandered back into the room, absorbed in a wine bottle label. 'I was sure we – ah!' She looked up and went sharply into reverse. 'Coffee, too, I think.' She bolted back into the kitchen.

Groaning with humiliation and anger, Phoebe tried groping for the taramasalata tub again, deciding to plop its remaining contents on to Felix's squeaky clean hair. But he was already pulling away, eyes blinking with remorse and self-loathing, lips releasing hers. As he let go of the back of her neck, he suddenly pressed his face tightly to her shoulder. 'Forgive me.'

Too furious and breathless to speak, she pressed herself back against the sofa, hating the feeling of his weight on top of her, of his thighs between hers. She could feel him breathing fast and furious, the warmth of his breath on her collar, the silk of his hair against her neck.

Still pinning her down, he started to kiss her throat – slowly at first, and so gently she could barely feel his touch. Then, shifting his weight on to one elbow, he freed her trapped arm and ran his hand from her fingertips to her shoulder, slipping beneath the silky strap of her dress. All the time his kisses covered her throat with desperate, apologetic tenderness.

The next moment his mouth was slipping downwards, and his fingers were sliding the strap of her dress free.

Phoebe suddenly felt so turned on, she was almost faint.

She closed her eyes, appalled at herself but unable to help the squirming, spiralling leaps of excitement from lapping heat into her thighs, hot air into her chest and a drumming pulse between her legs. She felt so horny, she was close to explosion.

In the bathroom, the loo flushed noisily with a croak of ancient ballcock.

As Felix shifted more snugly on top of her, kissing very slowly and deliberately towards one nipple, Phoebe tried to pull away, desperate to wrest control of the situation. But the feeling of his hips sliding against hers and his tongue circling her tight, hot skin made her gasp, her free hand climbing his side to his back with excited, digging fingers. God, she had to stop this.

Phoebe finally freed her other arm and pushed him off just as the lock of the bathroom door clicked undone. Dylan lurched back into the room, his hair on end, the tails of his striped shirt poking out of his fly.

'I think that dog's peed in there.'

As Phoebe pulled up her shoulder strap, Felix rolled onto the sofa beside her and sat up, running an angry hand through his hair. Grabbing a packet of cigarettes from the coffee table, he lit one with shaking fingers.

'Where's Fliss?' Dylan sagged down on the Papisan chair. 'Gosh, this is comfortable.' It promptly collapsed, leaving him sitting in a circular cushion boat on the floor.

The tension of the moment was instantly lightened by Dylan's astounded expression, his profuse, dumbfounded apology and consequent attempt drunkenly to mend the chair which rendered him helpless with giggles.

Fliss, dashing back out of the kitchen to see what the commotion was about, also developed the giggles, and dropped down on to the split brown sag-bag to recover.

'They're so drunk they'll be like that for at least an hour.' Felix turned to Phoebe. 'Let's have a fuck.'

She stared at him. His eyes were as cool as two cubes of ice in a glass of blue Bols. The playful, teasing brat was back with vengeance.

'What'll we do with the other fifty-nine minutes?' She lifted her chin and returned his steady gaze.

'I'll ask you what day it is and you'll think up the answer.'

'Do I have to spell it correctly?' Phoebe glared at him. 'Because I'll need more time.'

Fliss was crawling from the sag-bag to the sideboard now, still weeping with laughter.

'Does anyone fancy a game of cards?' she giggled, collapsing momentarily by the bookcase as she thought about Dylan and the chair again.

'Brilliant idea!' Dylan wiped his eyes and extricated himself from the last remnants of the chair. Looking around at the rest of the furniture, he chose the safer option of sitting on the floor.

'You guys'll play a game, won't you?' He looked up at Felix and Phoebe.

'We already are.' Phoebe stood up and went through to the kitchen to wash her taramasalata and ash-stained hand.

The puppy was back on her duffle bag now, snoring reedily, a chewed art pencil at her sleeping pink nose. Phoebe watched her for an indulgent moment, wondering how someone as capable of inflicting cruelty as Felix could want to give her something so profoundly personal, so uniquely capable of giving pleasure. Nothing would remove the terrible memories of poor little Rabbit and her dreadful death, but this tiny, pink-nosed creature was so like her that Phoebe could see her before the tragedy: the potty puppy, the rebellious young dog, the truculent middle-aged madam who wanted to sleep on the left hand side of the bed, thank you. In being handed this puppy, Phoebe had suddenly been handed back the pleasant memories, and not just the pain of one agonising night.

Why, when Felix seemed so intent on hurting her, had he just given her back a small bundle of childhood happiness? she wondered helplessly.

Grabbing a carton of juice from the fridge, she wandered into the sitting room again and perched back on the sofa, as far away from Felix's sprawling, desirable, loathsome body as possible. He was sharing a joint with Dylan now. The recent grapple on the sofa might never have happened.

In the raucous game of hearts that followed, Fliss and Dylan cheated mercilessly but were both too drunk to present any great threat to Phoebe, who seemed to be on a rare winning streak. She took almost every game. Felix lost them all and grew sulkier and sulkier, his verbal sparring matches with her increasingly acid as his losses mounted.

'You're bloody good at hearts, Phoebe,' Dylan hiccuped at one point, as he shuffled most of the cards on to the floor.

'Makes up for having such a cold one,' snapped Felix.

'Better than not having one at all,' she muttered.

'That way it can't get broken. Whilst yours, my darling, has a little target painted on it.'

'No one bothered to paint a target on your sensitive spot, I take it. That ego would take more red emulsion than the Forth Bridge.'

After another hour of winning the drinking race uncontested, losing at cards and drawing at bitching bouts, Felix retreated into a huffy, hammered silence, shooting Phoebe the odd cross-eyed look of both fury and admiration. He made no further attempts to bridge the sofa gap, however. When – taking her turn to shuffle – she leant across him for an errant card, he flinched away as though being felt up by a popcorn pervert in a cinema.

Drained by the effort of sparring with him, she felt almost too deflated to keep her chin up and her tears down. She couldn't shake the memory of how turned on she'd been earlier. How, despite his aggressive, manipulative unhappiness, she had still wanted him more than she'd ever wanted Dan. More, she suspected, than she'd ever wanted anybody. The realisation made her feel out of control and frightened.

When she and Fliss finally booted Felix and Dylan out in the early hours, Dylan turned back to Fliss and reeled around for a few seconds with his arm outstretched before he finally found her shoulder with it.

'I'll meet you for lunch on Thursday then,' he reminded her woozily. 'To draft this covering letter for the guests.'

'See you then.' Fliss smiled, scuttling away before the kiss Dylan was aiming at her cheek hit home. 'Bye. Er – 'bye, Felix,' she called over her shoulder before ricocheting her way off both sides of the doorframe and into the kitchen.

Felix flashed a vague, drunken smile at the spot she had just vacated and watched as Phoebe kissed Dylan on the cheek.

'You're not driving are you?' she asked anxiously.

He shook his head. 'We'll get a cab in Islington.'

'There's a mini-cab place round the corner – just keep turning left.' Phoebe doubted that either of them was capable of going very far. 'And thanks for the champagne.' She hugged his comforting, swaying bulk.

'Felix paid for it.' Dylan hugged her back and then, catching Felix's expression, quickly backed off. 'Thanks for setting this up, darling.' He winked gratefully. There was apology, as well as gratitude, in those devoted dog eyes.

Shrugging, she watching him step carefully down the stairs, holding the rail for support and looking down at his feet to check that he was getting the right one in front of the other.

Felix, the expert drink-holder, was close to passing out. Leaning against the landing wall, he uncrossed his eyes and, snatching Phoebe's arm, pulled her out of the flat. There he spun her round, pressed his long, lean body against hers and kissed her without any tenderness. He tasted of wine, cigarettes and dope. As he woozily dropped his lips to her throat, Phoebe closed her eyes and tried to pull away.

Felix held her tighter and pressed his face into her chest.

'Do you love Dan-druff more than me?' he muttered in a sad, slurred undertone.

'I don't love you, Felix,' she replied slowly, aching from the lie.

He laughed into her neck.

'So Dan's your man, is he?' he muttered, his lips moist against her skin. 'How fucking sweet. I'd offer to throw rice at the wedding, but I've missed it, haven't I? Oh, but then again, you weren't there either, were you? Still, I'm sure there's a video of the ceremony we can watch. Give you a chance to wear a hat and whip your hanky out. I bet you look gorgeous in hats. Kind of cute and kinky . . .' He rambled into an unhappy silence.

Phoebe took a deep, shuddering breath.

'It's over, Felix,' she whispered.

'No!' He gripped the sides of her jaw and pulled her head up so that she was looking into his anguished face. 'No, it fucking isn't over! Don't say that. Please don't say that. I know I've been shitty tonight, but I was so bloody hurt. Don't you dare tell me it's over. I love you, Phoebe.'

She looked into his tearful blue eyes and knew for certain that she had started to love him too.

'I was talking about me and Dan,' she breathed, weak with relief.

Felix took a few, drunken seconds to absorb this. Slowly, giddily, his eyes stopped sliding between hers as though staring into two barrels of a shot gun and started shining with sudden hope.

'You mean, – last night . . .' he asked shakily '. . . you weren't . . .'

'I told him it was over.'

Remembering she had been too cowardly to tell Dan at all, but had left a cruel, cold note, she dropped her gaze to Felix's shirt, staring at the buttons and wishing she still believed thimbles were kisses as she had when reading Peter Pan as a child. Life would be so much simpler then.

'For good?' Felix propped his chin on her head.

'For bad, forever.'

'For me?'

'Felix!' Dylan yelled up from below. 'Have you passed out on the stairs or something?'

'Coming!'

Slipping a finger under her chin, he gently tilted Phoebe's face up and kissed her very slowly on the mouth. The jabbing, angry assault of earlier had gone. The delicious, heart-stopping kiss of old was back.

Perhaps I don't want thimbles, she thought weakly. No, I definitely don't want thimbles. Oh, boy, stuff your bloody thimbles, Phoebe!

Slipping her hands inside his jacket and around to his warm, silk-covered back, she almost fell through the wall with desire and happiness. Excitement was making her pulse-points sizzle and her head feel hollow again. Her heart was trying to bang its way out of her chest via her pelvis.

Felix propped his elbows against the wall behind her head

and, gasping between takes, kissed her more urgently. As he pressed his hips against hers, she felt lust bubbling between her legs and kissed him back so furiously their breathless, tongue-tied excitement threatened to go horizontal there and then on the landing.

'Felix!' Dylan yelled up from the ground floor. 'I've read the *Thompson's Directory* twice down here.'

Phoebe and Felix ignored him, their kisses growing more and more unruly.

Downstairs, Dylan started to read the *Thomson's Directory* aloud.

'Emergency Services – Dial 999,' he read drunkenly. 'I mean, what sort of thick bastard would need to look that up if they'd just seen flames lapping at their bed? "Oh, look, darling – flames!" "Hang on, darling, I'll just fetch the *Thomson's Directory*."'

Felix's hand had started to creep up inside Phoebe's dress. Her skin shivered under the touch of his warm, sliding fingers.

'Animal Welfare.' Dylan boomed on in a monotone as he started reading again, 'Business, Community Services, Councils . . .'

Felix slipped his hands down Phoebe's stomach and around to her lower thighs. As she arched against him, he gripped her tightly and pulled her up the wall until she could coil her legs around him.

'Environment and Conservation, Government Offices, Health – I'm bloody worried about yours, Felix! Have you died up there?' There were a few lurching footsteps on the stairs.

As Felix slid her up the wall and kissed her shoulders, Phoebe pulled great hanks of silk shirt from his waistband and, slipping her hands beneath it, laughed with joy as she encountered stomach muscles as warm and hard as sun-drenched cobbles.

'Look, I'm coming up to see if you're okay, mate!' a slurred voice shouted from the first landing.

Very, very reluctantly, Felix pulled his head back and lowered Phoebe to the ground, his body still pressed to hers.

'Coming!' he shouted back, dropping his lips straight on to Phoebe's parted ones again.

Spluttering with mirth, she started to laugh. The next moment they had collapsed into giggles, leaning into one another for support.

'Shut up, out there!' yelled a muffled voice from behind a door on the second landing.

Widening his eyes in mock horror, Felix pressed his lips to Phoebe's chin and bit it teasingly.

'Come back with me.' He wrapped his arms around her. 'I can't bear to let you go now.'

'No, Felix.' She very carefully loosened his grip on her, fighting to get her breath and her resolve back on course.

'Then let me stay here tonight,' he breathed, chasing her mouth with his lips.

'I don't think so.' Phoebe shook her head guiltily and pulled away.

'Phoebe!' he pleaded, half laughing, half entreating. 'You can't do this.'

You don't know how easy it would be not to, she thought weakly, her heart still pounding like a fist on a door, her legs so wobbly with desire that she was walking like an hour-old foal.

Without her to hold on to, Felix reeled slightly and clutched at the wall for support, still extremely drunk.

'You just can't do this,' he repeated in a beseeching voice.

'I can do this, Felix – and I am,' Phoebe smiled as she reached behind her to check that the flat door was still off the latch.

'Why?' He leaned against the wall, his breath coming in short, excited bursts.

'You treated me like something you had stuck to your shoe tonight,' she said in a low voice.

'I know, but – '

'You may have thought you were justified,' she interrupted, determined to say her piece before she lost the will to do it. 'But you bitched me up, you ran me down and you deliberately set out to shred my confidence. You showed me no trust, no respect, no compassion. And, Christ, that hurt, Felix.'

'I – ' He blinked, totally astounded.

'I know you're drunk, I know you were hurt and uptight and

you felt vindicated,' she went on. 'And, believe me, I know I'm not some snow white virgin who deserves a coat over every puddle. But don't you ever, ever dare behave like that with me again.'

She could hear Dylan plodding very slowly and randomly up the penultimate flight of stairs now, seemingly taking more steps sideways than upwards.

Felix was still leaning against the landing wall and gaping at her, torn between head-hanging, self-loathing guilt, and drunken frustration that he was too slewed to argue back with anything matching Phoebe's lucidity.

'Goodnight, Felix.' She stepped forward and kissed him gently on the cheek, pulling away as he tried to make a grab for her. 'Thank you so much for the puppy – she's lovely. I'll call you tomorrow when you're sober.'

She backed through the door and reached across to close it.

'Promish?' Felix stumbled sideways and disappeared from view as he reeled across to the opposite wall. 'Wait! Christ, I'm never getting this pissed again.' He reeled back into view once more. 'Promise you'll call me tomorrow?'

Phoebe pressed her cheek to the side of the door and smiled. 'I promise.'

'Phoebe, I lo—'

She shut the door with a gentle click.

In the sitting room, Fliss had conked out on the sofa, fast asleep with her mouth open and an unlit cigarette tucked between the first fingers of her left hand.

Phoebe did some rudimentary tidying up around her, clearing the glasses, bottles, food debris and ashtrays into the kitchen, where Puppy was still snoring, belly-up, on the duffle-bag, her big pink bow acting as a pillow.

Back in the sitting room, Fliss had rolled over and her red curls were falling into an empty crisp bowl.

Phoebe knelt beside her and gently woke her up.

Grumpy, groggy and bewildered, Fliss barely said a word as she tottered drunkenly towards her room. At the door, however, she turned back.

'You were ace tonight, mate,' she smiled sleepily, her eyes barely open, red hair everywhere. 'Saskia will be made up when she hears about it. He really does love you, you know – I can tell.' She pitched sideways slightly.

'Thanks,' Phoebe looked away unhappily, her eyes resting on the gift-wrapped puppy box and spotting an unopened card Sellotaped to the top.

'You know,' Fliss was lurching into her room. 'I think Dylan quite fancies me.' She collapsed onto her bed, fully dressed, and conked out again.

Phoebe couldn't bring herself to open the card until she was washed, scrubbed, stripped and under her duvet.

Pulling it out of the envelope she realised that it was hand-made.

On the front of a stiff piece of red card, Felix had glued down an absurdly unflattering cut-out photograph of himself taken for a tube-pass. In it, he looked like a seedy hick with a sheep-fetish. Beneath it, he had drawn a slightly odd-shaped body which was definitely more naive art than Tom of Finland, but was nonetheless hugely funny in its outlandish proportions, dressed in a striped 1920s man's bathing suit and flexing football-shaped Popeye muscles. The feet were simply enormous, the knees gloriously knobbly, and the three-fingered hands tiny.

Surrounding this cartoon of Felix were lots of little labels written in tiny, neat capitals, with arrows pointing to specific parts of the body.

Phoebe laughed aloud as she read them.

'Slight paunch due 1998. Beer Belly arriving early c21', 'Birthmark shaped like small Hebridean island – forgotten which', 'Three hairs located here at seventeen. Bought champagne. No more have grown since. Still hoping', 'Scar shaped like upside down Y from experimenting too enthusiastically with girl-pulling disco-dancing techniques in bedroom aged thirteen. Knee made violent contact with bedside table. Success in girl-department remained elusive for years', 'Moles in extremely unfortunate places – don't laugh when you see them.'

Phoebe cocked her head. The arrow disappeared intriguingly behind the striped bathing costume. As she had seen pretty much all of Felix in Paris, she hadn't a clue where they could be. The thought of one day finding out, and the memory of her earth-quaking excitement at the top of the stairs earlier that night made her sink back on her pillows and smile until her face hurt.

She looked at the card again, reading the last few labels with a smile that ached even more happily. It was doubly touching that someone as physically perfect as Felix could point out all his blemishes – some of them gloriously embarrassing – with such open, self-deprecating humour.

Inside the card was a huge headline:

HAVE YOU SEEN THIS MAN?

Beneath it, like a copy-line for a Hollywood blockbuster, was written:

He's celebrating a birthday near you.

He's armed with a present.

She's dangerous.

She's gorgeous.

Dylan's getting the giggles.

And the bloody present is biting my ankle

as I write this.

Underneath, Felix had written: 'On front of card are a few geographical pointers just in case you fancy an expedition. Below is the self-confessed Notting Hill fault line. We both think that you're utterly, totally, unforgettably – 24. All my love, Felix. xxx.'

Beneath that was a cut-out holiday snap of Dylan's face resembling a photo-fit of a mad axe-man. Because there was only an inch or so between it and the bottom of the card, the cartoon body looked like a squat Tweedle Dee. There was only one little label with an arrow shooting out of it. It simply said 'Dylan.'

Beside it, Dylan had scribbled a message in unspeakably scruffy handwriting. Phoebe could only make out 'Happy', 'bag' and 'ancient'.

She read and re-read the card over and over again, finding herself still giggling and shivering with happiness each time.

She tip-toed through to the kitchen to peek at Puppy, who was now curled tightly into the duffle-bag like a hibernating mouse, a chewed paintbrush at the end of her pink nose.

Phoebe danced back to bed and read the card just twenty or so times before switching her light out.

Five minutes later she switched the light back on and read it again.

'I love him,' she laughed, kissing the little passport picture and wishing more than anything that she'd agreed to go back with him tonight.

Turning to snuggle her burning cheek into her pillow, she gazed at the phone by the bed and closed her eyes in horror.

I haven't phoned Saskia back, she remembered with such a lead-weight sinking feeling of guilt that her mattress seemed to plunge through three floors and land with a bump in the ground floor flat.

36

The next morning, having put it off for as long as she conceivably could, Phoebe phoned Saskia at work.

'She's in Berkshire again, darling,' Georgette told her sulkily. 'Something about dry cleaning of all things. She was supposed to be back yesterday. I'm snowed under here.'

'Sorry.'

'I should hope you are – you recommended her. No chance of Fliss helping me out, I suppose?'

'She's at the studio.'

'Damn. How's it going with Felix?'

'Fine. Look, I must go.'

'Don't be polite, darling – you want me to keep my nose out, I quite understand. See you for the Bank Holiday bust-up. Is it all still on schedule?'

'As far as I know.'

'Of course you know. You're the one doing the dirty. I must say, I can't wait. I'm bringing Dennis.'

'You're what?' Phoebe almost gagged.

'My husband, Dennis. He heard about it and thought it was a glorious idea.'

'The revenge?' Phoebe was almost on the ceiling with amazement.

'No, darling, the murder mystery weekend!' Georgette laughed. 'He's going to drive me down on Saturday night. He's really looking forward to it too.'

'Wish I felt the same way,' Phoebe snapped, hanging up.

When she called Deayton, she found herself chatting to Gin for ten minutes about the perils of trying to empty one's airing cupboard after nearly twenty years of simply ignoring its deeper recesses. In the background, she could hear Saskia hissing, 'Is that Freddy?'

'I'd forgotten such things as candlewick bedspreads existed,' Gin moaned.

'I hadn't.' Phoebe winced at the memory. 'They're back in fashion now.'

'Oh, in that case you wouldn't like some, would you, Freddy?' Gin offered excitedly. 'They'll only go to jumble if not.'

At that moment Saskia finally succeeded in wresting the phone from her mother.

'That was Felix who answered the phone last night, I take it?' Saskia asked as soon as she had raced into a private room out of maternal earshot.

'Oh God, was it you that called when he picked up? I thought it was Dan—'

'Were you two in bed?' Saskia interrupted curtly.

'No.'

'Don't lie to me.'

Phoebe decided to brave a tirade and confess all. Well, almost all.

'So he thought you were with Dan on Monday night?' Saskia whistled. 'Christ, I'm amazed he didn't just dump you.'

'He almost did.'

'You'll have to make up for it this week – spend as much time with him as you can. We'll have to meet up urgently and plan a few romantic surprises for you to spring on him. I don't suppose there's any chance of you borrowing a car?'

Phoebe found the thought of another plotting session with Saskia too depressing to contemplate. She looked at the pile of bills in front of her. 'Saskia, I must do something about getting a job.'

'Oh, don't worry about that – this is far more important,' she snapped impatiently, her blinkered vision impervious to life's trivial necessities like paying bills, eating and breathing. 'Oh, and can you get all Portia's clothes together this morning and tell me when it's safe to come round and collect them? She wants them back.'

'God, I think Milly's nabbed about half of them.' Phoebe bit her lip worriedly.

'Well, get them back as fast as you can, Freddy. Portia's hopping. I'm down here as an alibi, and now Mummy's roped me in to cleaning out my sodding room.'

'I'll see what I can do,' she promised. 'Oh, and Felix has given me a puppy for my birthday.'

'He what?' Saskia's voice dropped to an ominous growl.

'He gave me a puppy,' Phoebe repeated edgily. 'She's conked out on the sofa right now.'

'What sort?' Saskia demanded.

'Jack Russell – short-legged.' Phoebe watched indulgently as four little white paws twitched in a deep, yelping dream.

'Is that what's making a sound like a tortured hamster in the background?'

'Er – I guess so,' Phoebe cleared her throat. 'She hasn't got a name yet. I thought you might help me think of one?'

'Oh, grow up, Phoebe,' Saskia muttered unhappily. 'Stop offering me second-hand boiled sweets like consolation prizes. Call the little monster whatever you want, just keep it out of my sight. I'll collect that stuff this evening.'

That afternoon Phoebe walked down to Lancaster Gate and met Felix in Hyde Park.

He was waiting for them by the fountains, dressed in his old jeans and a faded navy sweatshirt, a green baseball cap shading his eyes from the lowering evening sun. Sitting on the back of a bench with his feet up on the seat and gazing into the water, he didn't see Phoebe as she wandered towards him, carrying Puppy in an old canvas bag over her shoulder. The dog, peering excitedly over the top of the bag at all around her, brown and white ears pricked tightly forwards, let out a series of delirious yelps as she spotted Felix.

He turned round and laughed, scooping the wriggling, yelping little bundle out of the bag and kissing Phoebe at the same time.

'How did she sleep?' He let the puppy down on to the grass where she raced around in ecstatic, sniffing circles.

'Not bad.' Phoebe looked at him. He had great black rings under his eyes and enough stubble on his face to sand down a chest of drawers. 'Better than you, I guess.'

Felix glanced away, staring at the fountain for what seemed an interminable amount of time, tired blue eyes unblinking, bottom lip drawn beneath those enviably straight upper teeth.

'Look, I'm seriously sorry about last night.' He turned back to her, eyebrows practically knotted together in apology. 'I behaved like a sod.'

'Yup.' Phoebe pulled her dark glasses up on to her head and smiled against the sun as she looked into his eyes.

'I was certain you wouldn't call me today.' He reached up and cupped her face, his thumb tracing her mouth with feather-light strokes.

'I was certain I would,' she laughed. 'I'm a persistent cow. And I told you off, so we're quits.'

'Not quitting?' He raised an eyebrow with a sly grin.

'Quintessentially not quitting,' she quipped. She pulled the peak of his baseball cap over his nose and ran, pursued by an overexcited, yapping Puppy.

'Has she had her jabs?' Phoebe asked as, catching her up, Felix slithered his arm under hers and pulled her back towards him.

Puppy, who seemed to have absolutely no nerves, had now trotted up to a mean-looking Staffordshire bull terrier and was bouncing around with stiff-legged, springy excitement as though the grass beneath her was a fun-time trampoline. The Staffy rolled its eyes wearily and ignored her, concentrating instead on ramming his snout into a tree root.

'I haven't a clue,' Felix shrugged, nicking Phoebe's dark glasses and donning them. 'I bought her from Harrods, so I guess she must have done.'

'You bought her from Harrods?' Phoebe couldn't help sneering slightly as she turned to look up at him.

God, he even looked handsome in her Jackie Onassis sun-specs, she marvelled.

'I know – stupidly flash,' he laughed. 'I went in to buy myself some socks, actually. I didn't know it was your birthday this weekend – I just saw her and thought about you and Rabbit, and the next thing I knew, she was pooping all over the mews.'

'Pets are nowhere near socks in Harrods, Felix,' Phoebe smiled, tucking herself tighter into him.

'So I wandered upstairs.' He grinned across at her. 'Okay, so I deliberately went up there to see what they had. Okay, so I ordered her. You have to admit, she's pretty damn bite-sized.'

'She's gorgeous,' Phoebe laughed, watching as Puppy, bored of the snooty Staffy, scuttled over to a laughing toddler, wagging her whole, tiny body with delight. The toddler clumsily threw her an ice-cream stick to fetch which she bounded after with her springy, trampoline gait before proudly trotting back towards them with it poking out of her mouth at a jaunty angle like The Penguin's cigarette holder.

'I found the card after you'd gone,' Phoebe stooped to collect the stick and threw it again. 'It's brilliant – I giggled for ages.'

'Dylan and I got completely stoned on Monday afternoon and fantasised we were Blue Peter presenters,' Felix admitted. 'I was afraid you'd think it was terribly uncool. I almost didn't give it to you, but Dylan insisted. He was particularly proud of his squashed Cyril Smith contribution.'

'I love it – it's not at all uncool,' Phoebe argued. 'Where are your unfortunate moles?'

'Ah – those. I'll show you later,' Felix promised.

Phoebe looked away towards the sparkling, orange reflection of the sun on the Serpentine, as fiery as burning petrol on the water.

I have to ask him, she told herself. I can't let this happen. Mustn't let it happen. I'm starting to love him and I'm not allowed. I *have* to ask him.

'Last night – I take it you've behaved like that before?' she said carefully.

Felix picked up the puppy and said nothing.

'Have you tried to end other relationships like that?' She stared across at him. 'By throwing verbal acid into someone's face?'

'Occasionally,' he muttered, pressing his chin to Puppy's warm head.

Phoebe took a deep breath, aware that she was drawing the sword to commit emotional hari-kiri. 'Did you do it to Saskia?'

Felix stopped in his tracks and spun around so quickly that Puppy, rolling her eyes in shock, almost suffered whip-lash.

'I saw her photograph in your bedroom the night Mungo invited me round – I'm sorry, I know I was snooping.' Phoebe realised that she was speaking far too quickly to be understood and forced herself to slow down, her heart hammering. 'I recognised her. Saskia Seaton. We were at school together.'

'I see.' Felix took off his baseball cap and rammed it into his back pocket then rubbed his hair, completely on edge.

'You were engaged, weren't you?'

'Yup.' He looked away. 'And yes, I threw "verbal acid" into her face too.'

Phoebe stared at the expressionless, heartbreaking face and almost heard her own heart crack. Years were being wiped off her life in the few seconds this was taking.

'Why?'

He laughed a silent, sardonic laugh, staring fixedly at a distant oak.

'Why, Felix?'

'Because,' he stared at her, huge blue eyes tortured, 'she was fucking Dylan.'

'What?' Phoebe almost passed out. She could feel the blood drain from her face to leave her skin cold and clammy, could feel her pulse skip and then pound out of control.

'She was sleeping with my best bloody friend, all right?' he yelled, glaring at her now. 'And, amazingly enough, I don't want to talk about it, I don't want to remember it, I don't want to think about it and I don't want to – shit, Phoebe!' He turned away, his shoulders hunched, one arm clutching Puppy, the other pressed to his head in turmoil. 'Why the hell did you have to bring this up now?'

Phoebe was totally confused. He was obviously terribly upset, and she was torn between appalled belief and seething distrust. Seeing his trembling shoulders, she wanted to wrap her arms around him and comfort him. At the same time, she wanted to hit him over his lying, self-loving tousled blond head for daring to use Saskia in such a blatantly deceitful way.

Puppy clearly just wanted to escape. She was wriggling furiously from Felix's grasp.

'I'm sorry,' Phoebe said, finally and lamely.

Felix shrugged, his back still hunched away from her.

'If you don't want to talk about it then – '

'No, I fucking don't!' he snapped, letting Puppy go. He stood up, grabbing behind him for her hand, and started to walk extremely fast.

Phoebe tripped and staggered for a few seconds as she stooped to gather a bewildered Puppy under one arm whilst being towed along by the other.

They marched on in silence for a few minutes. Clutching Puppy to her chest, Phoebe breathlessly tried to digest what he'd just said, tried to let the idea of Saskia and Dylan sink in, but she couldn't even begin to absorb a twist of such enormity. She simply couldn't match up the bloated, tearful, suicidal face on the hospital pillow a few weeks earlier with a double-sided one that would sleep with her fiancé's best friend for a thrill. The story seemed ludicrous, absurd, impossible. And yet, Felix was still shaking all over from the effort of telling her, his hand clamping hers as tightly as thumb screws. He had slowed their walk almost to normal pace now, but was staring straight ahead like a sleep-walker.

'What was she like at school?' he asked suddenly as they passed a couple of roller-bladers wobbling precariously, their equipment so spanking new that the plastic attachments from the price tags were still poking out.

It was Phoebe's turn to press her lips to Puppy's head.

'Popular,' she confessed, blinking hard at the memory of that taunting, snub-nosed face. 'Very pretty and sporty. Bright. Confident.'

'And you?'

Phoebe looked at him, but he was still staring ahead, his face visored, eyes crinkled against the sun

'Gawky, underdeveloped.' She rubbed her nose against Puppy's soft brown ear. 'Swotty. Crap at sport, worse at art. Always threw up when offered an Embassy Number 5 in the boathouse.'

'Sounds just like me,' he muttered, squeezing her hand and then dropping it as he reached up to stroke Puppy's dangling paw.

'We should have written to each other. Alleviated the agony. I was the only one who couldn't call her parents from the payphone on Fridays. I wasn't fast enough at ramming five-pence pieces in to get through to Dubai or wherever.'

'Same problem with the West Indies, I wish I'd known you then.'

'You wouldn't have fancied me – I had chainmail braces and a purely cosmetic teen bra that could take a lacrosse sock in each cup and still bagged.'

'I'd've fancied you rotten.' Felix turned to her suddenly and smiled. 'I'd've kept your photograph in my plastic cube – '

'You had one too?' Phoebe laughed.

'In my cube,' he went on, gathering Phoebe and Puppy into a hug, 'and then pretended to all my dorm-mates that I'd tonsil-tickled you and touched your nips. I might even have claimed to have had a quick grope up your skirt, although I'd have been deliberately vague in case they asked me what was actually up there which would have stumped me somewhat.'

'What age are we talking here?' Phoebe laughed. 'Sixth form?'

'Bog off!' he howled and then grinned. 'Third year at university.'

'I kept a cut-out picture of Rupert Everett in my cube – long before he was really well known – and pretended he was my boyfriend,' Phoebe remembered with an embarrassed grimace. 'Then *Another Country* came out and I had to pretend that fame had gone to his head and he'd decided to chuck me. I don't think anyone swallowed it.'

'Girls never swallow it at that age,' Felix said lightly.

'Probably think it's got too many calories in it.'

They started walking again.

'Did she bully you?' he asked after a while.

'Saskia?' Phoebe bit her lip, wondering how much to confess. 'Not much – our parents know one another, so we spent a lot of time pulling faces behind backs at drinks parties.'

'Gin and Tony Seaton?' Felix winced at the memory. 'I liked Gin Seaton.'

'So do I,' Phoebe sighed without thinking.

Felix shot her a speculative look but let it pass, choosing to switch topics abruptly instead.

'Are you and Dan really over?' He looked down at Puppy who had conked out in her arms.

'Completely.'

'I'm glad.'

Phoebe sighed and gazed at the Serpentine again. 'So am I.'

For the first time in forty-eight hours, she realised that she meant it.

Felix smiled, scratched Puppy's ears and moved away. 'Let's sit down.'

They settled on a bench and watched a couple of teenagers playing frisbee in the fading evening light. Puppy, tucked into Felix's lap now like a packed lunch, watched too for a few sleepy seconds, her head moving from side to side like a spectator at a tennis match. Then, with a tired sigh, she tucked her pink nose between Felix's legs and fell asleep.

'Dylan's really into this murder mystery thing.' He leant back against Phoebe and stared at the branches of the huge oak above them.

'Just the murder mystery?' She played with his hair absently, the subject of Dylan making her heart plunge anxiously towards her stomach.

'I think he's quite keen on Lady Euthanasia too,' laughed Felix. 'He was plotting to change his character to Colonel "Piggy" Pinchbottom, a boffish old roué – with an obligatory crush on Lady E – in the car last night.'

Phoebe smiled. 'How do you feel about Tess Tosterone?'

'Not keen on the bisexual stripper bit,' he groaned. 'Although I might not be able to make it that weekend anyway.'

'No?' She tried desperately hard to sound casual.

'This jeans deal thing – they want me over there for a screen test within the next fortnight, I think they're holding all the castings in September, but Piers is trying to be pre-emptive and set mine up for the end of August.'

'Is it really as big as he's making it out to be?'

'Huge.' Felix whistled. 'It'd make me into a star, baby. I could buy you a mock-French château on million-dollar-babe block and we could ask Babs Streisand round for poolside nibbles. Basically, she'd turn us down, but we could ask. Shannon Dougherty might roll up though. Madonna might even ask me out.'

Phoebe stroked Puppy unhappily.

'Do you want all that?'

'My mother certainly does – as we speak she's probably hiring an architect to design a Mummy-annex complete with mini-bar and mirrored ceilings,' Felix muttered, squinting up into the tree. 'No – make that a full-sized bar with a padded floor. She wants me in Hollywood so much, she's even conceding that I'm nineteen, not thirteen now, the bitch.'

'And you?'

'I'm twenty-six.'

'I mean, do you want to be an instant media star?'

'Who wouldn't?'

'I wouldn't.'

Felix twisted round to her, his lips against her neck. 'Really?'

'Definitely.' Phoebe watched as the teenagers threw the frisbee into a nylon duffle bag and headed off home. 'I really admire people who can cope with it. I can't face the milkman in the morning, let alone half a dozen paparazzi with two-foot zoom lenses trying to catch me pushing Richard Gere out of the back door.'

'I'm not planning on rogering Richard Gere. I'd rather roger you.'

'Saves you chanting a mantra afterwards, I guess.'

'What do you want to do?' He turned back to gaze at the tree again. 'I mean really want?'

'I'm quite happy being a nineties slacker.' She shrugged. 'I know it's as politically incorrect as a Jim Davidson joke, but I don't really care what I do as long as it makes me laugh. Ideally I'd like to get enough money together to travel the world and then find my conscience abroad, I guess.'

'Sounds good to me.'

'And you?'

'I want to be an actor.' He said without hesitation. 'I want to believe in it totally, to pull another person's personality around me like a complete, seamless body-suit, to forget about the lines and the blocking and the props and just be that person. I want to make buttocks clench on seats and hairs spring up on necks—'

'Not easy when you've got your bottom to the audience showing off the designer label on a pair of jeans,' Phoebe pointed out idly.

'My ideal show,' he went on, not really listening to her, 'would be one where there was nothing at the end. Silence. Complete hush in the audience.'

'What?' Phoebe looked at him in bemusement. 'No one claps?'

'Exactly.' Felix twisted around excitedly, his face alive with enthusiasm. 'There's just a shocked, stunned silence. Hush.' He paused weightily, gazing at her with sparkling eyes. 'You see? They believe in it so much, go with it so much, that they don't want it to end, can't accept that it has. No one claps. They can't.'

Phoebe knew for definite that he wasn't talking about the jeans deal.

'There's just one slight problem.' He pressed his nose to her shoulder.

'What?' Phoebe turned her face so that their eyes, just inches apart, almost crossed as they met.

Felix grinned. 'I can't bloody act!'

He started to laugh.

Holding her breath, Phoebe saw his total mirth and then joined in with surprised, amused amazement.

'I'm famished.' He sagged back against her again, tipping his head so that his hair tangled with hers.

'Me too.' Phoebe suddenly realised that her stomach had almost inverted with hunger.

With Puppy, still fast asleep, tucked in her canvas bag and swinging from Felix's shoulder, they wandered off to the base of the Serpentine to find a burger stand.

'Come back to the mews with me.' He rubbed his hair anxiously and started walking backwards in front of Phoebe, full of jumpy, hopeful energy. 'Dylan's working at the bar. He won't be back till after midnight.'

'And Mungo?' Phoebe laughed as Felix walked backwards into a tree, coming to an abrupt, wincing halt. There was an indignant growl from inside the canvas bag.

'Mungo,' Felix reached out and pulled Phoebe up against him, 'has found himself a flea-pit basement studio in Soho that he's immensely proud of. It's two minutes' crawl from the facilities house that he's a runner for at the moment, so he'll only be an hour late for work each day, instead of two.'

'Mungo works?' Phoebe widened her eyes and then, seeing Felix's insulted expression, crossed them apologetically.

'He thinks it adds to his mysterious sex appeal – a trustafarian with a wage,' Felix grinned, curling his fingers into her hair and then pressing his nose to it. 'You smell so delicious.'

Trying not to locate the delicious smell by sniffing along too, Phoebe realised that she'd forgotten to squirt on her Ysatis for today's meeting.

'It's Sainsbury's coconut shampoo,' she told him, feeling mildly uncool.

'Mmm.' Felix was kissing the soft skin between her hairline and her ear. 'Always wear it.'

'I'll dab it on morning and night.' She shivered happily.

There was another grumpy growl from inside the swinging canvas bag.

Laughing, she slid her arm around Felix and pulled him away from the tree. 'Let's go back. We can buy supper on the way.'

Weighed down by Puppy, Waitrose bags, Felix's post, milk bottles and three days' worth of uncollected newspapers, Phoebe and Felix creaked and crackled their way up the narrow mews stairs, laughing at daft jokes and dropping most of what they were carrying.

Puppy, recognising her old stomping ground, let out a series of delighted yaps and wriggled out of her canvas bag. Scuttling around the flat, she sniffed wildly and peed extensively in her excitement, small skewbald tail gyrating so frantically that she resembled a loose garden hose.

'No one's home,' Felix peered into the deserted kitchen.

'No,' Phoebe suddenly realised that she was so excited she was in danger of forgetting to breathe.

The plastic bags were dropped at the top of the stairs, supper forgotten.

She stretched her mouth up to meet his, her hand creeping around his waist, her fingers slipping beneath his belt into a lovely fug of cloth and skin. He placed a warm, smooth palm on each of her burning cheeks and pulled her to him, straight into that delicious, delving kiss which she never wanted to end. As his tongue snaked into her mouth and slipped between her teeth, he pressed his leg behind her knee and tipped her off balance, gathering her up into an unsteady lift. Still kissing her between laughs, they staggered through to the bedroom where he set her down on a bed covered with laundry, paired-up socks and paperback novels.

'Okay,' he backed away, smiling broadly. 'Seduce me.'

Still breathless from the kiss, Phoebe rolled over onto her stomach and cupped her chin in her hands.

The only thing Felix didn't drop was his steady, amused gaze as he discarded each item of clothing slowly and deliberately to the floor.

Phoebe bit her little finger with delight and smiled.

'Show me your moles,' she whispered.

'My moles?' he looked bemused as he reached down to pull off a sock.

'Two embarrassing moles,' she reminded him.

'Ah those,' he grinned, straightening up and pressing his fingers to his lips. 'Well, I have to confess, I put those in my diagram as a ruse.'

She lifted an eyebrow.

'I knew you wouldn't be able to resist finding out where they were,' he confessed. 'So I added it to my card. After all, you've seen the tattoo.'

Phoebe, her legs lolling behind her, started to kick her shoes off. She stretched out her arm and touched his warm, bare thigh, feeling the tremor beneath his skin. He shivered slightly as she ran her fingertip along the soft hairs on his leg.

Laughing, she pulled him onto the bed.

They shrieked and giggled and bit and nibbled as they play-fought their way out of the rest of their clothes, kicking them away as they went, along with the laundry and paperbacks. When Phoebe climbed on top of Felix and kissed between his nipples, alternating play-bites with flicks from her tongue, he looked down his chest at her, grinning broadly, his eyes veiled with lashes.

'Am I being mole-ested?' he laughed.

She slid her hands up the bumps of his ribs and along his arms until she was gripping the taut tendons of his wrists. Crossing them together behind his head, she held them there as she started to drop the kisses lower.

The sun sank behind the wall at the rear of the mews, the curtains stirred sleepily, traffic hummed in the distance, and the phone rang twice and was ignored while Phoebe and Felix crumpled the sheets, threw the pillows from the bed and explored one another with hands, tongues, eyes, lips and fingertips.

As soon as he was inside her, she let out a delighted gasp and bit back a riotous wail of pleasure. They worked together like a well-oiled machine. And boy, was she well oiled. She had never in all her recent Felix fantasies prepared herself for joy of this giddy degree, or anticipated that their bodies would slot so perfectly together. When she slid further beneath him, parting her legs wider so that his thrusts deepened within her, she moaned in bliss. When she rolled on top of him, pulling back her damp hair from her forehead, she let out a cry of pure delight.

Even so, by the time Felix's thrusts accelerated beyond control and he let out a final, ecstatic gasp, she herself hadn't come.

'I'm sorry,' he breathed into her chest as, hot and sated, he sank a kiss deep into her abdomen. 'I just couldn't hold back any longer.'

Phoebe ran her fingers down his shoulders and shook her head.

'I loved it,' she said honestly, stretching forwards to kiss his damp hair. 'Every second of it.'

'I wish to God we'd done this earlier.' He shifted his weight so that he could rest his head on her stomach, his hand gently stroking her breasts.

Phoebe curled a tuft of blond hair around her finger. It was now tinged with only the slightest trace of red. There had been no props, she realised. None of the acrobatics, crème fraîche, toys, scarves or dressing up that Saskia had spoken of, with Felix barking the orders and dictating the pace. There had been no showing off or one-upmanship with scores being awarded for originality and variety. Just sex. Lovely, earthy, simple, joyful sex.

'I wish we had, too.' She stretched back on the warm, creased sheets and quivered with a glowing, comforting happiness which enveloped her like a tight hug.

Later, they splashed around in a bath together, flicking foam and indulging in long, hot, soapy kisses. Outside the door, Puppy scratched and whined mournfully.

'She wants to be let in,' Phoebe glanced across to the gap beneath the door where a small, pink nose was snuffling anxiously.

'So do I,' Felix gazed straight at her and, very slowly, slipped his fingers between her legs.

As the water started to lap against the edges of the bath, his fingers worked carefully and intricately, tracing patterns, writing elaborate hieroglyphs and painting pictures that made her squirm and wriggle and laugh and cry out until she came with a delicious shudder. Afterwards they chatted, laughed and fought in the cold water and dispersing bubbles until Felix was coated in shampoo and Phoebe finished up totally submerged, her feet kicking in the air.

When they climbed out, he wrapped her in a squashy navy blue towel and, gathering another from a marble shelf, started to dry her hair so that it stuck up on end like a punk's.

'I'm starving,' she confessed, trying to flatten it as fast as he spiked it up.

'Me too,' he slipped the towel around her neck and tugged each end towards him so that she was drawn into another long kiss. Then, after writing I LOVE PHOEBE on the steam in the mirror, he headed, still completely naked, through to the kitchen, tripping over an ecstatic Puppy.

Lingering behind, Phoebe idly traced the letters with her fingers, seeing her face reflected through them, staring back at her. Beneath it, she wrote 'I love Felix', and then quickly wiped the words away before following him into the kitchen where he was complaining loudly that she'd forgotten to put fresh basil in the shopping basket.

They only managed the first five minutes of cooking pesto before they went to bed again, leaving Puppy, whose stomach was rumbling madly, to nose through the remainder of the shopping and chew her way into a packet of Parma ham.

When Dylan let himself into the mews cottage hours later, he was almost floored by the smell of burning. On the hob he found that a pan of pasta, having boiled dry, was now letting out clouds of smoke. The kitchen floor was covered with split carrier bags and chewed-up food packaging, contents either strewn liberally around the tiles or regurgitated into small piles. Perched on top of a canvas bag, Phoebe's puppy was looking decidedly jaded, its nose covered with blackcurrant jam.

As he helped himself to a beer and started to clear up, he could hear gasps and giggles coming from behind Felix's bedroom door.

The phone rang: a very curt Piers Fox was on the line.

'Where the hell is Felix? I've been trying him all evening.'

'He's – er – that is, I haven't a clue where he is.' Dylan glanced at the closed door from which muffled conversation and laughter could now be heard.

'And you didn't switch your bloody answermachine on.'

'It's broken. Look, can I pass on a message?'

'I really need to get hold of him tonight – I have to get back to a guy in LA before he leaves his office. Listen, if he comes in within the next hour, get him to call me. If not, tell him I've already agreed that he's flying to the States for a screen-test on the last Thursday in August.'

'I'll tell him.'

'Good.'

Piers rang off in his usual abrupt manner.

Felix, when he finally emerged to make himself and Phoebe a sandwich, wasn't as excited about the news as Dylan had anticipated.

'Shit, that's the weekend of Fliss's party, isn't it?' he called through to Phoebe, who appeared through the door wrapped in a towel, looking very pink in the face from her recent exertions.

'Yes it is,' she swallowed uncomfortably at the thought and then smiled at Dylan. 'Hello.'

'Hi, luvvy,' he grinned.

'You mustn't let that stop you going to the States, though,' Phoebe told Felix hastily. 'I mean, that is far more important.'

This was her escape hatch, she realised. If he was away for the party then she couldn't do what Saskia had asked of her. It gave her time and breathing space to call the whole thing off. Elated at the realisation, she scooped Puppy up into a tight hug and spun her around the kitchen, laughing with relief.

Puppy, despite her upset stomach, covered her face with kiss licks.

37

Bow-legged and flushed with the sort of delirious, excited happiness that was stitching a smile to her face like a teddy bear, Phoebe let herself quietly into the flat and danced inside.

Poking over the side of the sofa arm was a lot of red curly hair and the aerial of the cordless phone.

'Yes, Lucy mate – loads of dishy men. No, you don't have to be Meg O'Maniac if you don't want. Let's see . . . the Hon. Lucretia D'eath-Wyshe and Dizzy Okel are still free. Great. So I'll pencil you in for Lucretia, shall I? Now, d'you need a lift?'

Phoebe let Puppy down on the floor and tried to creep through the sitting room unnoticed, but a freckled nose emerged from the end of the sofa and two blue eyes rolled frantically at her.

'Hang on, Lucy.' Fliss held the receiver to her chest and pointed madly at Phoebe's bedroom, mouthing: 'Beware!'

Phoebe closed her eyes in horror. It could only be one of two people in there – Dan or Saskia. She prayed it was Dan. That way she could boot him out without remorse.

It was Saskia.

She was sitting on Phoebe's crumpled bed, holding Felix's now equally crumpled birthday card.

Her blonde hair was more khaki than ever, her baggy grey jogging suit was covered with stains and starting to hang like old elephant skin from her slimmed-down body. Her blue eyes were so black-rimmed and bloodshot they looked like two liquorice allsorts.

'You've been to bed with him, haven't you?' she howled, her face so twisted with hatred that it resembled a melting wax mask.

Quailing away with fear and guilt, Phoebe did the only thing she could: attack in self-defence. She felt anger pricking her skin like a deranged acupuncturist.

'He says you slept with Dylan behind his back,' she whispered, glancing over her shoulder in case Fliss was listening in.

'You've talked to him about me!' Saskia screamed in horror, her hand shooting to her mouth. 'You mentioned our – '

'I was trying to draw him out,' Phoebe bleated. 'Trying to get some answers to your – '

'You stupid, brainless fucking idiot, Freddy! Of all the – '

She covered her ears.

'– unthinking, ignorant, suicidal things to do. I told you never, ever to let on that you knew anything of what happened to me. You've deliberately fucked this thing up because you want him for yourself, haven't you?' Saskia had yelled herself into a hoarse croak.

'He said you were sleeping with Dylan,' Phoebe whispered again, quietly enough not to risk Fliss overhearing. 'He said you were sleeping with his best friend, Saskia.'

'And you believed him?' she laughed mockingly.

She's not looking at me, Phoebe realised in horror. She's not bloody looking into my eyes.

'When did it happen?' she asked slowly.

Saskia pressed her palms to her forehead, the laughter instantly silenced. Not crying or speaking, she started to rock backwards and forwards on the bed.

Phoebe, frozen to the spot as though standing on a patch of superglue, stared at her friend's swaying, shaking grey body. Watching her bleached white knuckles and hunched shoulders, she worried that Saskia had finally toppled over the edge into total, free-fall nervous breakdown. She looked totally insane with despair.

Pushing the door shut behind her, she sank down on the spot and hugged her knees tightly to her chest.

'Is it true?' she croaked, suddenly horribly uncertain.

Saskia carried on rocking.

'Is it true, Saskia?' Phoebe muttered. 'Did you sleep with Dylan?'

She made a noise into her hands.

'What?'

'Ysss.'

'*What*?'

'YES!' Saskia pushed her hands into her hair and glared at Phoebe as though she'd just extracted a confession from one of the Guildford Four.

Phoebe licked her dry lips and gazed at the ceiling, unable to bear looking at her any longer. She ached for Felix.

'When?' she whispered.

Saskia rubbed her running nose with the cuff of her sweat shirt and scrunched her eyes closed.

'When, Saskia?' Phoebe asked again. She felt icily calm and strangely detached, totally numbed against any reaction as though given a huge shot of heroin.

'When Felix went to visit his father in Barbados,' she mumbled, her lips quivering. 'Just before we broke up. I was so unhappy, so worried about his disappearance . . .' She started to sniff.

'And?' Phoebe continued staring at the ceiling.

'Dylan took me out and got me drunk to cheer me up.' She started to sob. 'We went to the Atlantic Bar and got truly, appallingly hammered. Dylan took a line of coke and just giggled for about two hours, talking absolute crap.' She shivered at the memory. 'He was so sweet and attentive. So desperate to make me laugh.'

'And you got off with the giggling chatterbox?' Phoebe hissed. 'Very loyal.'

'No!' Saskia howled. 'I mean, yes, but it wasn't like that at all. It was – oh, God, I can't explain.'

'Just try.' Phoebe cocked her head.

'You're even beginning to sound like fucking Felix!'

She looked so utterly pitiful that Phoebe fought hard against an urge to gallop across the room and comfort her.

'So you were trapped in the Atlantic Bar with the laughing gnome. What next?'

Saskia took a few seconds to swab her eyes with Phoebe's duvet cover and hiccup out a few more shuddering sobs.

'Back at the mews, we talked for a long time – about Felix mostly. And a bit about Dylan and his one and only true love.'

'Janey?'

'You know about that?' Saskia looked at her tearfully. 'Yes, Janey. I mean it's years ago now, but he's still really strung up about it. Banged on for hours. So we got even more drunk, and cried a bit together, and then he suddenly . . .' She started to sob again.

'Made a lunge for your bra strap?' Phoebe was aware that she was being deliberately cruel, but could feel every hair bristling on Felix's behalf.

'No!' Saskia wailed, crushing Felix's card under her fist. 'Dylan suddenly confessed that he'd always fancied me,' she carried on. 'He even said he loved me. I'm quite sure he didn't – I mean he was so pissed and melancholy and emotional by then that he'd have declared love to a lamp-post – but I was incredibly low and incredibly flattered and it seemed so natural to kiss him.'

She blew her nose on the duvet cover.

Watching her, Phoebe shuddered slightly, but was so engrossed in the story that she let it pass.

'He looked totally dumbfounded. I mean, really embarrassed,' Saskia hiccuped on. 'So we had another drink, said absolutely nothing to each other, and watched a video.'

'Which one?' Phoebe snapped sarcastically. '*Threesome?*'

Saskia sobbed out a sad laugh. '*Basic Instinct.*'

'Bad mistake.'

'Total, mind-blowing mistake,' Saskia sobbed. 'At about three in the morning we locked eyes and pounced. Afterwards, we couldn't move for apologies. It was too awful. We couldn't look at each other at all. Talked like strangers after a particularly seedy one night stand. All that lovely, chummy friendship had gone. I felt such a total bitch.'

'Dylan wasn't exactly blameless either,' Phoebe pointed out.

'I know, I know.' Saskia blew her nose on Phoebe's t-shirt nighty this time. 'But he always falls in love with Felix's girlfriends.' She looked up at Phoebe, blue eyes glowing red like an alien's from crying. 'I'm sure he's more than a bit in love with you.'

Phoebe glanced over her shoulder at the door. 'No, actually I . . .' She stopped herself, suddenly certain that Saskia didn't need to be told of Dylan's current pursuit of Fliss.

'He gets these big crushes – I mean, he even jokes about them.' Her voice disintegrated into a series of tearful spurts. 'But the reality is that they're just his daft, romantic ideal, like those bloody books he writes and thinks no one knows about. Act on them, like I did, and you're painting a moustache and glasses on his rose-tinted mental image of you.'

'So how did Felix find out?' asked Phoebe shakily.

Saskia buried her face in the nighty. 'He walked in on us.'

'Christ!' She bit her knees in horror. 'Not in – '

'No, not having sex.' Saskia's voice was muffled by several layers of cotton jersey, but nonetheless shrill with hysteria. 'But it was pretty obvious what we'd been doing.'

Phoebe closed her eyes and felt her heart blister into red-hot anger for Felix, who needed love and trust so desperately, sought unconditional, uncompromising honesty as others sought riches and power. Shivering with horrified compassion, she could imagine him walking in on the only two people he really trusted, groping for their clothes and feeble excuses, fresh from groping each other. The scenario was so painful and pitiful, she fought to breathe normally, to look at Saskia without screaming abuse.

'What did he do?' she asked, her voice a husk of dry fury. 'I take it he didn't show you his holiday snaps?'

Saskia flinched slightly.

'He walked out of the house. Dylan chased him but he'd

vanished. So Dylan came back and said sorry a lot and we had a cup of tea like all Brits do in a crisis, waiting up for hours. Then we went to bed.'

Phoebe gaped at her.

'Separately.' Saskia rolled her puffy red eyes. 'An hour or so later Felix came back, stripped off and climbed into bed without saying a word. We often made up in bed after rows, but nothing like this. He was all over me. We had the most incredible sex. It went on for hours, and then suddenly turned horrible – really violent and kind of frightening.'

'And you wonder why?' Phoebe propped her chin on her knees and ignored the tiny scrabbling paws on the door behind her. She was suddenly torn through with a seething mixture of fury and – although she could barely bring herself to admit it even to herself – jealousy.

Saskia mopped her eyes on the t-shirt nighty again and ignored the question.

'I take it that's his birthday present?' she hiccuped, nodding towards the plaintive whines and increased scrabbling at the bedroom door.

Phoebe nodded.

Saskia plucked the crumpled, creased card from the bed and peered at it with wet eyes.

'He never made anything like this for me,' she hiccuped.

'He said he was stoned,' Phoebe found herself shrugging it off embarrassedly. 'Dylan helped him.'

Wincing, Saskia let out a couple of deep, shuddery sighs to control her breathing and cast the card to one side.

'He had to side with someone, I guess, so he sided with Dylan.' She rubbed her forehead with the butt of her palm. 'I mean, for a while he acted as though nothing had happened. He was sulky and detached, but he can be like that anyway. There were no tantrums, no tears, no scenes, nothing. It was weird. I tried to bring it up a few times to apologise, to explain how drunk we'd been, but he'd just blank me out as though I hadn't spoken. I – I – ' she fought hard against another tirade of sobs '– I loved him so much that I simply hoped and prayed that he'd forgiven me; so much so, so blindly so, that I began to believe it. I mean, I loved him so much that I'd've forgiven him if he'd slept with my entire friends, family and social acquain—'

'Oh, come on!' Phoebe balked disbelievingly.

'I would!' Saskia howled. 'I loved him, Freddy. I still do. More than anything and anyone. Far more than my pride or self-respect. Far more than you ever could even imagine.'

Phoebe hugged her knees to her chest so tightly that her ribs were in danger of cracking.

'The rest of the story is like I told you,' Saskia said flatly. 'After a few days of holing himself up in the mews for one long drinking session and computer games marathon with Dylan, he seemed to snap out of his gloom and lay on the charm as though desperate to forgive and forget. I was ecstatic. The next minute, he turned around and dumped me like I was some cheap slut who had only ever fancied him because he was rich and pretty and a great fuck. He treated me as though I was some disposable piece of cheap pussy plastic with flat batteries.'

'You slept with his best friend,' Phoebe reminded her in a low voice.

Saskia stared at her in dismay, her voice a strangled breath of horror.

'You're in love with him, aren't you?'

'I'm not going to humiliate him,' she hissed, deliberately evading the question.

'You love him.' Saskia dug her palms into her eyes once more. 'Oh, Freddy, how could you? You know he'll crucify you, don't you?'

Phoebe found she couldn't argue any more. She was as played out as an arcade game flashing 'Game Over'.

'He'll do just the same thing to you as he did to me,' Saskia went on. 'I promise you he will. You're no different, Freddy. I know you think you are now, I know how lovely it is to have Felix, believe me I do. But he'll crucify you. He'll trash you like a brattish rock star in a hotel suite he's suddenly tired of.'

'I'm not actually planning to sleep with Dylan,' she whispered.

Saskia flinched.

'Do you really believe,' she said quietly, her voice shaking with anger, 'that was the only reason he dumped me? He'd done it before, after all. He'd have done it anyway. And he'll do just the same to you.'

'Why should he?'

Saskia stared at her, red eyes wide with raw fear. 'You simply have to do it to him, Freddy. Not for my sake, maybe, but for your own.'

'For my own sake?' She rubbed her face and sniffed deeply. 'I'm not sure I don't deserve a quick trip through the mill for going this far.'

'What about Jasmin?' Saskia argued. 'What about all the poor cows he picks on in bars? Fliss told me that he was slamming some sad, lonely wallflower only this week. Don't you think she deserves a bit of vengeance?'

'Maybe.' Phoebe couldn't look at her. 'But I can't do it for all of them. I might have done it for you, but I don't think I can any more. Not now.'

I love him too much, she added silently. I love him. I want to be with him now, not you. I want him here. I love him.

'You see, this is why I didn't tell you about the night with Dylan,' Saskia moaned in tearful despair. 'I knew you'd react like this. That you'd see some sort of vindication for his cruelty. Yes, I slept with his friend – a friend who spent half his life in our bed anyway, who was so much a part of Felix that it was sometimes hard to see him differently, a friend who'd always shared everything with him. Even lovers at one time. Even Janey.'

'What?'

'She was never really Dylan's girlfriend, Freddy. They were both screwing her. It was a competition between them to see who'd finally win. They'd played it before, with Dylan always good-naturedly conceding defeat. They did it for kicks. Felix's little party piece used to be a team game.'

'Not Dylan?' Phoebe glared at her. 'No way. I don't believe you.'

'They were pranking around at university, almost continually pissed or high. Dylan did a lot of coke,' Saskia sighed. 'They were nineteen, popular, spoilt, lusted-after, oversexed. And Dylan would have played Russian Roulette with only one empty chamber if Felix had asked him to then. He doted on him. He told me that.'

'So they both used to break hearts on purpose?' Phoebe bit her knuckles, tears starting to prickle.

'Yes. They called it Kiss Chase – like an innocent school playground game.' Saskia's tears had gone, replaced by hiccups that coursed through her throat at regular intervals. 'They singled out a girl, pursued and wooed her as a duo – you know how irresistible they are together, how they spark off each other. And when she chose one of them – chose Felix, rather – they both got bored and moved on to a new target, leaving her devastated.'

'Only Dylan fell in love with Janey, right?' Phoebe closed her eyes, remembering Felix disparagingly telling her that it had been hand-holding, skipping-together puppy love. He'd been so utterly dismissive, so upbeat and glib.

'Exactly.' Saskia pushed her greeny-blonde hair back from her face. 'This time, when Janey predictably chose Felix and the little bastard reacted true to form by telling her that he didn't want her any more, Dylan hung around. He mopped up her tears, listened to her ranting about how much she loved Felix and, in desperation, asked her to marry him. But she didn't want to know. She promptly dug out her passport and took her broken heart on a back-packing hiatus. Dylan never played the game with Felix again.

'So he's just carried on playing it alone, trying to find some sort of Nemesis for his screwed-up life. And Dylan has watched helplessly from the sidelines ever since, while his best friend still races around breaking hearts for a power kick. He told me all this that bloody night. He was trying to warn me.'

'The night you slept with him?'

'Yes, Freddy, I slept with Felix's best friend,' Saskia hissed in exasperation. 'Yes, I fucked up big time. Yes, Felix was hurt and angry and bitter. But no, I didn't deserve to have my life ruined as a consequence. I didn't deserve to be ripped apart. I didn't deserve to be humiliated and trashed and told I was worth shit. I didn't deserve it, Freddy.'

Phoebe winced, hearing her own words of twenty-four hours earlier, yet still finding them impossible to act upon. 'And does he?'

'Yes, he bloody does!' Saskia banged a fist on the bed. 'You didn't see him do it. He was smiling and calm and laid-back and revelling in it. He was enjoying himself. He was playing his fucking game again.'

'You'd just had sex with Dylan.' Phoebe buried her face in her hands in confusion.

'You just don't see it, do you?' Saskia howled. 'I chose Felix, not Dylan. The Kiss Chase had been won in traditional style. It was just like old times; Felix was on a high, he was soaring. He had no further use for me. He fired me, Freddy. And I promise you that he'll do it to you too. I know he will. You simply have to get in there first.'

'I can't,' she croaked. 'I just don't believe I'm justified.'

'If you don't do it,' Saskia warned, 'then I'll tell him what we've been up to.'

'You wouldn't!' Phoebe clasped a hand to her mouth disbelievingly.

'Oh, I would,' Saskia said with icy cool. 'And he won't be able to take it. I'll tell him about the planning meetings, the Felix file, the doctored invitation to that Showdown launch, the phone calls for advice. I'll tell him that the way you've dressed, talked, walked and acted since you've met him were all deliberately intended to seduce him. I'll tell him that he's looking a stalking horse in its laughing mouth. He'll simply hate you for it.'

Phoebe thought about it and closed her eyes in terror. She thought about the only alternative that Saskia was offering and opened them again to let the tears spill over.

'Would he hate me any the less for dumping him in front of all his friends?'

'He would if I told the press about our little sham too.'

'What?' Phoebe gaped at her.

'Evidently I could coin in a few zeros for this.' Saskia blinked her swollen eyes. 'England's favourite playboy duped by two old schoolfriends. How the model Casanova was cased over and won over by an unemployed ex-insurance salesgirl.'

Phoebe gasped.

'Dan could get a few little mentions too,' Saskia went on, the re-emerging tears belying her harsh, mocking tone. '"The Libel Detector and his Lying Belle Detective" – I'm sure the *News* main rivals would bid for the story.'

Phoebe pressed her hands to her head and stared at her.

'Saskia, you're mad.'

'I'm desperate, Freddy. Totally desperate.'

'You really want to hurt him that much?'

'No. I still love him. It will simply crucify me to see him hurt. But I want him to stop hurting other people. Don't pretend you haven't seen how easily he can do it, Freddy. He manipulates, seeks thrills, dares himself. Everything he does is a game. Why else d'you think I chose you?'

Phoebe dropped her forehead to her knees.

'I chose you because you have the nerve to play too. I knew he'd love you, and I guess I knew you'd love him too. I hated the idea, but I half expected it. That's why I'm being such a bitch now. It's my only chance.'

Phoebe pressed her eyes so tightly to her knees that her eyeballs ached and spun with kaleidoscopic colour.

'I was always jealous of you,' Saskia went on in a hollow, resentful voice.

'You?' Phoebe looked up in disbelief. 'Of me? Pul-ease.'

Saskia shrugged. 'You were always so bloody fuck-off and independent. You were the only one who never seemed to care, never followed the pack.'

'Defence mechanism.' She propped her chin on her knees once more, drained of energy and fight. 'I couldn't run away. I had no big sisters, no loyal gang, no chewing-gum-coterie of admirers. Even my parents were halfway across the globe. So I dyed my hair red, pierced every available fleshy bit and pretended I didn't care.'

'I wanted to be you,' Saskia said quietly, turning the card over and over in her hands.

'I wanted to be you too,' Phoebe sighed, close to tears again.

For a moment Saskia stared at her, blue eyes swimming, seemingly about to race across the room and hug her. Then she looked away and took a deep, shuddering breath.

'Well, it's your decision.' She heaved herself up off the bed, her voice as flat, cold and final as a mortician's slab. 'Either you do as I ask, or you open a tabloid over the next couple of weeks and see you, Felix, me, Dan and our raucous, revengeful romp dragged through the gutter.' She headed past Phoebe to the door.

'Don't make me do this, Saskia,' she whispered, her voice disintegrating into a whimper.

'I have to,' Saskia said between clenched teeth as she opened the door. 'If I don't, I'll go mad.'

As she opened the door wider, a tiny, waggling lump of ecstatic skewbald rapture fell through it and raced up to Phoebe, whimpering with relief and gratitude.

'She's lovely.' Saskia watched as Puppy clambered on to Phoebe's lap, her tail wagging so much that she promptly fell off again. 'She looks like that mangy little thing you used to have – Titbit.'

'Rabbit. Yes.'

'You should call her Rovenger,' Saskia suggested in barely more than a whisper, and, gathering the bin-bags containing Portia's clothes, she was gone.

38

'Felix, this is Susie.'

'Suse, darling. How the devil are you?'

'Fine. You sound very up.'

'I am. Did they like the Deus stuff?'

'They loved it, but that's not why I'm calling.'

'No? You're not calling to try and persuade me to shave my head and lie on a bed of burning coals for their new campaign? Because, I'm warning you, I've only just lost the Ranulph Fiennes look from last week, and my butt's still seriously sensitive.'

'Nope.'

'So you want me to stand around in designer trunks on a glacier in Norway for another *GQ* underwear feature? Wear a fur coat in the Cuban dry season for an Italian catalogue?'

'No, Felix.'

'Suse, are you okay, darling? You could almost be not trying to persuade me to do any work for you.'

'I'm not. Can we meet for lunch during the week? I don't want to do this over the phone.'

'Sounds saucily enticing, darling, but I've got other plans.'

'All week?'

'Every day. My diary's as jammed as a Lottery winner's post bag.'

'Then I'll just have to broach the subject now: Phoebe Fredericks.'

'Phoebe? You know her?'

'Not personally, no. It's rather complicated and rather delicate, Felix.'

'Yes?'

'Are you two – er – seeing one another?'

'Well, I've just seen her and I think she saw me. I guess that constitutes a mutual sighting, yes.'

'Don't joke, Felix. This is serious. You're rather keen on her, aren't you?'

'I rather love her, Susie. Not that it's any fucking business of yours!'

'Oh, Christ, I was afraid of this. I'm sorry, Felix, I know you think I'm a nosy old cow, but I think I have to warn you about something. I've left this far too late. Listen, Phoebe was until recently involved with a Daniel Neasham – he works for Satellite News and – '

'Look, Susie, I know all this. Anyway it's over between them. Phoebe – '

'Which is exactly why I'm calling. I just found that out today. I think Dan's on the warpath, Felix.'

'What? Is he going to come round here and beat me up? Hang on, I'll just check the window. Nope – can't see him.'

'Felix, he's gathering dirt on you. I know a guy who works in Satellite's PR department. He says Jasmin's been approached by hacks from the *News*. So has Saskia Seaton, I gather. Amongst other things, they were both asked about Topaz Fox.'

'Well, you know her name gets dropped more often than crockery in a Greek taverna these days, darling. I hardly feel – '

'Your parents' cuttings are being sifted through too.'

'Take longer to read than the Domesday Book, I should imagine.'

'Felix, aren't you at all worried?'

'Not unduly. Phoebe knows all the worst there is to know about me. That's one of the reasons I love her. Dan can't dig up anything I haven't already told her.'

'Christ, I didn't want to have to tell you this! Phoebe Fredericks is an old friend of Saskia's, Felix.'

'I know – they were at school together. So what? Look, is this conversation going anywhere? Only I'm knackered.'

'Phoebe is Saskia's agent provocateur. She's acting on Saskia's behalf. They've engineered this whole affair between them . . . Felix . . . are you still there? Felix?'

'I don't believe you.'

'Dan Neasham knows about it too and is pretty close to substantiating every quote against defamation or libel, I gather. He's now twisting the *News* corporate arm to run with the story on the same weekend that Saskia has earmarked for your comeuppance. It'll be picked up by every tabloid for the Sundays. Which means you can kiss Piers's mystery project goodbye at the same time as Phoebe Fredericks kisses you goodbye.'

'And I'm kissing you goodbye right now, Susie. I don't know what you think you're achieving by these lies, but let me tell you – the only fucking agent provocateur around here is me!'

'What?'

'Take this for a bit of provocation. You're fired! You're no longer my agent, darling.'

'Felix, you can't do this! Felix? Felix! . . . Felix? Shit!'

For the next fortnight, Phoebe saw Felix every day.

The only way she could cope was to see their relationship as a child that had a week to live. She could either cry for that week, or make it the best of her life. If she cried, then the child would suffer, might not even last until its allotted day to die. If she lived every minute to the full, enjoyed every second, made that week the best of her life, then she would never lose the hope that somehow a miracle might come along and save it.

So she crammed ten months' worth of sophisticated, tentative, creeping-together courtship into ten days' intense, delirious, laughing-together whirlwind.

What amazed her was that Felix seemed to match her desperation, her energy, her inexhaustible desire to do anything and everything together all at once. Between them, they seemed to have switched off two separate lives and turned on each other.

'What are we going to do today?'

'Have you ever read *The Dice Man*?'

'Okay, one for tea in Fortnum's, insisting we have fishpaste sandwiches and bags in mugs.'

'Very chic. Two for going to a fun fair and snogging at the top of a big dipper.'

'Three for staying in bed all day.'

'Four for staying in bed all day and ordering a pizza.'

'Five for going to the opera and walking out halfway through the last act saying we should have stayed in bed all day and ordered a pizza.'

'Six for going to Fred's and asking for Babychams with cocktail brollies, then sipping them with linked arms.'

They met up daily for breakfast or lunch or tea or drinks; they stayed together for films or plays or shopping or galleries; they hung on for kisses and hugs and play-fights and sex; they went out afterwards for walks or a swim or a work-out or a lie in the sun. They stayed in on the sofas for videos and endless chats. Then they went clubbing until the small hours and started with breakfast again. Sometimes, it seemed, they just met to stare at one another with the sort of gooey, romantic adoration that was acutely embarrassing to all around them. No one laughed at them more than they did at themselves.

'We're in serious danger of approaching a his-and-hers matching jumpers, watches and monogrammed love-heart pendant situation here, Fredericks.'

'Well, I am wearing your jeans, Sylvian.'

'You thief! Give them back at once.'

'We're in Bar Barella. I'm on my fifth tea break. This behaviour is rather frowned upon from employees. Stripping is in the Rule Book under Complete No-Nos.'

'Well no no one can see your legs under this table. We'll swap. I dare you.'

'Dinner in Kartouche if I do?'

'Okay, you calculating minx. Shit, I can't believe you're actually doing this – Ker-ist! I love you, Phoebe Fredericks.'

'Your turn. Hurry up. My legs are getting cold.'

They ate a lot, screwed even more, talked themselves hoarse and laughed like late-night, drunken lamp-post huggers.

Phoebe had never felt so utterly, anorak-friendly uncool in her entire life and she couldn't care less. She grinned at everyone and everything before, between, during and after Felix. She found herself beaming goofily at perverts on the tube, at businessmen in the street, at posters for heartstring-tugging charities. She had imaginary conversations with him whenever they weren't to-gether. Occasionally out loud on public transport. She also looked better than she could have believed on so little sleep and so much food. Eyes trailed her everywhere she went. One of the side effects of being in love, Phoebe began to realise, was being propositioned more often than an only-child supermodel heiress with kinky clothes, slack morals and terminally ill parents.

She and Felix didn't seem to need sleep. At three in the morning they would still be talking, or dancing, or laughing or screwing. Phoebe had never known anything like it without the aid of a Jackie Collins novel and recreational drugs.

Or anything as expensive. She was hitting the cash-point more often than a gambling junkie.

'Let me pay,' Felix insisted over and over again.

'No,' Phoebe bleated, aware of how much he had bought Saskia in the past and refusing to repeat the pattern.

'You,' Felix laughed, 'are a daft, screwed-up cow with funny ideas. And I just love you for it.'

On Saturday they moved on from small-hours drinking in the basement at Kartouche to dance for a few hours in Iceni and finally on to the Fox and Anchor in Smithfield market for a fried breakfast and Guinness at six in the morning.

'I love you.'

'No, you don't.'

'Do.'

'Don't.'

'Do you love me?'

'Is this a trick question? Do I get a clue?'

'You're going to leave me, Phoebe. Tell me you're not going to walk out on me?'

'Are we talking immediate future or long-term prospects here?'

'You're going to bloody crucify me. I've never wanted anyone this much. I'm so frightened of losing you.'

'I'm pretty hard to lose. Like snap.'

Phoebe went back to the Islington flat later that morning and cried for hours. It was one of the few occasions when she cracked. That afternoon, she went to Mothercare and bought Felix a coiled plastic wrist-lead for keeping hold of errant toddlers.

'So you know you won't lose me.'

He seemed absurdly touched by the gift and insisted on towing her and Yuppie around Hyde Park, both attached to him by a long lead.

Puppy had become Yuppie at some point during the week. While Phoebe and Felix were preoccupied in bed, she would stubbornly attempt to get under the duvet with them, her short legs failing her as she sought to ascend the two-foot sheer face to the wooden-framed love-pen she was missing out on. Finally conceding defeat, she'd clamber up on to a high pile of washing and peer grumpily at both of them.

'She wants to be upwardly mobile.'

'A Yuppie Puppy.'

On Friday, she became so irate during her bedside wall-climbing vigil that she chewed the aerial off Felix's seldom-used mobile phone.

'She's a hush puppy.'

'A hush yuppie. She's chewed off the send button.'

The name somehow stuck.

Phoebe occasionally bumped into Dylan while she was slopping out puppy food in the kitchen. He was as warm and friendly and disorganised as ever, giving her a hug and a kiss as he searched for his wallet or his socks or a credit card bill.

She always turned away, although she couldn't explain why. It was all part and parcel of some sort of unasked-for loyalty to Felix. Dylan nonetheless looked confused and hurt. He quickly stopped confiding in her about Fliss, she noticed. Soon, their sole conversations revolved around Yuppie.

'She gets better meals than I do.'

'She's a power-luncher.'

'She eats like a gift horse.'

'She's got bad teeth.'

'What?' Dylan gave her a sharp look.

'Her milk ones are shedding.'

'Oh.'

There was something about the way he occasionally looked at her that made Phoebe feel defensive even if he only wanted her to pass a tea bag. She so wanted to adore him unconditionally, but she sensed he mistrusted her. Thankfully, he spent a diplomatic amount of time away.

'Dylan's usually popping in to offer coffee every two minutes,' Felix noticed one day as they lay in bed. 'He's lying unusually low this week.'

'A habitual low liar, I'd say,' Phoebe muttered uneasily.

'Must be Yuppie. He hates dogs.'

'Mmm.' Phoebe guessed differently.

Yuppie had taken up more or less permanent residence at the mews, where she slept for far longer than any other of the residents, and now sat at the foot of the bed, growling disapprovingly while sex was in progress.

'Can't she wait outside?' Felix complained, looking up from between Phoebe's legs one day.

'She likes to feel included.'

'She's like Mary Whitehouse down there.'

'She's voicing her encouragement. They call it giving tongue in hunting circles.'

'Do they? Talk about His Master's Vice.' Felix laughed, dropping his head again.

'She feels neglected. She needs some love-toys. Oh, please don't stop.'

That afternoon, Phoebe and Felix took Yuppie shopping along the Fulham Road. Equipped with several squeaky balls, rubber rings and chew-sticks that were almost as large as she was, they paused outside an antique clothes shop where Phoebe had spotted a genuine nineteen-twenties dress of die-for-it sex appeal.

'That,' she whistled, 'would be simply perfect for Fliss's murder mystery.'

'You wear that and I warn you, I'll be walking around behind you all night to hide my hard on.'

'So you're coming?' She looked away, torn between delight and horror.

'Well, not right this minute. I mean, I'll need a bit more – '

'I meant, coming to the party.'

'Oh – that.' Felix grinned. 'I'm not sure. I think I'm flying back from LA on Friday night so I might make it for the Saturday night back-stabbing.'

Phoebe winced.

'Where's it being held? Dylan says it's some crumbling Berkshire pile without any furniture?'

'I'm not sure,' she muttered hastily. 'I mean, I can't remember off-hand.'

Felix flicked up one eyebrow. 'Let's look at this dress.'

They went into the shop and fell about trying on hats. The dress, it turned out, cost almost as much as Phoebe owed Fliss for the rent.

'I can't afford it,' she sighed despondently.

'I'll buy it for you.' Felix was swapping a flat cap for a deerstalker.

'No way!'

'Phoebe, I've seen your bank statement, for Chrissake. I thought I was dating a rich trust-fund babe until I noticed the D at the end of the summary of account phone number.'

'I won't take it from you.'

'Why not?'

'Because I'm a daft, screwed-up cow with funny ideas.'

'Try it on anyway,' he insisted, still wearing a deerstalker and looking absurdly sexy in it.

When Phoebe wore the dress, even she didn't recognise herself in the dusty, full-length mirror. She did a quick Charleston and then posed on tip-toes with a make-believe cigarette holder.

'Take it off,' Felix growled, watching the shop-keeper's bi-focals steaming up as he gazed at Phoebe with tongue-wetted lips. 'We're going home.'

Back at the mews, they screwed for hours.

Ignoring her new toys, Yuppie positioned herself at the foot of the bed and growled throughout.

Until Felix went to Los Angeles, he and Phoebe spent almost the entire few remaining days in bed. Yuppie's growling presence was banished to the kitchen as they tossed and turned and writhed and yearned.

'I want another day,' Felix breathed into Phoebe's stomach the day before he was due to fly.

'I want another lifetime,' she muttered into a pillow.

'Another what?'

'I want you.' She touched the soft silky hair she loved and stroked the warm, familiar neck she hadn't kissed nearly enough.

'I love you – no, I don't,' Felix laughed, pre-empting her denial. 'In fact I don't love you more than I've ever not loved anyone in my life. I don't love you very much indeed, Phoebe Fredericks.'

'I don't love you much either.' She kissed his head and knew the last few grains of sand were trickling to the bottom of their relationship.

Despite all her rigid attempts at self-control, tears started to stream down her cheeks to her hair.

'What is it?' Felix was suddenly up on one elbow, his lips frantically stemming the tide. 'Please tell me.'

Phoebe twisted away from him, feeling desperately alienated and hopelessly in need of comfort. The one thing she longed to tell him was the only subject she could never broach.

As the twenty-four-hour countdown to Wednesday's flight approached, he tried to persuade her to fly to LA with him.

'Piers is coming too – he's a control-freak from hell, but pretty harmless. He'll love you.'

'Fliss needs me around to help set up this party,' Phoebe explained, knowing she would die inside bit by bit without him.

'And I need you there to hold my hand.'

'I promised I'd help drive the stuff down,' she said with self-loathing finality.

'If I can't come on Saturday, I'll try to make it back for Sunday at least.'

'It's honestly not worth it. It'll be Alka-Seltzer sandwiches and clearing up till dawn by then. You're best out of it.'

'I'll want to see you.'

'I'm going pipe-smokingly dykey for the weekend, remember? I won't bat a false eyelash in Tess Tosterone's macho direction.'

'I'll just strip and muscle in. If necessary in a wig. And dress.'

It was inevitable. As he packed to leave, watched forlornly by both Phoebe and Yuppie, Felix asked where the party was going to be held.

'Saskia's house.' Phoebe suddenly wanted to give him the chance to guess, to be forewarned. She longed to give him the opportunity to escape. 'Deayton Manor Farm. Selbourne. It's empty at the moment.'

'Saskia's parents' place?' He froze.

'Yes. They've just sold it. It's going to be handed over to the new owners a few days after the party.'

'Will she be there?'

'Yes.'

He continued packing in stony silence.

A few minutes before his cab was due, Phoebe gathered together Yuppie and her debris and made to leave.

'Here.' Felix thrust a carrier bag at her as she headed for the stairs.

Inside, coated in more tissue paper than a pair of Versace shoes, was the bed-me nineteen-twenties dress she had tried on earlier that week.

She looked up at him, her eyes brimming with tears.

'Felix, I – '

'Don't thank me. Just piss off to Berkshire to put up fucking streamers,' he snapped so furiously that Yuppie shot down the stairs as though kicked.

Phoebe handed the carrier bag back to him, hating herself for being so proud.

'I wasn't going to thank you.' She stared into his eyes, knowing she'd never loved anyone this much in her life, never felt this completely terrified of losing them. 'I was going to tell you that I don't want it. I told you that when I tried it on. I can't take your expensive presents because I can't give any in return.'

'Oh, for Christ's – '

'I want you. Can't you get that into your thick head? Not the excess baggage, the trappings, the pretentious labels. I love them because they're a part of you, but I don't need them. I need you. 'Bye, Felix. Good luck.'

He caught her up at the bottom of the stair, where he kissed her as if they were heading off to the firing squad together. Phoebe kissed him back as though given her Four-Minute Warning, acutely aware that the one thing she couldn't afford to buy him as a present was any more time.

'Why do I feel this is so fucking final?' he laughed nervously. 'We're going to see each other in less than a week for God's sake.'

Phoebe pulled away, unable to stem her tears much longer. She stooped to gather Yuppie and pressed her wriggling warmth to her hollow chest.

Holding Felix's clear blue eyes just long enough to commit every lovely, symmetrical fleck to memory, she fled back to Islington.

In the Fox and Rabbit further along Douglas Street, Dylan had treated Fliss to seven Bailey's and Cointreau in an attempt to loosen her up towards seduction.

She now looked severely nauseous and barely conscious. The only thing he appeared to have loosened was her tongue and her twenty-buttoned frock-coat, worn outside a fifty-buttoned, fashion victim's dandy shirt.

'Felix will be over Ireland by now.' He looked at his watch.

But Fliss appeared to have passed out. Her red hair was falling on to his chest, her nose pressed against his shoulder. Dylan sat bolt upright, terrified by excitement.

As last orders were being called, he nudged her awake.

'Huh?' she squinted up at him with unfocused blue eyes, her freckled face scrunched against the pub's dim lighting like a hibernating dormouse taking her first peek at a spring sunrise.

'Are you okay to walk back, or shall I get a cab or something?'

'Is this a pub?' Fliss looked dazed.

Hating himself, Dylan took advantage. 'Can I kiss you?'

She peered woozily at him.

'Aren't you gay? I thought you fancied Felix. I fancy Mungo.' She grinned with soporific, unfocused delight. 'D'you know him?'

'Vaguely.' Dylan swallowed uneasily.

'Bet you fancy him too, huh?' Fliss giggled. 'What a man.'

39

Mungo grudgingly travelled down to Deayton on Friday evening with Dylan, who was also giving two girlfriends of Fliss's a lift in his rusty Renault 5.

'I wanted to go with Selwyn and his airhead model tomorrow,' Mungo grumbled. 'It's like being the very nice man in the AA van in here.'

The girls, squashed in the back seat between several old takeaway cartons, a rugby kit and a wilting inflatable banana that Dylan had used for a Caribbean promotion in his bar months ago, talked non-stop on the way down about mutual friends, their outfits and their ex-lovers. Only occasionally did they address Mungo or Dylan to request a loo stop or a light for their incessant Silk Cut habit. Mungo turned the radio up full volume, wound down the window and complained of carsickness. Behind him, Lucy and Claudia exchanged giggling looks and poked their tongues out at the back of his arrogant head. Both had secretly decided who they were going to murder given the chance.

It was late evening and they were driving west, straight into a blinding sunset, as they crawled along the M4 trapped amongst the Bank Holiday traffic. Dylan, his fingers drumming on the steering wheel, jaw clenched so tightly that his molars ached, was feeling more and more tense about the weekend ahead. He had wanted to give Fliss a lift down with the various props and murder weapons they'd assembled, but she had packed it all into Honk and set off that morning, stopping off in Soho on the way to collect several boxes of drinks from Bar Barella.

'I'm meeting Saskia's mother at the house at lunchtime to get the keys,' she'd told Dylan. 'I think it's probably best if you're not around.'

'Doesn't she know Felix and I are coming?' he had asked worriedly.

'Of course not.'

'But Saskia knows, surely?'

'Oh, yes. Saskia knows.'

Dylan hadn't liked the way she'd said that, but Fliss was far too preoccupied to elaborate. She'd just spent almost forty-eight hours non-stop at the studio finishing off her sculptures and packing them up ready to be transported to the gallery the following week. She looked diabolical.

'Have you known Fliss long?' he asked the two girls behind him.

'Ages,' they both chorused and collapsed into giggles.

Dylan shifted uncomfortably and reached for his cigarettes on the dashboard. He had an uneasy feeling that Fliss had told them he fancied her. From the way they were peering at Mungo in the rear-view mirror, it also seemed that she'd told them she fancied Mungo.

Almost slamming the Renault into a caravan as he tried to manoeuvre into the slow lane and turn off at Junction 14, Dylan wished he'd not bothered to pick the little squirt up.

He cheered up once they turned into Deayton's drive.

'Will you look at this? It's pure Toad Hall.' Mungo pushed his dark glasses on to the top of his head and whistled.

Behind him, the girls were letting out shrieks of excitement as they took in Deayton's squat, crumbling grandeur.

'Didn't you ever come here?' Dylan parked beside Fliss's dusty blue Peugeot. On the other side of the dented little car was a very tatty Dormobile which Dylan didn't recognise.

'No.' Mungo peered up at the house delightedly. 'Could never be bothered. Christ, Saskia's family must be loaded.'

'Hardly.' Dylan switched off the engine and sighed sadly. 'They've just sold this place, remember – there's Fliss.'

Looking even more pale and exhausted beneath her freckles, she wandered out of the house wearing ancient jeans and a vest-shirt with *Go on – Make My Friday* emblazoned across the front. Pulling back her red mane with one hand, she shielded her eyes with the other to see who had arrived.

'Oh hi.' She blushed to her roots as she saw Mungo clambering out of the car.

'Hi.' Still gazing up at the house, he didn't even glance at her.

No bad thing, Fliss reflected as she rushed across to kiss Dylan and her girlfriends hello. She hadn't had time to change yet.

'The place is completely barren,' she told Dylan as they headed inside. 'I mean, there aren't even any frigging chairs or beds.'

'No beds?' the girls groaned behind them.

Fliss nodded apologetically. 'Milly – that's Phoebe's little sister – and her boyfriend Goat are putting up a load of ex-army camp-beds that they brought down with them, and Gin Seaton has left us a pile of candlewick bedspreads and a few musty picnic chairs, but it's pretty basic. The Aga's still on, but there's no fridge for the food and drink. I've shoved it all in the cold cupboard. It's plastic cups and plates, I'm afraid.'

'What's that?' Mungo almost fainted as Goat loped out of the biggest drawing room and headed towards the green baize door carrying a hammer.

'Goat,' Fliss told him, blushing even more deeply.

'Yo!' he croaked, waving a cider can at them before disappearing towards the kitchen.

'I think I might put up in a local hotel,' Mungo sighed, gazing around the huge, empty hall. 'Does anyone have an RAC guide?'

Saskia insisted on driving Phoebe from London to Hexbury in Georgette's Merc.

'She won't let Fliss near it now,' Saskia announced proudly. 'Letting her look after it cost almost five hundred pounds in parking fees and paintwork repair. I had to arrange for the respray work.'

'And Georgette trusts you with it?'

'Only for the weekend. She's been unbelievably helpful. I mean, out of her way super. She's coming down tomorrow with loads of food. She hates driving anyway – no sense of direction.'

'Mmm.' Phoebe deeply suspected Georgette's motives, but said nothing. Saskia was too hyper to take it.

Phoebe was appalled by her appearance. On the surface, she looked better than she had in weeks. She had lost even more weight and her hair, professionally lightened to take away all traces of green, was now cut into a very chic layered bob, which fell seductively across her tanned face. She was almost too thin now, her body out of proportion from losing weight too quickly – her legs were like sticks, her chest as flat as a boy's, her face hollow, yet her midriff and bottom still bulged. She didn't look slim; she looked malnourished.

She'd also gone extremely trendy in new black Katherine Hamnett jeans and an elongated silk waistcoat which hid any last traces of a pudgy waist. But her skin, buried beneath a crust of fake tan and foundation, was as dry as cracking mud and covered with spots from eating practically nothing. Her hands shook constantly from taking so many appetite suppressants, her pupils were like pin-pricks in her reddened eyes and she took every quickened breath with the aid of a cigarette filter.

The drive down was a nightmare. Phoebe fought a continual urge to throw herself out of the passenger door, partly because she thought it would be safer than staying in the car with Saskia – who was driving like the last-placed competitor in the Monte Carlo Rally – and partly because the conversation made her want to scream. At her feet, Yuppie was whimpering, several small piles of regurgitated puppy food spotting the rubber mat beneath her. She looked up at Phoebe plaintively, her wall eye and brown eye glazed over with car-sickness, stumpy tail rammed between her quivering legs.

'You say you're pretty certain that Felix will turn up tomorrow?' Saskia asked again and again.

'I'm not sure,' Phoebe sighed, watching hundreds of cones slide by as they raced through a contraflow.

'He has to!' Saskia wailed, braking hard as they passed a police speed camera.

'We can't make him.'

'You can.'

'I don't have a number for him in the States,' Phoebe lied. 'And anyway, even he can't guarantee that he'll get a flight tonight.'

'He will,' Saskia muttered darkly. 'He loves you.'

Phoebe gazed unseeing at the cars they were overtaking. One hooted loudly.

Looking over her shoulder, she saw a Beetle being left behind in their slipstream, its passengers waving madly.

'There's Paddy and Stan.' She waved back as the Beetle flashed its lights in recognition.

'How many people has Fliss invited?'

'About ten tonight – the rest of the murder gang are arriving tomorrow lunchtime, I think. And then loads of friends for the party tomorrow night. Sixty or so, I'd say.'

'Lots of Felix's cronies, I hope.'

'A few,' Phoebe said cagily. 'I think Dylan invited quite a lot, but they can't all come. It's a bit far out of London. Is Portia coming?'

'She's gone abroad.' Saskia shot out of a slip-road without looking. 'Florence, I think she said. So how many of Felix's friends d'you reckon are coming down exactly?'

'Florence?'

'What?'

'You said Portia's in Florence?' Phoebe asked thoughtfully.

'Oh, yes. I think so. Can't remember.' Saskia raced around a roundabout on two wheels. 'So how many of Felix's friends, Freddy?'

'I really don't know.' Phoebe stared out of the windscreen. 'Maybe a dozen, twenty perhaps.'

'Enough to provide a decent audience, though?' Saskia hit eighty miles an hour on the Hexbury by-pass.

Phoebe closed her eyes. 'Plenty.'

*   *   *

Arriving at Deayton was heartbreaking. There were no dogs spilling out of the house to welcome them; no Gin bottom-up in the garden; no Sheila, red-faced from cooking, poking her head around the door to cry 'hello'. There were so many cars parked messily on the drive that Saskia decided the Merc would be safer behind the house in the stable yard. Phoebe got out and left her to park.

Fliss was delighted to see her but, walking into the kitchen behind her, almost bloodied her nose as she cannoned off her friend's back when Phoebe slammed to a shocked halt.

'Oh God.' She covered her mouth.

The dresser had gone, the huge warped table had gone, the mis-matched chairs had gone. Every scrap of Gin's presence, every messy Seaton mark, had gone. Phoebe wanted to weep. It was like looking at a skeleton of an old friend, all familiarity removed.

All that remained was the vast, four-doored cream Aga still burbling to itself in its tiled recess, the scrubbed enamel sinks and their dull, faded wooden drainers and the empty shelves stretching the length of one long wall. Shelves that had until recently groaned under an extraordinary collection of cooking implements, broken mugs, dog biscuits, stacks of plates, ring-marked vases and long-neglected post-cards.

Dumped on the wide, cracked expanse of quarry tiles were half a dozen boxes of bottles, a host of supermarket carrier bags bursting with food and plastic cups and, a box of 'murder weapons'.

'As there's no furniture in the house, there's absolutely nowhere to hide the knife, gun, rope and iron rod,' Fliss sighed, picking up a retractable dagger. 'Do you think Mungo would think it weird if I stick him in a bedroom on his own? Everyone else is sharing.'

'Shouldn't think so.' Phoebe peered into the larder, which was also stuffed with boxes of food and drink. 'Who am I with?'

'Saskia.'

Phoebe clung on to the door. 'But Felix is coming tomorrow night.'

'So?' Fliss said matter-of-factly. 'You'll have done the deed by the time we all go to bed. He's hardly going to want to share a room with you then, mate. I've put Paddy and Stan in with Lucy and Claudia to spice things up. What d'you think?'

'You look well,' Dylan lied. He and Saskia were wandering around the empty, soulless house, their feet echoing on dull floorboards which had until recently been covered with the Seatons' ancient threadbare rugs and carpets.

'Thanks.' Saskia peered into her old bedroom, her tanned face expressionless.

'Have you been away on holiday?'

'No, I've got a new job with a deranged party planner – she's coming down tomorrow. This is the Esteé Lauder instant week-in-the-Seychelles look,' she confessed. 'The clients don't go for the white mouse effect.'

'You're seeing Stan the artist now, I gather?' Dylan followed her along the landing to her parents' bedroom.

'That's right.' Saskia didn't look at him.

'What's going on, Saskia?' He cut her off at the door. 'You know Felix is coming here tomorrow night, don't you?'

'Of course I do.' She looked at him levelly. 'I'm over him, Dylan. It was all a horrible mistake we both regret – we all regret.' She gave him a sad half-smile. 'I bear no grudges.'

'Not even towards Phoebe?' Dylan asked disbelieving. 'You and she are old friends, aren't you?'

'Leave Freddy out of this.' She tried to push past him.

'How can I?' Dylan grabbed her arm. 'She's here, isn't she? She and Felix have hardly got out of bed for the past two weeks.'

Desperate not to react, Saskia pulled away and marched out of the room.

'I want to know what's going on.' Dylan chased after her. 'I'm really worried about you.'

'Worried about Felix you mean!' She turned on him. 'Let's face it, that's where your loyalties lie, isn't it? You certainly chose him over me last time.'

'Now that's not fair!'

'Yes, it fucking is!' she hissed, blonde hair falling across her angry face. 'You could have warned me what he was going to do. You could have – '

'I tried!' Dylan covered his face. 'Don't you think I bloody tried?'

'No, you didn't.' Saskia shook her head angrily. 'You were too bloody subtle. You have to shout it. Don't you think I've tried telling Phoebe how twisted he is? But she's got it into her head that he loves her. That he won't do it to her. That she's somehow – '

'I don't think he will.' Dylan dropped his hands from his face and stared at her, dark eyes suddenly melting with pitying apology. 'I really don't think he will do it this time.'

'No!' Saskia kept on shaking her head as though trapped in a bee swarm. 'No. He'll do it. He trashes everyone. He has to do it.'

'He loves her, Saskia.'

'He said he loved me!' She staggered to the landing wall and shouldered it in despair, pressing her forehead to it.

'And he thought he did, darling.' Dylan followed her, putting a tentative hand on her shoulder. 'He really thought he did. But you let him down. You – '

'*We* let him down, you mean?'

'Yes, we let him down.' Dylan removed his hand awkwardly. 'But it wasn't just that, as well you know. The rot was already starting to sour the eight-tier wedding cake long before that.'

'Was it?' Saskia wiped her nose on the back of her hand.

'Yes. Why d'you think he did a runner like that so soon before the wedding? It wasn't our fault,' Dylan said gently. 'It wasn't anyone's fault, really. He just felt smothered.'

'Smothered?' she laughed in amazement.

'The big loving family, the mammoth wedding plans, the constant gratification, the unconditional love. It was all too much for someone whose own family barely acknowledge him,' Dylan said softly. 'You gave it all up for him, didn't you? Your ambition, drive, that zany energy he was attracted to in the first place . . . all got jettisoned when you met him. You loved him so much that you couldn't see his faults, Saskia. You never once criticised him, argued with him, took issue with that great big swollen head of his. You just squandered every last ounce of love on him.'

'And he dumped me for *that*!'

'Partly.' Dylan shrugged, dropping his gaze to the scuffed floorboards. 'And partly because it was what he always does. He can't talk about these things, he just acts like a frightened dog – savages first and runs away second.'

'So you're saying it *was* my fault?' Saskia caught her breath tearfully.

'No.' Dylan raked his hair. 'You were just coming from different directions. He seems to ask for non-stop idol-worship, but do that and he despises you. I saw that at school, at university – all through our friendship, really. He gets frightened off by unqualified devotion; he sees his own howling flaws far too acutely to accept it. What he really strives for is trust, and who can trust someone who always flatters you – who always agrees with your arguments? You even told him he could act, for fuck's sake, Saskia. I loved you for it, adored you for it, but Felix couldn't cope with the lie.'

'Phoebe lies to him all the time,' she croaked, pressing her face tighter to the wall.

'And then admits to it.' Dylan turned to lean his back against the wall beside her, staring at a faded rectangle on the wall opposite, its picture hook still rusting at twelve o'clock. 'She's like him. They pretend it's all a game, but underneath it's as serious as Russian Roulette.'

'Is that what makes you think she's so bloody different?'

'Felix makes me think it.' Dylan let out a deep sigh. 'He trusts her because they're so similar, lets her into parts of his life that he keeps locked away from everyone else. Sometimes when they're together you feel like you're with one person – it's bloody weird. And he isn't playing this by any of his usual rules – she simply won't let him. He can't fool her like he has the oth—' Realising to whom he was speaking, Dylan coughed and looked at her, his soft brown eyes thoughtful. 'You haven't ever seen them together, have you?'

Saskia shook her head, staring fixedly at the wall.

He bit his lip, worried for her. 'You'll see what I mean when you do,' he said, almost apologetically. 'I'm so sorry, darling, I know it'll hurt like mad, but you'll see the way they just have to look at each other and the lights dim. They've found something in less than a month that I've been searching for all my life.'

'You really think it's so different?'

'Yes, I do. The pattern's changed. He's relaxed, he's honest, he's not posing around being fuck-off and arrogant, because she thinks he's a prat when he does. He's not going on benders or setting her tests. He's totally blown away by love that he believes in rather than wants. I've never known him like it. She's amazingly like him.'

'I know.' Saskia clenched her tearful eyes tightly shut.

'What's she going to do, Saskia?'

'Search me,' she said truthfully. 'I honestly don't know.'

'She's too volatile. I don't trust her.'

'Neither do I.' She turned towards him, pressing her forehead to his big, comforting shoulder. 'Your shirt needs washing, you old slob.'

'I know. I meant to do some washing last night, but I was working really late at the bar and I was too knackered.'

'You need a woman.'

'Maybe.' Dylan thought about Fliss and sighed sadly.

'Did you really love me for telling Felix he could act?'

'I wanted to make your tea forever, you old prima donna,' he laughed. 'It made me realise that you really could, whilst he can't. You looked so totally, believably sincere.' He ruffled her hair. 'I like this. It's much more you than the black mop.'

'It's my real colour,' she sniffed, unable to resist adding, 'Phoebe's naturally mouse.'

'I know.'

'You do?' She looked up, fighting a smile.

'There was a picture of her as a kid at her flat – with her parents and Milly, is it?'

'On a plastic tractor.' Saskia smiled bravely. 'I took it. She'd been in tears a few minutes earlier. God, I was such a bitch to her as a kid.'

'We're all pretty intolerable as kids. I once burned my brother's entire picture disc collection in a fit of pique.'

Saskia pulled her lips into her teeth. 'Do you love her too?'

'Not like I did you.' Dylan hugged her. 'You're gentler, more vulnerable. And prettier.'

'Really?'

'Definitely. She's all unchained sex appeal. You're much classier. You're my Kylie to her Madonna.'

Despite long-time *Neighbours* phobia, Saskia tried not to take the Kylie comparison as an insult. Dylan was, after all, one of the oldest, most devoted subscribers to the Kylie Minogue fan club. She looked up into those beautiful, trust-me brown eyes and felt her heart skip slightly.

'Do you think that we – '

'No.' He kissed her red nose. 'More water under that bridge than the Forth. Anyway, you're seeing Stan now.'

'Oh, yes, so I am.' Saskia wiped her wet eyes with a regretful laugh.

Dylan squeezed her shoulder and shot her a slanted look. 'You are seeing him, aren't you? At least Fliss said – '

'He's just on the tonic side of platonic.' She shrugged. 'We're still very much at the closed-mouth kissing stage. He used to date Phoebe as well as me, you know.'

'Talk about generation ex,' Dylan whistled. 'Don't tell me he went out with Fliss too?'

'No.' Saskia grinned. 'But there's a guy coming tomorrow who did – Iain.'

'I hate him already.' Dylan steered her towards the stairs. 'God, I'm so glad we're talking. I've missed you, you big granny.'

'I've missed you too, you dirty sod.'

'I'm your ex-husband tomorrow night, aren't I, Dame Bea Reeves?'

'Colonel Piggy Pinchbottom?' Saskia pounded down the

stairs beside him. 'One of the many, I believe – you old slime. But now you fancy Lady Euthanasia, my darling elder sister.'

'And you're closed-mouth kissing with the butler.'

'I do so love a grope below stairs.'

'Fancy a quickie in this cupboard for old slime's sake?'

'God, I've missed laughing this much.'

'I'm just so fucking pleased I can bring back the sensation.'

Phoebe felt distinctly unsociable as they all gathered in the scruffiest sitting room for a briefing from Fliss. It didn't feel like much of a party – to be lectured on behaviour, character and schedule before one knocked back one's first glass of punch. It was more like a briefing before an inter-school summer ball. She tried to sit in a dim corner and melt into a spider's web in true Black Widow fashion, but Mungo homed in on her and plonked himself beside her, passing across a can of Coke and an Ecstasy tab.

'We can boogie to Army of Lovers later. I brought my tape. Is your friend Paddy gay?'

Phoebe held the tablet away from Yuppie's snuffling pink snout and ignored him, appalled by the jealous, hurt looks Fliss was shooting her.

Clutching drinks, the others trooped in, looked for furniture and settled for the floor.

'Now here's how I think we should play it.' Fliss paced around as they all sat on the floorboards watching her, feeling like the Irish football squad facing up to Bobby Charlton the day before their first World Cup match.

Mungo, sitting with his arm around Phoebe, which she was loathing, started to giggle.

'I think we should get the place set up tonight,' Fliss looked at her watch in sergeant major synchronising style, 'work out the sleeping arrangements, check we all know what happens to-morrow night, and then go down to the local pub and get rat arsed. What d'you reckon?'

'Let's forget the first few things and get on with the last bit,' Paddy suggested, already halfway through a bottle of Newcastle Brown Ale.

'Hear, hear.' Mungo gave him a hot look.

Paddy – a skinny Irish artist with a number-one clipped haircut and ULSTER tattooed on his neck – grimaced and hissed across at Stan who was swigging from a Becks bottle beside him: 'Did she have to invite him?'

'She fancies him, doesn't she?' he whispered back.

'Christ give me hope!' Paddy took another swig of Newky Brown and looked sharply away as Mungo winked at him.

'Now does everyone know which parts they're playing? Are you all happy with them?' Fliss asked in the manner of a primary school headmistress asking whether everyone's happy with their assorted tambourines and triangles at morning assembly.

'I'm Dips "The Tips" O'Maniac now, right?' Paddy checked. 'Not that poofy film star's poofy cowing assistant?'

Mungo shuddered witheringly and played with Phoebe's hair. She ducked away and reached for her Coke, catching Fliss's wary eye. Opposite her, Saskia was keeping very quiet beside Dylan, her expression hidden behind Phoebe's Jackie-O specs. Dylan, meanwhile, was gazing up at Fliss like a cat at a queen.

'That's right, Paddy,' she was checking her list. 'You're Lady Euthanasia and Dame Bea's drunken, bankrupt racing manager. You have three daughters. Nymph, the spread-legged cellist – that's Milly,' Fliss shot her an evil smile before checking her list again, 'Meg, the frigid governess – that's whoever Selwyn's bringing. And Psyche, who – oh, hell, we haven't got a frigging Psyche! We'll have to say she's looking after your house-bound, crippled, estranged wife in Ireland or something.'

'And who's Selwyn?' Paddy scratched his head.

'He's Peregrine Fitzacoffin – Lady E's disinherited elder son. A gambling playboy who has you in his employ to nobble horses. It should be on your list.'

'No, I mean who *is* he?'

'Selwyn?' Fliss laughed. 'Selwyn Wolfe – my brother, Paddy.'

'I thought you said he was your son?' Paddy looked even more confused.

'For the party, yes,' she sighed despairingly. 'But he's my brother in real life. You must know that. You've met him. He's come to my parties before.'

'The idiot with the –?' Paddy swallowed. 'I mean, that dark-haired bloke with the dodgy northern accent? He's your brother?'

'Yes.' Fliss looked mildly irritated. 'He has been for most of my life, mate. And the accent's real.'

Mungo put up his arm.

'Yes, Mungo?' Fliss blushed, her standard reaction to him.

'Can I change from Otto Licher to Psyche O'Maniac, the loony Irish painter?' he chirruped. 'As no one's playing her?'

'Er – no,' Fliss croaked. 'I think it best if we stick to characters within our own sex.'

'Phoebe's a gender bender. Why can't I be?' he whinged.

'Shut up, Mungo,' Dylan snapped impatiently. 'Fliss has enough on her plate as it is without you changing characters at the last minute.'

'Oh, I'm bloody confused.' Paddy stood up and stretched his long, frayed denim legs. 'I can't be doing with all this. Who's coming down the pub for some grub?'

'I'm in.' Stan stood up.

'Us too.' Milly dragged Goat up.

'Wait on!' Claudia followed with Lucy.

'I'm free!' Mungo skipped after them, camping it up because he was bored stiff.

Fliss threw her clipboard down in despair and gazed from Saskia to Dylan to Phoebe.

'It's going to be a disaster, isn't it?' she moaned. 'No one understands what's going on.'

'Get them drunk and they'll all coast it,' Dylan assured her rather weakly.

'Er . . .' Claudia stuck her smooth, brown face around the door. 'Where exactly *is* the pub, Saskia?'

'The nearest one's about two miles away – on the far side of Selbourne village.' She grabbed her cigarettes. 'I'll come with you – we can probably all cram into a couple of cars. Are you three coming?' She looked back at the others.

'Oh, what the hell?' Fliss threw up her arms and followed. 'Dylan? Phoebes?'

'Count me out.' Phoebe wanted to dig herself a very big, very deep hole to die in tomorrow night. 'You go. I'll baby sit Yuppie.'

'She can come too.' Saskia lolled in the door, imploring her to come with a high, strained voice. 'They let dogs into the Axe and Compass. They wouldn't have any local drinkers if they didn't.'

Phoebe shook her head. 'Thanks, but I'm feeling a bit raggedy. I'll do some setting up while you're gone. Distribute a few blankets.'

'I'll stay too then.' Dylan nudged her arm kindly with his Sol bottle. Those devoted dog eyes crinkled as he smiled.

'No, you go with Fliss and the others,' she insisted edgily.

'I'll stay,' he said decidedly. 'I'm feeling a bit raggedy too. We can be raggedy together.'

Saskia's eyebrows shot up behind her dark glasses, but she said nothing.

As the sound of car engines faded away, Phoebe poured herself a huge glass of red wine and slugged almost half of it back in one.

'You *are* feeling raggedy,' Dylan whistled, following her through to the kitchen, and scratched his scruffy hair. 'You normally sip booze like a vinegar-taster.'

'It's seeing the place like this,' she admitted, hardly bearing to look around the kitchen once again. 'I used to come here so much as a kid – it was like a second home. Gin was a second mother. Seeing it like this is so unpleasant.'

'So you know Saskia pretty well then?' Dylan hopped up on the draining board, which was one of the only places to sit.

'Through our mutual families, yes,' she answered carefully. 'But we were never exactly friends. In fact, for a long time we loathed one another.'

'But you share the same birthday, yes?' Dylan hooked a patched knee up to his chin, dark eyes watching her closely.

Phoebe took another gulp of wine and nodded. 'You know that?'

'She just told me.'

'Oh – well, yes. We always joked that it was the only thing we had in common.'

He watched her as she started to unpack the boxes of drink. 'But weren't you going to be a bridesmaid at the wedding?'

Phoebe dropped a bottle of champagne which rattled, unbroken, into a corner, chased by Yuppie.

She slowly straightened up and rubbed her forehead with the back of her hand.

'Saskia told you that too?'

'No.' Dylan hooked his wrist over his knee and chewed at a frayed shirt cuff, peering at her over it with those irresistible brown eyes. 'I remember that bit. "Freddy" cropped up a few times in the last few weeks she was at the mews. She rather hero-worshipped you.'

'Oh, come!' Phoebe turned away.

'Straight up.' Dylan watched her pick up the champagne bottle and put it with the others in the cool room. 'She's almost as screwed up about you as she is about Felix.'

Saying nothing, Phoebe carefully stacked bottles of Bar Barella house red on the deserted wall shelves.

'What are you going to do to him, Phoebe?'

She looked down at Yuppie, who was searching around for something to sleep on. She finally settled for a pile of empty supermarket bags, curling around and around on them until they were scrunched up so tightly around her spiralling paws that she fell over.

'What I always do.' She looked up at him. 'What Saskia wants.'

'What does she want?'

Phoebe took a deep breath, opened her mouth, closed it again and then let the breath go. 'Guess.'

Dylan pushed his tongue behind his lower lip and, smiling unhappily, looked up at laundry rails suspended from the ceiling. 'You're going to trash him, aren't you? You're going to play Kiss Chase?'

Phoebe downed the rest of her wine and watched Yuppie settle for a discarded coat as a safer sleeping arrangement.

'Do you love him, Phoebe?'

'Oh God, Dylan!' She grabbed a pile of blankets and headed for the lobby door. 'Do your trousers do up at the front? Do you read from left to right? Has your nose got two nostrils? Your head got a squishy grey thing inside that occasionally comes to logical conclusions?'

'And you're still going to do what Saskia wants?'

Phoebe stood by the door, blankets in hand, unable to turn back to him for fear of breaking down.

'I promised I would.' She took a shaky breath. 'I swore I would. I really think she'll go mad if I don't.'

'And you?'

'This is driving me mad anyway. I've lied to him so much. I can't see anything ahead but hurting him. I might as well do it the way Saskia wants.'

'What if I warn him?' Dylan muttered.

Phoebe gripped the blankets tighter. 'I wish you would. I've been too much of a fucking coward. I love him, you see. It's kind of difficult to tell someone to burn in hell when you love both their broken heartbeats as though they were your own.'

She bolted up the back stairs to the main landing and threw all the blankets into the biggest bedroom before diving through what looked like a cupboard door and up to the attics where she wept desperately for Felix, sobbing into her knees with gulping, lung-tearing misery.

40

The others arrived at lunchtime on Saturday. Mungo was sunbathing in his boxer shorts in the garden, nursing a bottle of Chablis and conspicuously reading a Henrietta Holt romance novel to wind Dylan up; Paddy, Stan and Goat were raiding the outbuildings for old furniture; Milly and Claudia were stuffing blank cards into envelopes in the kitchen; Dylan was in the bath singing Sinatra hits in a remarkably good bass voice. Phoebe, Saskia, Lucy and Fliss were upstairs having a long, girly gossip about what they were going to wear that night.

When Iain and his girlfriend rolled up in a metallic black Saab convertible, their hair whipped into knotted peaks in sacrifice to stylish cruising, no one came out of the house to meet them. They sat in the car for several minutes, the stereo still blaring, in the hope of being noticed, but the only house guest to rush out and greet them was Yuppie, yapping frenziedly and spinning in pirouettes of excitement as she tried to wag herself to bits, chase her tail and attack a Saab tyre simultaneously.

The new arrivals weren't, however, without an audience.

'She's pre-pubescent!'

'She's bloody good-looking!'

The girlfriend was freckle-faced and red-headed. And stunning. Sitting in the Saab, she looked almost six feet tall and about twelve, appeared to have packed more luggage for one night than most political evacuees for an unknown lifetime, and she was in the driver's seat.

Fliss almost fell out of the window of Phoebe and Saskia's room, which afforded the best view of the drive.

'She looks like me, but without the fat, cellulite, bags and forced laughter lines.'

Phoebe craned past her, ever on the look-out for Felix.

'She hasn't got an iota of your sex appeal,' she assured Fliss. 'Her nappy line's bound to show in those hot-pants. Christ, is she young!'

'And she drives a frigging Saab,' wailed Fliss. 'I'm going to kill myself!'

Saskia, even more on the look-out for Felix, craned for a gawp too.

'She looks like Bonnie Langford on growth hormones. And her legs are seriously bandy.'

'Who's she playing?' Phoebe looked across at Fliss.

'Dizzy Okel, the toothless half-wit house maid.' Fliss smiled contentedly.

'Plenty of scope for a French maid's costume there,' Saskia pointed out. 'Frothy white pinny, black stockings, LBD, bow in that red hair.'

'I am definitely going to kill myself.'

Iain was immensely proud of Nadia, his date for the weekend, and dangled her from his wrist at all times like a new Rolex. He made a lot of fuss about not wanting to sleep on separate camp-beds until Goat finally offered him a double Lilo from the Dormobile.

'Don't you and he want that?' Phoebe asked Milly as they watched Goat huffing and puffing into a plastic tube on Iain's behalf.

'God, no.' Milly raised her eyebrows and whispered in her ear: 'It's got a tiny puncture – you go to sleep with it nice and bouncy; you wake up the next morning with your coccyx welded to the floor. It's Goat's idea of a joke.'

Fliss was surrounded by plastic shopping bags in the kitchen, valiantly trying to make lunch with nothing but plastic imple-ments to chop up meat, cheese and salad. On hearing that

Nadia didn't want butter in her sandwiches, didn't like pickle, preferred not to eat full-fat cheese and was allergic to tomatoes, she put a piece of white bread in between two slices of brown.

'A bread sandwich for the walking eating disorder. And if Iain tells me one more time that she's a former Miss Pears, I'm going to puke.'

'You did invite him,' Phoebe pointed out. 'You said you wanted to stay on friendly terms.'

'Nadia's a perfume girl in Harrods apparently.' Fliss curled her lip and hacked a cucumber with such violence that she broke the plastic knife. 'That's why you can smell her in the next room. She's one of those painted monsters that offers you a squirt as you walk past.'

'And dates them too,' Phoebe grinned.

'I just *have* to snog Mungo tonight,' Fliss muttered darkly. 'I am not being shown up by that wet fart parading around a scented twig with an inside leg measurement higher than her IQ!'

Selwyn phoned from the station to demand a lift just as Fliss's mound of sandwiches was threatening to topple from the paper plate she was stacking them on. Phoebe and Dylan, sitting side by side on the drainer, had been banished from trying to help after Dylan had distributed half a pound of cheese between just two sandwiches, and Phoebe had distractedly dolloped lemon curd into most of the ham ones in mistake for mustard.

Fliss, who had now snapped three plastic knives and vented a lot of anger on half a cooked chicken, was simmering with low-burning stress.

'Trust bloody Sel to want a lift now,' she fumed. 'These'll have gone as dry and curly as my hair by the time I've collected them.'

'I'll go,' Dylan offered, grabbing a couple of ham and pickle doorsteps from the top of the pile. 'I have to get some fags, anyway.'

'Get two hundred,' she suggested. 'All the smokers can chip in, then we won't run out all weekend.'

'I'd rather people don't smoke in the same room as me, actually,' Nadia breezed sweetly as she wandered in clutching a bottle of Pantène. 'Where are the towels, Felicity? I was hoping to wash my hair.'

'If you didn't bring one, tough,' she said through gritted teeth. 'And if you don't like smoking, I suggest you sit in another room. Or go outside. I'm coming with you, Dylan.' She grabbed the three slices of bread from beside her and handed them to Nadia. 'Bon appetit.'

The sandwiches had been raided and reduced to crumbs by the time Fliss and Dylan returned with the new arrivals.

Saskia, who hadn't eaten a thing, was sitting cross-legged on the quarry tiles with Stan, who had pickle smudges on his chin and a piece of cooked chicken hanging off his denim shirt. His thick blond mane was tied back with a bag tag. Both were busy making a big scoreboard for the final 'murderer poll' vote that night. They were surrounded by a cloud of cigarette smoke, marker pen fumes and a haze of pollen floating in from the open garden door.

'This is more like a Bangkok basement than Joanna Trollope's jam-making circle.' Selwyn squinted lazily around the door. 'Is that a spliff in your mouth, mate, or are you just pleased to see all eight of me?'

'It's a B and H,' Stan muttered uneasily, carefully finishing the drawing of a smoking pistol before looking up.

As the newcomers wandered in he assumed the fearful, slightly catatonic expression he always wore when looking at something ethereal, be it a painting, a custom Harley Davidson or a woman. Narrowing his eyes against the smoke, he sighed dreamily at an approaching vision of bone structure and not much else.

Following his gaze, Saskia caught her breath. Wavering in the door like a leaf skeleton shivering on a midwinter oak was Felix's ex-girlfriend, Jasmin.

With a fashionable black leather dress zipped like a plastic body-bag over her protruding bones, she followed a pensive-looking Fliss and Dylan through to the kitchen, pursued by a very smug Selwyn.

She looked so emaciated Saskia knew for certain she was anorectic. Her bones jutted out of her frail skin like bleached animal carcasses appearing through the mud of a dried-out African waterhole. Her creamy face had lost its exquisite beauty and sunk back into its skull. Despite the expertly applied make-up and ultra-trendy clothes, she looked haggard and dead-eyed, her brown hair dull, lank and starved of nutrients, her once-enviable legs like two lengths of thin string, knotted at the knees.

'Hi, Saskia.' Jasmin flickered a wary, red-lipped smile. 'How are you? You look loads better than the last time I saw you.'

'Thanks.' Saskia could barely look at her. She was utterly horrified by the image, suddenly realising that it was what she had been striving to become for weeks, and hating every broken, self-loathing inch of it.

'I didn't want to miss the side-show tonight,' Jasmin rattled on. 'I gather it'll be quite a crowd-puller. I was so pleased when Sel asked me along. I heard it was bring a bottle, so I've brought these.' She delved into a Timberland drawstring bag and pulled out a small brown bottle of Valium, hitching a very plucked, pencilled-in eyebrow and smiling broadly.

Selwyn, all blithe, dashing smoothness in cream chinos and a tobacco linen shirt that matched his amused eyes, laughed delightedly.

'Well, I'll certainly have a swig from that before tonight, darling – hi, Saskia sweetie.' He stretched down to kiss her on both cold, dry cheeks. 'Practising to present the Blue Peter appeal, I see.' He nodded at the votes scoreboard. 'Isn't that what all failed actresses secretly long to do? Grapple with a dead tortoise and sticky-backed plastic in the sunken garden?'

Saskia glared up at him. 'Here's one I prepared earlier, Selwyn.' She stuck up two fingers.

Georgette and Sir Dennis rolled up in their crow black Jaguar at tea-time, parking as far away from the Dormobile as possible and then eyeing it very suspiciously as they swung their hand-made shoes out on to the gravel and stood up. They gazed at the house with considerably more approbation.

Sir Dennis, a dab hand at delegating, quickly commandeered the entire troop of house-guests to carry in foil-covered trays of food from the Jag's boot while Georgette cornered Fliss for a briefing.

'I got Delia Fortescue's daughter to prepare all the grub, darling – a bit cheap and finger-buffetish, but, forgive me, I assumed your guests wouldn't be too discerning.'

'Er – no, they're not.' Fliss watched worriedly as Goat dropped a tray of pesto-stuffed tomatoes in a flower bed. 'This is really kind of you.'

'Nonsense, darling. I have a vested interest.' She flicked back her bob with a long red nail and winked.

'Huh?' Fliss yawned, only just remembering to cover her mouth before Georgette copped a close-up of her tonsils.

'Dennis – my vest-wearing voyeur,' Georgette smiled smoothly, 'he just loves young people.'

'I can imagine.' Fliss caught Sir D gawping lustily at Nadia's hot-pant-sporting rear as she teetered into the house, buckling under the weight of two miniature bread pudding ramekins.

'Is – er – Felix here yet?' Georgette peered short-sightedly as Stan trooped past with several foil trays under his chin.

'No.' Fliss batted away a wasp and rubbed her matted hair, wishing that she'd found time to wash it last night instead of hoping to do it this evening. She now doubted that she'd have time.

'And is Phoebe still planning to do the dirty?'

'Well, Saskia certainly hopes so.' Fliss dropped her voice as Dylan staggered into the house with a huge punch bowl.

'Gosh, what fun!' Georgette gushed insincerely. 'I've brought a smashing outfit for tonight. Dennis is going to be an assorted local yokel to add flavour.'

Fliss, barely listening, narrowed her eyes as Iain grabbed a very small foil tray from the Jag's back seat and wandered past them, blowing his floppy tortoiseshell forelock from his eye lashes, still looking horribly smug.

'Now,' Georgette went on, 'I thought Dora Mestick could be a fallen from grace ex-flapper who had her son, Mestick – a result of a drugged dalliance with the late Lord Fitzacoffin – very, very young in life. She was then taken on as the family housekeeper to save her from disgraced poverty, but has born a grudge ever since. What do you think?'

'Whatever you want.'

'Are you all right, darling? You look terribly tired.'

Fliss sighed. 'I *am* terribly tired.'

'Don't worry. You have a – over there, Dennis! No, not those ones! Have a rest, poppet. I'll take over from here.'

And she did.

While Fliss luxuriated in a deep, hot bubble bath and defluffed herself in Mungo's honour, Georgette ordered food into neat piles, drinks into serried ranks and plastic beakers on to assorted trays. Trotting around like girl guides, Stan, Paddy, Milly, Claudia, Lucy and Selwyn started to revise their choice of potential murder victim.

Mungo, still sunbathing in the garden, had fallen asleep, oblivious of newcomers, party-planning or food trays he could raid. His bottle of Chablis was now empty; his Henrietta Holt romantic novel had been devoured with unexpected appreciation. He was, in fact, rather pleased that he had come to this house party after all. It was proving gloriously restful.

Phoebe took Yuppie for a long walk.

Iain and Nadia spent the afternoon on their still-bouncy Lilo.

In the dining room, Sir Dennis was perching regally on a deck chair and peering lustily at Jasmin, his wise grey eyes scanning her body much as he speed-read a board meeting agenda, dwelling longest over matters arising. Sir Dennis liked things to be raised. He particularly liked the way that the wickedly short hem-line on this young thing's leather dress was rising up her slender thighs.

'So, my dear, do tell me about yourself,' he murmured kindly.

Sir Dennis liked his women lean of mind, body and morals. He was naturally drawn to scarcity of flesh and thought. He particularly liked verbal reserve, a quality not known to his wife.

'There's not much to tell, really.' Jasmin took in the fleece of white hair, the ruddy, baked biscuit tan and the hand-woven tweed and instantly thought: Silver Spoon, granulated, caster, Demerara, papa, père, father figure, six figure income, dirty old sod!

Three-quarters of an hour later, Dennis was still perched grandly and uncomfortably in the dining room, mentally running through a couple of important meetings he had scheduled for the following Tuesday morning. He'd stopped listening to Jasmin after five minutes, had stopped looking at that lush, red-painted mouth after ten, ceased to care about that slim-as-a-blade-of-grass body after fifteen. In fact, he now rather hoped a lawnmower would come along and crop the interminable flow of brainless self-pity.

Jasmin, still going strong, had so far only sketched her life up to five years old. She had another twenty to go – all far more eventful than the first fifth.

What a lovely, kind, sympathetic old darling, she thought tearfully.

Later, Phoebe prepared listlessly for the first full-dress drinks session, a towel wrapped around her freshly showered head, a vast, nervous spot welling up on the end of her nose.

Far from embodying Monika von Dyke, the cigar-puffing Czech poet, she felt more like crawling into her shredded sleeping bag and praying that Felix didn't turn up.

She fiddled with her spot unhappily and looked at her watch again. Six-fifteen. Please don't have got a flight, Felix, she prayed. Please let there be a bomb scare at Heathrow so that all transatlantic flights are landing in Manchester, or Aberdeen, or better still Greenland. Please don't turn up tonight, Felix. Please don't make me act the coward that does it with a kiss. She prodded her spot once more.

'Leave it alone, Phoebe, or it'll go shiny and form a head,' Saskia snapped, glancing at her in the unsteady reflection of her shaking mirror compact. 'Aren't you going to get dressed and put your slap on?'

'Sure.' She dug around in her bag for the dress she'd bought in Oxfam the previous morning. She had to dig carefully as Yuppie was snoring soundly on top of her flattened leather hold-all.

Saskia had blued a week's wages and hired a four-figure, figure-hugging Versace dress for the night. It was sensationally sexy and not at all what Phoebe had envisaged for Dame Bea Reeves. The twenties-style party-stopper was essentially a long, skintight tube of cream satin covered with row upon row of light-reflecting teardrop pearls that shimmered and swung as she moved. When she spun around, they flew out in lustrous, twirling arcs like the last flickers of a multi-layered Catherine wheel.

The dress ended demurely above the knee, where sheeny cream Wolford stockings took on the pearlised challenge and wrapped newly muscled, almost slender legs through to tapered ankles, ending in cream suede mules with very high Louis heels.

Matched with glossy blonde hair and glowing bronzed make-up, the final result was a spectacular mix of Essex raver fresh from the Hippodrome and Kensington deb fresh from Klosters.

'You look gorgeous.' Phoebe caught her breath as Saskia stood up. 'Way togs go, as we said at school. I mean it – you look really beautiful, Saskia.'

She wavered uncertainly in front of her, pearls rattling like maracas as she shook with nerves.

'You don't think I look a bit meringue-like?'

'Sexiest meringue I've ever seen.' Phoebe watched as Saskia arranged a pearl-encrusted headband on her sleek bob.

'Do you really think this is okay?' she asked uneasily.

'It's KO, not okay,' Phoebe smiled. 'It's breath-taking. Awesome. Pretty damn scrum. You've got the old pzazz back – and I don't mean the dress, hair and stuff. You look like the Saskia I hated at school again.'

She laughed delightedly, swooping on Phoebe with a soft clanking of pearls.

'That is simply the best compliment I could wish for,' she said, blue eyes gleaming rapturously. 'I feel a bit like the old Saskia again.'

The reaction when Phoebe wriggled into her Oxfam purchase and loosened her turban towel was somewhat more muted.

'What the fuck is that nylon sack?' Saskia gaped at Phoebe's bargain buy – a disastrous purple nylon handkerchief dress, as regularly modelled by Abba fans in the seventies. Three sizes too large, cut off at the knee, and sporting what appeared to be a large chili con carne stain – quite probably dating back to a yucca-and-brushed-denim seventies bring-a-course dinner party – it looked like Jane Torville's Bolero costume after a close shave with Christopher Dean's spinning skate blade. Even on Phoebe, Saskia reflected, it was monstrously unflattering.

Then her eyes slithered up to Phoebe's head.

'And why in hell has your hair suddenly gone from black to office carpet buff?'

'I thought we were all supposed to be revealing our true colours tonight,' she said in a small voice. 'This looked closest to my natural hue on the Boots charts.'

'It's the same shade as service station tea, Freddy!'

'So is my natural hair colour,' she muttered uneasily.

'Felix will hate it. Remember, he only fancies you because of the way you dress and the fact that you make him laugh. Face him like that and he'll run a mile.'

Phoebe winced. 'I don't think he's coming.'

Saskia ignored the remark and picked up a long purple scarf belt which was hanging out of Phoebe's bag.

'And what were you planning to do with this?' she asked despairingly.

'It came with the dress.' Phoebe shrugged. 'I thought I might wind it round my head or something.'

'Do me a favour and wind it round your neck instead.' Saskia sighed. 'Oh, Freddy, you're losing your edge. Are you deliberately setting out to get Felix to dump you? Christ, I knew I should have hired you something too. You look awful.'

The sound of Fats Waller suddenly crooning at top volume

from Fliss's stereo downstairs drowned out the crunch of tyres on gravel from outside. Yuppie, waking up with a startled series of barks, added to the confusion.

'I didn't have enough money to buy anything decent.' Phoebe perched on the edge of a camp-bed with Yuppie on her knee and stared up at Saskia imploringly. 'I mean, I know you wanted me to look stunning tonight, but I was in a hurry yesterday and it looked all right in the shop. I'm sure we can improve it a bit.'

'Well, we could start by torching it,' Saskia suggested bitterly, turning away in defeat. 'God, that sound system is distorted.' She listened to Fats crackling and fizzing downstairs.

It had to happen.

Phoebe was poised in a sprawled, leggy state of buff-haired, Oxfam-dressed, zit-nosed depression on the ledge of her re-assembled camp-bed. Standing in the middle of the room, Saskia was radiating glamorous, creamy-hued, sensually swathed disapproval from a perfect ballet first position. High-heeled, Bette Davis cool, Sharon Stone hot, she looked up as the door swung open, painted blue eyes batting their heavy, teased lashes like a Restoration fan across a flushed cleavage.

Pushing through the door with wide, worked-out shoulders and a leather suit-carrier, Felix looked sleepy, dishevelled, stubbled, and more desirable than ever. His hair had been cut into a crisp short-back-and-sides, his face tanned by the California sun, his long legs, swathed in white denim Strassi jeans, seemed to stretch forever and blur in front of her eyes.

Saskia caught her breath and held it there until her lungs felt like two overstuffed Hoover bags. Then he looked up at her and the Hoover bags burst open with a loud gasp as she fought hard not to sway on her high heels.

Phoebe, her back to the door, smelled the peppery aftershave and closed her eyes. Yuppie, meanwhile, threw herself off Phoebe's lap with suicidal momentum and raced to the door, where she was gathered up into a laughing hug.

'Hi there.' Felix clutched Yuppie and smiled uneasily at Saskia. 'How are you?'

Looking as she did, Saskia had the confidence not to lie. 'Miserable as hell.' She smiled back bravely. 'How are you?'

'Pretty much the same, but with jet lag.' Felix shrugged. Letting Yuppie down on to the floor again, he started to back out of the door. 'Look, I'm sorry to barge in – I was told Phoebe was in this room.'

'She is,' Saskia said with some satisfaction, torn between loving how repulsive her agent provocateur looked, and wishing she looked better for the sake of the revenge. She pointed towards her cowering friend.

Peering around the door, Felix eyed the mousy-haired oddity on the camp-bed with tired disinterest.

'Where?'

'You're looking at her.'

Saskia forced her biggest, most I'm-over-you-so-fuck-off smile, and then walked out, pearls rattling smoothly.

41

'God, I've missed you, Phoebe. Come here.'
 Felix dropped his bag on the floor and enveloped her in a tight hug. The warmth of his long body against hers was so snug and comforting; the feeling of his chin in the hollow of her collar and his arms wrapped tightly around her was so reassuring and longed-for, Phoebe wanted to stay there forever, winched out of the house by crane, still glued in that hug, and then lowered into a van like a sculpture and driven to London before being carried, still hugging, into the mews to hug somewhere safe.

Instead she pulled back, acutely aware that Saskia could walk back in at any second.

'I've missed you too.' She turned away, searching around for a distraction. She looked at Yuppie who had clambered on top of Felix's suit-carrier and was trying to tug off the flight tag.

'Good.' Felix pulled her back into a kiss. That Kiss. The Felix kiss which could floor her in seconds – literally had on a few occasions in the mews when they hadn't made it to the bed, or, once, even made it up the stairs from the front door.

Desperately fighting the punch of excitement between her legs, Phoebe kept half an eye on the door. Then, as Felix ran his hands down her back and pulled her tighter to him, she lost focus on the door, closed her eyes and kissed him back for heart-skipping joy, loving his mouth on hers, his body against hers, the strong, bristled warmth of his neck under her hands.

As they pulled apart for breath, he cocked his head and looked at her, biting his lip with a thoughtful grin.

He's noticed the hair, she realised suddenly. Wet, glossy, well-cut but undeniably mouse. He must hate it. And then she realised that he wasn't looking at her hair, he was looking straight into her eyes.

'I love the way you kiss. It's so firm and sexy and confident. You kiss like a man.'

Phoebe felt disturbed rather than flattered.

'Kissed a lot of men then, have you?'

'Of course I fucking haven't. You know what I mean.' Felix looked mildly huffy. 'It was a compliment.'

'Sure,' Phoebe smiled, although she was still uncertain if kissing like a man was a good thing. 'You kiss like a man too.'

'Thanks.'

'And,' she stroked his throat with a fingertip, 'you also kiss like a god.'

'Kissed a lot of gods, have you?' Felix's eyes played between hers delightedly.

'Snogged Apollo last week,' Phoebe nodded. 'Not a patch on Zeus, of course, but great with his tongue. Bacchus was okay – bit pissed. Cupid's a bit of a girl, really. Nope,' she cocked her head, 'I think you're the best of the lot.'

'I've missed you so fucking much.'

'And I've missed you too.'

'I've seriously pissed Piers off, coming back this early. He wanted to keep me on the West Coast for another week and tout me around like a pyramid-seller with a water-filter at a dinner party. But I was suffering Phoebe withdrawal symptoms. I started sleeping with the pillow lengthways beside me for the first time since I was a teenager, but I must say I much prefer groping you to a pile of duck down.' He slipped a hand to her buttocks.

Fats Waller was still chortling distortedly downstairs. Above the music various whoops and shrieks were echoing up from the hall as, one by one, the house guests descended in their murder mystery costumes, hammily acting their characters for all they were worth. Phoebe could hear corks popping, footsteps thumping on the stairs, could imagine Saskia, pearls rattling, knocking back wine in order to cope. Listening to the sound effects, her momentary bubble world with Felix suddenly popped as she realised that soon they would be expected to go down and join in.

'Did you come straight here from the airport?' She fingered his torn denim shirt collar, fighting to sound normal.

'No, I had to collect something from the mews first. I was in London at lunchtime. It took me sodding hours to get down here – the trains are appalling. Then my taxi driver took me to the wrong village. I'd forgotten the name of this place.'

'But you've been here loads of times before.' She stiffened, trying to pull away.

'Only twice.' Felix clutched on to her. 'And both times I was plastered, or stoned, or just too miserable to care – the fiancé with aisle phobia going off to meet his future in-laws who he wants to be out-laws. Christ, it's weird being here again – seeing Saskia. She looks good, doesn't she? I was so scared I'd fucked her up totally.'

Phoebe, riddled with doubt, jealousy and duplicity, couldn't answer.

'I only came here because I love you so bloody much, I can't think straight.' He pressed his chin back into her shoulder. 'I'm just praying that, come midnight, she's not the murderer. When the lights go out, I'm grabbing you and whisking you off to an attic for a cowardly snog. I might as well die well hung.'

Pressing her face tightly to his shoulder, Phoebe breathed in his familiar, warm smell and stifled a sob.

'What's wrong?' Felix drew away, cupping her face in his hands.

Phoebe stared at him. His eyes were bloodshot and squinting slightly from the long flight, underlined with tired smudges, but still he looked so lovely that she caught her breath, longing to cover his face with kisses and beg him to leave, to go back to London, to run away. More than anything she wanted to go with him. To escape from her pact with Saskia.

But she could still smell Saskia's perfume lingering in the room, could see her nighty hooked over the camp-bed and her hairbrush discarded on top of it, laced with blonde hairs. Phoebe could remember lying in her own camp-bed that morning listening to Saskia running her through the farewell Felix speech and telling her how utterly terrified she was of coming face to face with him.

'I'll probably crack up, Freddy,' she'd confessed tearfully. 'I mean, seeing him so close to after so long, and then seeing him with you as well, I think I'll crash and burn. I won't be able to talk to him without breaking down.'

But she had done it, had been incredibly calm and elegant and brave. Now Phoebe knew it was her turn.

She pulled away. 'I'm fine. Just a bit headachy. How did the test go?'

Felix grinned. 'Shit hot. Piers has heard a very, very off-the-record rumour that they're already drawing up contracts. I brought you back some jeans – here.' He dived into his bag and extracted three pairs of Strassi Workers – their most popular line – in garish shades of yellow, green and pink.

'Thanks.' Phoebe took them mindlessly. 'That's wonderful – about the job I mean. So you've almost definitely got it?'

Felix was still digging through his bag.

'Well, Piers clearly thinks so – he's even confident enough to start haggling about a price,' he said cheerfully. 'They certainly seemed pretty blown away. But I tell you, I was just a piece of meat out there. "Drop your strides, Felix – okay spin around, Felix – clench your butt, Felix – bend over." It was ten times worse than medicals at school.'

'I thought you were auditioning for a film too?' Phoebe watched him, drinking him in, trying to remember every beautiful angle before she lost him for good.

'Yeah, I read some of the script for them.' Felix dug out his dark silver Tess Tosterone shirt and threw it to one side. 'It stinks – but the character hardly has to say anything, so I'm away. I just have to chase pussy, read Proust in French, straddle a lot of babes and Harleys, love my Landed Gentry parents, solve the world's peace problems, play stud poker, say "oh golly gosh what I say" a lot, and drink Bud. It's all racy plot, product placement, arty shots and the Bay Watch boob, biceps and butt philosophy. Hugh Grant meets Micky Rourke; James Bond meets the Marlboro man. It'll be a cult smash. Here, take a couple of these.'

He handed her up a foil package of headache pills.

'Thanks.' Phoebe knocked two back with swigs from Saskia's big bottle of mineral water. She then sat cross-legged on the floor and started to towel dry her hair, listening to his amused, sardonic run-down, her stomach churning unhappily as she realised this might be their last decent conversation, the last time she heard that deep, drawling voice chatting to her easily and happily.

'They gave Piers and me this huge spiel about "the character criteria" – all market-share graphics and disposable income analyses,' he went on, still rooting through his bag. 'As if I fucking care! Basically, I'm only going along with this because Piers has been banging on about it for so – ah, there it is!' He withdrew a plastic bag from his suit-carrier. Putting it to one side, he twisted around to face her, yawning widely.

'Cover your mouth,' she joked listlessly.

'You cover it,' he grinned.

Phoebe dropped her head to her knees and started towelling the hair at the back of her neck.

A moment later, Felix had grabbed the towel and taken over, stretching long, white denim legs to either side of her.

'Now are you going to tell me what's bugging you?' he muttered, rubbing the towel gently on the soft hair behind her ears in almost a massage. 'Or do I have to start pulling out your stubby little fingernails?'

'I already chewed them off myself,' she mumbled, her face buried in towel. 'You haven't seen Dylan tonight?'

'Dylan?' The massaging strokes slowed. 'No – some thick red-head called Nadia showed me up. Why?'

Phoebe pushed the towel away and looked up at him. 'Saskia isn't your only ex here.'

'What?' Felix muttered edgily, rubbing a tired eye with his finger.

'Jasmin rolled up earlier with Selwyn.'

'Jasmin?' he looked amazed.

'Skinny model. You almost married her. Looks as though she stopped eating a couple of years ago.'

'I know who she bloody is,' he snapped. 'Christ, it's going to be quite a reunion, isn't it? God, I'm sorry, Phoebe. Talk about skeletons raiding their wardrobes.'

'That is not funny.' She looked away.

'I know, I know – I'm just jet-lagged and worried to distraction about you.'

'About me?' Her voice wobbled.

'You won't look at me.' Felix dropped the towel. 'I've thought about nothing but you for three days, dreamed about you, bored Piers to death about you, drummed my fingers, toes and heartbeat in anticipation of getting back to you. And suddenly I'm here and you're acting like you're yet another ex.'

'I should get ready.' She made to stand up.

Grabbing her arm, Felix dragged her down again.

'Something's happened, hasn't it?' he asked worriedly. 'Have you been talking to Saskia?'

'No more than usual.' Phoebe picked at the towel.

'You suddenly seem different.'

'Foul dress, office carpet hair, spotty nose. Changes a girl.'

'What?' he snapped in confusion.

Phoebe pulled up her head and glared at him.

'Look at me, Felix.'

He looked. He looked for a long, long time, eyes melting.

'I love you, Phoebe. I don't give a fuck what colour your hair is, what you're wearing, what your skin's like. I fancied you from the first moment I saw you, lolling drunkenly on a chair in a Kensington wine bar with your knickers showing.'

She gaped at him.

'You knew that was me?'

'Yup. And the Swedish barmaid with the Chris de Burgh t-shirt. I fancied her too. She had an arse from Heaven and could whizz through a crossword like smoke.'

Phoebe hung her head.

'If you'd care to look at me properly instead of gaping at my ear, you'd see that I'm actually looking far, far rougher than you.' He sighed. 'I'm dirty and unshaven and bug-eyed and spotty too.'

'You look lovely,' Phoebe mumbled. 'You always bloody do.'

'And so do you, you daft cow. You look lovely and beautiful and welcoming to me because you're you. Bright, funny, infuriating, sexy – you. You just look like you. Don't you see that? You'll always look fucking gorgeous to me because I love you.'

'No, you don't.'

'Don't fucking say that! Shit! You're always saying that.'

'That's because you're always saying you love me.'

'That's because I bloody do.'

'No, you don't.'

'When will you get it into your thick head that I've fallen rashly, stupidly, irreversibly in love with you, you stupid bitch?' He gripped her shoulders in despair. 'And that it's driving me demented that you never tell me how you feel for me – if you feel anything at all. It's why I get so insecure when you act like you are tonight.'

'I – ' Phoebe bit her lip, wanting to say it more than anything. 'Felix, I – '

'Yes?'

'Come here.'

She slid her hands on to his shoulders and pulled him closer, her eyes still glued to his.

Their mouths met and she almost dissolved into a fizzing puddle of unleashed libido as the instant, pounding sensation of free-fall lust took hold. Kissing Felix could turn her on as easily as a celebrity flicking the switch on the Regent Street Christmas lights. She coiled her arms around his neck and kissed him hungrily and frantically, certain that it was her last chance.

'Christ,' he breathed, 'I'm so glad I met you.'

He pressed her back against the floor, his hands searching for a zip in the monstrous dress. As they kissed more urgently and breathlessly, he gripped the collar and impatiently ripped the thin, cheap fabric from neckline to hemline.

'I'm sorry,' he gasped between kisses, 'I've been wanting to do that since I walked in.'

Phoebe couldn't care less. She stretched her mouth up to his again and reached for his belt.

It was an ungainly coupling, with Phoebe's ankles over Felix's shoulders and his boots jabbing into her armpits. But they laughed as they screwed and then, laughter dissolving, gasped with mounting pleasure, not giving a damn for the aesthetics of sex as dictated by Hollywood films, popular romantic fiction, tabloid magazines and Barry White. This was earthy, delightful, immediate sex at its most basic and satisfying – lights bright, legs cramping, semi-clothed bodies contorting and groins pumping with hot, fizzing, leaping pleasure.

Afterwards, Phoebe let Felix wrap his arms around her as she curled up into a tight ball and clenched her eyes shut, knowing that she had just been the stupidest cow on earth, if one of the most satisfyingly sated. Saskia could have walked in at any time. As could anyone. She just fancied this man so much, loved him so much, wanted him so much all the time. If horrified her that no one seemed to realise how much Felix meant to her.

And yet she always remained silent amongst her friends. Her burden of responsibility to Saskia was so great that she had failed over and over again to say out loud how much she loved Felix. Most of all to him because, once said, she would want to repeat it forever.

Headlights slid past the windows of the bedroom as another car pulled up in the drive.

'People are starting to turn up,' she muttered regretfully.

'I guess that means we should be on show.'

Phoebe looked across at the shredded purple monster dress and wondered if Monika von Dyke could get away with wearing pink Strassi jeans and a t-shirt.

Stretching behind him, Felix picked up the purple scarf belt and ran it across Phoebe's thigh.

'Let me dress you.' He kissed her hair.

'What?'

'Let me dress you,' he repeated quietly. 'After all, I don't think you have much choice.'

The next moment he was gently blindfolding her with the purple scarf.

The whole experience was incredibly sexy. Phoebe sat, blind and passive, while Felix slowly rolled hold-up silk stockings on to each of her legs with warm, cautious fingers, slipped a whisper-light camisole over her head, laid her back and rucked up her arse as he slithered French knickers past her hips. As he hooked a dress over her head and eased her arms through the shoulder straps, she recognised the faint, long-faded scent of cologne and slightly musty smell of long-term storage. It snaked down her body like a slow dive into a warm swimming pool.

'It's the Fulham Road frock!' she gasped, fingering the fragile gossamer. 'I can't believe you brought it down.'

'I had to go back to London to get it. No – don't take the blindfold off yet. I haven't finished.'

He disappeared for a few seconds, his footsteps fading from the room. Phoebe fingered the moth-wing thin silk chiffon of the dress and traced her fingers along the delicate, beaded embroidery, hand-sewn all those decades ago by some careful seamstress's hand.

Felix's footsteps padded back into earshot. At least Phoebe hoped it was Felix. She tensed slightly and battled with an urge to rip off the blindfold, terrified that it might be Goat or Stan, lurching in to ask where she had got to and offer her a glass of wine.

But the warm hands that touched her shoulders as he sat back down behind her were unmistakably Felix's. No one else could ever make her pulse leap like that.

The next moment, the hands were dripping with tepid water as they slicked her hair back.

'I've just dried that,' she grumbled.

'I'm damping the vamp.'

'I hope that's water.'

'Fresh from the tap. I just bumped into a rather shocked-looking girl with black hair, a string bag dress and a cello as I was heading back from the bathroom with a Duty Free bag full of warm water.'

'My sister,' Phoebe sighed. 'Although I can't imagine how you could possibly shock her.'

'I've got no shirt on and my flies are still undone.'

'She wouldn't bat an eyelid.'

'She didn't.' Felix dipped his hands in the Duty Free bag and slicked some more. 'She was shocked by the sudden appearance of a white-haired stick-man with awful teeth wearing a sack poncho and Hunter wellies.'

'Shaggy Okel.'

'Who?'

'Her boyfriend, Goat.'

'Christ.'

'He sharpens his teeth.'

'Saves on Crest, I should imagine. And the Barbour prat's here tonight. He's with Nadia the red-haired babelet who showed me up here. She's a call-girl.'

'She's what?' Phoebe reached for the blindfold.

'Don't take it off.' Felix covered her hands with his own. 'She's an escort. Piers has used her as a hostess at parties while Topaz is away. She's one of the best – Latymer education, fluent in Japanese, father's a member of the 1922 Committee. She was a deb a couple of years ago. Not cheap.'

'Christ!' Phoebe whistled. 'I wonder if Iain knows?'

'He should. He's hired her for the weekend.' Felix laughed. 'She told me earlier. Ten per cent off because he's pretty. She has to pretend to be his new lover.'

'Ohmygod! I can't wait to tell Fliss.' Phoebe bit her tongue in delight as Felix gently spun her around to clip on earrings, a choker and a bracelet, all heavy and cool against her hot skin.

He even made up her face – carefully and rather inexpertly applying red Cupid's bow lipstick before removing her blindfold and painting her eyes as huge, black and bruised as Marianne Faithful at her druggiest. He gripped the tip of his pink tongue with effort and concentration, leaning back occasionally to admire his handiwork as though putting the finishing touches to a water-colour portrait. Yuppie sat beside him and watched too, small head to one side, totally entranced.

'I thought you said you preferred me with no make-up on?' Phoebe grumbled as Felix applied the third coat of Saskia's Lancaster mascara, painting a lot of her cheek and eyebrow as he went.

'I do.' He wiped a smudge away with his fingers. 'God, this is much harder than it looks. I'm glad I'm a bloke. I'm doing this for you, not me. You were the one complaining you were spotty and badly dressed.'

'I *was* spotty and badly dressed.'

'I wouldn't want you any other way. I find you incredibly sexy when your clothes look as though you've dug your arm into the t-shirts for Rwanda post-box. Although, I must confess, you do look sensational tonight. Far too good to share, in fact.'

'We could hide all night,' she suggested hopefully. 'Or nick a car and drive back to London.'

'Tempting. But not quite as tempting as the opportunity to murder my little brother for the sake of entertainment.'

Felix dressed in minutes, stripping from his still-unbuckled white jeans to his jersey designer underpants then climbing into wide grey herringbone Oxford bags, a silver shirt, double-breasted black waistcoat and white cravat. With the short, floppy gold hair hidden under a very dapper squishy herringbone hat, he looked as twenties as the earthquake at Amalfi, Chanel and the bust flattener.

'Meeester Tosterone, you are ver' sexy man,' Phoebe purred in a husky Eastern European accent.

'Ms von Dyke.' Felix held out his arm for her to take. 'Shall we go down?'

Laughing, Phoebe scooped Yuppie under one arm and slotted the other through Felix's.

*   *   *

The drawing room was far less populated then she had feared. Drowned out by the Charleston, half a dozen couples were shouting polite conversation at one another and looking faintly ridiculous in their ad hoc costumes as they tried hard to stay in character. It was still light outside and the last red glow of a dropping sun was lending the room its enchanted grotto look, adding to the surreal quality of the gathering.

There was Goat and Milly, in the sack poncho and Phoebe's crocheted dress respectively, sharing a spliff in a cigarette holder. Milly had hacked the crocheted dress off above the knee and was trying to pull it down as she shot an annoyingly attentive Sir Dennis dirty looks. Beside them, Claudia – as Billie Havitawayday – was wearing a very nineties silver mini-dress, her concession to the twenties being an extraordinary rubber bathing hat – sprayed silver and trimmed with a glued-on hem of silver sofa fringe – crammed tightly over her corded hair. Sir Dennis was hovering nearby as a general yokel wearing a vast hessian smock, tied-ankle trousers and a squashy felt hat, a bottle of Krug in one hand.

In another corner, Stan was sporting his official butler's garb, hair scraped into a pony tail, looking immensely uncomfortable as he moved his head around to ease the itchiness of his wing collar. He had a bottle of red and white wine in each hand and was swigging from each at regular intervals, ignoring everyone's empty glasses. Chatting to him were Fliss's pretty blonde friend, Lucy, who was looking delightfully vampish as Lucrecia D'eath-Wyshe, and Iain, who was looking very slimy in a velvet smoking jacket, white silk evening scarf and satin cravat. He had slicked his floppy tortoiseshell forelock back and was sporting very small dark glasses in an attempt to look like Bart Stard, matinée idol and closet queen. The effect was very Rupert Everett, if slightly marred by digital watch, black trainers and can of draught Guinness.

As the doorbell rang in the hallway, almost everyone shrieked 'Door, Mestick!' with delighted hoots of laughter.

Saskia and Dylan were side by side.

Dylan's face lit up as soon as he spotted Felix, his false

moustache covered with beer froth, his monocle popping out of his eye socket.

'There you are, old boy!' he guffawed boffishly, tripping over the hem of his military trousers as he headed across the room. 'Jolly good show, what? Got a tipple yet?'

The very dashing uniform he was wearing was far too long and narrow for him, making him look rather like a Weeble crammed into Action Man's outfit.

'Borrowed it off a six-foot-six mate in the Life Guards,' he explained in an undertone. 'He'll kill me if I get so much as a crumb on it – he's got a full dress wedding next weekend. The medals are made of chocolate coins. Try one. They're already melting.'

'Later, perhaps.' Felix slipped his hand into Phoebe's to stop her from moving away. 'Who are you supposed to be, Dyldo?'

'Colonel Piggy Pinchbottom – and, before you say it, I know I've got a lieutenant's garb on,' Dylan swigged from his Sol bottle, moustache tilting dramatically, and eyed Phoebe nervously. 'You look gorgeous, poppet.'

'Tank you, darlink.' She smiled back, wishing she knew exactly what she did look like. From Saskia's amazed, eye-batting stare, she supposed it must be an improvement on the exploding purple blancmange outfit.

'How was the States, old boy?' Dylan asked Felix, pressing his loose moustache back on centre.

As they were chatting, Phoebe released her fingers from Felix's and, mouthing an apology, slipped away to fetch herself a drink.

Saskia was being accosted by Sir Dennis now, leaning away.

'Can you show me where the kitchen is, please?' Phoebe asked her politely. 'Please excuse me,' she apologised to Sir Dennis.

He opened his mouth to say 'Not at all, my dear', and no words came out. He carried on gaping at Phoebe, utterly transfixed, mouth still ajar, eyes steam-rolling her body.

Phoebe backed away sharply, treading on Yuppie who squealed in shock.

'Thanks, Freddy.' Saskia hugged her as soon as they were out of the room. 'I hope to God I'm not near that old letch when the lights go out at midnight. You look staggering.'

'So I've been told,' she sighed, clutching Yuppie and kissing her on the head to apologise for squashing her. 'I haven't had a chance to see myself yet.'

'What?'

'Felix did it.'

Saskia's eyes narrowed jealously. 'Felix dressed you up like this?'

'Yes. He wasn't too keen on the purple dress either.'

'Well, it explains why it leaves nothing to the imagination, I suppose,' Saskia muttered bitchily. 'He always did like everything to be on show.'

'You mean I've got something hanging out?' Holding Yuppie out in front of her, Phoebe looked down in horror. No wonder Sir Dennis had looked like a small boy peering into a large cleavage.

'No, but the dress is practically see-through, as are those undies. When you stand with your back to the light, it's pretty risqué. Not that I'm complaining. It'll make it all the more painful for Felix when you dump him – his doll turning around to stick pins in him.'

Phoebe put a hand to her damp hair and sighed uneasily, growing more and more certain that she wouldn't be able to do it.

'People are arriving already, and I still don't know who half the characters are,' she sighed.

'Common problem.' Saskia headed towards the baize door, pearls rattling. 'Mungo hasn't even appeared yet – apparently he's got terrible sun-burn from lolling about in the garden all day.'

'Serves him right.'

'And Paddy appeared for just five minutes as Dips "The Tips" O'Maniac, wearing *the* most extraordinary plus fours, before donning his leather jacket and heading off to the pub with Selwyn, Jasmin and Nadia – much to Iain's horror. Fliss is a bit stressed too.'

In the kitchen, Fliss looked exceptionally stressed. She was halfway down a very large gin and tonic and stuffing her face with sausage salad.

'It's a bloody disaster,' she moaned as they wandered in. 'Frigging Mungo hasn't even bothered to grace us with his gorgeous presence, Stan's got a bigger hump on than Quasimodo, Paddy's absconded with half my potential murderers, and my sodding tights keep falling down.'

Georgette – the most glamorous housekeeper ever in a Coco Chanel original – was taking over completely, arranging food on plates, drinks on trays, and paper tissues on hand for Fliss, who was descending towards a very rare show of tears.

'Girls!' Georgette sighed with relief, beaming at Saskia and Phoebe. 'Can you possibly do a bit of carrying through?'

'Sure.' Saskia grabbed a couple of plates of hors d'oeuvres and headed back into the throng.

Shutting Yuppie in the utility room with her duffle bag bed and some chews to distract her and keep her out of danger, Phoebe picked up a huge basket of home-made garlic crisps and nudged Fliss reassuringly as she passed. 'I think it's going superbly – everyone's really getting into it.'

'Thanks.' Fliss forced a brave smile. 'But how many times do I have to tell you to look someone straight in the eyes when you're lying to them?'

'Some more of your friends have just arrived.' Phoebe helped herself to a vast glass of Coke.

'Oh, God! Already?' Fliss swigged her gin. 'I told people half-seven.'

'It's quarter to eight, darling,' Georgette pointed out as she unwrapped two huge poached salmon. 'I think we should just – is Dennis behaving himself through there, Phoebe? – put all this stuff out and let people attack, don't you?'

'Yes,' Phoebe and Fliss said in unison, both answering different questions.

'You okay?' Fliss whispered to Phoebe.

'Is the Pope Jewish?'

'You'll be great.' Fliss wolfed some more sausage salad. 'Just give him hell. You're going to do it after the murder, yeah?'

Easing a salmon on to an oval plate, Georgette strained her ears to listen in.

'That's what Saskia is planning.' Phoebe drained most of her glass of Coke in one and helped herself to more.

'During the drawing-room interrogation?'

'S'the plan.' Phoebe closed her eyes.

'Good luck.'

'I don't think I can do it, Fliss.'

'Nonsense – you frigging well have to!' She polished off her gin and tonic, straightened her cloche hat, and picked up her pince nez. 'I'm going to get Mungo out of his room. I might be gone quite some time.'

After she had whisked out through the lobby, Phoebe clutched on to her basket of crisps and downed half a glass of wine for strength.

'So tonight's the night, huh?' Georgette whistled past her with a piping tube full of mayonnaise. 'All fired up for the final dénouement, darling?'

Phoebe poured herself the last of the Coke bottle, spilling most of it on the floor, and then looked up at her, the urge to splurge too great to hold back. If she didn't tell someone, she was going to go completely crackers.

'No.'

'Sorry, darling?' Georgette's piped mayonnaise suddenly went from neat twirls along one salmon's spine to a spaghetti junction of crazed loops on its flank.

'I love him, Georgette.' Phoebe sagged against the drainer. 'I love him too much to do it. I know it sounds crazy and egotistical and deluded, but I genuinely believe he won't try and hurt me in the same way he hurt Saskia. Doing this to him will cripple me.' She turned away, battling tears. 'And it'll just crucify him.'

'Then don't do it,' Georgette said simply.

'It's not that easy. Saskia is so desperate. And I gave her my word.'

Georgette wiped her hands on a tea towel and walked across to Phoebe, gripping her shoulders and coaxing her round to face those big, seal-brown eyes.

'Saskia will live if you don't do it,' she said firmly. 'She has a terrific family, a lot of friends and a lot of support, darling. She'll be hurt, but she'll also be fine. You'd be losing Felix, and you have to ask yourself if you can cope with that. Remember, you absolutely don't have to do it if you don't want. You can walk away now.'

'I can't.' Phoebe blinked hard. 'If I don't do it, she'll tell him everything anyway. And she'll tell the press, which will simply decimate his career.'

'Oh, God,' Georgette sighed, staring at the ceiling in sympathy. 'She's so obsessed. I was warned about this.'

'You what?'

Georgette took the basket from Phoebe and, casting it to one side, squeezed her hands apologetically. 'I've heard rumours that a story is bubbling in the gutter press, darling.'

'A story?'

'Well, more of a character assassination.'

'Oh God, poor Felix. I can't bear it.' Phoebe started to shake. She felt absolutely freezing cold, and her legs were threatening to give way under her. Gripping on to Georgette's hands for stability, she fought hard not to race straight through to the drawing room and throw herself in a penitent heap.

Georgette watched the beautiful, painted lips wobbling madly, the big green eyes swimming with unhappiness.

'You really do love him, don't you, darling?'

Phoebe nodded.

'Whichever way you look at it, tonight is our last, isn't it?' Her face crumpled. 'And I love him so much, I can barely look at him without breaking down. I've started counting the time we have together in minutes and it's killing me.'

'I think,' Georgette took a deep breath, 'that you should go back in there, grab him, and tell him everything. Absolutely everything, Phoebe. Right now.'

'I can't!' she gasped. 'Saskia will—'

'Bugger Saskia! You love him, darling. He loves you too, by all accounts. Susie says the story is coming out anyway. You have to rescue your—'

'Susie?'

'You have to tell him before it's too late, Phoebe.' Georgette clutched on to her hands more tightly, her voice low and urgent. 'If you confess what's been going on and how you now feel, there's a very good chance that, if and when this awful story comes out in the press, you and Felix can show a united front to disprove it – hold hands, smile at the cameras and laugh it off. It could even be good publicity for Felix. You have to—'

'Susie Middleton's your step-daughter, isn't she?' Phoebe snatched her hands away, backing off sharply. 'Has she put you up to all this?'

'No! I mean, yes, she's my step-daughter, but – '

'That's why you're down here helping Fliss.' Phoebe's eyes widened with horror. 'You're here as Susie's emissary, aren't you? Is that why you're suddenly sounding like Max Clifford on a PR damage limitation exercise?'

'I want to help you, Phoebe,' Georgette sighed. 'You're in a complete shambles of a situation, and I want to help.'

'By getting Felix some good publicity out of it? Very charitable.'

'Susie did ask me to keep an eye on things, yes.' Georgette tucked her neat black hair behind her ears and stared at Phoebe levelly. 'But not because of Felix's bloody career. He sacked her as his agent after all. She cares about the little sod, just as you do. Don't ask me why, but she's immensely fond of him – she's bailed him out of some pretty ghastly messes before.'

Phoebe pressed her palms to her eyes. 'Don't you think you've left it a bit late to intervene on her behalf?'

'Tell him, Phoebe. For both your sakes. I'll look after Saskia.'

'I say, is there any more white wine in here?' Dylan loomed through the door, moustache at a forty-five degrees. 'Spiffing jamboree out there. Where's that fine young filly, Euthanasia? Thought she'd be in here.'

Turning on her heel, Phoebe pushed past him and walked out.

Her heart thumping like a lead pendulum against her ribs, she survived the next hour by getting far too drunk and avoiding Felix. As more and more guests arrived, it became easier to dodge him. He was cornered by predatory female after predatory female; she was cornered by a few brave men, Sir Dennis being the most persistent.

'You really are a ravishing young thing,' he oozed, eyes threatening to cause a nuclear melt-down of Phoebe's see-through dress. 'Have you ever been to a London casino? I know a frightfully good one.'

'I'm more of a bingo girl.'

'Sounds enchanting. You must take me along with you very soon, my dear. Actually, I'm free on Tuesday.'

Phoebe glanced at her watch. Three hours and four minutes before she lost Felix forever. So why was she avoiding him totally? She was running away as she always did; burying her head in the fairy-tale sandcastles she had created in the hope that the tide would turn and not wash them away.

Still trapped amid his gaggle of friends in the sitting room, Felix was scratching under his floppy herringbone hat, hamming up his Tess Tosterone role and laughing delightedly as a friend's girlfriend felt his muscles with a girlish whoop. Dylan obviously hadn't warned him of his impending fate yet, Phoebe realised with an almost ruptured heart.

From the hall, she watched him through a crowd of mingling flappers, her ribs feeling as though they were interlocking and crushing her lungs to nothing.

Suddenly Felix looked up and gazed straight at her. He smiled his big, happy, gorgeous smile and mouthed, 'You okay?'

Phoebe turned away, her eyes swimming. Through a blurred haze, she saw Sir Dennis closing in fast and bolted in the opposite direction.

Retreating to a dark corner of the hall, she downed three glasses of white wine in a row. She knew that this was perilously close to her pass-out alcohol quota, but unconsciousness suddenly seemed preferable to responsibility. In fact, a life of alcoholism was increasingly tempting. She wanted to be the Olly Reed of Islington. No she didn't; she wanted Felix.

Suppressing a self-pitying sob, she allowed her plastic beaker to be topped up by a very drunken friend of Felix's who was wearing a striped blazer and clutching a bottle of Smirnoff Black Label in each hand.

'We met at Albany Mews,' he giggled, leaning so close to Phoebe that he knocked his boater off with her forehead. 'I'm Giles. You're the dyke, aren't you?'

'I'm sorry?' Phoebe blinked, too pissed to follow him.

'Knickers von Dyke – the Polish novelist?'

'Czech poet, yes.'

'Who are you going to murder, then?' He reeled around in front of her.

'Monika von Dyke, I think.' Phoebe sighed. 'The Czech poet.'

'Good one,' Giles nodded earnestly, pitching off to the left.

Phoebe knocked back some vodka and glanced at her watch. Two hours and forty-eight minutes.

Fliss had re-emerged with an extremely red Mungo. Dressed in white shorts, Aertex shirt and fluffy towelling head-band, Otto Licher looked as though he had been playing tennis in the Nevada desert. He was throwing out heat like a radiator and bright, angry red from platinum blond head to plimsolled foot. Even Fliss's recently applied layer of calamine lotion did nothing to calm the fiery radiance, although it had stained quite a lot of his outfit baby pink.

For the first time that night, Phoebe found herself bursting out laughing, the booze stripping away her misery, deadening her fear and giving her a strange carefree euphoric kick.

'It is *not* funny,' Mungo hissed. 'I'm in agony.'

'Well, if you're someone's victim, you'll be easily trapped.' Phoebe wiped her eyes. 'I'm sure you must glow in the dark.'

'No, I just glower.' Mungo huffed off, leaving Fliss beside Phoebe.

'I've gone off him,' she sighed sadly. 'He looks frigging awful.

And he told me that he thinks Iain is a closet gay who used me as a mother figure.'

Phoebe sighed with relief, taking another slug of vodka and choking, eyes streaming.

'Mungo's gay, Fliss.'

'What?' Fliss leaned against her woozily.

'I'm sorry.' Phoebe bit her lip apologetically and fought down a boozy, hiccupy burp. 'I know I should have told you weeks ago, but you were so wound up about him, and you know what you're like – you wouldn't have listened.'

'Oh!' Fliss's eyebrows shot up into her cloche hat and she peered at Phoebe for a few seconds, letting this sink in. Then she started to giggle. Hanging off Phoebe's arm and swinging towards the floor alarmingly, she hooted and giggled and tittered until she was clutching her ribs in pain.

'I'm such a bloody wally,' she cackled, clambering back up Phoebe's arm until she was upright again. 'No wonder he looked a bit put off when I daubed him in calamine. Poor bloke. I was enjoying it so much too. God, I'm a bit frigging squiffy, Phoebes – I think I just told him he was the sexiest man I'd ever met!'

Phoebe pulled a face. 'What did he say?'

'He just agreed with me!' Fliss shrieked with laughter again, clutching her stomach and plunging towards the floor once more. 'He looked completely serious and sincere; it really put me off. Christ, he's a frigging prat, isn't he?'

Phoebe grabbed her just before she toppled over.

Straightening up, Fliss wiped her eyes and grinned. 'I was lying when I said it anyway. Felix is far and away the sexiest man I've ever met, mate. And Dylan is quite the bloody nicest.'

'Kind, funny, loyal, talented,' Phoebe prompted. 'Even if he does look like Will Carling.'

'You know, I think I rather fancy him, Phoebes.' Fliss nodded thoughtfully. 'I always did think Will Carling had a certain something. Do you reckon I'm still in with a chance, mate? I think he's quite keen on Saskia.'

Phoebe looked at her flat-mate's earnest face and laughed,

pulling her into a hug. 'You're right – you are a bloody wally! Just go for it.'

At that moment Paddy burst back through the door with Selwyn, Jasmin and Nadia, fresh from shocking the locals in The Axe and Compass. Paddy's plus fours were matched with very holey socks which showed a lot of hairy leg at the top, sixteen-hole Doc Marten boots, a checked flat cap, denim shirt and his bovver boy leather jacket. He looked nothing like an alcoholic racing manager at all. He just looked rather frightening, his craggy face splitting into a huge, slightly deranged smile.

'Dips O'Maniac is back, so he is!' he announced from the door, clutching a large stock of carry-out Newcastle Brown Ale. 'I've brought me ravishin' daughter with me.' He clutched Jasmin to him, who almost snapped in two under the pressure of his long, sinewy arm. 'And there's the other young filly of my loins over there!' He pointed to Milly, who was snogging Goat under the staircase.

Most of the throng in the hall had started to gape at him.

'Oim op to me ears in debt, so oi am,' he boomed on in an extremely rough Irish brogue. 'And oi've just gambled me daughter Meg here away in a poker game to me auld friend, Peregrine Fitzacoffin.' He nodded towards Selwyn, who was looking very Bertie Wooster in tweeds. 'So oi'm going to shag this lovely house maid to cheer mesself op.' He nodded towards Nadia, who was predictably dressed in French maid's costume.

To a round of applause, he swaggered through to the sitting room just as Stan yelled in a market-stall voice that the silver salver was waiting for the potential murder suspects.

'Here goes.' Fliss leaned on Phoebe for support.

Phoebe leant back for support too and, as unsteadily balanced as two jokers in a house of cards, they lurched through to the sitting room.

Stan had silenced the jungle music. With sombre regality, he circulated around the sixteen murder suspects with his silver salver, chin and nose aloft.

One by one, the house guests took their sealed envelopes and sloped away to open them in private. Jasmin, dressed in a backless red tunic that made her look thinner than ever, clutched her card to her bony chest and headed for the door, pausing by Felix and his gang, her huge, tortured eyes almost burning his face off.

'Hello, Felix,' she said in a wavering attempt at a seductive purr.

'Jasmin.' He cleared his throat.

'Watch your back, darling.' She waved her unopened envelope in front of his nose, shaking from head to foot with loathing. She was so emaciated she almost seemed to rattle. 'I've been waiting for years for the chance to stick the knife in.'

'You'll have to join the queue,' he muttered uneasily.

'So I gather.' Jasmin's floodlight stare switched to Phoebe. 'We all know who's at the front of it, don't we?'

Phoebe stared back with drunken, jittery alarm.

Winking at her, Jasmin turned and walked out of the room, the bones of her back standing up through her white skin like tent poles under canvas.

Thinking this was all part of the murder mystery entertainment, a few people clapped and whooped delightedly. Knowing it wasn't but loving it all the same, Milly clapped and whooped too and winked at Saskia, who had turned as pale as her dress and was watching Felix's reaction nervously.

But he merely shugged the scene off, smiled reassuringly at Phoebe, and helped himself to another can of Coke. Jet-lagged and dehydrated, he wasn't drinking booze at all. That worried Saskia a lot. She could see Phoebe glazing over.

Phoebe found that she was swaying just feet away from Felix as she took her own envelope. She tried to make a bolt for the little study at the back of the scruffier Deayton sitting room, but he was too fast for her, catching her up within seconds and closing the door behind them.

'Why are you avoiding me?' he demanded.

'I'm not – I'm jusht,' Phoebe took a sharp breath, 'just circulating.'

'You're pissed.'

'Pissed and circulating, then.' She flopped down on the window seat. 'The two aren't incomparable.'

'Or even incompatible.' He sat beside her, ripping open his envelope.

Phoebe looked away and started shredding her own. It was a very complicated design, she realised. All those gummed flaps and paper panels; it was harder to open than a biscuit packet. She howled with frustration and attacked it with her teeth.

Felix calmly extracted it from her mouth and opened it for her before handing it back.

Peering at the card, Phoebe decided it was blank. She turned it over a couple of times and peered at it to make sure, not certain whether a small smudge in one corner was a cross or just, as it appeared, a bit of fag ash.

'We could have it carbon tested if you're still uncertain,' Felix laughed, watching her.

'We're not supposed to look at each other's.' She grumpily hid the card under her leg.

'Bit hard if someone's flapping it around like Paul Daniels saying "Memorise this card",' he pointed out.

She squinted at him grouchily, trying to blow her hair out of her face and finishing up making a farting noise. She took a couple of deep breaths in an attempt to sober up a little and think straight.

'Are you the – '

'No.' Felix planted a kiss on her lips. 'We're both victims, Ms von Dyke.'

'I always said I was a wictim of chance.' Phoebe pulled away, looking at her watch. Two hours and twenty-two minutes.

'Got a hot date?' Felix watched her closely.

'Mmm.' She swallowed, determined to forget, shakily re-solving to spend her last two hours with him, just as she had lived the last two weeks – in the cowardly, hedonistic, deluded pretence that all was well. She was certainly slewed enough to try, she realised.

'And who's this hot date with?' he demanded edgily.

'Viz a New York club owner called Tess Tickle.'

'Tosterone,' he laughed. 'I love you so much when you're pissed.'

'I just love you,' Phoebe said.

Felix froze.

'Do you mean that?'

'Mean what?' Phoebe hiccuped, listening to the dinner gong echoing through the house as Stan raced around the hall like the Rank Films intro man. She stretched out a hand and played with the fabric of Felix's Oxford bags.

'What you just said?'

'I always mean what I say.' She squinted at him woozily. 'To you, at least. Ask me anything – anything at all – and I'll give you an honest answer.'

Felix was staring at her intently now, his eyes unblinking. Such a lovely, honest face, Phoebe thought dreamily. I'll never wake up beside it again, never be able to watch it sleeping, drink in its beauty, wait for those long-lashed eyes to creep open and that kissable mouth to smile sleepily at me and then tell me off for nicking the duvet.

She didn't feel remotely hedonistic or deluded any more. She just felt unbearably sad, sober and frightened, her stomach so knotted with dread it ached as though kicked from inside by Rosemary's baby.

'Ask me what I'm planning to do tonight, if you want,' she gulped, suddenly trying to steer him towards the truth.

Felix ran his tongue nervously across his teeth.

'Ask me anything,' she urged.

He rubbed his mouth, not taking his eyes from her.

'Ask me, Felix,' Phoebe coaxed, her heart thumping unhappily.

'Anything I like?'

'Yes,' she whispered, looking away, certain she was about to cry.

'Will you come and live with me?'

'What?'

'Will you live with me?' He fingered the hem of her dress and smiled. 'In sickness and in health, in poverty, in London and in sin. For as long as we both shall live – er – together?'

Phoebe gazed at him in startled stupefaction.

'Is this a proposal?' she croaked, her head spinning, thoughts all over the place. 'Because if it is, I think you should take your hat off.'

'I don't believe in marriage.' Felix turned his hat back to front instead, his hands shaking with nerves. 'I don't think I ever have believed in it.'

'Neither do I,' Phoebe rattled. 'I never looked good in white – too bleaching. And besides, I wouldn't know what to do with three toasters and a matching Portmeirion set of gravy boats, lemon juicers and flan dishes.'

'I'm being serious.' Felix stared at her. 'I've never really wanted to marry anyone as much as I want to live with you. I always fucked up before – always felt stifled and trapped and miserable as hell. This is so different, it scares me shitless.'

Phoebe bit her lip. 'Me too.'

'Live with me then. We can be scared together.'

Every bone aching to say yes, she looked away, closing her eyes to stem any tears. 'I'm a terrible slut when it comes to house work.'

'I know. So am I.'

'I can't cook.'

'Nor can I.'

'I dry my knickers on the radiators.'

Sliding closer, Felix kissed the back of her neck very gently. 'I love you.'

'I love you too.'

He bit his way to her shoulder, kissing harder now, his hand creeping up her skirt, fingers easing under her stocking tops.

Phoebe pulled away, terrified by the way he could switch her on to near-senseless excitement within seconds.

'There's something I have to tell you,' she croaked, ramming herself against the thick window-frame and staring fixedly at the door.

'Oh, yes?' Felix backed off and rubbed his eyes uneasily.

Phoebe looked at him, suddenly churning with fear. She stared on in silence, taking in the calm, numb expression, the clever, anxious eyes, the whitened knuckles, drumming fingers, tautened spine.

Trying hard to cover up, Felix pulled his chin back and raised his eyebrows jokily. 'What?'

There was something in his eyes that told her. She couldn't explain why, but it hit her like a door in the face. He knew. He bloody well knew already!

Saying nothing, she stood up and walked out as fast as she could, dazed with shock, reeling with confusion.

Stumbling into the hall, she crashed straight into Milly.

'Grub's up, sis,' she croaked excitedly. 'Looks fabulous – there's loads of veggie stuff. I've sent Goat off to get a carrier bag so we can stock up for the squat. Did you know your dress is almost completely transparent?'

Phoebe gulped, shrugged, nodded, pushed past her and raced into the kitchen to sob on Georgette's shoulder.

The kitchen was full of drunken strangers in twenties garb, scoffing and swigging happily. Georgette was clearly mingling elsewhere.

Phoebe bolted out into the garden where the air was still soup thick with muggy warmth, the outside lights dancing with moths, the navy blue sky streaked with silvery clouds like fat in bacon rashers.

A couple were necking in the shadows by the kitchen wall. As Phoebe raced past them, she caught a glimpse of red hair and a glitter of swinging chocolate coins.

'Your moustache has gone down my cleavage now!' giggled a familiar voice.

'Don't panic,' a gruff voice laughed in return. 'I've been trained for this. I'm a professional. Believe me, I'm extracting absolutely no moustache from doing this – wow, these are simply gorgeous!'

Phoebe bolted up the steps to the lawn, ran past another necking couple and fell blindly through the door to the hot-house.

The furniture had been raided by Goat and his gang earlier that day. She crouched down on the floor in a bunched huddle and pressed her fists into her eyes, her breath coming out in sharp, painful rasps.

Five minutes later, Felix found her.

'Have you got a homing device or something?' she wailed.

'No, I just followed you,' he said simply. 'I've been hovering outside for ages debating whether or not to come in.'

'You've lost your hat.' Phoebe squinted up at him through the gloom.

'Hat – heart. What does it matter? Someone grabbed it in the hall. They're pretty raucous in there.' He dropped on to his haunches beside her, his face in shadow.

'Dylan's snogging Fliss against the kitchen wall.'

'I know, I saw them. Selwyn's necking Nadia in the garden as well.'

'That was Selwyn and Nadia?'

'Yup. I somehow doubt he's paying. Everyone will have passed out or copped off by the time this murder takes place,' he rattled on nervously. 'There could be mass carnage in there, and no one will . . . Oh, fuck this, Phoebe. What the hell is going on?'

'Sit down, Felix.' She pressed her fists to her forehead.

He sat down so close beside her that they connected from ankle to shoulder. She could feel his heart crashing, lungs moving, torso shaking.

'I do love you.' Phoebe's knuckles were indenting her forehead like stuck typewriter keys pressing into a ribbon. 'Believe me, I love you more than I've loved anyone. Three – four weeks after meeting you and I can't see a life without you. I'm mad. Totally mad.'

Smiling with relief, he pressed his mouth into the hollow of her neck.

'But I'm about two hours away from doing the stupidest thing I've ever done in my life.'

'No,' he whispered. 'No, Phoebe.'

'You know what's going on, don't you?' She stared blindly up at the moulded glass roof.

'I heard this rumour – '

'It's true.'

He pulled slowly away and sat beside her in silence for a few moments, his knees drawn up to his chin.

'I thought it was.'

'You knew?' Phoebe turned to him, gazing at his shadowed profile, the straight nose, the tense jaw.

'All those lies early on,' Felix tilted his face towards hers, 'and the way you seemed to know so much about me. Then you were so deliberately vague about your connection with Saskia. I finally figured it out in the States.'

'And you still came back?'

'I love you, Phoebe. I know this sounds totally fuck-witted, but I trust you.'

'I wish to God you didn't.'

'I don't believe you'll do it.' He touched her face with his finger, tracing the line of her jaw. 'I don't give a fuck why you got to know me, or who put you up to it, or what you know about me. I'll tell you anything, you know that. I just don't think you can do it, any more than I could do it when I tried.'

'Go back to London tonight, Felix,' she begged.

'No.'

'Please!'

'No, I'm not running away from this.' His finger ran over her forehead and around to her cheekbone. 'You're one of the few people in my life I've believed in enough not to run away from. I know you can't do it for her, not if you love me.'

'We could pretend,' Phoebe croaked deperately. 'For Saskia's sake.'

Felix pressed his chin to his knees again and fell silent. Outside a couple of girls had reeled out on to the lawn to smoke a spliff and discuss their love lives. One started shrieking with laughter as they compared notes.

'This isn't a game any more,' Felix said finally, his voice barely more than a breath. 'If you love me, you won't do it. It's as simple as that. You know it is.'

He ran a shaking hand through his hair and, standing up, walked out.

Phoebe watched his shadow moving across the lawn and heard the girls wolf whistling as he passed.

Moving around the house like a leading lady playing a command performance, Saskia counted the minutes until midnight as she acted her heart out, hammed up her vindictive character, held her chin up high in front of Felix's cronies, and occasionally helped Georgette to remove Sir Dennis from a distressed 'young thing'. It was extremely easy to caricature Dame Bea Reeves, the deranged crime novelist with a grudge against all her ex-husbands – Colonel 'Piggy' Pinchbottom amongst them. It was far harder to roam around the house and not crack up in the absence of both Phoebe and Felix.

Saskia had seen them together for the first time that night, and felt as though she'd been pushed off a high-rise building.

She now knew Dylan had been right. She was hurt, just as he'd predicted. She was so hurt and jealous and envious and angry, she wanted to punch walls as she passed them, kick doors, scream the ceilings down. She was also crippled with fear because, just as Dylan had warned, she'd seen the hold they had over one another and it had nailed forever her naive daydreams and hopes of a reconciliation with Felix.

42

At five to midnight, Dylan and Fliss, wearing lipstick and stubble rash respectively, came in from the garden, straightened their clothes, and rushed around warning everyone of the impending lights out.

'I'm going to announce the beneficiary of my estate at exactly midnight!' Fliss boomed, dashing around blowing out candles. 'I think there's an electric storm brewing up outside. Where's Mestic? We might need him to stand by the fuse box, just in case something blows.'

'What *is* she on about?' asked a few startled guests who weren't following the action.

'Ah – my grandfather's old hunting dagger!' Fliss peered at the retractable stage knife on the dining-room table. 'What *is* it doing here, I wonder?'

'I think she's been dropping acid,' muttered one of Fliss's artist friends from the Camden studio.

Most of the house guests' allotted characters had been long abandoned in the wake of heavy-duty partying, and had to be hastily resurrected. Mungo, who had lost his tennis racket, which he was planning to use to defend himself in the event of his being a victim, searched for it frantically, screaming: 'Vere ees my stringy bat, yah?' Georgette prised Sir Dennis away from a group of flappers and dusted him down. 'I expect you to protect me, Dennis dear, in case I'm the victim. I shall be holding your hand the entire time the lights are out.'

Sir Dennis watched Nadia smoothing a snagged black stocking as she wandered in from the garden and muttered 'Damn' under his breath.

Selwyn straightened Nadia's starched maid's cap and gave her a swarthy Latin smile. 'Who are you supposed to be again?'

'Dizzy Okel, I think – half-witted house maid. Who are you?'

'Peregrine Fitzacoffin – Lady E's gambling, disinherited elder son.'

'I can't remember if I'm the murderer or not.'

'Better bump someone off then, just to be on the safe side.'

Pushing his dark glasses on to his nose and shuddering, Iain shot Selwyn a look of pure loathing.

While Milly dusted down Goat's sacking poncho and took a swig of Strongbow, Paddy, who was the only person to have stayed consistently in character all night, was slapping Goat on the back.

'Well now, you little runt,' he boomed, 'Oi'll bet you fancy your chances with one of moi young fillies when the loights go out, huh? Well, oi'm telling you. Lay one finger on them and you'll be toid to one of me hosses and towed the auld mile at Leopardstown.'

Beneath his thick white fringe, Goat looked as though he was in imminent danger of fainting.

'Where are Phoebe and Felix?' Fliss asked Dylan just before midnight. 'Everyone else is here. I haven't seen either of them for hours.'

'Probably screwing, knowing those two.'

'Well, we can't wait any longer – Stan's standing by the fuse box with a watch. The lights'll go off at midnight whether they're here or not.'

'There's Phoebe.' Dylan nodded towards the door. 'Christ, the poor luvvy looks as though she's just given Count Vlad a drink.' Watching her, his veins suddenly felt like frozen pipes as his blood temperature seemed to plummet, and he gazed around desperately for Felix.

'I'm going to have to start.' Fliss looked at her watch. 'Here goes. Everybody! Friends, family, ex-lovers, new lovers, enemies, staff.' She shot Georgette a big smile. 'As you all know, I've gathered you here because, in my potty old age, I've decided to . . . bugger!'

They were plunged into complete darkness far earlier than she had anticipated.

From then on confusion reigned. Some people laughed, some screamed, others fondled, but most ran. They tripped over furniture, bottles, beakers, each other. They crashed into walls and doors, yelled loudly for their friends and groped furtively for interesting strangers.

In the fuse cupboard, Stan lit a fag and put his feet up, certain of five minutes' peace. Perhaps, he decided, he could just stretch it to ten before he turned the trip switch back on.

Phoebe was standing by the stairs when the lights went off. She clung tightly on to the banister and decided to stay put. But a drunk, tripping over the bottom step, knocked her sprawling. Someone else trod heavily on her arm and most of someone's drink landed on her back.

She made it to a wall and crawled along it until there were fewer people sprawling about, laughing and screaming. As she reached out to grip the wall and stand up, her hand made contact with the baize door to the back stairs. Clambering upright, she dusted herself down and slipped through it. Voices were laughing and giggling in the kitchen at the far end of the lobby. There was no one immediately around her. It was absolutely pitch dark. Groping around for a wall to get her bearings, Phoebe felt stupidly frightened and tearful, as though she was a gawky ten-year-old again, trapped at one of the Seaton girls' parties with a trick being played on her.

Turning left, she swung her hands around in the dark until she found the rail to the twisty back staircase. Very tentatively, she shuffled her feet to the bottom step and cautiously climbed up to the first back landing, listening to the gurgling of the hot pipes in the laundry ahead of her. The tiny window on the first landing let in a mean shaft of light. Looking down, Phoebe saw that her hands were shaking, the big amber ring Felix had slipped on her finger when he dressed her flickering like a firefly.

Suddenly she heard the baize door swinging open and closed beneath her, momentarily letting in the screaming, laughing din from the main house before muffling it once again to a burble. The next moment someone was starting to climb up the stairs, far more sure-footed than she had been.

Trying not to whimper, Phoebe tugged off her shoes and crept hastily along the narrow corridor to the second set of stairs. She paused at the baize door to the main landing, behind which she could hear Selwyn cooing 'Come here, little house maid', followed by a lot of screaming giggles. Several other people appeared to be wandering about out there, opening and shutting a lot of doors, laughing and talking and necking. Praying her pursuer would think she had gone out that way, Phoebe double-bluffed them by swinging the door open and then shot up the back stairs, wincing as several of them creaked like trees in a gale when she trod on them.

The footsteps were on the first back landing now, walking slowly and surely along it.

Phoebe made it on to the second and then froze as the footsteps paused. Her heart felt like a punch bag crashing back and forth in her chest, her breathing was short and shallow and terrified. She was drenched in freezing cold sweat.

This is ridiculous, she told herself firmly. It's only a game. Only a bit of fun.

But as the footsteps started clumping steadily up the second flight of back stairs, she almost screamed. This floor was entirely made up of attic rooms, some without proper floors laid. Phoebe knew it well having hidden up here countless times in her youth when sulking or crying or just avoiding the Seaton sisters' ridicule. She felt her way along the wall and crept up a couple of steps before slipping into a room on her right. At the far end she groped her way for the door to another small room, once undoubtedly belonging to an underpaid servant.

The footsteps were on the second landing now.

Phoebe dashed across the room, aiming to hide in a corner.

As she reached out for the far wall, her fingers made contact instead with the warm skin of someone's arm. The next moment a hand was being pressed tightly to her mouth as she was pulled quite roughly against someone.

Trying to scream against the hand, Phoebe suddenly felt the bumps of a hundred tear-drop pearls indenting themselves in her skin and relaxed slightly, realising it was Saskia.

'Shh!' she hissed. 'Whoever it is will hear us.'

Phoebe nodded and Saskia released her grip.

They stood in complete, frozen silence for what seemed like minutes. Phoebe's eyes had adjusted to the gloom enough now to see the outline of Saskia's shoulders, a glint of blonde hair, and the reflection of her pearls gleaming slightly in the dim, steely light from the ivy-covered window.

The footsteps on the landing shuffled around for a while, drew closer and then seemed to retreat.

'I think they've gone,' Saskia breathed. 'No one else knows the house well enough to find this room.'

'You're not the murderer then?' Phoebe whispered, sagging against the wall.

'Of course I'm bloody not!' Saskia snapped, lighting a cigarette. Her face was momentarily illuminated by the little lighter flame, her eyes dark with anxiety and excitement. 'Not long to wait now.'

'Yes, I'm sure someone will get bumped off in a minute.' Phoebe crept over to the window and peered out through the foliage.

'I wasn't talking about that. I was talking about Felix.'

Phoebe pressed her cheek to the window pane and took a deep breath.

'I'm sorry, Saskia,' she muttered. 'I'm not going to do it.'

'What?'

'I know you'll never forgive me, but I simply can't do it. I love him.'

Phoebe could hear the scratch of pearls against plaster as Saskia slid down the wall to sit on the floor, her knees jabbing into her chest.

'I said I'd go to the press, Phoebe,' she breathed unsteadily. 'I meant it.'

'The press already bloody know,' Phoebe sighed. 'The *News* is going to print the whole thing whether or not I do it. Georgette told me. But I'm bloody well not going to make it worse for Felix by feeding him a pack of lies in front of all his friends.'

'Shit!' Saskia banged her heel on the floor in utter frustration and despair.

'I love him, Sasky. Believe me, I hate myself to hell and back for doing this to you, but I love him.'

'I know you do. So do I.'

'I don't think you do,' Phoebe whispered. 'You love what he did for you once, the way he made you feel, the fact that you were so happy and beautiful and envied when you were with him and then afterwards felt worthless, miserable, ignored. You loved what he did for you. How he made you feel. You didn't love *him* – the bright, complicated, infuriating, selfish, vulnerable man. You loved his ability to make you feel good, and that's not fair. That's not love, Saskia. It's therapy.'

'I adored him!' she howled with furious indignation. 'I was obsessed by him, I thought about no one but him.'

'Who?' Phoebe turned to her. 'The dashing public school model with a jet-set social life, high-profile love-life, invites cramming his mantelpiece, girls' phone numbers cramming his pockets, who received so many freebies that his only use for his credit card was to cut coke? The man who screwed like a fantasy, lavished you with gifts, told you over and over again how crazy he was about you? That was the man you wrote to me about in New Zealand, Saskia.'

'He is like that,' she muttered. 'You know he's like that.'

Ignoring her, Phoebe carried on, 'Or did you love the mucked-up waster with no goals, no direction in life, with ghastly parents, a monumentally fucked-up brother, freeloading friends, a horrific, bullied childhood? Did you really love the man who's never held down a decent job, whose only long-term relationship is with a saint and a doormat, who's spent his life fighting a crippling, stultifying inability to trust people? Because that's the Felix I love, Saskia. For all his howling faults, I'm crazy enough to want to take him on. And I honestly don't think you

ever really knew that man. Or if you did look hard enough to see
him, then I don't think you liked him enough to pursue the
friendship, so you stuck with the sexy, charming, lethal philanderer who, for all his pseudo-intellectual graces, you assumed
to be about as deep as a puddle.'

'How dare you?' Saskia breathed venomously. 'How *dare* you
say all this on the basis of your short, dirty little shack-up? How
dare you suggest that I don't love Felix?'

'Because I don't think you'll ever get over him until you
realise that you don't,' Phoebe whispered. 'Because I think that
what you felt – what you feel now – is far more self-destructive,
more painful, more dangerous than love. And because, believe
it or not, I really do care about you. I've had to watch you try to
kill yourself by cutting your wrists, by drinking yourself stupid,
and now by starving yourself to death, and I can't bear what
you're doing to yourself, Saskia. Felix isn't doing this to you, *you*
are doing it. No one else. You have to see that.'

Saskia was crying quietly now, crumpled in a small, pearl-
encrusted heap by the wall.

Despising herself for being so deliberately cruel, Phoebe
rubbed her dry lips with her fingers and stared out of the
window. Down in the garden, the outside lights went on.

'Someone's been murdered,' she muttered, moving away.

'Can't have been nearly as painful as the slaughter that's just
gone on up here.'

Phoebe sank down beside her.

'Saskia, I can't do it, you see that, don't you? It wouldn't
assuage any of your unhappiness; it wouldn't be any sort of
revenge. The Felix you want to hurt has never really existed for
me. The only time I ever saw him like that was through your
eyes.'

The attic room was still as dark as soot. Through the gloom,
Phoebe could just make out that Saskia's hands were pressed
into her hair, her face hidden by her arms; her shoulders were
shuddering as though being vigorously shaken by invisible
hands.

Phoebe stretched out a hand to stroke her arm.

Lashing back, Saskia struck out and slapped her hard across the face.

Phoebe reeled away, cheek numb, eyes starting to stream.

'The Felix I want to hurt was alive and well and standing in his kitchen six months ago telling me I was a worthless, freeloading whore!' Saskia screamed, standing up as Phoebe clutched her face in pain and shock, the cheek beginning to burn. 'He did exist, Freddy. He existed so vividly that he's thoroughly wrecked my life. And he's alive and well now, too. He's downstairs. And you're going to dump him for me.'

'I can't do it!' Phoebe sobbed. 'I'm not going to do it to him.'

'Oh, yes you are,' Saskia headed for the door. 'Because if you don't, I'm going to kill myself. No revenge, no Saskia. Bye-bye, cruel world. And incidentally, whatever you like to believe, I did love Felix Sylvian. More than you ever could. I might be a worthless whore, but I've practised suicide like a good girl and I think I'm experienced enough to get it right this time.'

'No!' Phoebe screamed.

'I swear it.' Saskia turned back as she reached the door, her voice steely with determination, even though she was shaking uncontrollably. In the dim light from the window, her eyes shone like wet jet. 'And I'll do it properly this time. After all, I have nothing to lose but myself and I'm worth nothing anyway. If you don't do exactly what I ask, exactly the way I told you, then you're signing my death warrant. Is Felix's love worth more than Saskia's life? That's your poser for the next five minutes Freddy. Because that's how long you've got to make up your mind.'

In a room just along the corridor, Mungo Sylvian stubbed out his fourth cigarette in ten minutes and whistled. This house party was simply the most spectacular bit of entertainment he'd enjoyed in his life. He no longer minded the lack of male talent, the unwanted attentions from frumpy Fliss and the crippling sun-burn. This was one for his memoirs. He'd entitle the chapter 'Murder Mystery or Suicide History – the Mad Women in the Attic'.

He scratched the prickly heat on his chest thoughtfully and, pulling on his plimsolls, wandered downstairs to get a front seat for the show-down. If Phoebe didn't do 'it' – whatever 'it' was (Mungo had failed to extract the exact task from the overheard conversation) – then he wondered how Saskia was planning to kill herself. He hoped it showed a modicum more originality than she had ever displayed in the past. Something with silk scarves and a chandelier would be nice.

There had been two murder victims, not one. Nadia, the escort, and Fliss's brother, Selwyn, had both been 'murdered' and were now sharing a fag in the hall.

In the drawing room – now lit once more with flickering candles and the lowest setting of the dimmer switch – Dylan, as the colonel, was outlining the evidence at the scene of the crime. Beside him, Fliss was puce with excitement, both from a very long sexy lights-out snog with a man she now knew kissed better than anyone she had ever touched tongues with, and also from utter and total delight at the circumstances of the murder.

'Right, you chaps – settle down.' Dylan pressed his monocle to his left eye and, fishing in a pocket, extracted his moustache which he attached upside-down to his upper lip. 'There appears to have been a ghastly and grisly going on in this house tonight. Two of our delightfully spiffing house guests appear to have been murdered.'

There was a lot of theatrical gasping and gaping from the assembled drunks, and a small amount of tittering from those who already knew who'd been done in.

'I'm afraid it wasn't a pretty sight,' Dylan boomed on, hamming it up happily. 'But I'm trained in this sort of thing, so I was able to ignore the gore and jot down a few facts to help us deduce the dastardly culprat – I mean prit – behind this frightful crime.' He whipped out a notepad and flipped it open.

'Embarrassingly, Dizzy Okel, the half-wit housemaid, and Peregrine Fitzacoffin, the gambling bounder, have both been strangled whilst apparently *in flagrante delicto* on a deflated double Lilo in an upstairs bedroom. Indeflated delilo, one might say. The weapon was left at the scene of the crime.' Dylan reached for a gentleman's white silk scarf and held it aloft.

'As were these.' He held up a pair of small dark glasses.

'I believe,' Fliss butted in, loving the fact that Iain, minus his scarf and glasses, was halfway down a bottle of Southern Comfort in the corner and giggling drunkenly to himself, 'that the doctors have arrived to give us some forensic details and an exact time of death.'

She pointed at the door where Selwyn was hovering in a white coat, together with Nadia who had discarded the pinny and cap and was wearing just her black dress in an attempt to look medically trained. She was sporting a black Trilby and clutching a stethoscope, and looking far more Cabaret than Casualty, but nonetheless game to try.

As they headed, slightly red-faced, towards Fliss and Dylan's little stage in front of the mantelpiece, Felix wandered into the room behind them, looking as though he had suffered a real murder attempt, his eyes hollow, face bloodless.

'Right, chaps, just run everyone through a few of your findings,' Dylan told the doctors, before excusing himself and moving hastily across to Felix.

'Where have you been? You've been missing for hours.' Dylan pulled him out on to the landing.

'I went for a walk.' Felix swigged back some Coke. His hands were shaking so much that he spilled most of it down his front. 'I got lost. One field looks pretty much like another in the dark. Met a lot of cows. They all look the same in the dark too.'

Looking down, Dylan noticed that his trouser hems were coated with dew, grass seeds and dust. He looked back at Felix's face and bit his lip. It was shadowed, squinting, jet-lagged, and as bleached out as an overexposed photograph.

'You look fucking awful.'

'Frankly, I couldn't care less.'

In the sitting room, Selwyn had everyone in stitches with a description of the kinkiness of the sexual act immediately prior to death. Fliss, as the mother of kinky strangled Peregrine, was adding to the hilarity with a series of shocked swoons, faints and screams.

'Listen,' Dylan hastily pulled off his fake moustache and steered Felix into a quiet corner under the stairs, 'I've been trying to track you down all night. I have to – '

He tensed as Saskia stormed out of the lobby door to their right and marched across the hall, pearls rattling, mopping tears with a tissue and not seeing them as she slowed down outside the high drawing-room door and then crept inside, her pearl dress glittering like a honeycomb in the candlelight.

'I know what's going on,' Felix told him in a flat voice. 'You don't have to warn me.'

'You know?'

'I'd more or less guessed – and then Phoebe tried to warn me and the penance dropped.'

'You should get out of here then. Before she does it. Push off back to London for Chrissake – take my car. You've only drunk Coke all night, after all.'

'I'm not going anywhere.'

'But they're plotting to kick you in the teeth!' Dylan pleaded. 'Get out before she shreds you in front of everyone – in front of Mungo, Jasmin, Fliss, Selwyn. Everybody.'

'She won't do it,' Felix muttered.

'What makes you so sure?'

'I know her. I love her. She won't do it.'

'So why are you looking like a corpse if you're so certain she's not going to do it?'

'Because I'm so fucking scared that I've got it wrong, Dyldo. If she lets me down, I've lost my deposit on hope. She's so like me. If she fucks up, I know I'll never straighten out either. And I love her so bloody much.'

They both jumped as Mungo bounded down the main stairs, fag in mouth, tennis racket rotating jauntily. He was humming the 'Boat Song' and glowing more red than ever.

As his brother bounced excitedly into the drawing room, Felix sighed, rubbing his face with his hand and then downed another swig of Coke.

'Have you got a fag?'

Dylan handed him a Lucky Strike.

'Singularly inappropriate in the circumstances.'

'I'm certain she loves you.' Dylan lit himself one. 'Fliss is too. I'm equally certain Saskia's got some sort of emotional gun in her back.'

'If she does do it,' Felix dragged on his cigarette, 'I don't want you to do anything. I mean it. Keep out of it.'

'You're joking?' Dylan blinked. 'I just can't stand back and watch.'

'Then close your fucking eyes,' Felix muttered through gritted teeth.

'Go back to London, Felix,' Dylan tried one last time.

'We'd better go in and see whodunnit.' He tossed away his cigarette and headed for the noisy, crammed drawing room.

Chasing Felix's glowing stub and extinguishing it with his heel, Dylan followed him, running a despairing hand through his messy hair.

Questions and answers were in progress now, mostly concerned with the exact details of the last kinky sexual act and not the evidence left at the scene of the crime. Stan was grumpily holding up the voting scoreboard like a sulky model displaying the round number in a boxing match.

'I'd like to ask Dips O'Maniac what he was doing at the time of the murder?' someone shouted out.

'Whoi, oi was betting me other daughther on a game of tiddlywinks in the cellars, so oi was,' Paddy announced as he cracked open yet another bottle of Newcastle Brown.

'And what about the female victim's oddly reticent half-brother?' Sir Dennis asked, sounding frighteningly like Sherlock Holmes seconds away from solving the crime. 'What exactly were you doing at midnight, Mr Shaggy Okel?'

'Huh?' Goat took a swig of Strongbow and looked non-plussed. 'I wors on the bog, man.'

Several people laughed, thinking this a brilliant piece of characterisation, and Goat looked even more nonplussed.

Sir Dennis gave up his inquisition and ogled Nadia again

instead, wishing he could afford her services. But he was a Lloyd's Name – which had rather cut out the extra-marital opportunities of late.

'What ho, right, jolly good show. Are we ready to harry vote now, chaps?' Dylan boomed. 'Only I don't know about you lads, but I fancy wrapping this strangle fandango up and having another ruddy great snifter.'

Growing bored of the open and smut case, everyone cheered enthusiastically.

'Right.' Dylan took the unused poker 'weapon' from beside the fireplace and pointed at Stan's scoreboard with it. 'Now, hands up as I run through these names if you think the bugger did it. And I warn you, if you vote more than once, you're doing twenty press-ups and are confined to barracks for the duration of the ruddy weekend. Right – here goes. Mestick the Butler. Nasty piece of work. Slacks on the silver polishing and waters down the port. Hands up if you think he garrotted the besotted.'

Fliss counted the hands. 'Three, Piggy darling.'

'Three, Mestick darling – I mean, old boy,' Dylan ordered.

Stan huffily penned three stripes beside his own name on the score board, wishing he had stayed put in the fuse cupboard. He felt like Anthea Turner waiting for the Lottery balls to drop.

'And who thinks Billie Haveitawayday, the druggy blues singer, capable of such a heinous act?' Dylan was asking. 'Dodgy line in headwear – always a sign of homicidal tendencies or so Nanny told me. Press your buttons and flash your armpits if you think she choked the pokers.'

Fliss counted. 'One vote, Piggy, my love beast.'

'One, Mestick, old boy.' Dylan cleared his throat. 'What ho – now we come to Dame Bea Reeves, the potty crime novelist. Cast your votes now. Lady E's sister, remember, chaps. My ex-wife. Bit of a tartar. Scores on the drawers please, Euthy?'

'Twenty, Piggy, my mammoth manhood.'

'Thank you, my little itch tickler. That's twenty votes, Mestick. Twenty is four fives, so just count as high as you can four times, old boy. Shouldn't take long. I'll have a puff while I'm waiting, shall I?' He lit a cigarette.

'Twenty votes, Colonel, sir,' Stan nodded, applying twenty stripes to the scoreboard with the relish of one applying twenty strokes to a hated bottom.

'Next in your Eurovision score-calling bonanza is – er – Mr Tess Tosterone.' Dylan consulted the board. 'Runs a New York drinking club. Bit of a low profile tonight, but shifty nonetheless. Could have crept upstairs between country walks. Fond of cows.'

'One cow in particular,' murmured a voice from the door. Dylan froze.

In the middle of lighting another cigarette with trembling hands, Saskia looked up, eyes as bright as two blue flames with triumph and gratitude.

Phoebe was standing in the doorway, utterly stunning, utterly deadly, and totally dull-eyed with repressed misery.

'I'm certain he did it.' She walked into the room. 'After all, he's so poisonous he kills pretty much everything he touches.'

Clutching his Coke can with such force that it started to crumple, Felix didn't turn around or move.

Thinking this was all an additional twist to the murder mystery scenario, most of the room was watching her expectantly. Phoebe had her audience's rapt attention. The only person who didn't appear to be looking at her was Felix. She moved across so that she was equidistant between him and Saskia and then spun very slowly around to face him.

He was still staring fixedly at his Coke can. She looked quickly away, knowing that she simply couldn't go through with it if she watched his reaction, wouldn't be able to get out the words Saskia had rehearsed with her over and over again.

'Felix Sylvian,' Phoebe said slowly, 'is a complete and utter shit.'

Realising that she wasn't talking about an invented character, one or two people began to murmur in startled, hushed tones.

'He destroys people for a hobby,' she went on. 'Which would be admirably devilish if he weren't so pathetically inept.'

From behind Felix's hunched shoulder, Mungo was gaping at her in astonishment, the delighted smile dropping from his sunburnt face like a released bow string as he suddenly realised what it was that Saskia had forced Phoebe into doing.

'Felix sets out to seduce and traduce,' she went on, her voice as deadened as a morphine-pumped patient. 'Armed with a big toothpaste smile and a small, oiled dick, he beds girls who fall for his wittily original chat up lines – usually two powdered white ones on a mirror – and then tells them they're slags. Ironic, maybe. Sad, definitely. Tragic, certainly – coming as it does after he has. A singularly forgettable experience.'

As Phoebe paused for breath and audience laughter, Felix looked up at her for the first time since she'd walked in and immediately wished he hadn't. She'd slicked her hair back again, painted her lips afresh and drawn even darker lines around her blazing green eyes. She was so tall and still and poised in that spectacular dress that she would have made Louise Brookes smart with frumpy jealousy. With her chin up high and her shoulders squared, her long neck seemed to rise up forever in a slender, tendon-tight arc of anger. And she determinedly wasn't looking at him.

'I was unfortunate enough to be one of Felix's conquests,' Phoebe carried on, scanning her enthusiastic audience. 'He has, in the past few weeks, called me a cunt, bitch, bint and slut. Not particularly original, granted, but all single-syllable words which Felix finds easier to remember. He has screwed me with the lights off, and occasionally screwed me with the lights on so that I can tell when he's finished – although counting to ten usually solves that little dilemma. Alternatively, I just wait until he cries out his own name. He's so twisted he can kiss his own arse, which is useful because I'm certainly not going to any more. I'm fed up of him admiring his reflection in the silver spoon he was born with and I want out.'

Stop me someone, she screamed silently. Stop laughing and staring and whispering and drinking this in. Just stop me, for Chrissake. Stop me, Dylan.

But he was lighting another Lucky Strike and staring in tortured silence at Felix, doing absolutely nothing.

'I want him out of my life,' Phoebe continued, every word burning a hole in her heart like a torturer with a glowing brand.

'He's creepily persistent, but I really have had enough of his sick, twisted little mind and lack of guts.'

Argue back, Felix! For God's sake, fight me. Defend yourself.

'I don't want him any more,' she went on, her voice beginning to crack. 'He's shallow, he's vain, he's a loser, and he's far too in love with himself to give anyone else a look in. He thinks women can be disposed of alongside the used condom – fuck them and chuck them, hump them and dump them, blow them out then throw them out, that's his motto. Scratch the itch then ditch the bitch. Well, this is one bitch who's getting in there first. Rinse your hands of life's losers, that's my motto.'

She looked straight at him, desperate to provoke a reaction, but as she gazed into those achingly sad, desolate blue eyes, the only reaction she provoked was in herself. She just had to get out fast, before she cracked up for good.

As she walked towards the door and escape, she paused beside the person she loved most in the world and found she couldn't see him for tears.

'Goodbye, Felix,' she said, fighting hard against a wobbly voice. 'Idunnit.'

As soon as she was out of the room, she raced away from the cheers and claps and slapped through the baize door so fast that it clouted her in the face. Stumbling into the deserted kitchen, she dragged open the utility room door and gathered up an ecstatic Yuppie.

Holding her face away from the warm licks, Phoebe wrenched open the garden door and pelted across the lawns, kicking off her shoes as the heels plugged her into the dewy grass. At the far end of the garden, she ducked under the cast-iron railings and sprinted along an overgrown cart track, tripping and stumbling as she ran, not feeling the pain as stones bruised her heels and brambles ripped her legs.

Ten minutes later, she was racing along a sharp hoggin drive that shredded the soles of her feet. It seemed endless, but Phoebe stumbled on blindly, following the sound of dogs' muffled barking.

43

Encouraging the dogs to bark a little louder for once, Gin Seaton opened her front door a fraction. She was wearing her oldest nightdress and a motheaten cardigan in the hope that it would put off any potential rapist, and holding a large Georgian candlestick behind her back. She was also hopping mad because Tony, lying in bed with his pyjamas buttoned up to his several chins and his favourite Trollope open on his chest, had refused to come down and answer the desperate hammering on the door, sending her instead.

'Freddy!' she gasped in amazement as she took in the shuddering, tearstained girl on her doorstep.

Bursting into a fresh, heart-wrenching onslaught of tears, Phoebe was illuminated as Gin swung the door open, hopelessly fragile and distressed, her stockings laddered to shreds, shoeless feet bleeding on the Portland stone doorstep. She was clutching a wriggling skewbald puppy to her chest, which the Seaton dogs, surging forwards, all tried to befriend at once, jumping up so excitedly that they knocked Phoebe back on to the gravel drive where her bloodied feet were pierced once again by sharp little stones. She didn't even wince.

Gin steered her gently inside and, relieving her of the puppy, kicked an empty box from a chair and sat Phoebe down in the small, messy kitchen, flicking on the lights with her shoulder.

Posting the puppy through the door to the stairs, she fought her own dogs off and shut the little skewbald girl away, anxious to protect her from three boisterous Labradors and a sexually suspect Jack Russell.

'Hope you told whoever it was to piss off!' Tony yelled down from the bedroom.

'Shut up, Tonic,' Gin shouted back, opening the door a fraction again to post through a horse hoof cutting for the whining puppy to chew.

Turning back to Phoebe, she caught her breath. She looked utterly wrecked, as though she'd just escaped from a plane crash. Sitting forlornly at the huge Seaton kitchen table, which positively swamped the small, modern kitchen in the farmhouse, Phoebe was fighting a losing battle to mop her tears with the back of her hand. Her make-up had even run down on to her neck.

Gin hastily searched through the half-unpacked boxes and piles of crumpled newspaper on the loathsome fitted surfaces for the kitchen roll. Finally locating it under various parts of her ancient food processor, she handed it to Phoebe and grappled with the gas hob in order to put on the kettle.

The smell was awful, but no flame emerged. Gin twiddled a few more knobs.

'Press the ignition,' Phoebe sobbed. 'Red button to your right.'

Doing as she was told, Gin almost blasted her eyebrows off as a flame mushroomed up into the escaped gas.

'Oh, bugger this.' She twiddled enough knobs to extinguish the flame. 'I've got a bottle of wine around here somewhere – ah, here!' She grabbed a two-thirds full bottle of cheap Merlot with the cork rammed in the top. 'I used the rest in tonight's casserole, which that contraption also managed to ruin.' She shot the gas cooker an evil look before grabbing two glasses and sitting down opposite Phoebe.

'Okay.' She poured the wine and waited for Phoebe to finish blowing her nose. 'Tell me what you want to, and I promise not to pry about the rest.'

Half an hour later, Gin had drained all the Merlot and was starting on a bottle of Shiraz.

Phoebe hadn't once reached for her glass, although the kitchen roll had thinned dramatically from Superplus to Regular, and a pile of crumpled, damp tissue was snowballing beside it.

'I hope to God Saskia's all right,' she sobbed.

'I hope she's not.' Gin reached for her glass. 'I think she deserves to suffer in hell for what she's done to you, darling. I have every sympathy for her unhappiness; I've wept my way through sleepless nights for her, but I could quite honestly kill her for this.'

'Don't say that,' Phoebe shuddered.

''Course, she won't bloody do it,' Gin snapped. 'She's been threatening to kill herself from the day we refused to buy her a second pony. She's the youngest and therefore hopelessly spoiled. She came along when we had the most money so she always got more than the other girls, treated Tony and me like an endless tap for her whims and fads. She's so bright and talented, but even that's not enough. I love her to bits, but sometimes she asks for the moon.'

'She asked for Felix.' Phoebe ripped off another couple of leaves of kitchen roll.

'And he's your moon?'

Swabbing like mad, Phoebe shrugged.

'He'll come back to you.'

'He won't,' Phoebe pressed her eyes into the scratchy paper tissue. 'I know him. He's as finite as I am. He set the test and I failed it.'

'We'll see.' Gin reached across the table and squeezed Phoebe's hand. 'I liked Felix, although I know that's a dreadfully disloyal thing to say. I think I could even bring myself to like him again. If you love him, darling, then he's worthy of faith. I'll make up a bed for you. Finish your wine – start it even.'

Stifling a yawn, she battled the dogs away from the stairs door and creaked her way upstairs.

Phoebe stared into her wine glass and listened as Gin moved around overhead, treading on groaning floorboards and trying not to swear at Yuppie who was clearly dogging her every move.

When the phone rang, Phoebe knocked her wine all over the table.

It rang on for just three rings, before being intercepted upstairs. Phoebe's heart was thrumming out of control as she mopped up the wine spill with the last of the kitchen roll.

'Freddy!' Tony barked down the stairs. 'There's some anti-social young idiot called Dylan on the phone for you. Tell him not to call back.'

Phoebe searched frantically for a phone downstairs, scouring surfaces and walls until she finally tracked down a cordless one on the hall wall.

'Dylan.'

'Phoebe!' Dylan yelled gruffly over deafening background music. 'Christ, I'm glad we've tracked you down, at least. We thought Saskia might be there.'

'Saskia's gone missing?' Phoebe asked tearfully.

'Basically,' Dylan was puffing on a cigarette, 'you stalked out and all hell broke loose here. Felix walked across the room and slapped Saskia in the gob, and has now stormed off fuck knows where in Georgette Gregory's Merc which has *not* gone down well with the party concerned. Saskia went completely ape, cried a lot in the downstairs loo and then stormed off in Stan's Beetle, which has gone down even more badly. And Fliss is currently trying to prise a bottle of Valium out of one of Jasmin's bony hands and a bottle of Smirnoff Black Label out of the other. Apart from that, the party rages on oblivious.'

'I'm coming back.'

'No!' Dylan said hastily. 'You're better off there. It's a drunken orgy at this end – everyone's still milling around with drinks, grub and awful chat up lines. Stay there, get some sleep and I'll call you in the morning.'

'But what about Felix and Saskia?'

'Leave that to Fliss and me,' Dylan insisted, his tone acidly unfriendly. 'We'll keep calling the mews from here. No one's sober enough to drive except Georgette, who's already shot up to London in Dennis's Jag, but as she's been ringing on the carphone every five minutes since for directions, I don't hold out much hope – she's not even got out of Hexbury yet. None of us have a clue where Saskia would be headed.'

'She was staying at Sukey's flat,' Phoebe muttered.

'Do you have the number?'

'It's in the diary in my bag – upstairs in the big blue bedroom. You could try calling Portia's number too.'

'Okay, I'll get it in a sec.' He covered his mouthpiece to say something to an anonymous listener-in.

Phoebe picked at her shredded stockings and felt her raw, tattered feet starting to burn with hot, searing pain.

'Why the fuck did you do it?' Dylan was suddenly back in the phone, his anger all the more stinging because he displayed it so seldom.

'She said she'd kill herself if I didn't.'

'Christ. Bit of a mess, huh?'

'Bit meaning total.'

'I know it's a long shot, but try to get some sleep. I'll call you in the morning.'

When he'd rung off, Phoebe trailed upstairs to Gin, who had made up a bed in a small room crammed with packing cases, assorted furniture and suitcases full of bedlinen.

'Saskia's gone missing,' Phoebe whispered hoarsely from the door.

Gin looked up from tucking in a top blanket, her face pensive. Then she shook her head and shrugged.

'She should have come here, stupid girl. She'll be okay, Freddy. She'll be fine.'

Once Gin had returned to bed, Phoebe could hear her talking to Tony, her voice hushed, her tone fraught, clearly very worried indeed about Saskia. Then they fell silent and Phoebe started the agonising process of mental replay.

She spent the night in the curtainless room, clutching a snoring Yuppie and staring numbly out at the sky as it slowly lightened from black to blue like a fading bruise, her stomach trying to churn its way out through her mouth as she relived her awful speech over and over again, pausing as she reached the part where she looked across at Felix's stricken face and knowing what it felt like to burn in hell.

When Dylan called early the next morning, the news wasn't good.

'We haven't traced either of them,' he said in a hoarse, hungover voice. 'Although Georgette finally found London at six this morning, and is so relieved she's abandoned the car in Hammersmith and cabbed it home to Knightsbridge to recover. And you'd better get the Sunday papers.'

'Oh, God,' Phoebe groaned.

'Two hacks rolled up at eight this morning and freaked out Iain by peering through the window at him while he was throwing up in the kitchen sink. Paddy's just come back with the full quota of rags. It's pretty fucking sordid, I'm afraid.'

'I'll come over.'

'The journos are still hanging around outside – just a couple of local stringers, I think, but persistent enough to really bug you, darling.'

'I'll come the back way.' She tried not to sob. 'Christ, I'm so worried about Felix, Dylan.'

'Perhaps you should have thought of that last night. Or before you agreed to play this stupid charade of Saskia's in the first place.' He hung up.

Deayton was a mess. A few people were up, staggering around in t-shirts and underwear, complaining loudly about the absence of Alka Seltzers, bottled water and towels; most of the guests were still in their camp beds or improvised blanket beds. A few were sleeping in cars. Plastic cups, paper plates, empty bottles and food debris littered every surface. The kitchen was a polluted sea of squalor and drunken sluttishness. Someone had stubbed out a cigarette on the bony carcass of a poached salmon; another was poking out of a slice of strawberry cheesecake, like a chimney in the Wicked Witch's gingerbread cottage. Everything, it seemed, had been used as an ashtray – cups, plates, the sink, the floor. The room reeked of stale smoke, stale food and stale wine.

Three sleepy-looking girls Phoebe didn't recognise were

trying to make toast on the Aga when she wandered in through the garden door. They all stared at her in fascinated silence, trying hard to keep straight faces and not nudge one another. Dressed in one of Gin's ancient sweaters and a pair of jeans that were far too big and short, Phoebe ignored them and shivered, still feeling freezing cold. Her raw feet aching in Gin's old espadrilles, she headed along the lobby.

Dylan was wandering listlessly around the hall in his boxer shorts, carrying a clanking plastic bin bag and a mug of tea, his hairy chest full of toast crumbs. When he looked up at Phoebe, his set, angry expression lasted about two seconds before it melted into pity.

'I won't even ask you how you're feeling.' Dropping the bag, he raked his messy hair awkwardly and then hooked an arm around her shoulders. 'You don't look like a road accident, you look like a multiple pile up. Come in.'

He took Phoebe through to the little study where Paddy and Fliss, looking bug-eyed and wan, were sitting on the floor and ploughing through the Sunday papers, surrounded by sports supplements, Dixons catalogues, prize draw offers and television guides.

'Brace yourself.' Fliss looked up and winced as she saw Phoebe's haggard face and red, puffy eyes. 'I don't know who spilled the beans, but they could have been living with us for the past month. Christ, you look so awful, Phoebe.'

'Thanks.' Her voice trembled. 'I'll take that as a compliment since I certainly feel a whole lot worse.'

Paddy diplomatically heaved himself up and ushered Dylan back out of the room. 'Lots of tidying up to do, lad, can't slack now.'

Phoebe sank down beside Fliss, teeth chattering.

'Dylan told me what she said she'd do.' Fliss squeezed her hand.

Phoebe nodded silently, shaking more than ever. She didn't think she'd ever warm up.

'You and Dylan an item then?' she croaked, squinting at Fliss with sore, swollen eyes.

'Too early to tell. I hope so.'

'That's good,' Phoebe whispered numbly, picking up the nearest paper. She felt like a World War II army wife holding the dreaded telegram in her shaking hands.

All the tabloids had the story, although only the Satellite paper, the *News on Sunday*, had trailed it on the front page with a splash of a library photo of Felix looking staggeringly hunky and a headline that read:

SYLVIAN FEELS LICKED

Belle's randy boy has leg-over pulled by raven-haired stunner as jealous ex-lover, actress Saskia Seaton, ex-acts revenge on the blond model heartthrob.

Is revenge as sweet as Felix? See pages 15 and 16.

It was all in there, from Saskia's whirlwind courtship and the cancelled marriage, to the Felix file, the Parisian search, and Phoebe's last two heady weeks with him. There were even blurred, long-shot photographs of them walking in Hyde Park with Yuppie a few days earlier.

Someone extremely close to Phoebe and Saskia must have told all. And adding fuel to the story, someone with considerable sway at Satellite News had pulled the high-powered zooms out of the Kensington Palace shrubbery in its honour. It wasn't the sort of story that normally merited such attention or coverage – Felix, although a gossip column regular, simply wasn't well known enough for a double page, full-colour exclusive written in the style of a racy, romping airport novel. His parents featured in larger-than-life monster caricature to bump up the reader-appeal; there was even a gratuitous shot of Philomena gasping rapturously during one of her mini-series sex scenes.

Casting her blurred eyes over the other photographs, Phoebe groaned as she took in a shot of herself, tanned and oiled, posing sleazily in a bikini and giving the camera her most smouldering come-on. It looked as though it had been posed specifically for the paper. It hadn't. It had been taken amidst much giggling almost a year ago in Martha's Vineyard, and been kept in a desk drawer in a top office at the Satellite building ever since.

'Phoebe and Felix shared nights of sizzling passion in his Notting Hill flat', read the caption.

The story was compelling, trashy, entertaining, and immediately forgettable. It was a quick, cheap, voyeuristic fix, as easily consumed as a hot dog taken on the run. Whoever had written it had their tongue in their cheek and an eye on the clock. But whoever had supplied the information had extracted it with a fine-tooth comb and got their facts absolutely right, triple-checked and libel-free. It might look like a piece of entertaining fluff, but Phoebe could see the wolf hiding beneath it.

The other tabloids had abridged versions, consigned to higher numbered pages with fewer photographs, but were nevertheless agonising in their glib, alliterated, italicised dismissal of Felix, his family, his lovers, and his blind, gullible, duped love for Phoebe. Despite being lifted from the *News on Sunday*, their facts were far more hit-and-miss. One had Phoebe down as a call-girl, another as a soft-porn actress. All had lifted the bikini shot, reprinting it in a more blurred form, realising that it was perfect for their house style – possibly knowing, too, that they would never be sued for reprinting a non-syndicated photograph, as the snapper had no wish to reveal his identity. They were all too frightened of Daniel Neasham to name him, too aware that they would be decimated by him if they did. Dan covered his tracks with the care of Grizzly Adams; it might be common gossip amongst the crumpled-suited hacks that he'd once had an undressed, unvested interest in Phoebe, but it could never be proved in a crumpled libel suit. It was, however, made pretty clear by the other tabloids that Phoebe had even junked her 'well known' married lawyer lover for Felix's revenge.

Reading through them, Phoebe was reminded of the monk murdered by the abbot, slowly poisoned to death by the Holy

Bible itself as, licking his finger to turn each page while he read, he failed to notice the almond taste of cyanide, painted onto every leaf of his favourite read.

Phoebe had devoured the tabloids for years, giggling and gawping as she drank in the scandalous tales of sex-mad stars and kinky vicars, thinking it nothing more than a distracting hiatus between her Sunday morning fry-up and her coffee. When her own face stared back from those smudged, grainy pages, she realised their power to decimate lives.

'Do you think Saskia talked?' Fliss asked her.

Phoebe shook her head. 'They'd have quoted her if she had, angled the story differently. The only quotes are from Jasmin and a few freeloading friends. I don't think Saskia had any idea this was really going to happen.'

'Then who?'

'Dan.'

'No!' Fliss looked up from a horoscope page. 'Shit – of course! He works for them, doesn't he? Frigging Ker-ist.'

'He must have rumbled the whole thing.' Phoebe shrugged, scraping her hair back from her face. 'He was in the flat enough – he could easily have found the Felix file, heard Saskia's messages on the machine. He's a shrewd chap, remember. He's like a diviner when it comes to facts, knows precisely where to dig while others are turfing up soil here, there and everywhere. And he's seeing a lot of Portia Hamilton now. She knows pretty much everything, I'd say.'

'Christ!' Fliss's hungover eyes gaped to show a multitude of bloodshot veins. 'So he's been busy getting his own back on you for dumping him, while – '

'While I was getting revenge for Saskia.' Phoebe nodded. 'Exactly. And, let's face it, she wasn't exactly discreet about her plan. She told most of my friends in order to put pressure on me to do it. Anyone could have blagged over a boozy lunch.'

'I didn't, hon.' Fliss put an arm around her shoulder and kissed her on the forehead. 'God, you feel freezing!'

Phoebe gazed numbly at the ceiling, hardly feeling Fliss hug her vigorously, trying to warm her up.

Realising she was getting nowhere, Fliss stopped and licked her lips anxiously. She had never known Phoebe this glazed and spaced. It was like trying to comfort a junkie who's just shot up half a gram of high grade heroin. She was flat-voiced, dull-eyed and almost catatonic with misery.

'What are you going to do now?' she asked cautiously.

Phoebe rubbed her forehead and shook her head hopelessly. 'I don't know. Fall apart, I should think. Phone around a few friends, tell them I'll be out of action for a decade or so and then develop a couple of life-threatening habits. Fucking strangers and wandering about on the M4 should do it.'

'And Felix?'

'He won't want me within a million miles.' Phoebe looked away. 'I know him. Last night was absolutely my last chance. He's so screwed up about loyalty and trust. He wanted me to choose between him and Saskia to prove how much I loved him, and I picked her. Christ, I hope to God he's okay!'

'But you love him!' Fliss howled. 'Surely if you explain what Saskia said . . .'

'No!' Pulling violently away, Phoebe stood up. 'He'll never forgive me for this. Believe me, Fliss. He wouldn't give a damn what Saskia threatened – he won't see it like we do. And now it's all over the papers. That's my fault too, for being stupid enough to tell Dan I loved Felix. He'll never – oh God!' She started to cry again, burying her face in her hands and backing away.

'Crisis fuel.' Dylan burst in with three cracked mugs of tea balanced on a paper plate and almost up-ended them all as he banged into Phoebe, swinging his arm away just in time. 'Helps if you work in a bar,' he laughed, twirling the plate around flashily before holding it out in front of her, trying desperately to lighten the mood. 'Don't have the striped one – it's mine. Five sugars.'

'I'm going to collect my stuff,' she sobbed, reversing sharply out of the room. 'Then I'll go back to Gin's for Yuppie and head back to London or something. I can't bear – oh, shit!'

She fled.

*   *   *

Later that morning, Gin drove Phoebe to the station and hugged her tightly. She had tried to persuade her to stay on at Gayton's Farm, but Phoebe was determined to get back, desperate to get away from Selbourne and everything associated with it. Gin hated to leave her in such an overwrought state.

'You won't be alone, will you?'

'No,' Phoebe lied.

'Are you going to try and find Felix?' Gin asked cautiously.

Staring fixedly at the platform below, Phoebe didn't answer.

'Get him back.' Gin squeezed her shoulders.

'That's the moon.'

'Sometimes you get it, if you want it enough. And believe me Freddy, there are some occasional benefits from having nothing more to lose.'

44

From Paddington, Phoebe wandered aimlessly towards Notting Hill, not really knowing what she was doing. Carrying a rather dazed Yuppie in her canvas bag, she headed along Westbourne Grove with tears sliding on to her neck and her arms wrapped tightly around her for warmth.

It was a sweltering day. Fashion victims were out in force in jazzy bikini tops, crotch-length skirts and clumpy boots, their hair tucked into the latest craze in headwear, the oversized floppy straw beret. Dark glasses were glittering like fly's eyes on every face, shoulders were reddening and ankles were swelling as Bank Holiday revellers set out for the park to spend a day collecting blisters and wasp stings. Men with Atlantean shoulders and six-pack chests were taking the hot-house opportunity to show them off, wearing nothing between their birthday suit and fresh air but Calvin Klein underpants poking out of the waistbands of sawn-off jeans.

Open top cars were cruising up and down the Grove displaying their contents as though the carnival had come a month early. Cafés were cramming more and more chairs onto pavements for clients to soak in the sun and the sexual frisson as they sipped their coffee and peered at passing babes and babe-magnets from behind their designer dark glasses. It was a day to look and yearn, to pose and doze.

Scuttling past in her shapeless jumper and ill-fitting jeans, Phoebe saw nothing and turned no heads. It was as if she was existing in a parallel life to those around her. While palms swabbed sweating foreheads, Sunday supplements fanned faces and eyes squinted against the sun, she shivered, her teeth chattering, her body drenched in icy sweat, her goose bumps grating against the coarse wool of her jumper.

As she neared the mews, she slowed to a wavering snail's pace, her heart feeling as though it was rattling up and down behind her ribs. Creeping to the mews gate, she clutched on to an iron railing and peered along the little cobbled street.

Georgette's gold Mercedes wasn't parked amongst the XR6s and BMWs, but a couple of very dusty old wrecks were, and three or four men wearing ill-matched t-shirts and baseball caps were hanging around swigging from fizzy drink cans and scratching necks as they waited. Two of them had very phallic cameras slung around their bullish necks and huge, padded equipment bags sitting on the roofs of their dusty cars. Phoebe could hardly see Felix's cottage, could just make out the window boxes and a sideways slant of the glossy green door. Her heart was positively racing up and down her ribs now, clattering against them like a button on a washboard.

The next moment it was rammed into her throat as she caught sight of a tall blond man walking speedily towards the mews from the opposite direction, his face hidden behind dark glasses, his ripped jeans showing a lot of brown leg, a cream sweater tied around his lean waist. She dived behind a Mercedes jeep and, breathless with sickening fear and hope, peered around the edge.

But it was just Mungo, his face still glowing with sunburn, his overnight bag slung over his shoulder. He turned quickly into the mews and almost ran to the front door, ignoring the excited attentions of the doorsteppers. The press boys, clearly thinking that he was Felix, fired up their Dictaphones and raced around changing lenses.

Realising that he must just have come from Paddington too, but had been sensible enough to catch the tube, Phoebe crept back to the mews entrance railing and watched him leaning on the bell of number three.

The baseball caps, realising that he wasn't Felix after all, took a few shots and fired some half-hearted questions but Mungo just cut them dead and they weren't interested enough in him to persist. It was hot, it was Bank Holiday Sunday, and they couldn't really care less about some dumped, duped pip-squeak who would be forgotten about by the end of the week. They wanted to be given the 'topless sunbathing in Hyde Park on hottest Bank Holiday since 1976' assignment. Occasionally they checked the battery power on their mobile phones with a longing sigh.

After a few minutes of standing back, yelling and ringing the bell again, Mungo unhooked his bag from his shoulder and, digging around in it, finally extracted a set of keys and let himself in, telling the hovering, resurgent press guys to 'fuck off' in his withering drawl.

Turning on her heel, Phoebe headed dispiritedly back to Islington.

'Who was that?' asked one of the journos.

'Dunno – a fan perhaps. Looked a bit screwy if you ask me.'

There was someone sitting on Phoebe's doorstep in Douglas Street. As she turned into the road, she caught a glint of blond hair just above the front wall and sobbed with delirious, disbelieving relief. But as she raced forwards, Yuppie bouncing against her side, she slammed to a halt, suddenly seeing the rest of the doorstepper.

It was Saskia. She was still wearing her pearl dress, her party make-up streaked down her face. Further along the street, Stan's Beetle was parked at an acute angle to the pavement, one of its front wings crumpled from a prang.

Taking a deep breath, Phoebe headed for the front door, anger and disappointment coursing through her veins.

'You'd better come in.' She reached for her keys.

Saskia followed her in silence.

'How long have you been here?' Phoebe asked as she climbed wearily up the stairs.

'Since about five this morning. I went to the mews first.'

'Bit early to try for a reconciliation, isn't it?' Phoebe hissed bitterly. 'I should give him a couple of weeks to get over it if I were you.'

Starting to cry, Saskia followed her into the flat.

Phoebe was on auto pilot, but her instruments were giving out all the wrong readings. She turned on the central heating and cranked up the thermostat; she opened a can of red kidney beans with shaking fingers and forked out a third of it into a bowl before presenting it to a surprised Yuppie; she pressed the play button on the answer-machine as she passed it, half listening to a multitude of last-minute messages from party guests saying that they were going to be late or couldn't make it, couldn't find it, or needed to be picked up from Hexbury station. There were messages from Phoebe's mother, Fliss's exhibition gallery owner, the landlord and the bailiffs, which Phoebe didn't listen to. There was an urgent message from Dylan that made her pour scalding water all over the carpet until she realised that it had been left last night, before he'd tracked her down at the Seatons'. There were no messages from Felix. There was, however, one from Dan.

'I'm calling from Italy,' he said, not bothering to announce his name. The line crackled with long-distance interference. 'I got your birthday of reckoning card – sorry I've taken so long to write back. My letter's in the *Post*. It's also in the *Sunday Mirror*, the *News of the World*, the *People* and, of course, the *News on Sunday*. Bye.'

Hardly listening, Phoebe watered a few more plants and then put the kettle in the fridge before pouring herself a vast glass of Fliss's cooking brandy.

Wandering back into the sitting room, she faced up to Saskia, who was sitting on the sofa, still sobbing frantically and glistening with sweat from the stifling heat of the flat.

'Aren't you going to thank me then?' Phoebe asked coldly.

Saskia looked up at her with eyes as red as two pools of blood.

'I know you hate me. I hate myself,' she wailed. 'The moment you started doing it, I realised that what you'd said was right. It wasn't any sort of revenge – it was just a horrible, farcical mess and I couldn't bloody stop it.

'I wanted to,' she sobbed. 'I sat there watching you do what I'd asked and I just wanted to stop you the whole time, but I was too bloody frightened and guilty and messed up to move. I suddenly realised that your Felix was different to mine and it hurt so much, I couldn't do a thing, couldn't move, couldn't speak.'

'Oh, God,' Phoebe breathed, her throat choked with tears. 'Oh, God, Saskia, I wish you had.'

'When you rounded on me in the attic, told me that I didn't love Felix, I really wanted to kill you. I hated you so much for that, I played the dirtiest trick in the book and, Christ, I was so unwired I think I'd have gone through with it.'

Phoebe jumped as Yuppie, her pink nose stained with kidney beans, scrabbled at her legs, anxious for a bunk up.

'Then,' Saskia went on, 'I saw your face when you came into the room to do it, and I watched Felix's reaction, and I knew for certain that you were right. I didn't love the man you hurt. I'd hardly scratched his surface in all the time I knew him. You cut through to the core.'

'Peel away onion layers and you make yourself cry.' Phoebe gave a sad, tearful laugh.

'I went to the mews earlier to tell him how much you really love him – but he wasn't there.' Saskia gazed at her pleadingly. 'Please believe me, Freddy. I only went there to explain it was all my fault. That I'd set him up.'

'He already knew that.'

Saskia looked at her in bewilderment.

'He'd guessed, Sasky.' Phoebe looked away, unable to bear the scrutiny. 'He knew we were planning to humiliate him last night. He could have walked out hours before I did it. He hung around because he truly believed I wouldn't, even though he was the only one who did.'

'Oh, God,' Saskia wailed in horror, covering her face with shaking hands. 'And you wouldn't have, would you? Only I – oh, Christ, Freddy.' She stood up and stumbled into the kitchen to grab the brandy bottle, pressing her palms on the edge of the work surface and hunching her shoulders in despair before she turned back. 'I've been such a stupid, wasteful, self-destructive bitch, haven't I? I've trashed lives just to try and make myself feel better.'

Phoebe watched her wander shakily back into the sitting room before she spoke.

'Not entirely,' she said quietly. 'In the end, I had to do it to make you see straight, didn't I? I mean, if I had called your bluff, what would you have done?'

'The frame of mind I was in, I think I probably would have tried to kill myself.' Saskia pressed the brandy bottle to her lips. 'And, given my unsuccessful track record in that department, I guess I'd have spent a few weeks in hospital and then just carried on trying to get my own back on him *ad nauseam.*'

'And now?'

Saskia bit her lip and looked at Phoebe, realising where she was being led.

'I want to forget him, forget it ever happened, straighten myself out. I don't know if I can do it, but I really want to try. I'm still wallowing in self-pity, but, for the first time since it happened I want my life back. I guess it's like giving up smoking – you can only do it if you want to.'

'So it worked then, didn't it? For all the wrong reasons, it worked perfectly.' Phoebe pressed her wet eyes into Yuppie's warm, furry bulk. 'Ironic, huh?'

'And I want to get you and Felix back together,' Saskia said slowly. 'I'll never forgive myself unless I do. You've sorted me out, now it's my turn.'

'I don't think you can,' Phoebe mumbled.

About to protest, Saskia jumped as the phone rang beside her.

Frozen on the sofa, Phoebe stared at it as though, by gaping at it long enough, she might be able to tell who was calling.

'Answer it then,' Saskia said urgently.

'I can't.'

'It might be Felix.'

'And it might not be,' Phoebe sobbed. 'That's why I can't bear to answer it.'

As it rang for the tenth time, Saskia snatched the phone from the cradle.

'Hello?' she said in a low, wobbly voice. 'No, it's Saskia, Dylan. Yes, fine – I mean, no, awful, I'm cracking up – yes, she's here.' She looked up at Phoebe.

Shaking her head like mad, she sobbed and coughed into Yuppie's back.

'No, she can't speak right now.' Saskia's voice was climbing scales as she repressed her tears. 'Okay – yes – what? Shit! Oh, Christ, is he? I see. Okay. What time? I'll tell her. You too. 'Bye.' She hung up and walked across to Phoebe, dropping down on her haunches and giving her a cautious hug.

'He and Fliss are coming back to London this evening – they're leaving your sister and Goat in charge of house-partying and tidying up.'

'Do they know where Felix is?' Phoebe managed to splutter.

Saskia took a deep, shuddering breath. 'No, they can't trace him. But Georgette called. Apparently, the police have found her Merc wrapped around a lamppost on the Cromwell Road.'

Phoebe whimpered in terror, 'Oh, God, is Felix . . .'

'No. The car was empty when they found it.' Saskia hugged Phoebe tighter. 'Just a bit crumpled. He must have left it there and walked.'

'But walked where?' Phoebe sobbed. 'Christ, I'm insane with worry about him, Saskia. I can't bear the thought of him alone and tormented and hating me to hell. I'm going mad not knowing where he is, not knowing he's safe. He's so wound up he could be – '

As the phone rang again, she practically disintegrated in Saskia's arms.

'You get it, Sasky,' she whispered. 'Disguise your voice or something.'

''Ello?' Saskia picked up the call with a very tearful cockney accent. 'She can't come to the phone right now, I'm afraid.' She reverted to her normal voice, clearly talking to a stranger. Listening to the caller with a confused expression, she covered the mouthpiece and turned to Phoebe in bewilderment.

'It's someone called Greg Marston from the *News*,' she whispered. 'He wants to speak to you about an exclusive. He asked if you have a PR agent.' She held out her palms in total bafflement.

'Hang up on him,' Phoebe hissed urgently.

With a bemused shrug Saskia did as she was told. The phone rang again almost immediately.

Pushing Yuppie off her lap and diving across the room, Phoebe pulled the phone plug out of its socket and then, racing into her bedroom, yanked that one out too.

'What are you doing, Phoebe?' Saskia followed her. 'Who is Greg Marston?'

'I thought – I assumed – Oh, God, Saskia!' Phoebe looked up at her in horror, biting her lip hard. 'You haven't seen any Sunday papers yet, have you?'

Saskia shook her head. 'I've been sitting on your doorstep since five.'

'When you read them,' Phoebe sat forlornly on her bed, 'you'll realise why you haven't a hope in hell of getting me and Felix back together. I think I've just lost him the biggest break of his career.'

Dylan and Fliss did their best to look after Phoebe over the next two days, but both were too distracted really to take care of someone who was so hopelessly untogether that her seams were no longer just coming apart, they were gaping widely and gushing out stuffing.

Fliss spent most of Sunday night arranging for Gin Seaton to drive up to London and collect Saskia, who was so distraught with guilt and humiliation over the tabloid coverage that she couldn't stop crying. As Saskia moved on to her third absorbent loo roll, Gin finally arrived in a flurry of apologies and, giving her weeping daughter a huge hug, prised her away from a listless Phoebe, who was now totally dry-eyed and staring into space, seemingly oblivious of everything around her.

'She's cracking up,' Fliss told Dylan the following afternoon when they met up for a hasty drink in Camden. 'She's always been so sane, I just don't know what to do.'

'Stick with her, let her ramble on about it, remove all sharp objects from the bathroom.'

'I can't – and don't make sick jokes,' Fliss groaned in despair. 'My exhibition previews on Wednesday. I'm spending all tomorrow getting work transported and set up. I'm meeting the gallery admin manager tonight to write a last-minute catalogue because everyone forgot about it, and if the text doesn't get to the printers at eight tomorrow morning, people will be clutching a guide to Sly Stallone's paintings on Wednesday night. I'm stressed up to my eyeballs, I'm probably going to be up all night, Phoebe's going to be on her own again, and I feel a right frigging wreck.' She yawned widely, faded blue eyes closing like a new born puppy's.

'You are so gorgeous,' Dylan said suddenly. 'Really, utterly, fabulously gorgeous. You know I fancy you rotten, don't you?'

'And you gush too much.' Fliss blushed. 'But I quite fancy you too.'

'Where do you think Felix has got to?' she asked as they headed out on to Camden High Street, rubbing their dry, smoke-itched eyes as they walked into a blanket of bleaching afternoon sun.

Dylan shrugged. 'Christ knows. Mungo seems to have disappeared too. I was banking on his help, but I can't trace the little sod.'

At the tube, they had a short, rushed, fizzling kiss which left Fliss frustrated.

'Try and get someone round to keep Phoebe company tonight, huh?' Dylan said as he backed away from her towards the ticket barrier. 'And get a bit of sleep if you can. You look tired out, you poor darling.'

Yuppie, confused and disturbed by the non-stop hysteria and the increasingly odd meals she was getting, spent a lot of time in her canvas bag.

Phoebe was better when Fliss was with her, found that she could keep still for longer, but left alone she was climbing the walls, worried to jittery, moaning distraction for Felix yet too frightened to try and find him because she knew he wouldn't want her anymore, and too muddled with unhappiness to know where to start anyway. Time and time again, she plugged in the phone to try and call him, even though she knew he wasn't at the mews; grief had rendered her illogical. Every time she dialled, she hung up before the first ring, her heart blistering with unhappiness. Almost inevitably the phone would then ring as one of the weekday tabloids tried to get a quote for their follow-up stories.

They now knew that she had done the deed in style, and had plenty of quotes from Felix's freeloaders to testify to her character-assassinating speeches on Saturday night. Covering the story on Monday, they had eagerly and floridly described Felix's dramatic disappearance, crashing a £70,000 car in his wake.

By Tuesday, the story had been promoted to lower page numbers, had made the Comment sections, and had sourced a few more quotes:

·'*I just wish Saskia had asked me to do it.*' *Phoebe's buxom younger sister, Milly Fredericks, 19, told The* News *from her home in South London. 'I wouldn't have fallen in love with the b*******d like Phoebe did. I love my boyfriend, Goat.*'

Milly's partner, Gavin 'Goat' Reynolds, then went on to say, 'Phoebe is a horny babe. He must have really dug her, man. He looked gutted when it happened.'

Phoebe is still refusing to comment, or dispel rumours that she was paid £5000 to humiliate Felix, as reported in yesterday's 20p The News.

Somehow the story captured the nation's interest. The idea of a beautiful bastard, a vengeful ex-girlfriend, a ravishing decoy and an unfinished conclusion ignited their imaginations. Speculation was rife as to where Felix was; photos of him appeared everywhere, his name was suddenly synonymous with the perils of being a philanderer, the dangers of relying on the 'every woman loves a bastard' myth. Revenge, the cold dish, was the flavour of the day. Day-time television presenters joked about it on their pastel sofa and had a phone-in for viewers' getting-your-own-back anecdotes, DJs linked records with smug, light-hearted references to it, bars hummed with after-work gossip about it, columnists sharpened their pencils on the old 'woman scorned' cornerstone and thought up new angles to approach it from. It wasn't yet a media storm, but the thunder and lightning of real-life story and favourite topic were flashing and rumbling ever closer together.

Phoebe kept the phone unplugged and retired to her duvet with Yuppie to compose a hundred unwritten letters to Felix in her head.

Dylan scoured London for Felix, calling everyone he knew who might know where he was. No one had seen him. He trudged around bars and clubs and other Felix haunts to no avail, although it cost him a small fortune in entrance fees. He waited for hours at the mews, feeling hopeless. The tabloid door-steppers, far from drifting away as Dylan had been told they would, seemed to be breeding like gerbils out on the cobbled side street as public interest in one minor silly season story ran out of control. They lounged against their dusty cars, fending off clampers, yakking into their mobile phones, fiddling with their cameras, and taking it in turns to visit the sandwich shop around the corner. There hadn't been this sort of interest in a barely known celebrity's movements since Elizabeth Hurley wore That Dress to the première of That Film.

Dylan was so concerned about Felix, however, that he barely registered their presence.

On Tuesday night, he installed a new, working answerma-chine and set off to meet Fliss at the Gillam Gallery in South Kensington, where she had finally positioned the last of her sculptures and was waiting in an exhausted state of readiness for a quiet meal in a back-street restaurant before returning to Islington to Phoebe-sit and sleep for the first time in days.

Dylan would have liked to make a move and lure her back to the mews tonight, but hadn't had time to tidy up or have a bath, and guessed she was far too stressed and tired to cope with the rigours of a first bonk anyway, so planned to play it safe and not ask.

It was past ten and the mews was shadowy and silent when he banged the green front door behind him. The baseball caps had packed up for the night to make up a few fictional twists to a tale that was rapidly going nowhere, and to scour the photo-libraries for yet another shot of Felix looking like every girl's dream. Ironic, he reflected, that even though Felix was being painted in the press as the date from hell, Dylan had had several phone numbers pressed on him by girls in the bar today, asking him to pass them on to Felix, desperate to wipe his flat-mate's eyes and mend his broken heart.

When he got into his rusty Renault 5, he found that he'd left the lights on and the battery was flat. Kicking its balding tyres, he posted his car keys back through the mews cottage's letter box and headed out on to the Bayswater Road to catch a bus.

Felix rolled up at the mews twenty minutes later and leaned against his front door for almost ten more minutes as he searched for his key, dropped it in the shrubbery, fell over a milk bottle, banged his head on the wall, found his key again, stabbed it in the general direction of the lock and then finally fell into his hallway on top of Dylan's car keys which cut open his elbow.

Not even noticing, he lurched unsteadily up the stairs and, bouncing off the walls of the kitchen, made it through the narrow corridor before falling into his bedroom, nose-diving on to the bed. He then took a few deep breaths and upped himself again before staggering over to his clip frame and unhooking it from the wall. It slid from his fingers, landing on one of its right angles on the floor, the glass smashing.

Felix stooped over the debris of broken glass, metal clips and scattered photographs, blinking until he could focus on the photograph he wanted. Kicking glass out of the way with his foot and swaying dramatically as a result, he reached down for the snap he had taken of Phoebe last week, pitched sideways for a few steps and then reeled back out into the kitchen again.

Slumping down at the table, he took his lighter from his pocket and held it under the glossy rectangle, his thumb hovering over the flint wheel.

She was sitting on his bed dressed in nothing but his old grandad shirt, mouth wide open in that lovely, unconfined laugh which seemed to take over her whole face, big green eyes disappearing into two thick-lashed slits, long legs spread out, arms together in front of her with hands pressing into the duvet to hold down the tails of the shirt. Yuppie was sprawling over one of her feet, pink nose pressed to a mangled-looking squeaky toy, odd eyes bright red from the camera flash.

Felix's thumb struck down and a little flame lapped at the edge of the photograph.

A split second later he had thrown the lighter at the wall and was frantically trying to put out the small blue flames with his sleeve, pressing it on top of the rapidly disappearing photograph.

Flames extinguished, Felix peered down at it. He'd burned off her foot and most of Yuppie, but Phoebe still laughed up at him. He slumped back in his chair in despair, running a shaking hand through his hair and tipping his head back to gaze drunkenly at the ceiling. Suddenly he felt a lurching sensation as his stomach seemed to climb into his throat. The chair, propped on two legs, had carried on tipping. As it finally fell over backwards, Felix found himself staring at an upside down skirting board, his feet in the air.

'Shit!'

He closed his eyes.

Lurching into the mews at two in the morning, heady with lust, love and expectation, Dylan crashed straight on to his bed. At four, he woke momentarily and reached woozily down the duvet to remove his shoes before nodding off again, a smile plastered to his face as he indulged in carnal thoughts of Fliss.

He didn't notice the faint strains of 'Up the Junction' coming from the next room, or the occasional foray to the phone to dial a number which was never answered.

On Wednesday, Fliss flurried around in a state of panic, plugging the phone in to call every friend she could and badger them to come to her private view that evening. Each call took hours as everyone wanted to know about Felix and Phoebe. Redialling as soon as she'd hung up, she spent five solid hours on the phone.

Phoebe lay in the bath for almost as long, listening to Fliss talking in what she clearly thought were hushed enough tones not to be overheard.

'Off her rocker – yes, totally. Do you really think I should? Well, yes, I want her to be there, but I don't know if she could cope. Okay, I will – see you there.'

'Hi, Pads, it's me. Look it's my private pre – what? Oh, yes, she's in a terrible state. I just hope – '

Phoebe sat in a freezing cold bath, knowing that she was being a self-pitying weirdo and that she had to get her act together, face the fact that Felix now wanted her to burn in hell for mucking up his life, and stop frightening everyone by behaving so oddly. So she cried for another hour and washed her hair for a third time.

Oversleeping, Dylan headed off to work at the bar in a tearing hurry, still oblivious of Felix's presence in the mews.

The press boys greeted him in their usual raucous, chatty style.

'Still no sign of him, mate?'

'Nope.' Dylan smiled sadly.

'S'our last day on this job,' another said with relief. 'Not worth keeping us on if the fucker's done a runner for good. Latest rumour is he's gone to the States.'

Dylan spent the day in a preoccupied daze. The thought that Felix would do a complete bunk hadn't even occurred to him. He was so distracted that he spilled Jack Daniels all over his shirt while trying to hook up a new optic, which pissed him off even more as he was supposed to be going straight from work to Fliss's preview. He would stink like an old drunk now, and he knew that Fliss's parents were coming down from Manchester.

* * *

Three spliffs and half a bottle of vodka into the morning and Felix's hangover finally abated enough for him to stop crying and start drinking as though he meant it.

Hitting the last three inches of vodka, he suddenly knew that he had to see Phoebe face to two-faces.

He'd tried calling the Islington flat, but last night it was never answered and today the line was always engaged.

He decided to go round there, crashing into his room to pull on some clothes, so drunk that he put on two pairs of trousers, three t-shirts and odd shoes. Looking like a tramp who was wearing his entire summer wardrobe at once, he fell down the stairs and landed on a thick pile of post. Still on the floor, he scrabbled frantically through it, looking for an envelope addressed with Phoebe's funny, lop-sided handwriting. There wasn't one, although there appeared to be plenty of scented little pink, red and eau de nil envelopes addressed to him in other, much more loopy hands. Felix threw them at the side-door to the garage and scrambled upright with the aid of a cheeseplant which died for its efforts, its thick, rubbery central stem cracking in two.

But when he opened the front door about twenty mad yobs in shorts and baseball caps surged forward.

Terrified, pissed and stoned, Felix slammed the door on them and staggered back upstairs in a confused daze. He peered at them out of the sitting-room window. Several big lenses peered back and snapped him with his nose squished sideways on the glass. Felix backed off and scratched his head, spinning around several times in perplexed dilemma before collapsing on the sofa and picking up the phone. Still engaged. He hoped she wasn't calling her mother. Three solid hours was too much, even for the love of his life.

'Fucking bish – bitsssh – bi – Oh, shit!'

He closed his eyes and felt the room spinning around him. He had to talk to her, scream at her, cry at her; try and hate her enough to get through this thing.

The doorbell was ringing like mad now. Felix ignored it.

They flicked pebbles at the window, stood on the car roofs and yelled up at him. Felix moved into the bathroom with the rest of the vodka and the phone and tried a few more times. Engaged. It was no good. He was just going to have to brave them.

But as he yanked open the front door for the second time and listened to the machine gun click of film being shunted rapidly through motorised spools, he found himself face to face with his brother.

'Get inside,' Mungo hissed, pushing Felix back in. 'I've been leaning on the fucking doorbell for ages. I left my keys behind.'

He slammed the door behind him, pale blue eyes gleaming with irritation.

'How d'you know I'd be here?' Felix turned away and tripped up the stairs.

'I know one of the hacks out there,' Mungo said, pushing past him and storming into the kitchen. 'He just called me and said you'd finally turned up. Where the hell have you been?'

'Scotland.' Felix was still on the stairs and stumbling around alarmingly. 'I went to visit Granny.'

'She's dead,' Mungo snapped, pouring the remainder of Felix's vodka down the sink.

'I know.' Felix tripped up a couple more steps. 'But I didn't remember that until I got there. So I went to Aberdeen and got pissed instead.' He fell over the top step and crashed to the floor. 'And I'm proud to say I haven't sobered up since.' He passed out.

'Shit!' Mungo rushed forwards and dragged him upright.

'She did it, the bitch,' Felix whimpered groggily, and then started rambling drunkenly and incoherently: 'And I still bloody fucking love her – I hate her for it. I'm going to get Yuppie back. Yes, I'm going to have the dog – I want the bloody dog! If I can't have her, I'm having the dog.'

Mungo dragged him into the bathroom and pushed him under the shower, blasting him with cold water until he started screaming with some coherence: 'Turn that fucking deluge off, you bastard!'

Mungo relented.

His clothes dripping, his hair plastered to his head, shoes oozing water, Felix clambered out of the shower and wandered unsteadily back into the kitchen leaving a snail's trail of water in his wake. There, he paused to extract a sopping wet packet of Chesterfields from his pocket, removed one and popped it into his mouth with some dignity and poise, before lurching towards the stairs again, clearly about to fall down them once more.

Chasing him, Mungo steered him back into the kitchen and pushed him down onto a chair.

'Right, big brother,' he flicked on the kettle and helped himself to a biscuit. 'I'm going to sober you up and say something I never thought I could bring myself to say. I'm going to recommend a woman to you,' he winced at the thought.

'Forget it,' Felix spluttered. 'From now on I'm fucking celibate. If she'll have me.' He started to giggle. Then he started to cry.

'Ker-ist,' Mungo looked at the ceiling, realising the enormity of the task ahead.

When Fliss asked Phoebe to her private view, she predictably shook her head.

'I'll just be a dampener and a distraction,' she muttered miserably. 'You enjoy it – I'll come and see it tomorrow, when less people are around.'

'I want you to come tonight,' Fliss pleaded, hating the thought of leaving her alone again. 'Milly said she and Goat'll be there. And Clods, Paddy and Stan. Even old Iain might roll up, if he can get over the humiliation of the escort fandango – apparently, he got off with Lucy on Sunday evening, so he shouldn't be too red in the eggy face.'

'I don't think I could cope, to be honest,' Phoebe's voice trembled. 'It'd be like a reunion of the murder mystery lot, and they'll all be peering at my piggy eyes not your lovely sculptures. I think I'll tidy the flat a bit. Have a clean up.'

'Christ, you are really frigging losing it!' Fliss sighed in despair.

45

The Gillam Gallery was a huge, wide commercial showroom discreetly located in what had once been a bombed-out space between two elegant Georgian houses near Queen's Gate in South Kensington. Hidden behind a sympathetic architectural façade and a lot of wide glass windows, the exhibition space inside was just a vast, white box with glossy wooden floors and high white ceilings.

Fliss's sculptures, peopling the space before anyone at all arrived, gave the odd impression of a raucous party already in progress. Her cartoon-like characters with their distinctive pear-shaped bodies and ill-fitting clothes were clutching shopping baskets and toddlers and dogs and bags on wheels, yet their thickly textured, worldly faces bore the look of those who'd had a couple of stiff nips of gin before they came out. Fat, balding old men scratched their string vest paunches and eyed up ruddy-cheeked housewives with saucy-postcard cleavages and growing-out roots. Harassed young mothers with a kid on each hand and a pregnant bump in the middle looked from the corners of their eyes at slouch-hipped young thugs with number one cut hair, shiny nylon bomber jackets, and a can of Tennents in one tattooed hand.

When Fliss walked past on the opposite pavement, the lights were gleaming inside and a couple of waitresses were setting up a long table with trays of nibbles at one end and row upon row of champagne flutes at the other.

She paused for a moment to take in the sight. Her fat funny clay people who had started as a joke and ended up as a burgeoning career, were all looking far calmer than she was. A big poster bearing a photo of one of her felt hat and sheepskin boot pensioners, with her name above it in large self-important letters, was stuck up inside the wide glass frontage. Quaking with fear and excitement, Fliss bolted around the corner to the pub where she had arranged to meet her friends.

'Never arrive at your own private viewing on time or sober, girl,' Stan had warned her. Being an artist who had lived on the cusp of fame for almost five years, he was a veteran exhibitor. 'You roll up an hour late with a hell of a lot of friends and then, when you're whisked around VIPing, you've got to be bloody nice to everyone, just in case they've brought their Amex along or they're a critic.'

Fliss sat amidst her friends in the Ox and Yoke knocking back brandies and trying to stop hyperventilating. Just as they were about to set off for the viewing, she looked across at the bar and almost stopped breathing entirely.

'Do you see what I see?' she gasped.

'Shit!' Paddy followed her gaze. 'He's a focking cheek, now.'

Sitting at a small table in a dingy recess to the far end of the bar was a man with unmistakable blond hair, wide, sculptured shoulders and a profile to die for. He was nose-to-nose in conversation with another blonde – smaller, slighter, paler, but similar in classy good looks and clever blue eyes.

'I'm going over there.' Stan drained his pint. 'That berk deserves to – '

'No!' Fliss grabbed his arm to stop him. 'Leave it, Stan. It's not your fight. I think we should just go.'

All the excitement had drained out of her, the butterflies had flown away and the heady, fizzing energy had been replaced by a leaden, sickening feeling of dread. Her heart was bleeding for Phoebe.

As she waited for Stan, Paddy and Claudia to file out of the pub in front of her, Fliss gazed over her shoulder.

Felix and Saskia were so engrossed in conversation that they didn't once glance up. As Fliss stared, Felix stretched out a hand and stroked Saskia's cheek with a long finger before stretching over the table and kissing her there. Saskia looked elated, her eyes gleaming with tears of relief and gratitude.

Shuddering, Fliss raced out of the pub, desperately relieved that Phoebe hadn't been there to witness it.

Phoebe knew she was going totally demented when she found herself weeping with frustration because she couldn't quite scour all the mould from between the bathroom tiles immediately behind the bottom of the loo. The task had taken up hours of her time, and mould still sprouted everywhere like green furry lines on a graph.

Yuppie, sitting on the fluffy pink loo mat and looking disapproving, had long since tired of her mistress's caterwauling lamentations. There were only so many tears that a small pink postage stamp tongue could take. She whined with bored frustration, tiny stumpy tail gyrating hopefully.

'You're right.' Phoebe straightened up and looked at her, wiping her eyes with the back of her hands and almost blinding herself with the disinfectant on her Marigold glove. 'I'm going crackers in here. I couldn't care less about the mould. I couldn't care less about anything but Felix.'

Yuppie dipped her nose and rubbed it between her front paws, sneezing at the smell of bleach.

Phoebe kissed her on the head. 'Get your slap on, baby, we're going to look at some sculptures.'

Mungo finally staggered back from the bar with the drinks and plonked them on the table, slopping most of his pint over Saskia's lap.

'Sorry I took so long.' He straddled a bar stool. 'Service here is bloody lousy. How are you feeling?' He squinted at his brother.

Felix shuddered, rubbing his putty-pale face in his hands. 'Like I sobered up too fast. Like I wish I knew why the fuck you wanted to come to a dead-beat pub in the middle of South Ken to do this. Like I've just been hooked on to a life support machine after lying dead in a car crash for hours.' He glanced at Saskia whose eyes started to fill with tears again when he smiled that heart-stopping smile.

'Here's your morphine.' Mungo pushed a Bloody Mary towards him. 'I got you a cocktail, Saskia darling, because I couldn't remember what you asked for. Here – it's called a Loose Screw. Or is it a Screw Loose? I've forgotten. What an old fluffy head I am tonight.'

Saskia smiled ruefully, her red-rimmed eyes taking on his and showing no bitterness. 'Thanks, Mungo.'

'So why are we in this dump?' Felix said, knocking back most of his drink in one and lighting yet another Chesterfield.

'Not a bad place,' Mungo said airily, throwing out his arms to take in the arcade games, karaoke stage, satellite sports television, red-tiled food bar and huge oil painting of Margaret Thatcher.

'Fuck this – I can't wait any longer. I'm getting a cab to Islington.' Felix started to stand up.

'No, you're bloody not.' Mungo pulled him back down and looked at his watch. 'I reckon another twenty minutes should do it.' He winked at Saskia who nodded, swallowing the lump in her throat.

Phoebe was halfway to South Kensington before it occurred to her that she should have smartened herself up a bit for Fliss's sake. She was still dressed in the clothes she had clambered into after her earlier bath – a truly horrific black A-line mini-skirt that she'd bought on a schoolgirl kick before realising that it had a descending zip and was made of the sort of cheap fabric that combusted if put within three feet of a glowing cigarette, a shrunken pink t-shirt with bleach stains all over the front and a splitting seam on one shoulder, and a pair of scruffy old black boating shoes with no laces in them. Even Yuppie looked a bit moth-eaten, having chewed up the Hoover bag earlier, covering herself in dust, ash and fluff.

I'm simply not up to it, she realised in despair. I cry if I see a blond hair on a coat arm at the moment. I can't embarrass Fliss on the biggest night of her career by weeping all over the critics and wailing all over the nibbles.

She sat on the train until South Kensington anyway, feeling too wretched to bother going back. Then, because she was so near, she wandered towards the gallery and hovered across the road from it, watching the circulating, chattering guests, all clutching their catalogues and glasses of wine which necessitated a lot of fumbling and looking around for surfaces when a waitress wafted up with a tray of smoked salmon twists or miniature garlic tarts.

Phoebe could hardly see the sculptures for people, which she took to be a good sign. She spotted Fliss talking to her tall, sombre parents. She wasn't looking particularly cheerful, Phoebe noticed. In fact she was looking positively ashen under the freckles.

Milly and Goat were standing by the food table, stuffing their faces with mini tarts; Goat had a pilfered champagne bottle poking out of each of his overcoat pockets. Talking to them, Stan was also looking gaunt and serious. Even Paddy, the big, gangling joker, had a face like an iceberg.

Phoebe sat down on a low, tree-shadowed wall in front of the church opposite the gallery and bit her lip, hoping Fliss was all right.

A couple of minutes later Dylan loped up from the direction of the tube wearing a crumpled linen suit, his hair on end as ever, his tie over one shoulder from running most of the way there. He had a huge yellow stain on his stomach, she noticed.

Picking moss from the wall, Phoebe watched numbly as he fought his way over to Fliss and was hastily introduced to the tall, sombre duo before she pulled him to one side.

The next moment he was racing back out again and pelting towards the Brompton Road. Watching his lumping, lop-sided gait, Phoebe remembered Felix saying that Dylan moved like a gazelle with verrucas, and had another fit of the snivels.

Yuppie was growing increasingly frustrated with Phoebe's inertia and was now squirming around like a fish in a net, desperate for freedom. Still hiccuping and sniffing, Phoebe wandered into the grounds of the nearby church to let her have a run round the graves. She leant back against Beatrice Durant 1678–1702, who had a spectacularly ugly marble angel looking after her with no nose, a pigeon-dropping mob cap and a broken wing. The last red streaks were fading out of the sky now, and the old yews in the churchyard were huge, melancholy crows of shadow. The floodlighting beneath the church walls was starting to throw its buttresses into high relief as artificial light took over for the night shift.

'You snuffed it when you were my age, Beatrice,' Phoebe sighed, tapping the stone behind her. 'Was that from a broken heart, too?'

'Tuberculosis, actually.'

Phoebe screamed with ear-piercing clarity and leapt away, sending Yuppie off into a flurry of barking. A great, terrified whoosh of adrenaline sent her heart beat into orbit as she spun around to gape at the marble angel.

Standing just behind it, looking tired and tearful but far, far better than she had on Sunday, was Saskia. Her hair gleamed in the last of the evening's fading light; half obscured by the angel, her face was creamy and fake-tan free, her sloping nose slightly red from crying but those big blue eyes clear and brimming with a strange look of euphoria.

'Saskia! Shit, you scared me.' Phoebe found she could hardly speak for hyperventilating terror which was only just starting to ebb away. 'What on earth are you doing in the same graveyard as me?'

'Good question.' Saskia smiled nervously. 'I'm sorry I scared you, Freddy – I just couldn't resist it.'

'Well, you should have tried a bit bloody harder.' Phoebe rubbed her hair, most of which appeared still to be standing on end. 'Have you been at the viewing then?'

'No, I was about to go in when I spotted you sloping in here. I guessed you'd come out to support Fliss tonight.' Saskia stooped down to say hello to Yuppie, who had rushed up and was now bouncing around on her happiness trampoline at Saskia's feet.

'I wasn't actually going to go in.' Phoebe shifted uncomfortably. 'I can't face it. I thought I could, but now I'm here, I can't. I'm not exactly feeling sociable at the moment.' She battled to stop her voice wobbling up into a distressed squeak.

'Neither am I.' Saskia cleared her throat and straightened up, still hovering behind the angel's broken wing. 'We could go in together. Be unsociable together.'

Stepping forward, Phoebe eyed her curiously, taking in the clean hair, the smart black Armani trouser suit, the trendy Barbarella boots. She looked better than she had in months, her face still pinched with unhappiness, but her eyes were bright and her cheeks had the faintest streak of the old pink in them.

'You came up here from Berkshire to support Fliss?' she asked with tearful admiration. 'After everything that's happened this weekend, you still put on a brave smile and made it?'

'Well, I – ' Saskia wavered guiltily.

'God, I should pull myself together, shouldn't I?' Phoebe sagged back against Beatrice's marble guardian again, pressing her palms to her eyes to try and stem the inevitable tears. It amazed her that she had any left, having cried more than she'd drunk in the last three days. Yet still they kept welling up, and sprouting, and gushing, and leaking at the slightest provocation.

'Er – are you coming in then?' Saskia looked at her watch.

'Are you in a hurry or something?' Phoebe splayed her fingers and looked at her.

'No, no – it's just that I – er – ' Saskia stooped to pick up Yuppie. 'It might all be over soon.'

'These things go on for ages.' Phoebe blinked away one stray tear, rubbing her arms and trying to dispel the nervous goose-bumps that were popping up.

'Please come now, Freddy.' Saskia looked at her watch again.

'You go on ahead.' Phoebe started to feel the familiar oil-geyser rush of tears and panic coursing through her body again.

'I want you to come with me,' Saskia entreated.

'I can't,' Phoebe hiccuped. 'I can't – see that – looking at – looking at Fliss's – f-f-fat people is – going to help.'

'Please.'

'No!'

'Freddy – '

'Piss off!'

'Wait there,' Saskia rushed away.

'And b-bring back my dog!' Phoebe howled staggering back to Beatrice and sobbing onto her angel.

Mungo was waiting in the shadow of a huge plane tree to one side of the gallery and smoking a cigarette as Saskia crossed the road and headed back towards the pub.

'Saskia!' He raced after her, catching her up outside a noisy wine bar. 'Where the fuck is she?'

'In that bloody graveyard.' Saskia jerked her head towards the church opposite. 'I can't get her to come out. She just keeps crying. She looks pretty ghoulish too.'

'Christ!' Mungo looked frightened.

'And her clothes are absolutely awful – I'm a bit frightened this might not work.'

'It has to.' Mungo rubbed his hands together. 'It's so gloriously theatrical.'

'Well, there's just one thing.' Saskia squinted through the gallery windows, where the masses were still mingling amongst their clay fellows in rapidly dwindling numbers as invited guests started to drift away. 'Have you seen the sculptures, Mungo?'

He swung around and peered at them, his blue eyes stretching in horror. 'You said Fliss sculpted people, Saskia!'

'They are people. Very fat people.'

'And Phoebe is a very skinny bird.' Mungo rubbed a thumb around his lips anxiously. 'Quite. I see. God. Oh, bugger it – it's still worth a try. Make sure she's in there in exactly ten minutes. Dylan's spread the word already, so Fliss et al are pretty much in the know. If Felix gets any more difficult, I'll tell him Phoebe's gone to stay with her parents. Where do they live?'

'Hong Kong,' Saskia said in amazement.

'Hong Kong. Right. Ten minutes. See you there.'

Saskia headed back to the graveyard.

*   *   *

'Hi.'

'Oh, God, you're back, are you? Bit of a quick look round, wasn't it?'

'Wasn't the same without you.'

'Sure,' Phoebe sniffed. 'Don't tell me – you can't keep away from my scintillating, up-beat, dazzling repartee. After all, I cover so many subjects – like Felix and Felix and me and me and Felix and – '

'Please come over there with me.'

Phoebe sniffed stubbornly. 'Just give me the dog and go away.'

'You're being unreasonable.'

'I know. But I like to think I'm being justifiably unreasonable, don't you?'

Saskia walked up to her. 'Freddy, have you ever seen *The Winter's Tale*?'

'Once, I think. Y-years ago.' She blinked tearfully, slightly bewildered by the question.

'Do you remember what happens to Hermione at the end?'

'Look, Saskia.' Prickling with irritation, Phoebe railed against her, 'I am not in the mood to discuss English literature right now, okay? Now will you please hand over my dog and push off back to the exhibition you're so keen to get to.'

'But at the end,' Saskia persisted urgently, 'Hermione pretends to be a statue to—'

'I know what happens at the fucking end!' Phoebe howled. 'She pretends to be a statue and her repentant husband – who I always thought was an undeserving sod – really believes she is one, which just goes to show how thick he was.'

Saskia laughed tearfully. 'Then she comes alive in front of his eyes and – '

'In fact,' Phoebe stormed on, getting into her swing now, 'I always thought the end was a bit too bloody ridiculous for words, if you must know.'

'I think it's a lovely story.' Saskia looked at her with swimming eyes. 'A statue of a lover one thought one had lost coming to life.'

'Christ, you're seriously suggesting something here, aren't you?' Phoebe's tearful eyes stretched wide with appalled disbelief. 'What do you want me to do? Go over there and stand in amongst Fliss's fat old ladies and flat-capped pigeon fanciers, and strike a cute raver pose in the hope that Felix wanders in, cops me, and says: "That one looks like Phoebe – I think I'll knock its deceitful clay head off"?'

'Something like that,' Saskia cleared her throat. 'Though not the head-knocking bit, obviously.'

'Saskia, I am not going to march into Fliss's big, longed-for, slaved-over night and humiliate her by acting like a loon just to satisfy some dreamy romantic whim you have,' Phoebe spluttered on in furious disbelief. 'I've already made an exhibition of myself once this week, and that broke my heart. I have no intention of making myself part of an exhibition now and losing most of my friends as well.'

'If you don't do it, I'll kill – '

'Don't you *dare* tell me you're going to bloody kill yourself again!' Phoebe howled. 'Christ, I don't believe you, Saskia Seaton.'

'I was about to say I'd kill your dog,' Saskia muttered coldly, clutching tightly onto Yuppie, who tilted up her pink nose and gaped back at her.

Phoebe froze.

'Okay, hand over the dog and kill yourself,' she joked uneasily, not sure whether Saskia was telling sick jokes or genuinely certifiable ones. Yuppie was starting to look pretty concerned, her mismatched eyes bulging anxiously.

'Listen, Freddy,' Saskia said urgently, starting to speak so quickly it was difficult to follow her. 'This was supposed to be a surprise – some theatrical Vincent Price set-up Mungo's fixed his heart on. But I've got to tell you because we're running out of time. Felix is going to walk into that gallery in about five minutes ti—'

'Felix!' Phoebe clutched on to the stone angel. 'He's near here?'

'Very near, and he's hopping mad because he wants to hare off to Islington to pound on your door.'

She closed her eyes and moaned. 'Oh, Christ, he must hate me to hell and back now. No, hell and back is a short walk to the shops compared to how much he must hate me.'

'He loves you to bits, for Christ's sake,' Saskia howled irritably. 'We haven't got time to get into this now but he knows you would never have done it if I hadn't threatened to kill myself like that. Mungo was on the steps to the attic that night – he overheard everything,' Saskia wailed in frustration, looking at her watch. 'He's been trying to track Felix down all week. It doesn't even matter. Felix is going to be in that gallery in about one minute – Fliss knows about it, everyone does.'

'Fliss knows?'

'Yes! You weren't supposed to know but now you do, so for Christ's sake shut up, straighten your hair, wipe your nose, get a wiggle on and get over there!'

'But I let him down. He trusted me and I – '

'I told him everything, Freddy.' Saskia gripped her shoulder. 'I told him how hellish I was to you as a kid, how I bullied and teased and knocked you down at every opportunity. I told him what a jealous little demon I was. And that I started being the same when you wavered over this thing; I resorted to all the whining, spoiled, manipulative tactics I'd used to make you do things fifteen years ago. I was so jealous and resentful and fucked up about both of you that I forced you to do it in the end.' She winced, letting Phoebe's shoulder go and backing away, her face twisted with guilt.

'You told him all that?' Phoebe could hardly take it in. 'You painted yourself as a monster so that – '

'I *was* a monster, Freddy.' Saskia stared up at the sky, now a deep navy blue, glowing with the orange of London's street-lights. 'I was obsessed. He understands the grip your childhood has over you – he had such a hellish one himself, he knows that a bully has the power to come back and take over almost where they left off years later. I just made him realise that I was one of life's bullies, not victims. I know you say I hardly knew him when we were together, but he didn't really know me either; I was always so desperate to please him, always putting on an act.

He had no idea I could be so manipulative, and that I would pick the one person who would find it hardest to say no to me, however much they loved him.'

'But you told Felix,' Phoebe croaked. 'That must have hurt so much.'

'Well, I guessed I wasn't likely to be on his Christmas card list.' Saskia shrugged suddenly. 'So I figured I had nothing more to lose. Except you.' She looked up tearfully.

Phoebe stared at her in amazement.

They both jumped as voices drifted along the street, one purring and coercive, the other gruff and jolly. A third drawling, tetchy, irritated and reluctant.

'Just for five minutes,' purred one. 'She needs the support.'

'Knock back a drink and then push off, mate.'

'I want to fucking push off now. I'm DTing up to my shrunken eyeballs, I'm sweating like a pig, I loathe modern art, and the woman I love is, according to you, crying into a Shanghai Sling in fucking Hong Kong of all places. I have to get to a phone and try and get hold of her, fly out there, something – not eat a fucking nibble and look at Fliss's clay feet!'

Phoebe let out a whimper of joy, covering her mouth and starting to tremble.

'Now will you believe me?' Saskia sighed in exasperation, smiling even though tears were tipping over her lower lids. 'Christ, he took a hell of a lot less persuading than you did, Freddy. Now for Christ's sake get over there before he pushes off and tries to fly to Hong Kong. You don't want him turning up on your parents' doorstep.'

'Saskia, I—'

'Scram!' Saskia wailed, laughing through her tears and clutching tightly onto Yuppie, who let out a series of encouraging barks too, stump gyrating.

Phoebe paused for just a split second, then started to race towards the church gates like a sprinter out of the blocks. Almost at the road, she slammed to a halt and turned round. Wiping her eyes with the backs of her hands, she walked back towards Saskia.

'What are you doing, Freddy! Get over there,' Saskia screamed.

Phoebe looked at the heart-shaped face she had once envied so intensely, now streaming with tears, the cool blue eyes burning with anguish, the blonde hair gleaming almost white in the floodlights from the church.

'I think – ' she started, and then realised her throat was so choked up that her words were barely audible.

'Freddy, if you don't get over there now,' Saskia sobbed, 'I'm going to – '

'Kill the dog, I know.' Phoebe looked at Yuppie, her eyes blurring. 'Up until tonight, she was the most precious thing I had,' she pointed at the skewbald puppy and stroked a small white ear with a shaking hand, watching as the little dog tipped her pink nose back with self-indulgent bliss. 'Because she was the only part of Felix I knew I would be able to keep after last Saturday. I know you once accused me of offering you half-sucked boiled sweets as consolation prizes, but I want you to have her because, next to Felix, she's the only thing I can give you that shows you how much I love you. And,' Phoebe looked up at Saskia and smiled, 'I do love you, you old bag.'

Saskia laughed and sobbed at the same time, 'I love you too, you silly cow. Now get over there and put him out of his misery before I kill – '

'– the dog, I know.' Phoebe laughed, kissing Yuppie on the head, Saskia on the wet cheek and then running like smoke.

'I was going to say "you",' Saskia sighed, watching as she was almost flattened by a taxi.

As Phoebe raced towards the gallery, she caught sight of Mungo hovering near the door looking crestfallen. He glanced up from flicking his ash in a bay tree pot and almost whooped. Bounding forward, blue eyes blazing with relief, he checked nervously over his shoulder before intercepting her and pulling her to one side.

'About bloody time, too!' he hissed. 'And I can tell you didn't take all that time doing your make-up. Come here.' He wiped the last of the tears from her face, straightened her hair and winced as he took in the outfit. 'I can't do anything about the pit bull eyes and the port-drinker's nose, I'm afraid, but it's a bit better. And at least your hair's clean. You've ruined my plan, you know. We had it all worked out.'

'Shut up, Mungo,' Phoebe laughed, kissing him on both cheeks. 'And thank you so much. I had you all wrong. Tell me,' she dropped her voice, still battling not to shake all over, 'why are you doing this?'

He shrugged. 'You're the first one I've actually rather liked. And I could see how much it hurt you to do that Katharine Hepburn act on Saturday night. Everyone there saw it, even Felix. But he's a great stubborn mule with a huge *pomme frite* on his shoulder about broken promises and trust and this loyalty shit he bangs on about. Having heard your simply glorious cat fight with Saskia in the attic, I felt obliged to bawl him out and point out just how Hobsoned your choices were. He seems to be in quite a forgiving mood now, although I'd be a bit cautious if I were you, he's still a tad volatile – ie, hungover. And I have to warn you, the in-laws will be hell!'

Inside the gallery, Fliss nudged Dylan and nodded towards the door, her pale blue gaze glittering with excitement. He looked up from his catalogue and rolled his eyes, breathing, 'Thank Christ'.

Paddy had noticed her too, and glanced worriedly across at Felix. He stood as motionless as a statue, staring at a buxom earthenware swinger with flashing stocking tops as though her vast stomach hid some vital clue he had yet to fathom. He was looking as sulky as hell and riddled with tiny detox shudders, muscles quilting his cheeks, a tendon stretching taut in his neck.

When Phoebe walked in, he didn't register the movement, seemingly buried in his own private, stewing world of thought. He didn't even seem to notice that the low burble in the room had hushed to silence.

Phoebe ran her tongue over lips so dry they felt like a cracking pastry rim. She raked her hair back from her face and took such a deep breath that she had to let a little of it back out again to stop her lungs from bursting. Stepping out of her boating shoes so that her feet didn't squeak on the shiny floor, she walked slowly up behind him, shuddering with happiness and fear as she gazed at his lovely, familiar body and breathed in the faint, peppery smell that still punched her in the groin with longing as intensely as it had the first time she'd met him.

Creeping as stealthily as a cat burglar, she stole right up behind him, so close that she could feel the heat of his back just a few inches from her bursting lungs, could hear his tense, shallow breathing.

Phoebe lifted her hands, about to slip them around his waist.

'I hate to sound uncool,' Felix muttered, starting to shake, 'but is that Sainsbury's Coconut Shampoo?'

Even though he didn't turn round, Phoebe could tell from his voice that he was smiling.

'I dab it on my pulse points every day.' She pressed her forehead to the soft cotton on his back and slipped her hand beneath the tails of his shirt.

'I thought you were in Hong Kong.'

'I thought I was in purgatory.'

'I was there too. Funny we didn't meet. I was at the bar. Where were you?'

'Locked in the loo. I should have stuck my head around the door and asked to borrow your jumper.'

Laughing, he covered her hands with his and pulled her tighter.

Lurking behind the single mother with the bump, Fliss turned in bewilderment to Dylan and mouthed, 'What *are* they on about?'

He shrugged and mouthed, 'Fuck knows.'

As Felix pulled her round to face him, Phoebe looked into his eyes and almost exploded with happiness as she saw a clear blue gaze brimming over with relief and love.

'I am so, so, so sorry for what I did,' she said slowly, her voice hoarse with emotion. 'It hurt me so desperately to – '

'Shut up.' Felix smiled, covering her mouth with his own and wrapping his arms tightly around him.

Oh, that kiss. Phoebe shuddered ecstatically. That gorgeous bloody unforgettable bloody kiss. Unplug me from the mains, someone, peel me off the ceiling and then stop me sliding on to the floor in a great hot, sizzling puddle of horny love.

'I love you so much.' She pulled away, her gaze skipping between those huge blue eyes as she battled to make him believe her unequivocally. 'I've been hopelessly in love with you for weeks, since Paris really.'

'I knew that.' He kissed her nose.

'Arrogant bloody sod.' Phoebe widened her eyes. 'Like hell you did.'

Laughing delightedly, Felix indulged her in another of those kisses, far longer and gentler this time, and then slid his mouth to her ear.

'Do you get the feeling we're being watched?' he whispered.

Phoebe glanced over his shoulder and caught sight of Milly grinning at her from ear to ear. Beside her, Goat was blowing his nose on a paper napkin. Winking at her like a DOM in a pub, Paddy was draining both their glasses for them and munching the last of the smoked salmon.

'I think you're being paranoid,' she whispered back.

'I love you too, you know,' Felix breathed, 'but I can't say it in front of all these people. Unlike you, I'm not into public declarations.'

Phoebe winced.

'And,' he whispered, 'I can't move right now because I have the mother of all hard-ons.'

She laughed, propping her chin on his shoulder.

'It killed me saying all those things about you, you know,' she whispered, curling her arms tighter around him. 'All that awful stuff about you being a lousy lover, when really I've never met anyone who's made me feel so permanently horny and buzzing, and who has me soaring off into orbit every time he – '

'Thanks,' Felix butted in. 'That means you're stuck in this position for at least another five minutes. I'm definitely not going to say I love you out loud now.'

'Scared of admitting your feelings in front of witnesses?' Phoebe grinned.

'Hell, no.' Felix started kissing her ear.

'Coward.' She bit his.

'Er—quick announcement,' Felix said very loudly indeed, turning to peer around the room, 'I love Phoebe Fredericks. I love her. I plan to be in love with her for a very, very long time because, well – because I love her really. That is love with the usual four assortment of letters varying from l to e. Just the one syllable. I find that easier to remember.' He turned back to Phoebe and grinned. 'Okay?'

'Bit repetitive.' She wrinkled her nose, eyes brimming over with happiness.

'Christ, we're going to have such fucking fun,' he smiled, hugging her tightly.

'And then we can share a cigarette afterwards and have non-fucking fun.' Phoebe breathed him in, loving the warmth of his neck, the familiar smell. 'I think you're right about one thing, though.'

'What?'

'I think we *are* being watched.'

They leaned their heads back and stared at one another, eyebrows raised.

'Do you want to go home?' Felix asked, his eyes suddenly less cocksure.

'Home?' Phoebe bit her lip.

'Yes.'

'Er, which one is that exactly – your home or mine?'

'Ours,' Felix said very slowly, biting his lip too.

Phoebe felt the biggest, goofiest, most heart-skipping smile spread across her face as she watched the biggest, sexiest, most heart-stopping smile spread across Felix's.

'Home it is then.' She slid her hand around his waist and, feeling the weight of his arm hooking its way around her shoulders, they headed, still grinning like idiots, through the door and wandered off along Queen's Gate, their voices fading into the distance.

After they had disappeared from view, Saskia walked back from the shadowy gateway to the churchyard and kissed Beatrice's angel on its broken wing.

'Even broken-winged angels can do good deeds,' she whispered, standing back and looking up at him. 'Geeze, you're ugly. You need a nose job.'

Tightening her grip on the snoring puppy in her arms, she headed towards the road where she had left her mother's car, pausing in the gateway to look at the gallery once more. The last guests were spilling out now. Mungo was racing off towards the Brompton Road singing 'Everybody Needs Somebody'.

Saskia saw Fliss's red hair glint in the light of a street lamp as, tucked under Dylan's broad, comforting arm, they headed towards the tube. They were arguing like old spouses.

'But if they *have* gone back to the mews, there'll be no one at our flat, so we can have the place to ourselves . . .'

'But the mews is more comfortable.'

'Are you saying our flat's a dump?'

'You know it's a dump, Fliss!'

'But it's a comfortable dump. You can't say it's an uncomfortable dump.'

'Well that sofa leaves a lot to be desired. And I didn't have the best of luck with your papisan that time . . .'

Listening to them, Saskia laughed, but it turned into a half-sob and she covered her mouth as Claudia, Paddy, Milly and Goat walked out just as the gallery lights were switched off behind them. Plunged into shadows, they headed off behind Fliss and Dylan.

'Walk slowly, guys, they seem to be having snog stops every other paving stone. Christ they're rampant.'

'Nothing like as rampant as Phoebe and Felix – I think they'll spend most of their time joined at the hips.'

'You know, I don't think they've actually bonked yet . . .'

'C'mon! We all cringed under those madly creaking floorboards on Saturday night. They were at it two minutes after Felix arrived in that taxi . . .'

'I *mean* Fliss and Dylan – whoa, hold back, another snog stop.'

'I think that's sweet.'

'There's nothing sweet in that – Christ, will you look at that action. From the rate they're going they'll have bonked by the time they get home.'

'Goat, will you please stop crying. It wasn't that bloody romantic. Nowhere near as loving as the time at Womad where you carried me over all that thick mud to the latrines and . . .'

Saskia stared up at the sky. The Plough was out; she vaguely remembered teaching Phoebe how to identify it when they were kids.

'Don't wish on that big twinkling bugger – it's a 747,' called out a friendly voice.

Saskia looked down sharply and saw Stan standing on the opposite pavement, just in front of the darkened gallery. An alarm bleeper was shrilling dully behind him as a man in a suit locked the doors.

Stan crossed the road, carefully checking to either side for traffic although there was absolutely none about.

Saskia smiled, pressing her chin to Yuppie's small domed head. 'You always did cross the road as though the Green Cross Man was standing behind you.'

'Gotta be careful, girl,' Stan winked, checking over his shoulder for his companion, who was still grappling with a Fort Knox security system. 'Don't know why he bothers. It'd take an effing army of weight-lifters to make off with Fliss's podgy people.' He looked at Saskia again. 'She sold quite a few tonight.'

'That's good,' she shrugged. 'Look, I'm really sorry about your Beetle – I'll pay for the – '

'Doncha even give it a thought,' Stan grinned. 'After all, I can't drive it without a licence, can I? Bit of a bump won't kill it. Adds to the charm.'

Saskia smiled gratefully.

'You been standing out here all this time?' Stan gave the puppy a cautious pat.

She nodded.

'Why din' you come in for some grub and a chat?'

'You know why, Stan.' Saskia smiled bravely.

'Yeah – that.' Stan sucked on his teeth awkwardly and, plunging his hands into his pockets, rocked on his heels. 'Nice little dog – it's Phoebe's innit?'

'Was,' Saskia kissed Yuppie's head. 'She gave her to me tonight.'

Stan's sandy eyebrows shot up questioningly, but he just grinned and said, 'Good thing too – she didn't look after the poor little sod properly if you ask me. Spent the last few days using it as a handkerchief.'

'Stan!' yelled his companion from across the road, now hovering on the pavement and jangling a set of keys.

'You – er – you going back to Berkshire tonight?'

Saskia nodded.

'By car?'

'Yup.'

'Stan!'

Stan bit his lip and stared at her speculatively.

'I think your friend wants you,' Saskia laughed.

'Oh yeah – hang on a sec. Don't go away.'

Looking carefully to either side, he crossed back over the deserted road and went into a huddle with Henry Gillam, the gallery owner.

'Sorry about this, Henry, mate,' Stan whispered. 'But I don't need that lift after all.'

'No?' Henry's furry black eyebrow angled up in the middle as, with a knowing smile, he slid his eyes towards Saskia on the opposite pavement.

'No, no!' Stan said hastily, looking quite shocked. 'None of that monkey business. She's just been through a bit of a rough time lately. Needs a few friends on her side.'

'Sure,' Henry grinned. 'Anytime. Give me a call about Spring ninety-six, yeah?'

'Thanks, mate!' Stan dashed back to Saskia, stopping to look and listen at the kerb.

'Er – you couldn't possibly give me a life home, could you, Saskia?' he asked with an apologetic shrug. 'I know it's a bit effing rude of me, but I'm completely strapped for cash at the moment. Well, skint in fact. It's not really out of your way, is it?' he added, knowing that it was.

'No, not really,' Saskia smiled, knowing that it was too.

'Thanks, Sask mate. Thanks a lot.' Stan loped beside her as she headed for the Golf. 'If you like we can stop off on the way back and I'll buy you a coffee to say thanks. Have a bit of a natter.'

'That would be lovely,' Saskia smiled, too polite to remind him that he had just claimed to be penniless.

Only Stan, she reflected happily, was old fashioned enough to offer a girl coffee 'on the way' home, rather than luring her up to his flat with the offer of a superstrength Nescafé made with powdered milk in a mug that smelled of Cup-a-soup. And she really did need someone to talk to right now.

As she unlocked the driver's door and smiled across the roof at him, Saskia realised it was lovely to feel fancied again, even if one did have puffy eyes, a red nose and puppy slobber all over one's shirt.